WEIRD DETECTIVES:
RECENT INVESTIGATIONS

WEIRD DETECTIVES:
RECENT INVESTIGATIONS

Edited by Paula Guran

PRIME BOOKS

Contents

BEYOND RATIOCINATION, REASON, GUMSHOES, AND GUNS: WEIRD DETECTIVES

Paula Guran

The subgenre that came to be known as "urban fantasy" was the most popular type of fantasy—perhaps fiction as a whole—of the first decade of the twenty-first century. Although full of action-adventure and horror's supernatural beings—vampires, werewolves, shapeshifters, ghosts, witches, et al—it really owed more to mystery than any other genre, especially the hard-boiled or noir detective mystery. Raymond Chandler's Philip Marlowe, Dashiell Hammett's Sam Spade, and their fictional counterparts are close literary kin to today's vampire slayers, demon hunters, wizardly private eyes, and other paranormal protagonists.

Just as with urban fantasy's heroes and heroines, the hard-boilers were outsiders. They took a lot of physical punishment, and dished out just as much. They adhered to individual moral codes, even when doing so broke traditional societal rules. Their turf was the city: the epicenter of all that is unnatural, wicked, and perverse in the world. When you fight evil all the time, you wind up cynical and tend toward sarcasm and wisecracks . . .

But urban fantasy's protagonists are also related to another breed of shamus: the occult detective. These investigators of the supernatural had to counter what was, by definition, *outside* of the normal world, yet constantly invading it.

Detective fiction as we know it began in 1841 with Edgar Allen Poe's story "The Murders in the Rue Morgue." His investigator, Monsieur C. Auguste Dupin, also appeared in "The Mystery of Marie Roget" (1842-43) and "The Purloined Letter" (1845). The entertaining formula of a baffling crime or mystery being solved by a detective of superior intellect—often assisted by someone less brilliant who acts as a chronicler—was established.

It didn't take long for the uncanny to be combined with the fictional detective's rational analysis. Ghosts appear to Harry Escott in Fitz-James O'Brien's short story "The Pot of Tulips," published in *Harper's New Monthly Magazine* of November 1855. The specters help locate missing documents, and, consequently, right a wrong. In this brief tale, Escott seems to have made a study of the paranormal and is prepared to reconcile it with scientific theory. In 1859, Escott appeared again (in O'Brien's "What Was It? A Mystery," also published *Harper's*) and is attacked by a supernatural entity that is, itself, the mystery.

The occult detective had been born. Also known as psychic detectives or ghost hunters, they were more often portrayed as scientists or learned doctors than as true detectives. Rather than dealing with human crimes, these investigators were involved in cases dealing with ghosts, malevolent spirits, arcane curses, demons, monsters, and other supernatural events and entities. Occasionally, purported paranormality would be debunked.

A number of these sleuths made appearances in late nineteenth and early twentieth century fiction. We'll mention only a few of the most notable:

Although his publication debut came did not come until 1872, Joseph Sheridan Le Fanu's character Dr. Martin Hesselius is often cited as the original occult detective. If not *the* first, he was the first of significance and influence. Le Fanu's *In a Glass Darkly* collected five stories—the most famous of which is the novella *Carmilla*—which were purported posthumous reports of some of Dr. Hesselius's cases. An unnamed assistant supposedly compiled and edited his papers. He said of the rather shadowy physician, "His knowledge was immense, his grasp of a case was an intuition. He was the very man to inspire a young enthusiast, like me, with awe and delight."

In the novel *Dracula* by Bram Stoker (1897), the highly educated ("M.D., D. Ph., D. Lit., etc., etc.") Dr. Abraham van Helsing obviously knew something of vampires as he immediately suspected the true cause of Lucy Westenra's illness, and eventually displayed a knowledge of how to deal with the undead. He was not exactly a detective, but he did discover and destroy a vampiric mystery/problem.

Flaxman Low, created by E. and H. Heron (first appearance: 1898) is a contender for the title of the first *true* occult detective since he specialized in solving supernatural mysteries and was consulted specifically for the purpose. He used his vast knowledge of the uncanny as well as powers of observation and analysis similar to Sherlock Holmes to crack his cases.

Of Algernon Blackwood's Dr. John Silence (1908) it was said, " . . . though he would have been the last person himself to approve of the title, it was beyond question that he was known more or less generally as the 'Psychic Doctor'" who had undergone "a long and severe training, at once physical, mental, and spiritual. What precisely this training had been, or where undergone, no one seemed to know . . . but . . . it had involved a total disappearance from the world for five years . . . "

William Hope Hodgson's Thomas Carnacki (1913) was directly inspired by

Arthur Conan Doyle's Sherlock Holmes, but Carnacki dealt with supernatural rather than human mysteries. Primarily scientific, he also used modernized magical tools (like his electric pentacle), and sometime resorted to arcane rituals. His investigations resulted in finding both real and faked hauntings.

Aylmer Vance, created by Alice and Claude Askew (1914), was another Holmesian type, but his partner Dexter, a lawyer, had clairvoyant abilities.

Why occult detectives? The huge popularity of the adventures of Sherlock Holmes and Dr. Watson (beginning with *A Study in Scarlet*, published in 1887—and despite Arthur Conan Doyle's attempt at killing Holmes off in the *The Final Problem* (1893)—with stories appearing until 1927) combined with a societal interest in spiritualism and all things occult. Paranormal investigators were a natural outgrowth. For a while, readers wanted more and more.

Most stories tended to be mere variations on the same theme. This is exactly what readers wanted, of course, but eventually they tired of the formula and moved on to other types of fiction. Tales of psychic sleuths continued to be published by the pulps, but overall they were no longer in high demand. Or, like Seabury Quinn's Dr. Jules de Grandin and his narrator/assistant Dr. Trowbridge, their adventures remained popular, but were not of lasting literary quality. (Seabury's duo were featured in scores of usually supernatural, always over-the-top, and often poorly plotted stories published in *Weird Tales* magazine 1925-1951.)

In the 1930s and 1940s, there were a number of other fictional investigators whose adventures led to encounters with the supernatural, but the realities of World War II and the decline of pulp magazines further lessened interest in such stories.

Supernatural sleuths never completely disappeared. Characters like Clive Barker's Harry D'Amour, James Herbert's Harry Ash, and F. Paul Wilson's Repairman Jack (who is not exactly an occult detective, but "fixes" things in a world that contains supernatural adversaries)—have been protagonists in bestselling novels over the last few decades. Other weird detectives, like Manly Wade Wellman's creations—John the Balladeer, Judge Pursuivant, and John Thunstone—or Brian Lumley's Titus Crow are known only to horror or fantasy readers.

For reasons unknown (to us, at least) the zeitgeist of the late 1980s and early 1990s produced a new breed of weird investigator: the vampire detective. Maybe it was a natural combination. Vampires have a lot in common with noir/hard-boiled detectives: they both roam the streets at night, both tend to wear dark clothes and/or long coats, both usually have tragic personal histories, love never runs a true and easy course for either, and neither define morality in the same terms as society. Human detectives often seem to need to drink and, of course, vampires definitely need to "drink."

Although Marvel Comics introduced a vampire detective, Hannibal King, in *The Tomb of Dracula #25* (October 1974) and there are probably other examples previous to these, note:

In *Blood Hunt* (1987) and *Bloodlinks* (1988) by Lee Killough, homicide detective Garreth Mikaelian became a vampire. After tracking down his maker, he continued to fight crime using his vampiric powers. (A third novel, *Blood Games*, was published in 2001.)

Nick Knight, a TV movie released in 1989, featured Nick Knight (played by Rick Springfield), a vampire working as a police detective in modern-day Los Angeles. In 1992, CBS picked up the series and produced as *Forever Knight* with Geraint Wyn Davies as the vampire detective. It ran three seasons, ending in 1996.

Bloodlist (1990) by P. N. Elrod featured Jack Fleming as a good-guy vampire PI in 1930s Chicago. Supposedly hard-boiled, he's far too nice to be really boiled. Eleven other novels followed. *Dark Road Rising*, the most recent, was published in 2009.

Set in modern-day Toronto, Tanya Huff's *Blood Price* (1991) portrayed Vicki Nelson, an ex-cop going blind who turned to private detecting and teamed up with a vampire. It was adapted for television as *Blood Ties* (Lifetime, 2007). There were five Blood novels altogether.

There was also a trend toward vampire hunters . . . or at least characters who started out as such:

Guilty Pleasures by Laurell K. Hamilton (1993): The novel was a mix of horror, fantasy, mystery, action-adventure, and romance in which Anita Blake is a female hardboiled detective-type (contrary, sarcastic, and with a protective streak) necromancer who also hunts down criminal vampires. The series has now veered away from detection and into the erotic; the twenty-first full-length novel will be published this year.

Buffy the Vampire Slayer (TV series: 1997–2003): Darker than the original action-comedy/horror parody film of the same name (1992), the series also better embodied creator Joss Wheldon's concept of an empowered woman fighting monsters, which were metaphors for problems that teenagers, especially, face. Buffy was not a detective, but she did defeat supernatural meanies. She and her "Scooby gang" also employed detective-like investigation in some episodes. In the spin-off series, *Angel* (1999-2004), the title character does becomes a private detective who helps the helpless while battling his own demonic side.

. . .

The earliest occult detectives may have possessed arcane knowledge or special powers, but they were basically human. But after vampires became detectives and humans started needing more than bravery, common sense, and a solid stake to dispatch them—many occult investigators became paranormals themselves. By the time urban fantasy gained popularity in the twenty-first century, the protagonists were still solving supernatural mysteries and crimes—or at least righting preternatural wrongs—but they weren't always human detectives or even "scientific" crime-solvers who might know a few spells. Kim Harrison's Rachel Morgan, for example, is a "witch-born" demon who investigates all manner of paranormal badness. Harry Dresden, created by Jim Butcher, is a PI and a wizard. Patricia Briggs's Mercy Thompson is a Native American shapeshifter raised by werewolves.

The most popular urban fantasy characters sustained story lines for numerous serial novels that continue to be bestsellers.

Although they were not necessarily always urban fantasy, as part of the general popularity of this type of fiction some great short stories featuring a combination of the uncanny and detection or crime were published. This anthology compiles some of the best of them published from 2004 through 2011. In order to meet our definition of "weird detective story," a mystery had to be solved and/or actual detection involved, so supernatural crime- or adventure-only stories were not considered.

Fans of urban fantasy are likely to have already encountered some of our authors and the universes they have created. Most will know Jim Butcher's Harry Dresden in "Love Hurts," Quincey Morris of "Deal Breaker" is central to Justin Gustainis's Investigations novels, and Tony Foster ("See Me") appears in three Smoke novels by Tanya Huff. Even if set in a certain "universe," the selected stories do not always feature its best-known characters. Simon R. Green takes us to the Nightside, but John Taylor is nowhere in sight. Charlaine Harris's Dahlia Lynley-Chivers is part of the Sookieverse, but the famous telepathic waitress is not connected to "Death by Dahlia." Carrie Vaughn has written a number of novels about werewolf Kitty Norville, but Detective Jessi Hardin in "Defining Shadows" has appeared in only a couple of them. David Christiansen, in "Star of David," was only briefly mentioned in Patricia Briggs's *Moon Called,* the first of her bestselling Mercy Thompson books. Jane Yellowrock's presence in "Signatures of the Dead" by Faith Hunter takes place chronologically before her novel adventures begin.

The New York of Elizabeth Bear's "Cryptic Coloration" is very similar to our own, but it is also part of her Promethean Age continuity, where subtle and treacherous magic infests the real world throughout history—and is constantly fought—but is never noticed by most humans.

Some tales don't take place in alternative contemporary worlds. Lillian Stewart Carl takes us back to the sixteenth century with "The Necromancer's Apprentice." Richard Parks's "Fox Tails" is set even earlier—in Japan's Heian era (794 to 1185).

Some authors intentionally evoke both hard-boiled detectives and the noir-ish past. Both P. N. Elrod's "Hecate's Golden Eye" and Caitlín R. Kiernan's "The Maltese Unicorn" take place in the 1930s. "The Adakian Eagle" by Bradley Denton and "Swing Shift" by Dana Cameron have World War II-era settings. In "Mortal Bait" by Richard Bowes, the mystery occurs in the early fifties.

Über-detective Sherlock Holmes has also had a revival of late. And, fictionally at least, he has encountered the weird in numerous recent stories. We selected "The Case of Death and Honey" by Neil Gaiman and Simon Clark's "Sherlock Holmes and the Diving Bell" as two stand-outs. William Meikle pays tribute to an Edwardian era occult detective—who was initially inspired by Holmes—with "The Beast of Glamis."

We also present adventures of supernatural investigators who may go on to further adventures (or not). After appearing in short form, Dana Cameron's Fangborn are now being featured in novels. Jason Saunders (of Ilsa J. Bick's "The Key") appears in at least one other story. Joe Lansdale's Dana Roberts has appeared in two stories, both of which were originally published only in a limited edition chapbook, *The Cases of Dana Roberts*. Surely there are other cases? Sarah Monette has now written three stories with her odd detective couple of Jamie Keller and Mick Sharpton, and we certainly hope to see more. Jonathan Maberry's "Like Part of the Family" is a modern homage to noir fiction. Its PI Sam Hunter could easily become the protagonist of a novel.

Urban fantasy still has many readers, but lately its bubble has been somewhat deflated by a number of factors—including the fact that the public is inevitably fickle. We suspect the crossover of mystery into science fiction and fantasy—which was not exactly new, but has certainly been strengthened—will remain a major influence as we progress further into the century. Weird detectives may get weirder yet and find even stranger streets to walk. Not having psychic powers of our own, all we can do is wait and see. For now, we hope you enjoy these stories as much as we do.

Paula Guran
December 2012

The Case: *The body of a newborn is found by a jogger in a DC park. A strange tattoo and a small piece of cloth inscribed with arcane symbols are the only clues.*

The Investigators: *Kay Rollins and Jason Saunders, DCPD detectives. Both are good cops, but Saunders is still trying to shake the suicide of his last partner.*

THE KEY

Ilsa J. Bick

Kay said he was probably a week old. Two weeks, tops: the stub of the umbilical cord was still there. Found in a shallow grave, on the far side of a hill in Rock Creek Park, off Klingle Valley Parkway, not far from the National Zoo. The jogger was hunched in the back seat of a black-and-white, the golden retriever that went nuts over something that wasn't a chipmunk looking embarrassed, nose on its front paws, wondering what the hell it did wrong. There was a uniform with the jogger. We—my partner, Rollins, and I—passed them on our way down the hill that was high with grass and damp from last night's rain. The retriever looked up, hopeful, its tail thumping. The jogger's eyes slid past to stare at nothing.

The baby was a little white boy. Hair short and fuzzy, like a wool cap. Thick, sludgy purge fluid flowed from his nose and mouth. If you didn't know better, you'd think the stuff was blood. I know better. The purge meant the boy had been dead about three, four days. Luckily, it'd been a cold October so far; Halloween coming up that week, and Kay figured this slowed the rot. Still, there was that sick-sweet smell of death, and the baby's abdomen was huge with gangrene and greenish yellow, like a bruise changing color. Thick green-blue vessels showed beneath the skin of his chest, and his eyelids were bloated and black. Made me want to rip someone's head off.

"Anything?" I asked Kay.

"We won't know until we do the cut, Jason. Kid might have been delivered at home, though."

"Why?"

She pointed. "Not circumcised. These days, all hospitals circumcise unless parents specifically ask that they not."

"Anything else?"

"Nothing obvious. My guess is exposure and dehydration. Of course, there's the tattoo." Her gloved finger hovered over a blue smudge above the baby's left nipple. "I'd say gang-related, Jason."

I didn't buy it. "I don't buy it. I've lived in DC all my life. I've seen little babies in dumpsters, washed up along the Potomac. I've seen kids splattered in drive-bys while they're doing their homework. But a gang revenge killing? Of a baby? That'd be a first."

"But the tattoo . . . what else could it be?"

She had me there. I flipped to the page in my notebook where I'd written the symbols down. We used a magnifying glass: *L-M-Z-2-9,* as best we could make out. The *M* was done in cursive. The entire tattoo was smudged, like a rush job.

"Maybe they're Roman numerals," said Kay. "You know, *L* for fifty and *M* for a thousand."

"That makes sense," Rollins said. "*New Black Gangster Disciples Use a Roman Numeral Three.*"

"You see a Roman three?" I asked. "I don't see a three. And what's *Z?*"

Kay said, "Maybe it stands for twenty-six, the last letter of the alphabet."

"A code?" It wasn't a bad idea. I scribbled down the numbers. "Adds up to one thousand eighty-nine. No combination I know of."

We left Kay bagging the baby's hands and the crime scene techs crawling around for evidence. I picked my way up the slope. Burrs stuck to my black pea coat. "Listen," I said to Rollins. "I'll talk to the jogger, see what she says."

"Okay. What do you want me to do?"

"Run that tattoo. I'll sign off on the scene."

The jogger's name was Rachel Gold. She was twenty-seven and lived on the third floor of a townhouse off 26th, near George Washington University. "Across from the Watergate," she said. She was still sitting in the black-and-white, and she had to crane her neck. (Some people think I look like Patrick Ewing, except I only have the mustache and I'm about eighty gazillion bucks poorer.) Gold was wearing a black sweatshirt and black jogging sweats. The sweatshirt was speckled with vomit. She'd pulled her brown hair, which was very long and thick, into a ponytail that was taut against her scalp. A loop of gold chain spilled over the neck of her sweatshirt. Attached to the chain was a tiny gold key, maybe as big as my thumbnail. "Twenty-sixth and H."

"You're a student?"

"No." Gold's eyes were very dark and so large she looked like one of those porcelain figurines: all eyes. "I'm assistant curator of special collections at the Holocaust Museum."

"Special collections?"

"Yes. I just did an exhibition on Holocaust musicians, and I'm working on Eastern European folk art."

"Okay. Let's go through it again. What happened?"

She did. She'd left her apartment at eight to jog and, since her neighbor was away, to exercise her neighbor's golden retriever. Gold had planned to run to the turn-off for the National Zoo at Porter, and back. "Only I never made it," she said, her left hand slowly pulling the dog's ears. She flicked a couple of burrs from her fingers. "I let Rugby . . . the dog run free. All of a sudden, I'm running and she's not with me anymore. I call and then I hear her barking like, you know, she'd treed a squirrel. When she wouldn't come, I backtracked and then I saw her down there and . . . " She looked away, swallowed hard. "Rugby was standing over this mound. First, I think it's a groundhog. Then I get closer, and there's this . . . this little . . . f-foot." Tears tracked her cheeks. Her right hand snuck up to her neck and her slim fingers stroked the pendant. "I go a little closer to make sure, and then I see the leg and part of the fa-face . . . "

"You didn't touch anything?"

Shuddering, she gave her head a quick jerk from side to side. "After I saw, I couldn't . . . "

"And then you called nine-one-one? You got a cell?"

"No. There's an Exxon not far back," she gestured east, toward the Potomac and the Kennedy Center, "at Virginia, next to the Watergate. And then . . . " She trailed off. Toyed with her necklace.

A uniform huffed up. "Okay if they move the body?"

"Yeah." I tucked my notebook into an inside breast pocket. I was starting to feel the cold. My toes were icy. I craned my neck to see if Kay was starting up, but the angle of the hill was too steep.

Rachel Gold stood. "Is it okay if I go now? I'm cold and . . . " She glanced down at her stained sweatshirt. "I'm kind of a mess."

I made sure I had her home and office numbers and reminded her she'd get a call to come make a formal statement. As she turned to go, her pendant flickered in the sun.

"Pretty," I said.

"Oh," she said, glancing down. "It's old."

The key was modeled after those antique keys you see in old movies. At the top, I saw a single letter engraved in black. It looked like a *W,* but the ends were fashioned like the flames of tiny candles. "What is that?"

"Hebrew. A *shin.*"

All of a sudden, my chest got tight. "Unusual."

"Oh, it's old-country stuff. The charm's supposed to bring you luck." Her tears started again. "I guess it didn't work, did it?"

• • •

DC traffic's a bitch. The station's on Indiana, about two miles away from Rock Creek. So, I knew I could count on forty-five minutes, easy. That was okay because I needed to figure out why thinking about Adam made this knot, hard as a tennis ball, jam the back of my throat.

We did a case together last year, Adam Lennox—my first partner, my best friend—and me, right around this same time, Halloween. A bad case: nice girl murdered the day before her wedding, right behind her synagogue. Heart cut out. Swastika carved into the empty space. I thought it was the boyfriend because, as it happened, that nice Orthodox Jewish girl had a lover. A swastika's a good way to say *HATE* to a Jew, and I figured Adam, who was Jewish, would see it my way. He didn't. Instead, he dreamed up some theory about ritual Navajo shit, on account of the swastika being backward. Anyway, they buried that girl, and the case went cold.

Adam was never right afterward. Started talking to himself, and when I asked, he'd just say there was a ghost hitching a ride in his head and not to pay any attention. Then he decided, six months ago, that he liked the taste of gunmetal.

And, oh yeah—*he blew his brains out in Rock Creek Park.*

Coincidence? I'm superstitious. All cops are superstitious. Too much coincidence: Halloween, the Hebrew. Rock Creek. Bad karma, that's what.

God, I missed Adam. Damn him.

My phone sputtered as I turned left on Indiana. I thumbed it on. "Saunders."

"Jason." It was Kay. "We've started the cut."

"That was fast, Kay."

"It's a kid. Anyway, we found something."

The autopsy suite was cold and smelled of disinfectant. After I gowned and put on a blue surgical cap and paper booties, I walked over to the autopsy table where they were doing the boy. Kay was there, along with the chief ME, a guy named Strand who's been there about a thousand years.

"Detective Saunders." Strand held a small circular saw, and I could see that they'd done the baby's chest and abdomen. The boy's neck was braced with a block from a two-by-four, his scalp peeled from his skull front and back. Strand powered up the saw. The saw hissed, like the pneumatic drills they use in dentist's offices. "You're just in time. Tricky job on a newborn, on account of the skull being so soft."

"Uh-huh," I said. Strand is not my favorite person.

"Over here, Jason," Kay said. She thinks Strand's an asshole too. She stood at a stainless steel counter along the far wall.

I walked over. Behind us, the whine of the saw dropped as it bit bone. "What do you have?"

"This." She laid out an evidence bag. Inside the bag was a three-inch square of tan cloth. "We found it under the tongue."

"Tongue?"

"Folded nice and neat. You took so long, I called for someone to laser it."

"And?"

"No prints. Blood matches the baby's. There's something written on it. Drawn, anyway."

"You're kidding." I turned the bag over, and felt my stomach bottom out.

In the center of the cloth was a Star of David. In the center of the star and at the three uppermost points were Hebrew letters. Below the star was a crude drawing of a bull's-eye set atop a pole. Along the pole were six phalanges, curved up like scimitars: three to a side.

"First the tattoo," said Kay. "Now this. This case is getting weird, Jason."

I let my breath out a little at a time. "Yeah."

There was a Behavioral Sciences guy worked a case with Adam and me a few years back. A *holy shit* case is an FBI name for something religious. You know: seven deadly sins in blood, that sort of crap. If you're unsure, there's probably a movie in the multiplex, bring you right up to speed.

So here's what I had: a dead baby. A strange tattoo. A cloth with a Jewish star and Hebrew. Like I said, *Holy Shit.*

Before I left the morgue, I went into Kay's office and called Rollins. As I suspected, he'd come up empty on the tattoo. I told him about the cloth. "So I'm going to fax a copy. I want you to run it against the gang symbols we've got in our database. Start with the star. That ought to be easy. I can think of a couple groups right off the bat, like Gangster Disciples, or Folk Nation. The New Breed Black Gangsters use the star along with three *L*s. And I want you to call Gold. Tell her we want a formal statement. Have her there by four."

"But tomorrow mor—"

"Just call her."

"Okay. And you'll be . . . ?"

"Checking something out." I thumbed off, folded my phone, and tucked it into an inside pocket. Then I fed the fax.

Kay caught me as I left. "Photos of the tattoo and cloth *in situ,*" she said, handing over an envelope. "I'll call you soonest. But so far, he's clean."

"Thanks. Look, I want you to run something for me." I told her what I wanted.

"Looking for?"

"Maybe nothing. How long?"

"FBI developed a standard profile. We've got the setup. Say, three, four hours. You want a match with the FBI?"

"No, I just want it on file."

"Okay." Then: "You've got something."

"All I've got is coincidence. That's not something." *Yet,* I thought.

This case was worse than what I'd done with Adam. No matter what Adam said, I knew *that* case hadn't been about religion. But *this*—I corkscrewed the car down the parking garage, turned right on 23rd, and headed for the Lincoln Memorial—this case stunk to high heaven. Turning right on Constitution, I took the ramp past the E Street Expressway, the Kennedy Center on my right, and headed for Route 50 and Fairfax, Virginia.

When I found the place, I killed the engine and just sat. After all the junk last year, the congregation had relocated and built a new synagogue. As I watched, two men came out of a side door, their arms linked. They were arguing something, their free hands going like semaphores. They wore identical outfits: black overcoats that reached to their knees, black fedoras. One had a snowy white beard that reached his waist. The other was much younger, his beard full and black and bushy around his face, like a teddy bear.

There were security cameras mounted above the locked door, and I buzzed. They'd been vandalized, I heard. I selected a yarmulke from a wooden box mounted to the right of the door and patted it on. The rabbi's secretary, a woman named Miriam who wore a kerchief over her hair, long-sleeved shirt, and ankle-length skirt, told me to go on up.

The rabbi was seeing someone else out. The other man was very old, his beard like gray fringe. He said something in querulous Yiddish. The rabbi responded in Yiddish, patting the old man on the back, his tone soothing.

The rabbi watched the old man totter down the stairs. "Not a happy man," I said.

The rabbi, whose name is Dietterich, turned his brown gaze on me. "He doesn't have a reason to be happy." (Dietterich's from Queens, so I think Shea Stadium every time he opens his mouth.) "Yakov's daughter wants to marry a goy. Nice boy, I met him. He says he'll convert, but for Yakov, it's a calamity."

"How so?"

"Yakov survived Birchenau. He's the only one of his family left. For Yakov, his daughter does this, it's like Hitler won. That's why we Lubavitchers are so important. We keep the traditions alive, so people don't forget." Dietterich clapped his hands together as if to signal the subject closed. "So, Detective Saunders, come in, sit."

Dietterich's office was cramped, the shelves overflowing with books. He

offered coffee, and I accepted: black with two sugars. He handed me a mug
and then dropped into his seat with a slight groan. When we met last year,
I judged him to be my age, thirty-five or so. He'd aged. Gray streaked his
temples. Deep lines fanned the corners of his eyes and his face was pinched,
with a furrow chiseled into either side of his nose.

"So," he said, blowing on his coffee. "How can I help you?"

"I need your opinion." I showed him the drawings, and he studied them in
silence. I sipped coffee and waited. The coffee was worse than mine. I put the
mug on the floor.

When his eyes inched up again, he was frowning. "Where did you get
this?"

"I'm sorry, I can't tell you. It's an ongoing investigation. I can only ask the
questions, not answer them."

"All right." Dietterich placed his mug on a side table. "Yes, I know the
symbols. What this is, exactly, I'm not sure."

"What do you mean?"

"I mean it doesn't make sense. In essence, you have part of a formula."

"Formula?"

"Yes, for a protective amulet."

"Against what?"

Dietterich hesitated, then said. "Evil. You have to understand, Detective.
Judaism is a religion without a pantheon. In the distant past, calamities were
ascribed to evil demons and dark forces, whereas Judaism holds that these
things come from Hashem, from God. But illiterate and superstitious peasants
are slow to change. Superstitions persisted into the early half of the last
century."

I remembered Gold, and her key. "You're talking mysticism."

"Yes. Our Tanya, for instance, is based upon very ancient Kabbalah,
but only certain aspects, you understand. There are many obscure areas of
Kabbalah known only to very devout Jews, or to scholars. Most work is not in
translation, because of the dangers."

"Dangers."

"Of misinterpretation. Leading Jews to pursue paths that are specifically
prohibited because these practices are antithetical to our faith. How do I say
it?" Dietterich put a finger to his lips. "There is a branch of theory, and a
branch of practice. Devout scholars study, but that is all."

"Tell me about the practice."

Dietterich raised his hands, palms up. "What's to say? There are no Jewish
witches."

"Well, someone hasn't gotten the message."

"You think a *Jew* did this?" He moved his head firmly from side to side. "No. The prohibition in Exodus is very clear."

"But you said it yourself: superstitions persist. So, is this what the drawings are about?"

"These drawings are just bits and pieces." He went to a bookshelf, tilted out a book, and brought it back, flipping pages. I read the cover: *Amulets and Superstitions.* "Here," he said, then came to stand behind my right shoulder.

There was Hebrew text above and below a rectangle filled with crude, almost childish drawings. The rectangle was divided into two. On the left were what looked like bulbous birds with no wings, and bubble feet with no talons. On the right, there were two bizarre quadrangles, and then a drawing I recognized: the pole with the phalanges.

"What is that?"

"Part of a formula. This is a copy of a design for an amulet from a book that's in the British Museum, the *Book of Râzîêl.*" He pronounced it *RAY-zay-el.* "The formula's very precise. On the left are representations of three angels: Sanvi, Sanasanvi, and Samnaglof."

"And on the right?"

"Adam, Eve," and then he came to the pole, "and Lilith."

"Lilith?"

Dietterich sighed. "A myth. In Genesis, there is a curious section concerning creation. At the end of the first chapter, Hashem creates male and female. But, if you look at the second chapter, verse eighteen, Adam is alone again, and Eve is not created until verse twenty-two."

"So who is that first woman?"

"Lilith. The Mystics called her the First Eve. You find her in Midrash, in legends. According to Midrash, Lilith refused Hashem's injunction to submit to Adam. So she fled, using Hashem's Ineffable Name: Y–H–W–H. Hashem sent these three angels—Sanvi, Sanasanvi, and Samnaglof—to bring her back, but Lilith refused. In the end they let her go, but only if she agreed to leave whenever their names or images were invoked."

"Which is why they're on the amulet. You draw the angels, and Lilith has to obey and go away."

"Exactly. Anyway, Adam was lonely, and so Eve was created, and here is where things become very murky. According to some Midrash, Adam blamed Eve for the expulsion from Eden, and he reunited with Lilith. Some say he had relations with one of Lilith's daughters, Piznai, and produced many demon-children called *lutins.* Others say Lilith was Adam's consort, but then when Adam reconciled with Eve, Lilith vowed to take revenge by killing human children, primarily infant boys before their *bris milah,* their circumcision, on the eighth day after birth. The legends say that Hashem punishes Lilith by killing a hundred of *her* demon-children every day."

"Sounds like a soap."

"Yes," said Dietterich, tugging at his beard. "Demons, demon-children. All nonsense."

"But it's in your rabbinic tradition."

"No, it's Midrash. They're stories, not canonical."

I decided not to press. "So how does this figure in?"

"The amulet is protective. The Hebrew text at the top names the Seventy Great Angels who would protect in a general way. Sanvi, Sanasanvi, and Samnaglof protect the mother and her child. The text below is an incantation designed to ward off Lilith."

"How widespread was this practice?"

"Of the amulet? It varied. Eastern Europe, Germany. Jewish peasants had a custom called Watch Night, where women would stand guard over the baby the evening before his *bris*."

"And the drawing I showed you? It's protective?"

"No," he said, his tone almost fierce. He held up my notepad, shook it. "No, you see that's why I'm telling you: no Jew did this."

"But I thought you said—"

"It's *wrong*," he said, thrusting the notepad toward me. "They got it wrong. The Magen David? The Hebrew? Usually, the Hebrew stands for angels. But here, the Hebrew stands for demons: Ashmedi, Samael, and Azazel."

"Why would they be on the same amulet with Lilith?"

"Because whoever made this didn't want to keep Lilith *away*," said Dietterich, his eyes drilling me in place. "He *summoned* her."

My phone buzzed as I crossed the Roosevelt Bridge into DC. It was Kay. "Done," she said.

"Good. And the cut?"

"A big zero." She sounded tired. "Jason, that little boy . . . he just . . . died."

Rollins met me as I came off the elevator. "You're late. Gold's here. I put her in Room Three."

"Okay." I walked to my desk and retrieved a tape recorder from the bottom drawer.

Rollins watched. "I ran the drawings. Nothing matches."

I checked the batteries then tore the cellophane off two fresh ninety-minute cassettes. "Nothing's going to."

"You think Gold . . . ?"

I popped in a cassette. "I don't know."

"On the basis of?"

"Nothing. That's the problem."

"Yeah." Rollins eyed the recorder. "Should we advise her of her rights?"

"No. We don't have anything. For now, she's a wit, and I just want to talk with her, get a formal statement drafted. Very low key. We talk about rights, and she'll clam up."

We went in together. Gold was waiting, a Styrofoam coffee cup in one hand. She was dressed in blue jeans and a long-sleeved peasant blouse. I saw the key in the hollow of her throat. She didn't smile.

"You're looking better," I said, scraping a chair back from the table. Rollins dropped into a chair on my left.

"A hot shower does wonders," she said. "I had a heck of a time combing burrs out of Rugby's fur, though."

"Yeah, I'm still picking that stuff off my coat." I watched her face as I squared the recorder on the table.

Her eyes flicked to the recorder and back. "You don't use a court reporter?"

"No, that's for depositions, legal stuff. This is just a statement. I'll type it up later, and then you can sign it, okay? You want more coffee?"

She wrinkled her nose. "No. It's pretty bad, actually."

"It's cop coffee." I told her how we'd proceed then turned on the recorder. I recited my name, the date, our location, her name, and the purpose of the interview. Then I led her through her story again. She recited the same information, her voice a soft monotone. When she was done, I said, "I want to back up. You said you got ahead of the dog?"

"Yes. You know dogs."

"Okay. Then you turned back."

"Right. And that's when I heard her barking, to the left, and then I saw her down the hill."

"So you were on the path?"

"Uh-huh."

"Yeah, that's a problem," I said, doing my best Columbo. I looked at Rollins. "You see the problem?"

Rollins shrugged. "There's a problem?"

"Yeah, don't you remember that hill? I couldn't see a thing from the path. Hill's too steep."

"Really," said Rollins, and I could tell he saw where I was going. He played it just right. "You couldn't?"

"No," I said, and looked back at Gold, whose face was stony. "I couldn't, and I'm pretty tall. So how could you see the dog?"

A blotch of crimson stained Gold's throat. "Maybe I left the path. I don't remember."

"That would explain it," said Rollins.

"Yeah, maybe that's it," I said. "Because there's no way to see down that hill. But then . . . "

"Yes, Detective?" Gold's tone was neutral.

"Your clothes. You didn't have any burrs. I had burrs on my coat. The dog had burrs."

"I had burrs," said Rollins.

"You didn't have any burrs," I said to Gold. "But you should have. Your shoes weren't even wet."

Gold looked from me to Rollins and back again. "Are you accusing me of something, Detective? If you are, I should have a lawyer."

"I'm just trying to clear up a discrepancy, Miss Gold."

"No, you're not." She leaned forward, getting into my space, not intimidated in the slightest. "Listen to me. I did not kill that child. Now, I'm sorry if you and Detective Rollins can't find anyone to blame . . . "

"Hey," said Rollins.

Her gaze didn't waver, and I felt her take control. "But just because I may have made a mistake on where I was standing, or didn't have garbage on my clothes, doesn't mean I did anything wrong. Someone killed that little boy, and it wasn't me."

I tried to recoup. "You know who kills little babies, Miss Gold? It's not only their daddy, or their mommy's coked-up boyfriend, or some sick sex predator-creep. I'll tell who kills little babies: mothers. Sometimes that mother is depressed and suicidal and wants to take her child to a better place. Sometimes that mother wants attention. So she makes her child sick, and then there are all those doctors, and she feels important. And then there are mothers who are simply evil."

"Evil," said Gold. For the first time, I saw not defiance but astonishment cross Gold's features. "Is that what you think? You think that's *my* baby?"

Actually, until that moment, that's exactly what I'd thought. All I'd seen her in were baggy clothes, for one. And pieces of her story didn't fit. But Gold's reaction was genuine. You can't do a hundred million hours of interrogations and not know when someone's honestly amazed.

Gold gave a mirthless laugh. "I can't believe this. There are tests, right? To prove maternity?"

"Yes," I said, knowing already what we'd find. "DNA that we—"

"Fine." Gold held out her arms. "Which one?"

∎ ∎ ∎

She wasn't the mother.

My condo's off Lee Highway, in Arlington. I grew up in DC and now I work it. I can't live there. On the way home, I bought Thai takeout and then picked up a six-pack of icy-cold Bangkok beer. I ate my pad Thai out of the carton, had a beer. Then I popped a second beer, put on Mingus, and settled into my favorite—my only—recliner. I sleep there a lot. I don't know any single guy sleeps in his bed. We sleep on couches, chairs. Never the bed. And in our clothes, usually.

Rabbi Dietterich had given me a book on Kabbalah. Then, as we had shaken hands, he said, "I have often thought about Detective Lennox. His death, such a tragedy. You and I both know there are demons and monsters everywhere. Nazis, murderers. But what are not so easy are the monsters that are hidden." Dietterich bunched his fists and brought them to his chest. "The ones in here, in the dark chambers of the heart. Detective Lennox was a Jew, but he had no faith, and he found his monsters. Or they found him. Hashem can help, but a man must have faith, and he must work. We Jews are not like you Christians. We don't believe that Hashem makes everything better. Hashem can be harsh. Life is sometimes unfair. But we believe that Hashem gives us a fighting chance."

He clapped a hand to my right shoulder. "You're a good man, Detective Saunders. An honest man. Please take care not to let your monsters destroy you."

Now, thumbing to the index, I found a section on demons and paged there. The Kabbalists were big believers in an unseen spirit world, with some rabbis claiming that demons are consigned to a dark netherworld, and others stating that demons are born from sex between humans and demonic spirits. The rabbis agreed on six demonic attributes. In common with angels, demons have wings, can fly from one end of the earth to another, and tell the future. Like humans, however, they need food and water. They have sex. And, unlike the angels, they're mortal.

I flipped to a section on regional beliefs. I found North Africa, the Near East. But this leapt off the page:

> One of the most comprehensive works is the Zefunei Ziyyoni. Written in the late fourteenth century by Menachem Zion of Cologne, this book has the most extensive list of important demons and how they functioned. This German-born Kabbalist was influential in disseminating Arabic thought amongst the practical Kabbalists concentrated in Eastern Europe and Germany.

There it was: the *practical* Kabbalists. Translation: the witches. And Germany.

Something sparked in my brain. Quickly, I went to my coat and pulled out the packet of autopsy photos Kay had given me, flipping until I found the one of the tattoo.

To this day, I don't know how I got there. There was no logic. The sensation truly was a flash: like a bare bulb flaring to life in a dark basement. And then I knew.

I checked the index. But what I was looking for wasn't under *R*. It was under *G*: for "*gilgul.*"

I spent the rest of the night reading, thinking. I went online and did a search. It took time, but I found what I was looking for. Compared the information to what I had. As soon as the museums opened, I made a couple calls. The employment stuff was easy, even the call to Sydney, though it was evening there and the director a little grumpy until I went over what I wanted and why.

Then I called the Holocaust Museum. The information clerk funneled me to an archivist. When I explained, there was a moment's silence. Then the archivist said, "Not many people know about that. Unfortunately, those early records are lost. I'm sorry."

Then I made one last call. She picked up on the third ring. "Hello, Detective. No magic: caller ID. What do you want?"

I told her where to meet me. "Should I bring my lawyer?" she asked.

"No. I just want to talk."

"I'll be there," she said, and hung up.

My office away from the office: the bar's across the street from the Shakespeare Theatre on 7th and diagonal to Jaleo's, a Spanish tapas place where the beautiful people eat before going to the theatre. So I never go there.

I saw her come in, look around, start toward me. Her coat was open, and she wore a beige skirt that came to her knees, a cream linen blouse, and linen pumps. She had the pendant. When she'd slid onto the cushioned bench opposite mine and shrugged out of her coat, we did the waitress thing— bourbon for me, white wine for her.

Then she asked, "What did you want to see me about, Detective?"

"I want to tell you a story."

"Story?"

"Yeah, bear with me. See, there was once a terrible war. The people who suffered the most were the Jews."

The corners of her mouth quirked. "That could be all of Jewish history."

"But in this war, there was a demon. I believe devout Jews think of Hitler as Amalek, right?"

"That's right. Amalek was the great-great-grandson of Abraham, and there are specific injunctions to beware of Amalekites. Amalek has come to symbolize all evil."

"Okay. So Evil attacks the Jews. The Jews are expelled from their homes. Whole villages are destroyed; the Jews are killed, or sent to concentration camps. Some survive and they remember. But they're worried others will forget. And some can't let that past go. They wonder why they were spared. And they're lonely."

"This is," she began, then stopped when the waitress came with our drinks. The waitress tacked a napkin to the table with Gold's wine, slid one under my bourbon. When she'd gone, Gold said, "Do you have a point?"

I angled my glass toward a candle burning in a squat glass holder, liking the way the light shone gold through the liquor. "I'm getting to the best part. Isn't it true that the reason Chassids dress the way they do is to preserve a piece of their past?"

"That's one interpretation."

"So what keeps someone from preserving other customs, rituals?"

"Such as?"

"Magic."

She gave a very small half smile. She raised her glass, tipped wine into her mouth. "Jews don't believe in magic."

"Yes, they do." I flicked a finger at her pendant. "That thing, that's magic, right?"

"It's just a necklace."

"No. It's very specific. I know, because I looked it up." Reaching into my pocket, I pulled out my notepad and flipped. "Yeah, here it is. That *shin* is a really interesting letter. It means the Eternal Flame, and it reflects the fact that God is changeless, forever. There are some other things about *shin* I don't get."

"The mystical meanings."

"Right. And I have to admit I couldn't figure the key until I read about this very important angel named Râzîêl. Râzîêl sits at God's throne and takes notes, and he's written a book in which he recorded all celestial and earthly secrets. I've seen a picture from the book. To the Kabbalists, the book is a key. In fact, Râzîêl's book is supposed to hold the fifteen hundred keys to the secrets of the universe." I closed my notebook. "And Râzîêl's color is gold."

Her eyes were hooded. "And?"

"And Râzîêl, Rachel . . . the names are very close, don't you think?"

"Yes." She sipped wine. "Quite a coincidence."

"Know something else?"

"What?"

"You told the truth. You didn't kill that baby." I paused. "But you let evil destroy itself."

"And why would I do that?"

I slid out the photograph of the baby's chest. "The tattoo. We got it wrong, because of the numbers. And the location threw us: over the left breast, not the left forearm. The Germans didn't start putting tattoos on forearms until after 1942. So, that *L*—well, it's not an *L*. It's a triangle. And that letter we thought was a cursive *M*. It's two ones. And the *Z* is a seven. See, we don't put a horizontal line through our sevens and we don't have that long tail on our ones, but Europeans do. Germans do, except the German lady—and it was the ladies who did them—the one who did this tattoo was sloppy. Not all Germans cared, because these were Jews, after all. But this is a number, Miss Gold: a triangle, then 1-1-7-2-9. Auschwitz Prisoner 1-1-7-2-9."

I leaned forward. "Tell me about *gilguls,* Miss Gold."

Her face was unreadable. "What would you like to know?"

"Whatever you can tell me about reincarnation."

"Why don't *you* tell *me,* Detective? You're the one with the story."

I nodded. "Fair enough. Here's how I think it goes: the Kabbalists believed in reincarnation because they thought all souls came from one great big soul. An Oversoul, I guess you'd call it. Reincarnation isn't supposed to happen until a person dies. But the Kabbalists said there was *ibur,* meaning pregnant. That is, a person who already had a soul could house another: two for the price of one. But that was very rare and only happened when the person was very, very good."

"A *tzaddik.* A righteous person."

"But I also found a very obscure reference to an old ritual where a Kabbalist could conjure a soul to share, or take over another body. Here's the kicker: it's got to be a kid. Boys are best. The infant is to be left alone, outside, near water and within a week after birth, or if it's a boy, before his circumcision." I looked into her eyes. "I'll bet some of those Holocaust survivors would do just about anything to bring their families back. Even witchcraft."

"Yes, they would," she said, her voice calm. "But it's not their place. Only God can decide."

I nodded. "So, tell me, Rachel . . . your name *is* Rachel?"

Her lips curled slightly. "It'll do."

"I don't suppose you'd tell me who Prisoner 11792 was, would you? The records from 1941 aren't too good."

"I can't do that. That's for God now."

"I figured. But when they conjured the *gilgul* of their lost relative, it was *your* job to stop them. That's why you summoned Lilith to take the child."

She inclined her head. The key glittered in candlelight. "The child was an abomination."

"From where I'm sitting, it's murder even if you didn't do it. You could have saved that child. You could have taken it to a hospital." And yet, I had an involuntary thought: how many times had God killed in the name of justice? The great paradox of the Bible: a book that preaches against killing venerates one of the greatest mass murderers in history.

As if reading my mind—and maybe she could—Gold said, "There are choices, Detective. God can't rescue you every time you make the wrong one. There are consequences, and sometimes the consequences are unpleasant. Sometimes the consequences include death."

We were silent a moment. Then she asked, "How did you know?"

"Honestly? A leap of faith. Your employment record, for example. You've shown up in a lot of different places, but there's one thing those places all have in common. They have huge Orthodox populations, mostly German and Eastern European. I'll bet if I looked, there'd be a string of dead kids before you moved on. And there was that pendant, of course. But the clincher?" I took a sip of my bourbon, savoring the burn. "Your shoes. Like I said—no burrs. But they weren't muddy either, or wet. And then it hit me."

"What?"

"You didn't have to walk, and do you know why?" I grinned then, not quite believing I was going to say it until I did. "Because you flew."

When a body isn't claimed, the city buries it. Or volunteers: churches, synagogues, charities. So I wasn't surprised when Jews buried that baby the night before Halloween.

It's a year later now. October, again. Halloween. A lot of fall color left. The sky is gunmetal gray and the weatherman said rain, so it'll probably snow.

The cemetery's quiet. King David, it's called. There are stones, flowers. I don't know why I'm here. I stare down at a child's grave. The stone is new: *ben Judah,* son of Israel. A date. A tiny Jewish star.

I think about Rachel Gold. And I come back to the two questions I faced now that I faced then: how the hell do you prosecute an angel? How do you know you should even arrest her?

When we walked out of the darkness of that bar a year ago and into the late afternoon sun, Rachel had said, "What will you write in your report?"

"I don't know. Probably nothing. No one would believe it anyway, and I haven't got a shred of real evidence."

The sun glinted off her key. "But *you* believe."

"Yes." I stared down at her a few moments. "You're leaving." Not a question.

"Yes. It's a big world, Detective Saunders. A lot of monsters to hunt."

I nodded. "Mind if I ask you a question? Why did you stay? You had to know about Adam and Rabbi Dietterich. And the way you've left your tracks out there for anyone to see . . . you had to know that, eventually, I'd figure this out."

For the rest of my life, I will remember how she looked at me then: with great compassion and something very close to love.

"Detective, how do you know that *you* are not the one for whom I remained?" Then, before I could speak, she stepped forward and spread the fingers of her right hand over my heart, and a surge of emotion flooded my chest so that I had to fight for breath. It was like something had come alive in there and was being pushed, no, *forced* out—and I knew that when I was alone, I would cry in a way that I hadn't since I was a small child.

"Wounds of the heart are the most difficult to heal," she said gently. "There are many monsters, Detective. But there are the angels. We are here. All you need to do is know how to look."

And then I'd watched her move west, into the light of the setting sun. The light was so brilliant my eyes watered and I had to blink. When I'd opened them again, she was gone.

Since then, well, it's been a long year. One thing, though: I don't think about Adam as much, and when I do, I'm not as angry. I'm just sad, and even that's getting less over time, as if the past is bleaching out of my mind like an old photograph, the kind where people fade into ghosts and then penumbras—and then they're just gone, with only the suggestion of an outline to show that they'd been there at all. So that's probably good.

I hear the crunch of gravel. Then, a voice I recognize: "Detective Saunders."

"Rabbi." We shake hands. "What brings you here?"

Dietterich's in his standard uniform: long black coat, the hat. A quizzical look creases his features. "I don't really know. I visit cemeteries, though. I pay respect. There are so many," he gestures toward the markers, the flowers, "and never enough time to remember them all. And you?"

"Just thinking. Actually, I was getting ready to leave."

"Ah." He nods. We stare at the grave. Then, without looking up, he says, "Whatever happened with that case?"

"We didn't catch anyone." That's about as close to the truth as I can go, even with him—because he was right. There are some things people just aren't meant to handle.

He looks over, and his eyes are keen. "But you found an answer. You found some measure of peace."

"Yes. Yes, I did."

Dietterich nods. "Did you know that Detective Lennox came to see me a few months before he died?"

I'm genuinely taken aback. "No. Why?"

"I think he wanted to unburden himself, but he couldn't, or maybe he wouldn't. He came a few times. We had coffee. Then he just stopped coming, and I didn't call. Perhaps I should have."

"Adam had a choice." It's taken me a while, but now I can say it. "Adam may have had his monsters, but people have to want the help. They have to want to work at being free."

Dietterich sighs. "Yes. I see so many people in pain, Detective, more than you can know. Sometimes I think God asks the impossible."

"A leap of faith?"

"Nothing makes sense otherwise, does it?"

"I guess not." I stick out my hand. "I should go."

"Let's go together." Dietterich smiles. "We'll have coffee."

"I'd like that," I say, and mean it. "Cop coffee stinks."

Dietterich laughs. He loops his arm through mine, just like I've seen all those Chassids do. "I'll let you in on a secret. So does Miriam's."

We walk toward the entrance. As we step onto the sidewalk, into the world of the living, a sudden bolt of light knifes the clouds. Sun splashes gold upon the walk and touches the leaves with fire.

We walk, together, into the light.

Ilsa J. Bick is a child psychiatrist, as well as a film scholar, surgeon wannabe, former Air Force major, and an award-winning author of dozens of short stories and novels, including the critically acclaimed *Draw the Dark*; *Drowning Instinct*; *Ashes*, the first book in her YA apocalyptic thriller trilogy; and the just-released second volume, *Shadows*. Forthcoming are *The Sin-Eater's Confession* and the last installment in the Ashes Trilogy, *Monsters*. Ilsa lives with her family and other furry creatures near a Hebrew cemetery in rural Wisconsin. One thing she loves about the neighbors: they're very quiet and only come around for sugar once in a blue moon. Visit her at www.ilsajbick.com.

The Case: *Someone has been killed and the dead man wants to know who and why.*

The Investigators: *Larry Oblivion—with a name like that what else could he be but a private investigator?—and his partner and ex-lover, Maggie Boniface.*

THE NIGHTSIDE, NEEDLESS TO SAY

Simon R. Green

The Nightside is the secret, sick, magical heart of London. A city within a city, where the night never ends and it's always three o'clock in the morning. Hot neon reflects from rain-slick streets, and dreams go walking in borrowed flesh. You can find pretty much anything in the Nightside, except happy endings. Gods and monsters run confidence tricks, and all desires can be satisfied, if you're willing to pay the price. Which might be money and might be service, but nearly always ends up meaning your soul. The Nightside, where the sun never shows its face because if it did, someone would probably try to steal it. When you've nowhere else to go, the Nightside will take you in. Trust no one, including yourself, and you might get out alive again.

Some of us work there, for our sins. Or absolution, or atonement. It's that kind of place.

Larry! Larry! What's wrong?

The sharp, whispered voice pulled me up out of a bad dream; something about running in the rain, running from something awful. I sat up in bed, looked around, and didn't know where I was. It wasn't my bedroom. Harsh neon light flickered red and green through the slats of the closed shutters, intermittently revealing a dark dusty room with cheap and nasty furniture. There was nobody else there, but the words still rang in my ears. I sat on the edge of the bed, trying to remember my dream, but it was already fading. I was fully dressed, and there were no bedsheets. I still had my shoes on. I had no idea what day it was.

I got up and turned on the bedside light. The room wasn't improved by being seen clearly, but at least I knew where I was. An old safe house, in one of the seedier areas of the Nightside. A refuge I hadn't had to use in years. I still kept up the rent; because you never know when you're going to need a bolt-hole in a hurry. I turned out my pockets. Everything where it should be, and nothing new to explain what I was doing here. I shook my head slowly, then left the room, heading for the adjoining bathroom. Explanations could wait, until I'd taken care of something that couldn't.

The bathroom's bright fluorescent light was harsh and unforgiving as I studied my face in the medicine cabinet mirror. Pale and washed-out, under straw blond hair, good bone structure, and a mouth and eyes that never gave anything away. My hair was a mess, but I didn't need a shave. I shrugged, dropped my trousers and shorts, and sat down on the porcelain throne. There was a vague uneasy feeling in my bowels and then a sudden lurch as something within made a bid for freedom. I tapped my foot impatiently, listening to a series of splashes. Something bad must have happened, even if I couldn't remember it. I needed to get out of here and start asking pointed questions of certain people. Someone would know. Someone always knows.

The splashes finally stopped, but something didn't feel right. I got up, turned around, and looked down into the bowl. It was full of maggots. Curling and twisting and squirming. I made a horrified sound and stumbled backward. My legs tangled in my lowered trousers, and I fell full length on the floor. My head hit the wall hard. It didn't hurt. I scrambled to my feet, pulled up my shorts and trousers, and backed out of the bathroom, still staring at the toilet.

It was the things that weren't happening that scared me most. I should have been hyperventilating. My heart should have been hammering in my chest. My face should have been covered in a cold sweat. But when I checked my wrist, then my throat, there wasn't any pulse. And I wasn't breathing hard because I wasn't breathing at all. I couldn't remember taking a single breath since I woke up. I touched my face with my fingertips, and they both felt cold.

I was dead.

Someone had killed me. I knew that, though I didn't know how. The maggots suggested I'd been dead for some time. So, who killed me, and why hadn't I noticed it till now?

My name's Larry Oblivion, and with a name like that I pretty much had to be a private investigator. Mostly I do corporate work: industrial espionage, checking out backgrounds, helping significant people defect from one organization to another. Big business has always been where the real money is. I don't do divorce cases, or solve mysteries, and I've never even owned a trench coat. I wear Gucci, I make more money than most people ever dream of, and I pack a wand. Don't snigger. I took the wand in payment for a case involving the Unseelie Court, and I've never regretted it. Two feet long, and carved from the spine of a species that never existed in the waking world, the wand could stop time, for everyone except me. More than enough to give me an edge, or a running start. You take all the advantages you can get when you operate in the Nightside. No one else knew I had the wand.

Unless . . . someone had found out and killed me to try and get their hands on it.

I found the coffee maker and fixed myself my usual pick-me-up. Black coffee, steaming hot, and strong enough to jump-start a mummy from its sleep. But when it was ready, I didn't want it. Apparently the walking dead don't drink coffee. Damn. I was going to miss that.

Larry! Larry!

I spun round, the words loud in my ear, but still there was no one else in the room. Just a voice, calling my name. For a moment I almost remembered something horrid, then it was gone before I could hold on to it. I scowled, pacing up and down the room to help me think. I was dead, I'd been murdered. So, start with the usual suspects. Who had reason to want me dead? Serious reasons. I had my share of enemies, but that was just the price of doing business. No one murders anyone over business.

No; start with my ex-wife, Donna Tramen. She had reasons to hate me. I fell in love with a client, Margaret Boniface, and left my wife for her. The affair didn't work out, but Maggie and I remained friends. In fact, we worked so well together I made her a partner in my business. My wife hadn't talked to me since I moved out, except through her lawyer, but if she was going to kill me, she would have done it long ago. And the amount of money the divorce judge awarded her gave her a lot of good reasons for wanting me alive. As long as the cheques kept coming.

Next up: angry or disappointed clients, where the case hadn't worked out to everyone's satisfaction. There were any number of organizations in and out of the Nightside that I'd stolen secrets or personnel from. But none of them would take such things personally. Today's target might be tomorrow's client, so everyone stayed polite. I never got involved in the kinds of cases where passions were likely to be raised. No one's ever made movies about the kind of work I do.

I kept feeling I already knew the answer, but it remained stubbornly out of reach. Perhaps because . . . I didn't want to remember. I shuddered suddenly, and it wasn't from the cold. I picked up the phone beside the bed, and called my partner. Maggie picked up on the second ring, as though she'd been waiting for a call.

"Maggie, this is Larry. Listen, you're not going to believe what's happened . . . "

"Larry, you've been missing for three days! Where are you?"

Three days . . . A trail could get real cold in three days.

"I'm at the old safe house on Blaiston Street. I think you'd better come and get me."

"What the hell are you doing there? I didn't know we still had that place on the books."

"Just come and get me. I'm in trouble."

Her voice changed immediately. "What kind of trouble, Larry?"

"Let's just say . . . I think I'm going to need some of your old expertise, Mama Bones."

"Don't use that name on an open line! It's been a long time since I was a mover and shaker on the voodoo scene, and hopefully most people have forgotten Margaret Boniface was ever involved. I'm clean now. One day at a time, sweet Jesus."

"You know I wouldn't ask if it wasn't important. I need what you used to know. Get here as fast as you can. And, Maggie, don't tell anyone where you're going. We can't trust anyone but each other."

She laughed briefly. "Business as usual, in the Nightside."

I did a lot more pacing and thinking in the half hour it took Maggie to reach Blaiston Street, but I was no wiser at the end of it. My memories stopped abruptly three days ago, with no warning of what was to come. I kept watch on and off through the slats of the window shutters, and was finally rewarded with the sight of Maggie pulling up to the curb in her cherry-red Jaguar. Protective spells sparked briefly around the car as she got out and looked up at my window. Tall and slender, an ice-cool blonde with a buzz cut and a heavy scarlet mouth. She dressed like a diva, walked like a princess, and carried a silver-plated magnum derringer in her purse, next to her aboriginal pointing bone. She had a sharp, incisive mind, and given a few more years experience and the right contacts, she'd be ten times the operative I was. I never told her that, of course. I didn't want her getting overconfident.

She rapped out our special knock on the door, the one that said yes she had checked, and no, no one had followed her. I let her in, and she checked the room out professionally before turning to kiss my cheek. And then she stopped, and looked at me.

"Larry . . . you look half dead."

I smiled briefly. "You don't know the *half* of it."

I gave her the bad news, and she took it as well as could be expected. She insisted on checking my lack of a pulse or heartbeat for herself, then stepped back from me and hugged herself tightly. I don't think she liked the way my cold flesh felt. I tried to make light of what had happened, complaining that my life must have been really dull if neither Heaven nor Hell were interested in claiming me, but neither of us was fooled. In the end, we sat side by side on the bed, and discussed what we should do next in calm, professional voices.

"You've no memory at all of being killed?" Maggie said finally.

"No. I'm dead, but not yet departed. Murdered, but still walking around. Which puts me very much in your old territory, oh mistress of the mystic arts."

"Oh please! So I used to know a little voodoo . . . Practically everyone in my family does. Where we come from, it's no big thing. And I was never involved in anything like this . . . "

"Can you help me, or not?"

She scowled. "All right. Let me run a few diagnostics on you."

"Are we going to have to send out for a chicken?"

"Be quiet, heathen."

She ran through a series of chants in Old French, lit up some incense, then took off all her clothes and danced around the room for a while. I'd probably have enjoyed it if I hadn't been dead. The room grew darker, and there was a sense of unseen eyes watching. Shadows moved slowly across the walls, deep disturbing shapes, though there was nothing in the room to cast them. And then Maggie stopped dancing, and stood facing me, breathing hard, sweat running down her bare body.

"Did you feel anything then?" she said.

"No. Was I supposed to?"

Maggie shrugged briefly and put her clothes back on in a businesslike way. The shadows and the sense of being watched were gone.

"You've been dead for three days," said Maggie. "Someone killed you, then held your spirit in your dead body. There's a rider spell attached, to give you the appearance of normality, but inside you're already rotting. Hence the maggots."

"Can you undo the spell?" I said.

"Larry, you're *dead*. The dead can be made to walk, but no one can bring them all the way back, not even in the Nightside. Whatever we decide to do, your story's over, Larry."

I thought about that for a while. I always thought I would have achieved more, before the end. All the things I meant to do, and kept putting off, because I was young and imagined I had all the time in the world. Larry Oblivion, who always dreamed of something better, but never had the guts to go after it. One ex-wife, one ex-lover, no kids, no legacy. No point and no purpose.

"When all else fails," I said finally, "there's always revenge. I need to find out who killed me and why, while I still can. While there's still enough of me left to savor it."

"Any ideas who it might have been?" said Maggie. "Anyone new you might have upset recently?"

I thought hard. "Prometheus Inc. weren't at all happy over my handling of their poltergeist saboteur. Count Entropy didn't like what I found out about his son, even though he paid me to dig it up. Big Max always said he'd put me in the ground someday . . . "

"Max," Maggie said immediately. "Has to be Max. You've been rivals for years, hurt his business and made him look a fool, more than once. He must have decided to put an end to the competition."

"Why would he want to keep me around after killing me?"

"To gloat! He hated your guts, Larry; it has to be him!"

I thought about it. I'd rubbed Max's nose in it before, and all he ever did was talk. Maybe . . . he'd got tired of talking.

"All right," I said. "Let's go see the big man and ask him a few pointed questions."

"He's got a lot of protection," said Maggie. "Not at all an easy man to get to see."

"Do I look like I care? Are you in or not?"

"Of course I'm in! I'm just pointing out that Big Max is known for surrounding himself with heavy-duty firepower."

I smiled. "Baby, I'm dead. How are they going to stop me?"

We went out into the streets, and walked through the Nightside. The rain had stopped, and the air was sharp with new possibilities. Hot neon blazed on every side, advertising the kinds of love that might not have names, but certainly have prices. Heavy bass lines surged out of open club doors, reverberating in the ground and in my bones. All kinds of people swept past us, intent on their own business. Only some of them were human. Traffic roared constantly up and down the road, and everyone was careful to give it plenty of room. Not everything that looked like a car was a car, and some of them were hungry. In the Nightside, taxis can run on deconsecrated altar wine, and motorcycle messengers snort powdered virgin's blood for that extra kick.

Max's place wasn't far. He holed up in an upmarket cocktail bar called the Spider's Web. Word is he used to work there once. And that he had his old boss killed when he took it over, then had the man stuffed and mounted and put on display. Max never left the place anymore, and held court there from behind more layers of protection than some presidents can boast. The big man had a lot of enemies, and he gloried in it.

Along the way I kept getting quick flashes of déjà vu. Brief glimpses of my dream of running through the rain. Except I was pretty sure by now that it wasn't a dream but a memory. I could feel the desperation as I ran, pursued by something without a face.

The only entrance to the Spider's Web was covered by two large gentlemen with shoulder holsters, and several layers of defensive magics. I knew about the magics because a client had once hired me to find out exactly what Max was using. Come to think of it, no one had seen that client for some time. I murmured to Maggie to hang on to my arm, then drew my wand and activated it. It shone with a brilliant light, too bright to look at, and all around us the world seemed to slow down, and become flat and unreal. The roar of the traffic shut off, and the neon stopped flickering. Maggie and I were outside Time. We walked between the two bodyguards, and they didn't even see us. I could feel the defensive magics straining, reaching out, unable to touch us.

We walked on through the club, threading our way through the frozen crowds. Deeper and deeper, into the lair of the beast. There were things going on that sickened even me, but I didn't have the time to stop and do anything. I only had one shot at this. Maggie held my arm tightly. It would probably have hurt if I'd still been alive.

"Well," she said, trying for a light tone and not even coming close. "A genuine wand of the Faerie. That explains a lot of things."

"It always helps to have an unsuspected edge."

"You could have told me. I am your partner."

"You can never tell who's listening, in the Nightside." I probably would have told her, if she hadn't ended our affair. "But I think I'm past the point of needing secrets anymore."

We found the big man sitting behind a desk in a surprisingly modest inner office. He was playing solitaire with tarot cards, and cheating. Thick mats of ivy crawled across the walls, and the floor was covered with cabalistic symbols. I closed the door behind us so we wouldn't be interrupted, and shut down the wand. Max looked up sharply as we appeared suddenly in front of him. His right hand reached for something, but Maggie already had her silver magnum derringer out and covering him. Max shrugged, sat back in his chair, and studied us curiously.

Max Maxwell, so big they named him twice. A giant of a man, huge and lowering even behind his oversized mahogany desk. Eight feet tall and impressively broad across the shoulders, with a harsh and craggy face, he looked like he was carved out of stone. A gargoyle in a Savile Row suit. Max traded in secrets, and stayed in business because he knew something about everyone. Or at least, everyone who mattered. Even if he hadn't killed me, there was a damned good chance he knew who had.

"Larry Oblivion," he said, in a voice like grinding stone. "My dearest rival and most despised competitor. To what do I owe the displeasure of this unexpected visit?"

"Like you don't already know," said Maggie, her derringer aimed directly between his eyes.

Max ignored her, his gaze fixed on me. "Provide me with one good reason why I shouldn't have both of you killed for this impertinence?"

"How about: you already killed me? Or haven't you noticed that I only breathe when I talk?"

Max studied me thoughtfully. "Yes. You are dead. You have no aura. I wish I could claim the credit, but alas, it seems someone else has beaten me to it. And besides, if I wanted you dead, you'd be dead and gone, not hanging around to trouble me."

"He's right," I said to Maggie. "Max is famous for never leaving loose ends."

"You want me to kill him anyway?" said Maggie.

"No," I said. "Tell me, Max. If you didn't kill me, who did?"

"I haven't the faintest idea," said Max, smiling slowly, revealing gray teeth behind the gray lips. "Which means it isn't any of your usual enemies. And if I don't know, no one does."

I felt suddenly tired. Max had been my best bet, my last hope. He could have been lying, but I didn't think so. Not when he knew the truth could hurt me more. My body was decaying, I had no more leads, and I didn't have the time left to go anywhere else. So Maggie and I walked out the way we came in. Maggie would have killed Max, if I'd asked, but I didn't see the point. Feuds and vendettas are for the living; when you're dead you just can't be bothered with the small shit.

Maggie took me back to her place. I needed time out, to sit and think. I was close to despair. I didn't have enough time left to investigate all the enemies I'd made in my personal and professional life. A disturbing and depressing thought, for someone facing eternity. So many enemies, and so few friends . . . I sat on Maggie's couch, and looked fondly at her as she made us some coffee. We'd been so good together, for a while. Why didn't it work out? If f knew the answer to that, we'd still be together. She came in from the kitchen, carrying two steaming mugs. I took one, and held it awkwardly. I wanted to drink the coffee to please her, but I couldn't. She looked at me, puzzled.

"Larry? What's the matter?"

And just like that, I knew. Because I finally recognized the voice I'd been hearing ever since I woke up dead.

I was at Maggie's place, drinking coffee. It tasted funny. Larry? she said. Larry? What's wrong? I felt something burning in my throat, and knew she'd poisoned me. I stopped time with my wand, and ran. It was raining. I didn't dare go home. She'd find me. I didn't know where to go for help, so I went to ground, in my old safe house at Blaiston Street. And I died there, still wondering why my partner and ex-lover had killed me.

"It was you," I said, and something in my voice made her flinch. "You poisoned me. Why?"

"The how is more interesting," Maggie said calmly. She sat down opposite me, entirely composed. "An old voodoo drug in your coffee, to kill you and set you up for the zombie spell. But of course I didn't know about the wand. It interacted with my magic, buying you more time. The wand's magic is probably what's holding you together now."

"Talk to me, Maggie. We were lovers. Friends. Partners."

"That last one is the only one that matters." She blew on her coffee, and sipped it cautiously. "I wanted our business. All of it. I was tired of being the junior partner, especially when I did most of the work. But you had the name, and the reputation, and the contacts. I didn't see why I should have to go on sharing my money with you. I was the brains in our partnership, and you were only the muscle. You can always hire muscle. And . . . I was bored with you. Our affair was fun, and it got me the partnership I wanted; but, Larry darling, while you might have been adequate in bed, you were just so damned dull out of it.

"I couldn't split up the business. I needed the cachet your name brings. And I couldn't simply have you killed, because under the terms of your will, your ex would inherit your half of the business. And I really didn't see why I should have to go to all the trouble and expense of buying her out.

"So I got out my old books and put together a neat little package of poisons and voodoo magics. As a zombie under my control, you would have made and signed a new will, leaving everything to me. Then I'd dispose of your body. But clearly I didn't put enough sugar in your coffee. Or maybe you saw something in my face, at the last. Either way, that damned secret wand of yours let you escape. To a safe house I didn't even know we had anymore. You have no idea how surprised I was when you rang me three days later.

"Why didn't you remember? The poison, the spells, the trauma? Or maybe you just didn't want to believe your old sweetie could have a mind of her own and the guts to go after what she wanted."

"So why point me at Max?" I said numbly.

"To use up what time you've got left. And there was always the chance you'd take each other out and leave the field even more open for me."

"How could you do this? I loved you, Maggie!"

"That's sweet, Larry. But a girl's got to live."

She put aside her coffee, stood up, and looked down at me. Frowning slightly, as though considering a necessary but distasteful task. "But it's not too late to put things right. I made you what you are, and I can unmake you." She pulled a silver dagger out of her sleeve. The leaf-shaped blade was covered with runes and sigils. "Just lie back and accept it, Larry. You don't want to go on as you are, do you? I'll cut the consciousness right out of you, then you won't care anymore. You'll sign the necessary papers like a good little zombie, and I'll put your body to rest. It's been fun, Larry. Don't spoil it."

She came at me with the dagger while she was still talking, expecting to catch me off guard. I activated my wand, and time crashed to a halt. She hung over me, suspended in midair. I studied her for a moment; and then it was the easiest thing in the world to take the dagger away from her and slide it slowly into her heart. I let time start up again. She fell forward into my arms, and I held her while she died, because I had loved her once.

I didn't want to kill her, even after everything she'd done and planned to do. But when a man's partner kills him, he's supposed to do something about it.

So here I am. Dead, but not departed. My body seems to have stabilized. No more maggots. Presumably, the wand interacting with the voodoo magics. I never really understood that stuff. I don't know how much longer I've got, but then, who does? Maybe I'll have new business cards made up. Larry Oblivion, deceased detective. The postmortem private eye. I still have my work. And I need to do some good, to balance out all the bad I did while I was alive. The hereafter's a lot closer than it used to be.

Even when you're dead, there's no rest for the wicked.

Simon R. Green was born in Bradford-on-Avon, Wiltshire, England (where he still resides). He obtained an MA in Modern English and American Literature from Leicester University; he also studied history and has a combined Humanities degree. He is the bestselling author of several series, including twelve novels of The Nightside and The Secret Histories (book seven, *Casino Infernale*, is due out in 2013). His newest series, The Ghost Finders, will have a fourth novel, *Spirits From Beyond*, published this year.

The Case: *An eagle is found staked out and eviscerated on a mountain near a remote World War II base in the Aleutian Islands. The body of a murdered sailor is nearby.*

The Investigators: *An unnamed young private, and "Pop," a corporal who very closely resembles Dashiell Hammett, father of noir mystery fiction and creator of* Sam Spade (The Maltese Falcon) *and* Nick and Nora Charles (The Thin Man).

THE ADAKIAN EAGLE

Bradley Denton

I

The eagle had been tortured to death.

That was what it looked like. It was staked out on the mountain on its back, wings and feet spread apart, head twisted to one side. Its beak was open wide, as if in a scream. Its open eye would have been staring up at me except that a long iron nail had been plunged into it, pinning the white head to the ground. More nails held the wings and feet in place. A few loose feathers swirled as the wind gusted.

The bird was huge, eleven or twelve feet from wingtip to wingtip. I'd seen bald eagles in the Aleutians before, but never up close. This was bigger than anything I would have guessed.

Given what had been done to it, I wondered if it might have been stretched to that size. The body had been split down the middle, and the guts had been pulled out on both sides below the wings. It wasn't stinking yet, but flies were starting to gather.

I stood staring at the eagle for maybe thirty seconds. Then I got off the mountain as fast as I could and went down to tell the colonel. He had ordered me to report anything hinky, and this was the hinkiest thing I'd seen on Adak.

That was how I wound up meeting the fifty-year-old corporal they called "Pop."

And meeting Pop was how I wound up seeing the future.

Trust me when I tell you that you don't want to do that. Especially if the future you see isn't even your own.

Because then there's not a goddamn thing you can do to change it.

. . .

II

I found Pop in a recreation hut. I had seen him around, but had never had a reason to speak with him until the colonel ordered me to. When I found him, he was engrossed in playing Ping-Pong with a sweaty, bare-chested opponent who was about thirty years his junior. A kid about my age.

Pop had the kid's number. He was wearing fatigues buttoned all the way up, but there wasn't a drop of perspiration on his face. He was white-haired, brown-mustached, tall, and skinny as a stick, and he didn't look athletic. In fact, he looked a little pale and sickly. But he swatted the ball with cool, dismissive flicks of his wrist, and it shot across the table like a bullet.

This was early on a Wednesday morning, and they had the hut to themselves except for three sad sacks playing poker against the back wall. Pop was facing the door, so when I came in he looked right at me. His eyes met mine for a second, and he must have known I was there for him. But he kept on playing.

I waited until his opponent missed a shot so badly that he cussed and threw down his paddle. Then I stepped closer and said, "Excuse me, Corporal?"

Pop's eyes narrowed behind his eyeglasses. "You'll have to be more specific," he said. He had a voice that made him sound as if he'd been born with a scotch in one hand and a cigarette in the other.

"He means you, Pop," the sweaty guy said, grabbing his shirt from a chair by the curving Quonset wall. "Ain't nobody looking for me."

Pop gave him the briefest of grins. I caught a glimpse of ill-fitting false teeth below the mustache. They made Pop look even older. And he had already looked pretty old.

"Cherish the moments when no one's looking for you," Pop said. "And don't call me 'Pop.' 'Boss' will do fine."

"Aw, I like 'Pop,' " the sweaty guy said. "Makes you sound like a nice old man."

"I'm neither," Pop said.

"You're half right." The sweaty guy threw on a fatigue jacket and walked past me. "I'm gettin' breakfast. See you at the salt mines."

Pop put down his paddle. "Wait. I'll come along."

The sweaty guy looked at me, then back at Pop. "I think I'll see you later," he said, and went out into the gray Adak morning. Which, in July, wasn't much different from the slightly darker gray, four-hour Adak night.

Pop turned away from me and took a step toward the three joes playing poker.

"Corporal," I said.

He turned back and put his palms on the Ping-Pong table, looking across at me like a judge looking down from the bench. Which was something I'd seen before, so it didn't bother me.

"You're a private," he said. It wasn't a question.

"Yes, sir."

He scowled, his eyebrows pinching together in a sharp V. "Then you should know better than to call another enlisted man 'sir.' You generally shouldn't even call him by rank, unless it's 'Sarge.' We're all GI's pissing into the same barrels here, son. When the wind doesn't blow it back in our faces."

"So what should I call you?" I asked.

He was still scowling. "Why should you call me anything?"

I had the feeling that he was jabbing at me with words, as if I were a thug in one of his books and he were the combative hero. But at that time I had only read a little bit of one of those books, the one about the bird statuette.

And I had only read that little bit because I was bored after evening chow one day, and one of the guys in my hut happened to have a hardback copy lying on his bunk. I wasn't much for books back then. So I didn't much care how good Pop was at jabbing with words.

"I have to call you something," I said. "The colonel sent me to take you on an errand."

Pop's scowl shifted from annoyance to disgust. "The *colonel*?" he said, his voice full of contempt. "If you mean who I think you mean, he's a living mockery of the term *intelligence officer*. And he's still wearing oak leaves. Much to his chagrin, I understand. So I suppose you mean the *lieutenant* colonel."

"That's him," I said. He was the only colonel I knew. "He wants you and me to take a drive, and he wants us to do it right now. If you haven't eaten breakfast, I have a couple of Spam sandwiches in the jeep. Stuck 'em under the seat so the ravens wouldn't get 'em."

Pop took his hands off the table, went to the chairs along the wall, and took a jacket from one of them. He put it on in abrupt, angry motions.

"You can tell him I don't have time for his nonsense," he said. "You can tell him I'm eating a hot meal, and after that, I'm starting on tomorrow's edition. I'm not interested in his editorial comments, his story ideas, or his journalistic or literary ambitions. And if he doesn't like that, he can take it up with the brigadier general."

I shook my head. "The general's not in camp. He left last night for some big powwow. Word is he might be gone a week or more. So if I tell the colonel what you just said, I'm the one who'll be eating shit."

Pop snorted. "You're in the Army and stationed in the Aleutians. You're already eating shit."

He tried to walk past me, but I stepped in front of him.

He didn't like that. "What are you going to do, son? Thrash an old man?" He was glaring down at me like a judge again, but now the judge was going to throw the book. Which was something I had also seen before, so it didn't bother me.

"I'd just as soon not," I said.

Pop glanced back at the poker players. I reckoned he thought they would step up for him. But they were all staring at their cards hard enough to fade the ink, and they didn't budge.

"Did you see the boxing matches yesterday?" I asked.

Pop looked back at me. His eyes had narrowed again.

"There was a crowd," he said. "But yes, I watched from a distance. I thought it was a fine way to celebrate the Fourth of July, beating the snot out of our own comrades in arms. I hear the Navy man in the second match was taken to the Station Hospital."

I shrugged. "He dropped his left. I had to take the opportunity."

Pop bared those bad false teeth. "Now I recognize you. You KO'd him. But he laid a few gloves on you first, didn't he?"

"Not so's I noticed." Thanks to the colonel, I'd had two whole weeks during which my only duty had been to train for the fight. I could take a punch.

"So you're tough," Pop said. His voice had an edge of contempt. "It seems to me that a tough fellow should be killing Japs for his country instead of running errands for an idiot. A tough fellow should—" He stopped. Then he adjusted his glasses and gave me a long look. When he spoke again, his voice was quiet. "But it occurs to me that you may have been on Attu last year. In which case you may have killed some Japs already."

I didn't like being reminded of Attu. For one thing, that was where the colonel had decided to make me his special helper. For another, it had been a frostbitten nightmare. And seven guys from my platoon hadn't made it back.

But I wasn't going to let Pop know any of that.

"A few," I said. "And if the brass asked my opinion, I'd tell them I'd be glad to go kill a few more. But the brass ain't asking my opinion."

Pop gave a weary sigh. "No. No, they never do." He dug his fingers into his thick shock of white hair. "So, what is it that the lieutenant colonel wants me to assist you with? I assume it's connected with some insipid piece of 'news' he wants me to run in *The Adakian*?"

I hesitated. "It'd be better if I could just show you."

Pop's eyebrows rose. "Oh, good," he said. His tone was sarcastic. "A mystery." He gestured toward the door. "After you, then, Private."

It felt like he was jabbing at me again. "I thought you said enlisted men shouldn't call each other by rank."

"I'm making an exception."

That was fine with me. "Then I'll call you 'Corporal.'"

A williwaw began to blow just as I opened the door, but I heard Pop's reply anyway.

"I prefer 'Boss,'" he said.

III

We made our way down the hill on mud-slicked boardwalks. On Adak, the wind almost always blew, but the most violent winds, the williwaws, could whip up in an instant and just about rip the nose off your face. The one that whipped up as Pop and I left the recreation hut wasn't that bad, but I still thought a skinny old guy like him might fly off into the muck. But he held the rail where there was a rail, and a rope where there was a rope, and he did all right.

As for me, I was short and heavy enough that the milder williwaws didn't bother me too much. But as I looked down the hill to the sloppy road we called Main Street, I saw a steel barrel bouncing along at about forty miles an hour toward Navytown. And some of the thick poles that held the miles of telephone and electrical wires that crisscrossed the camp were swaying as if they were bamboo. We wouldn't be able to take our drive until the wind let up.

So I didn't object when Pop took my elbow and pulled me into the lee of a Quonset hut. I thought he was just getting us out of the wind for a moment, but then he slipped under the lean-to that sheltered the door and went inside. I went in after him, figuring this must be where he bunked. But if my eyes hadn't been watering, I might have seen the words *THE ADAKIAN* stenciled on the door.

Inside, I wiped my eyes and saw tables, chairs, typewriters, two big plywood boxes with glass tops, a cylindrical machine with a hand crank, and dozens of reams of paper. The place had the thick smell of mimeograph ink. Two of the tables had men lying on them, dead to the world, their butts up against typewriters shoved to the wall. A third man, a slim, light-skinned Negro, was working at a drawing board. It looked like he was drawing a cartoon.

This man glanced up with a puzzled look. "What're you doing back already, Pop?" He spoke softly, so I could barely hear him over the shriek of the williwaw ripping across the hut's corrugated shell.

"I don't know how many times I have to tell you," Pop said. "I don't like 'Pop.' I prefer 'Boss.'"

"Whatever you say, Pop. They run out of scrambled eggs?"

"I wouldn't know. My breakfast has been delayed." Pop jerked a thumb at me. "The private here is taking me on an errand for the lieutenant colonel."

The cartoonist rolled his eyes. "Lucky you. Maybe you'll get to read one of his novellas."

"That's my fear," Pop said. "And I simply don't have enough whiskey on hand." He waved in a never-mind gesture. "But we've interrupted your work. Please, carry on."

The cartoonist turned back to his drawing board. "I always do."

Pop went to an almost-empty table, shoved a few stacks of paper aside, and stretched out on his back. The stack of paper closest to me had a page on top with some large print that read: HAMMETT HITS HALF-CENTURY—HALF-CENTURY CLAIMS FOUL.

"Have a seat, Private," Pop said. "Or lie down, if you can find a spot." He closed his eyes. "God himself has passed gas out there. We may be here a while."

I looked around at the hut's dim interior. The bulb hanging over the drawing board was lit, but the only other illumination was the gray light from the small front windows. Wind noise aside, all was quiet. It was the most peaceful place I had been since joining the Army.

"This is where you make the newspaper?" I asked.

"You should be a detective," Pop said.

I looked at the two sleeping men. "It sure looks like an easy job."

Pop managed to scowl without opening his eyes. "Private, have you actually seen *The Adakian*? I suppose it's possible you haven't, since there are over twenty thousand men in camp at the moment, and we can only produce six thousand copies a day."

"I've seen it," I said. "I saw the one about the European invasion, and maybe a few others."

Pop made a noise in his throat. "All right, then. When have you seen it?"

"Guys have it at morning chow, mostly."

Now Pop opened his eyes. "That's because my staff works all night to put it out *before* morning chow. Starting at about lunchtime yesterday, they were typing up shortwave reports from our man at the radio station, writing articles and reviews, cutting and pasting, and doing everything else that was necessary to produce and mimeograph six thousand six-page newspapers before sunup. So right now most of them have collapsed into their bunks for a few hours before starting on tomorrow's edition. I don't know what these three are still doing here."

At the drawing board, the Negro cartoonist spoke without looking up. "Those two brought in beer for breakfast, so they didn't make it back out the door. As for me, I had an idea for tomorrow's cartoon and decided to draw it before I forgot."

"What's the idea?" Pop asked.

"It's about two guys who have beer for breakfast."

Pop grunted. "Very topical."

Then no one spoke. I assumed parade rest and waited. But as soon as I heard the pitch of the wind drop, I opened the door a few inches. The williwaw had diminished to a stiff breeze, no worse than a cow-tipping gust back home in Nebraska.

"We have to go, Boss," I said.

Pop didn't budge, but the cartoonist gave a whistle. "Hey, Pop! Wake up, you old Red."

Pop sat up and blinked. With his now-wild white hair, round eyeglasses, and sharp nose, he looked like an aggravated owl.

"Stop calling me 'Pop,'" he said.

Outside, as Pop and I headed down the hill again, I said, "That's something I've never seen before."

"What's that?" Pop asked, raising his voice to be heard over the wind.

"A Negro working an office detail with white soldiers."

Pop looked at me sidelong. "Does that bother you, Private? It certainly bothers the lieutenant colonel."

I thought about it. "No, it doesn't bother me. I just wonder how it happened."

"It happened," Pop said, "because I needed a damn good cartoonist, and he's a damn good cartoonist."

I understood that. "I do like the cartoons," I said.

Pop made a noise in his throat again.

"Would it be all right, Private," he said, "if we don't speak again until we absolutely have to?"

That was fine with me. We were almost to the jeep, and once I fired that up, neither of us would be able to hear the other anyway. The muffler had a hole in it, so it was almost as loud as a williwaw.

IV

Halfway up the dormant volcano called Mount Moffett, about a mile after dealing with the two jerks in the shack at the Navy checkpoint, I stopped the jeep. The road was barely a muddy track here.

"Now we have to walk," I told Pop.

Pop looked around. "Walk where? There's nothing but rocks and tundra."

It was true. Even the ravens, ubiquitous in camp and around the airfield, were absent up here. The mountainside was desolate, and I happened to like that. Or at least I'd liked it before finding the eagle. But I could see that to a man who thrived on being with people, this might be the worst place on earth.

"The Navy guys say it looks better when there's snow," I said. "They go skiing up here."

"I wondered what you were discussing with them," Pop said. "I couldn't hear a word after you stepped away from the jeep."

I decided not to repeat the Navy boys' comments about the old coot I was chauffeuring. "Well, they said they were concerned we might leave ruts that would ruin the skiing when it snows. After that, we exchanged compliments about our mothers. Then they got on the horn and talked to some ensign or petty officer or something who said he didn't care if they let the whole damn Army through."

Hunching my shoulders against the wind, I got out of the jeep and started cutting across the slope. The weather was gray, but at least it wasn't too cold. The air felt about like late autumn back home. And the tundra here wasn't as spongy as it was down closer to camp. But the rocks and hidden mud still made it a little precarious.

Pop followed me, and I guessed it had to be tough for him to keep his balance, being old and scrawny. But he didn't complain about the footing. That would have been far down his list.

"Tell me the truth, Private," he said, wheezing. "This is a punishment, correct? The lieutenant colonel stopped me on Main Street a few months ago and asked me to come to dinner and read one of his stories. But my boys were with me, so I said, 'Certainly, if I may bring these gentlemen along.' At which point the invitation evaporated. That incident blistered his ass, and that's why we're here, isn't it?"

I turned to face him but kept moving, walking backward. "I don't think so. When he sent me up here this morning, it didn't have anything to do with you. I was supposed to look for an old Aleut lodge that's around here somewhere. The colonel said it's probably about three-quarters underground, and I'd have to look hard to find it."

Pop was still wheezing. "That's called an *ulax*. Good protection from the elements. But I doubt there was ever one this far up the mountain, unless it was for some ceremonial reason. And even if there was an *ulax* up here, I can't imagine why the lieutenant colonel would send you looking for it."

"He has a report of enlisted men using it to drink booze and have relations with some of the nurses from the 179th," I said. "He wants to locate it so he can put a stop to such things."

Pop frowned. "Someone's lying. The 179th has twenty nurses here at most. Any one of them who might be open to 'such things' will have a dozen officers after her from the moment she arrives. No enlisted man has a chance. Especially if the lady would also be required to climb a mountain and lower herself into a hole in the ground."

"Doesn't matter if it's true," I said. "I didn't find no lodge anyway." I turned back around. We were almost there.

"That still leaves the question of why we're up here," Pop said.

This time I didn't answer. Although he was a corporal, Pop didn't seem to grasp the fact that an enlisted man isn't supposed to have a mind of his own. If an officer asks you to dinner, or to a latrine-painting party, you just say "Yes, sir." And if he tells you to go for a ride up a volcano, you say the same thing. There's no point in asking why, because you're going to have to do it anyway.

"Are we walking all the way around the mountain?" Pop shouted, wheezing harder. "Or is there a picnic breakfast waiting behind the next rock? If so, it had better not be another Spam sandwich."

"You didn't have to eat it," I said.

Pop started to retort, but whatever he was going to say became a coughing fit. I stopped and turned around to find him doubled over with his hands on his knees, hacking so hard that I thought he might pass out.

I considered pounding him on the back, but was afraid that might kill him. So I just watched him heave and thought that if he died there, the colonel would ream my butt.

Pop's coughing became a long, sustained ratcheting noise, and then he spat a watery black goo onto the tundra. He paused for a few seconds, breathing heavily, then heaved again, hacking out a second black glob. A third heave produced a little less, and then a fourth was almost dry.

Finally, he wiped his mouth with his sleeve and stood upright again. His face was pale, but his eyes were sharp.

"Water," he said in a rasping voice.

I ran back to the jeep, stumbling and falling once on the way, and returned with a canteen. Pop took it without a word, drank, then closed his eyes and took a deep breath.

"That's better," he said. He sounded almost like himself again. He capped the canteen and held it out without opening his eyes.

I took the canteen and fumbled to hang it from my belt. "What was that?" I asked. "What happened?" I was surprised at how shook-up my own voice sounded. God knew I'd seen worse things than what Pop had hacked up.

Pop opened his eyes. He looked amused. "'What happened?'" he said. "Well, that was what we call coughing."

I gave up on fixing the canteen to my belt and just held it clutched in one hand. "No, I mean, what was that stuff that came out?" I could still see it there on the tundra at our feet. It looked like it was pulsing.

"Just blood," Pop said.

I shook my head. "No, it ain't. I've seen blood." I had, too. Plenty. But none of it had looked this black.

Pop glanced down at it. "You haven't seen old blood," he said. "If this were red, that would mean it was fresh, and I might have a problem. But this is just old news coming up."

"Old news?" I asked.

"Tuberculosis, kid. I caught it during the *previous* war to end all wars. Don't worry, though. You can't catch it from me."

I wasn't worried about that. But I was confused. "If you were in the Great War, and you caught TB," I said, "then how could they let you into the Army again?"

Pop grinned. Those bad false teeth had black flecks on them now. "Because they can't win without me." He gestured ahead. "Let's get this over with, Private, whatever it is. I have to go back and start cracking the whip soon, or there might not be a newspaper tomorrow."

So I turned and continued across the slope. I could see the hillock I'd marked with rocks a few dozen yards ahead. I hoped Pop wouldn't go into another coughing fit once we crossed it.

V

Pop's eyebrows rose when he saw the eagle, but otherwise it didn't seem to faze him.

"Well, this is something different," he said.

I nodded. "That's what I thought, too."

Pop gave a small chuckle. "I'm sure you did, Private." He looked at me with his narrow-eyed gaze, but this time it was more quizzical than annoyed. "When I asked you what this was about, you said it would be better if you just showed me. Now you've shown me. So what the hell does the lieutenant colonel want me to do? Write this up for *The Adakian*?"

"I think that's the last thing he wants," I said. "He says this thing could hurt morale."

Pop rolled his eyes skyward. "Christ, it's probably low morale in the form of sheer boredom that did this in the first place. Human beings are capable of performing any number of deranged and pointless acts to amuse themselves. Which is precisely what we have here. The brass told us we couldn't shoot the goddamn ravens, so some frustrated boys came up here and managed to cut up a bald eagle instead. And they've expressed their personal displeasure with their military service by setting up the carcass as a perverse mockery of the Great Seal of the United States."

"The what?" I asked.

Pop pointed down at the bird. "There's no olive branch or arrows. But otherwise, that's what this looks like. The Great Seal. Aside from the evisceration, of course. But I suppose that was just boys being boys."

"You think it was more than one guy?" I asked.

Pop looked at me as if I were nuts. "How on earth would I know?"

"You said 'boys.' That means more than one."

"I was speculating. I have no idea whether this was a project for one man, or twenty."

I tossed the canteen from hand to hand. "Okay, well, do whatever you have to do to figure out who it was."

Now Pop looked at me as if I weren't only nuts, but nuts and stupid, too. "There's no way of knowing who did this. Or even why. Speculation is all that's possible. The bird might have been killed out of boredom, out of hatred, or even out of superstition. I have no idea."

None of that sounded like something I could report. "But the colonel says you used to be a detective. Before you wrote the books."

Pop took off his glasses and rubbed his eyes. "I was a Pinkerton. Not Sherlock Holmes. A Pinkerton can't look at a crime scene and deduce a culprit's name, occupation, and sock color. Usually, a Pinkerton simply shadows a subject. Then, if he's lucky, the subject misbehaves and can be caught in the act." Pop put his glasses back on and held out his empty hands. "But there's no one to shadow here, unless it's every one of the twenty thousand men down in camp. Do you have one in mind? If not, there's nothing to be done."

I looked down at the eagle. As big and magnificent as it might have been in life, it was just a dead bird now. What had happened here was strange and ugly, but it wasn't a tragedy. It wasn't as if a human being had been staked out and gutted.

But in its way, the eagle unnerved me almost as much as the things I'd seen and done on Attu. At least there had been reasons for the things on Attu. Here, there was no reason at all—unless Pop was right, and it had just been boredom. If that was the case, I didn't want to know which guys had been bored enough to do this. Because if I knew, I might get mad enough to hurt them. And then there'd be something else I'd have to see in my sleep over and over again.

"All right, Pop," I said, keeping my eyes on the eagle. "There's a can of gasoline strapped to the jeep. What if we tell the colonel that when you and I got up here, we found this thing burned up?"

Pop cleared his throat. "You'd be willing to do that, Private? Lie to the lieutenant colonel?"

I had never sidestepped an order before. The colonel had made me do some stupid things and some awful things, but this was the first time that it looked like he was making me do a pointless thing. Besides, Pop was older and smarter than the colonel—even I could see that—and if he thought the eagle was a waste of time, then it probably was.

Besides, we were enlisted men, and we had to stick together. As long as there weren't any officers around to catch us doing it.

"Sure," I said, looking up at Pop again. "I've lied before. Back home in Nebraska, I even lied to a judge."

Pop gave me a thin-lipped smile. "What did you do to wind up in front of a judge?"

I had done so much worse since then that it didn't seem like much of a fuss anymore. "I beat up a rich kid from Omaha for calling me a dumb Bohunk," I said. "Then I stole his Hudson, drove it into a pasture, and chased some cows. I might have run it through a few fences while I was at it."

Pop chuckled. "That doesn't sound too bad. Some judges might have even considered it justified."

"Well, I also socked the first deputy who tried to arrest me," I said. "But I think what really made the judge mad was when I claimed that I wasn't a dumb Bohunk, but a stupid Polack."

"Why would that make the judge angry?" Pop asked.

"Because the judge was a Polack," I said. "So he gave me thirty days, to be followed by immediate enlistment or he'd make it two years. That part was okay, since I was going to sign up anyhow. But the thirty days was bad. My old man had to do the hay mowing without me. I got a letter from my mother last week, and she says he's still planning to whip me when I get home."

I noticed then that Pop's gaze had shifted. He was staring off into the distance past my shoulder. So I turned to look, and I saw a man's head and shoulders over the top edge of another hillock about fifty yards away. The man was wearing a coat with a fur-lined hood, and his face was a deep copper color. He appeared to be staring back at us.

"Do you know him?" Pop asked.

I squinted. "I don't think so," I said. "He looks like an Eskimo."

"I believe he's an Aleut," Pop said. "And the only natives I've seen in camp have belonged to the Alaska Scouts, better known as Castner's Cutthroats. Although that may be for the alliteration. I don't know whether they've really cut any throats."

I was still staring at the distant man, who was still staring back.

"They have," I said.

"Then let's mind our own—" Pop began.

He didn't finish because of a sudden loud whistling noise from farther down the mountain. It seemed to come from everywhere below us, all at once, and it grew louder and louder every moment.

"Shit," I said. I think Pop said it, too.

We both knew what it was, and we could tell it was going to be a fierce one. And there were no buildings up here to slow it down. It was a monster williwaw whipping around the mountain, and we had just a few seconds before the wind caught up with its own sound. The jeep was hundreds of yards away, and it wouldn't have been any protection even if we could get to it. Our only option was going to be to lie down flat in the slight depression where the dead eagle was staked out. If we were lucky, the exposed skin of our hands and faces might not be flayed from our flesh. And if we were even luckier, we might manage to gulp a few breaths without having them ripped away by the wind. I had the thought that this wasn't a good time to have tuberculosis.

Then, just as I was about to gesture to Pop to drop to the ground, I saw the distant Cutthroat disappear. His head and shoulders seemed to drop straight into the earth behind the hillock. And in one of my rare moments of smart thinking, I knew where he had gone.

"Come on!" I shouted to Pop, and I dropped the canteen and started running toward the hillock. But I had only gone about twenty yards when I realized that Pop wasn't keeping up, so I ran back to grab his arm and drag him along.

He didn't care for that, and he tried to pull away from me. But I was stronger, so all he could do was cuss at me as I yanked him forward as fast as I could.

Then the williwaw hit us, and he couldn't even cuss. Our hats flew away as if they were artillery shells, and I was deafened and blinded as my ears filled with a shriek and my eyes filled with dirt and tears. The right side of my face felt as if it were being stabbed with a thousand tiny needles.

I couldn't see where we were going now, but I kept charging forward, leaning down against the wind with all my weight so it wouldn't push me off course. For all I knew, I was going off course anyway. I couldn't tell if the ground was still sloping upward, or if we were over the top of the hillock already. But if I didn't find the spot where the Cutthroat had disappeared, and find it pretty damn quick, we were going to have to drop to the ground and take our chances. Maybe we'd catch a break, and the williwaw wouldn't last long enough to kill us.

Then my foot slipped on the tundra, and I fell to my knees. I twisted to try to catch Pop so he wouldn't hit the ground headfirst, and then we both slid and fell into a dark hole in the earth.

■ ■ ■

VI

The sod roof of the *ulax* was mostly intact, but there were holes. So after my eyes adjusted, there was enough light to see. But Pop had landed on top of me, and at first all I could see was his mustache.

"Your breath ain't so good, Pop," I said. "Mind getting off me?"

At first I didn't think he heard me over the shriek of the williwaw. But then he grunted and wheezed and pushed himself away until he was sitting against the earthen wall. I sat up and scooted over against the wall beside him.

Pop reached up and adjusted his glasses, which had gone askew. Then he looked up at the largest hole in the roof, which I guessed was how we'd gotten inside. It was about eight feet above the dirt floor.

"Thanks for breaking my fall," he said, raising his voice to be heard over the wind. "I hope I didn't damage you. Although you might have avoided it if you'd told me what you were doing instead of dragging me."

I didn't answer. Instead, I looked around at the mostly underground room. It was maybe twenty feet long by ten feet wide. At the far end was a jumble of sod, timber, and whalebone that looked like a section of collapsed roof. But the roof above that area was actually in better shape than the rest. The rest was about evenly split between old sod and random holes. Some empty bottles and cans were scattered around the floor, and a few filthy, wadded blankets lay on earthen platforms that ran down the lengths of the two longer walls.

But there was no Cutthroat. I had watched him drop down into the same hole that Pop and I had tumbled into. I was sure that was what had happened.

But I didn't see him here now.

"What happened to the Eskimo?" I asked.

Pop scanned the interior of the *ulax* and frowned. "He must have gone elsewhere."

"There isn't any elsewhere," I said, almost shouting. I pointed upward. "Listen to that. And this is the only shelter up here."

Pop shook his head. "The man we saw was a native. He may know of shelters on this old volcano that we wouldn't find if we searched for forty years. Or he may even be so used to a wind like this that he'll stand facing into it and smile."

I looked up at the big hole and saw what looked like a twenty-pound rock blow past. "I saw him jump down here. That's how I knew where to go. And I think I would have seen him climb back out. Unless he can disappear."

And then, from behind the jumble of sod and whalebone at the far end of the *ulax,* the Cutthroat emerged. His hood was down, and his dark hair shone. He was in a crouch, holding a hunting knife at his side. A big one.

"Who the fuck are you people?" the Cutthroat asked. His voice was low and rough, but still managed to cut through the howling above us. This was a man used to talking over the wind.

Pop gave a single hacking cough. Then he looked at me and said, "Well, Private, it doesn't look as if he disappeared."

Right then I wanted to punch Pop, but it was only because I was scared. I wished the Cutthroat really had disappeared. I didn't recognize his dark, scraggly-bearded face, but that didn't mean anything. I didn't remember many living faces from Attu.

But I did remember the Cutthroats as a group. I remembered how they had appeared and vanished in the frozen landscape like Arctic wolves.

And I remembered their knives.

"I asked you two a question," the Cutthroat said, pointing at us with his knife. "Are you M.P.'s? And if you're not, what are you doing here?"

Pop gave another cough. This time it wasn't a tubercular hack, but a sort of polite throat-clearing. And I realized he didn't understand what kind of man we were dealing with. But maybe that was a good thing. Because if he had ever seen the Cutthroats in action, he might have stayed stone-silent like me. And one of us needed to answer the question before the Cutthroat got mad.

"We aren't M.P.'s," Pop said. "So if you've done something you shouldn't, you needn't worry about us."

"I haven't done a fucking thing," the Cutthroat said. Even though his voice was gravelly, and even though he was cussing, his voice had a distinctive Aleut rhythm. It was almost musical. "I just came up here because a guy told me there was a dead eagle. And I thought I'd get some feathers. I'm a goddamn native, like you said."

I managed to take my eyes off the Cutthroat long enough to glance at Pop. Pop had the same expression on his face that he'd had when I'd first seen him, when he'd been whipping the strong, shirtless kid at Ping-Pong. He was calm and confident. There were even slight crinkles of happiness at the corners of his eyes and mouth, as if he were safe and snug in his own briar patch, and anybody coming in after him was gonna get scratched up.

It was the damnedest expression to have while sitting in a pit on the side of a volcano facing a man with a knife while a hundred-mile-an-hour wind screeched over your head.

"I understand completely," Pop said. "We came up to find the eagle as well, although we didn't have as good a reason. We're only here because an idiot lieutenant colonel couldn't think of another way to make us dance like puppets. It's a stupid, pointless errand from a stupid, pointless officer."

The Cutthroat blinked and then straightened from his crouch. He lowered the knife.

"Fucking brass," he said.

"You're telling us," Pop said.

The Cutthroat slipped his knife into a sheath on his hip. "Colonel Castner's not too bad. He lets us do what we know how to do. But the rest of them. Fuck me, Jesus. They didn't listen on Attu, and they ain't listened since."

I knew what he was talking about. The Cutthroats had scouted Attu ahead of our invasion, so they had told the brass how many Japs were there and what to expect from them. But they had also warned that Attu's permafrost would make wheeled vehicles almost useless, and that we'd need some serious cold-weather boots and clothing. Plus extra food. Yet we'd gone in with jeeps and trucks, and we'd been wearing standard gear. Food had been C-rations, and not much of that. It had all been a rotten mess, and it would have been a disaster if the Cutthroats hadn't taken it upon themselves to bring dried fish and extra supplies to platoon after platoon.

Not to mention the dead Jap snipers and machine gunners we regular GI's found as we advanced. The ones whose heads had been almost severed.

"I cowrote the pamphlet on the Battle of the Aleutians," Pop said. "But of course it had to be approved by the brass, so we had to leave out what we knew about their mistakes. And we also weren't allowed to mention the Alaska Scouts. The generals apparently felt that specific mention of any one outfit might be taken to suggest that other outfits weren't vital as well."

The Cutthroat made a loud spitting noise. "Some of them *weren't*." He sat down with his back against the sod-and-whalebone rubble. "Don't matter. I was there, and I killed some Japs. Don't much care what gets said about it now."

The noise of the williwaw had dropped slightly, so when Pop spoke again his voice was startlingly loud.

"If you don't mind my asking," Pop said, "why are you on Adak? I was told the Scouts had gone back to Fort Richardson."

The Cutthroat's upper lip curled, and he pointed a finger at his right thigh. "I got a leg wound on Attu, and the fucking thing's been getting reinfected for over a year. It's better now, but it was leaking pus when the other guys had to leave. Captain said I had to stay here until it healed. But now I got to wait for an authorized ride. And while I wait, they tell me I'm an orderly at the hospital. Which ain't what I signed up for. So I tried to stow away on a boat to Dutch Harbor a couple weeks ago, and the fucking M.P.'s threw me off."

"I assume that means you're now AWOL from the hospital," Pop said. "Which explains why you thought that the Private and I might be police."

The Cutthroat shook his head. "Nah. The hospital CO don't really give a shit what I do. He let me put a cot in a supply hut and pretty much ignores me.

I'm what you call extraneous personnel." He jerked a thumb over his shoulder. "I just thought you might be M.P.'s because of this dead guy back here. I think it's the same guy who told me about the eagle, but maybe not. You people all look alike to me."

It took me a few seconds to realize what the Cutthroat had said. When I did, I looked at Pop. Pop's eyebrows had risen slightly.

"Would you mind if I have a look?" Pop asked.

The Cutthroat shrugged his shoulders. "What do I care? He ain't *my* dead guy."

Pop stood up stiffly, and I stood up as well. With the williwaw overhead now a somewhat diminished shriek, we walked, hunched over, to where the Cutthroat sat. And now I could see that the *ulax* had a second, smaller chamber whose entrance had been partially obscured by the fallen sod and bone.

We went around the pile of debris, through the narrow entrance beside the wall, and into the second chamber. It was about ten by eight feet, and its roof was also pocked by holes that let in light. But these holes were smaller, and they changed the pitch of the wind noise. The shriek rose to a high, keening whistle.

On the floor, a stocky man lay on his back, his open eyes staring up at the holes where the wind screamed past. His hair looked dark and wet, and his face was as pale as a block of salt except for a large bruise under his left eye. His mouth was slack. He was wearing a dark Navy pea jacket, dark trousers, and mud-black boots. His bare, empty hands were curled into claws at his sides.

Pop and I stared down at him for a long moment, neither of us speaking.

At first, I didn't recognize the man because he looked so different from how he had looked the day before. But then I focused on the bruise under his eye, and I knew who he was. My gut lurched.

Right behind me, the Cutthroat said, "Back of his head's bashed in."

Startled, I spun around, fists up.

The Cutthroat's knife shot up from its sheath to within two inches of my nose.

Then Pop's hand appeared between the blade and my face.

"Easy, boys," Pop said. "I'm the camp editor. You don't want your names in the paper."

I lowered my fists.

"Sorry," I said. I was breathing hard, but trying to sound like I wasn't. "It was just a reflex."

The Cutthroat lowered his knife as well, but more slowly.

"Now I recognize you," he said, peering at me intently. "You boxed yesterday. And you were on Attu. Okay, mine was just a reflex, too."

I still didn't know him, but that still didn't mean anything. The Cutthroats hadn't stayed in any one place very long when I had seen them at all. And some of them had worn their fur-lined hoods all the time.

Pop took his hand away, and then all three of us looked down at the body. I opened my mouth to speak, but suddenly had no voice. Neither Pop nor the Cutthroat seemed to notice.

"He's Navy," Pop said. "Or merchant marine. A young man, like all the rest of you." Pop's voice, although loud enough to be heard over the wind, had a slight tremble.

"Don't worry about it, old-timer," the Cutthroat said. "He's just another dead guy now. Seen plenty of those."

Pop got down on one knee beside the body. "Not on this island," he said. "Other than sporadic casualties generated by bad bomber landings, Adak has been relatively death-free." He gingerly touched the dead man's face and tilted it to one side far enough to expose the back of the head. The skull had been crushed by a large rock that was still underneath. The dark stuff on the rock looked like what Pop had coughed up earlier.

Feeling sick, I turned away and stared at the Cutthroat. I tried to read his face, the way I might try to read an opponent's in a boxing match. I'd been told that you could tell what another fighter was about to do, and sometimes even what he was only thinking about doing, just from the expression on his face.

The Cutthroat gave me a scowl.

"Don't look at me, kid," he said. "I would've done a better job than that."

Pop opened the dead man's coat, exposing a blue Navy work shirt. I could see his hands shaking slightly as he did it. "I believe you," he said. "Whatever happened here was sloppy. It may even have been an accident." He opened the coat far enough to expose the right shoulder. "No insignia. He was just a seaman." He opened the shirt collar. "No dog tags, either."

Then he reached into the large, deep coat pockets, first the left, then the right. He came up from the right pocket clutching something.

Pop held it up in a shaft of gray light from one of the ceiling holes.

It was a huge, dark-brown feather, maybe fourteen inches long. It was bent in the middle.

"That bird," Pop said, "is turning out to be nothing but trouble."

VII

We left the body where it was and went back into the larger room. The wind was still furious overhead, so we were stuck there for the time being. Pop and I sat back down against the wall at the far end, and the Cutthroat lounged on the earthen shelf along the long wall to our right.

Pop didn't look so good. He was pale, and he coughed now and then. I think he was trying to pretend that the dead man hadn't bothered him. He had probably seen death before, but not the way the Cutthroat and I had.

Still, this was different. In battle, death is expected. Back at camp, when the battlefields have moved elsewhere, it's something else. So I was a little shook up myself.

The Cutthroat didn't seem bothered at all. His mind was already on other things.

"This goddamn williwaw might take that eagle away," he said. "If it does, I won't get my feathers. I should have come in the other way, like you guys did. I saw you there with it, but then I felt the wind coming. I didn't think you two were gonna make it here."

"Neither did we," Pop said. "But if you want an eagle feather, you can have the one I took from that young man." He reached for his jacket pocket.

The Cutthroat made a dismissive gesture. "That one's bent in the middle. It's no good to me. The power's bent now, too."

"What sort of power do you get from feathers?" I asked. I immediately regretted it.

The Cutthroat gave me a look too dark to even rise to the level of contempt. "None of your fucking business. In fact, I'm wondering what you and your damn lieutenant colonel wanted with the eagle in the first place."

Pop coughed. "The private and I wanted nothing to do with it at all. But the lieutenant colonel seems to be curious about who killed it, gutted it, and staked it out like that. He incorrectly assumed I could help him discover that information."

The Cutthroat sat up straight. "Somebody killed it on purpose?"

"That's what it looks like," Pop said. "Couldn't you see it from over here?"

The Cutthroat's brow furrowed. "I just saw you two, and the eagle's wings, and then the wind hit me before I could come any closer. You say somebody pulled out its guts?"

"Yes." Pop's color was getting better. "And staked it to the earth with nails. Does that mean anything to you?"

The Cutthroat scowled. "Yeah, it means that somebody's a fucking son of a bitch. I ain't heard of nothing like that before." He scratched his sparse beard. "Unless maybe a shaman from a mainland tribe was here, trying to do some kind of magic."

Pop leaned toward the Cutthroat. His eyes were bright. "Why would killing an eagle be magic?"

The Cutthroat's hand came down to rest on the hilt of his knife. It made me nervous.

"The people along the Yukon tell a story about eagles," the Cutthroat said. "It's the kind of story you white people like to hear us savages tell. I even told it to some officers one night on Attu. Took their minds off the fact that they were getting a lot of kids killed. Got a promise of six beers for it. They paid up, too." He gave Pop a pointed look.

Pop gave a thin smile. "I don't have any beer at hand. Will you take an IOU?"

The Cutthroat answered Pop's smile with a humorless grin. "Don't be surprised when I collect." He leaned forward. "Okay. Long ago, a pair of giant eagles made their nest at the summit of a volcano. I'm talking about eagles nine, ten times the size of the ones we got now. They'd catch full-grown whales and bring them back to feed their young. And sometimes, if they couldn't find whales, they'd swoop down on a village and take away a few human beings. This went on for many years, with the giant eagles raising a new brood of young every year. These young would go off to make nests on other volcanoes and attack other villages."

Pop took a Zippo and a pack of Camels from a jacket pocket. "So they were spreading out like the Germans and Japanese."

The Cutthroat nodded. "Yeah, I guess so. Anyway, one day, one of the original eagles, the father eagle, was out hunting and couldn't find any reindeer or whales or nothing. So the father eagle said, fuck it, the babies are hungry. And he swooped down and took a woman who was outside her house. Carried her back to the volcano, tore her limb from limb, ripped out her guts, and fed her to his giant eaglets."

The pitch of the wind outside dropped, and the Cutthroat paused and listened. Pop lit a cigarette and then offered the pack to me and the Cutthroat. The Cutthroat accepted, but I declined. I'd promised my mother I wouldn't smoke.

The wind shrieked higher again as Pop lit the Cutthroat's cigarette, and then the Cutthroat went on.

"But this poor woman happened to be the wife of the greatest hunter of the village," he said, exhaling smoke. "And when the hunter returned and was told what had happened, he went into a rage. He took his bow and his arrows, and even though everyone told him he was a fool, he climbed the volcano."

"Most truly brave men *are* fools," Pop said. He gestured toward me with his cigarette. I didn't know why.

"I wouldn't know," the Cutthroat said. "In the Scouts, we try to be sneaky instead of brave. Works out better. Anyway, when the hunter got to the eagles' nest, he found six baby eagles, each one three times the size of a full-grown eagle today. They were surrounded by broken kayaks, whale ribs, and human bones. The hunter knew that some of those bones belonged to his wife, and that these eaglets had eaten her. So he shot an arrow into each of them, through their eyes, and they fell over dead. Then he heard a loud cry in the sky, which was the giant mother eagle returning. He shot her under the wing just as she was about to grab him, and then he shot her through the eyes. She tumbled off the mountain, and that was it for her. Then there was another loud cry, which was the father eagle—"

"And of course the hunter killed the father eagle as well," Pop said.

The Cutthroat glared. "Who's telling this fucking legend, old man? No, the hunter didn't kill the goddamn father eagle. The eagle dived at him again and again, and each time the hunter put an arrow into a different part of its body. But he never hit the father eagle in the eye. So, finally, pierced with arrows all over, and his whole family dead, the giant eagle flew away into the northern sky, and neither he nor any of his kind were ever seen again. But the eagles of today are said to be the descendants of those who had flown away in earlier times." The Cutthroat gave a loud belch. "At least, that's the story."

Pop leaned back again, looking up at the holes in the roof and blowing smoke toward them. "It's not bad," he said. "Not much suspense, though. I'm not sure it's worth six beers."

"I don't give a damn what you think it's worth," the Cutthroat said, tapping ash from his cigarette. "It ain't my story anyway. My mother heard it a long time ago from some Inuits on the mainland, and she told it to me when I was a kid. But we're Unangan. Not Eskimo."

"So you think an Eskimo might have killed this eagle too?" Pop asked. "Staked it to the ground, gutted it?"

The Cutthroat frowned. "Like I said, I ain't heard of anything quite like that. But I ain't heard of a lot of things. Some of those shamans might still hold a grudge against eagles. People can stay mad about crap like that for five, six hundred years. Or maybe some guy just thought if he killed an eagle, he could take its power. And then he could be a better hunter, or fisherman, or warrior. I've heard of that. And you white people like stuff like that, too. I'll toss that in for free."

Pop was giving the Cutthroat a steady gaze. "But you're saying it wouldn't have been you who killed the eagle. Or anyone else Unangan."

The Cutthroat shook his head. "Doubt it. Sometimes the eagles show us where the fish are. And sometimes we toss 'em a few in return. We get along all right."

Pop nodded, sat back against the earthen wall, and closed his eyes. He took a long pull on his cigarette. "I've been all over the post, both Armytown and Navytown, many times. But I've seen very few Aleuts or Eskimos. So just from the odds, I doubt that a native is our eagle-killer."

As much as I hated saying anything at all in front of the Cutthroat, I couldn't keep my mouth shut anymore. Pop was infuriating me.

"There's a dead man over there!" I yelled, pointing at the section of collapsed roof. "Who cares about the eagle now?"

Pop opened his eyes and regarded me through a smoky haze.

"Actually, I don't care much," he said. "But because of that dead man, the eagle has become slightly more interesting."

"Why?" I asked, still furious. "Just because he had a feather in his pocket? That doesn't mean anything. He might have found it."

Pop's eyebrows rose. "I don't think so. He and the eagle have both been dead less than a day. So the coincidental timing, plus the feather in his pocket, suggests a connection. Either he killed the eagle, and then had an unfortunate accident . . . "

He fixed his gaze on the Cutthroat again.

" . . . or whoever did kill the eagle, or helped him kill it, may have then killed him as well."

The Cutthroat ground out his cigarette butt. "I told you guys before. It wasn't me."

"And I still believe you," Pop said. "I'm just wondering if you might have any idea who it may have been."

"Nope," the Cutthroat said. There was no hesitation.

Pop leaned back against the wall again and looked up at the holes in the roof.

"I don't have any idea either," Pop said. "But I think you were right about one thing."

"Huh?" the Cutthroat said. "What's that?"

"Whoever it was, he's a fucking son of a bitch."

The wind seemed to scream louder in response.

VIII

The williwaw finally slacked off a little after noon, leaving only blustery gusts. The three of us stirred ourselves on stiff joints and muscles and rose from our places in the main room of the *ulax*.

Pop and the Cutthroat had both dozed after finishing their cigarettes, but I had stayed wide awake. I knew who the dead man was. But I hadn't told Pop yet for fear that the Cutthroat would hear me.

That was because, while I didn't recognize this particular Cutthroat, I knew who he was, too. On Attu, the Alaska Scouts had saved my life and the lives of dozens of my buddies, but they hadn't done it by being kind and gentle souls. They had done it by being cruel and ruthless to our enemies.

And I knew that a man couldn't just turn that off once it wasn't needed anymore. I knew that for a cold fact.

I boosted Pop up through the hole in the roof where we'd dropped in, and then I followed by jumping from the raised earthen shelf at the side of the room, grabbing a whalebone roof support, and pulling myself through.

I joined Pop on the hillock just beside the *ulax,* blinking against the wind, and then looked back and saw the Cutthroat already standing behind me. It was as if he had levitated.

"So this thing here is not our fucking problem," the Cutthroat said, speaking over the wind. "We all agree on that."

Pop nodded. "That's the body of a Navy man. So the private and I will tell the boys at the Navy checkpoint to come have a look. And if they ask our names, or if they know who I am, I'll be able to handle them. They're twenty-year-olds who've pulled checkpoint duty at the base of an extinct volcano. So they aren't going to be the brightest minds in our war effort."

I didn't like what Pop was saying. But for the time being, I kept my mouth shut.

The Cutthroat nodded. "All right, then." He turned away and started down the slope.

"We have a jeep," Pop called after him.

The Cutthroat didn't even glance back. So Pop looked at me and shrugged, and he and I started back the way we had come. A few seconds later, when I looked down the slope again, the Cutthroat had vanished.

When we reached the spot where the dead eagle had been staked, I thought for a moment that we had headed in the wrong direction. But then I saw the rocks I'd used as markers, so I knew we were where I thought we were. The eagle was simply gone. So were the nails. So was my canteen.

"The Scout was right," Pop said. "The wind took it."

If I tried, I could make out some darkish spots on the bare patch of ground where the bird had been staked, and when I looked up the slope I thought I could see a few distant, scattered feathers. But the eagle itself was somewhere far away now. Maybe the ocean. Maybe even Attu.

"This is a good thing," Pop said, continuing on toward the jeep. "Now when you tell the lieutenant colonel that the eagle was gone, you can do so in good conscience. Or good enough. It's certainly gone now. That fact should get me back to my newspaper until he thinks of some other way to torment me."

He looked at me and smiled with those horrible false teeth, as if I should feel happy about the way things had turned out. But I wasn't feeling too happy about much of anything.

"What about the man in the lodge?" I asked.

Pop frowned. "We're going to report him to the Navy."

"I know that," I said. "But what should I tell the colonel?"

Pop stopped walking and put his hand on my shoulder.

"Listen, son," he said. His eyes were steady and serious. "I'm not joking about this. Are you listening?"

I gave a short nod.

"All right." Pop sucked in a deep breath through his mouth and let it out through his nose. "When you see the lieutenant colonel, don't mention the dead man. You brought me up here to show me the eagle, as ordered, and it was gone. That's all. Do you understand?"

I understood. But I didn't like it.

"It's not right," I said.

Pop dropped his hand and gave me a look as if I'd slapped him. "Not right? How much more 'right' would the whole truth be? For one thing, there's no way of knowing how the eagle got into the state it was in. So there's no way to give the lieutenant colonel that information. But now it's gone, which means that problem is gone as well."

"You know I don't mean the eagle," I said.

Now Pop's eyes became more than serious. They became grim.

"Yes, we discovered a dead man," he said. "And the gutted eagle nearby, plus the feather in the dead man's pocket, raise some questions. But they're questions we can't answer. The simplest explanation? The sailor's death was an accident. He came up here, either alone or with comrades, got drunk, and hit his head when he passed out. But even if it was manslaughter or murder, he was Navy, and the guilty party is probably Navy as well. So we're telling the Navy. After that, it's out of our hands. Besides, Private, what do you suppose the lieutenant colonel would do if you did tell him about it?"

I didn't answer. I just stared back at Pop's grim eyes.

"I'll tell you what he'd do," Pop said. "He'd question us repeatedly. He'd make us trek back up here with M.P.'s. He'd order us to fill out reports in triplicate. He'd force me to run a speculative and sensational story in *The Adakian,* even though it's a Navy matter and affects our boys not at all. And then he'd question us again and make us fill out more reports. And all for what? What would the upshot be?"

I knew the answer. "The upshot," I said, "would be that the man would still be dead. And it would still be a Navy matter."

Pop pointed a finger at me. "Correct. And telling the lieutenant colonel wouldn't have made any difference at all."

I glanced back toward the *ulax.*

"It's still not right," I said.

The cold grimness in Pop's eyes softened. "There's nothing about a young man's death that's right. Especially when it was for nothing. But a lot of young men have died in this war, and some of those died for nothing, too. So the only thing to do is simply what you know *must* be done, and nothing more. Because trying to do more would be adding meaninglessness to meaninglessness." He stuck his hands into his jacket pockets. "And in this case, what we must do is tell the Navy. Period."

Then he started toward the jeep again. But I didn't follow.

"That won't be the end of it," I called after him.

He turned and glared at me. His white hair whipped in the wind.

"Why not?" he shouted.

I jerked a thumb backward. "Because I gave him that bruise on his face."

Pop stood there staring at me for a long moment, his stick-thin body swaying. I didn't think he understood.

"That's the guy I whipped in the ring yesterday," I said.

Pop just stared at me for a few more seconds. Then he took his right hand from his pocket and moved as if to adjust his glasses. But he stopped when he saw that he was holding the bent eagle feather he'd found on the dead man.

I saw his thin lips move under his mustache. If he was speaking aloud, it was too quietly for me to hear him over the wind. But I saw the words.

"Nothing but trouble," he said again.

IX

This time, I stayed in the jeep while Pop talked with the Navy boys at the checkpoint. He had said things would go better if I let him handle it. I thought they might give him a bad time, since that had been their inclination with me that morning. But Pop had given a weak laugh when I'd mentioned that. He assured me it wasn't going to be a problem.

It took twenty minutes or more. But eventually Pop came back to the jeep. Through the shack's open doorway, I could see one of the Navy men get on the horn and start talking to someone.

"Let's go," Pop said.

I still didn't feel right. I had known the dead man, even if it had only been for a few minutes in a boxing ring. And although I had seen what had happened to the back of his head, and I knew that it had to have happened right there where we'd found him, I couldn't shake the notion that my clobbering him had somehow led to his death.

Pop nudged my shoulder. "I said, let's go. We may have to answer a few questions for whoever investigates, but the odds are against it. Those boys told me that the *ulax* we found is well known to their comrades as an unapproved recreation hut. They've never even heard of Army personnel using it. So this really is a Navy matter."

I didn't respond. Instead I just started the jeep, which clattered and roared as I drove us back down to camp. I didn't try to talk to Pop on the way. I didn't even look at him.

He didn't say anything more to me, either, until I had stopped the jeep on Main Street near the base of the boardwalk that led up the hill to the *Adakian* hut. I didn't mean to shut off the engine, but it died on me anyway.

"You can go on back to work," I said, staring down Main Street at the long rows of Quonset huts interspersed with the occasional slapdash wood-frame building . . . at all the men trudging this way and that through the July mud . . . at the wires on the telephone poles as they hummed and swayed . . . and at the black ravens crisscrossing the gray air over all of it. I still wouldn't look at Pop. "I'll tell the colonel the eagle was a bust, like you said."

Pop coughed a few times. "What about the dead man?" he asked then. "Are you going to mention him, or are you going to take my advice and leave it to the Navy?"

Now, finally, I looked at him. What I saw was a scrawny, tired-looking old man. He might have been fifty, but he looked at least eighty to me. And I wanted to dislike him more than I did. I wanted to hate him.

"I'm going to tell him I found the body," I said. "But I'll leave you out of it. And I'll leave the Cutthroat out of it too, since that's what we said we'd do. I'll just say that I spotted the lodge and went to have a look, but you were feeling sick and headed back to the jeep instead. I'll tell him I found the dead guy and told you about it, but you never saw him. And that we went down and told the Navy."

Pop's eyebrows pinched together. "Not good enough. With a story like that, he'll want to play detective. So he'll try to involve me regardless."

I shrugged. "That's the best I can do. I found a dead man while I was doing a chore for the colonel, and I have to tell him. Especially since he arranged for me to fight that same guy. So even if the Navy handles it, he'll still hear about it. And once he knows where they found him, and when, he'll ask me about it. So I have to tell him. It'll be worse later, if I don't."

Pop bit his lip, and I saw his false teeth shift when he did it. He pushed them back in place with his thumb. Then he stared off down Main Street the way I just had.

"Ever since this morning, I've been puzzled," he said in a low voice. "How is it that a lieutenant colonel is using a private as an aide, anyway? Officers over the rank of captain don't usually associate with GI's lower than sergeant major. Unless the lower-ranking GI has other uses. As I do."

"Then I guess I have other uses too," I said. "Besides, I'm not his aide. He has a lieutenant for that. But when we got back from Attu, he said he was getting me transferred to a maintenance platoon so I'd be available for other things. And now I run his errands. I shine his shoes. I deliver messages. I box. And when he doesn't need me, I go back to my platoon and try not to listen to the shit the other guys say about me."

Pop gave another cough. He didn't sound good at all, but I guessed he was used to it.

"You haven't really answered my question," he said then. "You've explained what you do for him. But you haven't explained how you were selected to do it. Out of all the enlisted men available, what made him notice you in particular?"

He was jabbing at me yet again. I thought about dislodging his false teeth permanently.

Instead, I told him. As much as I could stand to.

"It was on Attu," I said. My voice shook in my skull. "Right after the Japs made their banzai charge. By that time some of those little bastards didn't have nothing but bayonets tied to sticks. But they wouldn't quit coming. My squad was pushed all the way back to the support lines before we got the last ones we could see. We even captured one. He had a sword, but one of us got him in the hand, and then he didn't have nothing. So we knocked him down, sat on him, and tied his wrists behind his back with my boot laces." I glared at Pop. "Our sergeant was gone, and by then it was just me and two other guys. Once we had the Jap tied, those guys left me with him while they went to find the rest of our platoon. Then the colonel showed up. He'd lost his unit, too, and he wanted me to help him find it. But I had a prisoner. So the colonel gave me an order."

Pop looked puzzled. "And?"

"And I obeyed the order."

Pop's eyes shifted away for a second, then back again. I thought he was going to ask me to go ahead and say it.

But then he rubbed his jaw, raised his eyes skyward, and sighed.

"All right," he said. "I'll go with you to speak with the lieutenant colonel. You won't have to tell him that I didn't see the corpse. But we'll still have to leave our friend from the Alaska Scouts out of it. And I'll have to go up to *The Adakian* first, to make sure the boys have started work on tomorrow's edition. There's nobody there over corporal, and they each refuse to take direction from any of the others unless I say so. I'm a corporal as well, of course, but our beloved brigadier general has given me divine authority in my own little corner of the war. He's an admirer. As were those Navy boys at Mount Moffett, as it turned out. Although I had the impression that what one of them really likes is the Bogart movie, while the other thinks I might be able to introduce him to Myrna Loy. But they were both impressed that I actually met Olivia de Havilland when she was here."

Pop liked to talk about himself a little more than suited me. But if he was going to do the right thing, I didn't care.

I got out of the jeep. "I'll go with you to the newspaper. In case you forget to come back."

Pop got out too. "At this point, Private," he said, "I assure you that you've become unforgettable."

After a detour to the nearest latrine, we climbed up to the newspaper hut. Pop went in ahead of me, but stopped abruptly just inside the door. I almost ran into him.

"What the hell?" he said.

I looked past Pop and saw nine men standing at attention, including the three I had seen there that morning. They were all like statues, staring at the front wall. Their eyes didn't even flick toward Pop.

Someone cleared his throat to our left. I recognized the sound.

I looked toward the table where Pop had napped that morning, and I saw the colonel rise from a chair. His aide was standing at parade rest just beyond him, glaring toward *The Adakian* staff. I had the impression they were being made to stand at attention as a punishment for something.

The colonel adjusted his garrison cap, tapped its silver oak leaf with a fingernail, then hitched up his belt around his slight potbelly and stretched his back. He wasn't a large man, but the stretch made him seem taller than he was. His sharp, dark eyes seemed to spark as he gave a satisfied nod and scratched his pink, fleshy jaw.

"It's about damn time," he said in his harsh Texas accent. Then he looked back at his aide. "Everyone out except for these two. That includes you."

The aide snapped his fingers and pointed at the door.

Pop and I stepped aside as Pop's staff headed out. They all gave him quizzical looks, and a few tried to speak with him. But the colonel's aide barked at them when they did, and they moved on outside.

The aide brought up the rear and closed the door behind him, leaving just the colonel, Pop, and me in the hut. To Pop's right, on the drawing board, I saw the finished cartoon of two soldiers having beer for breakfast. One soldier was saying to the other:

"Watery barley sure beats watery eggs!"

Pop's eyebrows were pinched together. He was glaring at the colonel.

"I don't know how long you made them stand there like that," Pop said. "But I'll be taking this up with the general when he returns."

The colonel gave a smile that was almost a grimace. "We'll cross that bridge when we come to it. At the moment, we're in the middle of another. I've received a call from a Navy commander who tells me a dead sailor has been found on Mount Moffett. He says the body was discovered by you, Corporal. I play cards with the man, and he's sharp. So I believe him."

Pop sat down on the cartoonist's stool, which still kept him several inches taller than me or the colonel.

"That's right," Pop said. He was still frowning, but his voice had relaxed into its usual cool, superior tone. "At your request, the private and I were looking for the dead eagle he'd found earlier. But it had apparently blown away. Then a williwaw kicked up, so we found shelter in an old Aleut lodge. That's where we found the unfortunate sailor."

The colonel turned toward me. "I understand it was the sailor you fought yesterday."

"Yes, sir," I said. I had gone to attention automatically.

"What happened?" the colonel asked. "Did he try to take another swing at you?" He was still smiling in what I guessed he thought was a fatherly way. "Was it self-defense, Private?"

It was as if an icicle had been thrust into the back of my skull and all the way down my spine.

"Sir," I said. I don't know how I managed to keep my voice from quaking, but I did. "He was dead when we found him, sir."

The colonel's fatherly smile faded. "Are you sure about that? Or is that what the corporal said you should tell me?"

Now Pop was staring at the colonel through slitted eyelids. And now he had a slight smile of his own. But it was a grim, knowing smile.

"Son of a bitch," he said.

The colonel turned on Pop with sudden rage. His pink face went scarlet.

"I wasn't speaking to you, Corporal!" he snapped. "When I need answers from a drunken, diseased has-been who hasn't written a book in ten years, you'll be the first to know. At the moment, however, I'll take my answers from the private."

Pop nodded. "Of course you will. He's just a kid, and he doesn't have a brigadier general in his corner. So you're going to use him the way you've used him since Attu. What happened there, anyway?"

"We won," the colonel said. "No thanks to the likes of you."

Pop held up his hands. "I'd never claim otherwise. At that time I was stateside having my rotten teeth pulled, courtesy of Uncle Sam."

The colonel stepped closer to Pop, and for a second I thought he was going to slap him.

"You're nothing but a smug, privileged, Communist prick," the colonel snarled. "The general may not see that, but I do. I've read the fawning stories you print about Soviet victories. You might as well be fighting for the Japs."

Pop's eyes widened. "Colonel, I realize now that your attitude toward me is entirely my fault. In hindsight, I do wish I could have accepted your dinner invitation. However, in my defense, by that time I had seen a sample of your writing. And it was just atrocious."

The colonel's face went purple. He raised his hand.

Then, instead of slapping Pop, he reached over to the drawing board, snatched up the new cartoon, and tore it to shreds. He dropped the pieces on the floor at Pop's feet.

"No more jokes in the newspaper about beer," he said. "They undermine discipline. Especially if they're drawn by a nigger."

Then he looked at me, and his color began draining back to pink.

"Private," he said, his voice lowering, "you and I need to talk. Unfortunately, I'm about to have lunch, and then I have to meet with several captains and majors. The rest of my afternoon is quite full, as is most of my evening. So you're to report to my office at twenty-one hundred hours. No sooner, no later. Understood?"

"Yes, sir," I said.

The colonel gave a sharp nod. "Good. In the meantime, I'm restricting you to barracks. If you need chow, get it. But then go to your bunk and speak to no one. While you're there, I suggest that you think hard about what happened today, and what you're going to tell me about it. If it was self-defense, I can help you. Otherwise, you may be in trouble." He glanced at Pop, then back at me. "And stay away from the corporal."

"Yes, sir," I said.

The colonel pointed at the door, so I turned and marched out. I caught a glimpse of the colonel's aide and the newspaper staff standing up against the wall of the Quonset, and then I headed down the boardwalk toward Main Street. The wind cut through me, and I shivered. I still had to return the jeep to the motor pool. Then get some chow. Then go to my bunk. One thing at a time. Jeep, chow, bunk. Jeep, chow, bunk.

The colonel seemed to think I had killed the Navy man. And that Pop had advised me to lie about it.

Jeep, chow, bunk.

Of course, Pop *had* advised me to lie, but not about that. Because that hadn't happened.

Or had it? Could I have done something like that and then forgotten I'd done it? Why not? Hadn't I already done things just as bad?

Jeep, chow, bunk.

All I knew for sure was that the colonel hated Pop, and that I had been in trouble ever since finding the eagle.

Jeep, chow, bunk. It wasn't working.

How I wished I had never seen the eagle. Or the *ulax*.

How I wished I had never met another Cutthroat after Attu.

How I wished I could have stayed in my combat unit.

How I wished I had never met Pop.

How I wished I had never been sent to the Aleutians in the first place.

How I wished I had never punched that rich kid from Omaha, and that I had stayed home long enough to help my old man with the hay.

X

I had my Quonset hut to myself while I waited for the afternoon to creep by. I didn't know what job the rest of my bunkmates were out doing, but it didn't matter. I would have liked to find them and do some work so I wouldn't have to think. But I was under orders to stay put.

Other than the truth, I didn't know what I would tell the colonel when 2100 finally came. Even if I included every detail, including the ones Pop and I had agreed not to tell, it still wasn't going to be the story the colonel wanted to hear. And whatever story that was, I knew I wasn't smart enough to figure it out.

I hadn't gotten any chow. My stomach was a hard, hungry knot, and I knew I should have eaten. But I was also pretty sure I wouldn't have been able to keep it down.

Sure, I had been in trouble before. But back then, I had just been a dumb Bohunk kid who'd gotten in a fight, swiped a Hudson, and insulted a judge. None of that had bothered me. But none of that had been anything like this.

I wasn't even sure what "this" was. But I did know that another kid, a kid just like me except that he was Navy, had gotten his skull bashed in. And the colonel thought that maybe I was the one who'd done it.

It all went through my head over and over again, and the knot in my stomach got bigger and bigger. I lay in my bunk and closed my eyes, but I couldn't sleep. Outside, the Aleutian wind whistled and moaned, and occasional short rat-a-tats of rain drummed against the Quonset tin. Every so often, I heard planes roaring in and out of the airfield. I tried to guess what they were, since the bombing runs from Adak had pretty much ended once we'd retaken Attu and Kiska. But I had never been good at figuring out a plane from its engine noise. If an engine wasn't on a tractor or jeep, I was at a loss.

"First impressions can be so deceiving," a low, smooth voice said.

I opened my eyes. Pop was sitting on a stool beside my bunk. He was hunched over with his elbows on his knees, his hands clasped under his chin, his dark eyes regarding me over the rims of his glasses. I hadn't heard him come in.

"How'd you know where I bunk?" I asked.

Pop ignored the question. "Why, just this morning, Private," he continued, "you seemed like such a tough young man. Such a hardened fighter. Yet here we are, scarcely nine hours later, and you're flopped there like a sack of sand. Defeated. Vanquished."

"Don't those mean the same thing?"

Pop gave me that thin smile of his. "My point is, you're taking this lying down. That doesn't sound like someone who'd dare to punch a rich kid from Omaha."

I turned away from him and faced the cold metal of the Quonset wall.

"I'm under orders," I said. "And I'm not supposed to be talking to you."

Pop laughed a long, dry laugh that dissolved into his usual hacking cough.

"Under orders?" he asked through the coughing. "Just how do you think you got into this confusing court-martial conundrum in the first place? You followed orders, that's how. Logically, then, the only possible way out of your current situation is to *defy* orders, just this once. It's only sixteen thirty, and the lieutenant colonel won't be looking for you until twenty-one hundred. You've already wasted more than two hours wallowing here, so I suggest you don't waste any more."

I turned back to face him.

"Just what am I supposed to do?" I asked. "My only choice is to tell him everything that happened, and the hell with our promise to the Cutthroat. So that's what I'm going to do."

Pop shook his head. "You can't tell him everything," he said, "because you don't *know* everything."

"And you do?"

"No." Pop stood and jerked his thumb toward the door. "But I know some of it, and I'm going to find out the rest. You see, unlike you, I've spent the past few hours doing something. My job is to get the news, and a large part of that involves getting people to talk. So for the past two hours, people have been talking to me and my boys a lot. But now the boys have to work on the paper. And my cartoonist has to draw a new cartoon, which has put me into a vengeful mood."

"So go get your revenge," I said. "What's it got to do with me?"

Pop leaned down and scowled. "It's your revenge, too. And I don't think I can find out the rest of what I need to know if you aren't with me."

I rose on my elbows and stared up at him. It was true that following orders hadn't really worked out for me. But I didn't see how doing what Pop said would work out any better.

"You say you know some of it already," I said. "Tell me."

Pop hesitated. Then he turned, crossed to the other side of the hut, and sat on an empty bunk.

"I know the lieutenant colonel placed a bet on your fight yesterday," Pop said. "A large one. And I know that your opponent had a reputation as a damn good boxer. He'd won eighteen fights, six by knockout. How many have you won?"

"Two," I said. "Yesterday was my second match. The first was with the guy whose bunk you're sitting on. It was a referee's decision."

Pop's eyes narrowed. "So any sane wager yesterday would have been on the Navy man. And I saw the fight, Private. He was winning. Until the third round, when he dropped his left. And as you told me this morning, you took advantage. Who wouldn't?"

I sat up on the edge of my bunk. In addition to the knot in my stomach, I now felt a throbbing at the back of my skull.

"You're saying it was fixed," I said.

"If I were betting on it, I'd say yes." Pop waved a hand in a cutting gesture. "But leave that alone for now. Instead, consider a few more things. One, we know that the *ulax* we found was used by Navy men for unofficial activities. The dead man is Navy. And the Navy boys we talked to said they didn't know of anyone but sailors having any fun up there. After all, they control access to that part of the island. Yet the lieutenant colonel sent you up because, he claimed, he had reports of Army GI's entertaining nurses there. Which doesn't quite jibe with the Navy's version."

"That's odd, I guess," I said. "But that's not anything you found out in the past two hours."

Pop looked down at the floor and clasped his hands again.

"No," he said. Now I could barely hear him over the constant weather noise against the Quonset walls. "I learned two more things this afternoon. One is that the lieutenant colonel will soon be up for promotion to full colonel. Again. After being passed over at least once before. And I know he wants that promotion very badly. Badly enough, perhaps, to do all sorts of things to get it."

Pop fell silent then, and kept looking down at the floor.

I stood. My gut ached and my head hurt. And I thought I knew the answer to my next question. But I had to ask it anyway.

"You said you learned two more things," I said. "What's the second?"

Pop looked up at me. His expression was softer than it had been all day. He looked kindly. Sympathetic. I had wanted to hit him earlier, but not as much as I did now.

"It's not really something new," Pop said. "It's what you already told me. Or almost told me. But of course I know the order that the lieutenant colonel gave you on Attu."

I clenched my fists. Maybe I would hit the old man after all. Maybe I wouldn't stop hitting him for a while.

"I won't say it aloud if you don't want me to," Pop said.

I turned and started for the door. I didn't know where I was going, but I knew I was getting away from Pop.

He followed and stopped me with a hand on my shoulder, so I whirled with a roundhouse right. He leaned back just in time, and my knuckles brushed his mustache.

"Jesus Christ, son," Pop exclaimed.

I grabbed his scrawny arms and pushed him away. He staggered back, but didn't fall.

"He was a Jap," I said. I was trembling. "He was trying to kill me not five minutes before. And it was an order. It was an order from a goddamn colonel."

Pop took a deep, quaking breath and adjusted his glasses.

"It was an order," I said.

Pop nodded. "I know. And now I need you to listen to me again. Are you listening, Private?"

I glared at him.

"Here it is, then," Pop said. "No one, and I mean no one—not your chaplain, not the general, not anyone back home, and sure as hell not me—*no one* would condemn what you did. If the circumstances had been reversed, that Jap would have done the same to you, and he wouldn't have waited for an order."

I could still see him lying there, his blood staining the thin crust of snow a sudden crimson. He had been as small as a child. His uniform had looked like dirty play clothes.

He was a Jap. But he was on the ground. With his hands tied behind his back. His sword was gone.

Pop wasn't finished. "The problem isn't that you followed the order. The problem is that out of the three thousand Japs you boys fought on Attu, we took only twenty-eight prisoners. I'm not saying that killing the rest was a bad thing. But prisoners can be valuable. Especially if they're officers. And a man with a sword might have been an officer. So someone would have wanted to ask him things like, what's your rank, who are your immediate superiors, where are your maps, what were your orders, what's your troop strength on Kiska, and where does Yamamoto go to take his morning shit. That sort of thing."

Pop was talking a lot, again. It wore on my brain. And Yamamoto's plane had been shot down a month before we'd hit Attu. But at least now I had something else to think about.

"You mean we need a supply of Japs?" I said.

Now Pop smiled his thin smile. "I mean that a lieutenant colonel in the Intelligence Section did a stupid thing. He wasn't even supposed to be near the fighting. But that banzai charge came awfully close. So in rage or fear, he forgot his job and ordered you to destroy a military intelligence asset. That's an act that could negatively affect his chances for promotion." Pop pointed at me again. "If anyone happened to testify to it."

I rubbed the back of my neck, trying to make the pain at the base of my skull go away.

"I don't understand how anything you just said adds up to anything we saw today," I told him.

Now Pop pointed past me, toward the door. "That's why there's more to find out, and that's why I need you to help me with it. There was one other man on the mountain with us this morning. And since you and he were freezing and fighting on Attu while I was elsewhere, I think he might be more willing to part with any answers if you're present."

That made some sense. The Cutthroat hadn't liked me, but he might respect me more than Pop.

Still, there was one thing that I knew Pop had left out in all his talk.

"What about the eagle?" I asked.

Pop bared his false teeth.

"That's the key," he said. "That's why we have to talk with the Scout again. Remember what he said about magic and power? Well, he also said that he told those same stories to officers on Attu." He went past me to the door. "Now, will you come along?"

I turned to go with him, then hesitated.

"Wait a minute." I was still trying to clear my head. "Are you saying the colonel believes in Eskimo magic?"

Pop held up his hands. "I have no idea. But magic and religion are based on symbols, which can be powerful as hell. And I know the lieutenant colonel *does* believe in that. After all, there's one symbol that he very much wants for his own."

I was still confused by most of what Pop had said. But this one part, I suddenly understood.

A full colonel was called a "bird colonel."

Because a full colonel's insignia was an eagle.

I went with Pop.

XI

The 179th Station Hospital wasn't just one building. It was a complex of Quonset huts and frame buildings, and it even had an underground bunker. When Olivia de Havilland had come to Adak in March, she had spent an entire day there, visiting the sick and wounded. There were a few hundred patients on any given day.

But all we needed to do was find the Cutthroat. So I waited outside the main building while Pop went in and charmed whomever he needed to charm to find out what he wanted to know. I was beginning to realize that there were some things, even in the Army, that superseded rank.

When Pop came out again, his hands in his jacket pockets, he tilted his head and started walking around back. I followed him to three Quonset huts behind the main building. He stopped at the lean-to of the first hut and looked one way and then the other as I joined him. There were a few GI's trudging along nearby with no apparent purpose. Maybe, I thought, they were just trying to look busy so they wouldn't be sent to the South Pacific.

"Do you see anyone you know?" Pop asked. "Anyone who might tell the lieutenant colonel we're here?" I tried to take a good look. But the usual gray light was dimming as evening came on, making all the soldiers appear gray as well.

"I don't think so," I said. "But everyone's starting to look alike to me."

Pop gave me an annoyed glance. "You sound like the Scout," he said. He stepped away, moved quickly to the center Quonset, and slipped into its lean-to. I followed. Then he barged into the hut without knocking.

The Cutthroat was in a small open space in the center of the hut, surrounded by shelves packed with boxes and cans. He was sitting on the edge of a cot under a single lightbulb that hung from the ceiling, leaning over a battered coffeepot on a GI pocket stove. The smell was not only of coffee, but of old beef stew, seaweed, and mud. My still-knotted stomach lurched.

The Cutthroat looked up, and his slick dark hair gleamed. "You guys." He didn't sound surprised. "Did you bring my beers?"

Pop and I stepped farther inside, and I closed the door behind us. There were two folding stools set up on our side of the pocket stove.

"I'll bring your beers tomorrow." Pop went to the right-hand stool and sat down. "In the meantime, I want you to know that both the private and I are doing our best to live up to this morning's agreements. For one thing, we haven't mentioned your presence on Mount Moffett to anyone else."

"I believe you," the Cutthroat said.

"But we have a problem," Pop continued. "So we may not be able to keep that confidence much longer. There's a lieutenant colonel who's trying to use that Navy man's death to make our lives hell."

The Cutthroat looked back down at his brew. "Yeah, I know." He rubbed his right thigh. "Goddamn, my leg is hurting tonight. I better not climb any more mountains for a while."

I sat down on the left-hand stool. The fumes from the stuff bubbling in the coffeepot were intense.

"What do you mean, you know?" I asked. "How could you know that?"

The Cutthroat glanced up at me. "Because I wasn't sure I trusted you guys. So I followed you. You didn't drive fast. I was outside the back wall of the newspaper hut when you got your asses chewed. I couldn't hear it all, but I got most of it. He's got it in for both of you. And I recognized his voice."

Pop's eyebrows rose. "That was quite stealthy of you."

The Cutthroat snorted. "I've snuck up on Japs in machine gun nests, and they knew I was coming. Buncha desk soldiers who don't expect me ain't a challenge."

"Nevertheless," Pop said. "I respect a man who can shadow that well. Especially if I'm the one he's shadowing."

The Cutthroat reached to a shelf behind him and brought down three tin cups. "You guys want coffee before you start bothering me with more questions?"

"Is that what that is?" I asked.

The Cutthroat gave me a look almost as dark as he'd given me in the *ulax*. "You need to work on your fucking manners."

Pop and I both accepted cups, and the Cutthroat poured thick, black liquid into both of them. It was something else that reminded me of what Pop had coughed up that morning.

Then the Cutthroat poured a cup for himself and set the pot back down on the pocket stove. He took a swig and smiled.

"That's good," he said. "This stuff will help you think better."

Pop took a swig as well, and I took a tentative sip of mine. It didn't taste as bad as it smelled, so I drank a little more. There was a hint of rotted undergrowth. But at least it was hot.

"Thank you," Pop said. He took a long belt. "But now I'm going to bother you, as you suspected. How did you recognize the lieutenant colonel's voice?"

The Cutthroat blew into his cup, and steam rose up around his face. "Because I've heard it before. On Attu, he was one of the shitheads who wouldn't listen to our scouting reports. But he loved our colorful stories. Here on Adak, I've been bringing him and his officer pals booze and coffee while they play poker right here in this hut. And when they get good and drunk, they want me to tell more stories. Like I said, you people can't get enough of that noble-savage crap."

"Do those poker pals include a Navy commander?" Pop asked.

"I guess that's what he is," the Cutthroat said. "He and the lieutenant colonel set up yesterday's boxing matches. They made a bet on the Army-Navy one." He pointed at me. "The lieutenant colonel bet on this guy."

"I know," Pop said. "For a lot of money, correct?"

The Cutthroat scowled and took a long drink. "Maybe there were side bets for money. But the bet between the lieutenant colonel and the Navy officer was for something else. See, the Navy guy has friends and family in high places. Like fucking Congress. So if the Army boxer won, the commander promised to have these friends pull strings and help with a promotion."

"What if the Navy man won?" Pop asked.

The Cutthroat grinned and shook his head. "Then the commander was going to have dinner with you, Corporal. That's what the lieutenant colonel promised. You must be famous or rich or something. Gotta say, it seemed like a lopsided bet to me."

Pop drained his cup and set it on the floor. He seemed to wobble on his stool as he did.

"Very lopsided indeed," he said, "since I wouldn't do a favor for the lieutenant colonel if my life depended on it."

I had been sipping the hot coffee and listening, but now I spoke up. "What about the eagle?"

The Cutthroat fixed me with an even gaze. "I still don't know about that. Not for sure. But nobody ever knows anything for sure. No matter who you ask, or what you find out, you'll never know all of anything that's already past."

The single lightbulb began to flicker. My stomach knot had relaxed, but now I found myself feeling lightheaded. I knew I should have had some chow.

"So I'm giving you both the opportunity to know as much as the lieutenant colonel," the Cutthroat said. "I told him the legend I told you. And once, he asked me about taking power from animals. I said I couldn't really explain that, since I didn't understand it myself. But if he were to take a spirit journey or have a vision, like some shamans do, he might have a chance to know all the secrets he wanted. He might die and be reborn. He might be torn apart and remade. He might meet his totem animal and be given its strength. He might gain whatever he desired. He might even see his entire life from his birth to his death." The Cutthroat shrugged. "Or he might go crazy. Or he might just pass out and sleep it off. It all depends on the individual."

The Cutthroat stood up from the cot, and he split into five men before me.

"Here," they all five said in harmony. They reached for Pop and grasped his forearms. "You take the cot. My mother got this recipe from the same people who told her the eagle story, and she always said that the most important part was to lie the fuck down. There's some mushrooms and other shit in it, and you don't want to know what I have to do to mix it right. But it hardly ever kills anyone."

The five Cutthroats put Pop on the bunk, and Pop curled up on his side. He looked like a toy made out of olive-drab pipe cleaners with a cotton-swab head. I could see his eyes behind his glasses, and they were like hard-boiled eggs.

Now the Cutthroat condensed into one man again, and he reached for me.

"You'll have to take the floor," he said. "But you're younger. It's fair."

As he grasped my wrist, I watched my tin coffee cup tumble from my numb fingers. It turned over and over, and brown droplets spun out and circled it. The cup turned into the sun.

The bright light was high above my eyes. I could see it between Pop's fingers.

"That's the best I can do for you," the Cutthroat's voice said. I couldn't see him anymore. He was far away. "Your enemy took this journey before you. But maybe you're better suited for it. I don't say that this means you'll beat him, or that you'll understand what he's done. But at least now you have the same magic. So it's a fair fight. You're welcome."

The earth shook with a deafening rumble, and the back of Pop's hand fell against my forehead.

Then, in brilliant flashes, in a cacophony of voices and noise and music, I began to see everything.

Everything.

I began to see both the past and present of every place I had ever been, every object I had ever touched, every thing I had ever done. It was as if I were a movie camera in the sky, looking down and watching it all.

Then, even as the past and present were flashing and roaring around me, I saw the future as well. And not just mine.

Pop's, too.

My advice: Never see the future.

Not anyone's.

I'm in my foxhole when the Japanese make their charge. I have to struggle for my helmet, for my weapon. When I make it out of the hole I run backward, firing as they come toward me. Some keep coming even after I hit them. One gets very close and sets off a hand grenade, trying to kill us both. But he trips and falls, his body covers it, and I'm all right. Then, to my left , I see my sergeant bayoneted. I shoot the one who did it. But it's too late.

A younger Pop, his hair not yet all white, is at a typewriter. It clacks and clatters, and the bell rings over and over again. He puts in page after page. He smokes cigarette after cigarette and drinks two bottles of whiskey dry, but he doesn't stop typing. He does this for thirty hours without a break. When he finally stops I can see his eyes. And I know he has emptied himself. There is nothing left.

The colonel points at the little man on the ground and shouts at me. I look at the little man and know he's a Jap who just tried to kill me. But now he's lying facedown, his hands behind his back. He hardly looks like a Jap now.

The colonel points and shouts again and again, louder and louder. I put the muzzle of the M1 at the base of the little man's skull and pull the trigger.

Pop, much, much younger, is wearing a uniform and walking into a hospital. He doubles over coughing as he climbs the steps. A pretty nurse rushes over and puts her arm around his shoulders.

I am much, much older, sitting in a tangle of metal and plastic. A young man is using huge steel jaws to push the metal apart and make a hole for me. You'll be okay, sir, he says. I'll get you out. I manage to take a small plastic rectangle from my pocket. It has little square buttons. I punch the buttons and call my daughter. You're right, I tell her. I shouldn't drive anymore.

The colonel is standing over the dead eagle. He is holding a knife. The sailor who fought me appears at the hillock beside the lodge, and the colonel goes to him. You'll have to trust me for an IOU, he says. It'll be a while before I can collect my winnings. But you did good. And thanks for the bird.

Pop, looking only a bit older, but wearing a nice suit, is being escorted from a bus by armed guards. They take him into prison and put him into a cell by himself. He stays in the prison for six months. He writes a lot of letters. But all his books go out of print. The radio money stops. When they let him out, he is sicker than ever and looks twenty years older. He is broke and goes to live in a tiny cottage owned by friends.

Guess I don't have any choice, the sailor says. But I know you're good for it, sir. Do I still get the date with the nurse? The blonde who swabbed my face and said I was handsome for a Navy man?

I am standing at the altar with my younger brother beside me, looking down at the far end of the aisle, when the pipe organ blares and all of the people on either side of the aisle stand up. A gorgeous woman in white appears on the arm of an older man, and they walk toward me, smiling. I can't wait for them to get here so I can find out what her name is.

You still get the date, the colonel says, holding out a bent eagle feather. Show this to her when she comes. It's dark down there, and she has to know it's you. She'll be here in a little while. Go on down and wait.

The heavy, sweating man with greasy, wormlike hair leans forward and looks *down from his high, long podium. I would like to ask, he says in a thick voice. Is Mr. Budenz being truthful when he told us that you were a Communist? So now Pop leans forward too, toward the microphones on the table where they've made him sit, and he says, I decline to answer on the grounds that an answer might tend to incriminate me. He is out of prison, and he is poor. But they won't leave him alone. They won't let him at least try to write.*

The sailor goes down into the lodge, and the colonel walks away, past the eagle. Another sailor approaches. He's in there, the colonel says, pointing back toward the lodge. Down where you boys have your fun. He threw the fight. He lost your money.

I am holding a baby. Her eyes look like mine. How the hell did this happen, I wonder. How did we finally have a girl after all these years? After all the bad things I've done, how did my life turn out to be this good?

The second sailor stops and stares down at the eagle. Never mind that, the colonel says. It's just a dead bird. It's none of your business. Go talk to your friend. He threw the fight.

In the hospital bed, Pop opens his eyes and he sees the woman. There have been dozens of women. Even a wife. But this is the one. The only one, really. She's there leaning over him.

In the lodge, the two sailors argue. You sold us out, the second sailor says. The first says, no, I'm going to share the winnings with you guys. I don't have any of it yet. But I will. Joe, calm down. Joe, no.

My daughter claps her hands the first time I walk to the mailbox and back without the crutches. You are one tough old bird, she says. Yes, I say. Yes I am. Guess what kind of tough old bird. I have its feather in my room. Have I ever shown you?

The woman leaning over Pop is at once plain and beautiful. That paradox was the first thing that drew him to her. And then her frighteningly sharp mind kept him there. More than thirty years now. She is his best friend, was several times his lover, has always been his savior. But he's been hers too, so that's only fair. She looks so frightened. Why? Pop wonders, and then he knows. That makes him frightened too. And angry. He's sixty-six. That's not old enough for this, is it?

The two sailors fight. The first catches the second with a punch to the jaw, but then the second shoves him back into the little room behind the jumble of sod and bone. He knocks him down, then slams his head back. He does it again.

Pop is frightened and angry for only a moment. Then he sinks away, down into warm black cotton, and can only hear the woman's sobs from far, far away. It's okay, Lilishka, he tries to say. It's okay.

My little grandson and granddaughter run out and throw their arms around my legs, and I drop all the mail. So I look up at my daughter on the porch and ask her to go get her mother to help me. But she frowns and says, Dad, don't you remember?

I don't. So she begins to tell me.

XII

Then Pop was slapping my face, hard, back and forth on both cheeks.

"That's enough," he said. "That's more than enough, goddamn it. Get up. Get your ass up right now, soldier."

He grabbed my collar and tried to pull me to my feet, but he wasn't strong enough. So he let me drop back down. My head thumped on the plywood floor, and then he started slapping me again. The light hanging above us shone around his wild white hair like a halo.

I almost slipped back into the visions, but Pop wouldn't stop slapping me. Finally, I came up from limbo enough to grab his right wrist with my left hand. My right fist clenched.

"Hit me again, old man," I said, my words slurring. "Hit me again, and I'll lay you out."

Pop sat down on the edge of the cot and ran his hand back through his hair. "All right," he said. "I'd like to see that. You tried to slug me once before, and all I got was a cool breeze. I'm beginning to think you aren't actually capable of hitting anyone who hasn't been paid to take a dive."

I struggled up to my knees, tried to make it all the way to my feet, and fell back onto one of the stools. It tipped, but Pop reached out and grabbed my sleeve to keep me from going over.

I didn't say thanks. I was mad at him for smacking me around. My cheeks were burning.

Pop let go of my sleeve and then shook his head as if trying to clear it.

"That may have been the worst coffee I've ever had," he said.

My head was muzzy, and Pop was going in and out of focus. But I was in the hospital's supply hut again. I was in the here and now. I looked around the room for the Cutthroat and didn't see him anywhere.

"He was gone when I came out of it," Pop said, anticipating my question. "Then I heard you talking to people who obviously haven't been born yet. So I decided that whatever you were experiencing, you'd better not experience any more of it. You're too young for family responsibilities."

I began to feel less angry toward Pop as I looked at him and remembered what I'd just seen. His hand had been touching my forehead, and I had seen everything about him.

Including his death.

"Did you . . . hallucinate?" I asked.

Pop looked at his wristwatch and stood. "We both know those were more than hallucinations. And I believe you and I saw and heard the same things, up to the point where I snapped out of it. But now it's eighteen thirty, and I have to piss like a thoroughbred. Then I have to go into Navytown and ask around for a certain commander. I understand he's an admirer of mine. Are you all right to take yourself to your bunk, or to mess, or wherever you need to go?" I stood too, but I was feeling considerably wobblier than Pop looked.

"Why aren't you shook up?" I asked. "If you'd seen anything like what I saw, you'd be shook up."

Pop smiled that thin smile. "I've seen a lot of things, Private. And they've all shook me up, even when they didn't involve Aleutian magic. But the key is to realize that it's all like that. It's all magic, it's all insane. So you make sense of what little you can, and you rely on alcohol for the rest." He gestured toward the door. "And now I really must be going."

"Are you sure you don't want me to go with you, Pop?" I asked. "I don't like the thought of you dealing with those Navy goons all by yourself. And I don't have to be at the colonel's office until twenty-one hundred."

I really wanted to stick with him so I could keep my mind off that meeting. I still had no idea what I was going to say to the colonel. What could I tell him? That I'd had a vision of what he'd done? I doubted that would go over too well with him. Or with a court-martial, either.

Pop shook his head. "No, Private, I don't want you with me this time. Frankly, you don't get along as well with those Navy people as I do. But while I'm gone, I would like you to do two things for me."

"Whatever you want," I said. "Shoot."

Pop held up an index finger. "One. Do not go to the lieutenant colonel's office at twenty-one hundred. I know he ordered you to be there. But again, ask yourself how well his orders have worked out for you so far. Stay in your barracks or hide somewhere. With luck, I'll be back before twenty-one hundred anyway. And I'll take care of all of this."

He stepped past me and headed for the door.

"How, Pop?" I asked. "How are you going to do that? We don't have proof of anything. All we have are hallucinations."

Pop paused at the door and looked back at me.

"No offense, Private," he said, "but that's all *you've* got. I plan to return with considerably more." He turned away and opened the door.

"Wait," I said. "You said you wanted me to do two things. What's the second?"

He held up two fingers and answered without looking back.

"Don't call me 'Pop,'" he said. Then the door swung closed behind him. I stepped out just a moment later and found that a thick Aleutian fog had fallen. The wind, for a change, had died. I looked down past the third storage hut. But between the fog and the dim light, I only caught a glimpse of Pop's thin, shadowy form before he disappeared.

XIII

My squad was back at our Quonset by the time I returned, and I went with them to mess. A couple of them tried to rib me by asking about what kind of soft duty I'd pulled that day, but I wouldn't even look at them. Pretty soon they got the idea and left me alone.

I made myself eat. I don't remember what it was. Some kind of gray Adak food that matched the gray Adak fog outside. I didn't want it. But I knew I had to put something in my stomach if I didn't want to collapse. I hadn't had anything to eat since the Spam sandwich more than twelve hours earlier. Besides, I wanted something to soak up whatever remained of the Cutthroat's black sludge. Whatever it had been.

The whole platoon had the evening off, which meant that my hut would be full of talking and card games. I didn't want to have to put up with any of that, so I took off after chow and slogged northward up Main Street, toward the airfield, in the opposite direction from Navytown. Pop had made it clear that he didn't want me around. So I didn't want to be tempted to go look for him.

I hadn't even met him before that morning, but now he seemed like the only friend I had on the whole island. I had considered my old sergeant to be my friend, but he had died on Attu. The closest I had gotten to anyone since then had been to the poor Navy guy at the Fourth of July boxing match. But apparently that hadn't been an honest relationship.

Somehow, I wandered my way eastward to the rocky shore of Kuluk Bay. The iron-colored, choppy water stretched out beyond the fog, and a frigid wind blew in and numbed my face. There weren't even any ships visible, since they were all anchored to the south in Sweeper Cove. So I had the feeling that I was alone at the edge of the world, and that all I had to do was step off into the cold dark water to be swallowed up, frozen and safe.

Then I glanced at my wristwatch, which my old man had given me as I'd left for basic. It was a lousy watch and lost almost fifteen minutes a day. Right now it said that it was 8:36, which meant that the actual time was about nine minutes before twenty-one hundred hours. Which was when the colonel had ordered me to be at his office. An order Pop had said I should disobey.

I thought about it.

Then I started back the way I had come, trudging through the muck as fast as I could. Maybe Pop was right, and I was an obstacle to the colonel's promotion. Maybe he was going to blame me for the sailor's death. Maybe he was going to have me court-martialed. Or maybe he was just trying to scare me into keeping my mouth shut no matter what anyone else might ask me.

It didn't matter. Whatever was going to happen to me now, I wasn't going to count on Pop to get me out of it. I had seen that he was going to have his own problems soon enough.

And I knew my life was going to be all right. I had seen that, too. I hadn't seen every day or every detail. And I knew there would be some tough times, too. But overall, it was going to be better than what most people got. Better than I deserved.

It was going to be better than what Pop had coming, anyway.

When I reached the small frame building that housed the colonel's office and living quarters, I had to stop and stare at it from across the road. The edge of the peaked roof was lined with ravens, stock-still except for a few ominous wing flaps. Normally, they would be swooping and squawking over my head. But now they were sitting on the colonel's roof in silence. There must have been fifty of them.

A few GI's walking by looked up, and one of them made a comment about "those weird birds." But otherwise, Main Street was almost empty. And that was weird, too.

I crossed the slop, went up the wooden steps, and wiped my feet on the burlap mat at the top. The real time was almost exactly twenty-one hundred. I knocked on the door and waited for the colonel's aide to let me in.

Instead, as if from a great distance, I heard the colonel's voice say, in a rough monotone, "Enter."

I opened the door and went in. The first small room was the colonel's aide's vestibule. The lamp on the desk was on, but the aide wasn't there. Beyond the desk, the door to the colonel's office was ajar. I crossed to it and hesitated.

Beyond the door, the colonel spoke again. "I said enter."

I pushed the door open just far enough and stepped into the colonel's office. The room was small and plain and lined with filing cabinets. The colonel's desk was dead center, with the overhead light shining down onto a small stack of papers between the colonel's hands. His garrison cap, its silver oak leaf shining, was flattened neatly beside the papers. The colonel's face was mostly shadowed, with just the tip of his nose glowing in the light.

I stepped smartly to within a foot of the desk, front and center, then saluted and stood at attention. It was the same thing I had done every time I had ever been summoned here.

"Thank you for coming, Private," the colonel said.

I almost laughed. He had never thanked me for coming before. But now he had thanked me as if we were equals and I had done him a favor. He had thanked me as if I weren't there because of a direct order that had been wrapped around a threat.

"Yes, sir," I said. "My pleasure, sir." I kept my eyes focused on an invisible point just over his head. But I could still see everything he did.

The colonel touched the top of the small stack of papers with his fingertips and pushed the top sheet across the desk toward me.

"I won't waste your time or mine, soldier," the colonel said. "This is a statement to the effect that this morning, 5 July 1944, you assisted your friend the corporal in a drunken escapade in which you killed an American bald eagle and then recklessly contributed to the accidental death of a Navy seaman. You are to sign at the bottom. I personally guarantee that you yourself will serve no more than one year in a stateside stockade, after which you'll receive a dishonorable discharge."

He placed a fountain pen atop the piece of paper.

I didn't even try to think. I just stayed at attention with my arms stiff at my sides and my eyes staring at that invisible spot above his head.

"Sir," I heard myself saying. "I decline to sign that statement on the grounds that signing it may tend to incriminate me."

I had heard words similar to those just a few hours before. But they wouldn't be spoken for a few years yet.

The colonel gave a growl. He picked up the pen, pushed across the next piece of paper, and put the pen down on top of it.

"Very well," he said. "This next statement is to the effect that you weren't intoxicated at all, but had an altercation with the sailor and committed manslaughter. And the corporal witnessed it."

"Sir," I heard myself saying again. "I decline to sign on the grounds that signing may tend to incriminate me."

The colonel stood, put his hands on the desk, and leaned forward into the light like a Nebraska judge. Now my eyes were focused on the top of his head. He had the same greasy, wormlike hair as the man at the high, long podium in my vision.

"Son, you'd best listen up and listen good," the colonel snarled. He pushed the remaining three pages onto the first two. "I have five confessions here, each with a slightly different version of what you and the corporal have done. You can sign any one of them. The consequences vary depending upon which one you choose. But if you don't choose one, then I'll choose one for you. And you won't like that. Nor will you like the way things go for you when both my aide and I swear that we witnessed the aftermath of your crimes as well as your signature."

I heard every word he said, and I knew what each one meant.

But what I said in reply was, "Sir, I decline to sign on the grounds—"

Then I heard the telltale sound of a hammer clicking back, and my eyes broke focus from the top of the colonel's head. I looked down and saw his .45 service automatic in his hand. It was pointing at my gut.

"Let me put this another way, Private," he said. His Texas accent slid into a self-satisfied drawl. "You can sign one of these pieces of paper, or I can tell the judge advocate that you went berserk when I confronted you with the evidence. I can tell him that you attacked a much superior officer, namely myself, and that the officer was therefore compelled to defend himself."

I stared at the muzzle of the .45 for what seemed like a long, long moment. Then I snapped my eyes back up to a point above and behind the colonel's head.

Maybe I hadn't seen the future after all. Maybe this was the future, right here. And maybe that was fair.

Maybe this would make me even again.

"Sir," I said. "I decline to sign. You already know why."

The colonel gave a disgusted groan. "That's a damn poor choice, son. But if that's the way you want it . . . "

Another hammer clicked.

This one was behind me. It was followed by a thick, hacking, tubercular cough. But that only lasted a second.

Then I heard that smooth, sophisticated voice.

"Speaking of damn poor choices," Pop said.

I looked down at the colonel again. His eyes were wide, and his face was twitching with mingled fury and fear.

But the fear won. He put his left thumb in front of the .45's hammer, let it down slowly, and then set the pistol on the stack of confessions.

"Lovely," Pop said, coming up on my right. He held up a fifth of Johnnie Walker Red with his free hand. God knows where he'd gotten it. "Now, let's have a drink."

XIV

Pop didn't even glance at me. He kept his eyes on the colonel, giving him the same thin smile I had been seeing all day. He had a .38 revolver in his right hand and the fifth of Johnnie Walker in his left.

"You can sit back down," he told the colonel. "But we'll stand."

The colonel sat down. He looked up at Pop with a mockery of Pop's thin smile. It was a repellent sneer.

"A Communist corporal holding a pistol on a lieutenant colonel," he said. "This is not going to end well for you."

Pop set the bottle of whiskey beside the stack of confessions. "Nothing ends well for anyone," he said. He picked up the .45 and dropped it into a small metal wastebasket on the floor beside the desk. "Do you have any glasses? I'd rather not pass the bottle."

The colonel nodded past my shoulder. "In the bottom drawer of the file cabinet beside the door. But don't touch my brandy."

Pop's eyes didn't move from him. "Private, would you mind?"

I took a few steps backward, bumped into the filing cabinet, and squatted down to open the drawer. There were two short glasses and a cut-glass bottle of liquor. I took out the glasses, closed the drawer, and brought the glasses to the desk.

"We need three," Pop said.

I set the glasses down beside the confessions. "I decline to drink," I said. My mother had asked me to avoid alcohol, too.

Pop still didn't take his eyes off the colonel, but he grinned. His false teeth didn't look so bad all of a sudden.

"You're an amusing young man, Private," he said.

The colonel crossed his arms. "Neither of you will be very amusing once my aide returns. You'll both be damned."

Pop shrugged. "We're damned anyway. Besides, I happen to know that your aide is at the movies with a nurse of my acquaintance. He'll be there at least another hour. I believe tonight's film is *They Died with Their Boots On*. Which isn't too surprising, since Olivia de Havilland has been popular here lately. Although the story of Custer's Last Stand might not be the most tasteful selection for an audience of GI's."

The colonel glowered. "If you shoot me, it'll be heard. There'll be dozens of men converging on this building before you're out the door."

Pop finally looked at me. His eyes were bright, and he laughed out loud.

"Can you believe this joker?" he asked. "*Now* he's worried about a shot being heard."

Pop turned back toward the desk, reached out with his left hand, and unscrewed the cap from the whiskey. He dropped the cap, picked up the bottle, and poured a hefty dose into each glass. Some of the booze splashed out onto the confessions.

"I have no intention of shooting you," he told the colonel. "I only brought the gun so you wouldn't shoot *us*." He tilted his head toward me. "That's right, Private. I knew you'd be here. You've hardly listened to me all day."

"Sorry," I said. "You're not an officer."

Pop put down the bottle and picked up one of the glasses. "I'll drink to that," he said, and downed the whole thing in three swallows. Then he set it down and refilled it. "Better have yours, sir." He said *sir* with deep sarcasm. "You're falling behind."

The other glass sat where it was, untouched, the amber liquid trembling.

The colonel bared his teeth. "I don't drink that stuff."

Pop picked up his glass again. "Ah. But I know something you do drink. You had a little belt of something cooked up by one of our Alaska Scouts, didn't you? But what you didn't know is that some men can hold their mystical potions, and some men can't. You see, to take a spiritual journey, you have to have a fucking soul to begin with. Otherwise, you just suffer from delusions of grandeur. Especially if that was your inclination to begin with." He downed his second glass of Johnnie Walker.

The colonel leaned forward. "Have another, corporal," he said. His voice was almost a hiss. "I really wish you would."

Pop poured himself another.

"Uh, Pop . . . " I said.

Pop picked up his glass a third time. "Mother's milk, son," he said. "And don't call me 'Pop.'"

As Pop slammed back the drink, the colonel lunged sideways and down, reaching for the wastebasket. But Pop kicked it away with the side of his foot, simultaneously draining his glass without spilling a drop. He moved as casually and smoothly as if he were swatting a Ping-Pong ball.

The colonel fell to his hands and knees. Pop leaned down and put the barrel of the .38 against the base of his skull.

"Feel familiar?" Pop asked.

The colonel made a whimpering sound.

"Bang," Pop said. Then he straightened, set down his glass again, and stepped over to the filing cabinet where the wastebasket had come to a stop. Pop picked up the wastebasket, brought it back, and set it on the corner of the desktop.

The colonel awkwardly hauled himself into his chair again. His face was florid and sweating.

"If you aren't going to shoot me," he said, "then what do you want?"

Pop scratched his cheek with the muzzle of the .38 before turning it back toward the colonel.

"I suppose I just want to see your face as I tell you what I believe I know," Pop said. "I want to see how close I am to the truth. And then I should return this pistol to the commander. Fine fellow, by the way. He says you stink at poker."

The florid color in the colonel's face began to drain. But the sweat seemed to increase. His wormlike hair hung in wet strands before his eyes.

"While you were drinking and playing cards," Pop said, shaking the .38 as if it were an admonishing finger, "you listened to stories told by our friend the Scout, some of which he'd told you before on Attu. And you decided you wanted to try out some of what he said for yourself. Well, that was fine with him. What did he care what a stupid white man might want to do to himself? Besides, you're a lieutenant colonel. If he crossed you, you might take him out of his hut behind the hospital and put him to work digging latrines.

"So he gave you the magic, and you drank it. But as I said, you and the magic didn't mix. So your overall unpleasantness became a more specific, insane nastiness. And you decided you were tired of waiting for that promised promotion. You decided you'd do a few things to make it happen.

"You'd kill the symbol of the power you desired, thus making its strength your own. And while you were waiting for that chance, you'd befriend a Navy commander with power of a different kind. The power of political connections.

"Finally, you'd eliminate some obstacles and settle some scores. And you'd use both the dead eagle and a fixed fight to do that. You'd set up the soldier who could testify to your panicked fuckup on Attu. And you'd set up the dirty, unjustly famous Marxist corporal who'd snubbed you and your talent—and who might also cause you trouble because of his habit of talking to every GI in camp. Including the occasional sailor."

Pop reached down with his free hand, picked up the confessions, and dropped them into the wastebasket on top of the .45. Then he pointed the .38 at the colonel's chest.

"Are there any carbons?" Pop asked. "Tell the truth, now. I was a Pinkerton."

The colonel, pale and perspiring, shook his head. Pop picked up the colonel's untouched glass of whiskey and poured it into the wastebasket.

"The one thing I can't figure," he said, "is how you arranged the timing and the murder. I know how you got your fall-guy sailor to show up at the *ulax* this morning—money and sex. But I don't know how you managed to have him capture an eagle for you to kill at almost the same time. And I don't know how you could be sure that the second sailor, even as angry as he was over being cheated, would go so far as to kill the boxer."

Now the colonel, still pasty and sweating, smiled. He looked happy. It was the scariest thing I'd seen since Attu.

"I saw the future," he said. His voice was as thick and dark as volcanic mud. "That's how."

Pop cocked his head. "Ah. Well, that wouldn't have made sense to me yesterday. But it's not yesterday anymore." He reached into a jacket pocket and brought out his Zippo. "So maybe you already saw this, too."

He lit the Zippo and dropped it into the wastebasket. Blue and yellow flames flashed up halfway to the ceiling, then settled to a few inches above the lip of the basket and burned steadily.

"We're going to leave now," Pop told the colonel. He picked up the bottle cap and replaced it on the Johnnie Walker. "You aren't going to bother us again. The private here isn't your slave anymore. And I don't have the time or stomach to read your stories." He picked up the bottle with his free hand and took a few steps backward toward the vestibule.

I hesitated, thinking that perhaps I should put out the fire. But neither Pop nor the colonel seemed concerned by it.

"You can't prove any of it," the colonel said. His voice was shaking and wild now. "You don't have anything you can tell anyone. You can't do a thing to me."

Pop stopped, then stepped forward again. He held out the bottle of whiskey toward mc. I took it.

Then Pop uncocked the .38 and slid it into in his right jacket pocket. He stepped up to the desk again. I could see the light of the flames dancing in his eyeglasses as he nodded to the colonel.

"You're partly right," Pop said. "No one can go to a court-martial and submit visions as evidence. But I do have a few things I can use in other contexts. I have a new friend in the Navy, a great admirer of my work, who has high connections. And I gave this same friend the name of a possible murderer. A sailor named Joe. I didn't have to tell him why or how I had the name. My reputation in matters of murder, fictional though those murders may be, seemed good enough for him.

"Now, the naval investigators might not find the right Joe, and even if they do, they might not be able to prove what Joe did. Especially if he's smart enough not to confess. But the Joe in question is a bit of a hothead. So, since those Navy boys will be questioning every sailor on Adak named Joe, it's possible that an angry Joe might reveal that one of yesterday's boxing matches was fixed. And he might tell them who else knows about that, and who he saw by that dead bird this morning. And then those Navy boys might come talk to some of their colleagues in the Army. Don't you think?"

The colonel began to rise from his chair again.

"Goddamn slimy Red—" he began.

As quick as a snake striking, Pop reached into his right jacket pocket and came up with the bent eagle feather. He thrust it across the desk and held it less than an inch from the colonel's nose.

"You," Pop said. "Will not. Fuck. With us. Again."

Then Pop reached down to the desk with his left and picked up the colonel's garrison cap. He dropped it into the wastebasket.

The flames shot higher, and something inside the basket squealed.

The colonel's mouth went slack. His eyes opened wide and stared at the fire without blinking. He looked like a wax statue. Or a corpse in rigor mortis.

Pop turned and put the feather back in his pocket. Then he gave me a glance and jerked his head toward the door. I turned and went out with him.

But Pop looked back toward the colonel one last time.

"By the way," he said. "If you've ever thought about asking for a transfer, now would be an excellent time. I understand MacArthur wants to get back to the Philippines in the worst way. And I'm sure he could use the help."

Then we went out. The fog was still thick, but we could see where we were going. Even this late in the day, there was a sun shining somewhere beyond the gray veil. It was summer in the Aleutians.

I looked back and saw that the ravens were gone.

XV

The lights were burning bright in the windows at the *Adakian* hut when Pop and I came up the hill. They were shining down through the fog in golden beams. And as we drew closer, I could hear the clatter of typewriters and the steady murmur of voices. Pop's staff was in there hard at work on the July 6 edition.

"I'm sorry your cartoonist has to draw his cartoon over again," I said as we climbed the last dozen yards.

Pop coughed. "He was upset. But between you and me, it wasn't his best work. I suspect he'll do a better one now. Unfair losses can be inspirational."

As we reached the entrance lean-to, a figure stepped out from behind it. It was the Cutthroat. Neither Pop nor I was startled.

"What took you guys so long?" the Cutthroat asked. "The colonel's shack ain't that far. I've been here five minutes already. Thought you might have died or something."

Pop and I exchanged glances.

"You were listening outside again, weren't you?" I asked.

He looked at me as if I were a moron. "What do you think? I wanted to know what you guys were gonna do. Which wasn't what I expected, but I guess it was okay. Might've been better if you'd gone ahead and shot him." He scratched his jaw. "You sure he's gonna let you be? More important, is he gonna let *me* be?"

"I suspect he'll have no choice," Pop said. "You see, I've already asked my new Navy comrade to inquire with his high-placed friends regarding a transfer for the lieutenant colonel. So whether he asks for one or not, one will soon be suggested to him. Assuming he doesn't find himself in Dutch before that happens. Because whenever the general returns, I may be having a conversation with him as well."

The Cutthroat gave a snorting laugh. "You are one strange fucking excuse for a corporal."

"That I am," Pop said. "And you brew the goddamnedest cup of coffee I ever drank. Next time, I'll make my own."

But the Cutthroat was already heading down the boardwalk. "Leave my six beers outside my shed," he called back. He glowed in the golden shafts of light from *The Adakian* for a few seconds, and then was gone.

Pop turned to me. "It was kind of you to walk back with me, Private. But unnecessary. I may seem like a frail old man. But despite my white hair and tuberculosis-ravaged lungs, I do manage to get around, don't I?"

"Yes, sir," I said.

"Jesus Christ," Pop said. He pointed at me with his bottle of Johnnie Walker. "What did I tell you about 'sir' and enlisted men?"

I held out my hand. "Well, I'm sure as hell not going to salute you."

He gave me a quick handshake. His grip was stronger than he looked.

"It's been a long and overly interesting day, Private," he said. "And I sincerely hope, you dumb Bohunk, that I only encounter you in passing from now on. No offense."

"None taken."

He turned to go inside. "Good night, Private."

But I couldn't let it go at that.

"That Navy boy is dead," I blurted. "It was the colonel's fault, and we're letting him get away with it."

Pop stopped just inside the lean-to. "Maybe so." He looked back at me. "But sometimes the best you can do is wound your enemy . . . and then let him fly away."

"Is that what happened?" I asked. "Is that what it meant when you showed him the feather?"

Pop rolled his eyes upward and grinned with those bad teeth.

"That didn't mean a thing to me," he said. "But it meant something to *him*." He checked his wristwatch. "And now I really do have a newspaper to put out. Any more silly questions?"

There was one.

"How can you do that?" I asked.

Pop frowned. "How can I do what?"

All the way back from the colonel's office, I had been struggling with the words in my head. I wasn't good with words. And Pop already thought I was stupid. So I knew I wouldn't say it right. But I had to try.

"How can you go back to what you did before?" I asked. "How can you do anything at all now that—" I closed my fist, as if I could grab what I wanted to say from the fog. "Now that you know what happens."

Pop's shoulders slumped, and his eyes drifted away from mine for a moment.

But only a moment.

Then his shoulders snapped up, and his eyes met mine again. They were fierce.

"Because I'm not dead *yet*," he said. He turned away. "And neither are you."

He opened the door with the words *The Adakian* stenciled on it. He raised the whiskey bottle, and a roar of voices greeted him. Then the door closed, and the long day was over.

I started back down the boardwalk. I thought I might go back to the bay and just watch the water all night. I'd probably get cold as hell without a coat, even in July. But as long as there wasn't a williwaw, I'd survive.

In the morning, at chow, I would tell my squad leader that I was all his.

Epilogue

There was buzz for the next several days about the Navy murder, and I eventually heard that they arrested a seaman named Joe. But no one ever questioned me, and I never heard what they did with him. And I didn't try to find out.

I saw the Cutthroat only once more, at a distance, just a few days after the fifth of July. He was boarding a ship at the dock in Sweeper Cove. It didn't look like he was sneaking on. So I think he probably made it back to Fort Richardson and finished the war with the Alaska Scouts. But I don't know.

The lieutenant colonel left Adak less than two weeks after that. I didn't hear where he had been sent. But a few years after V-J Day, my curiosity got the better of me, and I made some inquiries. I learned that he had gone to the Philippines and had died at the outset of the Battle of Leyte in October 1944. A kamikaze had hit his ship, and he had burned to death. He never received his promotion.

I never spoke with Pop again. I saw him around throughout the rest of July and the first part of August, because he was hard to miss. I even passed by him on Main Street a few times. Once he gave me a nod, and I gave him the same in return.

That was all that passed between us until Pop was transferred to the mainland. We had all heard it was happening, since he was the camp celebrity and there was a lot of debate as to whether it was a good thing or a bad thing that he was going. But no one seemed to know just when it would occur.

Then, one evening in August, I came back to my bunk after a long day of working on a new runway at the airfield. And there was a manila envelope on my pillow. Inside I found the bent eagle feather and a typed note:

CLEARING OUT JUNK. THOUGHT YOU MIGHT WANT THIS. YOU OWE ME A ZIPPO. P.S. WHEN YOU BRAG TO YOUR CHILDREN ABOUT HAVING MET ME, DO NOT CALL ME "POP." D. H.

I have not honored his request.

Toward the end of the war, I heard that Pop had made sergeant and been reassigned back to Adak in early 1945. But by then I was gone. I had been sent south to rejoin my old combat unit and train for an invasion of the Japanese home islands.

Then came the Bomb, and I was in Nebraska by Christmas.

Now, as an old man, I take the bent eagle feather from its envelope every fifth of July. Just for a minute.

My life has been good, but not much of it has been a surprise. I saw most of it coming a long time ago.

But then Pop slapped me awake. He slapped me awake, and he kept me from seeing the end.

I've always been grateful to him for that.

I don't know whether he was a Communist. I don't know whether he subverted the Constitution, supported tyrants, lied to Congress, or did any of the other things they said he did.

But I know he wore his country's uniform in two World Wars. And I know he's buried at Arlington.

Plus one more thing.

Just today, decades after I first saw that hardback copy on another guy's bunk . . .

I've finally finished reading *The Maltese Falcon*.

And you know what? I wish I could tell Pop:

It's pretty goddamn good.

Some of **Bradley Denton**'s stories have been collected in the World Fantasy Award-winning collections *A Conflagration Artist* and *The Calvin Coolidge Home for Dead Comedians*. His 2004 novella "Sergeant Chip" won the Theodore Sturgeon Memorial Award. His novels include *Wrack & Roll*, *Blackburn*, *Laughin' Boy*, *Lunatics*, and the John W. Campbell Memorial Award-winning *Buddy Holly Is Alive and Well On Ganymede* (soon to be a motion picture: www.aliveandwellmovie.com).

The Case: *Three apparently lovey-dovey couples commit dual suicide in the span of two weeks. But for the third pair . . . well, there are seriously irrational components to their behavior indicating mental tampering by black magic.*

The Investigators: *Harry Dresden—wizard-for-hire, private detective, and Special Investigations consultant for the Chicago Police Department—and Sergeant Karrin Murphy of the CPD.*

LOVE HURTS

Jim Butcher

Murphy gestured at the bodies and said, "Love hurts."

I ducked under the crime scene tape and entered the Wrigleyville apartment. The smell of blood and death was thick. It made gallows humor inevitable.

Murphy stood there looking at me. She wasn't offering explanations. That meant she wanted an unbiased opinion from CPD's Special Investigations consultant—who is me, Harry Dresden. As far as I know, I am the only wizard on the planet earning a significant portion of his income working for a law enforcement agency.

I stopped and looked around, taking inventory.

Two bodies, naked, male and female, still intertwined in the act. One little pistol, illegal in Chicago, laying upon the limp fingers of the woman. Two gunshot wounds to the temples, one each. There were two overlapping fan-shaped splatters of blood, and more had soaked into the carpet. The bodies stank like hell. Some very unromantic things had happened to them after death.

I walked a little further into the room and looked around. Somewhere in the apartment, an old vinyl was playing Queen. Freddie wondered who wanted to live forever. As I listened, the song ended and began again a few seconds later, popping and scratching nostalgically.

The walls were covered in photographs.

I don't mean that there were a lot of pictures on the wall, like at great-grandma's house. I mean covered in photographs. Entirely. Completely papered.

I glanced up. So was the ceiling.

I took a moment to walk slowly around, looking at pictures. All of them, every single one of them, featured the two dead people together, posed somewhere and looking deliriously happy. I walked and peered. Plenty of the pictures were near-duplicates in most details, except that the subjects wore different sets of clothing—generally cutesy matching T-shirts. Most of the sites were tourist spots within Chicago.

It was as if the couple had gone on the same vacation tour every day, over and over again, collecting the same general batch of pictures each time.

"Matching T-shirts," I said. "Creepy."

Murphy's smile was unpleasant. She was a tiny, compactly muscular woman with blond hair and a button nose. I'd say that she was so cute I just wanted to put her in my pocket, but if I tried to do it, she'd break my arm. Murph knows martial arts.

She waited and said nothing.

"Another suicide pact. That's the third one this month." I gestured at the pictures. "Though the others weren't quite so cuckoo for Cocoa Puffs. Or, ah, in medias res." I shrugged and gestured at the obsessive photographs. "This is just crazy."

Murphy lifted one pale eyebrow ever so slightly. "Remind me: how much do we pay you to give us advice, Sherlock?"

I grimaced. "Yeah, yeah. I know." I was quiet for a while and then said, "What were their names?"

"Greg and Cindy Bardalacki," Murphy said.

"Seemingly unconnected dead people, but they share similar patterns of death. Now we're upgrading to irrational and obsessive behavior as a precursor . . . " I frowned. I checked several of the pictures and went over to eye the bodies. "Oh," I said. "Oh, hell's bells."

Murphy arched an eyebrow.

"No wedding rings anywhere," I said. "No wedding pictures. And . . . " I finally found a framed family picture which looked to have been there for awhile, among all the snapshots. Greg and Cindy were both in it, along with an older couple and a younger man.

"Jesus, Murph," I said. "They weren't a married couple. They were brother and sister."

Murphy eyed the intertwined bodies. There were no signs of struggle. Clothes, champagne flutes, and an empty bubbly bottle lay scattered. "Married, no," she said. "Couple, yes." She was unruffled. She'd already worked that out for herself.

"Ick," I said. "But that explains it."

"Explains what?"

"These two. They were together—and they went insane doing it. This has the earmarks of someone tampering with their minds."

Murphy squinted at me. "Why?"

I spread my hands. "Let's say Greg and Cindy bump into Bad Guy X. Bad Guy X gets into their heads and makes them fall wildly in love and lust with one another. There's nothing they can do about the feelings—which seem perfectly natural—but on some level they're aware that what they're doing is not what they want, and dementedly wrong besides. Their compromised conscious minds clash with their subconscious and . . . " I gestured at pictures. "And it escalates until they can't handle it anymore, and bang." I shot Murphy with my thumb and forefinger.

"If you're right, they aren't the deceased," Murphy said. "They're the victims. Big difference. Which is it?"

"Wish I could say," I said, "But the only evidence that could prove it one way or another is leaking out onto the floor. If we get a survivor, maybe I could take a peek and see, but barring that we're stuck with legwork."

Murphy sighed and looked down. "Two suicide pacts could—technically—be a coincidence. Three of them, no way it's natural. This feels more like something's MO. Could it be another one of those Skavis vampires?"

"They gun for loners," I said, shaking my head. "These deaths don't fit their profile."

"So. You're telling me that we need to turn up a common denominator to link the victims? Gosh, I wish I could have thought of that on my own."

I winced. "Yeah." I glanced over at a couple of other SI detectives in the room, taking pictures of the bodies and documenting the walls and so on. Forensics wasn't on site. They don't like to waste their time on the suicides of the emotionally disturbed, regardless of how bizarre they might be. That was crap work, and as such had been dutifully passed to SI.

I lowered my voice. "If someone is playing mind games, the Council might know something. I'll try to pick up the trail on that end. You start from here. Hopefully, I'll earn my pay and we'll meet in the middle."

"Right." Murph stared at the bodies and her eyes were haunted. She knew what it was like to be the victim of mental manipulation. I didn't reach out to support her. She hated showing vulnerability, and I didn't want to point out to her that I'd noticed.

Freddie reached a crescendo which told us that love must die.

Murphy sighed and called, "For the love of God, someone turn off that damned record."

"I'm sorry, Harry," Captain Luccio said. "We don't exactly have orbital satellites for detecting black magic."

I waited a second to be sure that she was finished. The presence of so much magical talent on the far end of the call meant that at times the lag could stretch out between Chicago and Edinburgh, the headquarters of the White Council of Wizardry. Anastasia Luccio, Captain of the Wardens, my ex-girlfriend, had been readily forthcoming with the information the Council had on any shenanigans going on in Chicago—which was exactly nothing.

"Too bad we don't, eh?" I asked. "Unofficially—is there anyone who might know anything?"

"The Gatekeeper, perhaps. He has a gift for sensing problem areas. But no one has seen him for weeks, which is hardly unusual. And frankly, Warden Dresden, you're supposed to be the one giving *us* this kind of information." Her voice was half-teasing, half deadly serious. "What do you think is happening?"

"Three couples, apparently lovey-dovey as hell, have committed dual suicide in the past two weeks," I told her. "The last two were brother and sister. There were some seriously irrational components to their behavior."

"You suspect mental tampering," she said. Her voice was hard.

Luccio had been a victim, too.

I found myself smiling somewhat bitterly at no one. She had been, among other things, mindboinked into going out with me. Which was apparently the only way anyone would date me, lately. "It seems a reasonable suspicion. I'll let you know what I turn up."

"Use caution," she said. "Don't enter any suspect situation without backup on hand. There's too much chance that you could be compromised."

"Compromised?" I asked. "Of the two people having this conversation, which one of them exposed the last guy rearranging people's heads?"

"Touché," Luccio said. "But he got away with it because we were overconfident. So use caution anyway."

"Planning on it," I said.

There was a moment of awkward silence, and then Anastasia said, "How have you been, Harry?"

"Keeping busy," I said. She had already apologized to me, sort of, for abruptly walking out of my personal life. She'd never intended to be there in the first place. There had been a real emotional tsunami around the events of last year, and I wasn't the one who had gotten the most hurt by them. "You?"

"Keeping busy." She was quiet for a moment and then said, "I know it's over. But I'm glad for the time we had together. It made me happy. Sometimes I—"

Miss feeling that, I thought, completing the sentence. My throat felt tight. "Nothing wrong with happy."

"No, there isn't. When it's real." Her voice softened. "Be careful, Harry. Please."

"I will," I said.

■ ■ ■

I started combing the supernatural world for answers and got almost nothing. The Little Folk, who could usually be relied on to provide some kind of information, had nothing for me. Their memory for detail is very short, and the deaths had happened too long ago to get me anything but conflicting gibberish from them.

I made several mental nighttime sweeps through the city using the scale model of Chicago in my basement, and got nothing but a headache for my trouble.

I called around the Paranet, the organization of folk with only modest magical gifts, the kind who often found themselves being preyed upon by more powerful supernatural beings. They worked together now, sharing information, communicating successful techniques, and generally overcoming their lack of raw magical muscle with mutually supportive teamwork. They didn't have anything for me, either.

I hit McAnnally's, a hub of the supernatural social scene, and asked a lot of questions. No one had any answers. Then I started contacting the people I knew in the scene, starting with the ones I thought most likely to provide information. I worked my way methodically down the list, crossing out names, until I got to "ask random people on the street."

There are days when I don't feel like much of a wizard. Or an investigator. Or a wizard investigator.

Ordinary PIs have a lot of days like that, where you look and look and look for information and find nothing. I get fewer of those days than most, on account of the whole wizard thing giving me a lot more options—but sometimes I come up goose-eggs anyway.

I just hate doing it when lives may be in danger.

Four days later, all I knew was that nobody knew about any black magic happening in Chicago, and the only traces of it I *did* find were the miniscule amounts of residue left from black magic wrought by those without enough power to be a threat (Warden Ramirez had coined the phrase "dim magic" to describe that kind of petty, essentially harmless malice). There were also the usual traces of dim magic performed subconsciously from a bed of dark emotions, probably by someone who might not even know they had a gift.

In other words, goose eggs.

Fortunately, Murphy got the job done.

Sometimes hard work is way better than magic.

Murphy's Saturn had gotten a little blown up a couple of years back, sort of my fault, and what with her demotion and all, it would be a while before she'd be able to afford something besides her old Harley. For some reason, she didn't want to take the motorcycle, so that left my car, the ever trusty (almost always) *Blue Beetle*. It's an old-school VW Bug which had seen me through one nasty scrape after another. More than once, it had been pounded badly, but always it had risen to do battle once more—if by battle one means driving somewhere at a sedate speed, without much acceleration and only middling gas mileage.

Don't start. It's paid for.

I stopped outside Murphy's little white house, with its little pink rose garden, and rolled down the window on the passenger side. "Make like the Dukes of Hazzard," I said. "Door's stuck."

Murphy gave me a narrow look. Then she tried the door. It opened easily. She slid into the passenger seat with a smug smile, closed the door, and didn't say anything.

"Police work has made you cynical," I said.

"If you want to ogle my butt, you'll just have to work for it like everyone else, Harry."

I snorted and put the car in gear. "Where we going?"

"Nowhere until you buckle up," she said, putting her own seatbelt on.

"It's my car," I said.

"It's the law. You want to get cited? Cause I can do that."

I debated whether or not it was worth it while she gave me her cop look. And produced a ballpoint pen.

I buckled up.

Murphy beamed at me. "Springfield. Head for I-55."

I grunted. "Kind of out of your jurisdiction."

"If we were investigating something," Murphy said. "We're not. We're going to the fair."

I eyed her sidelong. "On a date?"

"Sure, if someone asks," she said, offhand. Then she froze for a second, and added, "It's a reasonable cover story."

"Right," I said. Her cheeks looked a little pink. Neither of us said anything for a little while.

I merged onto the highway, always fun in a car originally designed to rocket down the Autobahn at a blistering one hundred kilometers an hour, and asked Murphy, "Springfield?"

"State Fair," she said. "That was the common denominator."

I frowned, going over the dates in my head. "State Fair only runs, what? Ten days?"

Murphy nodded. "They shut down tonight."

"But the first couple died twelve days ago."

"They were both volunteer staff for the Fair, and they were down there on the grounds setting up." Murphy lifted a foot to rest her heel on the edge of the passenger seat, frowning out the window. "I found skee-ball tickets and one of those chintzy stuffed animals in the second couple's apartment. And the Bardalackis got pulled over for speeding on I-55, five minutes out of Springfield and bound for Chicago."

"So *maybe* they went to the Fair," I said. "Or maybe they were just taking a road trip or something."

Murphy shrugged. "Possibly. But if I assume that it's a coincidence, it doesn't get me anywhere—and we've got nothing. If I assume that there's a connection, we've got a possible answer."

I beamed at her. "I thought you didn't like reading Parker."

She eyed me. "That doesn't mean his logic isn't sound."

"Oh. Right."

She exhaled heavily. "It's the best I've got. I just hope that if I get you into the general area, you can pick up on whatever is going on."

"Yeah," I said, thinking of walls papered in photographs. "Me too."

The thing I enjoy the most about places like the State Fair is the smells. You get combinations of smells at such events like none found anywhere else. Popcorn, roast nuts, and fast food predominate, and you can get anything you want to clog your arteries or burn out your stomach lining there. Chili dogs, funnel cakes, fried bread, majorly greasy pizza, candy apples, ye gods. Evil food smells amazing—which is either proof that there is a Satan or some equivalent out there, or that the Almighty doesn't actually want everyone to eat organic tofu all the time. I can't decide.

Other smells are a cross-section, depending on where you're standing. Disinfectant and filth walking by the porta-potties, exhaust and burnt oil and sun-baked asphalt and gravel in the parking lots, sunlight on warm bodies, suntan lotion, cigarette smoke and beer near some of the attendees, the pungent, honest smell of livestock near the animal shows, stock contests, or pony rides—all of it charging right up your nose. I like indulging my sense of smell.

Smell is the hardest sense to lie to.

Murphy and I started in midmorning and started walking around the fair in a methodical search pattern. It took us all day. The State Fair is not a rinky-dink event.

"Dammit," she said. "We've been here all day. You sure you haven't sniffed out anything?"

"Nothing like what we're looking for," I said. "I was afraid of this."

"Of what?"

"A lot of times, magic like this—complex, long-lasting, subtle, dark—doesn't thrive well in sunlight." I glanced at the lengthening shadows. "Give it another half an hour and we'll try again."

Murphy frowned at me. "I thought you always said magic isn't about good and evil."

"Neither is sunshine."

Murphy exhaled, her displeasure plain. "You might have mentioned it to me before."

"No way to know until we tried," I said. "Think of it this way: maybe we're just looking in the exact wrong place."

She sighed and squinted around at the nearby food trailers and concessions stands. "Ugh. Think there's anything here that won't make me split my jeans at the seams?"

I beamed. "Probably not. How about dogs and a funnel cake?"

"Bastard," Murphy growled. Then, "Okay."

I realized we were being followed halfway through my second hot dog.

I kept myself from reacting, took another bite, and said, "Maybe this is the place after all."

Murphy had found a place selling turkey drumsticks. She had cut the meat from the bone and onto a paper plate, and was eating it with a plastic fork. She didn't stop chewing or look up. "Whatcha got?"

"Guy in a maroon tee and tan BDU pants, about twenty feet away off your right shoulder. I've seen him at least two other times today."

"Doesn't necessarily mean he's following us."

"He's been busy doing nothing in particular all three times."

Murphy nodded. "Five-eight or so, long hair? Little soul tuft under his mouth?"

"Yeah."

"He was sitting on a bench when I came out of the porta-potty," Murphy said. "Also doing nothing." She shrugged and went back to eating.

"How do you want to play it?"

"We're here with a zillion people, Harry." She deepened her voice and blocked out any hint of a nasal tone. "You want I should whack him until he talks?"

I grunted and finished my hot dog. "Doesn't necessarily mean anything. Maybe he's got a crush on you."

Murphy snorted. "Maybe he's got a crush on *you*."

I covered a respectable belch with my hand and reached for my funnel cake. "Who could blame him?" I took a bite and nodded. "All right. We'll see what happens, then."

Murphy nodded and sipped at her Diet Coke. "Will says you and Anastasia broke up a while back."

"Will talks too much," I said darkly.

She glanced a little bit away. "He's your friend. He worries about you."

I studied her averted face for a moment and then nodded. "Well," I said, "tell Will he doesn't need to worry. It sucked. It sucks less now. I'll be fine. Fish in the sea, never meant to be, et cetera." I paused over another bite of funnel cake and asked, "How's Kincaid?"

"The way he always is," Murphy said.

"You get to be a few centuries old, you get a little set in your ways."

She shook her head. "It's his type. He'd be that way if he was twenty. He walks his own road and doesn't let anyone make him do differently. Like . . . "

She stopped before she could say who Kincaid was like. She ate her turkey leg.

A shiver passed over the Fair, a tactile sensation to my wizard's senses. Sundown. Twilight would go on for a while yet, but the light left in the sky would no longer hold the creatures of the night at bay.

Murphy glanced up at me, sensing the change in my level of tension. She finished off her drink while I stuffed the last of the funnel cake into my mouth, and we stood up together.

The western sky was still a little bit orange when I finally sensed magic at work.

We were near the carnival, a section of the fair full of garishly lit rides, heavily slanted games of chance, and chintzy attractions of every kind. It was full of screaming, excited little kids, parents with frayed patience, and fashion-enslaved teenagers. Music tinkled and brayed tinny tunes. Lights flashed and danced. Barkers bleated out cajolement, encouragement, and condolences in almost-equal measures.

We drifted through the merry chaos, our maroon-shirted tail following along ten to twenty yards behind. I walked with my eyes half-closed, giving no more heed to my vision than a bloodhound on a trail. Murphy stayed beside me, her expression calm, her blue eyes alert for physical danger.

Then I felt it—a quiver in the air, no more noticeable than the fading hum from a gently plucked guitar string. I noted its direction and walked several more paces before checking again, in an attempt to triangulate the source of the disturbance. I got a rough fix on it in under a minute, and realized that I had stopped and was staring.

"Harry?" Murphy asked. "What is it?"

"Something down there," I said, nodding to the midway. "It's faint. But it's something."

Murph inhaled sharply. "This must be the place. There goes our tail."

We didn't have to communicate the decision to one another. If the tail belonged to whoever was behind this, we couldn't let him get away to give the culprit forewarning—and odds were excellent that the man in maroon's sudden rabbit impersonation would result in him leading us somewhere interesting.

We turned and gave pursuit.

A footrace on open ground is one thing. Running through a crowded carnival is something else entirely. You can't sprint, unless you want to wind up falling down a lot and attracting a lot of attention. You have to hurry along, hopping between clusters of people, never really getting the chance to pour on the gas. The danger in a chase like this isn't that the quarry will outrun you, but that you'll lose him in the crowd.

I had a huge advantage. I'm freakishly tall. I could see over everyone and spot Mr. Maroon bobbing and weaving his way through the crowd. I took the lead and Murphy followed.

I got within a couple of long steps of Maroon, but was interdicted by a gaggle of seniors in Shriners caps. He caught a break at the same time, a stretch of open ground beyond the Shriners, and by the time I got through, I saw Maroon handing tickets to a carnie. He hopped up onto a platform, got into a little roller-coaster style car, and vanished into an attraction.

"Dammit!" Murphy said, panting. "What now?"

Behind the attraction, advertised as the Tunnel of Terror, there was an empty space, the interior of a circle of several similar rides and games. There wouldn't be anyone to hide behind in there. "You take the back. I'll watch the front. Whoever spots him gives a shout."

"Got it." Murphy hurried off around the Tunnel of Terror. She frowned at a little plastic barrier with an Authorized Personnel Only notice on it, then calmly ignored it and went on over.

"Anarchist," I muttered, and settled down to wait for Maroon to figure out he'd been treed.

He didn't appear.

The dingy little roller coaster car came wheezing slowly out of the opposite side of the platform, empty. The carnie, an old fellow with a scruffy white beard, didn't notice—he was dozing in his chair.

Murphy returned a few seconds later. "There are two doors on the back," she reported, "both of them chained and locked from the outside. He didn't come out that way."

I inhaled and nodded at the empty car. "Not here, either. Look, we can't just stand around. Maybe he's running through a tunnel or something. We've got to know if he's inside."

"I'll go flush him out," she said. "You pick him up when he shows."

"No way," I said. "We stay with our wing—" I glanced at Murphy "—person. The power I sensed came from somewhere nearby. If we split up, we're about a million times more vulnerable to mental manipulation. And if this guy is more than he appears, neither of us wants to take him solo."

She grimaced, nodded, and we started toward the Tunnel of Terror together.

The old carnie woke up as we came up the ramp, let out a wheezing cough, and pointed to a sign that required us to give him three tickets each for the ride. I hadn't bought any, and the ticket counter was more than far enough away for Maroon to scamper if we stopped to follow the rules.

"Sir," Murphy said, "a man we're looking for just went into your attraction, but he didn't come out again. We need to go in and look for him."

He blinked gummy eyes at Murphy and said, "Three tickets."

"You don't understand," she said. "A fugitive may be hiding inside the Tunnel of Terror. We need to check and see if he's there."

The carnie snorted. "Three tickets, missy. Though it ain't the nicest room you two could rent."

Murphy's jaw muscles flexed.

I stepped forward. "Hey, man," I said. "Harry Dresden, PI. If you wouldn't mind, all we need to do is get inside for five minutes."

He eyed me. "PI, huh?"

I produced my license and showed it to him. He eyed it and then me. "You don't look like no private investigator I ever saw. Where's your hat?"

"In the shop," I said. "Transmission gave out." I winked at him and held up a folded twenty between my first and second finger. "Five minutes?"

He yawned. "Naw. Can't let nobody run around loose in there." He reached out and took the twenty. "Then again, what you and your lady friend mutually consent to do once you're inside ain't my affair." He rose, pulled a lever, and gestured at the car. "Mount up," he leered. "And keep your, ah, extremities inside the car at all times."

We got in, and I was nearly scalded by the steam coming out of Murphy's ears. "You just had to play along with that one."

"We needed to get inside," I said. "Just doing my job, Sergeant."

She snorted.

"Hey, Murph, look," I said, holding up a strap of old, worn leather. "Seatbelts."

She gave me a look that could have scoured steel. Then, with a stubborn set of her jaw, secured the flimsy thing. Her expression dared me to object.

I grinned and relaxed. It isn't easy to really get Murph's goat and get away with it.

On the other side of the platform, the carnie pulled another lever, and a moment later the little cart started rolling forward at the blazing speed of one, maybe even two miles an hour. A dark curtain parted ahead of us and we rolled into the Tunnel of Terror.

Murphy promptly drew her gun—it was dark but I heard the scratch of its barrel on plastic as she drew it from its holder. She snapped a small LED flashlight into its holder beneath the gun barrel and flicked it on. We were in a cramped little tunnel, every surface painted black, and there was absolutely nowhere for Maroon to be hiding.

I shook out the charm bracelet on my left wrist, preparing defensive energies in case they were needed. Murph and I had been working together long enough to know our roles. If trouble came, I would defend us. Murphy and her Sig would reply.

A door opened at the end of the little hallway and we rolled forward into an open set dressed to look like a rustic farmhouse, with a lot of subtle details meant to be scary—severed fingers at the base of the chicken-chopping stump, just below the bloody axe, glowing eyes appearing in an upstairs window of the farmhouse, that kind of thing. There was no sign of Maroon and precious little place for him to hide.

"Better get that seatbelt off," I told her. "We want to be able to move fast if it comes to that."

"Yeah," she said, and reached down, just as something huge and terrifying dropped onto the car from the shadows above us, screaming.

Adrenaline hit my system like a runaway bus, and I looked up to see a decidedly demonic scarecrow hanging a few feet above our heads, bouncing on its wires and playing a recording of cackling, mad laughter.

"Jesus Christ," Murphy breathed, lowering her gun. She was a little white around the eyes.

We looked at each other and both burst into high, nervous laughs.

"Tunnel of Terror," Murphy said. "We are *so* cool."

"Total badasses," I said, grinning.

The car continued its slow grind forward and Murphy unfastened the seatbelt. We moved into the next area, meant to be a zombie-infested hospital. It had a zombie mannequin which burst out of a closet near the track, and plenty of gore. We got out of the car and scouted a couple of spots where he might have been but wasn't. Then we hopped into the car again before it could leave the set.

So it went, on through a ghoulish graveyard, a troglodyte-teeming cavern, and a literal Old West ghost town. We came up with nothing, but we moved well as a team, better than I could remember doing with anyone before.

Everything felt as smooth and natural, as if we'd been moving together our whole lives. We did it in total silence, too, divining what each other would do through pure instinct.

Even great teams lose a game here or there, though. We came up with diddly, and emerged from the Tunnel of Terror with neither Maroon nor any idea where he'd gone.

"Hell's bells," I muttered. "This week has been an investigative suckfest for me."

Murphy tittered again. "You said 'suck.'"

I grinned at her and looked around. "Well," I said. "We don't know where Maroon went. If they hadn't made us already, they have now."

"Can you pick up on the signal-whatsit again?"

"Energy signature," I said. "Maybe. It's pretty vague though. I'm not sure how much more precise I can get."

"Let's find out," she said.

I nodded. "Right, then." We started around the suspect circle of attractions, moving slowly and trying to blend into the crowds. When a couple of rowdy kids went by, one chasing the other, I put an arm around her shoulders and drew her into the shelter of my body so that she wouldn't get bowled over.

She exhaled slowly and did not step away from me.

My heart started beating faster.

"Harry," she said quietly.

"Yeah?"

"You and me . . . why haven't we ever . . . " She looked up at me. "Why not?"

"The usual, I guess," I said quietly. "Trouble. Duty. Other people involved."

She shook her head. "Why not?" she repeated, her eyes direct. "All these years have gone by. And something could have happened, but it never did. Why not?"

I licked my lips. "Just like that? We just decide to be together?"

Her eyelids lowered. "Why not?"

My heart did the drum solo from "Wipeout."

Why not?

I bent my head down to her mouth, and kissed her, very gently.

She turned into the kiss, pressing her body against mine. It was a little bit awkward. I was most of two feet taller than she was. We made up for grace with enthusiasm, her arms twining around my neck as she kissed me, hungry and deep.

"Whoah," I said, drawing back a moment later. "Work. Right?"

She looked at me for a moment, her cheeks pink, her lips a little swollen from the kiss, and said, "Right." She closed her eyes and nodded. "Right. Work first."

"Then dinner?" I asked.

"Dinner. My place. We can order in."

My belly trembled in sudden excitement at that proposition. "Right." I looked around. "So let's find this thing and get it over with."

We started moving again. A circuit around the attractions got me no closer to the source of the energy I'd sensed earlier.

"Dammit," I said when we'd completed the pattern, frustrated.

"Hey," Murphy said. "Don't beat yourself up about it, Harry." Her hand slipped into mine, our fingers intertwining. "I've been a cop a long time. You don't always get the bad guy. And if you go around blaming yourself for it, you wind up crawling into a bottle or eating your own gun."

"Thank you," I said quietly. "But . . . "

"Heh," Murphy said. "You said, 'but.'"

We both grinned like fools. I looked down at our twined hands. "I like this."

"So do I," Murphy said. "Why didn't we do this a long time ago?"

"Beats me."

"Are we just that stupid?" she asked. "I mean, people, in general. Are we really so blind that we miss what's right there in front of us?"

"As a species, we're essentially insane," I said. "So, yeah, probably." I lifted our hands and kissed her fingertips. "I'm not missing it now, though."

Her smile lit up several thousand square feet of the midway. "Good."

The echo of a thought rattled around in my head: *Insane . . .*

"Oh," I said. "Oh, Hell's bells."

She frowned at me. "What?"

"Murph . . . I think we got whammied."

She blinked at me. "What? No, we didn't."

"I think we did."

"I didn't see anything or feel anything. I mean, *nothing*, Harry. I've felt magic like that before."

"*Look* at us," I said, waving our joined hands.

"We've been friends a long time, Harry," she said. "And we've had a couple of near misses before. This time we just didn't screw it up. That's all that's happening, here."

"What about Kincaid?" I asked her.

She mulled over that one for a second. Then she said, "I doubt he'll even notice I'm gone." She frowned at me. "Harry, I haven't been this happy in . . . I never thought I could feel this way again. About anyone."

My heart continued to go pittypat. "I know exactly what you mean," I said. "I feel the same way."

Her smile warmed even more. "Then what's the problem? Isn't that what love is supposed to be like? Effortless?"

I had to think about that one for a second. And then I said, carefully and slowly, "Murph, think about it."

"What do you mean?"

"You know how good this is?" I asked.

"Yeah."

"How right it feels?"

She nodded. "Yeah."

"How easy it was?"

She nodded energetically, her eyes bright.

I leaned down toward her for emphasis. "It just isn't fucked up enough to really be you and me."

Her smile faltered.

"My God," she said, her eyes widening. "We got whammied."

We returned to the Tunnel of Terror.

"I don't get it," she said. "I don't . . . I didn't feel anything happen. I don't feel any different now. I thought being aware of this kind of thing made it go away."

"No," I said. "But it helps sometimes."

"Do you still . . . ?"

I squeezed her hand once more before letting go. "Yeah," I said. "I still feel it."

"Is it . . . is it going to go away?"

I didn't answer her. I didn't know. Or maybe I didn't want to know.

The old carnie saw us coming and his face flickered with apprehension as soon as he looked at us. He stood up and looked from the control board for the ride to the entranceway to the interior.

"Yeah," I muttered. "Sneaky bastard. You just try it."

He flicked one of the switches and shambled toward the Tunnel's entrance.

I made a quick effort of will, raised a hand and swept it in a horizontal arc, snarling, "Forzare!" Unseen force knocked his legs out from beneath him and tossed him into an involuntary pratfall.

Murphy and I hurried up onto the platform before he could get to his feet and run. We needn't have bothered. The carnie was apparently a genuine old guy, not some supernatural being in disguise. He lay on the platform moaning in pain. I felt kind of bad for beating up a senior citizen.

But hey. On the other hand, he did swindle me out of twenty bucks.

Murphy stood over him, her blue eyes cold, and said, "Where's the bolt hole?"

The carnie blinked at her. "Wha?"

"The trap door," she snapped. "The secret cabinet. Where is he?"

I frowned and walked toward the entranceway.

"Please," the carnie said. "I don't know what you're talking about!"

"The hell you don't," Murphy said. She leaned down and grabbed the man by the shirt with both hands and leaned closer, a snarl lifting her lip. The carnie blanched.

Murph could be pretty badass for such a tiny thing. I loved that about her.

"I can't," the carnie said. "I can't. I get paid not to see anything. She'll kill me. She'll kill me."

I parted the heavy curtain leading into the entry tunnel and spotted it at once—a circular hole in the floor about two feet across, the top end of a ladder just visible. A round lid lay rotated to one side, painted as flat black as the rest of the hall. "Here," I said to Murph. "That's why we didn't spot anything. By the time you had your light on, it was already behind us."

Murphy scowled down at the carnie and said, "Give me twenty bucks."

The man licked his lips. Then he fished my folded twenty out of his shirt pocket and passed it to Murphy.

She nodded and flashed her badge. "Get out of here before I realize I witnessed you taking a bribe and endangering lives by letting customers use the attraction in an unsafe manner."

The carnie bolted.

Murphy handed me the twenty. I pocketed it, and we climbed down the ladder.

We reached the bottom and went silent again. Murphy's body language isn't exactly subtle—it can't be, when you're her size and working law enforcement. But she could move as quietly as smoke when she needed to. I'm gangly. It was more of an effort for me.

The ladder took us down to what looked like the interior of a buried railroad car. There were electrical conduits running along the walls. Light came from a doorway at the far end of the car. I moved forward first, shield bracelet at the ready, and Murphy walked a pace behind me and to my right, her Sig held ready.

The doorway at the end of the railroad car led us into a large workroom, teeming with computers, file cabinets, microscopes, and at least one deluxe chemistry set.

Maroon sat at one of the computers, his profile in view. "Dammit, Stu," he snarled. "I told you that you can't keep coming down here to use the john. You'll just have to walk to one of the—" He glanced up at us and froze in midsentence, his eyes wide and locked on Murphy's leveled gun.

"Stu took the rest of the night off," I said amiably. "Where's your boss?"

A door opened at the far end of the workroom and a young woman of medium height appeared. She wore glasses and a lab coat, and neither of them did anything to make her look less than gorgeous. She looked at us and then at Maroon and said, in a precise, British accent, "You idiot."

"Yeah," I said. "Good help is hard to find."

The woman in the lab coat looked at me with dark, intense eyes, and I sensed what felt like a phantom pressure against my temples, as if wriggling tadpoles were slithering along the surface of my skin. It was a straightforward attempt at mental invasion, but I'd been practicing my defenses for a while now, and I wasn't falling for something that obvious. I pushed the invasive thoughts away with an effort of will and said, "Don't meet her eyes, Murph. She's a vampire. Red Court."

"Got it," she said, her gun never moving from Maroon.

The vampire looked at us both for a moment. Then she said, "You need no introduction, Mr. Dresden. I am Baroness LeBlanc. And our nations are not, at the moment, in a state of war."

"I've always been a little fuzzy on legal niceties," I said. I had several devices with me that I could use to defend myself. I was ready to use any of them. A vampire in close quarters is nothing to laugh at. LeBlanc could tear three or four limbs off in the time it takes to draw and fire a gun. I watched her closely, ready to act at the slightest resemblance of an attack. "We both know that the war is going to start up again eventually."

"You are out of anything reasonably like your territory," she said, "and you are trespassing upon mine. I would be well within my rights under the Accords to kill you and bury your torso and limbs in individual graves."

"That's the problem with this ride," I complained to Murphy. "There's nothing that's actually *scary* in the Tunnel of Terror."

"You did get your money back," she pointed out.

"Ah, true." I smiled faintly at LeBlanc. "Look, Baroness. You know who I am. You're doing something to people's minds, and I want it stopped."

"If you do not leave," she said, "I will consider it an act of war."

"Hooray," I said in a Ben Stein monotone, spinning one forefinger in the air like a New Year's noisemaker. "I've already kicked off one war with the Red Court. And I will cheerfully do it again if that is what is necessary to protect people from you."

"That's irrational," LeBlanc said. "Completely irrational."

"Tell her, Murph."

"He's completely irrational," Murphy said, her tone wry.

LeBlanc regarded me impassively for a moment. Then she smiled faintly and said, "Perhaps a physical confrontation is an inappropriate solution."

I frowned. "Really?"

She shrugged. "Not all of the Red Court are battle-hungry blood addicts, Dresden. My work here has no malevolent designs. Quite the opposite, in fact."

I tilted my head. "That's funny. All the corpses piled up say differently."

"The process *does* have its side effects," she admitted. "But the lessons garnered from them serve only to improve my work and make it safer and more effective. Honestly, you should be supporting me, Dresden. Not trying to shut me down."

"Supporting you?" I smiled a little. "Just what is it you think you're doing that's so darned wonderful?"

"I am creating love."

I barked out a laugh.

LeBlanc's face remained steady, serious.

"You think that *this*, this warping people into feeling something they don't want to feel, is *love*?"

"What is love," LeBlanc said, "if not a series of electro-chemical signals in the brain? Signals that can be duplicated, like any other sensation."

"Love is more than that," said.

"Do you love this woman?"

"Yeah," I said. "But that isn't anything new."

LeBlanc showed her teeth. "But your current longing and desire is new, is it not? New and entirely indistinguishable from your genuine emotions? Wouldn't you say, Sergeant Murphy?"

Murphy swallowed but didn't look at the vampire. LeBlanc's uncomplicated mental attack might be simple for a wizard to defeat, but any normal human being would probably be gone before they realized their minds were under attack. Instead of answering, she asked a question of her own. "Why?"

"Why what?"

"Why do this? Why experiment on making people fall in love?"

LeBlanc arched an eyebrow. "Isn't it obvious?"

I sucked in a short breath, realizing what was happening. "The White Court," I said.

The Whites were a different breed of vampire than the Reds, feeding on the life-essence of their victims, generally through seduction. Genuine love and genuine tokens of love were their kryptonite, their holy water. The love of another human being in an intimate relationship sort of rubbed off on you, making the very touch of your skin anathema to the White Court.

LeBlanc smiled at me. "Granted, there are some aberrant effects from time to time. But so far, that's been a very small percentage of the test pool. And the survivors are, as you yourself have experienced, perfectly happy. They have a love that most of your kind seldom find and even more infrequently keep. There are no victims here, wizard."

"Oh," I said. "Right. Except for the victims."

LeBlanc exhaled. "Mortals are like mayflies, wizard. They live a brief time and then they are gone. And those who have died because of my work at least died after days or weeks of perfect bliss. There are many who ended a much longer life with less. What I'm doing here has the potential to protect mortalkind from the White Court forever."

"It isn't genuine love if it's forced upon someone," Murphy said, her tone harsh.

"No," LeBlanc said. "But I believe that the real thing will very easily grow from such a foundation of companionship and happiness."

"Gosh, you're noble," I said.

LeBlanc's eyes sparkled with something ugly.

"You're doing this to get rid of the competition," I said. "And, hell, maybe to try to increase the world's population. Make more food."

The vampire regarded me levelly. "There are multiple motivations behind the work," she said. "Many of my Court agreed to the logic you cite when they would never have supported the idea of strengthening and defending mortals."

"Ohhhhh," I said, drawing the word out. "You're the vampire with a heart of gold. Florence Nightingale with fangs. I guess that makes it okay, then."

LeBlanc stared at me. Then her eyes flicked to Murphy and back. She smiled thinly. "There is a special cage reserved for you at the Red Court, Dresden. Its bars are lined with blades and spikes, so that if you fall asleep they will cut and gouge you awake."

"Shut up," Murphy said.

LeBlanc continued in a calmly amused tone. "The bottom is a closed bowl nearly a foot deep, so that you will stand in your own waste. And there are three spears with needle-sized tips waiting in a rack beneath the cage, so that any who pass you can pause and take a few moments to participate in your punishment."

"Shut *up*," Murphy growled.

"Eventually," LeBlanc purred, "your guts will be torn out and left in a pile at your feet. And when you are dead, your skin will be flayed from your body, tanned, and made into upholstery for one of the chairs in the Red Temple."

"Shut up!" snarled Murphy, and her voice was savage. Her gun whipped over to cover LeBlanc. "Shut your mouth, bitch!"

I realized the danger an instant too late. It was exactly the reaction that LeBlanc had intended to provoke. "Murph! No!"

Once Murphy's Sig was pointing elsewhere, Maroon produced a gun from beneath his desk and raised it. He was pulling the trigger even before he could level it for a shot, blazing away as fast as he could move his finger. He wasn't quite fifteen feet away from Murphy, but the first five shots missed her as I spun and brought the invisible power of my shield bracelet down between the two of them. Bullets hit the shield with flashes of light and sent little concentric blue rings rippling through the air from the point of impact.

Murphy, meanwhile, had opened up on LeBlanc. Murph fired almost as quickly as Maroon, but she had the training and discipline necessary for combat. Her bullets smacked into the vampire's torso, tearing through pale flesh and drawing gouts of red-black blood. LeBlanc staggered to one side—she wouldn't be dead, but the shots had probably rung her bell for a second or two.

I lowered the shield as Maroon's gun clicked on empty, lifted my right fist, and triggered the braided energy ring on my index finger with a short, uplifting motion. The ring saved back a little energy every time I moved my arm, storing it so that I could unleash it at need. Unseen force flew out from the ring, plucked Maroon out of his chair and slammed him into the ceiling. He dropped back down, hit his back on the edge of the desk, and fell into a senseless sprawl on the floor. The gun flew from his fingers.

"I'm out!" Murphy screamed.

I whirled back to find LeBlanc pushing herself off the wall, regaining her balance. She gave Murphy a look of flat hatred, and her eyes flushed pure black, iris and sclera alike. She opened her mouth in an inhuman scream, and then the vampire hiding beneath LeBlanc's seemingly-human form exploded outward like a racehorse emerging from its gate, leaving shreds of pale, bloodless skin in its wake.

It was a hideous thing—black and flabby and slimy-looking, with a flaccid belly, a batlike face, and long, spindly limbs. LeBlanc's eyes bulged hideously as she flew toward me.

I brought my shield up in time to intercept her, and she rebounded from it, to fall back to the section of floor already stained with her blood.

"Down!" Murphy shouted.

I dropped down onto my heels and lowered the shield.

LeBlanc rose up again, even as I heard Murphy take a deep breath, exhale halfway, and hold it. Her gun barked once.

The vampire lost about a fifth of her head as the bullet tore into her skull.

She staggered back against the wall, limbs thrashing, but she still wasn't dead. She began to claw her way to her feet again.

Murphy squeezed off six more shots, methodically. None of them missed. LeBlanc fell to the floor. Murphy took a step closer, aimed, and put another ten or twelve rounds into the fallen vampire's head. By the time she was done, the vampire's head looked like a smashed gourd.

A few seconds later, LeBlanc stopped moving.

Murphy reloaded again and kept the gun trained on the corpse.

"Nice shootin', Tex," I said. I checked out Maroon. He was still breathing.

"So," Murphy said. "Problem solved?"

"Not really," I said. "LeBlanc was no practitioner. She can't be the one who was working the whammy."

Murphy frowned and eyed Maroon for a second.

I went over to the downed man and touched my fingers lightly to his brow. There was no telltale energy signature of a practitioner. "Nope."

"Who, then?"

I shook my head. "This is delicate, difficult magic. There might not be three people on the entire White Council who could pull it off. So . . . it's most likely a focus artifact of some kind."

"A what?"

"An item that has a routine built into it," I said. "You pour energy in one end and you get results on the other."

Murphy scrunched up her nose. "Like those wolf belts the FBI had?"

"Yeah, just like that." I blinked and snapped my fingers. "*Just* like that!"

I hurried out of the little complex and up the ladder. I went to the tunnel car and took the old leather seatbelt out of it. I turned it over and found the back inscribed with nearly invisible sigils and signs. Now that I was looking for it, I could feel the tingle of energy moving within it. "Hah," I said. "Got it."

Murphy frowned back at the entry to the Tunnel of Terror. "What do we do about Billy the Kid?"

"Not much we can do," I said. "You want to try to explain what happened here to the Springfield cops?"

She shook her head.

"Me either," I said. "The kid was LeBlanc's thrall. I doubt he's a danger to anyone without a vampire to push him into it." Besides. The Reds would probably kill him on general principles anyway, once they found out about LeBlanc's death.

We were silent for a moment. Then stepped in close to each other and hugged gently. Murphy shivered.

"You okay?" I asked quietly.

She leaned her head against my chest. "How do we help all the people she screwed with?"

"Burn the belt," I said, and stroked her hair with one hand. "That should purify everyone it's linked to."

"Everyone," she said slowly.

I blinked twice. "Yeah."

"So once you do it . . . we'll see what a bad idea this is. And remember that we both have very good reasons to not get together."

"Yeah."

"And . . . we won't be feeling *this* anymore. This . . . happy. This complete."

"No. We won't."

Her voice cracked. "Dammit."

I hugged her tight. "Yeah."

"I want to tell you to wait a while," she said. "I want us to be all noble and virtuous for keeping it intact. I want to tell you that if we destroy the belt, we'll be destroying the happiness of God knows how many people."

"Junkies are happy when they're high," I said quietly, "but they don't need to be happy. They need to be *free*."

I put the belt back into the car, turned my right hand palm-up and murmured a word. A sphere of white-hot fire gathered over my fingers. I flicked a hand, and the sphere arched gently down into the car and began charring the belt to ashes. I felt sick.

I didn't watch. I turned to Karrin and kissed her again, hot and urgent, and she returned it frantically. It was as though we thought that we might keep something escaping from our mouths if they were sealed together in a kiss.

I felt it when it went away.

We both stiffened slightly. We both remembered that we had decided that the two of us couldn't work out. We both remembered that Murphy was already involved with someone else, and that it wasn't in her nature to stray.

She stepped back from me, her arms folded across her stomach.

"Ready?" I asked her quietly.

She nodded and we started walking. Neither of us said anything until we reached the *Blue Beetle*.

"You know what, Harry?" she said quietly, from the other side of the car.

"I know," I told her. "Like you said. Love hurts."

We got into the *Beetle* and headed back to Chicago.

⎯◆⎯

Jim Butcher, a New York Times bestselling author, is best known for his The Dresden Files series. *Cold Days,* the fourteen in the series, was published last year. A martial arts enthusiast with fifteen years of experience in various styles including Ryukyu Kempo, Tae Kwon Do, Gojo Shorei Ryu, and a sprinkling of Kung Fu, he is also a skilled rider and has worked as a summer camp horse wrangler and performed in front of large audiences in both drill riding and stunt riding exhibitions. Butcher lives in Missouri with his wife, son, and a vicious guard dog.

The Case: *A crime against the world, against nature, against order—the death of Mycroft Holmes, in the specific, and Death in the general.*

The Investigator: *Sherlock Holmes, a "retired" British consulting detective, turned investigative apiarist.*

THE CASE OF DEATH AND HONEY

Neil Gaiman

It was a mystery in those parts for years what had happened to the old white ghost man, the barbarian with his huge shoulder bag. There were some who supposed him to have been murdered, and, later, they dug up the floor of Old Gao's little shack high on the hillside, looking for treasure, but they found nothing but ash and fire-blackened tin trays.

This was after Old Gao himself had vanished, you understand, and before his son came back from Lijiang to take over the beehives on the hill.

This is the problem, wrote Holmes in 1899: *ennui. And lack of interest. Or rather, it all becomes too easy. When the joy of solving crimes is the challenge, the possibility that you cannot, why then the crimes have something to hold your attention. But when each crime is soluble, and so easily soluble at that, why then there is no point in solving them. Look: this man has been murdered. Well then, someone murdered him. He was murdered for one or more of a tiny handful of reasons: he inconvenienced someone, or he had something that someone wanted, or he had angered someone. Where is the challenge in that?*

I would read in the dailies an account of a crime that had the police baffled, and I would find that I had solved it, in broad strokes if not in detail, before I had finished the article. Crime is too soluble. It dissolves. Why call the police and tell them the answers to their mysteries? I leave it, over and over again, as a challenge for them, as it is no challenge for me.

I am only alive when I perceive a challenge.

The bees of the misty hills, hills so high that they were sometimes called a mountain, were humming in the pale summer sun as they moved from spring flower to spring flower on the slope. Old Gao listened to them without pleasure.

His cousin, in the village across the valley, had many dozens of hives, all of them already filling with honey, even this early in the year; also, the honey was as white as snow-jade. Old Gao did not believe that the white honey tasted any better than the yellow or light brown honey that his own bees produced, although his bees produced it in meager quantities, but his cousin could sell his white honey for twice what Old Gao could get for the best honey he had.

On his cousin's side of the hill, the bees were earnest, hardworking, golden brown workers, who brought pollen and nectar back to the hives in enormous quantities. Old Gao's bees were ill-tempered and black, shiny as bullets, who produced as much honey as they needed to get through the winter and only a little more: enough for Old Gao to sell from door to door, to his fellow villagers, one small lump of honeycomb at a time. He would charge more for the brood-comb, filled with bee larvae, sweet-tasting morsels of protein, when he had brood-comb to sell, which was rarely, for the bees were angry and sullen and everything they did, they did as little as possible, including make more bees, and Old Gao was always aware that each piece of brood-comb he sold meant bees he would not have to make honey for him to sell later in the year.

Old Gao was as sullen and as sharp as his bees. He had had a wife once, but she had died in childbirth. The son who had killed her lived for a week, then died himself. There would be nobody to say the funeral rites for Old Gao, no one to clean his grave for festivals or to put offerings upon it. He would die unremembered, as unremarkable and as unremarked as his bees.

The old white stranger came over the mountains in late spring of that year, as soon as the roads were passable, with a huge brown bag strapped to his shoulders. Old Gao heard about him before he met him.

"There is a barbarian who is looking at bees," said his cousin.

Old Gao said nothing. He had gone to his cousin to buy a pailful of second-rate comb, damaged or uncapped and liable soon to spoil. He bought it cheaply to feed to his own bees, and if he sold some of it in his own village, no one was any the wiser. The two men were drinking tea in Gao's cousin's hut on the hillside. From late spring, when the first honey started to flow, until first frost, Gao's cousin left his house in the village and went to live in the hut on the hillside, to live and to sleep beside his beehives, for fear of thieves. His wife and his children would take the honeycomb and the bottles of snow-white honey down the hill to sell.

Old Gao was not afraid of thieves. The shiny black bees of Old Gao's hives would have no mercy on anyone who disturbed them. He slept in his village, unless it was time to collect the honey.

"I will send him to you," said Gao's cousin. "Answer his questions, show him your bees, and he will pay you."

"He speaks our tongue?"

"His dialect is atrocious. He said he learned to speak from sailors, and they were mostly Cantonese. But he learns fast, although he is old."

Old Gao grunted, uninterested in sailors. It was late in the morning, and there was still four hours walking across the valley to his village, in the heat of the day. He finished his tea. His cousin drank finer tea than Old Gao had ever been able to afford.

He reached his hives while it was still light, put the majority of the uncapped honey into his weakest hives. He had eleven hives. His cousin had over a hundred. Old Gao was stung twice doing this, on the back of the hand and the back of the neck. He had been stung over a thousand times in his life. He could not have told you how many times. He barely noticed the stings of other bees, but the stings of his own black bees always hurt, even if they no longer swelled or burned.

The next day a boy came to Old Gao's house in the village, to tell him that there was someone—and that the someone was a giant foreigner—who was asking for him. Old Gao simply grunted. He walked across the village with the boy at his steady pace, until the boy ran ahead, and soon was lost to sight.

Old Gao found the stranger sitting drinking tea on the porch of the Widow Zhang's house. Old Gao had known the Widow Zhang's mother, fifty years ago. She had been a friend of his wife. Now she was long dead. He did not believe any one who had known his wife still lived. The Widow Zhang fetched Old Gao tea, introduced him to the elderly barbarian, who had removed his bag and sat beside the small table.

They sipped their tea. The barbarian said, "I wish to see your bees."

Mycroft's death was the end of Empire, and no one knew it but the two of us. He lay in that pale room, his only covering a thin white sheet, as if he were already becoming a ghost from the popular imagination, and needed only eyeholes in the sheet to finish the impression.

I had imagined that his illness might have wasted him away, but he seemed huger than ever, his fingers swollen into white suet sausages.

I said, "Good evening, Mycroft. Dr. Hopkins tells me you have two weeks to live, and stated that I was under no circumstances to inform you of this."

"The man's a dunderhead," said Mycroft, his breath coming in huge wheezes between the words. "I will not make it to Friday."

"Saturday at least," I said.

"You always were an optimist. No, Thursday evening and then I shall be nothing more than an exercise in practical geometry for Hopkins and the funeral directors at Snigsby and Malterson, who will have the challenge, given the

narrowness of the doors and corridors, of getting my carcass out of this room and out of the building."

"I had wondered," I said. "Particularly given the staircase. But they will take out the window frame and lower you to the street like a grand piano."

Mycroft snorted at that. Then, "I am fifty-four years old, Sherlock. In my head is the British Government. Not the ballot and hustings nonsense, but the business of the thing. There is no one else knows what the troop movements in the hills of Afghanistan have to do with the desolate shores of North Wales, no one else who sees the whole picture. Can you imagine the mess that this lot and their children will make of Indian Independence?"

I had not previously given any thought to the matter.

"Will India become independent?"

"Inevitably. In thirty years, at the outside. I have written several recent memoranda on the topic. As I have on so many other subjects. There are memoranda on the Russian Revolution—that'll be along within the decade, I'll wager—and on the German problem and . . . oh, so many others. Not that I expect them to be read or understood." Another wheeze. My brother's lungs rattled like the windows in an empty house. "You know, if I were to live, the British Empire might last another thousand years, bringing peace and improvement to the world."

In the past, especially when I was a boy, whenever I heard Mycroft make a grandiose pronouncement like that I would say something to bait him. But not now, not on his deathbed. And also I was certain that he was not speaking of the Empire as it was, a flawed and fallible construct of flawed and fallible people, but of a British Empire that existed only in his head, a glorious force for civilization and universal prosperity.

I do not, and did not, believe in empires. But I believed in Mycroft.

Mycroft Holmes. Four-and-fifty years of age. He had seen in the new century but the Queen would still outlive him by several months. She was almost thirty years older than he was, and in every way a tough old bird. I wondered to myself whether this unfortunate end might have been avoided.

Mycroft said, "You are right, of course, Sherlock. Had I forced myself to exercise. Had I lived on birdseed and cabbages instead of porterhouse steak. Had I taken up country dancing along with a wife and a puppy and in all other ways behaved contrary to my nature, I might have bought myself another dozen or so years. But what is that in the scheme of things? Little enough. And sooner or later, I would enter my dotage. No. I am of the opinion that it would take two hundred years to train a functioning Civil Service, let alone a secret service . . . "

I had said nothing.

The pale room had no decorations on the wall of any kind. None of Mycroft's citations. No illustrations, photographs, or paintings. I compared his austere digs to my own cluttered rooms in Baker Street and I wondered, not for the first time, at Mycroft's mind. He needed nothing on the outside, for it was all on the inside—everything he had seen, everything he had experienced, everything he had read. He could close his eyes and walk through the National Gallery, or browse the British Museum Reading Room—or, more likely, compare intelligence reports from the edge of the Empire with the price of wool in Wigan and the unemployment statistics in Hove, and then, from this and only this, order a man promoted or a traitor's quiet death.

Mycroft wheezed enormously, and then he said, "It is a crime, Sherlock."

"I beg your pardon?"

"A crime. It is a crime, my brother, as heinous and as monstrous as any of the penny-dreadful massacres you have investigated. A crime against the world, against nature, against order."

"I must confess, my dear fellow, that I do not entirely follow you. What is a crime?"

"My death," said Mycroft, "in the specific. And Death in general." He looked into my eyes. "I mean it," he said. "Now isn't that a crime worth investigating, Sherlock, old fellow? One that might keep your attention for longer than it will take you to establish that the poor fellow who used to conduct the brass band in Hyde Park was murdered by the third cornet using a preparation of strychnine."

"Arsenic," I corrected him, almost automatically.

"I think you will find," wheezed Mycroft, "that the arsenic, while present, had in fact fallen in flakes from the green-painted bandstand itself onto his supper. Symptoms of arsenical poison are a complete red herring. No, it was strychnine that did for the poor fellow."

Mycroft said no more to me that day or ever. He breathed his last the following Thursday, late in the afternoon, and on the Friday the worthies of Snigsby and Malterson removed the casing from the window of the pale room and lowered my brother's remains into the street, like a grand piano.

His funeral service was attended by me, by my friend Watson, by our cousin Harriet and—in accordance with Mycroft's express wishes—by no one else. The Civil Service, the Foreign Office, even the Diogenes Club—these institutions and their representatives were absent. Mycroft had been reclusive in life; he was to be equally as reclusive in death. So it was the three of us, and the parson, who had not known my brother, and had no conception that it was the more omniscient arm of the British Government itself that he was consigning to the grave.

Four burly men held fast to the ropes and lowered my brother's remains to their final resting place, and did, I daresay, their utmost not to curse at the weight of the thing. I tipped each of them half a crown.

Mycroft was dead at fifty-four, and, as they lowered him into his grave, in my imagination I could still hear his clipped, gray wheeze as he seemed to be saying, "Now there is a crime worth investigating."

The stranger's accent was not too bad, although his vocabulary seemed limited, but he seemed to be talking in the local dialect, or something near to it. He was a fast learner. Old Gao hawked and spat into the dust of the street. He said nothing. He did not wish to take the stranger up the hillside; he did not wish to disturb his bees. In Old Gao's experience, the less he bothered his bees, the better they did. And if they stung the barbarian, what then?

The stranger's hair was silver-white, and sparse; his nose, the first barbarian nose that Old Gao had seen, was huge and curved and put Old Gao in mind of the beak of an eagle; his skin was tanned the same color as Old Gao's own, and was lined deeply. Old Gao was not certain that he could read a barbarian's face as he could read the face of a person, but he thought the man seemed most serious and, perhaps, unhappy.

"Why?"

"I study bees. Your brother tells me you have big black bees here. Unusual bees."

Old Gao shrugged. He did not correct the man on the relationship with his cousin.

The stranger asked Old Gao if he had eaten, and when Gao said that he had not the stranger asked the Widow Zhang to bring them soup and rice and whatever was good that she had in her kitchen, which turned out to be a stew of black tree-fungus and vegetables and tiny transparent river fish, little bigger than tadpoles. The two men ate in silence. When they had finished eating, the stranger said, "I would be honored if you would show me your bees."

Old Gao said nothing, but the stranger paid the Widow Zhang well and he put his bag on his back. Then he waited, and, when Old Gao began to walk, the stranger followed him. He carried his bag as if it weighed nothing to him. He was strong for an old man, thought Old Gao, and wondered whether all such barbarians were so strong.

"Where are you from?"

"England," said the stranger.

Old Gao remembered his father telling him about a war with the English, over trade and over opium, but that was long ago. They walked up the hillside, that was, perhaps, a mountainside. It was steep, and the hillside was too rocky to be cut into fields. Old Gao tested the stranger's pace, walking faster than usual, and the stranger kept up with him, with his pack on his back.

The stranger stopped several times, however. He stopped to examine flowers—the small white flowers that bloomed in early spring elsewhere in the valley, but in late spring here on the side of the hill. There was a bee on one of the flowers, and the stranger knelt and observed it. Then he reached into his pocket, produced a large magnifying glass and examined the bee through it, and made notes in a small pocket notebook, in an incomprehensible writing.

Old Gao had never seen a magnifying glass before, and he leaned in to look at the bee, so black and so strong and so very different from the bees elsewhere in that valley.

"One of your bees?"

"Yes," said Old Gao. "Or one like it."

"Then we shall let her find her own way home," said the stranger, and he did not disturb the bee, and he put away the magnifying glass.

The Croft East Dene, Sussex

August 11th, 1922

My dear Watson,

I have taken our discussion of this afternoon to heart, considered it carefully, and am prepared to modify my previous opinions.

I am amenable to your publishing your account of the incidents of 1903, specifically of the final case before my retirement, under the following conditions.

In addition to the usual changes that you would make to disguise actual people and places, I would suggest that you replace the entire scenario we encountered (I speak of Professor Presbury's garden. I shall not write of it further here) with monkey glands, or a similar extract from the testes of an ape or lemur, sent by some foreign mystery-man. Perhaps the monkey-extract could have the effect of making Professor Presbury move like an ape—he could be some kind of "creeping man," perhaps?—or possibly make him able to clamber up the sides of buildings and up trees. I would suggest that he could grow a tail, but this might be too fanciful even for you, Watson, although no more fanciful than many of the rococo additions you have made in your histories to otherwise humdrum events in my life and work.

In addition, I have written the following speech, to be delivered by myself, at the end of your narrative. Please make certain that something much like this is there, in which I inveigh against living too long, and the foolish urges that push foolish people to do foolish things to prolong their foolish lives:

There is a very real danger to humanity, if one could live forever, if youth were simply there for the taking, that the material, the sensual, the worldly would all prolong their worthless lives. The spiritual would not avoid the call to something higher. It would be the survival of the least fit. What sort of cesspool may not our poor world become?

Something along those lines, I fancy, would set my mind at rest.

Let me see the finished article, please, before you submit it to be published.

I remain, old friend, your most obedient servant,

Sherlock Holmes

They reached Old Gao's bees late in the afternoon. The beehives were gray wooden boxes piled behind a structure so simple it could barely be called a shack. Four posts, a roof, and hangings of oiled cloth that served to keep out the worst of the spring rains and the summer storms. A small charcoal brazier served for warmth, if you placed a blanket over it and yourself, and to cook upon; a wooden pallet in the center of the structure, with an ancient ceramic pillow, served as a bed on the occasions that Old Gao slept up on the mountainside with the bees, particularly in the autumn, when he harvested most of the honey. There was little enough of it compared to the output of his cousin's hives, but it was enough that he would sometimes spend two or three days waiting for the comb that he had crushed and stirred into a slurry to drain through the cloth into the buckets and pots that he had carried up the mountainside. Finally he would melt the remainder, the sticky wax and bits of pollen and dirt and bee slurry, in a pot, to extract the beeswax, and he would give the sweet water back to the bees. Then he would carry the honey and the wax blocks down the hill to the village to sell.

He showed the barbarian stranger the eleven hives, watched impassively as the stranger put on a veil and opened a hive, examining first the bees, then the contents of a brood box, and finally the queen, through his magnifying glass. He showed no fear, no discomfort: in everything he did the stranger's movements were gentle and slow, and he was not stung, nor did he crush or hurt a single bee. This impressed Old Gao. He had assumed that barbarians were inscrutable, unreadable, mysterious creatures, but this man seemed overjoyed to have encountered Gao's bees. His eyes were shining.

Old Gao fired up the brazier, to boil some water. Long before the charcoal was hot, however, the stranger had removed from his bag a contraption of glass and metal. He had filled the upper half of it with water from the stream, lit a flame, and soon a kettleful of water was steaming and bubbling. Then the stranger took two tin mugs from his bag, and some green tea leaves wrapped in paper, and dropped the leaves into the mug, and poured on the water.

It was the finest tea that Old Gao had ever drunk: better by far than his cousin's tea. They drank it cross-legged on the floor.

"I would like to stay here for the summer, in this house," said the stranger.

"Here? This is not even a house," said Old Gao. "Stay down in the village. Widow Zhang has a room."

"I will stay here," said the stranger. "Also I would like to rent one of your beehives."

Old Gao had not laughed in years. There were those in the village who would have thought such a thing impossible. But still, he laughed then, a guffaw of surprise and amusement that seemed to have been jerked out of him.

"I am serious," said the stranger. He placed four silver coins on the ground between them. Old Gao had not seen where he got them from: three silver Mexican pesos, a coin that had become popular in China years before, and a large silver yuan. It was as much money as Old Gao might see in a year of selling honey. "For this money," said the stranger, "I would like someone to bring me food: every three days should suffice."

Old Gao said nothing. He finished his tea and stood up. He pushed through the oiled cloth to the clearing high on the hillside. He walked over to the eleven hives: each consisted of two brood boxes with one, two, three or, in one case, even four boxes above that. He took the stranger to the hive with four boxes above it, each box filled with frames of comb.

"This hive is yours," he said.

They were plant extracts. That was obvious. They worked, in their way, for a limited time, but they were also extremely poisonous. But watching poor Professor Presbury during those final days—his skin, his eyes, his gait—had convinced me that he had not been on entirely the wrong path.

I took his case of seeds, of pods, of roots, and of dried extracts and I thought. I pondered. I cogitated. I reflected. It was an intellectual problem, and could be solved, as my old maths tutor had always sought to demonstrate to me, by intellect.

They were plant extracts, and they were lethal.

Methods I used to render them non-lethal rendered them quite ineffective.

It was not a three pipe problem. I suspect it was something approaching a three hundred pipe problem before I hit upon an initial idea—a notion, perhaps—of a way of processing the plants that might allow them to be ingested by human beings.

It was not a line of investigation that could easily be followed in Baker Street. So it was, in the autumn of 1903, that I moved to Sussex, and spent the winter reading every book and pamphlet and monograph so far published, I fancy, upon the care and keeping of bees. And so it was that in early April of 1904, armed only with theoretical knowledge, I took delivery from a local farmer of my first package of bees.

I wonder, sometimes, that Watson did not suspect anything. Then again, Watson's glorious obtuseness has never ceased to surprise me, and sometimes, indeed, I had relied upon it. Still, he knew what I was like when I had no work to occupy my mind, no case to solve. He knew my lassitude, my black moods when I had no case to occupy me.

So how could he believe that I had truly retired? He knew my methods.

Indeed, Watson was there when I took receipt of my first bees. He watched, from a safe distance, as I poured the bees from the package into the empty, waiting hive, like slow, humming, gentle treacle.

He saw my excitement, and he saw nothing.

And the years passed, and we watched the Empire crumble, we watched the Government unable to govern, we watched those poor heroic boys sent to the trenches of Flanders to die, all these things confirmed me in my opinions. I was not doing the right thing. I was doing the only thing.

As my face grew unfamiliar, and my finger-joints swelled and ached (not so much as they might have done, though, which I attributed to the many bee-stings I had received in my first few years as an investigative apiarist) and as Watson, dear, brave, obtuse Watson, faded with time and paled and shrank, his skin becoming grayer, his mustache becoming the same shade of gray, my resolve to conclude my researches did not diminish. If anything, it increased.

So: my initial hypotheses were tested upon the South Downs, in an apiary of my own devising, each hive modeled upon Langstroth's. I do believe that I made every mistake that ever a novice beekeeper could or has ever made, and in addition, due to my investigations, an entire hiveful of mistakes that no beekeeper has ever made before, or shall, I trust, ever make again. "The Case of the Poisoned Beehive," Watson might have called many of them, although "The Mystery of the Transfixed Women's Institute" would have drawn more attention to my researches, had anyone been interested enough to investigate. (As it was, I chided Mrs. Telford for simply taking a jar of honey from the shelves here without consulting me, and I ensured that, in the future, she was given several jars for her cooking from the more regular hives, and that honey from the experimental hives was locked away once it had been collected. I do not believe that this ever drew comment.)

I experimented with Dutch bees, with German bees and with Italians, with Carniolans and Caucasians. I regretted the loss of our British bees to blight and, even where they had survived, to interbreeding, although I found and worked with a small hive I purchased and grew up from a frame of brood and a queen cell, from an old Abbey in St. Albans, which seemed to me to be original British breeding stock.

I experimented for the best part of two decades, before I concluded that the bees that I sought, if they existed, were not to be found in England, and would not survive the distances they would need to travel to reach me by international parcel post. I needed to examine bees in India. I needed to travel perhaps farther afield than that.

I have a smattering of languages.

I had my flower-seeds, and my extracts and tinctures in syrup. I needed nothing more.

I packed them up, arranged for the cottage on the Downs to be cleaned and aired once a week, and for Master Wilkins—to whom I am afraid I had developed the habit of referring, to his obvious distress, as "Young Villikins"—to inspect the beehives, and to harvest and sell surplus honey in Eastbourne market, and to prepare the hives for winter.

I told them I did not know when I should be back.

I am an old man. Perhaps they did not expect me to return.

And, if this was indeed the case, they would, strictly speaking, have been right.

Old Gao was impressed, despite himself. He had lived his life among bees. Still, watching the stranger shake the bees from the boxes, with a practiced flick of his wrist, so cleanly and so sharply that the black bees seemed more surprised than angered, and simply flew or crawled back into their hive, was remarkable. The stranger then stacked the boxes filled with comb on top of one of the weaker hives, so Old Gao would still have the honey from the hive the stranger was renting.

So it was that Old Gao gained a lodger.

Old Gao gave the Widow Zhang's granddaughter a few coins to take the stranger food three times a week—mostly rice and vegetables, along with an earthenware pot filled, when she left at least, with boiling soup.

Every ten days Old Gao would walk up the hill himself. He went initially to check on the hives, but soon discovered that under the stranger's care all eleven hives were thriving as they had never thrived before. And indeed, there was now a twelfth hive, from a captured swarm of the black bees the stranger had encountered while on a walk along the hill.

Old Gao brought wood, the next time he came up to the shack, and he and the stranger spent several afternoons wordlessly working together, making extra boxes to go on the hives, building frames to fill the boxes.

One evening the stranger told Old Gao that the frames they were making had been invented by an American, only seventy years before. This seemed like nonsense to Old Gao, who made frames as his father had, and as they did across the valley, and as, he was certain, his grandfather and his grandfather's grandfather had, but he said nothing.

He enjoyed the stranger's company. They made hives together, and Old

Gao wished that the stranger was a younger man. Then he would stay there for a long time, and Old Gao would have someone to leave his beehives to, when he died. But they were two old men, nailing boxes together, with thin frosty hair and old faces, and neither of them would see another dozen winters.

Old Gao noticed that the stranger had planted a small, neat garden beside the hive that he had claimed as his own, which he had moved away from the rest of the hives. He had covered it with a net. He had also created a "back door" to the hive, so that the only bees that could reach the plants came from the hive that he was renting. Old Gao also observed that, beneath the netting, there were several trays filled with what appeared to be sugar solution of some kind, one colored bright red, one green, one a startling blue, one yellow. He pointed to them, but all the stranger did was nod and smile.

The bees were lapping up the syrups, though, clustering and crowding on the sides of the tin dishes with their tongues down, eating until they could eat no more, and then returning to the hive.

The stranger had made sketches of Old Gao's bees. He showed the sketches to Old Gao, tried to explain the ways that Old Gao's bees differed from other honeybees, talked of ancient bees preserved in stone for millions of years, but here the stranger's Chinese failed him, and, truthfully, Old Gao was not interested. They were his bees, until he died, and after that, they were the bees of the mountainside. He had brought other bees here, but they had sickened and died, or been killed in raids by the black bees, who took their honey and left them to starve.

The last of these visits was in late summer. Old Gao went down the mountainside. He did not see the stranger again.

It is done.

It works. Already I feel a strange combination of triumph and of disappointment, as if of defeat, or of distant stormclouds teasing at my senses.

It is strange to look at my hands and to see, not my hands as I know them, but the hands I remember from my younger days: knuckles unswollen, dark hairs, not snow-white, on the backs.

It was a quest that had defeated so many, a problem with no apparent solution. The first Emperor of China died and nearly destroyed his empire in pursuit of it, three thousand years ago, and all it took me was, what, twenty years?

I do not know if I did the right thing or not (although any "retirement" without such an occupation would have been, literally, maddening). I took the commission from Mycroft. I investigated the problem. I arrived, inevitably, at the solution.

Will I tell the world? I will not.

And yet, I have half a pot of dark brown honey remaining in my bag; a half a pot of honey that is worth more than nations. (I was tempted to write, worth more than all the tea in China, perhaps because of my current situation, but fear that even Watson would deride it as cliché.)

And speaking of Watson . . .

There is one thing left to do. My only remaining goal, and it is small enough. I shall make my way to Shanghai, and from there I shall take ship to Southampton, a half a world away. And once I am there, I shall seek out Watson, if he still lives—and I fancy he does. It is irrational, I know, and yet I am certain that I would know, somehow, had Watson passed beyond the veil.

I shall buy theatrical makeup, disguise myself as an old man, so as not to startle him, and I shall invite my old friend over for tea.

There will be honey on buttered toast served for tea that afternoon, I fancy.

There were tales of a barbarian who passed through the village on his way east, but the people who told Old Gao this did not believe that it could have been the same man who had lived in Gao's shack. This one was young and proud, and his hair was dark. It was not the old man who had walked through those parts in the spring, although, one person told Gao, the bag was similar.

Old Gao walked up the mountainside to investigate, although he suspected what he would find before he got there.

The stranger was gone, and the stranger's bag.

There had been much burning, though. That was clear. Papers had been burnt—Old Gao recognized the edge of a drawing the stranger had made of one of his bees, but the rest of the papers were ash, or blackened beyond recognition, even had Old Gao been able to read barbarian writing. The papers were not the only things to have been burnt; parts of the hive that the stranger had rented were now only twisted ash; there were blackened, twisted strips of tin that might once have contained brightly colored syrups.

The color was added to the syrups, the stranger had told him once, so that he could tell them apart, although for what purpose Old Gao had never enquired.

He examined the shack like a detective, searching for a clue as to the stranger's nature or his whereabouts. On the ceramic pillow four silver coins had been left for him to find—two yuan and two pesos—and he put them away.

Behind the shack he found a heap of used slurry, with the last bees of the day still crawling upon it, tasting whatever sweetness was still on the surface of the still-sticky wax. Old Gao thought long and hard before he gathered up the slurry, wrapped it loosely in cloth, and put it in a pot, which he filled with water.

He heated the water on the brazier, but did not let it boil. Soon enough the wax floated to the surface, leaving the dead bees and the dirt and the pollen and the propolis inside the cloth.

He let it cool.

Then he walked outside, and he stared up at the moon. It was almost full.

He wondered how many villagers knew that his son had died as a baby. He remembered his wife, but her face was distant, and he had no portraits or photographs of her. He thought that there was nothing he was so suited for on the face of the earth as to keep the black, bulletlike bees on the side of this high, high hill. There was no other man who knew their temperament as he did.

The water had cooled. He lifted the now solid block of beeswax out of the water, placed it on the boards of the bed to finish cooling. He took the cloth filled with dirt and impurities out of the pot. And then, because he too was, in his way, a detective, and once you have eliminated the impossible whatever remains, however unlikely, must be the truth, he drank the sweet water in the pot. There is a lot of honey in slurry, after all, even after the majority of it has dripped through a cloth and been purified. The water tasted of honey, but not a honey that Gao had ever tasted before. It tasted of smoke, and metal, and strange flowers, and odd perfumes. It tasted, Gao thought, a little like sex.

He drank it all down, and then he slept, with his head on the ceramic pillow.

When he woke, he thought, he would decide how to deal with his cousin, who would expect to inherit the twelve hives on the hill when Old Gao went missing.

He would be an illegitimate son, perhaps, the young man who would return in the days to come. Or perhaps a son. Young Gao. Who would remember, now? It did not matter.

He would go to the city and then he would return, and he would keep the black bees on the side of the mountain for as long as days and circumstances would allow.

⟨⇒⟩

Neil Gaiman is the *New York Times* bestselling author of novels *Neverwhere, Stardust, American Gods, Coraline, Anansi Boys, The Graveyard Book*, and (with Terry Pratchett) *Good Omens*; the Sandman series of graphic novels; and the story collections *Smoke and Mirrors* and *Fragile Things*. He has won numerous literary awards including the Hugo, the Nebula, the World Fantasy, and the Stoker Awards, as well as the Newbery medal. His next novel, *The Ocean at the End of the Lane*, will be published in June 2013.

⟨⇒⟩

The Case: *An apparent Manhattan suicide is actually murder by malevolent magic.*

The Investigators: *Dr. Matthew Szczegielniak, mage and guardian of the iron world by night, English professor by day. Other "detectives" include three of his female students who realize their mild-mannered prof is a tattooed hunk who seems to be able to appear and disappear at will—they are in hot pursuit.*

CRYPTIC COLORATION

Elizabeth Bear

Katie saw him first. The next-best thing to naked, in cutoff camouflage pants and high-top basketball sneakers and nothing else, except the thick black labyrinth of neo-tribal ink that covered his pale skin from collarbones to ankle-bones. He shone like piano keys, glossy-sleek with sweat in a sultry September afternoon.

Katie already had Melissa's sleeve in her hand and was tugging her toward the crosswalk. Gina trailed three steps behind. "We have *got* to go watch this basketball game."

"What?" But then Melissa's line of sight intersected Katie's and she gasped. "Oh my fuck, look at all that ink. Do you think that counts as a shirt or a skin?" Melissa was from Boston, but mostly didn't talk like it.

"Never mind the ink," Katie said. "Look at his *triceps.*"

Little shadowed dimples in the undersides of his arms, and all Katie could think of for a moment was that he wasn't terribly tall, and if she had been standing close enough when he raised his hands to take a pass she could have stood on tiptoe and licked them. The image dried her mouth, heated her face.

Melissa would have thought Katie silly for having shocked herself, though, so she didn't say anything.

Even without the ink, he had the best body on the basketball court. Hard all over, muscle swelling and valleying as he sprinted and side-stepped, chin-length blond hair swinging in his eyes. He skittered left like a boxer, turned, dribbled between his legs—quadriceps popping, calves like flexed cables—caught the ball as it came back up and leaped. Parabolic, sailing. Sweat shook from his elbows and chin as he released.

A three-point shot. A high geometric arc.

Denied when a tall black boy of eighteen or so tipped it off the edge of the basket, jangling the chain, and fired back to half court, but that didn't matter. Katie glanced over her shoulder to make sure Gina was following.

"God," Melissa purred. "I love New York."

Katie, mopping her gritty forehead with the inside of her T-shirt collar, couldn't have agreed more.

So it was mid-September and still too hot to think. So she was filthy just from walking through the city air.

You didn't get anything like the blond boy back home in Appleton.

Melissa was a tall freckled girl who wore her hair in red pigtails that looked like braided yarn. She had a tendency to bounce up on her toes that made her seem much taller, and she craned over the pedestrians as they stepped up onto the far curb. "There's some shade by the—oh, my god would you look at that?"

Katie bounced too, but couldn't see anything except shirts. "Mel!"

"Sorry."

Flanking Gina, two steps ahead of her, they moved on. Melissa was right about the shade; it was cooler and had a pretty good view. They made it there just as the blond was facing off with a white-shirted Latino in red Converse All-Stars that were frayed around the cuffs. "Jump ball," Gina said, and leaned forward between Katie and Melissa.

The men coiled and went up. Attenuated bodies, arching, bumping, big hands splayed. Katie saw dark bands clasping every finger on the blond, and each thumb. More ink, or maybe rings, though wouldn't it hurt to play ball in them?

The Latino was taller; the blond beat him by inches. He tagged the ball with straining fingertips, lofted it to his team. And then he landed lightly, knees flexed, sucked in a deep breath while his elbows hovered back and up, and pivoted.

It wasn't a boy, unless a man in his early thirties counted.

"Holy crap," said Gina, who only swore in Puerto Rican. "Girls, that's *Doctor S.*"

Wednesday at noon, the three mismatched freshman girls who sat in the third row center of Matthew Szczegielniak's 220 were worse than usual. Normally, they belonged to the doe-eyed, insecure subspecies of first-year student, badly needing to be shocked back into a sense of humor and acceptance of their own fallibility. A lot of these young girls reminded Matthew of adolescent cats; trying so hard to look serene and dignified that they walked into walls.

And then got mad at you for noticing.

Really, that was even funnier.

Today, though, they were giggling and nudging and passing notes until he was half-convinced he'd made a wrong turn somewhere and wound up teaching a high school class. He caught the carrot-top mid-nudge while mid-sentence (Byron, Scott), about a third of the way through his introductory forty minutes on the Romantic poets, and fixed her with a glare through his spectacles that could have chipped enamel.

A red tide rose behind her freckles, brightening her sunburned nose. Her next giggle came out a squeak.

"Ms. Martinchek. You have a trenchant observation on the work of Joanna Baillie, perhaps?"

If she'd gone any redder, he would have worried about apoplexy. She stared down at her open notebook and shook her head in tiny quick jerks.

"No, Doctor S."

Matthew Szczegielniak rubbed his nose with the butt of his dry-erase marker, nudging his spectacles up with his thumbnail. He wasn't enough of a problem child to make his students learn his last name—even the simplified pronunciation he preferred—though the few that tried were usually good for endless hours of entertainment.

Besides, Matthew was a Mage. And magic being what it was, he would be hard put to imagine a more counterproductive activity than teaching three hundred undergrads a semester how to pronounce his *name*.

Enough heat of embarrassment radiated from Melissa's body to make Katie lean on her opposite elbow and duck her head in sympathy. She kept sneaking looks at Doctor S., trying to see past the slicked ponytail, the spectacles, the arch and perfectly bitchy precision of his lecturing style to find the laughing half-naked athlete of the day before.

She'd thought he was probably gay.

Sure, books, covers, *whatever*. It was impossible to believe in *him* exultant, shaking sweat from his hair, even though she'd seen it, even though the image fumed wisps of intrigue through her pelvis. Even though she could see the black rings on every finger and each thumb, clicking slightly when he gestured. She couldn't understand how she had never noticed them before. And never noticed the way he always dressed for class, though it was still hotter than Hades; the ribbed soft-colored turtleneck that covered him from the backs of broad hands to the tender flesh under his throat, the camel- or smoke- or charcoal-colored corduroy blazer that hid the shape of his shoulders and the width of his chest.

It was maddening, knowing what was under the clothes. She wondered if the barbaric tattoos extended everywhere, and flushed, herself, at least as bright as Melissa. And then brighter, as she felt the prof's eyes on her, as if he was wondering what she was thinking that so discomfited her.

Oh, lord, but wouldn't that have hurt?

On the other hand, he'd had the insides of his arms done, and the inner thighs. And *that* was supposed to hurt like anything, wasn't it?

And *then* she noticed that his left ear was pierced top to bottom, ten or a dozen rings, and sank down in her chair while she wondered what else he might have had done. And why she'd never noticed any of it—the rings, the earrings, the ink, the muscles—any of it, before.

"Oh, God," she whispered without moving her lips. "I'm never going to make it through this class."

But she did. And leaned up against the wall beside the door afterwards, shoulder-to-shoulder with Melissa while they waited for Gina to come out. Quiet, but if anybody was going to do something crazy or brave or both, it would be her. And right now, she was down at the bottom of the lecture hall, chatting up the professor.

"Oh, God," Katie moaned. "I'm going to have to switch sections. I didn't hear a word he said."

"I did. Oh, God. He knows my name." Melissa blushed the color of her plastic notebook cover all over again. Her voice dropped, developed a mocking precision of pronunciation. "Ms. Martinchek, maybe you can tell me about Joanna Ballyhoo . . . "

"Baillie." Gina, who came up and stood on tiptoe to stick a purple Post-it note to Melissa's tit. "He wrote it down for me. This way you can impress him next week."

Melissa picked the note off her chest and stared at it. "He uses purple Post-it notes?"

"I was right," Katie said. "He's gay."

"Do you want to find out?"

"Oh, and how do you propose we do that? Check the BiGALA membership roster?" Melissa might be scoffing, but her eyes were alight. Katie swallowed.

Gina checked her wristwatch. She had thick brown-black hair swept up in a banana clip, showing tiny curls like inverted devil horns at her pale nape. "He's got office hours until three. I say we grab some lunch and drop off our books, and then when he leaves we see where he goes."

"I dunno." Katie crossed her arms over her notebook. "It's not like playing basketball with your shirt off is a crime . . . "

"It's not like following someone to see where they go is a crime, either," Melissa pointed out. "We're not going to . . . stalk him."

"No, just stalk him."

"Katie!"

"Well, it's true." But Melissa was looking at her, and . . . she had come to Manhattan to have adventures. "What if we get caught?"

"Get caught . . . walking down a public street?"

Right. Whatever. "We could just look him up in the phone book."

"I checked. Not listed, amigas. Maybe it's under his boyfriend's name."

Even Melissa blinked at her this time. "Jesus Christ, Gomez. You're a criminal mastermind."

Those same three girls were holding up the wall when Matthew left the lecture theatre, climbing up the stairs to go out by the top door. He walked past, pretending not to notice them, or the stifled giggles and hiccups that erupted a moment later.

He just had time to grab a sandwich before his office hours. Almost one o'clock; probably nothing left but egg salad.

He needed the protein anyway.

He supplemented the sandwich with two cartons of chocolate milk, a bag of sourdough pretzels and three rip-top packets of French's mustard, and spread the lot out on his desk while he graded papers for his Renaissance drama class. With luck, no students would show up except a lonely or neurotic or favor-currying PhD candidate, and he could get half of the papers done today.

He had twenty-four sophomores and juniors, and of the first ten papers, only two writers seemed to understand that *The Merry Wives of Windsor* was supposed to be funny. One of those was a Sociology major. Matthew was a failure as a teacher. He finished the sandwich, blew crumbs off his desk so he wouldn't leave mayonnaise fingerprints on the essays, and tore open the pretzels before he sharpened his red pencil one more time.

Honey mustard would have been better. He should get some to stick in his desk. Unless it went bad. Honey didn't go bad, and mustard didn't go bad. Logically, an amalgam would reflect the qualities of both.

The spike of ice and acid through the bones of his hands originated from his iron Mage's rings, and it not only made him drop a pretzel—splattering mustard across the scarred wooden desk—but it brought him to his feet before he heard the police sirens start.

He glanced at the clock. Five more minutes. "That which thou hast promised thou must perform," he said, under his breath.

He left his lunch on the desk and found his keys in his pocket on the way to the door.

■ ■ ■

Their quarry almost ran them over as *they* were on their way in to start stalking him. Katie sidestepped quickly, catching Gina across the chest with a straight left arm. Melissa managed to get herself out of the way.

Doctor S. was almost running. His corduroy jacket flapped along the vent as he skidded between pedestrians, cleared four concrete steps in a bounce, and avoided a meandering traffic jam of students with as much facility as he'd shown on the basketball court. And if Katie had begun to suspect that it was just a bizarre case of mistaken identity, the toreador sidestep around the lady with the baby carriage would have disabused her. Doctor S. moved with a force and grace that were anything but common to academia.

Katie turned to follow him. It was only a small gesture to catch Gina's wrist, and without more urging, Gina trotted along beside her. Which was good, because Gina was strong *and* stubborn, even if she was only three apples high. Melissa took two more beats to get started, but her longer legs soon put her into the lead. "Slow down," Katie hissed, afraid that he would notice them running after him like three fools in a hurry, but frankly, he was getting away.

So when Melissa glared at her, she hustled, like you do. And Gina actually broke into a trot.

Doctor S. strode east on 68th, against traffic, towards the park. He never glanced over his shoulder, but kept rubbing his hands together as if they pained him. Maybe the rings were the magnet kind, for arthritis or something. RSI.

"I can't believe I never noticed he wears all those rings."

"I can't believe I never noticed the muscles," Melissa answered, but Gina said "Rings?"

"On all his fingers?" Melissa was too busy dodging pedestrians to give Gina the *were you born that stupid or do you practice hard?* look, and Katie was as grateful as she could spare breath for. They were disrupting traffic flow, the cardinal sin of New York's secular religion. Katie winced at another glare. Somebody was going to call her a fucking moron any second.

Gina sounded completely bemused. "I never noticed any rings."

Doctor S. continued east on 68th past Park Avenue, down the rows of narrow-fronted brick buildings with their concrete window ledges. By the time he crossed Madison Avenue, she was sure he was headed for the park. Every so often he actually skipped a step, moving as fast as he possibly could without breaking into a purse-snatcher sprint.

. . . he wasn't going to the park.

Halfway between Park and Fifth Avenue—which, of course, unlike Park, was on the park—traffic was gummed up behind flashing lights and restraining police. Doctor S. slowed as he approached, stuffing his hands back into his pockets— "Would you look at that?" Gina said, and Katie knew she, too, had suddenly noticed the rings—and dropping his shoulders, smallifying himself. He merged with the gawking crowd; Katie couldn't believe how easily he made himself vanish. Like a praying mantis in a rosebush; just one more green thorn-hooked stem.

"Okay," Melissa said, as they edged through bystanders, trying not to shove too many yuppies in the small of the back. "Stabbing?"

"Sidewalk pizza," Gina the Manhattanite said, pointing up. There was a window open on the sixth floor of one of the tenements, and Katie glimpsed a blue uniform behind it.

"Somebody *jumped*?"

"Or was pushed."

"Oh, God."

Gina shrugged, but let her hip and elbow brush Katie's. Solace, delivered with the appearance of nonchalance. And then, watching Doctor S. seem to vanish between people, betrayed only by metallic gleams of light off slick hair. She could pick him out if she knew where to look, if she remembered to look for the tan jacket, the hair. Otherwise, her eyes seemed to slide off him. *Creepy*, she thought. *He's almost not really there.*

And then she thought of something else. And maybe Melissa did too, because Melissa said, "Guys? What's he doing at a crime scene?"

"Or accident scene," Gina said, unwilling to invest in a murder without corroboration.

"Maybe he's a gawker."

"Ew." Katie tugged Gina's sleeve. "We should see if we can get closer. He probably won't notice us." And then she frowned. "How did he know about it?"

"Maybe he has a police scanner in his office?"

"So he's a vulture."

"Maybe he's an investigator. You know. Secret, like."

Katie rolled her eyes. "Right. Our gay college prof is Spider-Man."

Gina snorted. "Hey. Everybody knows that Spidey and Peter Parker have a thing."

Melissa hunched down so her head wouldn't stick up so far above the crowd. Her hair was as bad as Doctor S.'s, and she didn't have his knack for vanishing into the scenery. "Gina," she said, "you go up, and tell us what's going on."

"I've seen dead people, chica."

"You haven't seen this one," Melissa said. "Go on. It might be important."

Gina shrugged, rolled her eyes, and started forward. And Melissa was right; a five foot tall Latina in gobs of eyeliner did, indeed, vanish into the crowd. "Criminal mastermind," Melissa said.

Katie grinned, and didn't argue.

• • •

This was the part of the job that Matthew liked least. There was no satisfaction in it, no resolution, no joy. The woman on the pavement was dead; face down, one arm twisted under her and the other outflung. She'd bounced, and she hadn't ended up exactly where she'd hit. She'd been wearing a pink blouse. Someone in the crowd beside him giggled nervously.

Matthew figured she hadn't jumped. He checked his wards—pass-unnoticed, which was not so strong as a pass-unseen, and considerably easier to maintain—and the glamours and ghosts that kept him unremarkable

His hands still ached; he really wished somebody would come up with a system for detecting malevolent magic that didn't leave him feeling like a B-movie bad guy was raking his fingerbones around with a chilled ice pick.

He pulled his cell phone from his pocket, buttoned the middle button on his jacket, and hit speed dial. He was one of five people who had the Promethean archmage's reach-me-in-the-bathtub number; he didn't abuse the privilege.

"Jane Andraste," she said, starting to speak before the line connected. He hadn't heard it ring on his end. "What's going on?"

"Apparent suicide at Fifth and Sixty-eighth." He checked his watch. "It tickles. I'm on the scene and going to poke around a little. Are any of the responders our guys?"

"One second." Her voice muffled as she asked someone a question; there was a very brief pause, and she was back on the line. "Marla says Marion Thornton is en route. Have you met her?"

"Socially." By which he meant, at Promethean events and rituals. There were about two hundred Magi in the Greater New York area, and like Matthew, most of them held down two jobs: guardian of the iron world by night, teacher or artist or executive or civil servant by day.

They worked hard. But at least none of them had to worry about money. The Prometheus Club provided whatever it took to make ends meet. "I'll look for her."

"She'll get you inside," Jane said. "Any theories yet?"

Matthew crouched amid rubberneckers and bent his luck a little to keep from being stepped on. The crowd moved around him, but never quite squeezed him off-balance. Their shadows made it hard to see, but his fingers hovered a quarter-inch from a dime-sized stain on the pavement, and a chill slicked through his bones. "Not in a crowd," he said, and pulled his hand back so he wouldn't touch the drip accidentally. "Actually, tell Marion to process the inside scene on her own, would you? And not to touch anything moist with her bare hand, or even a glove if she can help it."

"You have a secondary lead?"

"I think I have a trail."

"Blood?"

It had a faint aroma, too, though he wouldn't bend close. Cold stone, guano, moist rancid early mornings full of last winter's rot. A spring and barnyard smell, with an underlying acridness that made his eyes water and his nose run. He didn't wipe his tears; there was no way he was touching his face after being near this.

He dug in his pocket with his left hand, cradling the phone with the right. A moment's exploration produced a steel disk the size of a silver dollar. He spat on the underside, balanced it like a miniature tabletop between his thumb and first two fingers, and then turned his hand over. A half-inch was as close as he dared.

He dropped the metal. It struck the sidewalk and bonded to the concrete with a hiss, sealing the stain away.

"Venom," Matthew said. "I've marked it. You'll need to send a containment team. I have to go."

When he stood, he looked directly into the eyes of one of his giggly freshmen.

"Ms. Gomez," he said. "Fancy meeting you here. Sorry I can't stay to chat."

Gina was still stammering when she came back. "Did you see that? Did you *see* that?"

Katie hadn't. "Just the backs of a bunch of tall people's heads. What happened?"

"I was trying to stay away from him," Gina said. "And he just *appeared* right beside me. Poof. Poof!"

"Or you weren't looking where you were going," Katie said, but Melissa was frowning. "Well?"

"He did just pop up out of nowhere," Melissa said. "I was watching Gina, and he kind of . . . materialized beside her. Like he stood up all of a sudden."

"He's the devil." Gina shook her head, but she sounded half-convinced.

Katie patted her on the shoulder, woven cotton rasping between her fingertips and Gina's flesh. "He could have been tying his shoe."

"Right," Gina said, stepping out from under Katie's hand. She pointed back to the crowd. "Then where did he go?"

Even glamoured, he couldn't run from a murder scene. The magic relied on symbol and focus; if he broke that, he'd find himself stuck in a backlash that would make him the center of attention of every cop, Russian landlady, and wino for fifteen blocks. So instead he walked, fast, arms swinging freely, trying to look as if he was late getting back from a lunch date.

Following the smell of venom.

He found more droplets, widely spaced. In places, they had started to etch asphalt or concrete. Toxic waste indeed; it slowed him, because he had to pause to tag and seal each one.

How it could move unremarked through his city, he did not know. There were no crops here for its steps to blight nor wells for its breath to poison.

Which was not to say it did no harm.

These things—some fed on flesh and some on blood and bone. Some fed on death, or fear, or misery, or drunkenness, or loneliness, or love, or hope, or white perfect joy. Some constructed wretchedness, and some comforted the afflicted.

There was no telling until you got there.

Matthew slowed as his quarry led him north. There were still too many bystanders. Too many civilians. He didn't care to catch up with any monsters in broad daylight, halfway up Manhattan. But as the neighborhoods became more cluttered and the scent of uncollected garbage grew heavy on the humid air, he found more alleys, more byways, and fewer underground garages.

If he were a cockatrice, he thought he might very well lair in such a place. Somewhere among the rubbish and the poison and the broken glass. The cracked concrete, and the human waste.

He needed as much camouflage to walk here undisturbed as any monster might.

His hands prickled ceaselessly. He was closer. He slowed, reinforcing his wards with a sort of nervous tic: checking that his hair was smooth, his coat was buttoned, his shoes were tied. Somehow, it managed to move from its lair to the Upper East Side without leaving a trail of bodies in the street. Maybe it traveled blind. Or underground; he hadn't seen a drop of venom in a dozen blocks. Worse, it might be invisible.

Sometimes . . . often . . . *otherwise* things had slipped far enough sideways that they could not interact with the iron world except through the intermediary of a Mage or a medium. If this had happened to the monster he sought, *then* it could travel unseen. *Then* it could pass by with no more harm done than the pervasive influence of its presence.

But then, it wouldn't drip venom real enough to melt stone.

Relax, Matthew. You don't know it's a cockatrice. It's just a hypothesis, and appearances can be deceptive.

Assuming that he had guessed right could get him killed.

But a basilisk or a cockatrice was what made sense. Except, why would the victim have thrown herself from her window for a crowned serpent, a scaled crow? And why wasn't everybody who crossed the thing's path being killed. Or turned to stone, if it was *that* sort of cockatrice?

His eyes stung, a blinding burning as if he breathed chlorine fumes, etchant. The scent was as much *otherwise* as real; Matthew suffered it more than the civilians, who would sense only the miasma of the streets as they were poisoned. A lingering death.

He blinked, tears brimming, wetting his eyelashes and blurring the world through his spectacles. A Mage's traveling arsenal was both eclectic and specific, but Matthew had never before thought to include normal saline, and he hadn't passed a drugstore for blocks.

How the hell is it traveling?

At last, the smell was stronger, the cold prickle sharper, on his left. He entered the mouth of a rubbish-strewn alley, a kind of gated brick tunnel not tall or wide enough for a garbage truck. It was unlocked, the grille rusted open; the passage brought him to a filthy internal courtyard. Rows of garbage cans—of course, no dumpsters—and two winos, one sleeping on cardboard, one lying on his back on grease-daubed foam reading a two-month-old copy of *Maxim*. The miasma of the cockatrice—if it was a cockatrice—was so strong here that Matthew gagged.

What he was going to do about it, of course, he didn't know.

His phone buzzed. He answered it, lowering his voice. "Jane?"

"The window was unlocked from the inside," she said. "No sign of forced entry. The resident was a fifty-eight-year-old unmarried woman, Janet Stafford. Here's the interesting part—"

"Yes?"

"She had just re-entered secular life, if you can believe this. She spent the last thirty-four years as a nun."

Matthew glanced at his phone, absorbing that piece of information, and put it back to his ear. "Did she leave the church, or just the convent?"

"The church," Jane said. "Marion's checking into why. You don't need to call her; I'll liaise."

"That would save time," Matthew said. "Thank you." There was no point in both of them reporting to Jane *and* to each other if Jane considered the incident important enough to coordinate personally.

"Are you ready to tell me yet what you think it might be?"

Matthew stepped cautiously around the small courtyard, holding onto his don't-notice-me, his hand cupped around the mouthpiece. "I *was* thinking cockatrice," he said. "But you know, now maybe not certain. What drips venom, and can lure a retired nun to suicide?"

Jane's breath, hissing between her teeth, was clearly audible over the cellular crackle. "Harpy."

"Yeah," Matthew said. "But then why doesn't it fly?"

"What are you going to do?"

"Right now? Question a couple of local residents," he said, and moved toward the Maxim-reading squatter.

The man looked up as he approached; Matthew steeled himself to hide a flinch at his stench, the sore running pus down into his beard. A lot of these guys were mentally ill and unsupported by any system. A lot of them *also* had the knack for seeing things that had mostly dropped *otherwise*, as if in being overlooked themselves they gained insight into the half-lit world.

And it didn't matter how he looked; the homeless man's life was still a life, and his only. *You can't save them all. But he had a father and mother and a history and a soul like yours.*

His city, which he loved, dehumanized; Matthew considered it the responsibility that came with his gifts to humanize it right back. It was in some ways rather like being married to a terrible drunk. You did a lot of apologizing. "Hey," Matthew said. He didn't crouch down. He held out his hand; the homeless man eyed it suspiciously. "I'm Matthew. You have absolutely no reason to want to know me, but I'm looking for some information I can't get from just anybody. Can I buy you some food, or a drink?"

Later, over milkshakes, Melissa glanced at Katie through the humidity-frizzled curls that had escaped her braid and said, "I can't believe we lost him."

The straw scraped Katie's lip as she released it. "You mean he gave us the slip."

Melissa snorted. On her left, Gina picked fretfully at a plate of French fries, sprinkling pinched grains of salt down the length of one particular fry and then brushing them away with a fingertip. "He just popped up. Right by me. And then vanished. I never took my eyes off him."

"Some criminal mastermind you turned out to be," Katie said, but her heart wasn't in it. Gina flinched, so Katie swiped one of her fries by way of apology. A brief but giggly scuffle ensued before Katie maneuvered the somewhat mangled fry into her mouth. She was chewing salt and starch when Melissa said, "Don't you guys think this is all a little weird?"

Katie swallowed, leaving a slick of grease on her palate. "No," she said, and slurped chocolate shake to clear it off. Her hair moved on her neck, and she swallowed and imagined the touch of a hand. A prickle of sensation tingled through her, the same excitement she felt at their pursuit of Doctor S., which she had experienced only occasionally while kissing her boyfriend back home. She shifted in her chair. "I think it's plenty weird."

She wasn't going to ask the other girls. Melissa had a boyfriend at Harvard that she traded off weekends with. Gina was . . . Gina. She picked up whatever boy she wanted, kept him a while, put him down again. Katie would rather let them assume that she wasn't all that innocent.

Not that they'd hate her. But they'd laugh.

"What are we going to do about it?" she asked, when Melissa kept looking at her. "I mean, it's not like he did something illegal."

"You didn't see the body up close."

"I didn't. But he didn't kill her. We know where he was when she fell."

Gina's mouth compressed askew. But she nodded, then hid her face in her shake.

Melissa pushed at her frizzing hair again. "You know," she said, "he left in a hurry. It's like a swamp out there."

"So?"

"So. Do you suppose his office door sticks?"

"Oh, no. That *is* illegal. We could get expelled."

"We wouldn't take anything." Melissa turned her drink with the tips of her fingers, looking at them and the spiraling ring left behind on the tabletop, not at Katie's eyes. "Just see if he has a police scanner. And look for his address."

"I'm not doing that," Katie said.

"I just want to see if the door is unlocked."

Melissa looked at Gina. Gina shrugged. "Those locks come loose with a credit card, anyway."

"No. Not just no."

"Oh, you can watch the stairs," Gina said, sharp enough that Katie sat back in her chair. Katie swallowed, and nodded. Fine. She would watch the goddamned stair.

"You want to finish?" she asked.

Gina pushed her mangled but uneaten fries away. "No, baby. I'm done."

The man's name was Henry; he ate an extraordinary amount of fried chicken from a red paper bucket while Matthew crouched on the stoop beside him, breathing shallowly. The acrid vapors of whatever Matthew hunted actually covered both the odor of unwashed man and of dripping grease, and though his eyes still watered, he thought his nose was shutting down in protest. Perversely, this made it easier to cope.

"No," Henry said. He had a tendency to slur his speech, to ramble and digress, but he was no ranting lunatic. Not, Matthew reminded himself, that it would matter if he was. "I mean, okay. I see things. More now than when I got my meds"—he shrugged, a bit of extra crispy coating clinging to his moustache—"I mean, I mean, not that I'm crazy, but you see things out of the corner of your eye, and when you turn? You see?"

He was staring at a spot slightly over Matthew's left shoulder when he said it, and Matthew wished very hard that he dared turn around and look. "All the damned time," he said.

The heat of the cement soaked through his jeans; the jacket was nearly unbearable. He shrugged out of it, laid it on the stoop, and rolled up his sleeves. "Man," Henry said, and sucked soft meat off bones. "Nice ink."

"Thanks," Matthew said, turning his arms over to inspect the insides.

"Hurt much? You don't look like the type."

"Hurt some," Matthew admitted. "What sort of things do you see? Out of the corners of your eyes?"

"Scuttling things. Flapping things." He shrugged. "When I can get a drink it helps."

"Rats? Pigeons?"

"Snakes," Henry said. He dropped poultry bones back into the bucket. "Roosters."

"Not crows? Vultures?"

"No," Henry said. "Roosters. Snakes, the color of the wall."

"Damn." Matthew picked up his coat. "Thanks, Henry. I guess it was a cockatrice after all."

What happened was, Katie couldn't wait on the stairs. Of course she'd known there wasn't a chance in hell that she could resist Melissa. But sometimes it was better to fool yourself a little, even if you knew that eventually you were going to crack.

Instead, she found herself standing beside Gina, blocking a sight line with her body, as Gina knocked ostentatiously on Doctor S.'s door. She slipped the latch with a credit card—a gesture so smooth that Katie could hardly tell she wasn't just trying the handle. She knocked again and then pulled the door open.

Katie kind of thought she was overplaying, and made a point of slipping through the barely opened door in an attempt to hide from passers-by that the room was empty.

Melissa came in last, tugging the door shut behind herself. Katie heard the click of the lock.

Not, apparently, that that would stop anybody.

Katie put her back against the door beside the wall and crossed her arms over her chest to confine her shivering. Gina moved into the office as if entranced; she stood in the center of the small cluttered room and spun slowly on her heel, hands in her hip pockets, elbows awkwardly cocked. Melissa slipped past her—as much as a six foot redhead could slip—and bent over to examine the desk, touching nothing.

"There has to be a utility bill here or something, right? Everybody does that sort of thing at work . . . "

Gina stopped revolving, striking the direction of the bookshelves like a compass needle striking north—a swing, a stick, a shiver. She craned her neck back and began inspecting titles.

It was Katie, after forcing herself forward to peer over Gina's shoulder, who noticed the row of plain black hardbound octavo volumes on one shelf, each with a ribbon bound into the spine and a date penned on it in silver metallic ink.

"Girls," she said, "do you suppose he puts his address in his journal?"

Gina turned to follow Katie's pointing finger and let loose a string of Spanish that Katie was pretty sure would have her toenails smoking if she understood a word. It was obviously self-directed, though, so after the obligatory flinch, she reached past Gina and pulled the most recently dated volume from the shelf.

"Can I use the desk?" The book cracked a little under the pressure of her fingers, and it felt lumpy, with wavy page-edges. If anything was pressed inside, she didn't want to scatter it.

Melissa stood back. Katie laid the book carefully on an uncluttered portion of the blotter and slipped the elastic that held it closed without moving the food or papers. The covers almost burst apart, as if eager to be read, foiling her intention to open it to the flyleaf and avoid prying. The handwriting was familiar: she saw it on the whiteboard twice a week. But that wasn't what made Katie catch her breath.

A pressed flower was taped to the left-hand page, facing a column of text. And in the sunlight that fell in bars through the dusty blind, it shimmered iridescent blue and violet over faded gray.

"Madre de Dios," Gina breathed. "What does it say?"

Katie nudged the book further into the light. "14 October 1995," she read. "Last year, Gin."

"He probably has the new one with him. What does it *say*?"

"It says 'Passed as a ten?' and there's an address on Long Island. Flanagan's, Deer Park Avenue. Babylon. Some names. And then it says 'pursuant to the disappearance of Sean Roberts—flower and several oak leaves were collected from a short till at the under-twenty-one club.' And *then* it says 'Faerie money?' Spelled F-a-e-r-i-e."

"He's crazy," Gina said definitively. "Schizo. Gone."

"Maybe he's writing a fantasy novel." Katie wasn't sure where her stubborn loyalty came from, but she was abruptly brimming with it. "We are reading his private stuff totally out of context. I don't think it's fair to judge by appearances."

Gina jostled her elbow; Katie shrugged the contact off and turned the page. Another record of a disappearance, this one without supporting evidence taped to the page. It filled up six pages. After that, a murder under mysterious circumstances. A kidnapping . . . and then some more pages on the Roberts disappearance. A broken, bronze-colored feather, also taped in, chimed when she touched it. She jerked her finger back.

One word underneath. "Resolved." And a date after Christmastime.

Doctor S., it seemed, thought he was a cop. A special kind of . . . supernatural cop.

"It sounds like *Nick Knight*," Melissa said. Katie blinked, and realized she had still been reading out loud.

"It sounds like a crazy man," Gina said.

Katie opened her mouth, and suddenly felt as if cold water drained down her spine. She swallowed whatever she had been about to say and flipped the journal to the flyleaf. There was indeed an address, on West Sixtieth. "He's not crazy." *Not unless I am.*

"Why do you say that?" Melissa, gently, but Gina was looking at Katie too—not suspicious, or mocking, anymore, but wide-eyed, waiting for her to explain.

"Guys," Katie said, "He's a magician or something. Remember how he vanished on Gina? Remember the ink that you somehow just don't see? Remember the damned invisible rings?"

Melissa sucked her lower lip in and released it. "So did he kill that woman or not?"

"I don't know," Katie said. "I want him to be a good guy."

Gina patted her shoulder, then reached across to also pat the journal with her fingertips. "I say we go to his apartment and find out."

There were drawbacks to being a member of Matthew's society of Magi. For one thing, nobody else liked them. And with good reason; not only was the Prometheus Club full of snobs, Capitalists, and politicians, but its stated goal of limiting and controlling the influence of wild magic in the world put him in sworn opposition to any hedge-witch, Satanist, purveyor of herbs and simples, houngan, or priest of Santeria he might want to contract with for ritual supplies.

Such as, say, a white, virgin cockerel.

New York City was not bereft of live poultry markets, but given his rather specific needs, Matthew wasn't sure he wanted to trust one of those. He'd hate to find out at the last minute, for example, that his bird had had a few sandy feathers plucked. Or that it was, shall we say, a little more experienced than Matthew was himself.

And then there was the recent influenza scare, which had closed several poultry markets. And what he really needed, now that he thought about it, was an illegal animal; a fighting cock.

He booted his desktop system, entered an IP address from memory, wended his way through a series of logon screens, and asked about it on the Promethean message board.

Fortunately, even if Matthew didn't know something, it was a pretty good bet that *somebody* in Prometheus would.

Before close of business, he was twenty blocks north again, edging through a flaking avocado-green steel door into the antechamber of a dimly lit warehouse that smelled of guano and sawdust and corn and musty feathers. It drove the eye-watering stench of the cockatrice from Matthew's sinuses, finally, and seemed in comparison such a rich, wholesome smell that he breathed it deep and fast. He coughed, sneezed, and waved his hand in front of his face. And then he did it again, feeling as if the inside of his head were clean for the first time in hours.

There was a desk in a cage—not unlike the ones inhabited by the clucking, rustling chickens, but far larger—behind the half-wall at the far end of the dirty, hall-like room. Matthew approached it; a stout woman with her white hair twisted into a bun looked up from her game of solitaire.

He cleared his throat. "I need to buy a cockerel."

"I've got some nice Bantams," she said through the grate. "And a couple of Rhode Island Reds." Not admitting anything; those weren't fighting cocks. "You got a place to keep it? There are zoning things."

"It just needs to be pure white." He hesitated. "Or pure black."

She reached up casually and dropped the shutter in his face. Of course. He sighed, and rapped on the grate, rattling the metal behind it. No answer. He rapped again, and again.

Five minutes later she cracked it up and peered under the bottom, through the little hole for passing papers and money back and forth. He caught a glimpse of bright black eyes and a wrinkled nose. "I'm not selling you any bird for your Satanic rituals, young man."

No, but you'll sell me one for blood sports? Matthew sighed again and stuck his hand through the slot, nearly getting his fingers up her nose. She jerked

back, but he caught the edge of the shutter before she could slide it closed
again. His biceps bulged inside his shirt sleeve; his tendons dimpled his wrist.
She leaned on the shutter, and couldn't shift him.

"Young man." A level, warning tone. She didn't look intimidated.

Oh, what the hell. "It's for the cockatrice," he said.

Her hand relaxed, and the weight of the shutter lifted. She slid it up;
it thumped when it reached the top. "Why didn't you say so? About time
somebody took care of that thing. Though I notice you didn't give a shit when
it was just in East Harlem."

Matthew glanced aside. The cops were always the last to know.

She hesitated. "You'll need a human virgin too."

"Don't worry," he said, biting the inside of his cheek. "I've got that
covered."

When he returned home, there was a woman waiting in his apartment. Not
surprising in itself; Jane had a key and the passcode for the locks. But it wasn't
Jane. It was the homicide detective, Marion Thornton.

She had an outdoorswoman's squint and silky brown hair that framed her
long cheekbones in feathered wings; it made her look like a bright-eyed Afghan
hound. She showed him her badge and handed him back the keys before he
was fully in the door.

"The victim was an alcoholic," Marion said, re-locking the door as
Matthew put his chicken on the counter. It was in a cardboard animal carrier.
Occasionally a glossy jet-black beak or a malevolent eye would appear in one
of the holes along the top. It scuffed and kicked. He pushed it away from the
counter edge and it grabbed at him, as he thought of a line from a Russian fairy
tale: *Listen, Crow, crow's daughter! Serve me a certain service—*

"The nun was a drunk?"

"To put it crudely. And we found another possible for the same bogey,
about three days ago. Elderly man, never married, lived alone, drank like a
fish. We're continuing to check back for others." She flipped pages in her report
pad. "Here's something interesting. He was castrated in a farming accident
when he was in his teens."

"Oh," Matthew said. "It's always virgins, isn't it?"

"For dragons and unicorns, anyway," Marion answered. "But I'd guess you're
correct. And more than that. Heavy drinkers. Possibly with some talent; a link
my . . . secular . . . colleagues won't come up with is that Promethean records
show that we considered inviting both of these victims for apprenticeship when
they were young."

"So they saw things," Matthew said, thinking of Henry, living on the
monster's doorstep. If the thing had a preference for sexually inexperienced

prey, that would explain why it hadn't eaten him yet. Well, if Matthew was prepared to make a few conjectures. "Do you think it wanted them because they drank, or they drank because they saw things?"

"We operate on the first assumption." Marion picked her way around him, leaned down to peer into the animal carrier. She pulled back as a grabbing beak speared at her eye. "Vicious."

"I sure hope so."

"Jane said you had a possible ID on the bogey?"

He knelt down and began peeling the rug back, starting beside the inside wall of the living room. "The black cock isn't enough of a hint?"

"Basilisk."

"That's a weasel. Cockatrice, I'm guessing. Though how it lured its victim into hurling herself from her window is beyond me. You're describing very specialized prey."

She straightened up and arched, cracking her spine. She picked a spoon off the breakfast bar and turned it, considering the way the light pooled in the bowl. "Call it one in ten thousand? Then the Greater New York metropolitan area has, what, two thousand more just like 'em?"

"Something like that," Matthew said, and pinched the bridge of his nose. A dust bunny was stuck to the heel of his hand; he blew it off. When he opened his eyes, he found her staring at him, tongue-tip peeking between her lips.

"Want to make sure we're safe?" she said, with a grin. The spoon glittered as she turned it beside her face. "I'm off duty. And your chicken won't mind." She held up her left hand and showed him a plain gold band. "No hassles."

He bit his lower lip. Matthew had practice. And years of careful sublimation—which was, of course, the point: sacrifice made power. He also had a trick of flying under the gaydar, of making straight women think he was gay and gay men think he was straight. All just part of the camouflage.

He hated having to say no. "Sorry," he said. "That's a lovely offer. But I need a virgin for the cockatrice already, and it beats having to send out."

She laughed, of course.

They never believed him.

"Come on," he said. "Help me ensorcel this chicken."

Doctor S. lived in Midtown West, on Sixtieth near Columbus Avenue. It was kind of a hike, but they got there before sunset. It wouldn't get dark for an hour, but that was only because the afternoons were still long. By the time they paused down the block Katie's stomach was rumbling. That milkshake was only good for so long.

The spot they picked to loiter had a clear view of the front door of Doctor

S.'s brown brick apartment building. "Nice place for a junior professor," Melissa said, and for ten seconds she sounded like she was from Boston, all right.

Katie looked at Gina and made big eyes and whimpering noises, but it was Melissa who went and got convenience store hot dogs, Diet Pepsi, and a bag of chips. They ate in the shade on the north side of the building, the heat soaking from the stones, their hair lank and grimy with the city air. Katie scratched her cheek and brought her fingernails away sporting black crescents. "Ew."

"Welcome to New York," Gina said, which was what she said every time Katie complained.

Katie had nearly stopped complaining already. She scratched her nails against her jeans until most of the black came out and finished her hot dog one-handed, then wiped the grime from her face with the napkin before drying her hands. It worked kind of halfway—good enough, anyway, that when Melissa splashed ice water from a sport bottle into everyone's cupped hands and Katie in turn splashed it onto her face, she didn't wind up feeling like she'd faceplanted into a mud puddle.

The second handful, she drank, and only realized she had been carrying a heat headache when the weight of it faded. "All right," she said, and took the bottle from Melissa to squirt some on her hair. "Ready as I'll ever be."

"Unfortunately, apparently Doctor S. isn't," Melissa said, reclaiming the bottle to drink. She tilted her head back, her throat working, and as she lowered it a droplet ran from the corner of her mouth. "No, wait, spoke too soon."

Katie stepped behind the pole of a street lamp—silly, because Doctor S. wasn't even looking in their direction—and caught sight of his stiff little blond ponytail zigzagging through the crowd. He was wearing another sort-of costume—Katie wondered what he wore when he wore what he liked, rather than what suited his role—a well-cut gray suit with a fabulous drape. A woman in a navy pantsuit, whose light flyaway hair escaped its pins around a long narrow face, walked alongside him. Her stride was familiar. She had a white cardboard pet carrier slung from her left hand; Katie could not see what was in it, but it swung as if something was moving slightly inside.

"Isn't that the cop who showed up where the woman jumped?"

Katie glanced at Gina and back at the woman, a stuttering double take. It was. Not the same outfit, and her hair was clipped back aggressively now—though it wasn't staying restrained—but the woman was conspicuous. "Well," Katie said, feeling as if she watched the words emerge from a stranger's mouth, "we could follow him and find out where they're going."

Neither Matthew nor Marion was particularly sanguine about attacking on a cockatrice in the dark. They had to take the subway across the island (at least the cockerel was quiet, huddled in the bottom of its carrier) but still ascended to the surface with light to spare. It roused the bird; Matthew heard it shift, and Marion kept her fingers well clear of the air holes. It was, as promised, aggressive.

Matthew shoved down guilt and substantial apprehension. There was no other choice, and power grew out of sacrifices.

They found the courtyard without a problem, that tunnel-like entrance with its broken gate leaving rust on Matthew's clothes as they slipped through. He wasn't wearing his usual patrol clothes, a zipped camouflage jacket and boots enchanted to pass-unnoticed, but a gray silk suit with a linen shirt and a silver, red, and navy tie. A flask in an inside pocket tapped his ribs when he moved. He looked like a dot com paper millionaire on his way to a neck-or-nothing meeting with a crotchety venture capitalist who was going to hate his ponytail.

His clothes today, and the quick preliminary ritual they'd performed in his living room, were not designed to conceal him, to occlude his power, but rather to draw the right attention. If you squinted at him with otherwise eyes, he would shine. And other than his rings and the earrings and the pigment in the ink under his skin, he wasn't wearing any iron, as he might have been if they went to face something Fae.

Iron was of no use against a cockatrice. Except in one particular, and so two steel gaffs wrapped in tissue paper nested in the bottom of Matthew's trouser pocket. He touched them through fabric like a child stroking a favorite toy and drew his hand back when they clinked.

"This is it," he said.

Marion set the carrier down. "Nice place you've got here, Matthew. Decorate it yourself?" From the way her nose was wrinkling, she picked out the acid aroma of the monster as well.

Henry and his comrade at arms were nowhere to be seen. Matthew hoped they had taken his advice and moved on. He hated working around civilians.

Without answering Marion, he kicked aside garbage, clearing a space in the center of the court. The windows overlooking it remained unoccupied, and if for some reason they did not continue so, Marion had a badge.

She helped Matthew sketch a star overlaid on a circle in yellow sidewalk chalk. They left one point open, facing south by Marion's compass. When they were done, Matthew dusted his hands, wiped them on his handkerchief, and reached into his pockets for the spurs, the flask, and something else—a leather hood of the sort used by falconers to quiet their birds.

"Ready?"

She nodded. "Where's the lair?"

He patted himself on the chest—"the s.o.b. comes to us"—and watched her eyes widen. She had thought he was kidding.

They always did.

Well, maybe someday he could catch a unicorn.

"It's okay," he said, when her blush became a stammer. "Let's get the knives on this chicken."

It took both of them, crouched on either side, to open the box and hood the bird without harming it. It exploded into Matthew's grip as Marion pried open the flaps; he caught at it, bungled the grab and got pecked hard for his pains. Somehow he got the bird pressed to his chest, a struggling fury of iridescent black plumage, and caged it in his blunt hands. It felt prickly and slick and hotter than blood under the feathers. He smoothed its wings together and restrained the kicking legs, while Marion dodged the jabbing beak. Once in darkness it quieted, and Marion strapped the three-inch gaffs over its own natural spurs.

When they were done, it looked quite brave and wicked, the gleam of steel on rainbow-black. Marion stroked its back between Matthew's fingers, her touch provoking a tremor when she brushed the back of his hand. "Fucking abomination."

She meant cockfighting, not the bird. Matthew set the cockerel down and moved his hands away. It sat quietly. "How do you think I feel?"

She shrugged. Still crouched, she produced a pair of handcuffs and a silken hood from her tan leather handbag. Matthew bent over to pick up the flask. "God, I hate this part."

He prized it open with his thumb and upended it over his mouth. The fumes of hundred-and-fifty-proof rum made him gasp; he choked down three swallows and stopped, doubled over, rasping.

Matthew didn't often drink.

But that would be enough for the spell.

Light-headed, now, sinuses stinging from more than the reek of the cockatrice, Matthew handed Marion the flask and then his spectacles, feeling naked without them. He wiped his mouth on the back of his hand, fine hairs harsh on his lips. Four steps took him through the open end of the pentagram.

He turned back and faced Marion. With the silk of the hood draped over his forearm, he handcuffed himself—snugly: he did not want his body breaking free while he was not in it.

They weren't replaceable.

He took one more deep breath, closed his eyes on Marion's blurry outline, and with his joined wrists rattling pulled the hood over his head.

In the dark underneath, sounds were muffled. Concentrated rum fumes made his eyes water, but at least he could no longer smell the cockatrice. Chalk grated—Marion closing the pentagram. He heard his flask uncorked, the splash of fluid as she anointed the diagram with the remaining rum. Matthew tugged restlessly against the restraints on his wrists as she began to chant and a deep uneasy curdling sensation answered.

God, too much rum. He wobbled and caught himself, fretting the handcuffs, the tightness on the bones. The sensual thrill of the magic sparking along his nerves was accentuated by the blinding darkness. He wobbled again, or maybe the world did, and gasped at the heat in his blood.

Magic and passion weren't different. It was one reason sublimation worked.

The second gasp came cleaner, no fabric muffling his face, the air cooler if not fresher and the scent of rum less cloying. Marion seemed to have moved, by the sound of her chanting, and somehow the tightness had jumped from Matthew's wrists to his calves. He lay belly-down on rough ground.

He pushed with his arms to try to balance himself to his feet. The chanting stopped, abruptly, and someone was restraining him, folding his arms against his side gently but with massive cautious strength. "Matthew?"

He turned his head, seeking the voice. It echoed. The . . . arms? holding him retreated. "Matthew, if you understand me, flap once."

He extended odd-feeling arms and did so. A moment later, a half-dozen fists, it seemed, were unhooding him. He blinked at dizzy brilliance, and found himself staring into Marion's enormous face from only a few inches away. He hopped back and fouled himself on the gaffs. Fortunately, the needle point slipped between his feathers rather than stabbing him in the wing, and he stopped, precariously balanced, wings half-bent like broken umbrellas.

He clucked.

And flapped hard, surprised to find himself lifting off the ground. He flew the two feet to Marion's shoulder, landed awkwardly, facing the wrong way, and banged her in the eye with his wing. At least he had the sense to turn carefully, keeping the needle-tipped gaffs pointed away from her thin-skinned throat. He crouched on his heels, trying not to prick her with his claws, the alien body's balance far better than his own.

Only if he thought about it did he realize that the warm shoulder he nestled to Marion's warm cheek was feathered, that it was peculiar to be able to feel the beats of her heart through his feet like the footfalls of an approaching predator, that the colors he saw were abruptly so bright and saturated—so discriminate—that he had no names for them. That he balanced on her moving shoulder as easily as he would have roosted on a swaying branch, and that that was peculiar.

"Wow," he said. And heard a soft contemplative cluck. And laughed at himself, which came out a rising, tossing crow.

Marion flinched and put a hand up on his wing. "Matthew, please. My ears."

He ducked his head between his shoulders, abashed, and clucked *sorry*. Maybe she would understand.

His body stood stolidly, restrained, inside a wet circle of chalk and rum. The cockerel wearing it was quieted by the hood and the handcuffs, and Matthew turned his head right and left to center himself in his vision. He failed—he had the peripheral view, and only by turning to see it first with one eye and then the other could he reliably guess how far away it was. Almost no binocular vision, of course. But with a shock, he realized that he could see clearly around to the back of his head.

That was pretty tremendously weird. He'd have to practice that. And think about his small sharp body and its instincts, because the enemy could be along any moment.

Marion was pulling back, stepping into the shadows, an alcove near the gate concealing them. Matthew pressed against her warmth, feeling her heart beating faster. He clucked in her ear.

"Shh."

He hoped the cockatrice would come quickly. This could be very, very awkward to explain if something happened to the glamours. Still, they had brought alcohol, talent, and innocence—symbolically speaking—and left them, special delivery, in the thing's front yard. Wherever it was nesting, it should come to investigate before too long.

He was still thinking that when he heard the singing.

The three of them had been following for a long time, it seemed, when Doctor S. and the woman gave one another a conspiratorial glance and stepped through an archway, past a rusted gate. Gina drew up short, stepping out of the traffic flow into the shelter of a doorway. A moment later, Katie heard glass breaking and something kicked or thrown.

Katie ducked in behind Gina, rubbing her elbow nervously. This wasn't the best neighborhood at all. "That's a dead end, I bet," Gina said, when Melissa came up beside them. "Either they're going inside, or that's where they're going."

"Here?"

Gina winked. "Want to sneak up and peek through the gate?"

Katie and Melissa exchanged a glance, and Melissa angled her head and said, "What the heck." Side by side, the three stepped back out onto the sidewalk, picking their way over chewing gum spots and oily, indeterminate stains. Katie somehow found herself in the lead, as Gina and Melissa fell in single file behind her. She had to glance over her shoulder to make sure they were still with her.

She stopped two feet shy of the broken gate and tried to still her hammering heart. No luck, and so she clenched her hands at her sides and edged forward.

She could see through plainly if she kept her back to the wall and turned her head sideways. She saw Doctor S. and the cop sketch the diagram, saw them pull a black rooster from the box and do something to its head and feet. She flinched, expecting some bloody and melodramatic beheading, but instead Doctor S. went to the center of the star and began chaining himself up, which made her feel distinctly funny inside. And then he blindfolded himself with a hood, and the woman did some more sketching with the chalk and walked around the circle pouring something in between its lines from a flask.

A moment later, the rooster began to struggle, while Doctor S. stood perfectly still. The woman crouched down and unhooded it, and a moment later it flapped onto her shoulder and settled itself.

"This," Melissa whispered, a warm pressure against Katie's side, "is freaking weird."

"Gosh," Gina said, very loudly, "would you listen to that?"

Katie turned to shush her, and heard it herself. She took a deep breath, chest expanding against her shirt, as if she could inhale the music too. It seemed to swell in her lungs and belly, to buoy her. She felt Melissa cringe, and then fingers caught at her shoulder. "Fuck," Melissa said. "What is that?"

"Beautiful." Katie stepped forward, moving out of Melissa's grasp. Into the courtyard, toward the woman and the chicken and the blindfolded English professor. Katie lifted her arms and twirled, her feet light as if she walked on flowers. She strode through a pile of garbage that the magicians had piled up when they cleared the center of the courtyard and her airy foot came down on glass.

A cracked bottle broke further under her foot, shattering and crunching. The soft sole of Katie's tennis sneaker clung to broken glass; she picked it up again and stepped forward, to another crunch.

The noise was almost lost under the music. Rising chorales, crystalline voices.

"It sounds like a rat being shaken to death in a bag of hammers," Melissa groaned, and then sucked in a squeak. "Oh, fuck, Katie, your foot . . . "

There was something slick between her sole and the bottom of the shoe. She must have stepped in a mud puddle. She looked down. Or a puddle of blood.

Well, her foot was already wet. And the singers were over there somewhere. She took one more step, Melissa's fingers brushing her wrist as her friend missed her grab. Behind her, Melissa made funny sobbing noises, as if she'd been running and couldn't get a breath.

Somehow, Gina had gotten ahead of her, and was walking too, kicking rubbish out of the way with her sandaled feet, crunching through more glass, leaving red footsteps. The courtyard was filthy, the buildings moldy-looking, scrofulous: brick black with soot and flaking mortar.

Something moved against the wall. A gleam of brightness, like sun through torn cloth. And then—so beautiful, so bright, oh—a spill of jadevioletandazure, a trailing cloak of feathers, a sort of peacock or bird of paradise emerging like an image reflected in a suddenly lit mirror. Its crested head was thrown back, its long neck swollen with song. Its wings mantled and rays of light cracked from between its feathers.

Gina was still ahead of her, between her and the bird. Katie reached out to push her, but then suddenly she was gone, fallen down, and Katie stepped over her. It was the most beautiful thing she'd ever seen. It was the most beautiful thing she'd ever heard.

And oh, it was blind, the poor thing was blind. Somebody had gouged out its eyes, she saw now. The old wounds were scarred gray, sightless.

And still it sang.

She reached out her hand to touch it, and couldn't understand why Melissa was screaming.

Matthew saw both young women hurry across the glass and stones, faster than he could reach them—not that he could have stopped them. Even though he was airborne, and already on his way.

He saw his body react, too—it hurled itself at the edge of the pentagram, hurled and kept hurling, but the wards they'd so carefully constructed held him, and he bounced from them and slid down what looked like plain still air. So strange, watching himself from the outside. Marion and the red-haired girl both crumpled, Marion with her hands over her ears, belly-crawling determinedly toward the running children; Melissa Martinchek down in a fetal position, screaming.

And he saw the cockatrice.

The movement caught his eye first, a ripple of red like brick and gray like concrete, its hide patterned in staggered courses that blended precisely with the blackened wall behind it. It was bigger than a cock, but not by much, and his rooster's heart churned with rage at its red upright comb and the plumed waterfall of its tail. His wings beat in midair; he exploded after it like a partridge from cover.

It chameleoned from stone to brilliance, colors chasing over its plumage like rainbows over oil. The two girls clutched for it, their feet pierced with unnoticed shards, their hands reaching.

Matthew saw them fall, their bodies curled in around their poisoned hands. He saw the way they convulsed, the white froth dripping from the corners of their mouths.

He shrieked war, wrath, red rage, and oblivion. The spurs were heavy on his shanks; his wings were mighty upon the air. He struck, reaching hard, and clutched at the enemy's neck.

An eruption of rainbow-and-black plumage, a twist and strike and movement like quicksilver on slanted glass. Matthew's gaff slashed the cockatrice's feathers; the cockatrice whipped its head back and forward and struck like a snake. Pearl-yellow droplets flicked from fangs incongruous in a darting beak; the rooster-tail fanned and flared, revealing the gray coils of an adder.

Matthew beat wings to one side; his feathertips hissed where the venom smoked holes through them. He backwinged, slashed for the cockatrice's eye, saw too late that that wound had long ago been dealt it. A black cockerel was immune to a cockatrice's deadly glare, and to the poison of its touch. If he could hit it, he could hurt it.

Except it wasn't a cockatrice, not exactly. Because cockatrices didn't sing like loreleis, and they didn't colorshift for camouflage. Maybe it was hatched by a chameleon rather than a serpent, Matthew thought, beating for altitude, and then reminded himself that now was not the time for theory.

Some kind of hybrid, then.

Just his luck.

And now the thing was airborne, and climbing in pursuit. He dropped—the cockerel was not more than passably aerodynamic—and struck for its back, its wing, its lung. The breast was armored, under the meat, with the anchoring keel bones. His spurs would turn on those. But they might punch through the ribs, from above.

He missed when the monster side-slipped, and the blind cockatrice turned and sank its fangs into his wing. Pain, heat and fire, weld-hot needles sunk into his elbow to the bone. He cackled like a machine gun and fell after the monster; wing-fouled, they tumbled to stone.

It lost its grip at the shock of impact, and Matthew screamed fury and pain. The hurt wing trailed, blood splashing, smoke rising from the envenomed wound. He made it beat anyway, dragged himself up, his spurs scraping and sparking on stone. The cockatrice hissed as he rose; his flight was not silent.

They struck hard, breast to breast, grappling legs and slashing spurs. He had his gaffs; the cockatrice had weight and fangs and a coiling tail like a rubber whip. Wings struck, buffeted, thundered. The cockatrice had stopped singing, and Matthew could hear the weeping now. Someone human was crying.

The cockatrice's talons twined his. Left side, right side. Its wings thumped his head, its beak jabbed. Something tore; blood smeared its beak, his face. He couldn't see on his right side. He ripped his left leg free of its grip and punched, slashed, hammered. The gaff broke skin with a pop; the cockatrice's blood soaked him, tepid, no hotter than the air. A rooster's egg hatched by a serpent.

The cockatrice wailed and thrashed; he ducked its strike at his remaining eye. More blood, pumping, slicking his belly, gumming his feathers to his skin. The blood was venom too. The whole thing was poison; its blood, its breath; its gaze; its song.

The monster fell on top of him. He could turn his head and get his eye out from under it, but when he did, all he saw was Marion, each arm laced under one of Melissa's armpits, holding the redheaded girl on her knees with a grim restraint while Melissa tried to tear herself free, to run to the poisoned bodies of her friends. The bodies were poison too, corrupted by the cockatrice's touch. The very stones soaked by its heart's blood could kill.

It was all venom, all deadly, and there was no way in the world to protect anyone. Not his sacrifice, not the unwitting sacrifice of the black cockerel, made any goddamned difference in the end.

Matthew, wing-broken, one-eyed, his gaff sunk heel-deep in the belly of his enemy, lay on his back under its corpse-weight and sobbed.

The building was emptied, the block closed, the deaths and the evacuations blamed on a chemical spill. Other Prometheans would handle the detox. Matthew, returned to his habitual body, took the shivering black cockerel to a veterinarian with Promethean sympathies, who—at Matthew's insistence and Jane's expense—amputated his wing and cleaned and sewed shut his eye. Spared euthanasia, he was sent to a farm upstate to finish his days as a lopsided, piratical greeter of morning. He'd live long, with a little luck, and father many pullets.

Matthew supposed there were worse deaths for a chicken.

Marion did the paperwork. Matthew took her out to dinner. She didn't make another pass, and they parted good friends. He had a feeling he'd be seeing her again.

There were memorial services for his students, and that was hard. They were freshmen, and he hadn't known them well; it seemed . . . presumptuous to speak, as if his responsibility for their deaths gave him some claim over their lives. He sat in the back, dressed in his best black suit, and signed the guest book, and didn't speak.

Katherine Berquist was to be buried in Appleton, Wisconsin; Matthew could not attend. But Regina Gomez was buried in a Catholic cemetery in Flushing, her coffin overwhelmed with white waxy flowers, her family swathed in black crepe and summer-weight worsted, her friends in black cotton or navy.

Melissa Martinchek was there in an empire-waisted dress and a little cardigan. She gave Matthew a timid smile across the open grave.

The scent of the lilies was repellent; Matthew vomited twice on the way home.

Melissa came to see him in the morning, outside of his regular office hours, when he was sitting at his desk with his head in his heads. He dragged himself up at the knock, paused, and sat heavily back down.

Thirty seconds later, the locked door clicked open. It swung on the hinges, and Melissa stepped inside, holding up her student ID like a talisman. "The lock slips," she said. "Gina showed me how. I heard, I heard your chair."

Gina's name came out a stammer too.

"Come in," Matthew said, and gestured her to a dusty orange armchair. She locked the door behind her before she fell into it. "Coffee?"

There was a pot made, but he hadn't actually gotten up and fetched any. He waved at it vaguely, and Melissa shook her head.

He wanted to shout at her—*What were you thinking? What were you* doing *there?*—and made himself look down at his hands instead. He picked up a letter opener and ran his thumb along the dull edge. "I am," he said, when he had control of his voice again, "so terribly sorry."

She took two sharp breaths, shallow and he could hear the edge of the giggle under them. Hysteria, not humor. "It wasn't your fault," she said. "I mean, I don't know what happened." She held up her hand, and his words died in his open mouth. "I don't . . . I don't *want* to know. But it wasn't your fault."

He stood up. He got himself a cup of coffee and poured one for her, added cream and sugar without asking. She needed it. Her eyes were pink-red around the irises, the lower lids swollen until he could see the mucous membrane behind the lashes. She took it, zombie-placid.

"I was safe inside the circle," he said. "I was supposed to be the bait. Gina and Katie were unlucky. They were close enough to being what it wanted that it took them, instead. As well. Whatever."

"What did . . . it want?"

"Things feed on death." He withdrew on the excuse of adding more sugar to his coffee. "Some like a certain flavor. It might even . . . "

He couldn't say it. It might even have been trying to lure Matthew out. That would explain why it had left its safe haven at the north end of the island, and gone where Prometheus would notice it. Matthew cringed. If his organization had some wardens in the bad neighborhoods, it might have been taken care of years ago. If Matthew himself had gone into its court unglamoured that first time, it might just have eaten him and left the girls alone.

A long time, staring at the skim of fat on the surface of her coffee. She gulped, then blew through scorched lips, but did not lift her eyes. "Doctor S.—"

"Matthew," he said. He took a breath, and made the worst professional decision of his life. "Go home, Ms. Martinchek. Concentrate on your other classes; as long as you show up for the mid-term and the final in mine, I will keep your current grade for the semester."

Cowardice. Unethical. He didn't *want* to see her there.

He put his hand on her shoulder. She leaned her cheek against it, and he let her for a moment. Her skin was moist and hot. Her breath was, too.

Before he got away, he felt her whisper, "Why not me?"

"Because you put out," he said, and then wished he'd just cut his tongue out when she jerked, slopping coffee across her knuckles. He retreated behind the desk and his own cup, and settled his elbows on the blotter. Her survivor guilt was his fault, too. "It only wanted virgins," he said, more gently. "Send your boyfriend a thank-you card."

She swallowed, swallowed again. She looked him in the eyes, so she wouldn't have to look past him, at the memory of her friends. Thank God, she didn't ask. But she drank the rest of her too-hot coffee, nerved herself, licked her lips, and said, "But Gina—Gina was . . . "

"People," he replied, as kindly as he could manage with blood on his hands, "are not always what they want you to think. Or always what you think they ought to be."

When she thanked him and left, he retrieved the flask from his coat pocket and dumped half of it into his half-empty coffee mug. Later, a TA told him it was his best lecture ever. He couldn't refute her; he didn't remember.

Melissa Martinchek showed up for his next Monday lecture. She sat in the third row, in the middle of two empty desks. No one sat beside her.

Both Matthew and she survived it, somehow.

Elizabeth Bear is the author of over a dozen novels and a hundred short stories; she has been honored for some of them with the John W. Campbell Award, two Hugos, and a Sturgeon Award. Her second collection of short fiction, *Shoggoths in Bloom*, was published last year. Two novels, *Shattered Pillars* and *One-Eyed Jack*, will be published in 2013, as will *An Apprentice to Elves*, a novel written in collaboration with Sarah Monette. She currently lives in Massachusetts with a giant ridiculous dog.

The Case: *Lord Robert Dudley, Queen Elizabeth I's favorite since childhood, has been rumored as possible husband for the queen. But he is already married. When his wife is found at the foot of a staircase with her neck broken, Dudley's hopes for a royal marriage die too. How can a murderer wed a queen? Proof must be found that his wife's death was by chance or someone's evil design.*

The Investigators: *Dr. Erasmus Pilbeam, assistant to magician and alchemist Dr. John Dee, and Pilbeam's young apprentice Martin Molesworth.*

THE NECROMANCER'S APPRENTICE

Lillian Stewart Carl

Robert Dudley, Master of the Queen's Horses, was a fine figure of a man, as long of limb and imperious of eye as one of his equine charges. And like one of his charges, his wrath was likely to leave an innocent passerby with a shattered skull.

Dudley reached the end of the gallery, turned, and stamped back again, the rich fabrics of his clothing rustling an accompaniment to the thump of his boots. Erasmus Pilbeam shrank into the window recess. But he was no longer an innocent passerby, not now that Lord Robert had summoned him.

"You beetle-headed varlet!" his lordship exclaimed. "What do you mean he cannot be recalled?"

Soft answers turn away wrath, Pilbeam reminded himself. "Dr. Dee is perhaps in Louvain, perhaps in Prague, researching the wisdom of the ancients. The difficulty lies not only in discovering his whereabouts, but also in convincing him to return to England."

"He is my old tutor. He would return at my request." Again Lord Robert marched away down the gallery, the floor creaking a protest at each step. "The greatness and suddenness of this misfortune so perplexes me that I shall take no rest until the truth is known."

"The inquest declared your lady wife's death an accident, my lord. At the exact hour she was found deceased in Oxfordshire, you were waiting upon the Queen at Windsor. You could have had no hand . . . "

"Fact has never deterred malicious gossip. Why, I have now been accused of bribing the jurors. God's teeth! I cannot let this evil slander rest upon my head. The Queen has sent me from the court on the strength of it!" Robert dashed his fist against the padded back of a chair, raising a small cloud of dust, tenuous as a ghost.

A young princess like Elizabeth could not be too careful what familiar demonstrations she made. And yet, this last year and a half, Lord Robert had come so much into her favor it was said that her Majesty visited him in his chamber day and night . . . No, Pilbeam assured himself, that rumor was noised about only by those who were in the employ of Spain. And he did not for one moment believe that the Queen herself had ordered the disposal of Amy Robsart, no matter how many wagging tongues said that she had done so. Still, Lord Robert could hardly be surprised that the malicious world now gossiped about Amy's death, when he had so neglected her life.

"I must find proof that my wife's death was either chance or evil design on the part of my enemies. The Queen's enemies."

Or, Pilbeam told himself, Amy's death might have been caused by someone who fancied himself the Queen's friend.

Lord Robert stalked back up the gallery and scrutinized Pilbeam's black robes and close-fitting cap. "You have studied with Dr. Dee. You are keeping his books safe whilst he pursues his researches in heretical lands."

"Yes, my lord."

"How well have you learned your lessons, I wonder?"

The look in Lord Robert's eye, compounded of shrewd calculation and ruthless pride, made Pilbeam's heart sink. "He has taught me how to heal illness. How to read the stars. The rudiments of the alchemical sciences."

"Did he also teach you how to call and converse with spirits?"

"He—ah—mentioned to me that such conversation is possible."

"Tell me more."

"Formerly it was held that apparitions must be spirits from purgatory, but now that we know purgatory to be only papist myth, it must be that apparitions are demonic, angelic, or illusory. The devil may deceive man into thinking he sees ghosts or . . . " Pilbeam gulped. The bile in his throat tasted of the burning flesh of witches.

"An illusion or deception will not serve me at all. Be she demon or angel, it is Amy herself who is my best witness."

"My—my—my lord . . . "

Robert's voice softened, velvet covering his iron fist. "I shall place my special trust in you, Dr. Pilbeam. You will employ all the devices and means you can possibly use for learning the truth. Do you understand me?"

Only too well. Pilbeam groped for an out. "My lord, whilst the laws regarding the practice of magic are a bit uncertain just now, still Dr. Dee himself, as pious a cleric as he may be, has been suspected of fraternizing with evil spirits . . . my lord Robert, if you intend such a, er, perilous course of action as, well, necromancy . . . ah, may I recommend either Edward Cosyn or John Prestall, who are well known in the city of London."

"Ill-nurtured cozeners, the both of them! Their loyalty is suspect, their motives impure. No. If I cannot have Dr. Dee I will have his apprentice."

For a moment Pilbeam considered a sudden change in profession. His beard was still brown, his step firm—he could apprentice himself to a cobbler or a baker and make an honest living without dabbling in the affairs of noblemen, who were more capricious than any spirit. He made one more attempt to save himself. "I am honored, my lord. But I doubt that it is within my powers to raise your . . . er, speak with your wife's shade."

"Then consult Dr. Dee's books, you malmsey-nosed knave, and follow their instructions."

"But, but . . . there is the possibility, my lord, that her death was neither chance nor villainy but caused by disease . . . "

"Nonsense. I was her husband. If she had been ill, I'd have known."

Not when you were not there to be informed, Pilbeam answered silently. Aloud he said, "Perhaps, then, she was ill in her senses, driven to, to . . . "

" . . . to self-murder? Think, varlet! A fall down the stairs could no more be relied upon by a suicide than by a murderer. She was found at the foot of the staircase, her neck broken but her headdress still secure upon her head. That is hardly a scene of violence."

Pilbeam found it furtively comforting that Lord Robert wanted to protect his wife's reputation from hints of suicide . . . Well, her reputation was his as well. The sacrifice of a humble practitioner of the magical sciences, now—that would matter nothing to him. Pilbeam imagined his lordship's face amongst those watching the mounting flames, a face contemptuous of his failure.

"Have no fear, Dr. Pilbeam, I shall reward you well for services rendered." Lord Robert spun about and walked away. "Amy was buried at St. Mary's, Oxford. Give her my respects."

Pilbeam opened his mouth, shut it, swallowed, and managed a weak, "Yes, my lord," which bounced unheeded from Robert's departing back.

The spire of St. Mary's, Oxford, rose into the nighttime murk like a admonitory finger pointing to heaven. Pilbeam had no quarrel with that admonition. He hoped its author would find no quarrel with his present endeavor.

He withdrew into the dark, fetid alley and willed his stomach to stop grumbling. He'd followed Dr. Dee's instructions explicitly, preparing himself with abstinence, continence, and prayer made all the more fervid for the peril in which he found himself. And surely the journey on the muddy November roads had sufficiently mortified his flesh. He was ready to summon spirits, be they demons or angels.

The black lump beside him was no demon. Martin Molesworth, his apprentice, held the lantern and the bag of implements. Pilbeam heard no stomach rumblings from the lad, but he could enforce Dr. Dee's directions only so far as his own admonitory fist could reach. "Come along," he whispered. "Step lively."

Man and boy scurried across the street and gained the porch of the church. The door squealed open and thudded shut behind them. "Light," ordered Pilbeam.

Martin slid aside the shutter concealing the candle and lifted the lantern. Its hot-metal tang dispelled the usual odors of a sanctified site—incense, mildew, and decaying mortality. Pilbeam pushed Martin toward the chancel. Their steps echoed, drawing uneasy shiftings and mutterings from amongst the roof beams. Bats or swallows, Pilbeam hoped.

Amy Robsart had been buried with such pomp, circumstance, and controversy that only a few well-placed questions had established her exact resting place. Now Pilbeam contemplated the flagstones laid close together behind the altar of the church and extended his hand for his bag.

Martin was gazing upward, to where the columns met overhead in a thicket of stone tracery, his mouth hanging open. "You mewling knotty-pated scullion!" Pilbeam hissed, and snatched the bag from his limp hands. "Pay attention!

"Yes, Master." Martin held the lantern whilst Pilbeam arranged the charms, the herbs, and the candles he dare not light. With a bit of charcoal he drew a circle with four divisions and four crosses. Then, his tongue clamped securely between his teeth, he opened the book he'd dared bring from Dr. Dee's collection, and began to sketch the incantatory words and signs.

If he interpreted Dee's writings correctly—the man set no examples in penmanship—Pilbeam did not need to raise Amy's physical remains. A full necromantic apparition was summoned for consultation about the future, when what he wished was to consult about the past. Surely this would not be as difficult a task. "*Laudetur Deus Trinus et unus,*" he muttered, "*nunc et in sempiterna seculorum secula . . .*"

Martin shifted and a drop of hot wax fell onto Pilbeam's wrist. "Beslubbering gudgeon!"

"Sorry, Master."

Squinting in the dim light, Pilbeam wiped away one of his drawings with the hem of his robe and tried again. *There.* For a moment he gazed appreciatively at his handiwork, then took a deep breath. His stomach gurgled.

Pilbeam dragged the lad into the center of the circle and jerked his arm upwards, so the lantern would illuminate the page of his book. He raised his magical rod and began to speak the words of the ritual. "I conjure thee by the authority of God Almighty, by the virtue of heaven and the stars, by the virtue of the angels, by that of the elements. *Domine, Deus meus, in te speravi. Damahil, Pancia, Mitraton . . .* "

He was surprised and gratified to see a sparkling mist began to stream upwards from between the flat stones just outside the circle. Encouraged, he spoke the words even faster.

" . . . to receive such virtue herein that we may obtain by thee the perfect issue of all our desires, without evil, without deception, by God, the creator of the sun and the angels. *Lamineck. Caldulech. Abracadabra.*"

The mist wavered. A woman's voice sighed, desolate.

"Amy Robsart, Lady Robert Dudley, I conjure thee."

Martin's eyes bulged and the lantern swung in his hand, making the shadows of column and choir stall surge sickeningly back and forth. "Master . . . "

"Shut your mouth, hedge-pig!" Pilbeam ordered. "Amy Robsart, I conjure thee. I beseech thee for God his sake, *et per viscera misericordiae Altissimi,* that thou wouldst declare unto us *misericordiae Dei sint super nos.*"

"Amen," said Martin helpfully. His voice leaped upward an octave.

The mist swirled and solidified into the figure of a woman. Even in the dim light of the lantern Pilbeam could see every detail of the revenant's dress, the puffed sleeves, the stiffened stomacher, the embroidered slippers. The angled wings of her headdress framed a thin, pale face, its dark eyes too big, its mouth too small, as though Amy Robsart had spent her short life observing many things but fearing to speak of them. A fragile voice issued from those ashen lips. "Ah, woe. Woe."

Pilbeam's heart was pounding. Every nerve strained toward the doors of the church and through the walls to the street outside. "Tell me what happened during your last hours on earth, Lady Robert."

"My last hours?" She dissolved and solidified again, wringing her frail hands. "I fell. I was walking down the stairs and I fell."

"Why did you fall, my lady?"

"I was weak. I must have stumbled."

"Did someone push you?" Martin asked, and received the end of Pilbeam's rod in his ribs.

Amy's voice wavered like a set of ill-tempered bagpipes. "I walked doubled over in pain. The stairs are narrow. I fell."

"Pain? You were ill?"

"A spear through my heart and my head so heavy I could barely hold it erect . . . "

A light flashed in the window, accompanied by a clash of weaponry. The night watch. Had someone seen the glow from the solitary lantern? Perhaps the watchmen were simply making their rounds and contemplating the virtues of bread and ale. Perhaps they were searching for miscreants.

With one convulsive jerk of his scrawny limbs, Martin scooped the herbs, the charms, the candles, even the mite of charcoal back into the bag. He seized the book and cast it after the other items. Pilbeam had never seen him move with such speed and economy of action. "Stop," he whispered urgently, "Give me the book, I have to . . . "

Martin was already wiping away the charcoaled marks. Pilbeam brought his rod down on the lad's arm, but it was too late. The circle was broken. A sickly-sweet breath of putrefaction made the candle gutter. The woman-shape, the ghost, the revenant, ripped itself into pennons of color and shadow. With an anguished moan those tatters of humanity streamed across the chancel and disappeared down the nave of the church.

Pulling on the convenient handle of Martin's ear, Pilbeam dragged the lad across the chancel. His hoarse whisper repeated a profane: "Earth-vexing dewberry, spongy rump-fed skainsmate, misbegotten tickle-brained whey-faced whoreson, you prevented me from laying the ghost back in its grave!"

"Sorry, Master, ow, ow . . . "

The necromancer and his apprentice fled through the door of the sacristy and into the black alleys of Oxford.

Cumnor Place belonged not to Lord Robert Dudley but to one of his cronies. If Pilbeam ever wished to render his own wife out of sight and therefore out of mind, an isolated country house such as Cumnor, with its air of respectable disintegration, would serve very well. Save that his own wife's wrath ran a close second to Lord Robert's.

What a shame that Amy Robsart's meek spirit had proved to be of only middling assistance to Lord Robert's—and therefore Pilbeam's—quest. No, no hired bravo had broken Amy's neck and arranged her body at the foot of the stairs. Nor had she hurled herself down those same stairs in a paroxysm of despair. Her death might indeed have been an accident.

But how could he prove such a subtle accident? And worse, how could he report such ambiguous findings to Lord Robert? Of only one thing was Pilbeam certain: he was not going to inform his lordship that his wife's ghost had been freed from its corporeal wrappings and carelessly not put back again.

Shooting a malevolent glare at Martin, Pilbeam led the way into the courtyard of the house. Rain streaked the stones and timber of the façade.

Windows turned a blind eye to the chill gray afternoon. The odors of smoke and offal hung in the air.

A door opened, revealing a plump, pigeon-like woman wearing the simple garb of a servant. She greeted the visitors with, "What do you want?"

"Good afternoon, Mistress. I am Dr. Erasmus Pilbeam, acting for Lord Robert Dudley." He offered her a bow that was polite but not deferential.

The woman's suspicion eased into resignation. "Then come through, and warm yourselves by the fire. I am Mrs. Odingsells, the housekeeper."

"Thank you."

Within moments Pilbeam found himself seated in the kitchen, slurping hot cabbage soup and strong ale. Martin crouched in the rushes at his feet, gnawing on a crust of bread. On the opposite side of the fireplace a young woman mended a lady's shift, her narrow face shadowed by her cap.

Mrs. Odingsells answered Pilbeam's question. "Yes, Lady Robert was in perfect health, if pale and worn, up until several days before she died. Then she turned sickly and peevish. Why, even Lettice there, her maid, could do nothing for her. Or with her, come to that."

Pilbeam looked over at the young woman and met a glance sharp as the needle she wielded.

The housekeeper went on, "The day she died her ladyship sent the servants away to Abingdon Fair. I refused to go. It was a Sunday, no day for a gentlewoman to be out and about, sunshine or no."

"She sent everyone away?" Pilbeam repeated. "If she were ill, surely she would have needed an attendant."

"Ill? Ill-used, I should say . . . " Remembering discretion, Mrs. Odingsells contented herself with, "If she sent the servants away, it was because she tired of their constantly offering food she would not eat and employments she had no wish to pursue. Why, I myself heard her praying to God to deliver her from desperation, not long before I heard her fall."

"She was desperate from illness? Or because her husband's . . . duties were elsewhere?"

"Desperate from her childlessness, perhaps, which would follow naturally upon Lord Robert's absence."

So then, Amy's spear through the heart was a symbolic one, the pain of a woman spurned. "Her ladyship was of a strange mind the day she died, it seems. Do you think she died by chance? Or by villainy, her own or someone else's?"

Again Pilbeam caught the icy stab of Lettice's eyes.

"She was a virtuous God-fearing gentlewoman, and alone when she fell," Mrs. Odingsells returned indignantly, as though that were answer enough.

It was not enough, however. If not for the testimony of Amy herself, Pilbeam would be thinking once again of self-murder. But then, his lordship himself had said, *a fall down the stairs could no more be relied upon by a suicide than by a murderer.*

The housekeeper bent over the pot of fragrant soup. Pilbeam asked, "Could I see the exact staircase? Perhaps Lettice can show me, as your attention is upon your work."

"Lettice," Mrs. Odingsells said, with a jerk of her head. "See to it."

Silently the maid put down her mending and started toward the door. Pilbeam swallowed the last of his soup and followed her. He did not realize Martin was following him until he stopped beside the fatal staircase and the lad walked into his rump. Pilbeam brushed him aside. "She was found here?"

"Yes, master, so she was." Now Lettice's eyes were roaming up and down and sideways, avoiding his. "See how narrow the stair is, winding and worn at the turn. In the darkness . . . "

"Darkness? Did she not die on a fair September afternoon?"

"Yes, yes, but the house is in shadow. And her ladyship was of a strange mind that day, you said yourself, Master."

Behind Pilbeam, Martin muttered beneath his breath, "The lady was possessed, if you ask me."

"No one is asking you, clotpole," Pilbeam told him.

Lettice spun around. "Possessed? Why would you say such a thing? How . . . What is that?"

"What?" Pilbeam followed the direction of her eyes. The direction of her entire body, which strained upward stiff as a hound at point.

The ghost of Amy Robsart descended the steps, skirts rustling, dark eyes downcast, doubled in pain. Her frail hands were clasped to her breast. Her voice said, "Ah, woe. Woe." And suddenly she collapsed, sliding down the last two steps to lie crumpled on the floor at Pilbeam's feet, her headdress not at all disarranged.

With great presence of mind, Pilbeam reached right and left, seizing Martin's ear as he turned to flee and Lettice's arm as she swooned. "Blimey," said Martin, with feeling.

Lettice was trembling, her breath coming in gasps. "I did not know what they intended, as God is my witness, I did not know . . . "

The revenant dissolved and was gone. Pilbeam released Martin and turned his attention to Lettice. Her eyes were now dull as lead. "What have you done, girl?"

"They gave me two angels. Two gold coins."

"Who?"

"Two men. I do not know their names. They stopped me in the village, they gave me a parcel and bade me bring it here."

"A parcel for her ladyship?"

"Not for anyone. They told me to hide it in the house was all."

Pilbeam's heart started to sink. Then, as the full import of Lettice's words blossomed in his mind, it reversed course and bounded upwards in a leap of relief. "Show me this parcel, you foolborn giglet. Make haste!"

Lettice walked, her steps heavy, several paces down the hallway. There she knelt and shoved at a bit of paneling so worm-gnawed it looked like lace. It opened like a cupboard door. From the dark hole behind it she withdrew a parcel wrapped in paper and tied with twine.

Pilbeam snatched it up and carried it to the nearest windowsill. "Watch her," he ordered Martin.

Martin said, "Do not move, you ruttish flax-wench."

Lettice remained on her knees, bowed beneath the magnitude of her defeat, and made no attempt to flee.

Pilbeam eased the twine from the parcel and unwrapped the paper. It was fine parchment overwritten with spells and signs. Beneath the paper a length of silk enshrouded something long and hard . . . Martin leaned so close that he almost got Pilbeam's elbow in his eye. Pilbeam shoved him aside.

Inside the silk lay a wax doll, dressed in a fine gown with puffed sleeves and starched stomacher, a small headdress upon its tiny head. But this was no child's toy. A long needle passed through its breast and exited from its back—Pilbeam's fingertips darted away from the sharp point. The doll's neck was encircled by a crimson thread, wound so tightly that it had almost cut off the head. A scrap of paper tucked into the doll's bodice read: *Amy*.

Again Pilbeam could hear the revenant's voice: *A spear through my heart and my head so heavy I could barely hold it erect.* So the spear thrust through her chest had been both literal and symbolic. And Amy's neck had been so weakened it needed only the slightest jolt to break it, such as a misstep on a staircase. A misstep easily made by the most healthy of persons, let alone a woman rendered infirm by forces both physical and emotional.

It was much too late to say the incantations that would negate the death-spell. Swiftly Pilbeam re-wrapped the parcel. "Run to the kitchen and fetch Mrs. Odingsells," he ordered Martin, and Martin ran.

Lettice's bleak eyes spilled tears down her sunken cheeks. "How can I redeem myself?"

"By identifying the two men who gave you this cursed object."

"I do not know their names, master. I heard one call the other by the name of 'Ned' is all."

"Ned? If these men have knowledge of the magical sciences I should know . . . " She did not need to know his own occupation. "Describe them to me."

"One was tall and strong, his black hair and beard wild as a bear's. The other was small, with a nose like an axeblade. He was the one named Ned."

Well then! Pilbeam did know them. They were not his colleagues but his competitors, Edward Cosyn, called Ned, and John Prestall. As Lord Robert had said, they were ill-nurtured cozeners, their loyalty suspect and their motives impure.

Perhaps his lordship had himself bought the services of Prestall and Cosyn. If so, would he have admitted that he knew who they were? No. If he had brought about his wife's death, he would have hidden his motives behind sorrow and grief rather than openly revealing his self-interest and self-regard . . . *God be praised*, thought Pilbeam, he had an answer for Lord Robert. He had found someone for his lordship to blame.

At a step in the hall Pilbeam and Lettice looked around. But the step was not that of the apprentice or the housekeeper. Amy Robsart walked down the hallway, head drooping, shoulders bowed, wringing her hands.

Lettice squeaked in terror and shrank against Pilbeam's chest.

With a sigh of cold, dank air, the ghost passed through them and went on its way down the hallway, leaving behind the soft thump of footsteps and the fragile voice wailing, "Ah woe. Woe."

Pilbeam adjusted his robes and his cap. Beside him Martin tugged at his collar. Pilbeam jabbed the lad with his elbow and hissed, "Stand up straight, you lumpish ratsbane . . . "

"Quiet, you fly-bitten foot-licker," Lord Robert ordered.

Heralds threw open the doors. Her Majesty the Queen strode into the chamber, a vision in brocade, lace, and jewels. But her garments seemed like so many rags beside the glorious sunrise glow of her fair skin and her russet hair.

Lord Robert went gracefully down upon one knee, his upturned face filled with the adoration of a papist for a saint. Pilbeam dropped like a sack of grain, jerking Martin down as he went. The lad almost fumbled the pillow he carried, but his quick grab prevented the witching-doll from falling off the pillow and onto the floor.

The Queen's amber eyes crinkled at the corners, but her scarlet lips did not smile. "Robin, you roguish folly-fallen lewdster," she said to Lord Robert, her voice melodious but not lacking an edge. "Why have you pleaded to wait upon us this morning?"

"My agent, Dr. Pilbeam, who is apprenticed to your favorite, Dr. Dee, has discovered the truth behind my wife's unfortunate death."

Robert did not say "untimely death," Pilbeam noted. Then her Majesty turned her eyes upon him, and his thoughts melted like a wax candle in their heat.

"Dr. Pilbeam," she said. "Explain."

He spoke to the broad planks of the floor, repeating the lines he had rehearsed before his lordship: Cumnor Place, the maidservant overcome by her guilt, the death-spell quickened by the doll, and behind it all the clumsy but devious hands of Prestall and Cosyn. No revenant figured in the tale, and certainly no magic circle in St. Mary's, Oxford.

On cue, Martin extended the pillow. Lord Robert offered it to the Queen. With a crook of her forefinger, she summoned a lady-in-waiting, who carried both pillow and doll away. "Burn it," Elizabeth directed. And to her other attendants, "Leave us." With a double thud the doors shut.

Her Majesty flicked her pomander, bathing the men and the boy with the odor of violets and roses, as though she were a bishop dispensing the holy water of absolution. "You may stand."

Lord Robert rose as elegantly as he had knelt. With an undignified stagger, Pilbeam followed. Martin lurched into his side and Pilbeam batted him away.

"Where are these evildoers now?" asked the Queen.

"The maidservant is in Oxford gaol, your Majesty," Robert replied, "and the malicious cozeners in the Tower."

"And yet it seems as though this maid was merely foolish, not wicked, ill-used by men who tempted her with gold. You must surely have asked yourself, Robin, who in turn tempted these men."

"Someone who wished to destroy your trust in me, your Majesty. To drive me from your presence. My enemy, and yours as well."

"Do you think so? What do you think, Dr. Pilbeam?"

What he truly thought, Pilbeam dared not say. That perhaps Amy's death was caused by someone who intended to play the Queen's friend. Someone who wished Amy Robsart's death to deliver Lord Robert Dudley to Elizabeth's marriage bed, so that there she might engender heirs.

Whilst some found Robert's bloodline tainted, his father and grandfather both executed as traitors, still the Queen could do much worse in choosing her consort. One could say of Robert what was said of the Queen herself upon her accession, that he was of no mingled or Spanish blood but was born English here in England. Even if he was proud as a Spaniard . . .

Pilbeam looked into the Queen's eyes, jewels faceted with a canny intelligence. *Spain,* he thought. The deadly enemy of Elizabeth and protestant England. The Spanish were infamous for their subtle plots.

"B-b-begging your pardon, your Majesty," he stammered, "but I think his lordship is correct in one regard. His wife was murdered by your enemies. But they did not intend to drive him from your presence, not at all."

Robert's glance at Pilbeam was not encouraging. Martin took a step back. But Pilbeam barely noticed, spellbound as he was by the Queen. "Ambassador Feria, who was lately recalled to Spain. Did he not frequently comment to his master, King Philip, on your, ah, attachment to Lord Robert?"

Elizabeth nodded, one corner of her mouth tightening. She did not insult Pilbeam by pretending there had been no gossip about her attachment, just as she would not pretend she had no spies in the ambassador's household. "He had the impudence to write six months ago that Lady Robert had a malady in one of her breasts and that I was only waiting for her to die to marry."

His lordship winced but had the wisdom to keep his own counsel.

"Yes, your Majesty," said Pilbeam. "But how did Feria not only know of Lady Robert's illness but of its exact nature, long before the disease began to manifest itself? Her own housekeeper says she began to suffer only a few days before she died. Did Feria himself set two cozeners known for their, er, mutable loyalties to inflict such a condition upon her?"

"Feria was recently withdrawn and replaced by Bishop de Quadra," murmured the Queen. "Perhaps he overstepped himself with his plot. Or perhaps he retired to Spain in triumph at its—no, not at its conclusion. For it has yet to be concluded."

Lord Robert could contain himself no longer. "But your Majesty, this hasty-witted pillock speaks nonsense, why should Philip of Spain . . . "

" . . . wish for me to marry you? He intended no compliment to you, I am sure of that." Elizabeth smiled, a smile more fierce than humorous, and for just a moment Pilbeam was reminded of her father, King Henry.

Robert's handsome face lit with the answer to the puzzle. "If your Majesty marries an Englishman, she could not ally herself with a foreign power such as France against Spain."

True enough, thought Pilbeam. But more importantly, if Elizabeth married Robert then she would give weight to the rumors of murder, and might even be considered his accomplice in that crime. She had reigned for only two years, her rule was far from secure. Marrying Lord Robert might give the discontented among her subjects more ammunition for their misbegotten cause, and further Philip's plots.

Whilst Robert chose to ignore those facts, Pilbeam would wager everything he owned that her Majesty did not. His lordship's ambition might have outpaced his love for his wife. His love for Elizabeth had certainly done so. No, Robert Dudley had not killed his wife. Not intentionally.

The Queen stroked his cheek, the coronation ring upon her finger glinting against his beard. "The problem, sweet Robin, is that I am already married to a husband, namely, the Kingdom of England."

Robert had no choice but to acknowledge that. He bowed.

"Have the maidservant released," Elizabeth commanded. "Allow the cozeners to go free. Let the matter rest, and in time it will die for lack of nourishment. And then Philip and his toadies will not only be deprived of their conclusion, they will always wonder how much we knew of their plotting, and how we knew it."

"Yes, your Majesty," said Lord Robert. "May I then return to court?"

"In the course of time." She dropped her hand from his cheek.

He would never have his conclusion, either, thought Pilbeam. Elizabeth would like everyone to be in love with her, but she would never be in love with anyone enough to marry him. For then she would have to bow her head to her husband's will, and that she would never do.

Pilbeam backed away. For once he did not collide with Martin, who, he saw with a glance from the corner of his eye, was several paces away and sidling crab-wise toward the door.

Again the Queen turned the full force of her eyes upon Pilbeam, stopping him in his steps. "Dr. Pilbeam, we hear that the ghost of Lady Robert Dudley has been seen walking in Cumnor Park."

"Ah, ah . . . " Pilbeam felt rather than saw Martin's shudder of terror. But they would never have discovered the truth without the revenant. No, he would not condemn Martin, not when his carelessness had proved a blessing in disguise.

Lord Robert's gaze burned the side of his face, a warning that matters of necromancy were much better left hidden. "Her ghost?" he demanded. "Walking in Cumnor Park?"

Pilbeam said, "Er—ah—many tales tell of ghosts rising from their graves, your Majesty, compelled by matters left unconcluded at death. Perhaps Lady Robert is seeking justice, perhaps bewailing her fate. In the course time, some compassionate clergyman will see her at last to rest." *Not I,* he added firmly to himself.

Elizabeth's smile glinted with wry humor. "Is that how it is?"

She would not insult Pilbeam by pretending that she had no spies in Oxfordshire as well, and that very little failed to reach her ears and eyes. And yet the matter of the revenant, too, she would let die for lack of nourishment. She was not only fair in appearance, but also in her expectations. He made her a bow that was more of a genuflection.

She made an airy wave of her hand. "You may go now, all of you. And Dr. Pilbeam, Lord Robert will be giving you the purse that dangles at his belt, in repayment of his debt to you."

"Yes, your Majesty." His lordship backed reluctantly away.

What an interesting study in alchemy, thought Pilbeam, *that with the Queen the base metal of his lordship's manner was transmuted to gold.* "Your Majesty. My Lord." Pilbeam reversed himself across the floor and out the door, which Martin contrived to open behind his back. Lord Robert followed close upon their heels, his boots stepping as lightly and briskly as the hooves of a thoroughbred.

A few moments later Pilbeam stood in the street, an inspiringly heavy purse in his hand, allowing himself a sigh of relief—ah, the free air was sweet, all was well that ended well . . . Martin stepped into a puddle, splashing the rank brew of rainwater and sewage onto the hem of Pilbeam's robe.

Pilbeam availed himself yet again of Martin's convenient handle. "You rank pottle-deep measle! You rude-growing toad!" he exclaimed, and guided the lad down the street toward the warmth and peace of home.

Lillian Stewart Carl (www.lillianstewartcarl.com) is the author of numerous mystery and fantasy novels and short stories, all available in electronic and paper form. *The Mortsafe,* sixth and most recent of the Alasdair Cameron/Jean Fairbairn series, takes place in mysterious underground Edinburgh. Of *The Blue Hackle,* fifth in the series, *Publishers Weekly* said, in " . . . Carl's spirited fifth mystery featuring American travel journalist Jean Fairbairn and her Scottish fiancé, retired detective inspector Alasdair Cameron . . . [a] ghostly ancestress . . . interacts with Jean and [a visiting American antique dealer's] young daughter, Dakota, to diverting effect."

The Case: *A haunted woods, an eerie tree, a shadowy threat, malevolent strangeness . . .*

The Investigator: *Dana Roberts, a detective of the supernormal. Now famous for her work with the supernatural (although she does not consider what she does as dealing with the supernatural), this was her first "case."*

THE CASE OF THE STALKING SHADOW

➤

Joe R. Lansdale

I've mentioned Dana Roberts before, though with less kindness than I do now, and if anyone would have told me that I would be defending, even supporting, someone who in layman's terms might be known as a ghost breaker, or a dealer in the supernatural, I would have laughed them out of the room.

It should also be noted that Dana does not consider what she does as dealing with the supernatural, which she believes is a term that often assigns some sort of religious aspect to her work. She believes what others call the supernatural is an unknown reality of this world, or some dimensional crossover that has yet to be explained, and if it were truly understood would be designated as science.

But here I go trying to explain her books, which after her first visit to our club I have read extensively. That said, I should also note that my conclusions about her observations, her work, might be erroneous. I'm a reader not a scholar, and above all, I love a good story.

The first time she was with us, she told us of an adventure she called *The Case of the Lighthouse Shambler*. At the end of her tale, or her report, if you take it as fact—and I do—she showed us something trapped in a mirror's reflection that was in my view impossible to explain away. She was also missing the tip of her right index finger, which went along nicely with the story she had just finished.

Her visit to our club was, without a doubt, a highlight.

Though I suppose I've gotten a little out of order, I should pause and tell you something about our group. It now stands at twelve—three women and nine men. Most of us are middle age or better. I should also mention that during our last meeting I recorded Dana's first story for our gathering, unbeknownst to her. My intent was to do so, and then replay parts of it to our treasurer, Kevin, with the intent of obvious ridicule and a declaration that dues spent on spook hunters as guests was money wasted.

Instead, I was so captivated with Dana's story that I went home forgetting I had recorded her. Of course, Kevin had heard it all firsthand and had been as captivated with her adventure as I was.

A few weeks later I was finally brave enough to call Dana's business, which is registered simply, Dana Roberts, Supernormal Investigations, and tell her what I had done. There was no need for it, as she would never know, but I harbored a certain amount of guilt, and liked the idea of having contact with her. I encouraged her to come to the club again.

To my relief, she found my original skepticism more than acceptable, and asked if I might like to transcribe my recording for publication in her monthly newsletter. I not only agreed, but it appeared in the April online magazine, *Dana Roberts Reports*. And so, here is another story, recorded and transcribed with her enthusiastic permission.

The night she came to us as a speaker, she was elegantly dressed, and looked fine in dark slacks and an ivory blouse. Her blond hair was combed back and tied loosely at her neck, and she wore her usual disarming smile.

She took her place in the large and comfortable guest chair, and with a tall drink in her hand, the lights dimmed, a fire crackling in the fireplace, she began to tell a story she called *The Case of The Stalking Shadow*.

It follows.

Since most of the events of the last few months have turned out to be hoaxes or of little interest, and because I am your invited guest, I decided tonight to fall back on one of my earlier cases—my first in fact—and the one that led me into this profession. Though at the time I didn't know I was going to become a serious investigator of this sort of thing, or that it would require so much work, as well as putting myself continually in the face of danger. I've done more research for my current job than I ever did gaining my PhD in anthropology. Mistakes in what I do can have dire consequences, so it's best to know what one is doing, at least where it can be known.

I was not paid for this investigation. It was done for myself, with the aid of a friend, and it happened when I was still in college. In the process of discovering my lifelong occupation, I nearly lost my life on more than one occasion, for there were several touchy moments. Had this particular case gone wrong, I would not be here today to entertain you with my adventures, nor would my friend and cousin Jane be alive.

Simply put, I come from what must be defined as a wealthy family. There were times when there was less wealth, but there was always money. This was also true of my close relatives, and so it was that my Aunt Elizabeth, on my father's side, invited us each year to her home for the summer. It was a kid event, and children of both my mother and father's siblings were gathered each year when school let out to spend a week with Aunt Elizabeth, whose husband was in oil, and often gone for months at a time. I suppose, having no children of her own, she liked the company, and in later years when her husband—my then Uncle Chester—ran off with a woman from Brazil, it became more clear to me why she looked forward each year to a family gathering, and why she surrounded herself with so many other activities, and spent Uncle Chester's money with a kind of abandon that could only speak to the idea of getting hers while there was something to be got.

But that is all sour family business, and I will pass over it. I'm sure I've told too much already.

The year I'm talking about, when I was thirteen, my Aunt and Uncle had moved from their smaller property upstate and had bought what could only be described as a classic estate, made to look very much like those huge British properties we see frequently in older movies and television programs. It was in America, in the Deep South, but it certainly had the looks of a traditional upper-level British residence, with enormous acreage to match. In the latter respect, it was more common to America's vast spaces. One hundred acres, the largest portion of it wooded, with a house that had no fewer than forty-five rooms, and a surrounding area dotted with gardens and shrubs trimmed in the shape of animals: lions and tigers and bears.

It was overdone and overblown. For a child, those vast rooms and that enormous acreage were a kind of paradise. Or so it seemed at the time of that initial gathering of my cousins and myself.

After arrival, and a few days of getting to know one another—for in some cases our lives were so different, and things had changed so dramatically for each of us in such a short period of time—it was necessary to reacquaint. We were on the verge of leaving childhood, or most of us were, though some of us were younger. For me, this year was to be particularly important, and in many ways the last year of what I think of as true childhood. Certainly, I was not grown after this year passed, but my interests began to move in other directions. Boys and cars and dating, the whole nine yards. And, of course, what happened changed me forever.

But this summer I'm talking about, we spent a vast amount of time playing the old childhood games. It was a wonderful and leisurely existence that consisted of swimming in the pool, croquet, badminton, and the like. At night, since my aunt would not allow television, we played board games of all varieties, and as there were a huge number of us cousins, we were often pitted against one another in different parts of the house with different games.

One night, perhaps three days into my visit, my cousin Jane and I found ourselves alone in a large room where we were playing chess, and between moves she suddenly asked, without really waiting for a reply: "Have you been in the woods behind the estate? I find it quite queer."

"Queer?" I said.

"Strange. I suppose it's my imagination, being a city girl, I'm not used to the proximity of so many trees."

I didn't know it at the time, and would probably not have appreciated it, but those trees had been there for hundreds of years. And though other areas had been logged out and replaced with "crops" of pines in long rows, this was the remains of the aboriginal forests.

Jumping ahead slightly—the trees were not only of a younger time, but they were huge, and they grew in such a way the limbs had grown together and formed a kind of canopy that didn't allow brush and vines to grow beneath them. So when someone says there are as many trees now as there once were, you can be certain they are describing crop trees, grown close together without the variance of nature. These trees were from a time when forests were forests, so to speak.

Anyway, she said perhaps a few more words about the trees, and how she thought the whole place was odd, but I didn't pay any real attention to her—and there was nothing in her manner that I determined to be dread or worry of any kind. So, her comments didn't really have impact on me, and it wasn't until later that I thought back on our conversation and realized how accurately impressionable Jane had been.

There was something strange about those woods.

After another day or so, the pool and the nighttime games lost some of their appeal. We did some night swimming, lounging around the pool; but one moonlit night one of the younger children among us—Billy, who was ten— suggested that it might be fun to play a game of tag in the woods.

Now, from an adult standpoint this seems like a bad choice, mucking about in the woods at night. But we were young and it was a very bright night, and it seemed like a wonderful idea.

We decided a game would be delicious. We chose up teams. One team constituted eight cousins, the other seven. The game was somewhere between hide-and-go-seek and tag. One team would hide, the other would seek. The trick was to chase down the hiding team and tag them, making them a member of the hunting team. In time, the idea was to tag everyone into the chasing team, and then the game would switch out.

How we started was, the chasing team was to stay at the swimming pool while the hiding team had a fifteen minute head start into the woods. It was suggested that the more open part of the woods was to be our area, but that no one should go into the thicker and darker part, because that was a lot of acreage and more difficult.

At the signal, we shot off like quail, splitting up in the woods to hide, each of us going our own route.

I went through the trees, and proceeded immediately to the back of the sparser woods and came to the edge where it thickened. The trees in the sparser area were of common variety, but of uneven shape. They didn't grow high, but were thickly festooned with sickly widespread branches, and beneath them were plenty of shadows.

As if it were yesterday, I remember that as soon as I came to that section of trees, I was besieged by an unreasonable sensation of discomfort. The discomfort, at this point, wasn't fear—it was more a malaise that had descended on me heavy as a wool blanket. I thought it had to do with my overextending myself while on vacation, because I was used to a much more controlled environment and an earlier bedtime.

The trees seemed far more shadowy than they had appeared from a distance, and I had the impression of being watched. No, that isn't quite right. Not of being watched so much as of a presence in the general locale. Something so close, that I should be able to see it, but couldn't.

I marked this down to exhaustion, and went about finding a good place to hide. I could hear the seekers beginning to run toward the woods, and then I heard someone scream, having been tagged immediately. I chose a place between two trees that had grown together high and low in such a way as to appear to be a huge letter H placed on a pedestal; the trees met in such tight formation they provided a near singular trunk and the bar of the H was an intermingled branch of both trees. I darted behind them, scooted down, and put my back against the trunk.

No sooner had I chosen my spot than it occurred to me that its unusual nature might in fact attract one of the seekers. But by then, I felt it was too late and pressed my back against the tree, awaiting whatever fate might come.

From where I sat, I could see the deeper woods, and I had an urge to run to them, away from the grove of trees where I now hid. I also disliked the idea of having my back against the tree and being discovered suddenly and frightened by the hunters. I didn't want that surprise to cause me to squeal the way I had heard someone squeal earlier. I liked to think of myself as too mature for a child's game to begin with, and was beginning to regret my involvement in the matter.

I sat and listened for footfalls, but the game went on below me. I could hear yelling and some words, and I was bewildered that no one had come to look for me, as my hiding place wasn't exactly profound.

After awhile, I ceased to hear the children, and noticed that the moonlight in the grove, where the limbs were less overbearing, had grown thinner.

I stood up and turned and looked through the split in the H tree. It was very quiet now, so much in fact, I could almost hear the worms crawling inside the earth. I stood there peeking between the bars of the H, and then I saw one of the children coming toward me. I couldn't make out who it was, as they were drenched in shadow, but they were coming up the slight rise into the ragged run of trees. At first, I felt glad to see them, as I was ready for my part in this silly game to be over, and planned to beg off being a seeker.

However, as the shape came closer, I began to have a greater feeling of unease than before. The shape came along with an unusual step that seemed somewhere between a glide and a skip. There was something disconcerting about its manner. It was turning its shadowed head left and right, as I would have expected a seeker to do, but there was a deeply ingrained part me that rejected this as its purpose.

The closer it came, the more my nervousness was compounded, for the light didn't delineate its features in any way. In fact, the shape seemed not to be a shadow at all, but the dark caricature of a human being. I eased behind the trunk and hid.

Dread turned to fear. I was assailed with the notion that I ought to run away quickly, but to do that, I would have to step out and reveal myself, and that idea was even more frightening and oppressive. So I stayed in my place, actually shivering. Without seeing it, I could sense that it was coming closer. There was a noise associated with its approach, but to this day, I can't identify that noise. It was not footfalls on leaves or ground, but was a strange sound that made me fearful, and at the same time, sad. It was the kind of sound that reached down into the brain and bones and gave you an influx of information that spoke not to the logical part of your being, but to some place more primal. I know that is inadequate, but I can't explain it any better. I wish that I could, because if I could imitate that sound, most of this story would be unnecessary to tell. You would understand much of it immediately.

I spoke of shivering with fear, but until that day, I didn't know a person's knees could actually knock together, or that the sound of one's heart could be so loud. I was certain both sounds would be evident to the shadow, but I held my ground. It was fear that held me there, as surely as if my body had been coated in an amazingly powerful glue and I had been fastened and dried to that tree with it.

Eventually, I steeled my courage, turned and peeked between the trunks of the H tree. Looking right at me was the shadow. Not more than a foot away. There wasn't a face, just the shape of a head and utter blackness. The surprise caused me to let out with a shriek—just the sort I'd tried to avoid—and I leapt back, and without really considering it, I broke around the tree and tore through the woods toward the house as if my rear end were on fire.

I looked back over my shoulder, and there came the thing, flapping its arms, its legs flailing like a wind-blown scarecrow.

I tripped once, rising just as the thing touched my shoulder, only for a moment. A cold went through me as it did. It was the sort of cold I imagined would be in the arctic, a sensation akin to stepping out of a warm tent, soaking wet, into an icy wind. I charged along with all my might, trying to outrun the thing I knew was right behind me. It was breathing, and its breath was as cold as its touch on the back of my neck. As it ran, the sound of its feet brought to mind the terrors I had felt earlier when I first saw it making its way through the woods—that indescribable sound that held within it all the terrors of this world, and any world imagined.

I reached the edge of the woods, and then I was into the clearing. I tried not to look back, tried not to do anything that might break my stride, but there was no stopping me. I couldn't help myself. When I looked back, there at the line of the woods, full in the moonlight, stood the thing waving its arms about in a frustrated manner, but no longer running after me.

I thundered down a slight rise and broke into the yard where the topiary animals stood, then I clattered along the cobblestone path and into the house.

When I was in the hallway, I stopped to get my breath. I thought of the others, and though I was concerned, at that moment I was physically unable to return to those woods or even the yard to yell for the others.

Then I heard them, upstairs. I went up and saw they were all in the Evening Room. When Jane saw me, her eyes narrowed, but she didn't speak. The others went about joshing me immediately, and it was just enough to keep me from blurting out what I had seen. It seemed that everyone in the game had been caught but me, and that I had been given up on, and that switching the game about so that the other side might be the pursuer had been forgotten. Hot chocolate was being served, and everything seemed astonishingly normal.

I considered explaining all that had occurred to me, but was struck with the absurdity of it. Instead, I went to the window and looked out toward the forest. There was nothing there.

Jane and I shared a room, as we were the closest of the cousins. As it came time for bed, I found myself unwilling to turn out the light. I sat by the window and looked out at the night.

Jane sat on her bed in her pajamas looking at me. She said, "You saw it, didn't you?"

She might as well have hit me with a brick.

"Saw what?" I said.

"It," she said. "The shadow."

"You've seen it too?"

She nodded. "I told you the woods were strange. But I had no idea until tonight *how* strange. After the game ended, the others thought it quite funny that you might still be hiding in the woods, not knowing we were done. I was worried, though."

How so? I thought, but I didn't want to interrupt her train of thought.

"I actually allowed myself to be caught early," Jane said. "I wanted out of the game, and I planned to feign some problem or another and come back to the house. It was all over pretty quick, however, and this wasn't necessary. Everyone was tagged out. Except you. But no one wanted to stay in the woods or go back into them, so they came back to the house. I think they were frightened. I know I was. And I couldn't put my finger on it. But being in the woods, and especially the nearer I came to that section where it thinned and the trees grew strange, I was so discomforted it was all I could do to hold back tears. Then, from the window, I saw you running. And I saw it. The shadow that was shaped like a man. It stopped just beyond the line of trees."

I nodded. "I thought I imagined it."

"Not unless I imagined it too."

"But what is it?" I asked.

Jane walked to where I stood and looked out the window. The man-shaped shadow did not appear and the woods were much darker now, as the moon was beginning to drop low.

"I don't know," she said. "But I've heard that some spots on earth are the homes of evil spirits. Sections where the world opens up into a place that is not of here."

"Not of here?"

"Some slice in our world or their world that lets one of us, or one of them, slip in."

"Where would you hear such a thing?" I asked.

"Back home, in Lansdale, Pennsylvania. They say there was an H tree there. Like the one in these woods. I've seen it in the daytime and it makes me nervous. I know it's there."

"I hid behind it," I said. "That's where the shadow found me."

"Lansdale was home to one of the three known H trees, as they were called."

This, of course, was exactly what I had called the tree upon seeing it.

"It was said to be a portal to another world," Jane said. "Some said hell. Eventually, it was bulldozed down and a housing project was built over the site."

"Did anything happen after it was torn down?" I asked.

Jane shrugged. "I can't say. I just know the legend. But I've seen pictures of the tree, and it looks like the one in the woods here. I think it could be the same sort of thing."

"Seems to me, pushing it over wouldn't do anything." I said.

"I don't know. But the housing division is still there, and I've never heard of anything happening."

"Maybe because it was never a portal to hell, or anywhere else," I said. "It was just a tree."

"Could be," Jane said. "And that could be just an odd tree in the woods out there." She pointed out the window. "Or, it could be what the one in Lansdale was supposed to be. A doorway."

"It doesn't make any sense," I said.

"Neither does a shadow chasing you out of the woods."

"There has to be a logical explanation."

"When you figure it out," Jane said. "Let me know."

"We should tell the others," I said.

"They won't believe us," Jane said, "but they're scared of the woods. I can tell. They sense something is out there. That is why the game ended early. I believe our best course of action is to not suggest anything that might involve those woods, and ride out the week."

I agreed, and that's exactly what we did.

The week passed on, and no one went back in the woods. But I did watch for the shadow from the backyard, and at night, from the window. Jane watched with me. Sometimes we brought hot chocolate up to the window and sat there in the dark and drank it and kept what we called The Shadow Watch.

The moon wasn't as bright the following nights, and before long if we were to see it, it would have had to stand underneath the back yard lights. It didn't.

The week came to an end, and all of us cousins went home.

There was an invitation the next summer to go back, but I didn't go. I had tried to dismiss the whole event as a kind of waking nightmare, but there were nights when I would awaken feeling certain that I was running too slowly and the shadow was about to overtake me.

It was on those nights that I would go to the window in my room, which looked out over a well-lit city street with no woods beyond. It made me feel less stressed and worried to see those streets and cars and people walking about well past midnight. And none of them were shadows.

Jane wrote me now and again, and she mentioned the shadow once, but the next letter did not, and pretty soon there were no letters. We kept in touch by email, and I saw her at a couple of family functions, and then three years or so passed without us being in communication at all.

I was in college by then, and the whole matter of the shadow was seldom thought of, though there were occasions when it came to me out of my subconscious like a great black tide. There were times when I really thought I would like to talk to Jane about the matter, but there was another part of me that felt talking to her would make it real again. I had almost convinced myself it had all been part of my imagination, and that Jane hadn't really seen anything, and that I misremembered what she had told me.

That's how the mind operates when it doesn't want to face something. I began my studies with anthropology as my major, and in the process of my studies I came across a theory that sometimes, instead of the eye sending a message to the brain, the brain sends a message to the eye. It is a rare occurrence, but some scientists believe this explains sincere ghostly sightings. To the viewer, it would be as real as you are to me as I sit here telling you this story. But the problem with this view was that Jane had seen it as well, so it was a nice theory, but not entirely comforting.

And then out of the blue, I received a letter from Jane. Not an email. Not a phone call. But an old fashioned letter, thin in the envelope, and short on message.

It read: *I'm going back on Christmas Eve. I have to know.*

I knew exactly what she meant. I knew I had to go back too. I had to have an answer.

Now, let me give you a bit of background on my Aunt's place. She and her husband separated and the house and property were put up for sale. I knew this from my mother and father. They had been offered an opportunity to buy the house, but had passed due to the expense of it all.

Interestingly enough, I learned that Jane's family, who had later been offered the opportunity, could afford it, and plans had been made. Jane's father had died the year before, and a large inheritance was left to Jane's mother. No sooner had the house been bought than her mother died, leaving Jane with the property.

Perhaps this was the catalyst that convinced Jane to go back.

I acquired Jane's phone number, and called her. We talked briefly, and did not mention the shadow. It's as if our conversation was in code. We made plans: a time to arrive and how to meet, that sort of thing.

Before I left, I did do a bit of research.

I didn't know what it was I was looking for, but if Jane was right, her hometown of Lansdale, Pennsylvania, was a former home to an H tree. I looked it up on the Internet and read pretty much what Jane had told me. As far back as the Native Americans there had been stories of Things coming through the gap in the H tree. Spirits. Monsters. Demons. Shadows.

As Jane had said, the H tree had been destroyed by builders, and a subdivision of homes was built over it. I looked for any indication that there had been abnormal activity in that spot, but except for a few burglaries, and one murder of a husband by a wife, there was nothing out of the average.

Upon arrival at the airport I picked up my rental car and drove to a Wal-Mart and bought a gas can, two cheap cigarette lighters, and a laser pointer. Keep in mind, now, that I was doing all of this out of assumption, not out of any real knowledge of the situation. There was no real knowledge to be had, only experience that might lead to disappointment, the kind of disappointment that could result in a lack of further experience in all matters. I had that in mind as I drove, watching the sun drop in the west.

When I arrived at the property and the house, it had changed. The house was still large and regal, but the yards had grown up and the swimming pool was an empty pit lined at the bottom with broken seams and invading weeds. The topiary shrubs had become masses of green twists and turns without any identifying structure.

I parked and got out. Jane greeted me at the door. Like me, she was dressed simply, in jeans, a T-shirt, and tennis shoes. She led me inside. She had bought a few sandwich goods, and we made a hasty meal of cheese and meat and coffee, and then she showed me the things she had brought for "protection" as she put it.

There were crosses and holy water and wafers and a prayer book. Though I don't believe that religion itself holds power, the objects and the prayers, when delivered with conviction, do. Symbols like crosses and holy water and wafers that have been blessed by a priest who is a true believer, contain authority. Objects from other religions are the same. It's not the gods that give them power, it is the dedication given them by the believer. In my case, even though I was not a believer, the idea that a believer had blessed the items was something I hoped endowed them with abilities.

I placed great faith in the simple things—like gasoline and fire starters.

Shortly after our meal, we took a few moments to discuss what we had seen those years ago, and were soon in agreement. This agreement extended to the point that we admitted we had been, at least to some degree, in denial since that time.

Out back we stood and looked at the woods for a long moment. The moon was rising. It was going to be nearly full. Not as full as that night when I saw the shadow, but bright enough.

Jane had her crosses and the like in a small satchel with a strap. She slung it over her shoulder. I carried the gas can, and had the lighters and laser pointer in my pants pocket. By the time we reached the bleak section of woods and the H tree was visible, it was as if my feet had anvils fastened to them. I could hardly lift them. I began to feel more and more miserable. I eyed Jane and saw there were tears in her eyes. When we were to the H tree, I began to shake.

We circled the tree, seeing it from all angles. Stopping, I began to pour gasoline onto its base, splashing some on the trunk from all sides. Jane pulled her wafers and holy water and crucifixes from her bag, and proceeded to place them on the ground around the tree. She took out the prayer book and began to read. Then, out of the gap between the trees, a shadow leaned toward her.

I tried to yell, to warn her, but the words were frozen in my mouth like dead seals in an iceberg. The shadow grabbed her by the throat, causing her to let out a grunt, and then she was pulled through the portal and out of sight.

I suspected there would be danger, but on some level I thought we would approach the tree, read a prayer, stick a cross in the ground, set the tree on fire, and flee, hoping the entire forest, the house, and surrounding property wouldn't burn down with it.

I had also hoped, for reasons previously stated, that the religious symbols would carry weight against whatever it was that lay inside that gateway, but either the materials had not been properly blessed, or we were dealing with something immune to those kinds of artifacts.

Now, here comes the hard part. This is very hard for me to admit, even to this day. But the moment Jane was snatched through that portal, I broke and ran. I offer as excuse only two things: I was young, and I was terrified.

I ran all the way to the back door of the house. No sooner had I arrived there than I was overcome with grief. It took me a moment to fortify myself, but when that was done, I turned and started back with renewed determination.

I came to the H, and with a stick, I probed the gap between the trees. Nothing happened, though at any instant I expected the shadow to lean forward and grab me. I picked up the bottle of holy water that Jane had left, hoping it might be better than a prayer book. I climbed over the communal trunk, ducked beneath the limb that made the bar on the H, and boldly stepped through the portal.

■ ■ ■

It was gray inside, like the sun seen through a heavy curtain, but there was no sunlight. The air seemed to be fused with light, dim as it was. There were boulder-like shapes visible. They were tall and big around. All of them leaned, and not all in the same direction. Each was fog-shrouded. There were shadows flickering all about, moving from one structure to another, being absorbed by them, like ink running through the cracks in floor boards.

Baffled, I stood there with the bottle of holy water clutched in my fist, trying to decide what to do. Eventually, the only thing that came to me was to start forward in search of Jane. As I neared the boulders, I gasped for breath. They were not boulders at all, but structures made of bones and withering flesh. The shadows were tucked tight between the bone and skin like viscera. I stood there staring, and then one of the bones—an arm bone—moved and flexed its skeletal fingers, snatched at the air, and reached for me.

Startled, I let out a sharp cry and stepped back.

The structure pivoted, and a thousand eyes opened in the worn skin. It was a living thing made of bone and skin and shadow. As it slid along, a gray slime oozed out from beneath it like the trail of a slug.

I flung the holy water violently against the thing, but the only reaction I got was a broken bottle and water leaking ineffectually down its side. As it turned, I saw sticking out from it a shape that had yet to become bone and dried skin. It writhed like a worm in tar. Then it screamed and called out.

It was Jane, attached to the departing thing like a fly stuck to fly paper.

Other mounds of bone and shadow and flesh were starting to move now, and they were akin to hills sliding in my direction. They were seeking me, mewing as they went, their sliding giving forth that horrid shuffling sound I had heard years before from the running shadow. The sound made me ill. My head jumped with all manner of horrid things.

I realized escape was impossible—that no matter which way I turned, they were there.

Now the shadows, as if greased, slipped out of gaps in the bones and skin, moved toward me, their dark feet sliding, their arms waving, their odd, empty, dark faces turning from side to side.

I knew for certain that it was over for Jane and me.

And then I remembered the laser pointer in my pocket. I had brought it because shadows are an absence of light, and if there is one thing that is the enemy of darkness, it is the sharp beam of a laser.

That said, I was unprepared for the reaction I received when I snapped it on. The light went right through one of the shadows, entering it like the thrust of a rapier. The shadow stopped moving, one hand flying to the wound. The beam, still directed to that spot, clipped off its hand at the wrist. It was far more than I expected; my best-case plan had been that the light would be annoying.

I knew then that I had a modern weapon to combat an ancient evil. I swung the light like a sword, and as I did, the shadows came apart, fell in splashes of inky liquid, and were absorbed by the gray ground. Within moments, the shadows were attempting to leap back inside the structures, but I followed them with my beam, discovering I could cut flesh and bone with it as well, for what had once been human had been sucked dry of its essence, and was now a fabric of this world.

As I cut through them, the bones were dark inside, full of shadow, and the skin bled shadows; the ground was sucking them up like a sponge soaking up water.

I darted to the beast that held Jane. It was sliding along at a brisk pace. I grabbed one of Jane's outreaching hands and tugged. I was pulled to my knees as the thing flowed away. I didn't let go. I went dragging along, clinging to Jane with one hand, the laser with the other.

Eventually, I lost my grip, stumbled to my feet, and pursued the monster as it moved into a gray mist that nearly disguised it. A shadow came out of the mist and grabbed me. When it did, an intense coldness went over my body. I almost passed out.

I cut with the laser. The shadow let go and fell apart. I had split it from the top of its head to the area that on a human would have been the groin.

I ran after Jane. The mist had become so thick I almost lost her. I ran up on the creature without realizing it, and when I did, its stickiness clung to me and sucked at me. I was almost lifted off my feet, but again I utilized the laser, and it let me go.

Aware of my determination, it let go of Jane, too. She fell at my feet. My last sight of the thing was of it moving into the mist, and of bony arms waving and eyes blinking and shadows twisting down deep inside it.

I pulled Jane upright, and it was purely by accident that I saw a bit of true light—a kind of glow poking through the mist.

Yanking her along, I ran for it. As we neared the light, it became brighter yet, like a large goal post. We darted through it and fell to the ground in a tumble. Making sure Jane was all right, I cautioned her away, and stuck the laser in my pocket.

I pulled out one of the cigarette lighters I had bought. Shadowy arms reached through the gap in the trees, into the light. The dark fingers snapped at me like the fangs of a snake. I avoided them with an agility I didn't know I possessed.

I bent low and clicked the lighter and put the flame to the spot where I had poured gasoline. A blaze leaped up and engulfed the tree in a ball of fire.

With a shaking hand, I went around to the other side of the H tree and put a lick of flame to it. Coated in gasoline, it lit, but weakly.

I flicked off the lighter and grabbed the can with its remaining gas and tossed it toward the fire. The can exploded.

My ears rang. The next thing I knew I was on the ground and Jane was beating out tufts of fire that had landed on my pants and the front of my shirt.

We watched as the tree burned. Shadow shapes were visible inside the H, looking out of the gray, as if to note us one last time before the fire closed the gateway forever.

The tree burned all night and into the next morning. We watched it from where we sat on the ground. The air was no longer heavy with foreboding. It seemed . . . how shall I say it? . . . *empty*.

I feared the flames might jump to the rest of the trees, but they didn't. The H tree burned flat to the ground, not even leaving a stump. All that was left was a burned spot, dark as a hole through the center of the earth.

Jane and I parted the next morning, and for some reason we have never spoken again. At all. Maybe the connection at that time of our young life, that shared memory, was too much to bear.

But I did hear from her lawyer. I was offered an opportunity to buy the house and property where the H tree had been. Cheap.

It was more than I could manage, actually—cheap as it was—but I acquired a loan and bought the place. I felt I had conquered it, and buying it was the final indicator of this.

I still own it. No more shadows creep. And that spot of woods where the tree grew? I had it removed by bulldozer. I put down a stretch of concrete and built a tennis court, and to this day there has not been a single inkling of unusual activity, except for the fact that my tennis game has improved far beyond my expectations.

Finished, Dana leaned back in her chair and sipped from her drink.

"So, that's how I got my start as an investigator of the unusual. Beyond that revelation, I suppose you might want me to explain exactly what happened there inside that strange world, but I cannot. It is beyond my full knowledge. I can only surmise that our ideas of hell and demonic regions have arisen from this and other dimensional gaps in the fabric of time and space. What the things did with stolen flesh and bone is most likely nothing that would make sense to our intellect. I can only say that the shadows appeared to need it, to absorb it, to live off of it. However, their true motivation is impossible to know."

With that, she downed her drink, smiled, stood up, shook hands with each of us, and left us there in the firelight, stunned, contemplating all she had told us.

⇒—

Joe R. Lansdale is the author of over thirty novels and numerous short stories. His novella, *Bubba Ho-tep*, was made into an award-winning film of the same name, as was *Incident On and Off a Mountain Road*. Both were directed by Don Coscarelli. His works have received numerous recognitions, including the Edgar, eight Bram Stoker awards, the Grinzane Cavour Prize for Literature, American Mystery Award, the International Horror Award, British Fantasy Award, and many others. *All the Earth, Thrown to the Sky*, his first novel for young adults, was published last year. His most recent novel for adults is *Edge of Dark Water*.

⇒—

The Case: *Mabel Weaver's grandmother left her a family heirloom passed down through generations of women—a nearly flawless yellow diamond, Hecate's Golden Eye, said to kill any man who touches it. Her cousin Agnes has stolen it and Mabel needs help to get it back.*

The Investigators: *Jack Fleming—a former reporter who is now a vampire and private investigator—and his British partner, Charles Escott, private agent and former theatrical actor.*

HECATE'S GOLDEN EYE

P. N. Elrod

Chicago, June 1937

Hanging around this alley gave me the creeps because it looked exactly like the one where I'd seen a man gunned down in front of me. That had been shortly before my own murder.

The man in front of me tonight was my partner, Charles Escott, who was unaware of my thoughts while we waited for his client to show. I didn't like the meeting place, but the client had insisted, and Escott had to earn a living. At least he'd invited me along to watch his back. Too often he ignored risks and bulled ahead on his own, which was damned annoying when it wasn't scaring the hell out of me.

The air was muggy to the point of settling down in your lungs and forgetting to pay rent. I had no need to breathe regularly anymore, but still found the heaviness uncomfortable in this hot, windless place. A car cruised by, briefly visible in the alley opening. The faint wash of light from its headlamps allowed Escott to see my face.

"Stop worrying, old man," he said, speaking quietly, knowing I could hear. "Miss Weaver just wants to be careful."

That would be Miss Mabel Weaver, his prospective client, who was late. She'd made the appointment hours ago when the sun was up and I lay dreamless and, for all other purposes, dead in the basement under Escott's kitchen.

Yeah, dead. I'm undead now, the way Bram Stoker defined it, but don't ask me to turn into a bat. He got that wrong, among other things.

I moved closer so Escott could hear. "Careful? Wanting to meet you in a dark alley is nuts."

"Less so than wanting to meet you."

He had a point, but Miss Weaver didn't know I was a vampire, so it didn't count. "Charles, this has to be a setup. Someone with a grudge paid some pippin to get you here. They figured you wouldn't be suspicious if a dame called asking for help."

"I considered that, but there were notes of hope, anger, frustration, and desperation in her voice that are difficult to convincingly feign . . . I think I know when someone is lying or not."

He was uncannily good at reading people, even when there was a telephone in between. I could trust his judgment; it was this damned alley that put my back hairs up. Just like the other place, it had stinking trash barrels, a scrawny cat nosing through the garbage, and sludgy water tricking down the middle.

This one didn't have a body in it yet, but my mind's eye could provide.

"I have my waistcoat on," Escott added, meaning his bulletproof vest. His business occasionally required dealing with all sorts of unsavory characters—I was considered by a select few to be one of them—so I was grateful he'd bothered. How he could stand the extra weight of those metal plates in this heat was a mystery, though.

"You think you need it?"

He gave a small shrug, fingers twitching once toward the pocket where he kept his cigarettes. That told me he had some nerves after all. A smoke would have calmed him, but it was also a distraction. For a meeting with an unknown client in a dark alley he'd keep himself focused.

We glanced up at the sound of thunder rumbling a long, slow warning. I couldn't smell the rain yet, but change was in the sky. It would get worse before it got better. Storms coming down off the lake from Canada were like that.

"Crap," I said.

He grunted agreement. "If she doesn't appear before—"

We jumped when the door in the building on my left abruptly opened, filling the alley with the noise and brightness of a busy kitchen. A large man in a sweat-stained undershirt banged out with two buckets of leavings. The scrawny cat went alert and darted toward him with an impatient *meow*, tail up. This was a regular event. Escott must have come to a similar conclusion, but he relaxed only slightly.

The stink of cooked food fought against the rotting stuff in the garbage cans a few yards away. Fresh or foul, unless it was blood, all food smelled sickening to me. Coffee was the one exception; I'd yet to figure out why.

The big man dumped the buckets' contents more or less accurately into a trash barrel and tossed a large scrap of something to the eager cat, who seized it and ran off. The man fit one bucket inside the other, giving Escott and me a hard once-over.

We had no legitimate reason to be here, and I looked suspicious. Escott was respectably dressed, but I was in my sneaking-around clothes, everything black and cheap, because sneaking around can be rough work. The man would be within his rights to tell us to clear out or dump us into the barrel with the leavings—he had the size for it.

"You waitin' for someone?" he finally asked.

It was Escott's turn to take the difficult questions. I made sure the guy didn't have a gun or friends with guns.

"I'm from the Escott Agency, waiting for a Miss Weaver. Is she an acquaintance of yours?"

He gave no answer, going back into the kitchen. A second later, a tall, sturdily built woman hastily emerged.

She was too big-boned to be fashionable, but there was grace in her simple blue dress. A matching hat teetered on her head, barely held in place by several hatpins stuck in at various angles. The hat was an oddball thing with a brim that was supposed to sweep down to cover one eye, but now askew, as though she'd pushed it out of the way and then forgotten. She had a small purse, but no gloves. My girlfriend never left her flat without them.

"Miss Weaver?" Escott stepped forward into the spill of light.

"Yes, but not here," she whispered. She shut the door, moved toward him, and promptly skidded on something in the sudden dark. I caught her before she could fall. She gave a gasp of surprise. I can move fast when necessary, and this alley murk was like daylight to me. I decided to be kind and not tell her what she'd slipped in. Maybe that cat would come back later and eat it.

"Sorry," I said, letting go when she got her balance.

"Mr. Escott?" She squinted at me, uncertain because my partner and I have nearly identical builds, tall and lean. Our faces are very different, and I look about a decade younger even though I'm not.

"The skinny bird with the English accent and banker's suit is who you want. I'm just here for the grouse hunt."

Escott shot me a *pipe down* look. "I am Charles Escott. This ill-mannered fellow is my associate, Jack Fleming."

I tipped my hat.

"Mabel Weaver," she said, and ladylike, extended a hand to let us take turns shaking her fingers. She had dusty red-brown hair, a long, narrow, humped nose in a long face, and a lot of freckles no amount of makeup could conquer.

"May I inquire—?" began Escott.

"We have to be quick and not attract attention," she said, glancing toward the kitchen door. Her strong husky voice sounded unused to whispering. "The owner's an old friend and let me sneak out the back."

"Toward what purpose?"

"I'm ostensibly having dinner with my boyfriend and his parents. They're my alibi—no one else should know about any of this. I'll tell you why if you take the job."

"Which is . . . ?"

"I heard about you through Mrs. Holguin. She said you pick locks, recover things, and can keep quiet. She said I could trust you."

Escott does everything a private detective does, except divorce work, calling himself a private agent instead. It's a fine point, allowing him to bend the law when it's in the interests of his client. He'd found it profitable.

"Mrs. Holguin's assessment is accurate. How may I assist you?"

"I need you to recover something my cousin Agnes stole from me. She's my first cousin on my late mother's side. We've never liked each other, but this time she's gone too far."

"What was taken?"

"This . . . "

Miss Weaver wore a long necklace with a heavy pendant dangling from it. She held it up. Escott struck a match to see. Set in the pendant's ornate center was an oval-cut yellow stone the size of a big lima bean.

She pointed at the stone just as the match went out. "This is *supposed* to be a nearly flawless, intense-yellow diamond. That color is rare, and one this size is *really* rare. Sometime in the last week my cousin Agnes got into my *locked* room and switched them. She had a copy made of this pendant, a good one—that's real white gold, but around a piece of colored glass. She thinks I'm too stupid to notice the difference."

"You want to recover the original?"

"And substitute this one, but I'll handle that part. I happen to know she is too stupid to know the difference. When I get the real one back I'll put it in a safety deposit box so she can't steal it again, but it has to be done tonight. Can you help me?"

"Before I undertake such an errand I need proof of your ownership of the diamond."

She gave a flabbergasted stare, mouth hanging wide. "Isn't my word good enough?"

"Miss Weaver, please understand that for all I know, you—"

I put a hand on his arm before he could finish. Accusing a client of being a thief using us to do her dirty work was a good way to get slapped. She looked solid enough and angry enough to pack quite a wallop.

Another, louder rumble of thunder rolled over our little piece of Chicago. A stray gust of cool air made a half-assed effort to clear the alley stink, but failed and died in misery.

"Tell us a little more," I suggested.

For a second it was even money whether Miss Weaver would turn heel back into the kitchen or give Escott a shiner, but she settled down. "All right—just *pretend* you believe me. The diamond is called Hecate's Golden Eye. It's been in my family for generations, passed down from mother to daughter. There's no provenance for *that*."

"What about insurance? Is your name on a policy?"

"There is none, and before you say so, yes, that's stupid, but I can't afford the premium. The family used to have money, but it's gone. I work in a department store, and it's been enough until now because I lived in the family home, then Grandma Bawks died and left the house to Agnes, so I've had to start paying rent."

"Your cousin charges you rent?"

"With a big simpering smile. One of these days I'll rearrange her teeth. I'm moving out. I'd rather live in a Hooverville shack than under the same roof with her and that smirking gigolo she married."

"Could you put events in their order of occurrence?" Escott asked.

"Yes, of course. I know all this, but you don't. Hecate's Eye belonged to Grandma Bawks—my late mother's mother—and in her will left it to me. Agnes got the house. It's a big house, but the Eye could buy a dozen of them."

"It's that valuable?"

"And then some, but Grandma Bawks knew I would always keep the gem and someday pass it down to my daughter. She couldn't trust Agnes to do that. Hecate's Eye has been in our family for generations; it's always brought good luck to those who respect it."

"Interesting name," I said.

"It's for the one flaw in the stone. It looks like a tiny eye staring at you from the golden depths."

"Hecate, traditionally the queen of witches," Escott murmured. "Does this diamond have a curse?"

"Yes. It does."

For all that Escott's own friend and partner was a vampire, he had a streak of skepticism about other supernatural shenanigans. He'd also apparently forgotten that the customer is always right. "Really, now . . . "

She put her fists on her hips, ready for a challenge. Most women fall all over themselves once they hear Escott's English accent, but she seemed immune. "There are stories I could tell, but suffice it to say that any man who touches the Eye dies."

Her absolute conviction left him nonplussed for a moment. I enjoyed it.

"That's why I have to be along, to protect you from the curse."

"Keep going, Miss Weaver," I said in an encouraging tone. She favored me with a brief smile. It didn't make her pretty, but she was interesting.

"Grandma Bawks passed on two weeks ago. Before she went, she gave me the pendant. She put it into my hand and gave her blessing the way it's been done for who knows how long. I'm not the eldest granddaughter, but she said the stone wanted to be with me, not Agnes."

"Agnes didn't agree with that?"

"Hardly, but she wouldn't say anything while Grandma was alive or she'd have been cut from the will. Agnes got the Bawks house and most everything in it; I got a little money, some mementos, and Hecate's Eye, but that's more than enough for me. My cousin wanted everything, so she stole the Eye. I had it well-hidden in a locked room, but somehow she found it."

"Being female, your cousin is exempt from the curse?"

"She doesn't believe in it, neither does that rat she married, but if he so much as breathes on it, he'll find out for sure. Her being female might not matter: Grandma gave it to me. The stone will know something's wrong."

"Curses aside, these are tough times," I said. "A rock like that could buy a lot of money for you."

"That's how Agnes thinks. She's never had a job, and her husband's too lazy to work. She's selling the stone to live off the proceeds. It would never occur to her to try earning a living."

I liked Miss Weaver's indignation.

"I don't want the *money*, I want my grandmother's gift back." She looked at Escott. "You can go through the history of the family at the library, look up old wills wherever they keep those things, and I can show you Grandma Bawks's will and her diary, and it will all confirm what I've just told you, but there's no *time*. Agnes is selling the stone tonight to a private collector, then it's gone forever. I *must* switch it before he arrives. Will you help me?"

Escott glanced my way, though he couldn't have seen much more than my shape in the dark. I knew what he wanted, though.

Damnation.

"I believe her," I said, hoping to get out of things.

"Best to be absolutely certain, though."

He was right. Neither of us needed to be involved in a jewel theft, though my instincts were with Miss Weaver being on the up and up. She'd gotten truly angry having her word questioned. Honest people are like that.

"Miss Weaver? Over here a moment," I said, moving toward the kitchen door. Might as well get it over with.

"What for?"

"A private word." I opened the door just enough to provide some light to work with. She had to be able to see me.

"Will you do this or not?" she demanded.

I looked her hard in the eyes, concentrating. "Miss Weaver, I need you to listen to me very carefully . . . " I'd not smelled booze on her breath. This is difficult to do when they're drunk or even just tipsy. Or insane.

Fortunately, she was neither and went under fast and easy. That was fine with me; hypnotizing people gave me a headache, and lately it had been worsening. Even now it felt like a noose encircling my skull, drawing tight.

Escott stepped in close. "Miss Weaver, are you the rightful owner of Hecate's Eye?"

"Yes." Her voice was strangely softened. Her eyes were her best feature, nearly the same color as her hair, a darker red brown. At the moment they were dead looking. I hated that.

The rope twisted tighter.

"Did your cousin Agnes steal it from you?"

"Yes."

He glanced my way again, questioning. It was up to me. He'd need my help and not just to watch his back.

"Count me in," I said. I wanted to see what a cursed jewel looked like.

He nodded and turned to our new client. "You may trust us, Miss Weaver." It was both acceptance and an instruction.

"All right," she agreed, almost sounding normal.

I quietly shut the door. The darkness crowded close around us. She'd wake on her own shortly. My head hurt. I think it had to do with guilt. The more guilt, the sharper the pain. I didn't like doing that to people, but especially to women. I have my reasons.

Miss Weaver would not recall the interlude. Just as well. She might have popped me one, and I'd have deserved it.

Escott was satisfied we weren't being duped into committing a criminal act—not much of one, anyway. When Miss Weaver woke, they shook hands, clinching the deal.

Stealing back a stolen item was nothing new to him. The work was no great mental challenge, but paid his bills. This would be a legal cakewalk. Agnes the thief wouldn't dare report it to the cops, especially since Miss Weaver's boyfriend and his family would swear she was with them all evening, wearing the heirloom pendant.

The cat shot out of the dark, lancing between us for the street. I shoved our client behind Escott and rushed the other way, pulling my gun from its shoulder holster. Yeah, I'm a vampire, but Chicago is a tough town . . . and I have bad memories concerning alleys.

A man crouching behind the garbage barrels slowly stood, hands out and down, his hat clutched in one of them. He had an egg-shaped balding head, thick arching black eyebrows, and plenty of teeth showing in his smile. "Easy, there, friend. No need to get bothered. Me an' Charlie over there are old acquaintances. You just be askin' him."

An Irish accent combined with a sardonic tone. I didn't turn to check on Escott; he'd moved next to me and had his own gun out, a cannon disguised as a Webley. A small flashlight was in his other hand, the beam on the man's face.

"Riordan," my partner said. "What the devil are you doing here?"

"That would be tellin'. We two bein' in the same line, I'm sure you understand I have to maintain a bit of hush about me business." He spoke fast with a glint in his eye, as though daring the world to call him a liar, even if it was true.

Escott held his gun steady. "Following Miss Weaver, are you? Working for Cousin Agnes?"

Riordan didn't blink, just kept grinning. "Now is that civilized, asking a man questions he can't answer while tryin' to blind him? Not to mention threatenin' him with no less than two deadly weapons. I ask you now, is it?" When he got no reply, he looked my way, squinting against the light in his eyes. "So you're the mystery fellow who's been keepin' this lad out of the red. Pleased to meet you. Shamus Riordan, me name is me game, spell it the same." He put a hand out.

I took my cue from Escott and kept him covered.

Miss Weaver came cautiously forward. "Is that true? Agnes hired that man to follow me?"

"Circumstances favor it," said Escott. He looked tense and—rare for him—unsure of himself.

Riordan raised his hat. "Pleased to meet you, Miss. We appear to be at a partin' of the ways, so if you don't mind I'll be takin' me leave."

"Jack . . . " I'd seen this coming, even if I wasn't clear on the why behind Escott's caution. Gun holstered, I stepped forward to grab Riordan and pin his arms, but he bolted an instant ahead of me. He dragged a garbage can down to block my path, but I had enough speed when I jumped it to land square on his back and tackle him. That should have finished him, but he twisted like a snake, hammering short, powerful blows under my ribs with one hand, while his other covered my face, pushing me away, his fingers curled for eye-gouging.

Before that happened I vanished.

I'm good at it. It drains me, but damnation, it's the second best thing about my change from living to undead. The first best has to do with my girlfriend, but I'll talk about that some other time.

My abrupt absence didn't faze Riordan; he scrambled up and sprinted, but by then I'd reformed in front of him and landed a solid fist to his gut that almost stopped him cold.

Struggling for air, he staggered and stubbornly kept going, but I swung him face-first against a brick wall and hauled his arms back just short of dislocation. I was fresh for more fight. Vanishing heals me: no bruises in my middle. Even my headache was gone.

Escott caught up, our client in his wake.

"What do we do with him?" I asked. Let him go and he'd phone Cousin Agnes.

"I suggest a refreshing nap." Escott held the light; I turned Riordan around and made myself calm. I couldn't let myself get emotional. It adds extra pressure to things that can permanently damage a mind.

Riordan was gasping, his face red under the sweat, but his brown eyes were alert and suspicious, his forearms raised to ward off a physical attack. I fixed my gaze hard on him and told him to listen to me, just as I'd done with Miss Weaver. Only nothing happened. The noose went tight around my head from the effort, but Riordan stayed conscious. His breath told me he was sober, leaving one alternative. "Charles . . . he's crazy."

Riordan grinned. "We Irish . . . are a mad race . . . or so I'm told," he puffed out. "What concern . . . is it t'you?"

Escott snorted. "I'm not surprised. He still wants a nap."

"No problem," I said, and popped Riordan one the old-fashioned way. His eyes rolled up, and he slithered down the bricks as his legs gave out.

Miss Weaver gaped. "My God, did you kill him?"

"Not yet." I hauled him up over one shoulder like a sack of grain. He was heavy, all of it muscle. "Let's find his car."

Escott knew the vehicle—a battered black Ford—got the keys from Riordan's pocket, and opened the trunk. It was full of junk, but there was just room enough to stuff him in.

"He'll suffocate in this heat," she said.

She had a point. I found a tire iron in the junk and used the prying end to punch half a dozen air holes into the trunk lid before slamming it shut. They looked like bullet holes but larger.

"He can get help in the morning if he yells loud enough," I said, trying for a reassuring smile.

The businesses along this street behind the restaurant were closed. There was little chance of a stray pedestrian passing by, especially with a storm looming.

"Who is he?" Miss Weaver asked, voicing my own question.

"No one important," Escott said. He took the tire iron from me, dropping it and the car keys on the front seat of the Ford. "He fancies himself to be a private investigator, but his methods are sloppy and his personal ethics questionable. If you offered him a dollar more than your cousin's payment, he would cheerfully switch sides until such time as he could solicit her for a counteroffer."

I'd talk to Escott later about Riordan. The way he grabbed the crowbar while glaring at the car trunk told me that it was just as well there was a locked steel barrier between them.

Escott drove us to Bawks House; Miss Weaver—Mabel now, she insisted—sat next to him. I had the backseat to myself, slumping low in case she noticed I wasn't reflecting in the rearview mirror.

She fussed with her hat, trying to secure it better. She was cheerful, almost relaxed, and made a point of turning around to beam at me now and then as we talked. Escott had instructed her to trust us. With her, trust must also include liking a person. She acted as though we were all old friends. I'd have been uncomfortable, but she'd forget it in a few weeks.

We had the windows down on his Nash; the hot air blowing in was viscous as tar. Through breaks in the buildings we saw restless clouds thickening, making plans. Lightning defined their shifting forms for an instant, thunder grumbled, and they went dark until the next flash. We headed north, right into it.

Escott gently plied questions under the guise of conversation.

Since discovering the fake gem, Mabel had been careful not to give anything away to her cousin, otherwise the real diamond would evaporate to a safer hiding place. For the present, it was still in the house, cached in a shoe in her cousin's bedroom closet.

"How did you find that out?" he asked.

"Agnes is always eavesdropping on the extensions, but until now I had no reason to do the same to her. She thinks I'm too goody-goody. Well, I started listening, too, and got an earful on everything."

"You must have had opportunity to switch pendants prior to this."

"No, I have not. One or the other of them is always home, they keep their bedroom door locked, and I don't have a key. I'm sorry I couldn't give you more time, but only this morning did I learn about the collector coming tonight.

Agnes's husband found him. Agnes married him just a few months ago. He saw the big house, met our sick grandmother, and assumed he'd be coming into big money soon enough. Agnes didn't set him straight. She and Clive were made for each other: both sly, greedy Philistines."

Escott came subtly alert. "Is he English? That's not a common first name in America."

"Clive Latshaw's no more English than I'm Greta Garbo. He puts on a good show, though. He'll high-hat anyone if he thinks he can get away with it. He even charmed Grandma, but not enough so she'd change her will."

"Who is this private collector?"

"I didn't get a name, but they're meeting at Bawks House at ten. We'll be able to sneak in with no trouble. Agnes and Clive are always in the parlor with the radio on. She won't go up for the Eye unless she sees the money."

"This is very uncertain, if they should catch us—"

"Then I came home early from dinner, and you're my invited guests. If we're caught, I'll be embarrassed, but I'm getting my property back. If it was me facing just Agnes I'd be fine, but Clive would step in, and he can be mean. I can't fight them both."

"Your gentleman friend did not put himself forward as a protector?"

"Bartie's a good egg but no Jack Dempsey. Clive won't try anything with you there, but if we're careful, we can be in and out, and they'll never know a thing. I just wish I could see Agnes's face when she tries to palm off a piece of glass as a diamond."

A reviving gust of cooler air hit my face. "What about this curse?"

Mabel was thoughtful. "I know it sounds silly, but I've always believed it. Grandma told stories, lots of them, about what happened whenever someone tried to take Hecate's Eye away from its . . . well, Grandma called herself and the other women before her its guardians."

"It kills people?"

"Men. It kills men. The Eye has always brought bad luck to them and good luck to women, but I don't want to trust that too much."

"How so?"

"If Agnes sells it, I think something terrible will happen to her. I don't like her, but she's family. I have a duty to try to protect her from herself."

The storm hit just as we made the turn to Bawks House, and even I couldn't see much of the joint through the heavy gray sheets of rain. It was big, and a single vivid lightning flash made it look haunted.

Mabel directed Escott to a branching in the drive that went around to the rear. He cut the headlamps, and we had to trust to luck that more lightning wouldn't suddenly reveal us to anyone watching from the house.

She pointed toward a porte cochère serving the back door.

Escott glided under its shelter, parking next to a snappy-looking Buick coupe, which was parked pointing outward. The rain drumming on our roof ceased. We'd put the windows up to keep out the water and rolled them down again to let in the air.

"Feels like winter," said Mabel in a more normal tone, sounding pleased.

"Whose vehicle?" Escott asked.

"Clive's. He never uses the garage. Likes to leave quick when he has someplace to go."

"Aren't we a bit obvious here?"

"They'll stay in the parlor so they can watch for their big buyer."

"I'm curious about this providentially wealthy collector of rare gems—how would Clive Latshaw find such a person?"

"He must have asked around. Maybe he went to a jewelry store."

"What about his background?"

She shrugged. "He said he was from New England—but his accent says Detroit. We must get moving. For all I know, Agnes might have brought the Eye down early, and all this effort will be wasted."

I cleared my throat. "Say she did. We can still get it."

Mabel gave me a sideways look. "What do you mean?"

"Nothing violent, but I can have a talk with them, make them see reason."

"If it's nothing violent, why mention it?"

"My associate has a very persuasive and calming manner even with the most obstreperous of types," Escott explained. "You always talk like that?"

"Like what?"

She waved a hand. "All right, but let's try my way first. I'll get the door open and you two follow. And be *quiet*."

On the drive over, she'd given us her plan of attack, which was to sneak upstairs, have Escott pick the bedroom lock, and I'd keep lookout. Of course, I had my own way into the room that involved vanishing and sieving under the door, but Mabel Weaver didn't need to witness it. This was her party; let her have her fun. She left the car, carefully not slamming the door. Escott and I did the same, following her through the back entry into a sizable mudroom. I had no need of an invitation to cross the threshold. Bram Stoker, go jump in a lake.

Mabel took her shoes off and gestured for us to do likewise.

Escott leaned close to whisper. "We're shod in gumsoled shoes, Miss Weaver."

"Really? I thought that was just in the movi—" She clapped a hand over her mouth, apparently remembering her own order about silence.

The mudroom opened to a dim kitchen, also large. There were dinner leavings forgotten on the table in the dining room on our left. The parlor was the next room over, visible through an open door; a comedy show played on the radio.

In silence, Mabel led us to a plain hall with stairs going up. The house had been built for a large family with a lot of servants, all long gone and moved on. It seemed a shame to have it wasted on two thieves, but I was just the hired help and not entitled to an opinion about the wisdom of Grandma Bawks's bequest.

There were walls between us and the parlor, but I heard Rochester making a comment to Jack Benny and getting a huge laugh despite static from the storm affecting reception. The noise would mask our own movements, and just as well—the old wooden stairs squeaked.

We took them slow. Mabel would stop and listen, anxious, then move up a few more steps. She finally made the landing, and then padded down the hall on tiptoe. Escott kept up with her, not quite so silent as I, but damned close. He had the small flashlight in one hand, but enough ambient glow from an uncurtained window allowed them to navigate. The lightning flashes were getting more frequent, the thunder insistently louder. Mother Nature wanted to let everyone know who was in charge tonight.

Mabel stopped before a door and pointed. Escott gave her the flashlight and dropped to one knee, reaching for his inside coat pocket. He drew out his lock-pick case, opened it, and went to work.

I eased toward a second staircase that curved down to the entry foyer. White marble, lofty columns, paneled walls—nice place, but I couldn't see myself ever living in anything this fancy. Maybe Grandma Bawks hadn't done Agnes any favors. The property taxes would be steep, and with a husband who was allergic to work . . . I suddenly wanted a look at those two.

It was easy to build a mental picture of them from Mabel's talk, but I knew better than to trust such things. The parlor was temptingly close, just off the entry to judge by the radio volume.

Escott performed his magic, listening and feeling his way as he attacked the lock. With the thunder and rain, it was taking longer than usual. Mabel held the flashlight, her fingers covering most of the beam, letting just enough escape so Escott could work. Neither noticed when I vanished.

Escott would know I'd be reconnoitering and not worry, but he'd have a tough time convincing Mabel to do the same. What the hell, he could use the practice.

Formless, I drifted downstairs, hugging the wall for orientation. When I ran out of wall, I bumbled toward the radio noise. When invisible, I can't see and my hearing's muffled, but I've no shins to crack. I flowed gently along, working around, and sometimes under, furniture until I was in the parlor next to the radio.

It crossed my mind that this would be a perfect night to suddenly go solid and yell boo, but I restrained myself.

A quick circuit gave me a sense of where various obstacles like chairs were located, as well as where Agnes and Clive had roosted. She sat close to the radio; he stood by a wall.

Pushing away, I found what I hoped was the opposite wall and forced myself to go high until I hovered against the ceiling.

I hate heights, but most people don't look up. If luck was with me, Clive and Agnes would be doing what I did myself: watching the radio. The thing isn't a movie screen, but you get into the habit of staring at the glowing dial as though it's a face.

Slowly I took on solidity and got some of my sight back, though the view was faded and foggy. The more solid, the better my vision, but the more weight. If I didn't hold to a semitransparent state, I'd drop like a brick.

Agnes flipped through a picture magazine, her head down. She had dark hair and looked more lightly built than Mabel.

Clive was at a window, holding the curtain to one side. Maybe he liked storms, but my money was on the gem collector's arrival being the object of his interest. He was a square-looking specimen, clear featured, nothing unpleasant about him. They were not the shifty-eyed, snarling crooks with pinched and ugly mugs my mental picture had conjured. They were as ordinary as could be, enough so I doubted Mabel's assessment.

An important message interrupted Jack Benny's show. Before the announcer could make his point over the increasing static, Agnes shut the sound down. "He won't arrive faster for you watching," she said, flipping a magazine page.

Clive grunted. "I'm sure I saw a car turn in."

"If it did, then it went out again. We're near the end of the lane. They use the drive for that all the time. It's too early, anyway."

"What if that was Mabel coming back?"

"She'd be inside by now, and we'd have heard her big feet clomping up the stairs. I'll be glad when she goes."

"Taking her rent money with her."

Agnes looked up. "You're a funny one. The money we're making tonight and you're worried about her five-and-dime rent?"

"The deal's not a sure thing, I've told you a hundred times."

"Then why's he coming over if not to buy? Once he sees the diamond, he'll want it."

"Don't be too confident about that."

She slapped the magazine shut. "And you don't be too anxious to sell or he won't make a good offer. I know what the thing's worth, and if he isn't up for that, then you'll just have to find another man."

"Listen, crazy collectors who don't ask questions aren't falling out of trees. I had to hustle to find this one."

"But it's not like we're in a hurry. Mabel's not caught on yet, and she never will."

He chuckled. "Did you see her going out?"

"You know I did. I nearly broke something trying not to laugh. The way she was sweeping around like some queen in the crown jewels, the big snob. One of these days I'm going to tell her about this."

There was a white flash from the window, and thunder boomed like a cannon a bare second after. Agnes yelped, Clive jumped, the lights flickered, and I vanished altogether. It startled me, too. Just as well—people tend to look up when that happens.

"Come away from the window before you get electrocuted," Agnes said, shaken. "It's right over us. Did you feel that? Shook the whole house."

"I'll get a candle before we blow a fuse." She passed under me, using the doorway into the dining room. She fumbled around and returned. "That's better," she said some moments later. "Makes it cozy. Want a drink?"

"Not until this is over."

"Then I'll wait, too."

"What are you doing?"

"Grandma was always gabbing on about the good old days and how it looked by candlelight. I want to see."

"Put it up."

"The yellow goes away in this light. The old bat was right. It looks like a real diamond now—come see."

"No thanks."

"Don't tell me you believe that crock about the curse."

"You were just telling me not to be too anxious. What's Taylor going to think when he walks in and sees you waving that thing around like a Cracker Jack prize?"

"That maybe I have some sentimental attachment to it and will be reluctant to sell. I'll make sure he hears my heart breaking."

"Go easy on the Sarah Bernhardt act—this isn't his first time. He'll know if you're trying to—" I missed the rest, being too busy finding and shooting back up the stairs. I moved along the hall, bumping into someone who gave a sudden shiver. Escott once compared the kind of cold I inflict in this form to that feeling you get when someone waltzes on your grave.

"Problem?" Escott whispered, evidently recognizing the chill. I hung back, not knowing where Mabel might be. "Miss Weaver isn't here."

I resumed form and weight. Gravity's always an odd shock, like climbing out of a swimming pool after a long float.

The door he'd been working on was open. I looked in. The flashlight was on the floor. Its beam took in Mabel, who was on her knees by a closet going through dozens of pairs of women's shoes. They have only two feet, why is it dames need so many things to put them in?

Mabel stopped when she heard my *psst*. She hastily got up.

"We're skunked," I whispered. "Agnes has the rock with her. You want to try the next plan?"

She scowled. "You'll never talk her out of it. No matter what, there's going to be a fight."

"Jack has a winning way with people," Escott assured. "This won't take long. We can wait in the car."

"Oh, this I've got to see."

"No." I was decisive. "You two clear out." But— "I promise not to break anything. Hand over the fake. I'll trade them."

"But if you touch the real one . . . the curse—I can't." She was absolutely serious.

"Please." I put a little pressure on. Since she'd been under so recently, it didn't take much. If the real diamond killed men, it was too late for me.

Reluctantly, Mabel slipped the pendant off its chain. "You're sure?"

I jerked my head toward the scattered shoes. "Put those back so she won't know."

While she made repairs, I turned to Escott. "You hear of any gem collectors named Taylor?"

He shook his head. When it came to various criminals working in Chicago and points east and south, he was an encyclopedia. Honest citizens held little interest for him.

Mabel came out, easing the door shut; Escott locked it again. We took the back stairs down. The vulnerable spot on our exit was the dining room door, still wide open with a view through to the parlor. Anyone looking our way would see us passing.

I put an eye around the edge. The coast was clear. A quick gesture, and Escott and Mabel slipped by, heading for the mudroom. Thunder covered the sounds they made.

The coast was still clear, so I ducked into the dining room, staying solid and sneaking up on the parlor door.

Standing behind it, I could peer through the crack on the hinge side.

Agnes was in her chair with the magazine; Clive was back staring out the window.

If they'd split up, the job would be easy. I could hypnotize them one at a time into a nap. Both at once would necessarily be violent. I'd have to physically restrain one while working my evil eye whammy on the other. Not impossible, but it's noisy, exasperating, and never goes smoothly.

My best bet was to draw one of them from the room long enough to get to the other. A of couple spoons from the uncleared dinner table would do. I'd toss them at the marble in the foyer. Clive was already up and more or less pointing in the right direction . . .

The doorbell rang.

"It's him," said Clive, excited.

Crap. I didn't want to have to take out three of them.

"Didn't you see him drive up?" Agnes asked.

"It's like Niagara out there. You can't see anything."

She put the magazine to one side, stood, smoothed her dress, and sat down again, ankles crossed, hands in her lap they way they teach girls to do in finishing schools. She had a little black box in one hand, not hard to guess what was in it. "When this is done I want a real honeymoon," she said with a spark in her eyes. She was as tall as Mabel, but finer-boned and more aristocratic in features.

"You got it, baby!" He hurried to the foyer.

I had my chance. He'd be busy with the guest, finding a place for his hat and umbrella. I'd have the moment I needed to steal in and put her out.

Only Agnes did something odd, and that made me hesitate. While looking toward the foyer with the box in her left hand, her right hand left her lap briefly, brushing against a pocket on her dress. It was swiftly and deftly done. She'd checked to make sure something was where it was supposed to be.

What's in your pocket, Mrs. Latshaw?

Then my opportunity was gone. Clive led the buyer in and introduced William D. Taylor (the Fourth) to his wife. I guess they make eccentric collectors in all types and sizes, but this one looked as average as Clive. Taylor wore a nice suit, a stuffy expression behind his wire-rimmed glasses, and had a briefcase.

Pleasantries were exchanged about the terrible weather. Mr. Taylor apologized and was forgiven for arriving early. "You'll pardon if I'm in a rush, Mrs. Latshaw, but I've a train to New York to catch. The sooner I make a decision on this stone, the sooner I may leave. This dismal rain . . . "

"I understand."

"Excellent. I came prepared." He produced a jeweler's loupe. "Mr. Latshaw, may I trouble you to move a lamp to this table?"

When the lamp was in place, Agnes stepped forward. "This is my family's prize heirloom: Hecate's Golden Eye," she said with a well-calculated dose of hushed respect as she opened the box.

Taylor accepted the box, held it under the lamp's light, peered at the contents, and set it down on the table. He pulled on a pair of white gloves, and only then picked up the pendant. I wondered if they'd be enough to protect him from the curse. He screwed the loupe in one eye and spent several minutes examining the gem. Clive and Agnes exchanged worried looks, but resumed their poker-playing faces when Taylor grunted. "The genuine thing. Superb clarity for its size. I can see that legendary flaw quite clearly. A perfect eye with pupil and even lashes. Extraordinary."

"My dear grandmother often mentioned it. She loved the piece very much."

"No doubt. I'm sure you would rather keep it in the family."

Clive worked hard to hide his alarm. "You're not interested?"

"I am, sir, but cannot offer you much for it. I collect with the intent of appreciation of value as well as for a gem's unique beauty. Without provenance—you were clear this diamond has none beyond private family records which, forgive me, can be forged—I cannot easily resell it in the future for as much profit as I would like."

"You could to another private collector."

"Humph. That would be that so-and-so Abercrombie. I'd never give him the satisfaction. I'm glad he's moved to Switzerland or he might have gotten wind of this first. I'm sorry, but I can offer you only so much and no more. You may take it or leave it as you choose." Then he said a number that made my jaw drop.

The Latshaws failed to hide their gleeful satisfaction. Clive recovered first. "My wife and I assure you that we would be very pleased for Hecate's Eye to become part of the Taylor collection."

"Very good."

They shook hands.

"A check will suffice, and once it clears you may take possession."

"Mr. Latshaw, my train won't wait for the banks to open, but I am prepared to conclude this transaction now." He put the briefcase on the table and opened it to reveal a respectable load of wrapped banknotes. The Latshaws were appropriately impressed.

My jaw kept swinging. I'd seen bigger stacks of cash, but only in gangster-controlled gambling clubs. I drew breath for a silent whistle and could actually smell the ink.

"How can you carry all that?" Agnes asked. "What if you're robbed?"

"I can take care of myself, ma'am." Taylor opened his suit coat just enough to give her a glimpse of his shoulder rig and whatever gun it held. "If Mr. Latshaw would count the money and sign a receipt, I'll be off to catch my train."

Clive counted, and Agnes poured sherry into three stemmed glasses, making small talk with Taylor. Alone on the table was the open black box with the Eye still in it.

Even across the room I could tell it was a real gem. The glass imitation in my pocket was a vulgar peasant compared with the elegant royalty over there. Simply lying on its white silk padding, the stone glowed like molten gold. It took light and set it on fire. When I shifted, futilely trying to move closer for a better view—I swear it—the thing winked at me.

That was eerie. The longer I stared, the less I liked it. The damned thing was just a chunk of crystallized carbon in an unexpected color with a fancy name, and for some reason, people had decided it was worth something. They killed and died for such shiny baubles. Insane.

Despite that, I wouldn't have minded having a few locked up in the safe at home. Just not this one.

Hecate's Eye twinkled goldly at me, and I fought down a shiver.

Clive finished his count and closed the briefcase. Taylor said he could keep it along with the cash. Taylor picked up the Eye and peered through his loupe. Wise of him. He'd been distracted by Agnes; Clive could have slipped a fake in.

"It is beautiful," Taylor said. "I've seen its equal only at the British Museum, and that one had two inclusions, but neither like this simulacrum."

They made a toast, and everyone looked pleased. Agnes gently took the pendant from Taylor—to have one last look at her darling grandmother's pride and joy, she said. "I shall miss you," she said, holding the stone to the light, gravely wistful.

Clive and Taylor exchanged glances, two men in silent agreement about the frail sentiment of the fair sex, shaking their heads and smiling.

By the time they turned back, Agnes had made the switch. She'd practiced; she was so fast, I almost missed it. She put a pendant in the box and closed the lid, handing it to Taylor. The real stone was still in her palm so far as I could tell. While the men shook hands, she slipped it into her dress pocket. Slick, but foolish. Sooner or later, Taylor would take another gander at his toy and call the cops. How could she think she'd get away with it?

Someone eased up behind me, and I did not trust it to be Escott checking to see what was taking so long.

I ducked and twisted in time to avoid the full force of the crooked end of a tire iron on my skull. It smashed into my left shoulder square on the bone joint. Most of the time a regular person hasn't got the strength to damage me, but the application of raw kinetic force on a single spot with an unbreakable tool—something's going to give. I heard it do just that with a sickening, meaty pop and dimly knew that it hurt, but was too busy to register how much. I spun the rest of the way around to face Riordan. He was ready and punched the iron hard into my gut. It had a hell of a lot more force than a bare fist. I doubled over.

Not needing to breathe, I wasn't yet on the mat, and I lunged forward to tackle him. He danced back and almost made it, but collided violently into the dining table, tumbling it and himself over with a satisfyingly noisy crash. A woman screamed.

My left arm was completely useless and hanging. I grabbed at Riordan with my right, but he didn't stop, cracking the tire iron smartly on the back of my hand. I heard bones snap, but again felt no pain, which meant serious, crippling damage. Before he caught me another one—dammit, he was *fast*—I got a fist in his belly. It was a lighter tap than I wanted, since I was forced to use my right. No pain—things were moving too quick.

Riordan *did* have to breathe, and slowed just enough that I had time to stun him silly with an openhanded slap on the side of his head. Again, not my full muscle behind it, but it got the job done so well that I wanted to scream as my shattered bones ground against one another under the skin.

The starch left him, but he fought it, his eyes going in and out of focus. I grabbed the iron. It took effort to pry from his grip, and I had to drop it immediately as my fingers gave up working. Everything came to roaring, agonizing life. One arm dead, the other much too alive, I needed to vanish so I could heal.

"Hands up!"

William D. Taylor (the Fourth) had me covered with an efficient-looking semi-auto. A .32 or .38, it gave the impression of being field artillery from my angle on the floor.

I froze. I *hate* getting shot. It hurts like hell, I lose precious blood, and the bullets go right through to hit anything and anyone with the bad luck to be behind me. I also tend to involuntarily vanish. With the damage I already had, I'd not be able to stop the process.

Couldn't risk it in front of this bunch. None of them needed to know that much about me. In the spirit of cooperation, I tried to raise my one moving arm. Pain blazed down it like an electric shock. I gasped and hunched over it, suddenly queasy. My left arm wasn't responding at all; a major nerve or something was gone, couldn't feel it except as a heavy dragging weight. I smelled blood where the skin was broken on my shoulder, but the black shirt hid it.

Clive Latshaw, the outraged man of the house, demanded to know who I was and what I was doing there.

Not having a good answer for either, I told him to call the cops.

Their reaction was interesting. When trespassers demolish your home, most folk are eager to turn them in.

This trio hesitated with an exchange of uncomfortable glances.

Taylor spoke first. "I *have* to be on that train tonight. It's vital to my business."

Clive slowly nodded. "Of course. I can take care of this. We don't need the police."

Not too strangely, given the switch she'd pulled and the fact that she'd stolen the gem in the first place, Agnes did not utter a single reasonable objection to this extraordinary statement. Instead, she glared at the wreckage that happens to a nice room when two grown men try to kill each other in it.

"Who *are* they?" she asked, somehow taking me and Riordan in at the same time.

She'd shown no recognition at all for him, but then neither had Clive. They were both competent enough liars. Were they in on it together or separately? Did she have a reason not to tell her husband about hiring a man, or had Clive retained him and not shared with her?

Visible through the parlor curtains, lightning flashed bright. Thunder boomed, shaking the whole house again. We all jumped a little under flickering lights.

Her hand was in her pocket, nervously touching Hecate's Golden Eye, and I wondered briefly about the curse. This weather had me spooked.

I'd only *looked* at the damned thing and had a bushel basket of bad luck dropped on me. Had I been normal, I'd be maimed for life.

I needed to vanish; a few seconds out of their sight would be enough. My best option was to hypnotize them into a nap on their feet, but attempting to take all three at once while they were on guard was bound to fail. I was too distracted by pain, which was getting worse.

Get them separated.

"Call the cops," I said, looking at Clive, willing him to listen. If just one of them left, I had a chance. "I'm a burglar and this is another burglar. We came here to steal everything, and we should be jailed."

Riordan roused himself enough to mutter, "Y'daft b'sturd." He was soaked through from the storm. He might have entered the house from some other door than the one in the mudroom, but it wasn't likely. Worry for Escott and Mabel stabbed through me, breaking my concentration. If he'd gotten the drop on them . . .

Riordan won his struggle back to consciousness and dragged himself to a sitting position. "Jesus, Mary, an' Joseph, for a skinny git, you know how to scrap."

"Where are they?" I snarled.

"If you're meanin' the Holy Family, take yourself to a church, they'll be glad to inform you. If it's Charlie an' his new sweetheart, you'll find them tight as sardines in the boot of his car."

Clive looked ready to choke. "*Quiet!*"

As if to punctuate him, thunder boomed over the house, rattling everything and everyone.

Riordan squinted up at him. "Friends in high places, have ye?" With a groan, he found his unsteady feet.

Agnes instinctively retreated behind her husband. "Clive . . . "

"Stay right there," Taylor ordered, reminding us he was armed.

"I'm no burglar, missus, not t'worry." Riordan looked at me. "Don't kid yourself, mate, I had a great pleasure in bustin' you up, but it happens I'm here on me own business."

"What business?" Taylor's aim was steady. A man used to firearms.

Riordan rubbed the side of his head. "Me ears are ringing, but I've no time for that phone. It's you"—he looked at Clive Latshaw—"I want a word with."

Clive had a good poker-playing face, but not good enough. Riordan was the last person he wanted here, that was plain.

"Clive—do you know that man?" Agnes stared at him.

"Indeed he does, missus. Pleased to meet you. Shamus Riordan, me name is me game, spell it the same. Pardon me manners, but I've had a bad night. I want a word with your mister about me payment."

"Who *is* he?"

Clive did his best. "He's a man I hired to follow Mabel. It's nothing important."

He was desperate for her to take the hint. Mention of Mabel could bring out that she was the real owner of the Eye. Taylor might not care, but then again, he might.

"An' paid well for it," Riordan added. "Very well indeed from a man with holes in his shoes. Polish on top, holes on the bottoms, an' I'll not mention too loudly the shockin' state of your heels. You had work for me, that's all I care about. But I began wonderin' how you got hold of so much lovely money, when it was clear you were in such need for yourself—"

Clive told him to shut up. I had to read his lips; the thunder drowned him out.

Despite the agony, I started to laugh, getting a collective glare from them.

Perversely, I enjoyed the moment. It happens when the adrenaline's running and certain oddities suddenly make sense.

"Would you let us in on the hilarity?" Riordan asked.

"You already got the joke." I let the laughter run down. Continuing was too painful.

"I don't consider it t'be all that amusin'."

He wouldn't. No one would.

It was hard to read Taylor's eyes behind those wire glasses. My guess was that I'd said too much already. We were in dangerous waters.

Riordan started to speak, but I caught his eye and gave a fast wink, hoping the others would miss it and that he'd take the warning. If I got shot, I'd vanish. Riordan would bleed out and die. He gave a snort of contempt, muttered about "bloody Yankee Doodles," and subsided, turning away.

Good man.

Another exchange of looks between Taylor and Clive. I pretended not to see, but Agnes had picked up on things. She backed off to watch them both, her eyes sharp and suspicious. Clive took charge, speaking slowly, his voice thick. "Mr. Taylor, as this has nothing to do with you, I think you should leave. If you would give me the loan of your gun, I can take care of this situation. I'll return it later; I have your address." Thinking it over, Taylor finally nodded, but didn't move right away. He blinked several times and rubbed his eyes. Clive extended a hand sideways toward him, but there was an unusual sluggishness to the action.

"I have . . . your address," he repeated.

Taylor made no reply.

Agnes stepped forward and took the gun from Taylor's hand.

Neither of the men protested; their faces had gone slack in what to me was a too-familiar dead-eyed stare.

She rounded on me and Riordan, scowling. "What am I going to do with you two?" she wanted to know.

One to one, the odds were in my favor. I pushed away the pain and concentrated on her.

But there was still some bad luck left in the barrel. Another lightning flash edged the curtains with white fire for a breathless moment. Thunder boomed seemingly right over the house. The lights failed.

Skunked again, dammit. At least when it came to hypnosis. But if the power stayed off long enough . . .

The parlor candle was far enough away to leave the dining room sufficiently dark. I went out like the lights, and for a few precious seconds the gray nothingness swept me from the weight and pain of physical burdens. It was a little bit of heaven, tempting me to linger. Alas, no.

When I came back, my arms worked just fine again; I was also right behind Agnes, grabbing for her gun. Taylor and Clive continued to stand in their tracks, oblivious as a couple of store-window mannequins. I caught a of glimpse of a gleeful Riordan grinning like a maniac in the face of all the impossibilities taking place.

Agnes put up a hell of a fight, screaming, clawing, hissing, kicking, and not letting go of the gun, not giving an inch as we danced around. With a ferocious twist, she broke free and fired at me, the gun's roar matching the thunder for sheer eardrum-breaking sound.

At less than ten feet she missed, but you can do that if you're excited and don't know how to shoot.

However, even an excited, inexperienced shooter can get lucky. Time to leave.

I retreated in haste to the dining room. Riordan, no fool, was just ahead, scrambling toward the kitchen.

She fired again, screaming something abusive. We dashed toward the mudroom, jamming shoulders in the doorway, fighting to be the first out. Riordan slipped sideways and won, slamming through the back door into the rain with me at his heels.

He took off down the drive, presumably to reclaim his car. We should have tied and gagged him. He was too good an escape artist.

He looked back once, teeth white in the darkness. "Till the next round!" he yelled, then sprinted away.

Escott's Nash was still there, the keys and his Webley on the front seat. Mabel and Escott were indeed inside the trunk, to tell by the muffled shouts and thumping, but they could wait.

I got the car started, shifted gears, and shot out from under the porte cochère. Rain once more pounded the roof with brutal force, but the heavy fall and general darkness would obscure the vehicle from Agnes, hopefully throwing off her aim. I didn't stop to look.

When I judged the distance to be far enough, I cut the motor, vanished, and bee-lined my invisible way back to the house. Wind buffeted me, and the rain was a startling unpleasantness. I usually get that kind of quivering discomfort when sieving through solid walls. When it stopped, I made the reasonable assumption I was under shelter.

With great caution, I took on just enough solidity to get my bearings. Clive's flashy coupe was in front of me. I let myself float up into a dim corner to watch.

In the few moments since Riordan and I escaped, Agnes had been busy.

Wearing hat and gloves, she emerged from the back door, the leather case with the money in one hand, a travel suitcase in the other. She tossed them into the passenger side of Clive's coupe and hopped in herself. She was laughing, a free and easy sound of pure delight and triumph.

I half expected a fateful bolt of lightning to strike just then, but nothing happened. The storm seemed to be letting up. Agnes revved the motor, shifted gears, and roared off into the rain.

Escott had past experience at being locked in car trunks, so he was more sanguine about it than our client. That, or maybe he'd enjoyed being stuffed into a small space with a healthy young woman on top of him. I'd kept a straight face when I'd let them out, though they were rather badly rumpled.

Mabel was livid and ready to strangle Riordan, but I explained he was long gone. I had a lot of explaining to do, but first had her give me the location of the fuse box so I could get the lights working. She was none too pleased at the state of the dining room, appalled and aghast at the sight of Clive and Taylor literally asleep on their feet, and furious with me on general principles. She visibly fumed as I eased each man flat on the floor. They were breathing okay, hearts pumping steadily, so they didn't seem to be in any immediate danger.

"Some kind of curare?" Escott ventured, studying them with his own brand of cold-blooded curiosity. "If so, they might well be aware of everything we're saying."

I shrugged. "Just don't touch the sherry. It might be a good idea to empty all the open bottles into the drain. Agnes could have left a booby trap behind."

Mabel was ready to explode. "*What* happened?"

I sat down because I was damned tired. Before dawn, rain or no, I'd have to stop at the Stockyards and have a long drink. With the promise of fresh beef blood in my near future, I told them everything that happened, including Riordan's badly timed interruption and the fight, leaving out the part about my injuries. I'd tell Escott later. He'd need to know just how violent his acquaintance had gotten.

"You let her go?" Mabel's throaty voice rose. I held up a hand.

"She didn't get away with anything."

"Only with Hecate's Eye and all that money. She'll never come back."

I took the pendant—the real one—from my pocket and held it out to her.

Mabel gaped, then reached for it, fingers shaking. "You switched them!"

"Said I would. It took long enough, what with Agnes fighting me every inch of the way."

"You mustn't touch it. My God, put it down before something horrible happens."

I put it into her hand and told her how I'd played pickpocket during the tussle. Agnes must have thought I was some kind of masher since I'd had to keep my hands moving. No wonder she'd shot at me.

"She still got away with the payment—Taylor will set the police on her."

"No, he won't. He brought a case full of funny money to buy the gem. It's as counterfeit as the pendant he got. Agnes had two fakes made. Maybe the jeweler cut her a deal for making two."

That took them both a moment to digest. I used the pause to take the little box from Taylor's coat pocket and spilled *his* fake pendant onto the table.

"But how did you know about the money?" Escott asked. "You couldn't have gotten a close look at it."

"It was the smell. Ever smell uncirculated cash straight from the bank? Nothing like that fresh ink, only this was just too fresh. It was strong enough that I picked up on it in the next room, but its importance didn't click until Riordan showed up wanting to talk with Clive. When he hired Riordan to follow Mabel, he paid with counterfeit bills."

"How did *he* get them?" she asked. "Oh—oh, it couldn't be."

"It could. He and Taylor are partners, working a long confidence game. Clive the gigolo marries an heiress with expectations. I wouldn't be surprised if he's left a number of wives in his wake."

"A bigamist?" Mabel stared at Clive as though he were an exotic zoo specimen.

"It's likely. Marriage is a tool of the trade. I bet this time the deal wasn't as sweet as he'd hoped. Agnes got the house, but it was worthless to him. A family heirloom like a rare diamond was much better. He probably put a few words in her ear about how unfair it was that you got it, unless it was her idea to start with. When the time was right, he called in Taylor to pose as a wealthy gem collector. The hard part for them was probably finding really good counterfeit cash. The printer should have let it dry longer."

More gaping from Mabel; then she began to hoot with laughter. There was no love lost between her and her cousin. That Agnes had married a confidence man and possible bigamist bothered Mabel not at all. Tears ran down her face, and she had to blow her nose.

When she got her breath, I continued. "Neither of them knew that Agnes had her own angle, which was to drug them, switch the gems, and drive off with both brass rings. Clive would wake in the morning with no wife and no cash. Maybe Taylor would crash his car in the rain or not, but . . . " I let it hang.

That sobered Mabel up. "I can't believe she'd have gone that far."

"She might have planned to delay him long enough for the mickey she slipped to put them out. Riordan interrupted when he tried to crack my skull open."

"You're sure you're not hurt?"

"It'll take more than a crazy Irishman with a stick to do that." I turned to Escott. "You're going to tell me more about him, right?"

He looked pained. "Not just now."

"I suppose I'll have to call the police," said Mabel about the supine mannequins on the parlor floor.

"Don't worry about it. I've a friend who will want to meet these jokers." My friend was a gang boss of no small influence who owed me a favor or three. Northside Gordy would be very interested in hearing Taylor and Clive's life stories and why they were operating in his city without his permission, thus denying him his cut of their deal. If they were lucky, he might let them go with most of their body parts intact.

"Poor Agnes." Mabel snickered. "When she starts spending that fake money . . . "

"She could go to jail," Escott completed for her.

"It'd serve her right, but I better let the police know that she stole a car."

Mabel put Hecate's Eye in its little box and went to the kitchen to make the call.

Escott and I looked at the gem, neither of us disposed to get closer.

A last bit of lightning from the fading storm played hob once more with the house lights. They flickered, leaving the one candle to take up the slack for an instant before brightening again.

"Did you see that?" I asked. "Tell me you saw that."

"Trick of the light, old man, nothing more." But Escott looked strangely pale. "It absolutely did *not* wink at us."

P. N. Elrod is best known for her Vampire Files series featuring wiseacre undead gumshoe, Jack Fleming. She's the prize-winning editor of several successful anthology collections for St. Martin's Griffin and is branching into steampunk with a new series for Tor Books. More info on her toothy titles may be found at vampwriter.com.

The Case: *The lower half of a woman's body is found standing in a shed. There is no sign of the upper half, and no further clues.*

The Investigator: *Detective Jessi Hardin, the only officer currently assigned to the new Denver PD Paranatural Unit (one of the first in the country). Her experience with the magical is minimal, but it is more than the other cops have.*

DEFINING SHADOWS

=◆=

Carrie Vaughn

The windowless outbuilding near the property's back fence wasn't big enough to be a garage or even a shed. Painted the same pale green as the house twenty feet away, the mere closet was a place for garden tools and snow shovels, one of a thousand just like it in a neighborhood north of downtown Denver. But among the rakes and pruning shears, this one had a body.

Half a body, rather.

Detective Jessi Hardin stood at the open door, regarding the macabre remains. The victim had been cut off at the waist, and the legs were propped up vertically, as if she'd been standing there when she'd been sliced in half and forgotten to fall down. Even stranger, there didn't seem to be any blood. The gaping wound in the trunk—vertebrae and a few stray organs were visible in a hollow body cavity from which the intestines had been scooped out—seemed almost cauterized, scorched, the edges of the flesh burned and bubbled. The thing stank of rotting meat, and flies buzzed everywhere. She could imagine the swarm that must have poured out when the closet door was first opened. By the tailored trousers and black pumps still in place, Hardin guessed the victim was female. No identification had been found. They were still checking ownership of the house.

"Told you you've never seen anything like it," Detective Patton said. He seemed downright giddy at stumping her.

Well, she had seen something like it, once. A transient had fallen asleep on some train tracks, and the train came by and cut the poor bastard in half. But he hadn't been propped up in a closet later. No one had seen anything like *this*, and that was why Patton called her. She got the weird ones these days. Frankly, if it meant she wasn't on call for cases where the body was an infant with a dozen broken bones, with deadbeat parents insisting they never laid a hand on the kid, she was fine with that.

"Those aren't supported, are they?" she said. "They're just standing upright." She took a pair of latex gloves from the pocket of her suit jacket and pulled them on. Pressing on the body's right hip, she gave a little push—the legs swayed, but didn't fall over.

"That's creepy," Patton said, all humor gone. He'd turned a little green.

"We have a time of death?" Hardin said.

"We don't have shit," Patton answered. "A patrol officer found the body when a neighbor called in about the smell. It's probably been here for days."

A pair of CSI techs were crawling all over the lawn, snapping photos and placing numbered yellow markers where they found evidence around the shed. There weren't many of the markers, unfortunately. The coroner would be here soon to haul away the body. Maybe the ME would be able to figure out who the victim was and how she ended up like this.

"Was there a padlock on the door?" Hardin said. "Did you have to cut it off to get inside?"

"No, it's kind of weird," Patton said. "It had already been cut off, we found it right next to the door." He pointed to one of the evidence markers and the generic padlock lying next to it.

"So someone had to cut off the lock in order to stow the body in here?"

"Looks like it. We're looking for the bolt cutters. Not to mention the top half of the body."

"Any sign of it at all?" Hardin asked.

"None. It's not in the house. We've got people checking dumpsters around the neighborhood."

Hardin stepped away from the closet, caught her breath, and tried to set the scene for herself. She couldn't assume right away that the victim lived in the house. But maybe she had. She was almost certain the murder had happened somewhere else, and the body moved to the utility closet later. The closet didn't have enough room for someone to cut a body through the middle, did it? The murderer would have needed a saw. Maybe even a sword.

Unless it had been done by magic.

Her rational self shied away from that explanation. It was too easy. She had to remain skeptical or she'd start attributing everything to magic and miss the real evidence. This wasn't necessarily magical, it was just odd and gruesome. She needed the ME to take a crack at the body. Once they figured out exactly what had killed the victim—and found the rest of the body—they'd be able to start looking for a murder weapon, a murder location, and a murderer.

* * *

The half a body looked slightly ridiculous laid out on a table at the morgue. The legs had been stripped, and a sheet laid over them. But that meant the whole body was under the sheet, leaving only the waist and wound visible. Half the stainless steel table remained empty and gleaming. The whole thing seemed way too clean. The morgue had a chill to it, and Hardin repressed a shiver.

"I don't know what made the cut," Alice Dominguez, the ME on the case, said. "Even with the burning and corrosion on the wound, I should find some evidence of slicing, cutting movements, or even metal shards. But there's nothing. The wound is symmetrical and even. I'd have said it was done by a guillotine, but there aren't any metal traces. Maybe it was a laser?" She shrugged, to signal that she was reaching.

"A laser—would that have cauterized the wound like that?" Hardin said.

"Maybe. Except that it wasn't cauterized. Those aren't heat burns."

Now Hardin was really confused. "This isn't helping me at all."

"Sorry. It gets worse. You want to sit down?"

"No. What is it?"

"It looks like acid burns," Dominguez said. "But the analysis says salt. Plain old table salt."

"Salt can't do that to an open wound, can it?"

"In large enough quantities salt can be corrosive on an open wound. But we're talking a lot of salt, and I didn't find that much."

That didn't answer any of Hardin's questions. She needed a cigarette. After thanking the ME, she went outside.

She kept meaning to quit smoking. She really ought to quit. But she valued these quiet moments. Standing outside, pacing a few feet back and forth with a cigarette in her hand and nothing to do but think, let her solve problems.

In her reading and research—which had been pretty scant up to this point, granted—salt showed up over and over again in superstitions, in magical practices. In defensive magic. And there it was. Maybe someone *thought* the victim was magically dangerous. Someone *thought* the victim was going to come back from the dead and used the salt to prevent that.

That information didn't solve the murder, but it might provide a motive.

Patton was waiting at her desk back at the station, just so he could present the folder to her in person. "The house belongs to Tom and Betty Arcuna. They were renting it out to a Dora Manuel. There's your victim."

Hardin opened the folder. The photo on the first page looked like it had been blown up from a passport. The woman was brown skinned, with black hair and tasteful makeup on a round face. Middle-aged, she guessed, but healthy. Frowning and unhappy for whatever reason. She might very well be the victim, but without a face or even fingerprints they'd probably have to resort to DNA testing. Unless they found the missing half. Still no luck with that.

Ms. Manuel had immigrated from the Philippines three years ago. Tom and Betty Arcuna, her cousins, had sponsored her, but they hadn't seemed to have much contact with her. They rented her the house, Manuel paid on time, and they didn't even get together for holidays. The Arcunas lived in Phoenix, Arizona, and this house was one of several they owned in Denver and rented out, mostly to Filipinos. Patton had talked to them on the phone; they had expressed shock at Manuel's demise, but had no other information to offer. "She kept to herself. We never got any complaints, and we know all the neighbors."

Hardin fired up the Internet browser on her computer and searched under "Philippines" and "magic." And got a lot of hits that had nothing to do with what she was looking for. Magic shows, as in watch me pull a rabbit out of my hat, and Magic tournaments, as in the geek card game. She added "spell" and did a little better, spending a few minutes flipping through various pages discussing black magic and hexes and the like, in both dry academic rhetoric and the sensationalist tones of superstitious evangelists. She learned that many so-called spells were actually curses involving gastrointestinal distress and skin blemishes. But she could also buy a love spell online for a hundred pesos. She didn't find anything about any magic that would slice a body clean through the middle.

Official public acknowledgement—that meant government recognition—of the existence of magic and the supernatural was recent enough that no one had developed policies about how to deal with cases involving such matters. The medical examiner didn't have a way to determine if the salt she found on the body had had a magical effect. There wasn't an official process detailing how to investigate a magical crime. The Denver PD Paranatural Unit was one of the first in the country, and Hardin—the only officer currently assigned to the unit, because she was the only one with any experience—suspected she was going to end up writing the book on some of this stuff. She still spent a lot of her time trying to convince people that any of it was real.

When she was saddled with the unit, she'd gotten a piece of advice: the real stuff stayed hidden, and had stayed hidden for a long time. Most of the information that was easy to find was a smoke screen. To find the truth, you had to keep digging. She went old school and searched the online catalog for the Denver Public Library, but didn't find a whole lot on Filipino folklore.

"What is it this time? Alligators in the sewer?"

Hardin rolled her eyes without turning her chair to look at the comedian leaning on the end of her cubicle. It was Bailey, the senior homicide detective, and he'd given her shit ever since she first walked into the bureau and said the word "werewolf" with a straight face. It didn't matter that she'd turned out to be right, and that she'd dug up a dozen previous deaths in Denver that had been attributed to dog and coyote maulings and gotten them reclassified as unsolved homicides, with werewolves as the suspected perpetrators—which ruined the bureau's solve rate. She'd done battle with vampires, and Bailey didn't have to believe it for it to be true. Hardin could at least hope that even if she couldn't solve the bizarre crimes she faced, she'd at least get brownie points for taking the jobs no one else wanted.

"How are you, Detective?" she said in monotone.

"I hear you got a live one. So to speak. Patton says he was actually happy to hand this one over to you."

"It's different all right." She turned away from the computer to face the gray-haired, softly overweight man. Three hundred and forty-nine days to retirement, he was, and kept telling them.

He craned around a little further to look at her computer screen. "A tough-nut case and what are you doing, shopping for shoes?"

She'd cultivated a smile just for situations like this. It got her through the Academy, it got her through every marksmanship test with a smart-ass instructor, it had gotten her through eight years as a cop. But one of these days, she was going to snap and take someone's head off.

"It's the twenty-first century, Bailey," she said. "Half the crooks these days knock over a liquor store and then brag about it on MySpace an hour later. You gotta keep on top of it."

He looked at her blankly. She wasn't about to explain MySpace to him. Not that he'd even dare admit to her that he didn't know or understand something. He was the big dick on campus, and she was just the girl detective.

At least she had a pretty good chance of outliving the bastards.

Donning a smile, he said, "Hey, maybe it's a vampire!" He walked away, chuckling.

If that was the worst ribbing she got today, she'd count herself lucky.

Canvassing the neighborhood could be both her most and least favorite part of an investigation. She usually learned way more than she wanted to and came away not thinking very highly of people. She'd have to stand there not saying anything while listening to people tell her over and over again that no, they never suspected anything, the suspect was always very quiet, and no, they never saw anything, they didn't know anything. All the while they wouldn't meet her gaze. They didn't want to get involved. She bet if she'd interviewed the Arcunas in person, they wouldn't have looked her in the eyes.

But this was often the very best way to track down leads, and a good witness could crack a whole case.

Patton had already talked to the neighbor who called in the smell, a Hispanic woman who lived in the house behind Manuel's. She hadn't had any more useful information, so Hardin wanted to try the more immediate neighbors.

She went out early in the evening, after work and around dinnertime, when people were more likely to be home. The neighborhood was older, a grid of narrow streets, eighty-year-old houses in various states of repair jammed in together. Towering ash and maple trees pushed up the slabs of the sidewalks with their roots. Narrow drives led to carports, or simply to the sides of the houses. Most cars parked along the curbs. A mix of lower-class residents lived here: kids living five or six to a house to save rent while they worked minimum-wage jobs; ethnic families, recent immigrants getting their starts; blue collar families struggling at the poverty line.

Dora Manuel's house still had yellow tape around the property. When she couldn't find parking on the street, Hardin broke the tape away and pulled into the narrow driveway, stopping in front of the fence to the back lot. She put the tape back up behind her car.

Across the street, a guy was on his front porch taking pictures of the house, the police tape, her. Fine, she'd start with him.

She crossed the street and walked to his porch with an easy, non-threatening stride. His eyes went wide and a little panicked anyway.

"I'm sorry, I wasn't hurting anything, I'll stop," he said, hiding the camera behind his back.

Hardin gave him a wry, annoyed smile and held up her badge. "My name's Detective Hardin, Denver PD, and I just want to ask you a few questions. That okay?"

He only relaxed a little. He was maybe in his early twenties. The house was obviously a rental, needing a good scrubbing and a coat of paint. Through the front windows she could see band posters on the living room walls. "Yeah . . . okay."

"What's your name?"

"Pete. Uh . . . Pete Teller."

"Did you know Dora Manuel?"

"That Mexican lady across the street? The one who got killed?"

"Filipino, but yes."

"No, didn't know the lady at all. Saw her sometimes."

"When was the last time you saw her?"

"Maybe a few days ago. Yeah, like four days ago, going inside the house at dinnertime."

Patton's background file said that Manuel didn't own a car. She rode the bus to her job at a dry cleaners. Pete would have seen her walking home.

"Did you see anyone else? Maybe anyone who looked like they didn't belong?"

"No, no one. Not ever. Lady kept to herself, you know?"

Yeah, she did. She asked a few more standard witness questions, and he gave the standard answers. She gave him her card and asked him to call if he remembered anything, or if he heard anything. Asked him to tell his roommates to do the same.

The family two doors south of Manuel was also Filipino. Hardin was guessing the tired woman who opened the door was the mother of a good-sized family. Kids were screaming in a back room. The woman was shorter than Hardin by a foot, brown-skinned, and her black hair was tied in a ponytail. She wore a blue T-shirt and faded jeans.

Hardin flashed her badge. "I'm Detective Hardin, Denver PD. Could I ask you a few questions?"

"Is this about Dora Manuel?"

This encouraged Hardin. At least someone around here had actually known the woman. "Yes. I'm assuming you heard what happened?"

"It was in the news," she said.

"How well did you know her?"

"Oh, I didn't, not really."

So much for the encouragement. "Did you ever speak with her? Can you tell me the last time you saw her?"

"I don't think I ever talked to her. I'm friends with Betty Arcuna, who owns the house. I knew her when she lived in the neighborhood. I kept an eye on the house for her, you know, as much as I could."

"Then did you ever see any suspicious activity around the house? Any strangers, anyone who looked like they didn't belong?"

She pursed her lips and shook her head. "No, not really, not that I remember."

A sound, like something heavy falling from a shelf, crashed from the back of the house. The woman just sighed.

"How many kids do you have?" Hardin asked.

"Five," she said, looking even more tired.

Hardin saw movement over the mother's shoulder. The woman looked. Behind her, leaning against the wall like she was trying to hide behind it, was a girl—a young woman, rather. Sixteen or seventeen. Wide-eyed, pretty. Give her another couple of years to fill out the curves and she'd be beautiful.

"This is my oldest," the woman said.

"You mind if I ask her a few questions?"

The young woman shook her head no, but her mother stepped aside. Hardin expected her to flee to the back of the house, but she didn't.

"Hi," Hardin said, trying to sound friendly without sounding condescending. "I wondered if you could tell me anything about Ms. Manuel."

"I don't know anything about her," she said. "She didn't like kids messing in her yard. We all stayed away."

"Can you remember the last time you saw her?"

She shrugged. "A few days ago maybe."

"You know anyone who had it in for her? Maybe said anything bad about her or threatened her? Sounds like the kids around here didn't like her much."

"No, nothing like that," she said.

Hardin wasn't going to get anything out of her, though the girl looked scared. Maybe she was just scared of whatever had killed Manuel. The mother gave Hardin a sympathetic look and shrugged, much like her daughter had.

Hardin got the names—Julia Martinal and her daughter Teresa. She gave them a card. "If you think of anything, let me know."

Two houses down was an older, angry white guy.

"It's about time you got here and did something about those Mexicans," he said when Hardin showed him her badge.

"I'm sorry?" Hardin said, playing dumb, seeing how far the guy would carry this.

"Those Mexican gang wars, they got no place here. That's what happened, isn't it?"

She narrowed her gaze. "Have you seen any Mexican gangs in the area? Any unusual activity, anything you think is suspicious? Drive-bys, strange people loitering?"

"Well, I don't get up in other people's business. I can't say that I saw anything. But that Mexican broad was killed, right? What else could have happened?"

"What's your name, sir?" Hardin said.

He hesitated, lips drawing tight, as if he was actually considering arguing with her or refusing to tell. "Smith," he said finally. "John Smith."

"Mr. Smith, did you ever see anyone at Dora Manuel's house? Anyone you'd be able to pick out of a line up?"

He still looked like he'd eaten something sour. "Well, no, not like that. I'm not a spy or a snitch or anything."

She nodded comfortingly. "I'm sure. Oh, and Mr. Smith? Dora Manuel was Filipina, not Mexican."

She gave him her card, as she had with the others, and asked him to call her.

Out of all the people she'd left cards with today, she bet Smith would be the one to call. And he'd have nothing useful for her.

She didn't get much out of any of the interviews.

"I'm sorry, I never even knew what her name was."

"She kept to herself, I didn't really know her."

"She wasn't that friendly."

"I don't think I was surprised to hear that she'd died."

In the end, rather than having any solid leads on what had killed her, Hardin walked away with an image of a lonely, maybe even ostracized woman with no friends, no connections, and no grief lost at her passing. People with that profile were usually pegged as the killers, not the victims.

She sat in her car for a long time, letting her mind drift, wondering which lead she'd missed and what connection she'd have to make to solve this thing. The murder wasn't random. In fact, it must have been carefully planned, considering the equipment involved. So the body had been moved, maybe. There still ought to be evidence of that at the crime scene—tire tracks, footprints, blood. Maybe the techs had come up with something while she was out here dithering.

The sun was setting, sparse streetlights coming on, their orange glow not doing much to illuminate past the trees. Not a lot of activity went on. A few lights on in a few windows. No cars moving.

She stepped out of the car and started walking.

Instead of going straight through the gate to the backyard, she went around the house and along the fence to the alley behind the houses, a narrow path mostly haunted by stray cats. She caught movement out of the corner of her eye; paused and looked, caught sight of small legs and a tail. She flushed and her heart sped up, in spite of herself. She knew it was just a cat. But her hindbrain thought of the other creatures with fur she'd seen in back alleys. The monsters.

She came into Manuel's yard through a back gate. The shed loomed before her, seeming to expand in size. She shook the image away. The only thing sinister about the shed was her knowledge of what had been found there. Other houses had back porch lights on. She could hear TVs playing. Not at Manuel's house. The lights were dark, the whole property still, as if the rest of the street had vanished, and the site existed in a bubble. Hardin's breathing suddenly seemed loud.

She couldn't see much of anything in the dark. No footprints, not a stray thread of cloth. She didn't know what she was hoping to find.

One thing she vowed she'd never do was call in a psychic to work a case. But standing in the backyard of Manuel's residence at night, she couldn't help but wonder if she'd missed something simply because it wasn't visible to the mundane eye. Could a psychic stand here and see some kind of magical aura? Maybe follow a magical trail to the person who'd committed the crime?

The real problem was—how would she know she was hiring an actual psychic? Hardin was ready to believe just about anything, but that wouldn't help her figure out what had happened here.

The next day, she made a phone call. She had at least one more resource to try.

Hardin came to the supernatural world as a complete neophyte, and she had to look for advice wherever she could, no matter how odd the source, or how distasteful. Friendly werewolves, for example. Or convicted felons.

Cormac Bennett styled himself a bounty hunter specializing in the supernatural. He freely admitted he was a killer, though he claimed to only kill monsters—werewolves, vampires, and the like. A judge had recently agreed with him, at least about the killer part, and sentenced Bennett to four years for manslaughter. It meant that Hardin now had someone on hand who might be able to answer her questions. She'd requested the visit and asked that he not be told it was her because she didn't want him to say no to the meeting. They'd had a couple of run-ins—truthfully, she was a little disappointed that she hadn't been the one who got to haul him in on charges of attempted murder at the very least.

When he sat down and saw her through the glass partition, he muttered, "Christ."

"Hello," she said, rather pleased at his reaction. "You look terrible, if you don't mind me saying." It wasn't that he looked terrible; he looked like any other con, rough around the edges, tired and seething. He had shadows under his eyes. That was a lot different than he'd looked the last time she'd seen him, poised and hunting.

"What do you want?"

"I have to be blunt, Mr. Bennett," she said. "I'm here looking for advice."

"Not sure I can help you."

Maybe this had been a mistake. "You mean you're not sure you *will*. Maybe you should let me know right now if I'm wasting my time. Save us both the trouble."

"Did Kitty tell you to talk to me?"

As a matter of fact, Kitty Norville had suggested it. Kitty the werewolf. Hardin hadn't believed it either, until she saw it. It was mostly Kitty's fault Hardin had started down this path. "She said you might know things."

"Kitty's got a real big mouth," Bennett said wryly.

"How did you two even end up friends?" Hardin said. "You wanted to kill her."

"It wasn't personal."

"Then, what? It got personal?" Hardin never understood why Kitty had just let the incident go. She hadn't wanted to press charges. And now they were what, best friends?

"Kitty has a way of growing on you."

Hardin smiled, just a little, because she knew what he was talking about. Kitty had a big mouth, and it made her charming rather than annoying. Most of the time.

She pulled a folder from her attaché case, drew out the eight-by-ten crime-scene photos, and held them up to the glass. "I have a body. Well, half a body. It's pretty spectacular and it's not in any of the books."

Bennett studied the photos a long time, and she waited, watching him carefully. He didn't seem shocked or disgusted. Of course he didn't. He was curious. Maybe even admiring? She tried not to judge. This was like Manuel's shed; she only saw Bennett as sinister because she knew what he was capable of.

"What the hell?" he said finally. "How are they even still standing? Are they attached to something?"

"No," she said. "I have a set of free-standing legs attached to a pelvis, detached cleanly above the fifth lumbar vertebra. The wound is covered with a layer of table salt that appears to have caused the flesh to scorch. Try explaining that one to my captain."

"No thanks," he said. "That's your job. I'm just the criminal reprobate."

"So you've never seen anything like this."

"Hell, no."

"Have you ever heard of anything like this?" She'd set the photos flat on the table. He was still studying them.

"No. You have any leads at all?"

"No. We've ID'd the body. She was Filipina, a recent immigrant. We're still trying to find the other half of the body. There has to be another half somewhere, right?"

He sat back, shaking his head. "I wouldn't bet on it."

"You're sure you don't know anything? You're not just yanking my chain out of spite?"

"I get nothing out of yanking your chain. Not here."

Scowling, she put the photos back in her case. "Well, this was worth a try. Sorry for wasting your time."

"I've got nothing but time."

He was yanking her chain, she was sure of it. "If you think of anything, if you get any bright ideas, call me." As the guard arrived to escort him back to his cell, she said, "And get some sleep. You look awful."

Hardin was at her desk, looking over the latest reports from the crime lab. Nothing. They hadn't had rain, the ground was hard, so no footprints. No blood. No fibers. No prints on the shed. Someone wearing gloves had cut off the lock in order to stuff half the body inside—then didn't bother to lock the shed again. The murderer had simply closed the door and vanished.

The phone rang, and she answered, frustrated and surly. "Detective Hardin."

"Will you accept the charges from Cormac Bennett at the Colorado Territorial Correctional Facility?"

It took her a moment to realize what that meant. She was shocked. "Yes, I will. Hello? Bennett?"

"*Manananggal,*" he said. "Don't ask me how to spell it."

She wrote down the word, sounding it out as best she could. The Internet would help her find the correct spelling. "Okay, but what is it?"

"Filipino version of the vampire."

That made no sense. But really, did that matter? It made as much sense as anything else. It was a trail to follow. "Hot damn," she said, suddenly almost happy. "The victim was from the Philippines. It fits. So the suspect was Filipino, too? Do Filipino vampires eat entire torsos or what?"

"No," he said. "That body *is* the vampire, the *manananggal*. You're looking for a vampire hunter."

Her brain stopped at that one. "Excuse me?"

"These creatures, these vampires—they detach the top halves of their bodies to hunt. They're killed when someone sprinkles salt on the bottom half. They can't return to reattach to their legs, and they die at sunrise. If they're anything like European vampires, the top half disintegrates. You're never going to find the rest of the body."

Well. She still wouldn't admit that any of this made sense, but the pieces fit. The bottom half, the salt burns. Never mind—she was still looking for a murderer here, right?

"Detective?" Cormac said.

"Yeah, I'm here," she said. "This fits all the pieces we have. Looks like I have some reading to do to figure out what really happened."

He managed to sound grim. "Detective, you might check to see if there've been a higher than usual number of miscarriages in the neighborhood."

"Why?"

"I used the term *vampire* kind of loosely. This thing eats the blood of fetuses. Sucks them through the mother's navel while she sleeps."

She almost hung up on him because it was too much. What was it Kitty sometimes said? Just when you thought you were getting a handle on the supernatural, just when you thought you'd seen it all, something even more unbelievable came along.

"You're kidding." She sighed. "So, what—this may have been a revenge killing? Who's the victim here?"

"You'll have to figure that one out yourself."

"Isn't that always the way?" she muttered. "Hey—now that we know you really were holding out on me, what made you decide to remember?"

"Look, I got my own shit going on and I'm not going to try to explain it to you."

She was pretty sure she didn't really want to know. "Fine. Okay. But thanks for the tip, anyway."

"Maybe you could put in a good word for me," he said.

She supposed she owed him the favor. Maybe she would after she got the whole story of how he ended up in prison in the first place. Then again, she pretty much thought he belonged there. "I'll see what I can do."

She hung up, found a phone book, and started calling hospitals.

Hardin called every hospital in downtown Denver. Every emergency room, every OB/Gyn, free clinic and even Planned Parenthood. She had to do a lot of arguing.

"I'm not looking for names, I'm just looking for numbers. Rates. I want to know if there's been an increase in the number of miscarriages in the downtown Denver area over the last three years. No, I'm not from the EPA. Or from *Sixty Minutes*. This isn't an exposé, I'm Detective Hardin with Denver PD and I'm investigating a case. *Thank* you."

It took some of them a couple of days to get back to her. When they did, they seemed just as astonished as she was: Yes, miscarriage rates had tripled over the last three years. There had actually been a small decline in the local area's birth rate.

"Do I need to worry?" one doctor asked her. "Is there something in the water? What is this related to?"

She hesitated about what to tell him. She could tell the truth—and he would never believe her. It would take too long to explain, to try to persuade him. "I'm sorry, sir, I can't talk about it until the case is wrapped up. But there's nothing to worry about. Whatever was causing this has passed, I think."

He didn't sound particularly comforted, and neither was she. Because what else was out there? What other unbelievable crisis would strike next?

Hardin knocked on the Martinal's front door. Julia Martinal, the mother, answered again. On seeing the detective, her expression turned confused. "Yes?"

"I just have one more question for you, Mrs. Martinal. Are you pregnant?"

"No." She sounded offended, looking Hardin up and down, like how dare she.

Hardin took a deep breath and carried on. "I'm sorry for prying into your personal business, but I have some new information. About Dora Manuel."

Julia Martinal's eyes grew wide, and her hand gripped the edge of the door. Hardin thought she was going to slam it closed.

Hardin said, "Have you had any miscarriages in the last couple of years?"

At that, the woman's lips pursed. She took a step back. "I know what you're talking about, and that's crazy. It's crazy! It's just old stories. Sure, nobody liked Dora Manuel, but that doesn't make her a—a—"

So Hardin didn't have to explain it.

The daughter, Teresa Martinal, appeared where she had before, lingering at the edge of the foyer, staring out with suspicion. Her hand rested on her stomach. That gesture was the answer.

Hardin bowed her head to hide a wry smile. "Teresa? Can you come out and answer a few questions?"

Julia moved to stand protectively in front of her daughter. "You don't have to say anything, Teresa. This woman's crazy."

"Teresa, are you pregnant?" Hardin asked, around Julia's defense.

Teresa didn't answer. The pause drew on, and on. Her mother stepped aside, astonished, studying her daughter. "Teresa? Are you? Teresa!"

The young woman's expression became hard, determined. "I'm not sorry."

"You spied on her," Hardin said, to Teresa, ignoring her mother. "You knew what she was, you knew what that meant, and you spied to find out where she left her legs. You waited for the opportunity, then you broke into the shed. You knew the stories. You knew what to do."

"Teresa?" Mrs. Martinal said as exclamation, her disbelief growing.

The girl still wouldn't say anything.

Hardin continued. "We've only been at this a few days, but we'll find something. We'll find the bolt cutters you used and match them to the cut marks on the padlock. We'll match the salt in your cupboard with the salt on the body. We'll make a case for murder. But if you cooperate, I can help you. I can make a pretty good argument that this was self-defense. What do you say?"

Hardin was making wild claims—the girl had been careful and the physical evidence was scant. They might not find the bolt cutters, and the salt thing was pure television. And while Hardin might scrounge together the evidence and some witness testimony, she might never convince the DA's office that this had really happened.

Teresa looked stricken, like she was trying to decide if Hardin was right, and if they had the evidence. If a jury would believe that a meek, pregnant teenager like her could even murder another person. It would be a hard sell—but Hardin was hoping this would never make it to court. She wasn't stretching the truth about the self-defense plea. By some accounts, Teresa probably deserved a medal. But Hardin wouldn't go that far.

In a perfect world, Hardin would be slapping cuffs on Dora Manuel, not Teresa. But until the legal world caught up with the shadow world, this would have to do.

Teresa finally spoke in a rush. "I had to do it. You know I had to do it. My mother's been pregnant twice since Ms. Manuel moved in. They all died. I heard her talking. She knew what it was. She knew what was happening. I had to stop it." She had both hands laced in a protective barrier over her stomach now. She wasn't showing much yet. Just a swell she could hold in her hands.

Julia Martinal covered her mouth. Hardin couldn't imagine which part of this shocked her more—that her daughter was pregnant, or a murderer.

Hardin imagined trying to explain this to the captain. She managed to get the werewolves pushed through and on record, but this was so much weirder. At least, not having grown up with the stories, it was. But the case was solved. On the other hand, she could just walk away. Without Teresa's confession, they'd never be able to close the case. Hardin had a hard time thinking of Teresa as a murderer—she wasn't like Cormac Bennett. Hardin could just walk away. But not really.

In the end, Hardin called it in and arrested Teresa. But her next call was to the DA about what kind of deal they could work out. There had to be a way to work this out within the system. Get Teresa off on probation on a minor charge. There had to be a way to drag the shadow world, kicking and screaming, into the light.

Somehow, Hardin would figure it out.

Carrie Vaughn is the author of the *New York Times* bestselling series of novels about a werewolf named Kitty, the most recent of which is *Kitty Rocks the House.* She's also the author of young adult novels (*Voices of Dragons, Steel*) and contemporary fantasy (*Discord's Apple, After the Golden Age*). A graduate of the Odyssey Fantasy Writing Workshop, she's a contributor to the Wild Cards series of shared world superhero books edited by George R. R. Martin, and her short stories have appeared in numerous magazines and anthologies. An Air Force brat, she survived her nomadic childhood and managed to put down roots in Boulder, Colorado. Visit her at www.carrievaughn.com.

The Case: *Hilda Beyers, a junior at Rutgers, has been missing for four months . . . Sarah Culpepper thinks her husband, Avery, is cheating on her . . . but that's far from all . . .*

The Investigator: *Sam Grant, a New York City private investigator, former cop, and decorated veteran of World War I.*

MORTAL BAIT

Richard Bowes

When I think of death what comes to mind is the feel of an ice-cold knife racing up my leg like I'm a letter being sliced open. When that happens in my nightmares I wake up. In real life, just before the blade of ice reached my heart, the medic got to me where I lay in that bloody field at Aisne-Marne, tied and tightened a tourniquet above my left knee and stopped the flow before all my blood ran onto the grass.

That memory of my war came out of nowhere as I sat in my little office in Greenwich Village on a sunny October afternoon. It felt like someone had riffled through my memories and pulled out that one. Beings that my Irish grandmother called the Gentry and the Fair Folk walk this world and can do things like that to mortals. A shiver ran through me.

My name's Sam Grant and I'm a private investigator. Logic and deduction come into my line of work. So do memory and intuition. My grandmother always said a sudden shiver meant someone had just stepped on the spot where your grave would be.

I could have told myself it was that or a stray draft of cold air. But I'd felt this before and knew what it meant. Some elf or fairy had shuffled my memories like a card deck. And that wasn't supposed to happen to me.

At that moment I was writing a letter to my contact, Bertrade le Claire. It was Bertrade who had worked a magic to shield me.

An intruder would see her image, her long dark hair, beautiful wide eyes—a face that seemed like something off a movie screen. She wore a jacket of red and gold and a look that said "Step back!" She was a law officer in the Kingdom Beneath the Hill.

The letter I was writing concerned new clients, the Beyers, a couple from Menlo Park, New Jersey. He worked for an insurance company; she taught Sunday School. In my office she talked; he studied the photos I keep on my wall and they both clung to hope and the arms of their chairs.

They were the parents of Hilda, a junior at Rutgers and currently a missing person. Hilda, according to her mother, was a sensitive girl who wrote poetry, was due to graduate in June of 1952 and become an English teacher. She'd had a few boyfriends over the years but nothing serious as far as anyone knew. Not the kind of young lady to run off on a whim. But four months back it seems that she did.

While his wife talked, Mr. Beyer looked at the signed photo of Mayor LaGuardia with his honor mugging for the camera as he shook my hand and thanked me for civilian services to New York City during the Second War to End All Wars.

The one where I'm getting kissed by Marshal Foch I leave in the drawer because some guys in this neighborhood might get the wrong idea.

But I display Douglas MacArthur, executive officer of the Rainbow Division in 1918, pinning a Distinguished Service Cross on the tunic of a soldier on crutches. I'm not that easy to make out. But Colonel MacArthur with his soft cap at a jaunty angle and a riding crop under his arm, you'd recognize anywhere. I figure it's got to be worth something that I served under Dugout Doug and lived to tell about it.

Mrs. Beyer told me how the New Jersey cops couldn't find a lead on Hilda. After other private eyes struck out, my name came up.

Mrs. Beyer paused then said, "We have heard that she could have gone to another . . . " and trailed off.

" . . . realm," I offered and she nodded. "It's possible," I said. Mr. Beyer's eyes widened at hearing a man who'd been decorated by MacArthur say he believed in fairies.

After that we closed the deal quickly. My initial fee is $250. It's stiff but I think I'm worth it: especially since I wore my good suit and a fresh starched shirt for the occasion. I didn't promise them their daughter back. I did promise I'd do everything I could to find her. On their way out, I shook hands with him. Put my left hand on hers for reassurance.

Playing baseball as a kid, I was a switch hitter and I could field and throw with both my right and my left. I even learned to write with either hand. These days the left's the only thing about me that still works the way everything once did. And I tend to save it for special occasions.

In the Beyer's presence I walked tall. But I still have metal fragments in my knee. With the clients gone I limped a bit on my way back to the desk.

I took a sheet of paper and a plain envelope out of the desk, stuck in a high school yearbook photo of Hilda, scribbled a few lines about the case, dated and signed it. Then I felt the intrusion and added the PS, "Some stray elf or fairy just got into my memories." On the envelope I wrote Bertrade's full name and her address in The Kingdom.

The phone rang and a woman said, "Sam," and nothing more. She sounded tired, flat.

"Annie." Anne Toomey is the wife of my buddy Jim. He and I were in France together. "How's Jimmy?" Since she was calling I knew the answer. Knew what she was going to ask.

"Not feeling great, Sam. We wondered if you could handle the Culpepper case today."

"We" meant that Anne was doing this on her own.

"Sure I'll do it. Nothing changed from Jim's report yesterday right?"

"You're a saint, Sam."

I picked up the phone and dialed the Up To the Minute Answering Service. Gracie was on duty. Behind her I could hear half a dozen other girls at switchboards.

"Doll," I said, "I'll be out for most of the afternoon. Anyone wants me I'll be back after six."

Under her operator voice Gracie talks Brooklyn like the Queen speaks English. "Be careful, you," she said. She gets her ideas of private detectives from paperback novels.

We've never met. Going down in the elevator I thought of Gracie as being maybe in her mid-thirties—which seems young to me now. I imagined her as blond and nicely rounded sitting at the switchboard in a revealing silk robe.

I imagined the other Up To the Minute ladies sitting around similarly dressed. This is the privilege of a divorced and decorated veteran who once got kissed by a French Field Marshall.

My office is on the fifth floor. With a couple of errands to do, I crossed the vestibule and stepped outside. They tore down the elevated line before World War II but better than a decade later Sixth Avenue still looked naked in the October afternoon sunlight.

Across the way, the women's prison stood like a black tower as all around it paddy wagons unloaded their cargo. Some parents find out their daughters have run off to Fairyland. Others discover them at the Women's House of Detention.

They use the old Jefferson Market Court House next door to the prison as the Police Academy now. Sergeant Danny Hogan was showing a couple of dozen cadets in their gray and green uniforms how to write out parking tickets.

Hogan and I did foot patrol in the old Fourteenth Precinct back when we were both starting out. He spotted me and rolled his tired eyes.

As I headed towards the subway I saw the headlines and front pages of the afternoon papers. My old pal MacArthur had landed at Inchon a couple of weeks before. Maps of the Korean Peninsula showed black arrows pointing in all directions.

On the subway stairs, I felt something like the opposite of forgetting. A stray sprite with nothing better to do had tried to probe me. The mental image of Bertrade appeared and whatever it was immediately broke contact. I continued down the stairs, stuck a dime in the slot and got on the uptown A train.

Early in life I heard about fairies. My mother's mother saw leprechauns in the coal cellar and elves under the bed. Mostly I ignored her once I turned into a hard guy at the age of eight.

My mother was born and raised in the Irish stretch of Greenwich Village. She learned stenography, got a job in an import/export office, and married late. Sam Grant Senior was part Irish and not very Catholic. He had been on the road as a salesman for many years before my mother forced him to settle down. I was the only kid.

I remember my old man a little sloshed one night telling me about having been on the night train to Cincinnati with "the crack women's apparel salesman on that route."

This guy was very smashed and told the old man how he'd gone down the path to Fairyland when was young, stayed there for a few years, learned a few tricks. My father told me, "He said some of the ones there could read your mind like a book."

I heard about The Kingdom Beneath the Hill a few more times over the years. As a legend it was slightly more believable than Santa Claus and a bit less likely than the fabled speakeasy that only served imported booze.

Then almost ten years ago, an elf almost killed me and a couple of fairies saved my life. One of them was a young lady named Bertrade.

The two errands I had were within a few blocks of each other. I rode the A train up to Penn Station and used the exit on Thirty-third and Eighth. First I went to the General Post Office. The place is like a Mail Cathedral. I climbed the wide stairs and the knee complained.

Inside under the high vaulted ceilings were big posters commemorating the pilots who had died flying mail planes thirty years back. I walked past the window that said "Overseas Mail" to the small window that said nothing.

It was there that I always mailed my letters to the Kingdom. The man on duty had a slight crease on the left side of his head—a veteran of something I thought. I'd spoken to him a couple of times, asked him questions, and never got more than a shrug or a shake or nod of the head.

He took the letter. Right then another mind touched mine, saw the image of Bertrade that I flashed and bounced away.

The clerk eyes widened. He'd caught some of it too. I took back the letter, picked up a pen and wrote, "Urgent—contact!" on the envelope. The clerk nodded, stuck a stamp I'd never seen before, one with a falcon in flight on it, turned and put it down a slot behind him.

"They'll have it by midnight," he said in an accent I couldn't catch. "Keep your head down. Tall elves are questing today." Then he stepped away from the window.

I waited for a minute for him to come back. When he didn't I turned and walked the length of the two-block-long lobby all the way to Thirty-first Street. Maybe it was just an elf lost and a stranger in the big city who kept trying to bust into my head, and I was overacting. Maybe I was lonely and wanted to see Bertrade.

Going down stairs was tougher on my knee than going up stairs. I walked two blocks south on my errand for Jim and Anne. Thinking it was good to have a simple assignment to occupy my mind I bought a late edition of the *Journal American*. It was 4:35. Some people were already heading for the subway.

Just west of Sixth Avenue on the south side of Thirtieth Street stood the Van Neiman, a nondescript office building. Across the street was a luncheonette. The only other customer was hunched over his paper; the counterman and waitress were cleaning up.

I ordered coffee, which was old and tired at this time of day, and sat where I could await the appearance of Avery J. Culpepper, CPA. His wife, Sarah, a jealous lady out in Queens was convinced that he was stepping out on her. Private investigators in one-man offices like Jim Toomey and me need to form alliances with other guys in similar circumstances.

For the two of us it went beyond that. In France I was the one who got to smell the mustard gas, take out the machine gun nest, and get my leg chewed up. For me the real war lasted about two weeks. I got decorated and never fired another shot for Uncle Sam.

Jimmy passed unharmed right up through Armistice Day, won few medals, got to see every horror there was to see. I was hard to deal with when I got back, and my marriage to the girl I'd left behind only lasted as long as it did because she was very Catholic.

But Jim still woke up at night screaming. It drove Anne crazy and it broke her heart but she stuck with him. For a while things got better. Lately they seemed to have gotten worse.

I thought about that as Avery J. Culpepper, wearing a light gray suit, a dark felt hat, carrying a briefcase and looking just like the photos his wife had supplied came through the revolving door of the Van Neiman Building. A punctual guy Mr. Culpepper: in his late thirties and in better shape than your average philanderer.

This was the first time I'd tailed him. Twice before Jim Toomey had followed Culpepper and ended up riding the crowded F train all the way out to Forest Hills. When Jimmy talked to me about it on the phone even that routine assignment had him ready to jump out of his skin.

The time with me was a little different. Mr. C came out the door and headed west along Thirtieth Street. I followed him for a few blocks through the rush hour crowds pouring out of offices and garment factories.

He turned south on Ninth Avenue then turned west again on Twenty-ninth. These blocks had warehouses and garages, body shops, but also some rundown apartment houses. Here the crowds heading east for the subways were longshoremen, workers from the import/export warehouses. I stayed on the other side of the street, kept an eye on him and watched the sky, which was getting dark and cloudy.

Culpepper crossed Tenth Avenue. A long freight train rolled over the elevated bridge halfway down the block. On the North corner of the avenue was an apartment house that must once have been a bit ritzy when this was mostly residential but now looked run down and out of place. That's where he turned and went in.

I glanced over as I passed to make sure he wasn't lingering in the entryway, waiting to pop out and give me the slip. As I did, a light went on up on the third floor. I noted it and wondered if that's where he was. Then I continued walking till I was under the train tracks. Already the streets and sidewalks were getting empty.

At the end of the next block, beyond Twelfth Avenue, was a pier with a tired-looking freighter moored and beyond that the river. A string of barges each with its little captain's shack went by pulled by a tug.

It was growing dark and all the warmth had been in the sun. I paused and turned like I'd forgotten something. Culpepper had not come out of the apartment house.

I crossed the street then walked back to the building he'd gone in. I spotted no one watching me. The outer door was open. One side of the entry hall was lined with mailboxes—twenty-four of them. I took out my notebook and copied the names. Many times when the husband strays it's with someone the wife already knows.

The third floor was where I'd seen a light go on. So I gave those mailboxes my special attention. Apartment #15 in particular had a recently installed nameplate. *Mimi White* it read. If that's where Culpepper was, the name seemed too good to be true.

Somebody upstairs had the news on the radio. In the first floor back, the record of "If I Knew You Were Coming, I'd Have Baked a Cake" got played a few times.

As I finished copying the names, an old lady came in carrying an armload of groceries. Like the building itself she looked like she'd seen better days. I held the door for her, said my name was Tracy, that I was from the National Insurance Company, and was looking for a Mr. Jameson who was listed as living at this address in apartment #15.

She thought for a moment then said #15 had been occupied for years by an Asian couple. They had moved out and it had stayed empty for a while. A young lady had moved in just recently. I thanked her and noted that.

As she headed upstairs, I heard footsteps and voices coming down. I went outside, crossed the street, turned and walked slowly back towards Tenth Avenue. I noticed the third floor light was off.

When I paused on the corner I saw the couple. Mr. Culpepper had left his briefcase upstairs. The lady he was with wore a short camel hair coat, a nice black hat set on her blond hair and high heels. She looked like her name could easily be Mimi and that you could take her places.

Culpepper glanced neither left nor right as they walked to the corner and he hailed a cab. In my experience, a guy stepping out with a good-looking woman usually wants to see who else notices. Culpepper apparently was made of sterner stuff.

Walking back across town, I was amazed at how easy this assignment was and wondered why that bothered me. I'd detected no presence of the Gentry in the last couple of hours. That probably meant the one or ones I'd felt earlier had found whoever they were looking for.

Or maybe they had discovered I was right where I was supposed to be and doing what they wanted me to. Being involved with the Fair Folk had always left me feeling like a dollar chip in a very big game.

I remembered a face, elongated and a little blurred, that I'd once seen. It was a tall elf with a smile that said, "How stupid these mortals are."

On the A train downtown, I got a seat and thought over that first time I felt an alien presence and how close I came to dying from it.

In '41 I did undercover work, none of it strictly official. My old regiment was the 69th, "The Fighting Irish," and our colonel was Donovan—the one they called "Wild Bill."

Later he was the guy who started the OSS and became the U.S. intelligence chief in World War II. But even before that war he had connections in Washington and an interest in foreign espionage in New York City. He got to do something about it.

The colonel remembered me. I got called down to his office on Wall Street. Right then my marriage was over and there was a limit to how long the wedding of the Police Department and me was going to last.

So, I got seconded to Wild Bill along with half a dozen other chewed up old vets on the force. Most of what we investigated turned out to be minor stuff: crazy little Krauts up in Yorkville who wore Kaiser Wilhelm helmets and sent out ham radio reports about freighters leaving the port of New York, German bars out in New Hyde Park on Long Island where the neighbors reported the patrons said "*Sieg Heil*," gave the Nazi salute, and had pictures of Hitler up above the bar.

Rumors and stories about mysterious strangers came in from all over the city. We went crazy trying to keep up with them. Then we stumbled on a sleeper operation out on the Brooklyn waterfront. They were accumulating operatives, waiting for the great day when we'd be at war and they could start blowing up bridges. We nabbed a couple of them. But the rest melted away.

Right after that a call came in one night about activity on a pier in Red Hook. We were stretched thin. I had no backup. Maybe I was tired and that made me careless. Maybe part of me wanted to use up whatever leftover life I had. But I went out there without even a driver.

The one who'd made the call must have dreamed about someone like me showing up: a dumb asshole with plenty of information about Wild Bill and his band of veterans. The gate on the street was open. A long wooden shed stood on the pier. A dim light shone in a window. I knocked. Nothing. I tried the door and it swung open. A light shone somewhere at the end of an empty two hundred foot shed.

I took a step inside. Someone had me by the throat and started to choke me. I spun around. No one was behind me. I drew my .38. Something knocked me flat and the gun fell on the floor. My arm could as well have gone with it. I couldn't feel it, couldn't make it move.

That long face with that amused smile flickered. It wasn't a thing I saw with my eyes. It was inside my head. And I felt every bloody memory get sucked out of me: Colonel Donovan, the other cases I'd worked on, friends and family, the telephone number of a waitress I was seeing, my batting average when I played twilight baseball as a kid in 1914.

When the one that had me found all it wanted, my lungs stopped, my lights started going out. I wasn't coming back, and thought I was stupid enough that I probably deserved to die. But to go like this pissed me off royally.

A little later I came to and found myself in a movie. The light was dim and this woman and guy, tall and slim, who looked like the stars of this movie, crouched over me, elegant and seeming to flicker slightly around the edges.

As that came into my mind they looked at each other and smiled. I realized they knew what I saw and thought. Her name was Bertrade and his was Darnel. I knew all that without being told. Still being mostly numb probably made everything easier to accept.

"You'll be well," she said. There was an accent I couldn't place. "We have taken care of your friend."

Bertrade turned her head and somehow I had a glimpse of what she saw. The one who'd attacked me, a tall guy with his head shaved, sat on the floor, leaned against the wall glassy eyed. I understood they had him under a kind of spell.

"An elf on a mission," Darnel said, "And a mutual enemy." I knew without them speaking that they were Fey, loyal subjects of the King Beneath the Hill. They were lovers, tourists in the city. Even half in shock I knew that the first was true and the second was a cover. They were operatives.

Things weren't good between their people and The King of Elfland. My city, my world was a kind of buffer between the two countries. Elfland favored Germany in the war going on in Europe.

They'd been watching our elfin friend when I showed up and they nailed him as he smothered me. From thinking this was a movie, I gradually decided it was a dream and a crazy one. I tried to push myself up.

As a kid I'd thought I was right handed. Then I broke some fingers when I was maybe twelve and learned I was better with my left. Now it was like the left arm was gone. I fell back and banged my head. "I'm useless," I said.

They touched my memories of my short, bad war and long lousy marriage. She frowned and shook her head at my misfortunes. "I'd want you to be in any unit where I served," he said. First Darnel and then Bertrade touched my dead arm, quietly spoke words I didn't understand. The two said good-bye and that we'd meet again. Then they were gone and the elf with them.

Feeling came back and my arm was better than new. I never told anyone else what had happened that night. Walking up Sixth Avenue to the Bigelow Building ten years later it felt like a movie and a dream.

I let myself into my office, sat down and called the answering service. It was night now and Gracie was off duty. The young lady who answered gave me a few messages. A call about a case that was going nowhere, one from somebody who wanted to sell me things, a couple of calls from people who wanted me to pay them: all calls that were going to wait.

Then there was a message from Anne Toomey asking me to call. I looked over my case notes, scribbled a few more details, and dialed the Toomey's number. I let it ring three times and three more to be sure. They didn't have an answering service and I decided they could wait until tomorrow.

Instead I went out and had a bite to eat and a drink or two at McNulty's where the cops go. After that I spent some more of the Beyers' fee at Moe's on Third Street where the cops and the hookers go. I finally settled in at the Cedar Tavern over on University Place because Lacy Duveen who tends bar there would rather talk to me than listen to painters arguing.

Lacy got his nickname for working over Tiger Shaughnessy's face with the laces of his gloves after Tiger hit him in the groin during a preliminary bout at the Garden. He and I go back to when we played pick-up ball games on the East River as kids.

We talked about the time he was catching, and all the way from deep center I tossed out a skinny Italian guy at home plate. It was twilight baseball, the light was fading and the other guy claimed I hadn't thrown anything and that Lacy had pulled a ball out of his pocket. In fact I'd thrown a perfect left-handed strike right over the plate. Naturally, it ended in a fight that we won.

Next morning I woke up in my room with that throw on my mind. I've awakened in worse shape and there was still a bit of the morning left. I'd had a dream of Bertrade that got away from me as I grabbed for it.

Out the window I saw it was a chill drizzling day on Cornelia Street. When I had washed and shaved and dressed, I put on my trench coat and wide-brimmed fedora.

When I came downstairs Mrs. Palatino, the landlady, had her door on the first floor open and her television on as usual. She liked to show off that TV. Some guy in a chef's hat was chopping celery and talking in a French accent.

Mrs. Palatino knew my late mother from church and that's why she rented to me even though I'm not Italian. She sat on the couch in her robe and slippers and looked at me long and hard. This was a woman who thought the worst of everyone and never saw anything that made her doubt her judgment.

"You decided to dress like a detective today," she said, like she couldn't decide why this was wrong. I nodded and tipped my hat. Mr. Palatino died some years ago. I pegged him as a coward who took the easy way out.

On the way to my office I thought about Bertrade and the dream and how in it she had told me some things I couldn't quite remember.

For some years after that encounter in Red Hook in '41, I didn't see Bertrade. When she reappeared she was still beautiful and young despite being a couple of decades older than me. But she looked maybe frayed and Darnel wasn't with her.

They had both served in something called The War of the Elf King's Daughter—fairies versus elves. At one time the idea would have made me laugh. But not after Bertrade let me see a bit of what she'd gone through.

Her war occurred at about the same time as WWII and looked in some ways just as bad. Spells and magic: getting tortured to the point of suicide by hideous nightmares, seeing friends with enemy minds in theirs who tore their own throats out. Darnel hadn't come back. He wasn't dead because the Fair Folk never die. "Lost to this world," was how she put it and I knew it made her sad.

For other guys maybe it was Garbo or Hayworth they thought about. For me, ever since that first encounter, it had been Bertrade. And whenever she came back here and wanted to be with me it was like a daydream became real.

She knew more, had seen more, than anybody I'd ever met. Something she once showed me which I thought about as I walked to work that day was a whole unit of trolls, ordinary soldiers like I had been if you ignored how they looked, caught by tall elves. Rifles fell from their hands as their minds were seized and twisted by the Gentry. They fell dead wiped out without a sound made or a shot fired.

Weapons were beneath the Fair Folk she told me. You could walk up to one, pull out a gun and shoot him, provided you could somehow keep all thought of what you were about to do out of your mind.

At the Bigelow Building I went into the big pharmacy on the first floor, got a few black coffees to go and took those upstairs, drinking one on the elevator. It was still just short of noon. My energy and purpose amazed me.

The mail had already been delivered: a couple of bills, a few flyers and a report on the whereabouts of a bum who had skipped out on the alimony and child support he owed a client of mine. All but the last got tossed in the wastebasket. I'd had nothing from Bertrade except maybe that foggy dream.

I called Up to the Minute and got Gracie. "You have six calls including four so far this morning from Anne Toomey." She paused. "Mr. Grant, this is none of my business. But a couple of times a man, I think it was her husband, was yelling at her. It sounded bad."

"Thanks." This time Jim must really have jumped the rails.

I hung up and made the call. Anne answered halfway through the first ring. She spoke softly like she didn't want someone to overhear. "Sam, I'm sorry I didn't get back to you." She did sound very sorry. "And I'm going to have to ask if you'll do it again today. I promise I'll get . . . "

"I was going to volunteer. How's Jim? The operator says he was shouting at you."

"He's quiet right now. Sam, this whole case is strange. I've tried half a dozen times to call Mrs. Culpepper, you know while her husband's at work. No answer. They're not listed in the telephone book. Jim's the only one she's talked to. And he's . . . not good. Last night he was talking, yelling at someone who wasn't there. And he told me someone was in his head. He's been saying that for the last couple of days. It's never been this bad."

"Was it more than just shouting at you, Anne?"

She said, "This is what I've been afraid of."

"Anne, I'll be out there as fast as I can. Is there some place you can go meanwhile?

"My aunt's a few blocks over."

"Go there right now. Don't talk to Jim. Just leave. Understand?"

Anne said she did. I doubted her.

Then I made a call to Police Chaplain Dineen. Young private Kevin Dineen served as an altar boy in France for the famous Father Duffy of the 69th. He came back home and found a vocation. It was said that Father Dineen spiked the sacramental wine with gin and he was reputed to get a bit frisky with the widows he comforted.

But it was Dineen who got called when O'Malley at the Ninth Precinct, a fellow vet, was at the Thanksgiving table eating mashed potatoes with the barrel of his loaded revolver while all his children looked on. Dineen got O'Malley to hand the weapon over and had the kids smiling at the game he and their daddy were playing.

When I explained as much of the situation as he needed to know all Dineen asked was, "Do we need an ambulance or a squad car?"

"Both," I said. Before going downstairs to meet the chaplain I took my service .38 and holster out of the locked drawer, cleaned and loaded the revolver, buckled on the holster. It seemed I remembered doing the same thing in my dream the night before.

I called Up to the Minute and told Gracie I wouldn't be back until late and not to wait up. She laughed. As I adjusted my hat and went out the door, I remembered something from the dream. Bertrade lay among pillows and bedclothes, looked right at me and spoke about bait and traps.

Ten minutes later Father Dineen and I were in his brand new Oldsmobile four-door headed through the drizzle for Windsor Terrace in Brooklyn. His car had a siren and a flashing light. We went through red lights; traffic cops waved us on at intersections. Dineen was on the radio to a squad car out in Park Slope as we crossed the Bridge with a motorcycle escort and he cursed because we weren't going faster.

Anger was what I felt: anger at the one who had maybe screwed around with Toomey's mind and caused Anne pain. They weren't even the object of this operation. I probably wasn't either. It struck me that they and I were just bait in some game the Gentry were playing.

When we arrived at Sixteenth Street, a crowd had gathered in the drizzle and homicide was out in force. Anne Toomey must have tried one last time to talk to Jim. She was at the bottom of the stairs. Jim had stood halfway up when he shot her twice in the face before pumping two shots into his open mouth.

For the young homicide detective who took my statement this was open-and-shut murder/suicide. The second bullet in the shooter's mouth was nothing more than a dying twitch, not the sign someone else was operating Jim's hand. And this young man was confident his career was not going to end like Toomey's or mine.

What I wanted to tell him was, "The creature that had James Toomey in its control used Toomey's own hand to eliminate him and cover its tracks." My actual statement stuck strictly to the facts with nothing more than a brief mention of the Culpepper case.

Father Dineen drove like a cop—that is, as if he owned the road. He knew something was up but not even a couple of belts from the ecclesiastic flask made me talk. An image of Anne and Jimmy dead in their house was burning a hole in my brain.

It was very late afternoon that the chaplain dropped me off in front of the Main Post Office, told me to go home and get some rest.

On the ride back from the Toomey's I'd thought about the dream and Bertrade. Usually dreams are vivid when you wake up but as you try to grab them they turn to nothing and disappear. This one started out vague but seemed to linger.

Climbing the post office stairs I remembered another fragment. Bertrade, lovely as I've ever seen her, wore nothing but a silver moon on a chain around her neck and touched my arm. So slippery was the memory that I began to wonder if this dream might have been something planted in my head by an enemy.

The little unmarked window was where I always picked up mail from the Kingdom Beneath the Hill. And I wanted to talk to that clerk and find out what he knew. The window was shut, which had never happened before.

The guy at the Overseas window didn't know what I was talking about when I asked about the window next door. He said this wasn't his regular assignment and that I should try the next day.

Walking slowly across that lobby, I thought of the ice-cold knife racing up my leg like I was a letter being sliced open and I felt real small and insignificant. But I started to put things into some kind of order.

The elves had set up Jim and Anne Toomey as bait for me. First they invented the Culpepper job and hired Jim, who needed the work. Then they made sure he couldn't function and put it in his head and Anne's that they should ask me. And I was the bait to lure Bertrade.

Taking my seat in the coffee shop across from the Van Neiman Building, it occurred to me that maybe on our first encounter Bertrade and Darnel had used me as bait to catch the elf. Knowing the ways of the Gentry, that seemed quite possible.

The waitress and counter man didn't notice that I was a repeat customer. I figured that the elves wouldn't probe as long as I was doing what they wanted. They didn't have to worry. My memory of Anne and Jimmy had burned a hole in my brain. And that may have been what the elves expected when they killed them.

That they were keeping me in play, letting me stay alive, could mean they'd made Bertrade aware that I was in danger. And it would also mean they weren't sure where she was or what she was going to do. That Bertrade avoided direct contact with me was a sign that she relied on me to play my part, walk into the trap, and ensnare the trapper. It would also mean she knew that the spell that shielded my thoughts could be broken by the enemy.

Just then Culpepper, whoever he was, came through the doors of the Van Neiman Building with his briefcase. I got up and followed him. It went like before. He walked west and I followed on the other side of the street. I wondered how much Culpepper knew, what promises and rewards had they made to him?

Seeing him go through this routine reminded me of seeing the enemy in France, just before we saw action. I saw a couple of German prisoners, starving, flea-bitten men, cramming army rations into their mouths while our guys stared like they were exhibits in a zoo. That sight took away all of the enemy's mystery.

I stopped on the east side of Tenth Avenue, watched from a doorway when Culpepper crossed and went into the apartment building. As I waited, a light went on in the third floor window.

A rhythmic pounding came from over on the river. It sounded like they were driving piles. The earlier drizzle had become rain. Workers headed home at a brisk pace. The streets were getting empty.

Stake-out work is fine, outdoor labor, good for the health and spirits. But I'd noticed a bar on the corner with a clear view of the apartment house.

It was a Wednesday night with a moderate-sized crowd and a cowboy movie on the TV above the bar. The guys drinking spotted a cop and looked away when I stepped inside. I ordered a rye and water and kept my eye on the apartment house doorway.

I was pretty sure they wouldn't leave without me. There was a good chance I'd be dead before long. But death hadn't yet happened and I'd given it several very good chances.

In the dark, a long freight train ran south on the elevated tracks. When I looked further west beyond Twelfth Avenue the pier at the end of the street seemed lit up.

About the time I began to wonder if I was crazy and Culpepper really was just a guy stepping out on his wife I saw through someone else's eyes. They were moving uptown along the river's edge, I saw a pier and a big yacht all lit up. Suddenly that disappeared. Was this skirmishing between elves and fairies?

Like it was a signal, the one called Culpepper came out the door of the apartment house. He carried an umbrella and held it over Mimi White. The game was on. They headed west and I followed them.

A good detective recognizes a pattern. Once more I was heading onto a pier at night to encounter one of the Gentry.

As we crossed Eleventh Avenue a big ocean liner sailed up the Hudson with every light on board shining. It looked like a floating city block. The tugboats guiding it honked at each other. I saw the liner and then for an instant I saw it again from the viewpoint of someone down at the river. The pile driving paused briefly and all was as quiet as Manhattan ever gets.

Approaching Twelfth Avenue I saw that the old freighter from the day before was gone. In its place was the ocean going yacht with lights on deck that I'd seen through another's eyes.

At certain moments time gets fluid. At Aisne-Marne, the platoon was pinned by machine gun fire. The gunners had waited until we were within a hundred yards. The lieutenant was dead. Someone was screaming. Later I found out the whole company was pinned; the battalion had gone to earth. The minutes we were down went by like hours.

The machine guns fired a short burst right over me; fired a burst to my left, another further along. I knew that it was rat-like little guys going through the motions. It would be a bit before they'd come back my way.

I pulled a pin with my right hand. I jumped up with a grenade in my left. The Krauts were firing from a gap in an embankment a hundred yards away. I'd hurled dummy grenades in practice, knew their weight. I judged the arc and tossed. "Get down," someone yelled. The grenade hit the side of the gap, bounced in the air.

As I dove for cover I was knocked flat and the cold knife raced up my leg. A muffled bang sounded, a man screamed, another cried out, the machine gun fire stopped and my war was over.

Crossing Twelfth Avenue, walking into the trap, I told myself that all I needed was a few seconds of clarity, like I'd had thirty-two years before.

Maybe Bertrade had given me up. But I was going to deal out payment for Jim and Anne. All I needed was those few seconds.

Culpepper and Mimi stopped just inside the gates at the end of the pier. A couple of hundred feet beyond them the yacht had lights on the gangplank, atop the cabins, shining through the portholes.

A figure—tall and thin, wavering slightly—stood on the deck leaning on the rail. He was faced away from me. But I could recognize one of the Fair Folk, whether elf or fairy. He was too far away to hit with a hand gun. I wished I had a grenade.

A scream in the night came from downriver. At almost the same moment the pile driver started up out in the water. Distant sirens sounded but they were on fire trucks and going the wrong way. The Fair Folk didn't want any human interference.

A breeze blew the rain in my face as I crossed the Avenue with my raincoat open. My arms were at my side. The .38 in my hand was hidden by the coat flapping.

The ones I knew as Culpepper and Mimi faced me as I approached. I was going to tell them to get out of my way before they got hurt.

But their eyes were blank. For an instant I saw myself from their viewpoint as I walked past them. Someone was looking out through them like they were TV cameras. Someone was in my head.

Figures moved in the darkness beyond the lights. Fair Folk were out there. For an instant I caught an image of long, thin figures on a small power boat.

The lights on the yacht flickered for a moment. The tall elf on the deck looked my way. He seemed amused. Bertrade's image telling intruders to stay out got knocked aside like it was cardboard. He was in my mind. My feet moved without my willing them and my body shambled forward to the foot of the gangplank.

I saw myself in his eyes, an old man—stunned and confused in a trench coat and battered hat—staring up at him. He sent that image out in all directions. The elf knew I had the gun and knew I was in his power.

Then the lights flickered fast. Out in the dark amid the noise of the pile drivers there were cries and gunshots. Suddenly Bertrade was inside me, "My lefthand man!"

Under a spell my arm moved. The elf couldn't stop it. The left arm was magic. He blocked my breath and sent a bolt of pain through my head, stopped my eyes from seeing. But the arm rose. I couldn't see him but I fired. Nothing. My head spun.

For an instant my sight cleared. I saw the elf. I squeezed the trigger as my sight went dark. Nothing happened.

Blind, I fired to the left and there was a scream. My breath came back. My sight returned. Up the gangplank the elf grasped his shoulder. I felt him stop my heart. But I blew his jaw off and my heart started again. I shot him in the head before I passed out.

The morning was long gone and done when I came home. Mrs. Palatino had actually turned off her television, put on street clothes and was headed out to Thursday afternoon bingo at Our Lady of Pompeii Church. She gave me a look full of disapproval and shook her head.

I needed to go upstairs and change my clothes, stop around at the office. In my jacket pocket was a letter to the Beyers from Hilda, saying she was alive and well and thinking of them.

Bertrade had brought that with her from the Kingdom Beneath the Hill. Our business relationship was still intact.

We'd parted half an hour before. That night was spent at the Plaza: part of our reward for smashing the elf and his espionage crew. After he went down, three of his fellow Gentry came out of the dark and surrendered to Bertrade and her friends.

Culpepper and Mimi and a couple of other mortals the elves had recruited bore the body into the back of a panel truck.

That dream I'd half-remembered had been sent by Bertrade. In the game of cat and mouse she and the big elf had played, some of his magic was stronger than hers.

"Askal is his name. We met in the Kingdom," she said, "and he was able to read me enough to know how I felt about you. He wanted to use you to draw me. I wanted to use that magic arm Darnel and I gave you to do away with him."

It seemed to me like the kind of game in which mortals were just breakable objects. Bertrade winced when I thought that.

Askal, of course, didn't completely die. I heard him shrieking; saw his shadow moving around the pier after his corpse had been taken away in the truck.

It isn't likely I'll ever go back to that spot on the Hudson. And it isn't likely I'll ever completely trust Bertrade. What I feel for her may not be love. But I know that when I'm with her this mortal life of mine gets torn open by magic, and when she's gone that's all I remember.

But when we parted outside the Plaza that morning and kissed, she told me she'd be back before long. And I look forward to it.

Tomorrow evening Jim and Anne Toomey will be waked out in Brooklyn. Their connection with me is what killed them, and I'll think of that.

My life may not run out of me into a big red puddle, but someday my life will run out. And before that happens in this world of bait and traps I'll see Bertrade again.

Richard Bowes has won two World Fantasy, an International Horror Guild, and Million Writer Awards. His new novel *Dust Devil on a Quiet Street* will appear on May Day 2013 from Lethe Press, which is also republishing his Lambda Award-winning novel *Minions of the Moon*. Additionally two short story collections will be published in 2013: *The Queen, the Cambion and Seven Others* from Aqueduct Press and *If Angels Fight* from Fairwood Press.

Recent and forthcoming appearances include: *The Magazine of Fantasy & Science Fiction, Icarus, Lightspeed,* and the anthologies *After, Wilde Stories 2012, Bloody Fabulous, Ghosts: Recent Hauntings, Handsome Devil, Hauntings,* and *Where Thy Dark Eye Glances.*

The Case: *Sixteen-year-old Devonte allegedly wrecks his foster parents' home. The damage is far more than one lone human boy could inflict. The kid's not talking, but Stella Christiansen, whose agency placed Devonte, senses he is in danger.*

The Investigator: *David Christiansen, a werewolf and mercenary, as well as Stella's estranged father.*

STAR OF DAVID

Patricia Briggs

"I checked them out myself," Myra snapped. "Have you ever just considered that *your boy* isn't the angel you thought he was?"

Stella took off her glasses and set them on her desk. "I think that we both need some perspective. Why don't you take the rest of the afternoon off?" *Before I slap your stupid face.* People like Devonte don't change that fast, not without good reason.

Myra opened her mouth, but after she got a look at Stella's face she shut it again. Mutely she stalked to her desk and retrieved her coat and purse. She slammed the door behind her.

As soon as she was gone, Stella opened the folder and looked at the pictures of the crime scene again. They were duplicates, and doubtless Clive, her brother the detective, had broken a few rules when he sent them to her—not that breaking rules had ever bothered him, not when he was five and not as a grown man nearing fifty and old enough to know better.

She touched the photos lightly, then closed the folder again. There was a yellow sticky with a phone number on it and nothing else: Clive didn't have to put a name on it. Her little brother knew she'd see what he had seen.

She picked up the phone and punched in the numbers fast, not giving herself a chance for second thoughts.

The barracks were empty, leaving David's office silent and bleak. The boys were on furlough with their various families for December.

His mercenaries specialized in live retrieval, which tended to be in and out stuff, a couple of weeks per job at the most. He didn't want to get involved in the gray area of unsanctioned combat or out-and-out war—where you killed people because someone told you to. In retrieval there were good guys and bad guys still—and if there weren't, he didn't take the job. Their reputation was such that they had no trouble finding jobs.

And unless all hell really broke loose, they always took December off to be with their families. David never let them know how hard that made it for him.

Werewolves need their packs.

If his pack was human, well, they knew about him and they filled that odd wolf-quirk that demanded he have people to protect, brothers in heart and mind. He couldn't stomach a real pack, he hated what he was too much.

He couldn't bear to live with his own kind, but this worked as a substitute and kept him centered. When his boys were here, when they had a job to do, he had direction and purpose.

His grandsons had invited him for the family dinner, but he'd refused as he always did. He still saw his sons on a regular basis. Both of them had served in his small band of mercenaries for a while, until the life lost its appeal or the risks grew too great for men with growing families. But he stayed away at Christmas.

Restlessness had him pacing: there were no plans to make, no wrongs to right. Finally he unlocked the safe and pulled out a couple of the newer rifles. He needed to put some time in with them anyway.

An hour of shooting staved off the restlessness, but only until he locked the guns up again. He'd have to go for a run. When he emptied his pockets in preparation, he noticed he had missed a call while he'd been shooting. He glanced at the number, frowning when he didn't recognize it. Most of his jobs came through an agent who knew better than to give out his cell number. Before he could decide if he wanted to return the call, his phone rang again, a call from the same number.

"Christiansen," he answered briskly.

There was a long silence. "Papa?"

He closed his eyes and sank back in his chair feeling his heart expand with almost painful intentness as his wolf fought with the man who knew his daughter hated him: didn't want to see him, ever. She had been there when her mother died.

"Stella?" He couldn't imagine what it took to make her break almost forty years of silence. "Are you all right? Is there something wrong?" Someone he could kill for her? A building to blow up? Anything at all.

She swallowed. He could hear it over the line. He waited for her to hang up.

Instead, when she spoke again, her voice was brisk and the wavery pain that colored that first "Papa" was gone as if it had never been. "I was wondering if you would consider doing a favor for me."

"What do you need?" He was proud that came out evenly. Always better to know what you're getting into, he told himself. He wanted to tell her that she could ask him for anything—but he didn't want to scare her.

"I run an agency that places foster kids," she told him, as if he didn't know. As if her brothers hadn't told her how he quizzed them to find out how she was doing and what she was up to. He hoped she never found out about her ex-boyfriend who'd turned stalker. He hadn't killed that one, though his willingness to do so had made it easier to persuade the man that he wanted to take up permanent residence in a different state.

"I know," he said because it seemed like she needed a response.

"There's something—" she hesitated. "Look, this might not have been the best idea."

He was losing her again. He had to breathe deeply to keep the panic from his voice. "Why don't you tell me about it anyway? Do you have something better to do?"

"I remember that," she said. "I remember you doing that with Mom. She'd be hysterical, throwing dishes or books, and you'd sit down and say, 'Why don't you tell me about it?'"

Did she want to talk about her mother now? About the one time he'd needed to be calm and failed? He hadn't known he was a werewolf until it was too late. Until after he'd killed his wife and the lover she'd taken while David had been fighting for God and country, both of whom had forgotten him. She'd been waiting until he came home to tell him that she was leaving—it was a mistake she'd had no time to regret. He, on the other hand, might have forever to regret it for her.

He never spoke of it. Not to anyone. For Stella he'd do it, but she knew the story anyway. She'd been there.

"Do you want to talk about your mother?" he asked, his voice carrying into a lower timbre; as it did when the wolf was close.

"No. Not that," she said hurriedly. "Nothing like that. I'm sorry. This isn't a good idea."

She was going to hang up. He drew on his hard-earned control and thought fast.

Forty years as a hunter and leader of men had given him a lot of practice reading between the lines. If he could put aside the fact that she was his daughter, maybe he could salvage this.

She'd told him she ran a foster agency like it was important to the rest of what she had to say.

"It's about your work?" he asked, trying to figure out what a social worker would need with a werewolf. Oh. "Is there a—" His daughter preferred not to talk about werewolves, Clive had told him. So if there was something supernatural she was going to have to bring it up. "Is there someone bothering you?"

"No," she said. "Nothing like that. It's one of my boys."

Stella had never married, never had children of her own. Her brother said it was because she had all the people to take care of that she could handle.

"One of the foster kids."

"Devonte Parish."

"He one of your special ones?" he asked. His Stella had never seen a stray she hadn't brought home, animal or human. Most she'd dusted off and sent home with a meal and bandages as needed—but some of them she'd kept.

She sighed. "Come and see him, would you? Tomorrow?"

"I'll be there," he promised. It would take him a few hours to set up permission from the packs in her area: travel was complicated for a werewolf. "Probably sometime in the afternoon. This the number I can find you at?"

Instead of taking a taxi from the airport, he rented a car. It might be harder to park, but it would give them mobility and privacy. If his daughter only needed this, if she didn't want to smoke the peace pipe yet, then he didn't need it witnessed by a cab driver. A witness would make it harder for him to control himself—and his little girl never needed to see him out of control ever again.

He called her before setting out, and he could tell that she'd had second and third thoughts.

"Look," he finally told her. "I'm here now. Maybe we should go and talk to the boy. Where can I meet you?"

He'd have known her anywhere though he hadn't, by her request, seen her since the night he'd killed his wife. She'd been twelve and now she was a grown woman with silver threads running through her kinky black hair. The last time he'd seen her she'd been still a little rounded and soft as most children are—and now there wasn't an ounce of softness in her. She was muscular and lean—like him.

It had been a long time, but he'd never have mistaken her for anyone else: she had his eyes and her mother's face.

He'd thought you had to be bleeding someplace to hurt this badly. The beast struggled within him, looking for an enemy. But he controlled and subdued it before he pulled the car to the curb and unlocked the automatic door.

She was wearing a brown wool suit that was several shades darker than the milk and coffee skin she'd gotten from her mother. His own skin was dark as the night and kept him safely hidden in the shadows where he and people like him belonged.

She opened the car door and got in. He waited until she'd fastened her seatbelt before pulling out from the curb. Slush splattered out from under his tires, but it was only a token. Once he was in the traffic lane the road was bare.

She didn't say anything for a long time, so he just drove. He had no idea where he was going, but he figured she'd tell him when she was ready. He kept his eyes on traffic to give her time to get a good look at him.

"You look younger than I remember," she said finally. "Younger than me."

"I was thirty-five or thereabouts when I was Changed. Being a werewolf seems to settle physical age about twenty-five for most of us." There it was out in the open and she could do with it as she pleased.

He could smell her fear of him spike and if he'd really been twenty-five, he thought he might have cried. Being this agitated wasn't smart if you were a werewolf. He took a deep breath through his nose and tried to calm down—he'd earned her fear.

"Devonte won't talk to me or anyone else," she said, and then as if those words had been the key to the floodgate she kept going. "I wish you could have seen him when I first met him. He was ten going on forty. He'd just lost his grandmother, who had raised him. He looked me right in the eye, stuck his jaw out and told me that he needed a home where he would be clothed and fed so he could concentrate on school."

"Smart boy?" he asked. She'd started in the middle of the story: he'd forgotten that habit of hers until just now.

"Very smart. Quiet. But funny, too." She made a sad sound, and her sorrow overwhelmed her fear of him. "We screen the homes. We visit. But there's never enough of us—and some of the horrible ones can put on a good show for a long time. It takes a while, too, before you get a feel for the bad ones. If he could have stayed with his first family, everything would have been fine. He stayed with them for six years. But this fall she unexpectedly got pregnant and her husband got a job transfer . . . "

They'd abandoned the boy like he was an old couch that was too awkward to move, David thought. He felt a flash of anger for this boy he'd never met. He swallowed the emotion quickly; he could do that these days. For a while. He was going to have to take that run when he got back home.

"I was tied up in court cases and someone else moved him to his next family," Stella continued, staring at her hands, which were clenched on a manila folder. "It shouldn't have been a problem. This was a family who already has fostered several children—and Devonte was a good kid, not the kind to give anyone problems."

"But something happened?" he suggested.

"His foster mother says that he just went wild, throwing furniture, breaking things. When he threatened her, his foster father stepped in and knocked him out. Devonte's in the hospital with a broken wrist and two broken ribs and he won't talk."

"You don't believe the foster family."

She gave an indignant huff. "The Linnfords look like Mr. and Mrs. Brady. She smiles and nods when he speaks and he is all charm and concern." She huffed again and spoke very precisely, "I wouldn't believe them if all they were doing was giving me the time of day. And I know Devonte. He just wants to get through school and get a scholarship so he can go to college and take care of himself."

He nodded thoughtfully. "So why did you call me?" He was willing to have a talk with the family, but he suspected if that was all she needed it would have been a cold day in hell before she called him—she had her brothers for that.

"Because of the photos." She held up the folder in invitation.

He had to drive a couple of blocks before he found a convenient parking place and pulled over, leaving the engine running.

He pulled six photos off a clip that attached them to the back of the folder she held and spread them out to look. Interest rose up and he wished he had something more than photos. It certainly looked like more damage than one lone boy could do: ten boys maybe, if they had sledge hammers. The holes in the walls were something anyone could have done. The holes in the ten foot ceiling, the executive desk on its side in three pieces and the antique oak chair broken to splinters and missing a leg were more interesting.

"The last time I saw something like that . . . " Stella whispered.

It was probably a good thing she couldn't bring herself to finish that sentence. He had to admit that all this scene was missing was blood and body parts.

"How old is Devonte?"

"Sixteen."

"Can you get me in to look at the damage?"

"No, they had contractors in to fix it."

His eyebrows raised. "How long has it been?"

"It was the twenty-first. Three days." She waved a hand. "I know. Contractors are usually a month wait at least, but money talks. This guy has serious money."

That sounded wrong. "Then why are they taking in a foster kid?"

She looked him in the eye for the first time and nodded at him as if he'd gotten something right. "If I'd been the one to vet them I'd have smelled a rat right there. Rich folk don't want mongrel children who've had it rough. Or if they do, they go to China or Romania and adopt babies to coo over. They don't take in foster kids, not without an agenda. But we're desperate for foster homes . . . and it wasn't me who approved them."

"You said the boy wouldn't talk. To you? Or to anybody?"

"To anybody. He hasn't said a word since the incident. Won't communicate at all."

David considered that, running through possibilities. "Was anyone hurt except for the boy?"

"No."

"Would you mind if I went to see him now?"

"Please."

He followed her directions to the hospital. He parked the car, but before he could open the door she grabbed his arm. The first time she touched him.

"Could he be a werewolf?"

"Maybe," he told her. "That kind of damage . . . "

"It looked like our house," she said, not looking at him, but not taking her hand off him either. "Like our house that night."

"If he was a werewolf, I doubt your Mr. Linnford would have been about to knock him out without taking a lot of damage. Maybe Linnford is the werewolf." That would fit, most of the werewolves he knew, if they survived, eventually became wealthy. Children were more difficult. Maybe that was why Linnford and his wife fostered children.

Stella jerked her chin up and down once. "That's what I thought. That's it. Linnford might be a werewolf. Could you tell?"

His chest felt tight. How very brave of her: she'd called the only monster she knew to deal with the other monsters. It reminded him of how she'd stood between him and the boys, protecting them the best that she could.

"Let me talk to Devonte," he said trying to keep the growl out of his voice with only moderate success. "Then I can deal with Linnford."

The hospital corridors were decorated with garland and green and red bulbs. Every year Christmas got more plastic and seemed farther and farther from the Christmases David had known as a child.

His daughter led him to the elevators without hesitation and exchanged nods with a few of the staff members who walked past. He hated the way his children aged every year. Hated the silver in their hair that was a constant reminder that eventually time would take them all away from him.

She kept as much distance between them as she could in the elevator. As if he were a stranger—or a monster. At least she wasn't running from him screaming.

You can't live with bitterness. He knew that. Bitterness, like most unpleasant emotions, made the wolf restless. Restless wolves were dangerous. The nurse at the station just outside the elevator knew Stella, too, and greeted her by name.

"That Mr. Linnford was here asking after Devonte. I told him that he wasn't allowed to visit yet." She gave Stella a disappointed look, clearly blaming her for putting Mr. Linnford to such bother. "What a nice man he is, looking after that boy after what he did to them."

She handed Stella a clipboard and gave David a mildly curious look. He gave her his most harmless smile and she smiled back before glancing down at the clipboard Stella had returned.

David could read it from where he stood. *Stella Christiansen and guest.* Well, he told himself, she could hardly write down that he was her father when she looked older than he did.

"He may be a nice man," Stella told the nurse with a thread of steel in her voice, "but you just keep him out until we know for sure what happened and why."

She strode off toward a set of doors where a policeman sat in front of a desk, sitting on a wooden chair, and reading a worn paperback copy of Stephen King's *Cujo.* "Jorge," she said.

"Stella," he buzzed the door and let them through.

"He's in the secured wing," she explained under her breath as she walked briskly down the hall. "Not that it's all that secure. Jorge shouldn't have let you through without checking your ID."

Not that anyone would question his Stella, David thought. Even as a little girl, people did what she told them to do. He was careful not to smile at her; she wouldn't understand it.

This part of the hospital smelled like blood, desperation, and disinfectant. Even though most of the scents were old, a new wolf penned up in this environment would cause a lot more excitement that he was seeing: and a sixteen-year-old could only be a new wolf. Any younger than that and they mostly didn't survive the Change. Anyway, he'd have scented a wolf by now: their first conclusion was right—Stella's boy was no werewolf.

"Any cameras in the rooms?" he asked in a low voice.

Her steady footfall paused. "No. That's still on the list of advised improvements for the future."

"All right. No one else here?"

"Not right now," she said. "This hospital isn't near gang territory and they put the adult offenders in a different section." She entered one of the open doorways and he followed her in, shutting the door behind them.

It wasn't a private room, but the first bed was empty. In the second bed was a boy staring at the wall—there were no windows. He was beaten up a bit and had a cast on one hand. The other hand was attached to a sturdy rail that stuck out of the bed on the side nearest the wall with a locking nylon strap—better than handcuffs, he thought, but not much. The boy didn't look up as they came in.

Maybe it was the name, or maybe the image that "foster kid" brought to mind, but he'd expected Devonte to be black. Instead, the boy looked as if someone had taken half a dozen races and shook them up—Eurasian races, though, not from the Dark Continent. There was Native American or Oriental in the corners of his eyes—and he supposed that nose could be Jewish or Italian. His skin looked as if he had a deep suntan, but this time of year it was more likely the color was his own: Mexican, Greek or even Indian.

Not that it mattered. He'd found that the years were slowly completing the job that Vietnam had begun—race or religion mattered very little to him anymore. But even if it had mattered . . . Stella had asked him for help.

Stella glanced at her father. She didn't know him, didn't know if he'd see through Devonte's defiant sullenness to the fear underneath. His expressionless face and upright military bearing gave her no clue. She could read people, but she didn't know her father anymore, hadn't seen him since . . . that night. Watching him made her uncomfortable, so she turned her attention to the other person in the room.

"Hey, kid."

Devonte kept his gaze on the wall.

"I brought someone to see you."

Her father, after a keen look at the boy, lifted his head and sucked in air through his nose hard enough she could hear it.

"Where are the clothes he was wearing when they brought him in?" he asked.

That drew Devonte's attention and satisfaction at his reaction slowed her answer. Her father's eye fell on the locker and he stalked to it and opened the door. He took out the clear plastic bag of clothes and said, with studied casualness, "Linnford was here asking about you today."

Devonte went still as a mouse.

Stella didn't know where this was going, but pitched in to help. "The police informed me that Linnford's decided not press assault charges. They should move you to a room with a view soon. I'm scheduled for a meeting tomorrow morning to decide what happens to you when you get out of here."

Devonte opened his mouth, but then closed it resolutely.

Her father sniffed at the bag, then said softly, "Why do your clothes smell like vampire, boy?"

Devonte jumped, the whites of his eyes showing all the way round his irises. His mouth opened and this time Stella thought it might really be an inability to speak that kept him quiet. She was choking a bit on "vampire" herself. But she wouldn't have believed in werewolves either, she supposed, if her father weren't one.

"I didn't introduce you," she murmured. "Devonte, this is my father, I called him when I saw the crime scene photos. He's a werewolf." If he was having vampire problems, maybe a werewolf would look good.

The sad blue-gray chair with the ripped Naugahyde seat that had been sitting next to Devonte's bed zipped past her and flung itself at her father—who caught it and gave the boy a curious half-smile. "Oh I bet you surprised it, didn't you? Wizards aren't exactly common."

"Wizard?" Stella squeaked regrettably.

Her father's smile widened just a little—a smile she remembered from her childhood when she or one of her brothers had done something particularly clever. This one was aimed at Devonte.

He moved the chair gently between his hands. "A witch's power centers on bodies and minds, flesh and blood. A wizard has power over the physical—" The empty bed slammed into the wall with the open locker, bending the door and cracking the drywall. Her father was safely in front of it and belatedly she realized he must have jumped over it.

He still had the chair and his smile had grown to a wide, white grin. "Very nice, boy. But I'm not your enemy." He glanced up at the clock on the wall and shook his head.

"Someone ought to reset that thing. Do you know what time it is?"

No more furniture moved. Her father made a show of taking out his cell phone and looking at it. "Six-thirty. It's dark outside already. How badly did you hurt it with that chair I saw in the photo?"

Devonte was breathing hard, but Stella controlled her urge to go to him. Her father, hopefully, knew what he was doing. She shivered, though she was wearing her favorite wool suit and the hospital was quite warm. How much of the stories she'd heard about vampires was true?

Devonte released a breath. "Not badly enough."

On the tails of Devonte's reply, her father asked, "Who taught you not to talk at all, if you have a secret to keep?"

"My grandmother. Her mother survived Dachau because the American troops came just in time—and because she kept her mouth shut when the Nazis wanted information."

Her father's face softened. "Tough woman. Was she the Gypsy? Most wizards have at least a little Gypsy blood."

Devonte shrugged, rubbed his hands over his face hard. She recognized the gesture from a hundred different kids: he was trying not to cry. "Stella said you're a werewolf."

Her father cocked his head as if he were weighing something. "Stella doesn't lie." Unexpectedly he pinned Stella with his eyes. "I don't know if we'll have a vampire calling tonight—it depends upon how badly Devonte hurt it."

"Her," said Devonte. "It was a her."

Still looking at Stella, her father corrected himself. "Her. She must have been pretty badly injured if she hasn't come here already. And it probably means we're lucky and she is alone. If there were others they'd have come yesterday or the day before—they can't afford to let Devonte live with what he knows about them. Vampires haven't survived as long as they have by leaving witnesses."

"No one would have believed me," Devonte said. "They'd have locked me up forever."

That made her father release her from the grip of his gaze as he focused his attention on Devonte. The boy straightened under the impact—Stella knew exactly how he felt.

"Is that what Linnford told you when his neighbors came running to see why there was so much noise?" her father asked gently. "Upscale apartment dwellers aren't nearly as likely to ignore odd sounds. Is that why you threw around so much furniture? That was smart, boy."

Devonte was nodding his head—and he straightened a little more at her father's praise.

"Next time a vampire attacks you and you don't manage to kill it, though, you shout it to the world. You may end up seeing a psychologist for the rest of your life—but the vampires will stay as far from you as they can. If she doesn't come tonight, you tell your story to the newspapers." Her father glanced at Stella and she nodded.

"I know a couple of reporters," she said. "'Boy Claims He Was Attacked by Vampire' ought to sell enough papers to justify a headline or two."

"All right then," her father returned his attention to her. "I need you to go out and find some wood for us: a chair, a table, something we can make stakes out of."

"Holy water?" asked Devonte. "They might have a chapel here."

"Smart," said her father. "But from what I've heard it doesn't do enough damage to be worth running it down. Go now, Stella—and be careful."

She almost saluted him, but she didn't trust him enough to tease. He saw it, almost smiled and then turned back to Devonte. "And you're going to tell me everything you know about this vampire."

Stella glanced in the room next to Devonte's, but, like his, it was decorated in early Naughahyde and metal: no wood to be found. She didn't bother checking any more but hurried to the security door—and read the note on the door.

"No, sir. She lived with them—they told me she was Linnford's sister." Devonte stopped talking when she came back.

"Jorge's been called away, he'll be back in a few minutes."

Her father considered that. "I think the show's on. No wooden chairs?"

"All the rooms in this wing are like this one."

"Without an effective weapon, I'll get a better chance at her as a wolf than as a human. It means I can't talk to you though—and it will take a while to change back, maybe a couple of hours." He looked away, and in an adult version of Devonte's earlier gesture, rubbed his face tiredly. She heard the rasp of whisker on skin. "I control the wolf now—and have for a long time."

He was worried about her.

"It's all right," she told him. He gave her the same kind of keen examination he'd given Devonte earlier and she wondered what information he was drawing from it. Could he tell how scared she was?

His face softened. "You'll do, my star."

She'd forgotten that he used to call her that—hated the way it tightened her throat. "Should I call Clive and Steve?"

"Not for a vampire," he told her. "All that will do is up the body count. To that end, we'll stay here and wait—an isolation ward is as good a place to face her as any. If I'm wrong, and the guard's leaving isn't the beginning of her attack—if she doesn't come tonight, we get all of us into the safety of someone's home, where the vampire can't just waltz in without invitation. Then I'll call in a few favors and my friends and I can take care of her somewhere there aren't any civilians to be hurt."

He looked around with evident dissatisfaction.

"What are you looking for?" Devonte asked so she didn't have to.

"A place to hide." Then he looked up and smiled at the dropped ceiling.

"Those panels won't support your weight," she warned him.

"No, but this is a hospital and this is the old wing. I bet they have a cable ladder for their computer and electric cables . . . " As he spoke, he'd hopped on the empty bed and pushed up a ceiling panel to take a look.

"What's a cable ladder?" Stella asked.

"In this case, it's a sturdy aluminum track attached to the oak beam with stout hardware." He sounded pleased as he replaced the ceiling panel he'd taken out. "I could hide a couple of people up here if I had to."

He was a mercenary, she remembered, and wondered how many times he'd hidden on top of cable ladders.

He moved the empty bed away from the wall and climbed on it again and removed a different panel. "Do you think you can get this panel back where it belongs after I get up here, boy?"

"Sure." Devonte sounded thoroughly pleased. If anyone else had called him "boy" he'd have been bristling. He was already well on the way to a big case of hero worship, just like the one she'd had.

"Stella." Her father took off his red flannel shirt and laid it on the empty bed behind him. "When this is over, you call Clive, tell him everything and he'll arrange a cleanup. He knows who to call for help with it. It's safer for everyone if people don't believe in vampires and werewolves. Leaving bodies makes it kind of hard to deny."

"I'll call him."

Without his shirt to cover him, she could see there was no softness in him. A few scars showed up gray on his dark skin. She'd forgotten how dark he was, like ebony.

As he peeled off his sky-blue undershirt he said, with a touch of humor, "if you don't want to see more of your father than any daughter ever should, you need to turn your back." And she realized she'd been staring at him.

Devonte made an odd noise—he was laughing. There was a tightness to the sound and she knew he was scared and excited to see what it looked like when a man changed into a werewolf. For some reason she felt her own mouth stretch into a nervous grin she let Devonte see just before she did as her father advised her and turned her back.

David didn't like changing in front of anyone. He wasn't exactly vulnerable—but it made the wolf edgy and if someone decided to get brave and approach too closely . . . well, the wolf would feel threatened, like a snake shedding its skin.

So to the boy he said quietly, "Watching is fine. But wait for a bit if you want to touch . . . " He had a thought. "Stella, if she sends the Linnfords in first, I'll do my best to stay hidden. I can take a vampire . . . " Honesty forced him to continue. "Maybe I can take a vampire, but only with surprise on my side. Her human minions, if they are still human enough to walk in daylight, are still too human to detect me. Don't let them take Devonte out of this room."

He tried to remember everything he knew about vampires. Once he changed, it would be too late to talk. "Don't look in the vampire's eyes, don't let her touch you. Unless you are really a believer, don't plan on crosses helping you out. When I attack, don't try and help, just keep out of it so I don't have to worry about you."

Wishing they had a wooden stake, he knelt on the floor and allowed himself to change. Calling the wolf was easy, it knew there was a fight to be had, blood to be shed, and in its eagerness it rushed the change as if called by the moon herself.

He never remembered exactly how bad it was going to hurt. His mother had once told him that childbirth was like that for women. That if they remembered how bad it was, they'd lack the courage to face the next time.

But he did remember it was always worse than he expected, and that somehow helped him bear it.

The shivery, icy pain slid over his bones while fire threaded through his muscles, reshaping, reorganizing and altering what was there to suit itself. Experience kept him from making noise—it was one of the first things he learned: how to control his instincts and keep the howls, the growls, and the whines inside and bury them in silence. Noise can attract unwanted attention.

His lungs labored to provide oxygen as adrenaline forced his heart to beat too fast. His face ached as teeth became fangs and his jaw extended with cheekbones. His eyesight blurred and then sharpened with a predatory clarity that allowed him to see prey and enemy alike no matter what shadows they tried to hide in.

"Cool," said someone. Devonte. He-who-was-to-be-guarded.

Someone moved and it attracted his attention. Her terror flooded his senses like perfume.

Prey. He liked it when they ran.

Then she lifted her chin and he saw a second image, superimposed over the first. A child standing between him and two smaller children, her chin jutting out as she lifted up a baseball bat in wordless defiance that spoke louder than the her terror and the blood.

Not prey. Not prey. His. His star.

It was all right then. She could see his pain—she had earned that right. And together they would stop the monster from eating the boy.

For the first few minutes after the change, he mostly thought like the wolf, but as the pain subsided he settled back into control. He shook off the last of unpleasant tingles with the same willpower he used to set aside the desire to snarl at the boy who reached out with a hand . . . only to jerk back, caught by the strap on his wrist.

David hopped on to the bed and snapped through the ballistic nylon that attached Devonte's cuff to the rail and waited while the boy petted him tentatively with all the fascination of a person touching a tiger.

"That'll be a little hard to explain," said Stella.

He looked at her and she flinched . . . then jerked up her chin and met his eyes. "What if the Linnfords ask about the restraint?"

It had been the wolf's response to seeing the boy he was supposed to protect tied up like a bad dog, not the man's.

"They haven't been here," said Devonte. "Unless they spend a lot of time in hospital prison, they won't know it was supposed to be there. I'll cover the cuff on my wrist with the blanket."

Stella nodded her head thoughtfully. "All right. And if things get bad, at least this way you can run. He's right, it's better if the restraint is off."

David let them work it out. He launched himself off Devonte's bed and onto the other—forgetting that Devonte was already hurt until he heard the boy's indrawn breath. David was still half-operating on wolf instincts—which wasn't very helpful when fighting vampires. He needed to be thinking.

Maybe it had only been the suddenness of his movement though because the boy made the same sound when David hopped through the almost-too-narrow opening in the ceiling and onto the track in the plenum space between the original fourteen-foot ceiling and false panels fitted into the flimsy hangers that kept them place. The track groaned a little under his sudden weight, but it didn't bend.

"My father always told us that no one ever looks up for their enemy," Stella said after a moment. "Can you replace the panel? If you can't I—"

The panel he'd moved slid back into place with more force than necessary and cracked down the middle.

"Damn it."

"Don't worry, no one will notice. There are a couple of broken panels up there."

She couldn't see any sign that her father was hiding in the ceiling except for the bed. She grabbed it by the headboard and tugged it back to its original position, then she did the same with the chair.

She'd forgotten how impressive the wolf was . . . almost beautiful: the perfect killing machine covered with four-inch-deep, redgold fur. She hadn't remembered the black that tipped his ears and surrounded his eyes like Egyptian kohl.

"If you'll get back, I'll see what I can do with the wall," said Devonte. "Sometimes I can fix things as well as move them."

That gave her a little pause, but she found that wizards weren't as frightening as werewolves and vampires. She considered his offer, then shook her head.

"No. They already know what you are." She gathered her father's clothes from the bedspread and folded them neatly. Then she stashed them—and the plastic bag with Devonte's clothes—into the locker. "Just leave the wall. We only need to hide the werewolf from them, and you might need all the power you've got to help with the vampire."

Devonte nodded.

"Right then." She took a deep breath and picked up her catch-all purse from the floor where she'd set it.

Her brothers had made fun of her purses until she'd used one to take out a mugger. She'd been lucky—it had been laden with a pair of three-pound weights she'd been transporting from home to work—but she'd never admitted that to her brothers. Afterwards they'd given her Mace, karate lessons, and quit bugging her about the size of her purse.

Unearthing a travel-sized game board from its depths she said, "How about some checkers?"

Five hard-won games later she decided the vampire either wasn't coming tonight, or she was waiting for Stella to go away. She jumped three of Devonte's checkers and there was a quiet knock on the door. She turned to look as Jorge, the cop who'd gotten babysitting duty today, stuck his head in.

"Sorry to leave you stuck here."

"No problem. Just beating a poor helpless child at checkers."

She waited for him to respond with something funny—Jorge was quick on his feet. But his face just stayed . . . not blank precisely, but neutral.

"They need you down in pediatrics, now. Looks like a case of child abuse and Doc Gonzales wants you to talk to the little girl."

She couldn't help the instincts that brought her to her feet, but those same instincts were screaming that there was something wrong with Jorge.

Between her job and having a brother on the force, she'd gotten to know some of the cops pretty well. Nothing bothered Jorge like a child who'd been hurt. She'd seen him cry like a baby when he talked about a car wreck where the child hadn't survived. But he'd passed this message along to her with all the passion of a hospital switchboard operator.

In the movies, vampires could make people do what they wanted them to—she couldn't remember if the people were permanently damaged. Mostly, she was afraid, they just died.

She glanced down at her watch and shook her head. "You know my rules," she said. "It's after six and I'm off shift."

Her rules were a standing joke with her brothers and their friends—a serious joke. She'd seen too many people burn out from the stress of her job. So she'd made a list of rules she had to follow, and they'd kept her sane so far. One of her rules was that from eight in the morning until six in the evening she was on the job, outside of those hours she did her best to have a real life. She was breaking it now, with Devonte.

Instead of calling her on it, Jorge just processed her reply and finally nodded. "All right. I'll tell them."

He didn't close the door when he left. She went to the doorway and watched him walk mechanically down the hall and through the security door, which he'd left open. Very unlike him to leave a security door open, but he closed it behind him.

"That was the vampire's doing, wasn't it?" she asked, looking up.

The soft growl that eased through the ceiling was somehow reassuring—though she hadn't forgotten his reservations about how well he'd do against a vampire.

She went back to Devonte's bed and made her move on the board. Out in the hall the security door opened again, and someone wearing high heels *click-click*ed briskly down the hall.

Stella took a deep breath, settled back on the end of the bed and told Devonte, "Your turn."

He looked at the board, but she saw his hand shake as whoever it was in the hallway closed in on them.

"King me," he said in a fair approximation of triumph.

The footsteps stopped in the doorway. Devonte looked over her shoulder and his face went slack with fear. Stella inhaled and took her first look.

She'd thought a vampire would be young, like her father. Wasn't that the myth? But this woman had gray hair and wrinkles under her eyes and in the soft, white skin of her neck. She was dressed in a professionally tailored wine-colored suit. She wore a diamond necklace around her aging neck, and diamond-and-pearl earrings.

"Well," said Stella. "No one is going to think you look like a cuddly grandma."

The woman laughed, her face lighting up with a cheer so genuine that Stella thought she might have liked her if only the laughter didn't showcase her fangs. "The boy talked, did he? I thought for sure he'd hold his tongue, if only to keep his own secrets. Either that or broadcast it to the world, and then you and I wouldn't be in this position."

She gave Stella a kindly smile that showed off a charmingly mismatched pair of dimples. "I am sorry you had to be involved. I tried to get you out of it."

But Stella had been dealing with people a long time, she could smell a fake a mile away. The laughter had been real, but the kind concern certainly wasn't.

"Separating your prey," Stella said. She needed to get the vampire into the room where her father could drop on top of her, but how?

The vampire displayed her fangs and dimples again. "More convenient and easier to keep the noise down," she allowed. "But not really necessary. Not even if you are a—" she took a deep breath "—werewolf."

The news didn't seem to bother her. Stella fought off the feeling that her father was going to be over-matched. He'd been a soldier and then a mercenary, training his own sons and then grandsons. Surely he knew what he was doing.

"Hah," sneered Devonte in classic adolescent disdain. "You aren't so tough. I nearly killed you all by myself."

The vampire sneered right back and, on her, the expression made the hair on the back of Stella's neck stand up and take notice. "You were a mistake, boy. One I intend to clear up."

David crouched motionless, waiting for the sound of the vampire's voice to indicate she had moved underneath him.

Patience, patience, he counseled himself, but he should have been counseling someone else.

If the vampire's theatrics scared Stella, they drove Devonte into action. The bed he tried to smash her father with rattled across the floor. He must have tired himself out with his earlier wizardry because it was traveling only half as fast as it had when he'd tried to drive her father through the wall.

The vampire had no trouble grabbing it . . . or throwing it through the plaster wall and into the hallway where it crashed on its side, flinging wheels, bedding, mattress and pieces of the arcana that distinguished it from a normal bed.

She was so busy impressing them with her Incredible Hulk imitation, she didn't see the old blue-gray chair. It hit her squarely in the back, driving her directly under the panel Devonte had cracked.

"Now," whispered Stella diving toward the hole the vampire had made in the wall, hoping that would be out of the way.

Even though Devonte's chair had knocked the vampire to her knees, Stella's motion drew her attention. The thing was fast, and she lunged for Stella in the same motion she used to rise. Then the roof fell on top of her, the roof and a silently snarling redgold wolf with claws and fangs that made the vampire's look like toys.

For a moment she was twelve again, watching the monster dig those long claws into her mother's lover and she froze in horror. The woman looked frail beneath the huge wolf's bulk—until she pulled her legs under him and threw him into the outer wall, the one made of cinder blocks and not plaster.

With an inhuman howl the vampire leaped upon her father. She looked nothing like the elegant woman who had walked into the room. In the brief glimpse she'd had of her face, Stella saw something terrible . . . evil.

"Stella, behind you!" Devonte yelled, hopping off the bed, his good arm around his ribs.

She hadn't been paying attention to anything except the vampire. Devonte's warning came just a little late and someone grabbed her by the arm and jerked her roughly around—Linnford. Gone was the urban smile and *GQ* posture; his face was lit with fanaticism and madness. He had a knife in the hand that wasn't holding her. She reacted without thinking, twisting so his thrust went past her abdomen, slicing though fabric but not skin.

Something buzzed between them, hitting him in the chest and knocking him back to the floor. He jerked and spasmed like a skewered frog in a film she'd once had to watch in college. The chair sat on top of him, balanced on one bent leg, the other three appearing to hover in the air.

It took a moment for her to properly understand what she was seeing. The bent chair leg was stuck into his ribcage, just to the left of his sternum. Blood began spitting out like a macabre fountain.

"Honey?" Hannah Linnford stood in the doorway. Like Stella, she seemed to be having trouble understanding what she was seeing.

Muttering, "Does no one remember to shut the security doors?" Stella pulled the mini-canister of Mace her youngest brother had given her after the mugging incident out of her pocket and sprayed it in the other woman's face.

If she'd been holding Linnford's knife she could have cheerfully driven it through Hannah's neck: These people had taken one of her kids and tried to feed him to a vampire.

Thinking of her kids made Stella look for Devonte.

He was leaning against the wall a few feet from his bed, staring at Linnford—and his expression centered Stella because he needed her. She ran to him and tugged him to the far corner of the room, away from the fighting monsters, but too close to the Linnfords. Once she had him where she wanted him, she did her best to block his view of Linnford's dying body. If she could get medical help soon enough, Linnford might survive—but she felt no drive to do it. Let him rot.

Mace can in hand, she kept a weather eye on the woman screaming on the floor, but most of her attention was on the fight her father was losing.

They fought like a pair of cats, coming together clawing and biting, almost too fast for her eyes to focus on, then, for no reason she could see, they'd retreat. After a few seconds of staring at each other, they'd go at it again. Unlike cats, they were eerily silent.

The vampire's carefully arranged hair was fallen, covering her face, but not disguising her glittering . . . no, glowing red eyes. Her arm flashed out in a jerky movement that was so quick Stella almost missed it—and the wolf twitched away with another wound that dripped blood: the vampire was still virtually untouched.

The two monsters backed away from each other and the vampire licked her fingers.

"You taste so good, wolf," she said. "I can't wait until I can sink my fangs through your skin and suck that sweetness dry."

Stella sprayed Hannah in the face again. Then she hauled Devonte out the door and away from the vampire, making regrettably little allowance for his broken ribs. Dead was worse than in pain.

It's working, David thought, watching the vampire lick his blood off her fingers. Though he was mostly focused on the vampire, he noticed when Stella took the boy out of the room. Good for her. With the vampire's minions here, one dead and one incapacitated, she shouldn't have trouble getting out. He hoped she took Devonte to her home—or any home—where they'd be safe. Then he put them out of his mind and concentrated on the battle at hand.

He'd met a vampire or two, but never fought one before. He'd heard that some of them had a strange reaction to werewolf blood. She seemed to be one of them.

He could only hope that her blood lust would make her stupid. He'd heard that vampires couldn't feed from the dead. If it wasn't true, he might be in trouble.

He waited for her to come at him again—and this time he stepped into her fist, falling limply at her feet. She hit him hard, he felt the bone in his jaw creak, so the limp fall wasn't hard to fake. He'd wait until she started feeding, and the residual dizziness from her blow left, then he'd take her.

She fell on him and he waited for her fangs to dig in. Instead she jerked a couple of times and then lay still. She wasn't breathing and her heart wasn't beating—but she'd been like that when she walked into the room.

"Papa?"

Stella was supposed to be safely away.

He rose with a roar, making an audible sound for the first time so the vampire would pay attention to him and leave his daughter alone. But the woman's body rolled smoothly off of him and lay on the floor—two wooden chair legs stuck through her back.

"Are you all right? Jorge left the security door open, I knew it when the Linnfords came in. We broke the legs off Jorge's chair and used whatever he used to toss the furniture around to drive them into her back."

The soldier in him insisted on a full and quick survey of the room. Linnford was dead, the abused chair was the obvious cause of death. A woman, presumably his wife, sobbed harshly, her face pressed into Linnford's arm: a possible threat. Stella and Devonte were standing way too close to the vampire.

They'd killed her.

For a moment he felt a surge of pride. Stella didn't have an ounce of quit in her whole body. She and the boy had managed to take advantage of the distraction he'd arranged before he could.

"Everyone was gone, Jorge and everyone." He looked at the triumph in Stella's face, not quite hidden by her worry for her friends.

She thought the vampire was finished, but wood through the heart didn't always keep the undead down.

"Are you all right?" Stella asked. And then when he just stared at her, "Papa?"

He'd come here hoping to play hero, he knew, hoping to mend what couldn't be mended. But the only role for him was that of monster, because that was the only thing he was.

He pulled the sheet off the bed and ripped it with a claw, then tossed it toward Linnford's sobbing woman. Stella took the hint and she and Davonte made a rope of sorts out of it and tied her up.

While they were working at that, he walked slowly up to the vampire. Stella had called him Papa tonight, more than once. He'd try to hold on to that and forget the rest.

He growled at the vampire: her fault that he would lose his daughter a second time. Then he snapped his teeth through her spine. The meat of her was tougher than it should have been, tougher than jerky and bad tasting to boot. His jaw hurt from the hit he'd taken as he set his teeth and put some muscle into separating her head from her body.

When he was finished, the boy was losing his last meal in the corner, an arm wrapped around his ribs. Throwing up with broken ribs sucked: he knew all about that. Linnford's woman was secured. Stella had a hand over her mouth as if to prevent herself from imitating Devonte. When she pulled her eyes away from the vampire's severed head and looked at him, he saw horror.

He felt the blood dripping from his jaws—and couldn't face her any longer. Couldn't stay while horror turned to fear of him. He didn't look at his daughter again as he ran away for the first time in his long life.

When he could, he changed back to human at the home of the local werewolf pack. They let him shower, and gave him a pair of sweats—the universal answer to the common problem of changing back to human and not having clothes to put back on.

He called his oldest son to make sure that Stella had called him and that he had handled the cleanup. She had remembered, and Clive was proceeding with his usual thoroughness.

Linnford was about to have a terrible car wreck. The vampire's body, both parts of it, were scheduled for immediate incineration. The biggest problem was what to do with Linnford's wife. For the moment she seemed to be too traumatized to talk. Maybe the vampire's death had broken her—or maybe she'd come around. Either way, she'd need help, discreet help from people who knew how to tell the difference between the victim of a vampire and a minion and would treat her accordingly.

David made a few calls, and got the number of a very private sanitarium run by a small, very secret government agency. The price wasn't bad—all he had to do was rescue some missionary who was related to a high-level politician. The fool had managed to get kidnapped with his wife and two young children. David's team would still get paid, and he'd probably have taken the assignment anyway.

By the time he called Clive back, his sons had located a few missing hospital personnel and the cop who'd been guarding the door. David heard the relief in Clive's voice: Jorge was apparently a friend. None of the recovered people seemed to be hurt, though they had no idea why they were all in the basement.

David hung up and turned off his cell phone. Accepting the offer of a bedroom from the pack Alpha, David took his tired body to bed and slept.

Christmas day was coming to a close when David drove his rental to his son's house—friends had picked it up from the hospital for him.

Red and green lights covered every bush and railing as well as surrounding all the windows. Knee-high candy canes lined the walk.

There were cars at his son's house. David frowned at them and checked his new watch. He was coming over at the right time. He'd made it clear that he didn't want to intrude—which was understood to mean that he wouldn't come when Stella was likely to be there.

He'd already have been on a flight home, except that he didn't know how to contact Devonte. He tapped the envelope against his leg and wondered why he'd picked up a Christmas card instead of just handing over his business card. Below his contact information he'd made Devonte an open job offer beginning as soon as Devonte was eighteen. David could think of a thousand ways a wizard would be of use to a small group of mercenaries.

Of course, after watching David tear up the vampire's body, Devonte probably wouldn't be interested, so more to the point was the name and phone number on the other side of the card. Both belonged to a wizard who was willing to take on a pupil; the local Alpha had given it to him.

Clive had promised to give it to Devonte.

David had to search under the giant wreath on the door for the bell. As he waited, he noticed that he could hear a lot of people inside, and even through the door he smelled the turkey.

He took a step back, but the door was already opening.

Stella stood in the doorway. Over her shoulder he could see the whole family running around preparing the table for Christmas dinner. Devonte was sitting on the couch reading to one of the toddlers that seemed to be everywhere. Clive leaned against the fireplace and met David's gaze. He lifted a glass of wine and sipped it, smiling slyly.

David took another step back and opened his mouth to apologize to Stella . . . just as her face lit with her mother's smile. She stepped out onto the porch and wrapped her arms around him.

"Merry Christmas, Papa," she said. "I hope you like turkey."

Patricia Briggs is the #1 *New York Times* bestselling author of the Mercy Thompson series, the seventh novel of which—*Frost Burned*—has just been published. Briggs also writes the Alpha and Omega series, which is set in the same world as the Mercy Thompson novels. Starting with a novella, "Alpha and Omega," three full-length novels have followed. She has also penned eight other fantasy novels. Briggs lives in Washington State with her husband, children, and a small herd of horses. For more information about the author, feel free to visit www.patriciabriggs.com.

The Case: *People are going crazy and killing themselves . . . but people don't just "go crazy" out of the blue.*

The Investigators: *Jamie Keller—black, built like a Mack truck, gentle as a lamb—and Mick Sharpton—white, queer, clairvoyant, Goth as Goth can be—both agents of the Babylon, Tennessee, branch of the Bureau of Paranormal Investigation.*

IMPOSTORS

Sarah Monette

They were pulling out of the parking lot of St. Dymphna's Psychiatric Hospital when the radio crackled into life. Mick Sharpton answered. Dispatch said, "There's been another one."

"Shit," Jamie said. They'd developed a rule that the partner not holding the handset did the swearing for both of them. Mick said to Dispatch, "Give us an address, and we're on our way."

There was a hesitation, infinitesimal, but years long in Dispatch-time, which they understood when the dispatcher said, "Langland Street subway station. He jumped."

"Christ," Mick said, racking the handset.

"That makes what, three jumpers?"

"Three jumpers, a bullet to the brain, and Mrs. Coulson back there in St. Dymphna's. I think the police are right. This one's paranormal."

"Evidence or hunch?"

"Hunch mostly. But. People don't just 'go crazy' out of a clear blue sky, you know. And here's four people—five now, I guess—no history of mental illness, going zero to psychosis in sixty seconds flat. Something is very definitely wrong with this picture. And it feels paranormal to me."

Mick's 3(8) esper rating wasn't quite high enough for his intuition to be admissible legal evidence, but Jamie had never known him to be wrong. "Then we'd better start trying to figure out what these people had in common."

"Nothing," Mick said, pale blue eyes staring an angry hole in the dashboard. "Absolutely fuck all. Aside from the fact that they all went crazy, of course."

"Well, and crazy in the same way," Jamie said, determined not to let this blow up into a fight, not even to make Mick feel better.

"Yeah." Mick sighed, offered Jamie a sidelong, apologetic smile. "What did she say? 'I stole her life.'"

"Yeah," Jamie Keller echoed softly and shivered, trying not to imagine what it would be like to wake up one morning believing himself to be an impostor. He didn't blame any of them for committing suicide, nor Mrs. Coulson for trying.

"Must be hell on earth," Mick said, and they drove the rest of the way to Langland Street in troubled silence.

Paul Sinclair was brought up off the subway tracks one piece at a time. Jamie kept a weather eye on the progress of that operation and its delicate balance between speed and thoroughness; the last thing anyone wanted was for ghouls to be drawn out of the tunnels by the smell of blood. But although dealing with the ghouls if they appeared would be his and Mick's responsibility, they'd only be in the way of the morgue workers if they went over there now. They were listening to witnesses instead.

Eyewitness testimony was notoriously volatile, but allowing for the inevitable variations in what individual witnesses perceived, Jamie was getting a fairly clear picture of the last two minutes of Paul Sinclair's life.

The witnesses agreed that he'd been nervous and jerky in his movements when he came down the stairs from the street. A homeless woman who panhandled in the station on a regular basis remembered noticing him the day before, and he hadn't looked well then, either. Jamie would have dismissed that as embellishment, a natural desire to stay in the limelight a little longer, but Mick said she was telling the truth.

Paul Sinclair—bank manager, aged thirty-two, single—had advanced to the edge of the platform, where he'd set down his briefcase and waited, attracting attention by his fidgeting and the way he moved sharply apart from the other people on the platform. "Like we were dirty and he didn't want to touch us," said a teenage boy who probably should have been in school, but that wasn't Jamie's problem and he wasn't asking. When the 10:43 D train made itself heard approaching the station, its ghoul-ward howling, Paul Sinclair said, very audibly, something like, "Don't try to save me. I'm not me." And he jumped straight into the path of the D train, which tore him to pieces.

When the police opened his briefcase, it contained nothing but a suicide note along all too familiar lines. Paul Sinclair, in handwriting Jamie had no doubt would be proved conclusively to be that of Paul Sinclair, asserted that he was an impostor. *I have stolen his life,* he wrote, echoing Marian Coulson and the other victims. *I don't deserve his life.* The note was not signed—poor bastard, Jamie thought, what name could he use?—but scrawled at the bottom, a painful afterthought: *Please take care of Mr. Sinclair's dogs. Their names are Leo and Bridget.*

"Just like the others," Mick said. He sounded–and looked—ill. "Even the same phrasing."

"Definitely paranormal."

"You say that like you think it helps."

"It is the first thing Jesperson told us to do."

"Well, hooray for us." But there was no anger in him now; he just sounded defeated.

"It's better than nothing."

"Tell that to Paul Sinclair," Mick said, and Jamie was glad to be called away to talk to the morgue crew.

After a hurried and unenthusiastic lunch, they spent the afternoon going through the case files again, correlating and cross-checking, trying to narrow down the possibilities. Mick remained subdued, which increased their efficiency, but Jamie found himself perversely wishing for Mick's usual argumentative and scattershot approach to this kind of work. It did not reappear, and Thursday was more of the same, as they conducted interviews with witnesses and survivors and Marian Coulson's bewildered husband, and if Mick strung three words together into a sentence, it was as much as he did all day.

At 3:32 Friday morning, Jamie's cellphone rang, waking him from a confused dream in which the Bureau of Paranormal Investigations was being moved into his old elementary school. He had the phone open and to his ear before he was even sure where he was, and his "Foxtrot-niner" was as clear and crisp as if he were in his office rather than up on one elbow groping for the lamp on the nightstand.

Lila mumbled something, but Jamie's attention was focused on the silence from his cellphone. "Hello?"

More silence, but the distinct sound of someone breathing, too rapidly and hard.

"Who is this? Look, if you don't say something, I'm going to have to assume you have hostile intent, and we don't none of us want that paperwork. So come on. What do you want?"

Thin thread of a voice: "Jamie?"

"Mick? What the fuck?"

"Jamie, how do you know you're you?"

Jamie felt every separate blood vessel in his body go cold. "Where are you, blue eyes?"

"I, um, I don't know. On a bridge."

Jamie rolled out of bed, yanking sweatpants on over his boxers, shrugging into a flannel shirt one arm at a time, so he didn't have to put the phone down. "Which bridge, blue eyes? Come on. How'm I supposed to come get you if I don't know where you are?"

"You're going to come get me?"

Mick sounded dazed, the way he did when his esper hit him hard.

"Course I am." Shoes. Shoes. Goddammit, they had to be here somewhere. "Can't leave you freezing your ass off all night."

"But I'm not . . . "

"Yes, you are," Jamie said, as forcefully as he thought he could without spooking Mick. "You're just confused, blue eyes, that's all."

"Are you sure? Are you sure I'm me?"

It was all too easy to imagine Mick standing on one of Babylon's bridges, hunched around his cellphone, his long dyed-black hair straggling across his face. Jamie tried to keep that imaginary Mick firmly on the pavement, but it was even easier to imagine him standing on the railing, one arm wrapped around a stanchion, teetering out over the black water.

"I am absolutely certain you're you," Jamie said, cramming his feet into his sneakers. "You trust me, don't you?"

"Yes," Mick said promptly.

"Good, blue eyes, that's good. Now can you tell me where you are?"

"I, um . . . "

"Jamie," Lila hissed, "what on earth is going on?"

"Mick's in trouble," he said over his shoulder, heading down the short hallway to the living room to find his keys. The Saturn was Lila's, and he didn't normally drive it, relying on buses and subway trains to get him to and from work, but there were no buses this time of night, and he couldn't leave Mick out there in the state he was in.

"I should have guessed. God knows you wouldn't race off like this for your mother." Mick and Lila had not taken to each other the one time they'd met.

"Can you find a street sign?" he said to Mick.

A long pause, during which Jamie did not panic because he could still hear Mick breathing. He and Lila stood staring at each other, neither one of them quite willing to have the argument they were on the brink of.

"Rossiter!" Mick said triumphantly. "I'm on the Rossiter Street Bridge."

One of the jumpers had gone off the Rossiter Street Bridge; Jamie wondered if Mick had remembered that, or if this was just unhappy coincidence. "Good, blue eyes. Now, don't hang up, okay? It'll take me ten minutes to get to you, but I'll stay on the phone the whole time. You can talk to me. Okay?"

"Okay," Mick said. He sounded lost again. "But why would you . . . "

"Why would I what, blue eyes?" Jamie asked, buttoning a couple of random buttons on his shirt. Lila tsked, rolled her eyes, and came over to do the buttons up properly.

"I stole his life. Why would you help me?"

There was the confirmation Jamie hadn't needed. "Because you need me," he said. "Besides, remember you trust me? And I don't think you stole anybody's life."

Lila finished buttoning his shirt, stepped back with a firm pat to his chest. "You can make it up to me later," she said in a sultry whisper and turned to make her way back to bed.

"Blue eyes?" Jamie said. "You still with me?" He left the apartment, took the stairs two at a time.

"I, um . . . yeah. You'd tell me, wouldn't you? If you really thought I wasn't me?"

"Course I would," Jamie said. "But that's not what I think. I think you are you." Out into the crisp night air, around to the back of the building and the parking lot.

"Oh," Mick said, a barely voiced exhalation.

Jamie unlocked the Saturn, wedged himself in. "Talk to me," he said to Mick. "When did you start feeling funny?"

"I've always been fake," Mick said, his voice thin and desolate and eerie. "Glass eyes."

It was something Jamie had thought more than once himself, pale as Mick's eyes were against his unnaturally black hair. "You didn't think you were fake yesterday."

"Of course I did. I've always been fake. It just didn't . . . it didn't bother me before."

Jamie whipped the car around in the tightest three-point turn that parking lot had ever seen, and put his foot down. This time of night, traffic was sparse, and he drove hard and fast, all the while encouraging Mick to keep talking, asking questions, trying both to keep him from jumping—for there was never the slightest doubt in Jamie's mind that that was why Mick was on the Rossiter Street Bridge—and to get more information, some hint as to the parameters of the thing they were dealing with. He wondered if it was Mick's esper that had made it hit so hard, so quickly. Wondered if in another three or four days, it would be him on the bridge.

He left the car half on the sidewalk on the north bank of the river and walked, carefully not allowing himself to run, out to the midpoint where Mick was standing, leaning against the railing like a drunk.

At least he wasn't on the railing, and Jamie took what felt like the first breath he'd had in years.

He hung up the phone only when he saw Mick glance at him, and in another three strides, he was standing beside his partner. The Rossiter Street Bridge wasn't very high, but it was high enough.

"Hey, blue eyes."

Mick was looking carefully at his hands where they rested on the bridge railing. He whispered something.

"Sorry, what?"

"You can tell now, can't you? That I'm an impostor?"

"Oh, Christ, Mick," Jamie groaned, although it wasn't Mick's fault, and he knew it. Except, said a mean and entirely reasonable voice in the back of his head, that he won't go for the esper training like Jesperson's been on at him . . .

A sudden, blessed inspiration. "Come on. We're going to go see Jesperson."

"Jesperson?"

"You remember, the nice man we work for? Class nine necromancer. No impostor could ever get by him."

And to his relief, Mick said, "Okay," and let himself be shepherded to the car.

At 8:30 that morning, Jamie was leaning against the wall of the BPI clinic, watching Mick sleep the sleep of the heavily drugged. Jesperson had wasted no time in calling out the night-shift decon team, and then had torn strips out of Jamie's hide for not thinking to do the same. Jamie was too relieved to mind, too relieved, now, to do anything but stand and watch Mick sleep and occasionally remember to take a mouthful of lukewarm coffee.

"Well," said Jesperson, scaring the living daylights out of him, "at least we know considerably more than we did." And he added, almost under his breath, "Damn and blast the boy," making the ritual sign to nullify his words with his free hand.

Jamie eyed the stack of reports in his other hand with foreboding. "What do we know, sir?"

"It's definitely a curse, and it was definitely laid on Sharpton, rather than being transmitted by a curse-vector. But there's no structure to it."

"Meaning?"

"This isn't the work of a magic-user," Jesperson said grimly. "It's not even really a curse, in the technical sense. More like an extremely powerful ill-wishing."

"Thought those went out with the bustle."

"That's just the problem, Keller. Ill-wishing is much less common these days, thanks mostly to improvements in public education, but by its nature it will always happen—if only among the ill-educated and the very young."

"You don't think a child did this?"

"I was speaking in general terms. And, no, this curse is not the product of a child's psyche."

"So it must be someone without much education?"

"Or someone whose mind is not well-controlled at the moment. There is a reason necromancers fear senile dementia above all other illnesses, you know."

Jamie frowned, trying to figure out where Jesperson was headed. "Mrs. Coulson? But—"

"She and Sharpton are the only two who have survived. And Sharpton only survived because something—training or motherwit or God knows what—impelled him to call you before he—"

"Did anything stupid," Jamie finished hastily; his memories of the Rossiter Street Bridge were still too vivid for comfort. "So you want me to go see Mrs. Coulson again?"

"At the very least, that ill-wishing needs to be raised. I'm giving you Juliet-seven until Sharpton's back on his feet. She can take care of that part."

"Yessir," Jamie said without enthusiasm. Juliet-seven was Marie-Gabrielle Parker, one of this year's crop of rookies.

"She's a class two necromancer," Jesperson said, amused. "And someone has to blood the tyros, Keller."

"Yessir. But Mick's gonna be okay?"

"Oh, yes. The ill-wishing is lifted. Dr. Sedgwick just wants to let him sleep off the residue. He should be gadflying about again by tomorrow."

"Thank you, sir." Jamie pushed off from the wall. He might as well go find Parker and get this over with.

"Oh, and Keller—"

"Yessir?"

"Be careful. I don't know if our ill-wisher is Mrs. Coulson or not, but whoever it is, he or she is . . . " He hesitated a moment, as if he could not find the right word. "Ill-wishing is made of anger. Someone out there is very angry indeed."

"Yessir," Jamie said. "I'll keep it in mind."

But Jesperson's suspicions were wrong.

Primed with the knowledge gained from Mick's case, Parker lifted the ill-wishing, if not easily, then at least without making a huge production number out of it. And she and St. Dymphna's staff magic-user—a lowly class three magician, but good at his job—agreed: Marian Coulson was a victim here, not a perpetrator. Parker said pithily, "She doesn't have the strength of will to ill-wish a mosquito." And looking at the soft-eyed, frightened woman blinking around at her strange surroundings, Jamie could only agree. She hadn't succeeded in committing suicide because she didn't have the guts.

He questioned her gently; she was afraid of him, but eager to help, willingly telling him everything she could remember about the events of the previous week. Jamie took notes, although he had no real hope that Mrs. Coulson would remember anything useful, working on autopilot until the words *Langland Street* brought him back with a thump.

"How did you get to Langland Street, ma'am?"

"Oh, I took the subway." Remembered irritation creased her forehead and made her voice peevish. "I really wish the city would do something about cleaning up the subway stations. There was a dirty old woman there, asking everyone for money—"

"Thank you, ma'am, you've been a great help," Jamie said, scrambling to his feet, and led the bewildered Parker nearly at a run back to the car.

He was lucky enough to get Avery when Dispatch patched him through to Records, and Avery didn't fuss or ask questions, but found out what Jamie needed to know. What he already knew.

All of the victims had been on Langland Street in the week before their deaths.

"Son of a *bitch*," Jamie said. "All right, Parker, hang on." And he floored it, wondering how many people, like Paul Sinclair, he was going to be too late to save.

She was a dirty old woman, as Mrs. Coulson had said, and Jamie was ashamed to realize he didn't remember her name. Avery in Records had that, too: Veronica Braggman. Old and dirty and shapeless beneath layers and layers of ragged clothes, her eyes small and bright and half-mad. She was tucked into a corner of the Langland Street Station, her crudely lettered cardboard sign in front of her like a shield: *Cant Work / Gov took my penshon / please help.*

She saw him coming—he would have had to be a class nine necromancer like Jesperson to have any hope of concealing himself—and heaved herself to her feet. "You stay away from me, nigger!" she cried. "I was respectable once—I don't have to talk to you!"

That answered one question: why her ill-wishing had landed on Mick instead of him. He hadn't been worth her anger.

"Miz Braggman?" he said politely, carefully. "We just need to ask you a few more questions."

"I ain't talking to you!" she said, still with her high voice pitched to carry.

"Ma'am, there's four people dead. You don't have a choice."

Her head lowered, and she looked at him sidelong, like an ill-tempered, cunning animal. "Ain't my doing. I didn't push 'em."

"Yes, you did, and you know it," Jamie said. The stench of her body was nothing compared to the stench of her mind, and he didn't need esper to feel it. "You hexed 'em."

Hex was an old word, his Great-Granny May's word, and he saw from the way she blinked that it was Veronica Braggman's word, too. "I can't hex nobody, nigger. Just a poor old lady, that's all I am."

He cut her off before she could get well-launched into that rehearsed whine. "Why'd you do it?"

"Didn't do nothing," she said sullenly. Then suddenly, she was shouting again, "Get him away from me! Get this nigger away from me! Ain't there no decent God-fearing folks anymore?" Jamie realized they'd attracted an audience, and one of them was a woman in the uniform of the Babylon Metropolitan Police Department, who was already pushing her way through the crowd toward him.

He turned carefully, not letting Veronica Braggman out of his sight, and said, "I'm with the BPI. If you'll give me a moment, I can show you my ID."

"He's a liar!" shouted Veronica Braggman. "A filthy liar!"

Jamie slowly reached into his hip pocket, slowly brought out his ID folder, slowly opened it for the policewoman's inspection. He saw her face change, and Veronica Braggman saw it, too, for she changed her tactics. "They're all against me, all the gummint! Just want to keep a poor old lady down so the niggers and the white-trash can walk all over me. They took it all away from me, so I ain't got nothing. And now they gonna take that, too!"

The policewoman said, "Do you need any help, Mr. Keller?"

He saw the incandescent fury light Veronica Braggman's face and instinctively backed away from her. But nothing seemed to happen; she slumped back against the wall, muttering, "It ain't no use, none of it. Can't never get back my rights. Can't never get what they stole from me."

Marie-Gabrielle Parker's voice said, from the midst of the crowd, a little unsteady but admirably clear, "Keller, we've got the evidence we need. And we need to get you back to headquarters before that ill-wishing has time to sink in. I don't think I can handle it myself."

He turned back to Veronica Braggman. "You just hexed me?"

Her head came up; there was nothing sane in her eyes at all. *"You stole my life,"* she said, and it was the snarl of an animal goaded past endurance, the wail of a lost child, the cry of a woman who had nothing left, nothing, and who sat on the cold tiles of the Langland Street subway station every day, watching people go past, people with jobs and families and homes to go to, people with lives . . . people who saw her, if they saw her at all, merely as a nuisance, as dirt to be cleaned up.

She lunged at him; he had played football from the time he was an eight-year-old bigger than most ten-year-olds, and he could read her body language. She expected him to fall back, to leave her space to twist through the crowd, to throw herself off the edge of the platform like Paul Sinclair. And part of him wanted to let her do it. Even if she didn't break her neck in the fall, and she didn't land on the third rail, and a train didn't kill her, the ghouls would take care of her before she'd gone half a mile in the darkness of the subway tunnels. Like a garbage disposal.

Jamie put his hands out and caught her—and narrowly avoided being bitten to the bone for his pains. And then Parker was there, and they were getting handcuffs on her; she went limp, weeping great maudlin crocodile tears, and Jamie knew no matter how long he spent in the shower, he'd never really get the stink of her off him: madness and hate and despair and the terrible bewilderment of not knowing how she had ended up like this. He did not want empathy with her, but he could not help understanding. Blame the government at first, but the government is faceless, far away. It's the people who walk by you every day and don't make eye-contact, who call you names and talk about needing to "clean up" the subway stations; they're right there, and it must be their fault. They're the ones with lives they don't deserve; they're the ones who have stolen your life. They're the impostors, because under their clothes and makeup, their cellphones and iPods and the hard shell of security, they're *just like you*.

Jamie shuddered, and Parker said, with surprising authority, "Come on, Keller, move your ass."

She was all right, Parker was.

He ended the day where he'd begun it, in the BPI clinic. Mick was awake now, a little owlish still with the sedative and somewhere between mortified and furious at what Veronica Braggman had done to him.

The decon team had lifted the ill-wishing off Jamie, although it had taken them three tries before they were sure they had all of it, and somewhere else in the BPI's sprawling bulk, that lady was doubtless being fingerprinted and tested and, Jamie hoped, fed.

"Ironic that she's probably going to end up better off," Mick said.

" 'Less she goes to the electric chair."

Mick shook his head. "She'll be found insane, and they'll put her in Leabrook."

"You sound awful sure."

"I was . . . well, I wasn't in her head, exactly, but something like it. The reverse of it, maybe. She's insane."

"And four people are dead."

Mick raised his eyebrows. "You sound like you think your halo's a little tarnished on this one."

"Fuck off, Mick." He couldn't leave—they wanted to keep him under observation overnight, and Lila'd had a fit about that, too—but he got up to pace. Up and back, the room not really long enough to accommodate his stride, but it was better than sitting still with Mick sneering at him.

"Jamie?"

He swung round to give Mick a glare, and maybe a piece of his mind, but Mick was looking at him wide-eyed, solemn and a little taken aback, and Jamie's anger drained out of him.

"I'm sorry," Mick said. "You wanna tell me what I did?"

"You were just being your usual charming self. I'm sorry. Shouldn't've flown off the handle like that."

"I don't mind. Except you usually don't. It's more my speed, isn't it?"

Jamie thought of some of the tantrums Mick had pitched and grinned reluctantly. "I just . . . she's not a nice old lady, you know."

"Parker gave me the highlights," Mick said, rather dryly. "But I don't see why that's got your tail in a knot. You caught her, you know. Justice will be served."

"Yeah, but she was right."

"I'm sorry?"

"All those people walking past her every day. Probably most of them ain't nice, either. Who says they have any right to good clothes and a warm place to sleep? Who says they deserve it more than her?"

"Nobody," Mick said. He was eyeing Jamie cautiously now. "You still feeling like yourself, Keller?"

"It ain't that," Jamie said and started pacing again. "It's just, how come she ended up the villain here?"

"Because she started killing people."

"You said it yourself. She's crazy. And she's crazy because somehow she got fucked over and spat out in little pieces. Blame The Victim isn't a nice game, Sharpton."

"Nor is Pin The Blame On The Donkey." Mick slid off the bed, gawky and angular in the clinic's ugly gown. He approached Jamie slowly, put one bony hand on Jamie's biceps. "Jamie, it isn't your fault."

"I know that. Nobody's fault, really. Or everybody's. Just another clusterfuck of modern life."

"We do the best we can, instead of the worst," Mick said. "That's all we can do."

· "I know," Jamie said, not turning to face Mick, because he knew the particular kind of courage it took for Mick to offer comfort and just how fragile that courage was. "I just hate it that that's not enough sometimes, you know?"

"Yeah," Mick said, his hand warm and heavy and vital on Jamie's arm. "I know."

⊰⊱

Sarah Monette lives in a 106-year-old house in the Upper Midwest with a great many books, two cats, and one husband. Her first four novels were published by Ace Books. Her short stories have appeared in *Strange Horizons*, *Weird Tales*, and *Lady Churchill's Rosebud Wristlet*, among other venues, and have been reprinted in several Year's Best anthologies. *The Bone Key*, a 2007 collection of interrelated short stories, was re-issued last year in a new edition. A non-themed collection, *Somewhere Beneath Those Waves*, was published in 2011. Sarah has written three novels (*A Companion to Wolves*, *The Tempering of Men*, and the soon-to-be-published *An Apprentice to Elves*) and several short stories with Elizabeth Bear. Her next novel, *The Goblin Emperor*, will come out under the name Katherine Addison. Visit her online at www.sarahmonette.com.

⊰⊱

The Case: *A man who believes he's sold his soul has, for ten years, received just what he bargained for: success. But now the decade is drawing to an end, he's in despair, and needs some professional help.*

The Investigator: *Quincey Morris, occult investigator and great-grandson of Quincey P. Morris, who had a hand in destroying a certain Count Dracula in the nineteenth century.*

DEAL BREAKER

Justin Gustainis

"You're not an easy man to find, Mr. Morris," Trevor Stone said. "I've been looking for you for some time."

"It's true that I don't advertise, in the usual sense," Quincey Morris told him. "But people who want my services usually manage to get in touch, sooner or later—as you have, your own self." Although there was a Southwestern twang to Morris's speech, it was muted—the inflection of a native Texan who has spent much of his time outside the Lone Star State.

"I would have preferred sooner," Stone said tightly. "As it is, I'm almost . . . almost out of time."

Morris looked at his visitor more closely. Trevor Stone appeared to be in his mid-thirties. He was blond, clean-shaven, and wearing a suit that looked custom made. There was a sheen of perspiration on the man's thin face, although the air conditioning in Morris's living room kept the place comfortably cool— anyone spending a summer in Austin, Texas without air conditioning is either desperately poor or incurably insane.

Morris thought the man's sweat might be due to either illness or fear. "Are you unwell?" he asked.

Stone gave a bark of unpleasant laughter. "Oh, no, I'm fine. The picture of health, and likely to remain so for another"—he glanced at the gold Patek Philippe on his wrist—"two hours and twenty-eight minutes."

Fear, then.

Morris kept his face expressionless as he said, "That would bring us to midnight. What happens then?"

Stone was silent for a few seconds. "You ever play Monopoly, Mr. Morris?"

"When I was a kid, sure."

"So, imagine landing on Community Chest and drawing the worst Monopoly card of all time—one that reads *Go to Hell. Go directly to Hell. Do not pass Go. Do not collect $200.*"

It was Morris's turn for silence. He finally broke it by saying, "Tell me. All of it."

The first part of Trevor Stone's story was unexceptional. A software engineer by training, he had gone to work in Silicon Valley after graduation from Cal Tech. Soon, he had made enough money out of the Internet boom to start up his own dot-com company with a couple of college buddies. They all made out like bandits—until the bottom fell out in the Nineties, taking most of the dot-commers with it.

That was how, Trevor Stone said, he had found himself sitting alone in his company's deserted office one afternoon—bankrupt and broke, under threat of lawsuits from his former partners and of divorce from his wife. He was just wondering if his life insurance had a suicide clause when a strange man appeared, and changed everything.

"I never heard him come in," Stone said to Morris. "Which was kind of weird, because the place was so quiet you could have heard a mouse fart. But suddenly, there he was, standing in my office door.

"I looked at him and said, 'Buddy, if you're selling something, have you ever come to the wrong place.' And he gave me this funny little smile and says "I suppose you might consider me a salesman of a sort, Mr. Stone. As to whether I am in the wrong place, why don't we determine that later?' "

"What did he look like?" Morris asked.

"Little guy, couldn't have been more than five foot five. Had a goatee on him, jet black. Can't vouch for the rest of his hair, because he kept his hat on the whole time, one of those Homburg things, which I didn't think anybody wore anymore. Nice suit, three-piece, with a bow tie—not a clip on, but one of those that you tie yourself."

"Did he give you a name?"

"He said it was Dunjee. What's that—Scottish?"

"Maybe." Morris's voice held no inflection at all. "Could me any number of things." After a moment he continued, "So, what did he want with you?"

"Well, he was one of those guys who take forever to get to the point, but what it finally came down to was that he wanted me to play *Let's Make a Deal.*"

Morris nodded. "And what was he offering?"

"A way out. A change in my luck. An end to my problems, and a return to the kind of life I'd had before."

"I see. And your part of the bargain involved . . . "

"Nothing much." Another bitter laugh. "Just my soul."

"Doesn't sound like a very good deal to me," Morris said gently.

"I thought it was just a *joke*, man!" Stone stood up and started pacing the room nervously. "I only listened to the guy because I had nothing else to do, and it gave me something to think about besides slitting my wrists."

Morris nodded again. "I assume there were . . . terms."

"Yeah, sure. Ten years of success. Ten years, back on top of the world, right where I liked it. Then, at the end of that time, Dunjee said, he'd be back. To collect."

"And your ten years is up tonight, I gather."

"At midnight, right. That's actually a few hours over ten years, since it was the middle of the afternoon when I talked to him, that day. But he said he wanted to 'preserve the traditions.' So midnight it is."

"Did he have you sign a contract?"

"Yeah."

"Something on old parchment, maybe, smelling of brimstone?"

"No, nothing like that. He had the template on a disk in his pocket. He asked if he could use my PC to fill in the specifics, so I let him. Then he printed out a copy, and I signed it."

"In blood?"

"No, he said I could use my pen. But then he pulled out one of those little syrettes they use in labs, still in the sterile wrapper, and everything. Dunjee said he would need three drops of blood from one of my fingers. I said okay, so he stuck me, and let the three drops fall onto the contract, just below my signature."

"Then what happened?"

"He said he'd see me in ten years plus a few hours, and left. I told myself the whole thing was going to make a great story to tell my friends, assuming I had any friends left."

"You felt it was all just an elaborate charade."

"Of *course* I did. I wouldn't have been surprised if one of my former partners had sent the little bastard, just to mess with my head. I mean, deals with the devil—come on!"

Morris leaned forward in his chair. "But now you feel differently."

"Well . . . yeah. I do."

"Why? What changed your mind?"

Stone flopped back in the chair he had left. "Because it *worked*, that's why. My luck changed. Everything turned around. *Everything.* My partners dropped their lawsuits, some former clients who still owed me money decided to pay up, a guy from Microsoft called with an offer to buy a couple of my software patents, my wife and I got back together—six months later, it was like my life had done a complete one-eighty."

"So you decided that your good fortune meant that your bargain with the Infernal must have been real, after all."

"Yeah, eventually. It took me a long time to finally admit the possibility. Denial is not just a river in Egypt, you know what I mean?"

"I do, for sure."

"But the bill comes due at midnight, and I'm scared, man. I have to admit now that I am really, big-time terrified. Can you help me? I mean, I can pay whatever you want. Money's not a problem."

"Well, I'm not sure what—"

"Look, you're some kind of hotshot occult investigator, right? There's a story about a bunch of vampires, supposed to have taken over some little Texas town. I heard you took care of that in four days flat. And, yesterday, I talked to a guy named Walter LaRue, he's the one told me how to find you. He said you saved his family from some curse that was, like, three centuries old, but he wouldn't tell me more. Christ, you must deal with this kind of stuff all the time. There's got to be a way out of this box I've got myself in, and if anybody can find it, I figure it's you. Please help me. *Please*."

Morris looked at Trevor Stone for what seemed like a long time. Unlike his unexpected visitor, Morris was dressed casually, in a gray Princeton Tigers sweatshirt, blue jeans, and sandals. There were a few touches of gray in his closely trimmed beard, but none at all in the black hair above it. Finally, he said, "You're probably pretty thirsty after all that talking—how about something to wet your whistle, before we talk some more?"

Stone asked for bourbon and water, and Morris went to a nearby sideboard to make it, along with a neat Scotch for himself. Although well into his forties, Morris moved easily, like someone who still likes to make hard use of his body from time to time.

Morris gave Stone his drink and sat down again. "You know, my profession, if you want to call it that, isn't exactly well organized. There's no union, no licensing committee, no code of ethics we're all expected to follow. But my family has been in this business going back four generations, and we have our own set of ethical standards."

Stone took a pull on his drink but said nothing. He was watching Morris with narrowed eyes.

"And it's a good thing too," Morris went on. "Because it would be the simplest thing in the world for me to go through a bunch of mumbo-jumbo, recite a few prayers over you in Latin, maybe splash a little holy water around.

Then I could tell you that you were now safe from the forces of Hell, charge an outrageous amount of money, and send you on your way. You would be, too."

Stone shook his head in confusion. "I would be—what?"

"Safe, Mr. Stone. You'd be safe, no matter what I did, because you were never in any danger to begin with."

After a lengthy silence, Stone said, "You don't believe I made a deal with the Devil."

"No, I don't. In fact I'm sure you didn't."

Hope and skepticism chased each other across Stone's face. "Why?" he asked sharply. "What makes you so certain?"

"Because that kind of thing just doesn't happen. It's the literary equivalent of an urban legend. I don't know if Marlowe's *Doctor Faustus* was the start of it or not, but bargaining away your soul to a minion of Hell has become a . . . a cultural trope that has no basis in actual practice. Sort of like the Easter bunny, but more sinister in its implications."

"You're saying you don't believe in Hell?"

Morris shook his head slowly. "I'm saying no such thing, no sir. Hell really exists, and so does Satan, or Lucifer, or whatever you want to call him. And the other angels who fell with him, who were transformed into demons as punishment for their rebellion—they exist, as well. And sometimes one of them *can* show up in our plane of existence, although that's rare. But selling your soul to the devil?" Morris shook his head again. "Just doesn't happen."

"But how can you be *sure*?"

"Because, among other things, it makes no sense theologically. The disposition of your soul upon death is dependent on the choices you make throughout your life. We all sin, and we all have moments of grace. The way the balance tips at the end of your life determines whether you end up with a harp or a pitchfork, to use another pair of cultural tropes."

"What makes you such an authority?" Stone asked.

"Apart from what I do for a living, you mean? Well, I suppose my minor in Theology at Princeton might give me a little credibility, along with the major in Cultural Anthropology. But far more important is the fact that we're talking about the essence of the Judeo-Christian tradition, Mr. Stone. The ticket to Heaven, or to Hell, is yours to earn. You don't determine your spiritual fate by playing *Let's Make a Deal*—with anybody."

"But it *worked*, goddammit! I bargained for a return to success, and success is what I got."

"What you got was confidence. You may have had a little good luck, too, but most of it was just you."

"Are you *serious*?"

"Of course. You must know how important confidence is in business. If you believe in yourself it shows, which causes other people to believe in you, too. And that's where success usually comes from. You were convinced your business problems were going to be fixed, and thus you acted in such a way as to fix them. You assumed your failing marriage could be repaired, and so you went and repaired it. And so on. They call that a 'self-fulfilling prophecy.' Happens all the time."

"My God." Stone sat back in his chair, relief spreading over his face like a blush. But in a moment, he was frowning again. "Wait a minute—Dunjee, with his contract and the rest of it. I didn't imagine that, I didn't dream it, and I don't do drugs that would give me those kinds of hallucinations."

"I have no doubt he was there. That's why I asked you what name he was using, and what he looked like. Your description was very accurate, by the way."

"You've heard of him?"

"Oh, yeah," Morris said, with a broad smile. "When you deal with the occult, it pays to keep track of the various frauds who pretend to supernatural powers. A lot of my work involves debunking con artists."

"Con artists? That's what Dunjee was—nothing but a *con artist*?"

"Exactly. His real name, by the way, is Manfred Schwartz, and he ran that particular scam very lucratively for a number of years. He would look for successful people who had fallen on very hard times. He'd show up, go through the routine he used on you, get a signed contract, then fade away."

Stone's brow had developed deep furrows. "I don't get it—how could he make money off that kind of thing? He didn't ask me for a dime."

"Not at the time, no. His approach, as I remember, was to visit a number of people, across a wide geographical area. He would go through his 'deal with the devil' act, then wait."

"Wait for what?"

"For his 'clients' ' fortunes to improve. Some of them would never recover from their adversity, of course. Those folks would never see 'Dunjee' again. But Manny chose his victims carefully—people with brains, guts, and ambition, who had just been dealt a few bad hands in life's poker game. People who might very well start winning again, especially if Manny convinced them that the powers of Hell were now on their side. Then, after they started to pull themselves out of their hole, Manny would show up again."

"Before the ten years were up?"

"Oh, yes, long before. He'd say he was just checking to confirm that they were receiving what he had promised—and to remind them what the ultimate price would be. Then he'd sit there, looking evil, and wait for them to try to buy their way out of their contract."

"Oh, my God," Stone said. "I see what he was doing, the little bastard."

"Sure. Manny would act reluctant, which would usually prompt the victim to offer even more money, which he would finally accept—in cash, of course. Then he'd make a ritual of tearing up the contract, and go off to spend his loot. It's a perfect example of the long con, because the mark never knows that he's been ripped off."

"Wait a minute—Dunjee never came back to see me. Never!"

"I'm not surprised," Morris said. "Because Manfred Schwartz was picked up by the FBI on multiple counts of interstate fraud—something like nine and half years ago."

"Son of a bitch!"

"Manny never came back to extort money out of you after your life got better, because Manny's life took a turn for the worse. He's currently serving fifteen to twenty-five in a federal pen—Atlanta, I think."

"But I never heard a thing—the feds never asked me to testify."

"Probably because Manny hadn't received any money from you yet, so technically he hadn't committed a crime. Besides, I expect the government had plenty of other witnesses to present at his trial."

Stone leaned back in the easy chair and appeared to relax for the first time since he had shown up at Morris's door.

"Feeling better?" Morris asked with a quiet smile.

"*Better* doesn't begin to describe it," Stone said. "I feel like . . . like I can take a deep breath for the first time in ten years."

"Well, then, I'd say that calls for another libation."

Morris took their empty glasses back to the sideboard. While mixing Stone's bourbon and water, he unobtrusively opened a small wooden box and removed a couple of capsules. Using his body to shield what he was doing, he popped open the capsules and poured their contents into the drink he was making. He stirred the contents until the powder dissolved, then poured a Scotch for himself.

Morris gave Stone his drink and sat down again. The two of them talked desultorily for a while, then Stone said, "Man, I suddenly feel really wiped out."

"Not surprising," Morris said. "With the release of all that tension, you're bound to feel pretty whipped. Anyone would."

A few minutes later, Stone's speech started to slur, as if he had consumed far more than two drinks. His eyelids began to droop, and then they closed all the way. Stone's head fell forward onto his chest, and the nearly empty glass dropped from his fingers and rolled across the carpet, before coming to rest against a leg of Morris's coffee table.

Morris called Stone's name at a normal volume, then again, more loudly. Receiving no response, he slowly stood up and went over to the unconscious man. He put two fingers on the inside of Stone's wrist and held them there for several seconds. Satisfied, he gently released Stone's arm.

Morris then went into his bedroom and came back carrying a small, square-shaped bottle with a gold stopper. Back at the sideboard, he poured several ounces of a clear liquid from the bottle into a clean glass. He stoppered the bottle, then took the glass back over to his chair. He put the glass on a nearby end table, but did not drink from it. Then he glanced at his watch, picked up the latest issue of *Skeptical Inquirer* from the end table, and settled down to wait.

Morris did not check his watch again, but he knew the witching hour had arrived when a gray Homburg suddenly plopped onto the middle of his coffee table. Looking up, Morris saw a small man in an elegant suit and bow tie sitting on the sofa. The man absently stroked his goatee as he frowned in Morris's direction.

"I was about to say that I'm surprised to see you, Quincey." The little man's voice was surprisingly deep. "But, on reflection, I really shouldn't be. My last client tried to hide out in a cathedral, for all the good it did him. So I suppose it was only a matter of time before one of them came crying to you for protection."

"I'm surprised you even bothered with this one, Dunjee," Morris said. "He was contemplating suicide when you showed up to make your pitch, so you guys would have had him anyway."

The little man shook his head. "Our projections were that he wouldn't have given in to his suicidal ideations, more's the pity. Even worse, there was a seventy-thirty probability that, after hitting rock bottom a year or so later, he was going to enter a monastery and devote the rest of his life to prayer and good works. Ugh."

Dunjee stood up. "I hope we're not going to have any unpleasantness over this, Quincey." He reached inside his jacket and produced a sheet of paper, which he waved in Morris's direction. "I have a contract, duly signed of his own free will. My principals have lived up to their part of the agreement, in every respect." He glanced over at Stone, and the expression on his face reminded Morris of the way a glutton will look at a big plate of prime rib, medium rare. "Now it's his turn."

"You know that contract of yours is unenforceable in any court, whether in this world or the next," Morris said. "The only thing you've got working for you is despair. The client thinks he's damned, and his abandonment of hope in God's mercy ultimately makes him so."

Dunjee shrugged. "Say you're right. It doesn't matter a damn, you should pardon the expression. If it's despair that makes him mine, so be it. Bottom line: the wretch *is* mine."

"Not this time," Morris said quietly.

"Surely you're not claiming he didn't accept the validity of the deal. Did he come running to you because he was eager to hear stories about that ancestor of yours who helped kill Dracula all those years ago? I don't think so, Quincey. He *knew* he was damned, and he was hoping you could find him an escape clause."

"You're absolutely right," Morris told him.

Dunjee stared at him, as if suspecting a trick. "So, why are we talking?"

"Because I found one."

"Impossible!"

"Not at all. Despair is the key, remember? Well, he doesn't despair any more. I convinced him that the soul is not ours to sell—which you admit yourself. Further, I spun him a yarn about how you were a con artist planning to come back when his luck changed and extort money from him, except you got arrested before you could return." Morris shook his head in mock sympathy. "He doesn't believe in the deal anymore, and that means there's no deal at all."

Dunjee's eyes blazed. "He doesn't believe?" Before Morris's eyes, the little man began to grow and change form. "*Then I will MAKE him believe!*" The voice was now loud enough to rattle the windows, and Dunjee's aspect had become something quite terrible to behold.

Morris swallowed, but did not look away. He had seen demons in their true form before. "That won't work, either. I slipped him a mickey—120 milligrams of chloral hydrate, combined with about four ounces of bourbon. He'll be unconscious for hours, and all the legions of Hell couldn't wake him."

Morris stood up then, facing the demon squarely. "The hour of midnight has come and gone, Hellspawn," he said, formally. "You have failed to collect your prize, and consequently any agreement you may have had with this man is now void, in all respects and for all time."

Morris picked up the glass he had prepared earlier. Pointing the index finger of his other hand at the demon he said, in a loud and resolute voice, "I enjoin you now to depart this dwelling, and never to enter it again without invitation. Return hence to your place of damnation, where the worm dieth not, and the fire is never quenched, and repent there the sin of pride that caused your eternal banishment from the sight of the Lord God!"

Morris dashed the contents of the glass—holy water, blessed by the Archbishop of El Paso—right into the demon's snarling face, and cried, "*Begone!*"

With a scream of frustration and agony, the creature known as Dunjee disappeared.

Morris took in a deep breath and let it out slowly. He carefully put the glass down, then pulled out his handkerchief to mop his face. His hands were trembling, but only a little.

He looked over at Trevor Stone, who had started to snore. He would never know what Morris had accomplished on his behalf, but that was all right. In the ongoing war that Morris fought, what mattered were the victories, not who received credit for them.

He sniffed the air, noting that the departing demon had left behind the odor characteristic of its kind.

He hoped the sulfuric scent of brimstone would be gone from his living room by morning.

⊏⊷⊐

After earning both Bachelor's and Master's degrees, **Justin Gustainis** was commissioned a Lieutenant in the U.S. Army. Following military service, he held a variety of jobs, before earning a PhD. Gustainis currently lives in Plattsburgh, New York where he is a Professor of Communication at Plattsburgh State University. Outside of his academic publications, he has authored three novels and two novellas of occult investigator Quincey Morris and his "consultant," white witch Libby Chastain; three novels featuring Stan Markowski and the Scranton [PA] Police Department's Occult Crimes Investigation Unit—the most recent is *Known Devil*—as well as a standalone novel, *The Hades Project*. He also edited *Those Who Fight Monsters: Tales of Occult Detectives*.

⊏⊷⊐

The Case: *An FBI agent, with troubles of his own, needs help uncovering a treasonous leak of secrets to the Nazis. He calls on an old friend for assistance . . . and gets far more than he bargained for.*

Investigator: *Jake Steuben, a former deputy sheriff whose family—including cousins Vic, Rosalie, and Olivia—is particularly talented and quite used to saving humankind.*

SWING SHIFT

Dana Cameron

Jake Steuben knew it would be easy to find Harry amid the crowd at North Station. All he had to do was find the highest density of pretty girls; his friend would be within fifteen feet.

Sure enough, there he was, ten feet away from a group of secretaries by the newsstand, watching as they chattered about the stars on the cover of *Life*. Jake picked up his valise and edged his way through the crowd. He leaned over and whispered into Harry's ear.

"If you get into trouble and you can't get out, it'll be because of a girl."

"There are worse reasons." Harry startled, his morose stare gone, and stood up to shake Jake's hand. "Train was on time. Any trouble?"

"What trouble would there be? It was crowded but quiet; I stood in the vestibule most of the way."

Harry looked askance. "No doubt the conductor made you stand out there—that's the ugliest hat I've seen in quite some time, my friend."

Jake took off his hat to look at it fondly. It was a little shiny, stretched, and the brim needed reblocking. "It's just getting broken in."

They walked out of the train station, past drunken sailors staggering to Scollay Square, then a few blocks to the Boston Common.

Harry said, "How's the wife?"

"Sophia is fine, thanks. How's the war effort in Washingt—?"

"And the baby's doing well?"

Jake couldn't help smiling. "Cutting his first tooth, so he's a handful. Say, Harry, what is it you—?"

"Good, glad to hear it. And everyone in Salem?"

Jake looked around. There was no one to overhear their conversation, so why did Harry keep interrupting? Politeness was all well and good, but he had come to Boston on the double. "Real good," he said slowly. "Thanks for asking."

They settled on a bench on the Common. The leaves on the trees were starting to turn, and would soon fall, but for now, the sun was warm and high.

Harry looked around carefully, then sighed. He shoved his hat back, mopped his forehead with his handkerchief. He sat forward, clapped his hands together, but didn't say anything.

Jake had had enough of waiting. "So, what's the problem you couldn't wire me about?"

Harry shifted uneasily. "I got a case I can't crack. It's a doozy. You've got a knack for getting into the tough ones, seeing angles I don't."

"Tell me." They'd worked occasionally as deputies for the Essex County sheriff until Harry started with the Bureau, and Jake inherited his family's farm near Salem.

Harry hesitated. "It's not easy. You know I deal with . . . government secrets."

"Are you sure you should tell me, then?" Jake enjoyed the sun on his face. His feet ached inside his shoes. The grass of the Common looked inviting.

"It's okay," Harry said, a little impatiently. "I cleared it upstairs. And got you clearance, too." He took a deep breath. "It's one of the research facilities, over in Cambridge. There's a bad leak. I can't pin it down."

"And what do you think I can do that the FBI can't?"

"I . . . I think I'm too close to it. You're outside." Harry looked up. "Like I said, you see angles no one else would. Remember the Beverly Slasher, how you knew he was the guy who found the first body? I wouldn't ask, but we got two strikes, two outs, bottom of the ninth. I don't find a DiMaggio soon, it's gonna be my fat in the fire."

"Sure, Harry. You know, I'll do whatever I can."

"Thanks, Jake." Harry smiled for the first time since Jake had gotten off the train, but it didn't reach his eyes. "The security is tight enough, I've been watching for weeks. I just don't know how the information is getting out."

"What do you think's going on? They've somehow learned to walk through walls? Use *magic* to whisk the secrets away?"

"Stop razzin' me, Jake." Harry shook his head, dead serious. "You know the Krauts are involved with some pretty unsavory investigations into the paranokermal and mystical. The trips to Tibet, the archaeology, their obsession with skulls . . . don't even joke about it. My boss, Mr. Roundtree, has stories that would curl your hair." Harry shuddered. "Nope, I'm hoping like heck it's good old human sneakiness and greed. I want you to get in there, see what I'm not seeing."

Harry pulled an envelope out of his jacket and handed it to Jake. "Your credentials, the location of a boardinghouse, description of your job. And a new name; we're not going to suddenly introduce a new guy with a German name. No offense."

Jake nodded. "Where will I be, and what will I be doing?"

"Janitor at a computational research lab. We want someone who will blend in, who no one will take too seriously. It's all in the file." He stood up, began to pace. "I should get going."

Jake was surprised. He wondered when his friend last slept through the night, ate a square meal, or bathed: his aftershave was faintly, nauseatingly sweet. "Hey, wait a minute! What do you think will happen, someone will go 'Psst, hey bud, want some government secrets?' You're gonna have to give me a few more—"

"Look, it's all in the file!" Harry said. "Wise up! I called you in because I need help. I can't sit around babysitting you; I got a job to do, an *important* job. There's a war on."

He mopped his face again. "Sorry, Jake. The pressure's killing me. I'll stop by your room in a couple of days. We can talk then. Okay?"

Harry stood and held out his hand. Jake stared at his friend, nodded slowly, and shook. He was genuinely worried now. His friend wasn't telling him the entire truth.

"Yeah, sure. Don't take any wooden nickels, Harry."

Later that night, Jake sat on the quilt-covered bed in his rented room, reading the file. Harry was right. He'd covered all the bases—waste disposal, deliveries, repairs—and checked some less obvious ways. Harry was a good agent for the same reason he'd been a good deputy: he had a mind like a criminal, and though he went to extremes, he was thorough. Harry had already followed several of the potential suspects: the secretary who'd been complaining about the rationing complained about everything else. The technician who seemed to have an unlimited supply of gasoline for a car with an A sticker was found to be siphoning fuel from his brother's trucking business. No one was obtaining the information any way he could see.

It was time to call in reinforcements, Jake decided. He went down to the drugstore and called his cousin Vic, arranging to meet him at the boarding-house in two hours.

When Vic arrived, the cousins set out for a walk along the Charles River. Jake explained everything, not sparing the details. "I want you to follow up on what Harry started. You and Rosalie tail the employees, sniff around, see what you turn up. It can't be magic that's getting those secrets out."

"Hey, there could be vampires," Vic said. He waggled his fingers, widened his eyes. "Turning into mist and going under the doors."

Jake shot his cousin a dirty look. "Stop clowning." Then he began to worry that Vic might not be too far off the mark.

Vic nodded. "Okay, you want Rosie's sister—you remember Olivia?—to cuddle up to anyone? She's got a real knack for making men want to please her."

Jake thought about it. Olivia might get Harry to reveal what he hadn't told Jake. As badly as he wanted to know, he shook his head. "No, thanks. Best not to raise our profile, now of all times, if we can avoid it."

After confirming their plans, Vic left for downtown, and Jake went about assuming his new identity.

Every day for two weeks, Jake—wearing Coke-bottle-bottom glasses and coveralls—swept, emptied the trash, and did odd jobs at the research facility. Even though he had access to almost everyone and everything, he still couldn't figure out how the information was leaving the lab. Rosalie and Vic had no better luck.

After two weeks working the day shift, Jake switched to the swing shift. The second night, he was mopping up in the office area when he heard a hiss from the doorway to Section Sixteen.

"Psst! Hey, buddy!"

Half convinced Harry was playing a joke on him, he looked up from the bucket to see a stacked redhead in a white lab coat beckoning to him. He recognized her as one of the computers, the women who operated the large, impossibly complicated analytical machines that were behind the locked door.

He made a point of looking over his shoulder, turned back, and raised his eyebrows—surely *she* couldn't mean *him*? She nodded vigorously, waved at him to hurry. He could barely believe his luck at this break. Supposedly, all the computers, mostly women, had the highest clearance, but maybe—

"Hey, I'm not trying to borrow money," she whispered. "I just need someone with good, strong hands."

Jake knew what she meant, but stayed in character. He backed away a step or two, holding his hands up. "Sister, I may be on the dumb end of the mop, but you move too fast for me."

The redhead blushed six different shades of mortified. "I . . . I didn't . . . I never . . . oh, golly, I just need you to help me fix something, and quick!"

"I'm not supposed to go in there," Jake said. No sense appearing too eager. "I don't have clearance."

"I've hidden all the sensitive material," she said, bouncing a little with impatience. "Unless you think a bearing that's come out of a rotor is top secret. And you're cleared to be *here*, right? I need to finish this set of calculations tonight, mister! Please?"

Jake shrugged. "You're the boss."

When he entered the long, wide room, the racket almost floored him. One side of the room were rows of shelves of electronics, bulbs and dials like ten thousand radios. The other side, a spaghetti mess of wires, all the way down the wall. The heat from the analytical machines was oppressive; a few curls stuck limply to the redhead's cheek.

"It's over here," she said and handed him a screwdriver. "If you could get that bearing back on track, I'd owe you."

Jake saw the problem right away. He grimaced; his hand was too big to fit comfortably, but she was right. All it took was brute strength to get the bearing reset. When it snapped into place, the woman's face lit up.

"Oh, thanks a million! I'd just gotten the—well, I can't really say. But if you hadn't been there, a lot of hard preparation would have gone down the drain, and some of our boys would have been in a real jam." Satisfied the machine was in order, she ushered Jake back to the administrative area.

The door safely shut behind her, she exhaled. "Phew! Thank goodness you were there. Those machines are so twitchy! Anyway, thanks."

"My pleasure." An idea blossomed. "Say, how do you manage when I'm not here?"

"Oh, I'm usually on the day shift. There's a supervisor to help out then. And funny, they don't think they need one after five o'clock. Sometimes the fireman on duty—you saw how hot it gets? Sometimes he helps me." She stuck out her hand. "I'm Ginny."

Jake shook her hand, being careful not to crush her delicate fingers. "Stuart." He grinned. "Call me Stu."

"Well, Stu, I'd be happy to buy you a cup of coffee. I've got a ten-minute break coming up."

Good thing he'd hidden his wedding band under the lining of his bag at the boardinghouse. "Why, thanks, Ginny. That sounds fine."

They drank the coffee, didn't even miss the sugar. Ginny unwrapped a piece of newspaper, offered Jake a molasses cookie.

Sighing deeply, Jake said, "I sure am glad we met! What a treat."

Suddenly shy, Ginny said, "I'm covering for my friend Ida. Her boyfriend got the night off. They went to see Duke Ellington at the Roseland. And tomorrow, they'll see Sabby Lewis at Le Club Martinique."

Jake perked up; he was a fan of jazz and the local bands. "The boyfriend's either missing a leg, an eye, or is about a hundred and forty-seven."

Ginny laughed. "It's not that bad. He tried to sign up—three different recruitment stations—but they all caught on to his gimpy leg and marked him 4-F. But we can use every pair of hands we get. This place is always humming, always something new. Eddie—that's the boyfriend—he's the head of grounds services, here." She smiled, compressing her lips hard together. "So many boys gone . . . if a gal gets the chance to go on a date, you help her out."

There was such a wistfulness in her voice, Jake asked, "And your young man?"

"It shows, huh?" She nodded. "Italy. Or last I heard, two months ago."

"That's tough. War won't last forever, though." Jake thought a minute. "Ida and Eddie must get to take lunches, breaks, together, though. He helps her out with the, er, machinery in there?"

"Oh." Ginny looked around, nervously. "That's how they met, actually. And that's why they keep it quiet. We're supposed to be really strict about access."

"Mum's the word," Jake said. He mimed turning a key in front of his lips, then throwing it away.

"But you and he couldn't even be in this building if you didn't check out, right?" she said, now obviously wondering whether she'd made a mistake. "And I'm usually pretty good at telling the good eggs from the bad."

Jake believed her; he was good at reading people, too. He laughed. "I got more papers than a show dog, and to do what? Push a broom, wash windows. Even with these cheaters, I can barely see three feet in front of me. Nah, just be careful with everyone else." He stood up. "Thanks for the coffee, Ginny."

"Thanks for the company," she replied. Then she winked. "And the help."

Jake finished his shift, then went back to the boardinghouse. He had warmed-over dinner—meatloaf and green beans—for breakfast, went up to his room, took off his shoes, and stared at the peeling paint on the tin ceiling. After about an hour, he thought he had it pretty well figured out.

It was all just a little too easy, like it had all been laid out for him. And that made him nervous. He decided he needed to go to Le Club Martinique that evening.

Jake crossed the bridge over the Charles River to Boston, and walked down Massachusetts Avenue. The neighborhood was still bustling six hours after the close of regular business. The clubs and bars on this end of town drew whites and Negroes, all dressed in their finest. Music seemed to create places where Jim Crow occasionally blinked. Jake appreciated that; he knew something about not fitting in.

Down toward Columbus Avenue, past the Savoy and the Hi-Hat, was the place Jake was looking for. Le Club Martinique might not have had the size or the garish splendor of the Roseland Ballroom, but it was hopping. Every time the door opened, a blast of swinging trumpet music threatened to knock passing pedestrians off their feet. Jake put it on his list to visit, after this job—maybe he'd even be able to talk the tin-eared Harry into coming with him. It was the kind of place where famous musicians would come after their sets to jam until morning.

A uniformed doorman tipped his braided hat as Jake entered. A big band was playing on the stage; they were good, not cluttering up the music with an unnecessary vocalist. The dancing couples got more and more daring with flips and twirls, putting aside care for a few hours, banishing worry with the joy and audacity of the music. They'd pay for it in the morning, but for now, it was worth every sore foot and hangover-to-be.

Inside the club, Jake saw a number of extravagantly long and baggy zoot suits. He wondered whether the uniformed soldiers there would call out the wearers as unpatriotic and wasteful as the beer flowed and the evening grew more raucous—

Jake's attention was drawn suddenly to a couple sitting alone. They matched Ginny's description of Ida and her boyfriend, Eddie.

The band tore into a version of "Cotton Tail" that would have done Ellington proud. Drinks were set aside, and the dance floor was mobbed.

The couple sat still, though Ida looked like she wanted to dance, too. Eddie, a weasely looking fellow, said something to her. She pouted; he refilled her coupe with champagne—Jake could see the French label—and patted her hand. Ida smiled, and Eddie limped over to another table.

Jake thought about Eddie the groundskeeper pouring French champagne.

Unless the dolly sitting at the table was Eddie's sister, Jake thought, Ida was right to pout. The other girl was all done up in blue satin and had on more rouge than was smart. Jake couldn't really tell—the smell of beer and chicken mingled with cigarettes and liquor sweat—but he would have bet she was wearing too much perfume, too. Eddie was leaning in a little too close; she let him. When their hands disappeared under the table simultaneously and stayed there for too long, Jake began to understand.

The drum solo ended, the horns jumped in, and a burst of energy surged through the club. Eddie stuck something into his pocket. The girl put an envelope into a satin clutch with rhinestones bigger than a Packard's headlights. Everyone's eyes were on the dancers or the band; Jake was the only one who'd seen the transaction.

The couple, Eddie and Ida, left then; she was protesting, but he was having none of it. Jake thought about following them, but realized there were bigger fish to fry. He had to keep his eyes on the glamour puss in blue satin. He waited about twenty minutes.

When Harry came into the club, Jake cussed and ducked behind a pillar.

If things had been so plain to him—how Eddie was working and why—why hadn't they been plain to Harry? And what was he doing here now? He *hated* jazz.

Afraid he'd queer his friend's plans, Jake stayed hidden, watched his friend go through a similar routine with Glamour Puss, hands under the table, swapping envelopes. Only this time, the girl wasn't so pleased. She and Harry exchanged heated words, to judge by their expressions. They were lucky the band had started in on a rowdy version of "Bugle Blues," drowning them out. Finally, Harry left, the girl looking more irked than ever.

Jake knew he could come back any night and find the girl sitting in her evening gown at that same table; he'd only have this one chance to find out what was up with Harry. He decided to follow Harry, intending to straighten this out, once and for all.

Two toughs grabbed Harry as soon as he reached the front door. As they dragged him outside, the song ended, and the dancers mobbed the bar. Jake struggled to get through the packed ballroom.

When he reached the street, Jake paused. It had rained briefly while he was indoors, but that wasn't what stopped him. What was a guy supposed to do? Let his best friend get roughed up—maybe even killed—or blow his cover? Jake knew a thing or two about discretion, and knew it was just as important to Harry the G-man.

If it took blowing his cover to save a friend, Jake would do it. The risk came with the job.

But he was going to pick his moment, if he could. No sense in undue haste.

Jake spat out his gum and followed the two goons who had Harry—they were professionals, no doubt about it, keeping things quiet while they were among the crowds on the street. Had Harry done something so stupid he'd gotten on the wrong side of a mobster? Jake recalled the glamour puss in the club. Harry should have known better, doing the work he did. Dames like that didn't sit alone for no reason.

If you get into trouble and can't get out, it'll be because of a girl.

Jake picked up speed; the trio was heading into a shady-looking neighborhood, even darker than normal because of the enforced blackouts. Things would happen quickly.

They were in an alleyway, now, and it wasn't to talk. At first, Harry played it smart and got in a few good punches; Jake hoped he could keep himself out of it. But two against one was too much, and Harry faltered, went down. The darkness made it the perfect place for trouble; there'd be no rescue from anyone on the street.

Jake couldn't wait any longer. He had to get in there.

Jake took a deep breath and concentrated, Changing only halfway. Tissue rippled, and bone stretched; the slack of his suit was filled with new muscles and thick, rough fur. The wolf-self, contained too long by the city, by the cheap shoes, by Jake's cover, was let loose. The joy of the Change ran through his body, from lengthening teeth and pointing ears to sharpened nails. Jake couldn't resist chuckling, a guttural, inhuman noise. The stink of evil was strong on the two goons.

He felt traces of power crawling through his system as he sized up the men. One, a guy the size of a moose, had a shiv that looked a mile long, sharp as sharp could be. The shorter one—Jake thought of him as "Cagney"—had just laid a cosh upside Harry's head. Harry looked like he was down for the count.

Good, Jake thought. *That will make this easier.*

Jake growled. The goons ignored him. Guys like that don't scare easy, and they were busy.

He hurled himself on them. They couldn't ignore that.

Jake landed on the back of Moose; best to lose the knife first, especially if the thug was any good with it. Moose kept his head, even as he found himself slammed into the brick wall, slimy with rain and God knows what else. He twisted fast, ignoring the blood pouring from the side of his forehead. He held onto the knife, tore it along Jake's arm. Jake pressed his face close, so the other man could see the teeth that didn't belong in a human mouth, feel the heat of a lupine mouth as it tore his ear.

Moose yowled and clutched his head, as Jake took the steel blade and snapped it like a cheap toy. It fell to the ground with a tinny clink. Moose turned and ran, screaming bloody murder and bleeding like a stuck pig.

No time to waste; even in this crummy a neighborhood their racket would bring unwanted attention. His hat went flying as Jake bounded to the end of the alley and tackled Moose. Jake tore out his vocal cords with another slash. There was only a wet gargling noise, now.

Jake turned to Cagney, who was going through Harry's pockets. The guy must have feared whoever he was working for more than he feared what was happening to Moose, because he had worked all through the fight—

Cagney suddenly looked up. His eyes were wide and unfocused, and his face slack. At first Jake thought he might be drunk, or a little soft in the head, but then the sweetish smell worked its way past the filth of the alley. Jake knew Cagney was high on opium.

Jake recognized another smell now. This was a stronger version of Harry's sickly aftershave.

Jake knocked the cosh out of Cagney's hand with one paw while raking claws down his cheek with the other. Cagney screamed, his hands flying up to his face as much to block as to hide from the Anubis-like monster before him. Jake's face had lost nearly all trace of humanity: elongated snout, fangs and a row of jagged teeth, ears sharply extended above his head. The fur wasn't the worst, or the whiskers, Jake had been told. It was his eyes. Somehow it was wrong that such human eyes should be set into the face of a slavering animal.

But Moose's screams had brought interest; Jake heard automobile engines and police sirens moving closer. He couldn't just leave Harry in the alley; one way or another, he was responsible for getting him out of the trouble he was now in.

Jake leaned over, grabbed his hat, and picked Harry up effortlessly. He slung him over his shoulder and turned to leave when a car pulled across his path, blocking his exit. He loped to the other end of the alley, but a Cadillac screeched to a stop there. The headlights from both cars lit the narrow lane; Jake was trapped in the middle near a couple of rank-smelling ash cans. The five men who spilled out of the cars brandished revolvers, aiming them at Jake and the unconscious Harry. Crazy shadows made many-armed monsters on the walls.

The three toughs at one end stumbled over the bodies Jake had left behind. There were exclamations, and one of the men retched at the sight and smell.

"That's the guy, Mr. MacLaren." At the other end of the alley, Eddie limped behind a large man in a flashy, double-breasted suit. He gestured to where Jake was trying to melt back into the shadows. "I'd recognize that cheap suit anywhere. I watched him eyeballing Sadie at the club while she was dealing. Then I followed him here, when I saw *him* trailing Sid and Joey as they hauled off that deadbeat Harry Gray."

Then Eddie got a look at what was left of Sid and Joey at the far end of the alley. He moved farther behind MacLaren.

"Wait a minute," MacLaren said. "Gray is the junkie? He's a Fed—he was at the big bust two years ago! The new boss is going to be very interested in what Gray knows about us!"

Jake was in a bind. He could run for his life, but leaving Harry behind with these goons would be tantamount to killing him. Jake could Change back to his human form, maintain his cover, and although he'd be able to fight, the chances of Harry and him surviving the armed gang were slight.

Jake adjusted Harry over his shoulder and pulled his hat lower. He'd try to make a break, hoping that in the mayhem, no one would notice a werewolf too much.

Fat chance.

He tensed himself, ready to spring, when he heard the clatter of ladies' shoes on the pavement at the top of the alley.

He froze. It was Rosalie and her sister Olivia.

It wasn't until the ladies called out that the gunmen noticed the two women had passed the cars and were right smack in the middle of things.

"Jake? You there, Cousin Jake?" Their voices couldn't have been more out of place in that dirty alley.

MacLaren didn't lower his pistol. "Ladies, this is a private party. Best you turn right around and get yourselves home."

"I think not," Rosalie said. "Not without Jake and his friend." She and Olivia were dressed for an evening out. They stood primly, in their best coats and hats, between the two groups of gangsters. Their arms were linked, their gloved hands folded over their handbags. They might have been strolling to church.

The other gunmen didn't bother stifling their laughter. Even MacLaren grinned at the ridiculousness of the situation. He snapped his fingers. "Walt, Jonesy, Studs."

The men moved forward quickly. Walt stepped behind Rosalie and shoved her hard to the ground. She didn't raise her head, and she was shaking.

At the same time, Jonesy grabbed Olivia by the arm.

"Take your hands off me!" Olivia demanded.

Jonesy laughed again but did as he was told.

"Jonesy! What are you doing!" MacLaren said.

When Jonesy realized what had happened, he looked at his hand and shook his head. "I don't know! It was like . . . I didn't have any choice!"

"Well, get them out of here," MacLaren said. "Or shoot 'em. We ain't got time for this."

Jonesy grabbed Olivia again and yanked her into him. "C'mon, you! You'd better scram—argh!"

Olivia had turned in to Jonesy and latched onto his neck with her mouth. As he screamed, perhaps Jake was the only one of the men capable of seeing her skin change, becoming violet snake scales. Her eyes enlarged, her nose diminished, and her teeth became . . . vampiric.

Studs and Walt tried to pull Olivia off Jonesy; she lashed out at them with razor-like claws. With a growl, Rosalie hurled herself from the ground and landed on top of the men attacking her cousin. Rosalie's face was like Jake's, now: furred, fanged, furious. Her little hat fell to the mud as she and Olivia shredded the gangsters. Bones crunched, blood ran.

As surreptitiously as he could, Jake deposited Harry behind the ash cans.

MacLaren was smarter than his men. He stared for only a moment, then aimed his pistol at Jake.

Jake rose up and threw an ash can at MacLaren, bowling him over. Jake turned to Eddie, who had the sense to run. Jake hesitated: Eddie now knew Harry was a government officer with an opium problem. Jake couldn't let him get away. But MacLaren was already scrambling up, his pistol cocked and ready—

A flash of fur. Something bounded over the Cadillac, knocking Eddie over. A large wolf, wearing a red union suit, grabbed the dope dealer by the back of the head and shook.

Jake dove for MacLaren, who managed to fire a shot. Jake clutched his shoulder but landed on top of MacLaren. The mobster screamed, the fear widening his eyes as Jake lowered his wolfy head toward him and snarled . . .

"Jake, no!" Olivia placed her hand on his back. "Don't kill him!"

Jake growled, thinking what MacLaren was: he would have killed Harry, he was a poison to his community, he was betraying his country by stealing secrets. "Since when are you squeamish?" Jake said, his voice made harsh by his elongated jaw.

"We need him for the FBI to quethtion. So Harry can wrap up his cathe." She, too, spoke awkwardly around a mouthful of sharpened teeth and two long fangs.

MacLaren, unable to see past Jake's head, still had it in him to be offended by mercy from a lady. "What makes you think I'll talk, sister?"

Olivia leaned down so MacLaren could see her. Her black eyes narrowed, and her head swayed slightly, fixing MacLaren with her gaze. He almost screamed, but stiffened, stared as if in a trance.

"You'll thing like a canary, when I get done with you," she said. No one hearing her would have doubted her, even with her hissing lisp.

A thrill of power rushed through the air. Vic had Changed back to human form, shivering in the night air wearing only his union suit. "Hey, Jake, we got to finish up quick. I left the car a few blocks back after I dropped off the girls, and tried to make sure the coast was clear for us to join you. But we won't stay alone forever."

"Right," Jake said. He got up and Changed back skin-self, handed the shivering Vic his jacket. "You and Rosalie move the bodies so it looks like they were fighting each other. The big guy down the end was a knife man; use that to cover up the worst of the claw and bite wounds." He turned to Olivia. "And how about you lay one of your Lamont Cranston–Shadow whammies on MacLaren? Suggest he remember this was a fight among his own men, and we were never here. And that he's dying to confess to the FBI, starting with who the 'new boss' is. I'm willing to bet he's a Nazi, or linked to them, if he's dealing in top secret calculations."

"Right, Jake." She pulled MacLaren up by the lapels and slammed him against the wall. "I know what evil lurks in the hearts of men."

She sank her fangs into his neck; MacLaren went limp, his eyes wide.

"Jake?" There was a weak voice from the sidelines; Harry struggled to pull himself upright. "Jake, what the heck—?"

"Harry, it's all right!" Jake tried to reassure him, but Vic was standing in his long underwear and a borrowed suit coat, and Rosalie was Changing back from her wolf-self, mourning a run in her last whole pair of stockings. Olivia, still a purple vampiress in a muddied coat, was whispering to MacLaren, who nodded eagerly.

Harry rubbed his head woozily. "Jake, there was a wolf-man. And he was wearing your ugly hat . . . "

"Harry," Jake said. "We're Fangborn. And we're here to help. Give us a hand, Olivia?"

She turned from MacLaren, delicately licking the blood from her fangs.

"We need to clean up my friend. And please give him a good story about how he followed Eddie from the club just in time to see the fight among MacLaren's men. How he flagged down the local cops and brought them here."

Olivia cocked her head. "It'll be tricky. It's harder to alter the blood chemistry of an opium addict. And he's concussed." It sounded like "concuthhhed."

"Do your best. We'll alert the Family down in Virginia to keep an eye on him. They'll give him more forget-me juice, if he shows signs of remembering us too well."

After they rearranged the bodies to suit their story, they loaded the still-dazed Harry in the back of MacLaren's Cadillac, his head cradled in Olivia's lap.

Jake handed Rosalie into the front seat and, after she smoothed her skirt around her knees, got in beside her and shut the door. He leaned around to the backseat. "Hey, Harry? How'd you like a kiss from my cousin Olivia?"

Harry's head ached from the beating, and the need for a fix was almost crippling. He looked up woozily at the lady who was stroking his hair in the dark. He couldn't see her well, but he knew, somehow, she was pretty.

He did like a pretty girl.

"Okay," Harry said. Was it his imagination, or was the pain that consumed him lessening?

Olivia leaned down to him, her lips slightly parted. Harry imagined a glint of white teeth. She brushed right past his lips and went for his neck.

By the time her fangs had pierced his skin and his blood was flowing into her mouth, Harry was so overwhelmed by a sense of wellbeing and comfort, the pain and the call of the opium needle was as remote as Shangri-La. There was room for only one thought:

That's some A1 kissing . . .

In the front seat, Vic peered into the night, navigating their way back to his car. "So the girl, the computer—Ida? She was letting her boyfriend, Eddie there, into the lab?"

"She thought Eddie was just helping her out," Jake said. "But he was helping himself to the calculations *and* the information about who they were for. We were looking for some criminal mastermind, not Eddie trying to keep his junk supplier happy. MacLaren's men, well, let's say they didn't just deal drugs. I'll be surprised if they weren't being encouraged to expand their businesses by the Nazis. The Bureau will track down the rest, shut them down, as soon as they find MacLaren's 'new boss.'"

Jake continued. "Harry couldn't afford to reveal himself as a Fed to MacLaren's men. He couldn't admit to his boss that he was taking opium. So he brought me in to get the evidence, while he kept himself out of the picture."

A voice came from the backseat, as if from a great distance. "Wow," Harry said.

"How you doing, Harry?" Jake asked. Vic and Rosalie exchanged tense glances.

"Well, I don't mind telling you, Jakey, I'm feeling pretty fine. But, tonight I saw a wolf-man wearing your darned hat. I saw a giant dog kill that cut-rate hood Eddie. And Olivia, well, apparently, she's a vampire—but nothing like what you see in the movies, let me tell you! At first, I thought I was high—who knows what that lovely, wicked Sadie has been giving me?—but I hadn't fixed. And it all seems so clear now. Like that time, up in Salem, when you—"

Time for Jake to step in. "Yes, Harry, my Family is full of werewolves and vampires, but not like in the movies. We're the good guys."

"Gee." Harry sighed. "That's swell."

"Olivia?" Vic said quietly. "You got the mix a little off. A little rich on the truth-telling serums and light on the memory blockers."

"Hey, it's a complicated case," she said, weaving a little. She was drained and giddy from the night's work. "But I'll take another crack at it." She smiled blearily and regarded Harry. "C'mere, lover boy."

A week later, Harry was back in Washington, whistling his way down Pennsylvania Avenue, his second-best suit cleaned and spruced up, a brand-new fedora cocked jauntily on the back of his head. There was a spring in his step that would have been out of place during wartime, save that everyone who saw him was suddenly filled with encouragement. Everything about his attitude shouted: *We can do it!*

Something had changed him in Boston. Maybe it was solving the case, maybe it was seeing his old friend, maybe it was getting hit on the head in that filthy alley, but Harry hadn't had the urge to use since then. It was days before he even noticed. Before Boston, he would have described himself as possessed by opium.

No more of that, now. Never again.

He'd already convinced his boss, Mr. Roundtree, to keep him on the job. In a month or two, Harry'd be back on track to run his own projects. Heck, he'd win the war from this side of the Atlantic!

He was still whistling as he entered the Department of Justice. He'd be hunting and pecking his way through another night at the old Smith Corona, and his fingers would be sore and stiff from jabbing the heavy keys. But his work—with Jake's help—had been a significant break, uncovering a major conduit for drugs and industrial-military espionage in the Northeast.

Something stopped him in his tracks. It took one minute to realize he wasn't ill, another to wonder what the problem was. But there was no problem. It was the image of the family sitting at the cloth-covered table, joined in company, sharing food, giving praise. On the left-hand side was a large, scruffy, shepherd-like dog, his head happily uptilted to the woman serving coffee.

He had passed the murals every day, had never really taken the time to examine them. Too tied up with work and then the pursuit of the needle, he'd barely bothered to look up. He did now. Amazing.

It was the dog that caught his attention. He wasn't much for dogs, didn't like the way they slobbered and jumped all over you—

In the alley. In Boston. Something had attacked MacLaren's men. Harry had been rattled, his head half-caved in, but he hadn't been high, and he knew what he saw. A wolf, standing on two legs, wearing a suit and one damned ugly hat—

The hat had been Jake Steuben's. He'd have recognized it anywhere.

As Harry stared at the mural, he remembered it all.

Jake had pulled a Lon Chaney in the alley, turned into a wolf-man. And Jake's friend Olivia had bitten him in the neck, just like Dracula. Only Harry was in better shape than he had been in years, and clean, to boot.

The first thing he thought was: *Oh, no. I don't want to want to have to get high again . . .*

And when he realized the idea left him with distaste, rather than that burning desire, he took a deep breath and considered. He'd done shady things to feed his addiction, seen horrors on the job. And now he realized Jake and his family were something out of a Saturday matinée.

But he'd trusted Jake with his life on more than one occasion. And Jake had always come through. Olivia had taken the most terrible burden from him, given him his life back.

Jake and his family *were* the good guys. They were patriotic, and discreet, too. Had to be.

Harry decided that there was nothing monstrous about them. He was eternally grateful to them.

It took him a while to find out the name of the mural—*Society Freed Through Justice,* by George Biddle. It stuck him as particularly appropriate. He wondered why the artist had included the dog. Wondered how many more—Fangborn?—there might be out there.

Harry thought long and hard. If Jake and his family could defeat MacLaren, and save a lost cause like Harry, imagine what they could do with a little help from the Federal Bureau of Investigation . . .

He made an appointment to discuss the matter with Mr. Roundtree. He had a feeling that after hearing what they could do, these Fangborn would suit his boss down to the ground.

⟫—⟨

Whether writing noir, historical fiction, urban fantasy, thriller, or traditional mystery, **Dana Cameron** draws from her expertise in archaeology. Her fiction, including stories featuring the Fangborn—who were introduced in "The Night Things Changed"—has won multiple Agatha, Anthony, and Macavity Awards as well as earning an Edgar Award nomination. The first of three novels set in the Fangborn universe, *Seven Kinds of Hell,* was published earlier this year by 47North. Dana lives in Massachusetts with her husband and benevolent feline overlords.

⟫—⟨

The Case: *A terrifying bogle starts haunting a Scottish laird's castle after the birth of the laird's youngest daughter.*

The Investigator: *Thomas Carnacki, a British occult detective with a penchant for ghostbusting gadgets like his "electric pentacle"—quite "high-tech" for his era.*

THE BEAST OF GLAMIS

➖✦➖

William Meikle

I arrived in Cheyne Walk that Friday evening in response to a very welcome card from Carnacki. It had been several weeks since our last supper together, and I knew that Carnacki had not been at home for a fortnight at least. Such an absence told of an adventure and I admit to a certain degree of anticipation as he showed me in.

"So what is it this time, old chap?" I asked as he took my overcoat. "A haunt or just another gang of criminals bent on deception?"

He smiled.

"Oh, there was certainly a degree of deception involved," he said. "But never fear . . . it is a fine tale that will be a whole evening in the telling. I hope you have a full pouch of tobacco at hand."

It was not long before Carnacki, Arkwright, Jessop, Taylor, and I were all seated at Carnacki's ample dining table. As ever he brooked no discussion as to why we had been asked to supper, and we all knew from long experience that he would not say a single word until the meal was over and he was good and ready.

At table we exchanged cordialities, and Arkwright entertained us with his tales of the goings on in the corridors of Westminster. Carnacki kept us waiting until we retired to the parlour and charged our glasses with some of his fine Scotch.

Jessop's palate was the first to notice a new addition to Carnacki's drinks cabinet.

"I say old man, isn't this the Auld Fettercairn?"

Carnacki smiled.

"Indeed it is, old chap. And thirty-five years old at that, one of only twenty bottles in existence. It was part of my payment for my recent sojourn. If you will all be seated, I shall tell you the tale as to how it was procured."

■ ■ ■

"It begins with a letter," he started as we fell quiet. "It was delivered on the Monday three weeks past, delivered by hand from those same Westminster corridors that Arkwright has so successfully lampooned. It was a simple note, requesting my attendance for lunch with a certain Claude Bowes-Lyon. Of course I knew the chap, knew his family history, and his reputation. I wondered what a Scottish lord from one of the old families would want with me.

"I did not have to wait long to find out. Lunch was served on the terrace, a fine breast of duck and an even finer Chablis. The lord, although he looked to be in rude good health, took none of it. But he had the good manners to wait until the meal was over before getting to the reason I had been brought here.

"'There are two things in this world I love above all others,' he said by way of preamble. 'My castle at Glamis, and my youngest daughter. To have both under threat at the same time is almost more than I can bear.'

"I lit a pipe and waited. I knew when a proud man needs to talk, and this was one of those occasions.

"'I have heard the stories of course,' he continued. 'All of us who live in and around the estate have lived with them all our lives; about the *beast* in the hidden room or the card game being played with Auld Nick for the player's souls. I put no credence in such matters. I have seen men dead . . . and they stay that way. The dead do not come back.

"'At least that is what I have always believed, and I continued to believe it right up until the birth of my youngest, Lisabet. Our troubles started on the night she came into the world.'

"He must have seen my shock, and was quick to allay any fears I might have shown.

"'Oh no. You misunderstand me. There is nothing wrong with Lisabet. A more even-tempered girl you will never find. No. The problems arose within the walls of the old castle itself. At first it was merely knockings in the night, doors opening and closing, that sort of thing. I tried to write it off as merely the old stone itself settling and aging. But soon the servants began to rebel, refusing to go to the second floor, and I had a mutiny on my hands when I tried to force the issue.

"'We took to ignoring the second floor completely, and that was that for several years. But we came to notice that things got worse when Lisabet was around. Matters came to a head just last month. I woke to the child's screams, and when I got to her room she was almost hysterical. It tooks us hours to calm her down. All she could tell us was that the bogle had tried to take her.

"'I have brought the girl to London in the meantime, but I need your help, Carnacki. I understand you have experience of this kind of thing, and I will *not* be forced from my own home. I need you to find out what this dashed thing is . . . and rid my family of it once and for all.' "

Carnacki paused to re-light his pipe before continuing.

"I could not with all conscience refuse," he said. "There was the fact that he was a lord, of course. But more interesting to me than that was the opportunity it gave me. I had a chance to get to the bottom of an age-old mystery, and by Jove, I meant to take it.

"I set off the next morning, taking the Flying Scotsman as far as Edinburgh then another train on to Dundee where I had telegraphed ahead to have a carriage waiting. I needed one, you see, as I had ensured that I took a great deal of equipment with me, not knowing what might be required at the other end. A further twenty miles of rough road later and I arrived at the castle itself. It sits in a beautiful position with a wide, open aspect but, although it was still only late afternoon, a chill seemed to emanate from the very walls.

"The feeling of oppression only grew stronger as I was shown inside. The lord, or laird as they knew him here, had given me a letter of introduction to show to his housekeeper. The woman seemed to have been built from the same stuff as the castle itself, and indeed gave off a similar chill. She perused the laird's letter twice before she deigned to allow me over the threshold. Even then she was at pains to inform me that I would be spending my nights in the servant's quarters, being clearly, in her eyes, a mere tradesman in the laird's employ.

"I was so enthused at the mere prospect ahead of me that I did not put up an argument. She showed me to a back room that was little bigger than a closet, and contained no more than a camp bed, a sink, and a bedside cabinet.

" 'I shall make you some breakfast in the morning,' she said. "But only the once. After that you can do for yourself.'

"Again I did no more than agree. So far she had only showed me an icy coldness, but I am afraid I shattered that bastion completely with my next, and last, question.

" 'Can you show me to the room please?' I asked. "The child Lisabet's room? I need to find the bogle.'

"At the merest mention of the word she went as white as a sheet. She made a quick movement with her right hand, warding off the evil eye.

" ''Tis on the second floor,' she said, already leaving the room. I could see she was trying hard not to appear to be hurrying. 'You can find your own way there I am sure, a fine *gentleman* such as yourself.'

"And with that I was left to my own devices. The first order of business was to inventory what I had brought with me. I had, of course, a copy of the Sigsand MS at hand, along with my defense kit. I checked the vials of holy water, the bulbs of garlic, the chalk, and the string—all were present and correct. As the castle fell quiet around me I also checked the apparatus of the electric pentacle. All the valves had remained intact despite the rattling of the carriage over the hard roads of Tayside. Satisfied that I had everything at hand if the need should arise, I headed forth into the castle proper.

"My first surprise came when I had barely gone ten yards. I walked up a staircase, intent on reaching the second floor when I realized the import of the window directly ahead of me. It was at least fifteen feet tall, and the glass glowed where moonlight hit it, like silver melted in a furnace. The leaded glass was imprinted with the finest of mosaics, and showed a figure standing on a border. On the left hand side of the window was a winter scene, a snow-covered landscape that twinkled with frost and reflected harsh moonlight in dark shadows that seemed to creep across the view.

"On the right-hand side it was summer. Children played in a field of green with lambs and foals. A glorious sun lit everything in deep gold that seemed almost warm against my face.

"The watcher himself had two faces. An old wrinkled visage watched the summer scene, while a fresh faced youth watched the snowfall in winter."

Carnacki paused again, this time to pack fresh tobacco in his pipe. The rest of us took our cue from him and did likewise.

"Here is a fact for you chaps to ponder," he said. "Did you know that in the eighth century, the Arab chemist Jabir ibn Hayyan described forty-six original recipes for producing colored glass in *The Book of the Hidden Pearl*? It is directly from him that the whole history of stained glass windows, from then to now, descends. His name was also Latinized as *Geber*. He wrote in a mangled verse that was so convoluted and strange that it coined a new word, *gibberish*. And since him, alchemists have always hidden their secrets in code."

"Alchemy?" Jessop said, and guffawed. "Fairy tales and hokum."

Carnacki merely smiled.

"We shall see," was all he said.

He waited until we were settled again, then continued.

"That window had given me pause, for I had not thought to find something so arcane decorating the hallway of the staid lord I had met in London.

"The second floor of the castle intrigued me further. The floor, unlike the others I had traversed, was uncarpeted and my footsteps echoed on old wooden boards. And it did not take me long to pinpoint the young girl's room. It was the only one on the whole floor that looked as if it had been recently occupied, and it was decorated as if the occupant wished to be a princess straight from the days of chivalry; all satin drapes and lush tapestries.

"This was where the child had apparently seen the bogle, and this was where my investigations must begin. I did not, in that first instance, set up any protections at all, for I was unsure as yet as to what I was dealing with, and I did not want to show my own hand until it was absolutely necessary. I sat on a chair that was several sizes too small to accommodate me comfortably, lit a pipe, and waited to see what the night might bring.

"By now, the castle had fallen completely silent around me, and the only sound was the soft whistling of the wind outside. I began to consider that I might be dealing with a bhean sidhe, a portent of doom for the clan chieftain. But the very involvement of the child had me confused, for a banshee would not make a corporeal appearance such as that reported by Lisabet.

"I was not left wondering for very long.

"The first intimation I had was a sudden lowering of temperature—not in itself an unusual occurrence of a Scottish evening, but what set this one apart was the tracing of frost that ran across the inside of the window as if laid there by some manic spider. Light footsteps came towards the room from out in the corridor. I stood, thinking myself ready for whatever would enter.

"I expected a person, but what entered was little more than a pale shadow, as insubstantial as the infamous Scotch mist. It hovered in the doorway then came forward, looming over the empty bed where the child would have lain. Then, with no sound other than more accompanying footsteps, the mist left the room and returned to the corridor, paying no heed whatsoever to my presence. I followed, several yards behind at first, then closer when I realized there was no threat to my person.

"I was led to the furthest reaches of the second floor, to a back corridor where there was only a single gas lamp flickering wanly on one wall. The mist went through a closed door as if it wasn't there. If I wanted my answers, I had no option but to follow.

"The door handle near froze to my palm, and the cold took my breath away as I pushed my way into a small unlit room no more than eight feet square, and with only a single table for furniture. The mist hovered over the table for a second, then faded to nothingness, leaving not even a patch of dampness behind.

"There was something lying on the table, a thin journal bound in brown calfskin with raised letters on the surface. I tried to read the title but it was too dark in the room to make it out. Besides, although the spectre, if that it what it had been, had gone, yet the chill remained. I took the book with me and returned to my Spartan, but relatively warm, quarters.

"I studied the volume at my leisure over another very welcome pipe of tobacco.

"The book was no more than eight inches in length, and was a slim volume. As I have said, it was bound in dark brown calf over wooden boards, heavily ornamented and gold tooled. The frontispiece inscription read as follows:

"*Ye Twelve Concordances of ye Red Serpent. In wch is succinctly and methodically handled ye stone of ye philosophers, his excellent effectes and admirable vertues; and, the better to attaine to the originall and true meanes of perfection, inriched with Figures representing the proper colours to lyfe as they successively appere in the practise of this blessed worke.*

"Once again I had a reference to the Great Work. Somehow my bogle was intimately connected with a work of alchemy.

"Inside, the book was an illuminated manuscript on parchment, some thirty leaves or so. Each page contained a drawing in a high degree of precision and a commentary done in a neat tidy hand.

"The first caught my eye immediately.

"*Extractio Animae Solis: or a Triall upon Sol, for the Extraction of Philosophical earth. The Author has putt doon the consequences of his Experiments therein, from the beginning to the end, by way of Journal; in the sure and sertin hope of the resurrection and the life of Our Lady, in this year of oor lord fifteen hunner an eichty seven. Putt doon here in the Castle of The Lions.*

"The accompanying picture was titled *MALAGMA*, and showed a fiery red serpent eating the world which was depicted as a shining golden disc.

"Strictly speaking of course, this wasn't part of the process at all, rather, this picture was a symbolic representation of the whole process. As you chaps are aware *malagma* is Latin, meaning *amalgamation*. And the whole process of alchemy, the quest if you like, is to amalgamate the soul, the *microcosm*, with the universe, the *macrocosm*."

Carnacki paused.

"Would you like to recharge your glasses?" he said. "The tale is a long one, and we have a ways to go yet."

As we helped ourselves to more of the fine Scotch, Jessop cornered Carnacki by the fireplace.

"I'm sorry, old chap," he said. "You've lost me already. What was that about *amalgamation*?"

Carnacki laughed.

"I thought that might confuse matters. The symbolism was obscure even when it was written. But all we need to concern ourselves with is the larger picture. We all exist together in one huge womb that is the universe, the macrocosm, while we inhabit the lower regions, this Earth, in our daily lives, the microcosm. Alchemists were convinced that they could transcend both states, both above and below, both life and death. It came to symbolize the transformation required to reach illumination and eternal life."

"Illumination?" Jessop asked, clearly perplexed.

"Let us not get ahead of ourselves," Carnacki said smiling. "I just wanted you to get some idea what I was getting into. As I have already said, the tale has only just begun to unravel."

He allowed us time to light fresh smokes then, settled in his chair once more, he continued his tale.

"I found another picture I recognized in the book. *Solutio*, the heading above the picture read. It showed a tall figure with two faces, one old, one young. The young one looked over a winter scene, the old one over summer. The bottom half of the figure seemed to be melting into a deep black pool, but both faces were smiling.

"It was the same as I had seen in the stained glass, only this time the figure looked thinner, more feminine. But I knew something of its import. This was one of the main steps in the great journey. The active principals from the microcosm are subsumed and dissolved by oil of mercury, the last vestiges of the old removed, preparing the way for the rise to the new beginning in the macrocosm."

"The remainder of the folio was as I have already described, a series of pictures describing the steps of alchemy. I do not pretend to understand it all, but even so, I failed to see how it helped in any way with my investigation. I tossed the book aside in disgust. It hit the side of my cramped bed and fell to the floor. As it did so, the spine of the folio split, revealing a folded sheet of paper cunningly hidden inside. I removed it as carefully as I was able. It was a short note, undated and unsigned.

"*I hae done whit wis requested. Something hae been brocht back. Whever it be fit fur the task will hae to be seen. She is confused and sair afflicted, but it is her. There is nae doobt o' that. It is a great blasphemy, but it needed done, and I am content to await the accountability of God alone. It will be wurth a' the trials if it brings the end o' tyranny and the return o' that which wis taken from us.*

"As you can imagine, that did not enlighten me to any great extent. An examination of the paper showed it to be of a similar date to the *Concordances*, but more than that I could not ascertain.

"By now it was well into the reaches of the night and I had more than enough to think on. I spent the hours through until morning in fitful sleep on a bed that was scarcely worthy of the name. As soon as the sun came up I rose, made what ablutions I could, and went in search of some breakfast.

"The housekeeper was in the kitchen, and proved as irascible as before. I was unceremoniously served with a thick porridge that looked like gray paste but was surprisingly tasty, and a pair of smoked kippers that were as divine as anything ever served in any fine hotel in town.

"I thanked her profusely, but still she did not soften . . . not until I mentioned the child, Lisabet.

" 'I have no time for you poking around in the lady's room,' she said. 'That girl is the only reason I stay in this godforsaken place. A sweeter child you will never meet.'

"And at that I do believe I saw a tear in the housekeeper's eye. But when I looked again, the steely glint had returned. I tried to ask about the back room on the second floor, and the calf-bound journal, but she brooked no discussion of either that, or the bogle.

" 'It is the laird's place to tell any stories, not mine.'

"She would say no more, and as I moved around the lower floors of the castle I realized there were no other servants there for me to question. I resolved that I would put my questions to the source, the bogle itself, that very night.

"That left me with a day to fill. I took myself off for a walk around the castle grounds. The laird kept a fine garden, full of plants drawn from all quarters of the globe, and the views across the valley were clear and bright on a fine sunny day such as this. Later I left the castle itself and wandered into the small town that butted up against the main exterior wall of the grounds. Several locals eyed me warily, but I managed to loosen tongues in the local inn when I spent a guinea buying those present some ale and whisky.

"Yet again my attempt to find information was to be foiled. All present had indeed heard of the bogle in the castle, but theories about its origins were as many as the number of flagons I had bought. There was only one statement that stayed with me as I returned to my small billet. It was something the landlord of the inn said as I left.

" ' 'Tis a shame we only have the laird and the bairn,' he said. 'For yon castle is fit for bigger than that. 'Tis fit for royalty.'

Carnacki stopped, tapped out the pipe in the grate and refilled it.

"I wonder if any of you are beginning to understand what was ahead of me?"

Arkwright raised a hand, like a boy in a schoolroom, but Carnacki waved him down.

"No. Let us save theories and explanations until the story is done.

"Let me just say that as I waited for night to fall, I was starting to have an inkling as to the nature of the bogle."

■ ■ ■

"I began the evening by setting up the pentagram in the child's bedroom. I was by no means sure that any such defenses were necessary but discretion is usually the better part of valor. I overlaid the electric pentacle on the pentagram, attached it to the battery, and settled down to wait, eschewing the child's chair this time, preferring to sit inside the pentagram on the hard wood floor.

"And once again I did not have to wait long. I was still on my first pipe when the air chilled and soft footsteps echoed in the corridor outside. I do not know whether it was the presence of the pentagram or not, but this time the mist that came through the doorway seemed more solid, more in a shape representing a human figure. And there was something more—the faintest hint of a high heady perfume.

"The mist entered and again paid no heed to me. As it drifted over to the child's bed the azure valve brightened slightly, but there was none of the blazing intensity I would have expected had the apparition been less than benign.

"The odor of the perfume grew stronger still, and beneath that, something else I recognized; the dank dead smell of the grave.

"Whispers came from within the mist as it loomed over the bed, and I had to strain to make out the words.

"'It was mine by right,' a soft voice said. 'Mine by birth. She shall not have it again.'

"As the figure turned away from the bedside it brushed against the outer edge of my electric pentacle. The azure valve brightened and at the same instant the mist *thickened* until it had taken the form of a tall, painfully thin figure. A woman stood looking sadly back at the small bed. She was dressed in a long black robe of a thick velvet, and a hood partly obscured her features so that all I could see was a flash of white at her cheek and a thin, aquiline nose. As she turned further the robe encroached on my defenses. She *jolted* as if struck, the hood fell back, and by Jove I took one heck of a fright I can tell you.

"It was not the empty stare from the eyes that shocked me, nor the cold gray tongue that looked like a piece of old stone. No, the thing that took me aback and near robbed me of my senses was the red scar that ran clear round her neck just above the shoulders . . . a scar that still wept blood down her chest.

"I shuffled backwards across the pentacle, but she showed no sign of approaching me, nor of trying to breach the defenses. She had one last look at the bed, and whispered again.

"'Mine by birth. She shall not have it.'"

Carnacki sat back in his chair and smiled.

"I do believe I have given you quite enough clues now," he said. "But please, let me finish the story. It is time now for you chaps to recharge your glasses for the final push."

By this time I was also coming to some conclusions as to the nature of Carnacki's bogle, and I was keen to see if I had guessed correctly. I believe everyone present felt the same, for we refilled our snifters in record time and were soon ready for Carnacki to continue.

"She left the room, footsteps fading along the corridor. Silence fell but I sat there a while longer before rising, pondering my next move. I knew it would cause consternation in the household, but the way ahead was clear to me. I had to persuade the laird to return to the house, and to bring his daughter with him. For only by direct confrontation could this business be finished once and for all.

"Getting the man back to the castle was easier said than done. It required a series of terse telegrams between the post office in Forfar and London which caused a great deal of chatter in the town and cost me several guineas in bills for a carriage to and from Glamis itself. Finally we reached agreement, and all I could do was wait for their return.

"That was to take more than a week, during which time I took in a trip around the Perthshire Hills and met an adversary who was much less benign. But that is a tale for another evening. Suffice to say I spent the time fruitfully and on the day the laird arrived from London with his retinue I was at the door of the castle waiting for him.

"A child I guessed was Lisabet held him tightly by the hand, but as they approached the door she let go and ran past me, heading inside.

"'She seems to have forgotten all about the bogle,' the Laird said as he shook my hand. 'Perhaps it is best to keep it that way?'

"'I doubt that very much sir,' I replied. 'I have some questions I need you to answer, then you will have a decision to make.'

"He nodded curtly and went inside.

"It was my turn to mind my manners, and I held my peace through a fine supper of salmon and pheasant, washed down with some excellent port. I waited until everyone else had retired, and we were sat in armchairs around a fireplace before I broached the matter at hand.

"The laird seemed surprised at the questions I put to him, but not as much as I would have thought. He poured us a snifter of brandy each, and it seemed he was buying time to muster his thoughts, as if deciding what to reveal to me.

"'There were rumors,' he finally said. 'Tales that an attempt such as you describe had been made. You have seen the window . . . you know already that this place has a history in such matters?'

"I nodded in reply.

" 'But what in Jesu's name is my daughter's part in all of this?' he asked me. 'She is only a child, and innocent of any hurts done in centuries past.'

" 'The coincidence of the names at least is obvious,' I replied. 'But answers may only become clear in time. It may be something in the child's future that has brought this attention on her.'

"The laird looked pensive at that, but said nothing.

" 'With your permission,' I said softly. 'I would like to give the lady some rest. I think you will agree that she deserves that at least?'

"It was his turn to nod in agreement.

"We made our way to Lisabet's room and found the child examining the chalk markings I had made on the floor. She was most excited when I brought out the electric pentacle. Her father gave her a stern warning to *haud her wheesht* and she fell quiet as I first repaired the defenses, then set the pentacle to work.

"The three of us sat, pressed close together

" 'What is it we are waiting for?' Lisabet asked.

Her father replied for me.

" 'A princess,' he said. 'Just like you.'

"He ruffled her hair, and at that very same moment the soft footsteps echoed in the corridor outside. We smelled the heady perfume even before she walked through the doorway.

"This time she was almost fully formed. The black velvet robe looked like a hole in the very fabric of space itself, her pale face hovering like a moon above it. The dead eyes turned and stared at the child.

" 'You took it,' she whispered. 'It is mine by right, and you took it from me.'

Lisabet stiffened but did not cry out, merely stared back at the thing before her.

" 'I do not know you, madam,' she said, so prim and proper that I had to stifle a laugh. 'Kindly be so good as to introduce yourself.'

The robed figure loomed over us. Once again the only activity from the pentacle was a slight brightening of the azure valve.

" 'Madam,' I said softly. 'This is not your sister. She has been dead these three centuries and more. There is no place for you here.'

"The darkness thickened slightly and the blank eyes turned towards me. Bloody tears ran from them.

" 'Go?' she whispered. 'That is my dearest wish. But I know not how.'

" 'Let me help,' I said softly, and uttered the prayer of passing.

" '*Adjuro ergo te, omnis immundissime spiritus, omne phantasma, omnis incursio satanæ, in nomine Jesu Christi.*'

"She broke apart, like smoke taken by wind. At the last, a wispy tendril reached towards the child.

" 'Lisabet,' came a whisper.

"Then she was gone.

" 'What did that lady want with me?' the girl asked as I packed away the pentacle and cleaned the chalk from the floor.'

" 'She was dead, but did not know it,' I replied. 'And she thought you were someone she knew a long time ago.'

" 'Well I'm not going to die,' Lisabet said loudly. 'I shall live till I'm a hundred.'

"And do you know something, chaps? I do believe she might just do it."

Carnacki sat back in his chair, a wide grin on his face.

"Before we get to *who* the apparition might have been, I suppose I had better tell you *how* it came about.

"You chaps all know that I do not believe in the soul as such," he continued. "And at first, this bogle almost made me doubt my own convictions. But having thought long and hard, I believe I may have the truth of it.

"It starts in the late sixteenth century, with an attempt by a Scottish alchemist to revive a dead lady. Now I have studied the Great Work to some degree, and have already this evening commented on the amalgamation of the microcosm with the macrocosm. What no one, not the alchemist, nor I, had considered, was what effect the transformation would have on a body already dead. What was transformed was not capable of ascension to the Outer Realms, the macrocosm. It was forced to remain, rooted to its earthly plane, doomed for eternity to roam, seeking something it could never find.

"And you came along and freed it?" Jessop piped up.

"Freed *her*," Carnacki said softly. "For there was still something there of the lady she had once been."

"And who was she exactly, Carnacki?" Arkwright said. "Lady Macbeth?"

Carnacki laughed loudly at that.

"No. Not that one, but the lady I sent to her rest was also of noble birth. Come, chaps. Have I not given you enough clues? The date of the journal alone should give you some idea? And the place, the seat of an ancient Scottish family? If you have not the wit to work it out for yourself then I have not the inclination to enlighten you. All I shall say is we should look out for the name Elizabeth Bowes-Lyon in the years ahead, for I believe she has a destiny that the whole country will come to understand in time."

At that Carnacki rose from his chair, the time honored signal that our evening was over.

"Out you go," he said jovially at the door.

As we left Carnacki whispered just one word in my ear, but it was enough for me to consider on the way back along the Embankment. By the time I reached home I had confirmed my own earlier guess as to the identity of the Beast of Glamis.

Carnacki's whispered word stayed in my mind even as I drifted to sleep. *Fotheringay.*

William Meikle is a Scottish writer now resident in Canada. He has fifteen novels published in the genre press and over two hundred and fifty short story credits in thirteen countries. More of his stories featuring William Hope Hodgson's Carnacki have been collected in *Heaven and Hell*. His work appears in many professional magazines and anthologies and he has recent short story sales to *Nature's* science-fiction section *Futures*, *Penumbra*, and *Daily Science Fiction* among others. He now lives in a remote corner of Newfoundland with icebergs, whales, and bald eagles for company. In the winters he gets warm vicariously through the lives of others in cyberspace, so please check him out at www.williammeikle.com.

The Case: *The McCarleys, a family of five, are found brutally slaughtered and partially eaten. It looks like the work of vampires.*

The Investigators: *Molly Everhart Trueblood, an earth witch; Jane Yellowrock, a shape-changing Cherokee skinwalker and sometimes vampire hunter with other special talents; Paul Braxton, retired from the New York City PD, now a sheriff detective in North Carolina.*

SIGNATURES OF THE DEAD

—◆—

Faith Hunter

It was nap time, and it wasn't often that I could get both children to sleep a full hour—the same full hour, that is. I stepped back and ran my hands over the healing and protection spells that enveloped my babies, Angelina and Evan Jr. The complex incantations were getting a bit frayed around the edges, and I drew on Mother Earth and the forest on the mountainside outback to restore them. Not much power, not enough to endanger the ecosystem that was still being restored there. Just a bit. Just enough.

Few witches or sorcerers survive into puberty, and so I spend a lot of time making sure my babies are okay. I come from a long line of witches. Not the kind in pointy black hats with a cauldron in the front yard, and not the kind like the *Bewitched* television show that once tried to capitalize on our reclusive species. Witches aren't human, though we can breed true with humans, making little witches about 50 percent of the time. Unfortunately, witch babies have a poor survival rate, especially the males, most dying before they reach the age of twenty, from various cancers. The ones who live through puberty, however, tend to live into their early hundreds.

The day each of my babies were conceived, I prayed and worked the same incantations Mama had used on her children, power-weavings, to make sure my babies were protected. Mama had better-than-average survival rate on her witches. For me, so far, so good. I said a little prayer over them and left the room.

Back in the kitchen, Paul Braxton—Brax to his friends, Detective or Sir to the bad guys he chased—Jane Yellowrock, and Evan were still sitting at the table, the photographs scattered all around. Crime scene photos of the

McCarley house. And the McCarleys. It wasn't pretty. The photos didn't belong in my warm, safe home. They didn't belong anywhere.

Evan and I were having trouble with them, with the blood and the butchery. Of course, nothing fazed Jane. And, after years of dealing with crime in New York City, little fazed Brax, though it had been half a decade since he'd seen anything so gruesome, not since he "retired" to the Appalachian mountains and went to work for the local sheriff.

I met Evan's gray eyes, seeing the steely anger there. My husband was easygoing, slow to anger, and full of peace, but the photos of the five McCarleys had triggered something in him, a slow-burning pitiless rage. He was feeling impotent, useless, and he wanted to smash things. The boxing bag in the garage would get a pummeling tonight, after the kids went to bed for the last time. I offered him a wan smile and went to the Aga stove; I poured fresh coffee for the men and tea for Jane and me. She had brought a new variety, a first flush Darjeeling, and it was wonderful with my homemade bread and peach butter.

"Kids okay?" Brax asked, amusement in his tone.

I retook my seat and used the tip of a finger to push the photos away. I was pretty transparent, I guess, having to check on the babies after seeing the dead McCarleys. "They're fine. Still sleeping. Still . . . safe." Which made me feel all kinds of guilty to have my babies safe, while the entire McCarley family had been butchered. Drunk dry. Partly eaten.

"You finished thinking about it?" he asked. "Because I need an answer. If I'm going after them, I need to know, for sure, what they are. And if they're vamps, then I need to know how many there are and where they're sleeping in the daytime. And I'll need protection. I can pay."

I sighed and sipped my tea, added a spoonful of raw sugar, stirred and sipped again. He was trying to yank my chain, make my natural guilt and our friendship work to his favor, and making him wait was my only reverse power play. Having to use it ticked me off. I put the cup down with a soft china clink. "You know I won't charge you for the protection spells, Brax."

"I don't want Molly going into that house," Evan said. He brushed crumbs from his reddish, graying beard and leaned across the table, holding my eyes. "You know it'll hurt you."

I'm an earth witch, from a long family of witches, and our gifts are herbs and growing things, healing bodies, restoring balance to nature. I'm a little unusual for earth witches, in that I can sense dead things, which is why Brax was urging me to go to the McCarley house. To tell him for sure if dead things, like vamps, had killed the family. How they died. He could wait for forensics, but that might take weeks. I was faster. And I could give him numbers to go on, too, how many vamps were in the blood-family, if they were healthy, or as healthy as dead things ever got. And, maybe, which direction they had gone at dawn, so he could guess where the vamps slept by day.

But once there, I would sense the horror, the fear that the violent deaths had left imprinted on the walls, floor, ceilings, furniture of the house. I took a breath to say no. "I'll go," I said instead. Evan pressed his lips together tight, holding in whatever he would say to me later, privately. "If I don't go, and another family is killed, I'll be a lot worse," I said to him. "And that would be partly my fault. Besides, some of that reward money would buy us a new car."

"You don't have to carry the weight of the world on your shoulders, Moll," he said, his voice a deep, rumbling bass. "And we can get the money in other ways." Not many people know that Evan is a sorcerer, not even Brax. We wanted it that way, as protection for our family. If it was known that Evan carried the rare gene on his X chromosome, the gene that made witches, and that we had produced children who both carried the gene, we'd likely disappear into some government-controlled testing program. "Moll. Think about this," he begged. But I could see in his gentle brown eyes that he knew my mind was already made up.

"I'll go." I looked at Jane. "Will you go with me?" She nodded once, the beads in her black braids clicking with the motion. To Brax, I said, "When do you want us there?"

The McCarley house was on Dogwood, up the hill overlooking the town of Spruce Pine, North Carolina, not that far, as the crow flies, from my house, which is outside the city limits, on the other side of the hill. The McCarley home was older, with a 1950s feel to it, and from the outside, it would have been hard to tell that anything bad had happened. The tiny brick house itself with its elvish, high-peaked roof, green trim, and well-kept lawn looked fine. But the crime scene tape was a dead giveaway.

I was still sitting in the car, staring at the house, trying to center myself for what I was about to do. It took time to become settled, to pull the energies of my gift around me, to create a skein of power that would heighten my senses.

Brax, dressed in a white plastic coat and shoe covers, was standing on the front porch, his hands in the coat pockets, his body at an angle, head down, not looking at anything. The set of his shoulders said he didn't want to go back inside, but he would, over and over again, until he found the killers.

Jane was standing by the car, patient, bike helmet in her hands, riding leathers unzipped, copper-skinned face turned to the sun for its meager warmth on this early fall day. Jane Yellowrock was full Cherokee, and was much more than she seemed. Like most witches, like Evan who was still in the witch-closet, Jane had secrets that she guarded closely. I was pretty sure I was the only one who knew any of them, and I didn't flatter myself that I knew them all. Yet, even though she kept things hidden, I needed her special abilities and gifts to augment my own on this death-search.

I closed my eyes and concentrated on my breathing, huffing in and out, my lips in an O. My body and my gift came alive, tingling in hands and feet as my oxygen level rose. I pulled the gift of power around me like a cloak, protection and sensing at my fingertips.

When I was ready, I opened the door of the unmarked car and stepped out onto the drive, my eyes slightly slit. At times like this, when I'm about to read the dead, I experience everything so clearly, the sun on my shoulders, the breeze like a wisp of pressure on my face, the feel of the earth beneath my feet, grounding me, the smell of late-blooming flowers. The scent of old blood. But I don't like to open my eyes. The physical world is too intense. Too distracting.

Jane took my hand in her gloved one and placed it on her leather-covered wrist. My fingers wrapped around it for guidance and we walked to the house, the plastic shoe covers and plastic coat given to me by Brax making little shushing sounds as I walked. I ducked under the crime scene tape Jane held for me. Her cowboy boots and plastic shoe covers crunched and shushed on the gravel drive beside me. We climbed the concrete steps, four of them, to the small front porch. I heard Brax turn the key in the lock. The smell of old blood, feces, and pain whooshed out with the heated air trapped in the closed-up home.

Immediately I could sense the dead humans. Five of them had lived in this house—two parents, three children—with a dog and a cat. All dead. My earth gift, so much a thing of life, recoiled, closed up within me, like a flower gathering its petals back into an unopened bloom. Eyes still closed, I stepped inside.

The horror that was saturated into the walls, into the carpet, stung me, pricked me, like a swarm of bees, seeking my death. The air reeked when I sucked in a breath. Dizziness overtook me and I put out my other hand. Jane caught and steadied me, her leather gloves protecting me from skin-to-skin contact that would have pulled me back, away from the death in the house. After a moment, I nodded that I was okay and she released me, though I still didn't open my eyes. I didn't want to see. A buzz of fear and horror filled my head.

I stood in the center of a small room, the walls pressing in on me. Eyes still closed, I saw the death energies, pointed, and said, "They came in through this door. One, two, three, four, five, six, seven of them. Fast."

I felt the urgency of their movements, faster than any human. Pain gripped my belly and I pressed my arms into it, trying to assuage an ache of hunger deeper than I had ever known. "So hungry," I murmured. The pain grew, swelling inside me. The imperative to eat. Drink. The craving for blood.

I turned to my left before I was overcome. "Two females took the man. He was surprised, startled, trying to stand. They attacked his throat. Started drinking. He died there."

I turned more to my right, still pointing, and said, "A child died there. Older. Maybe ten. A boy."

I touched my throat. It wanted to close up, to constrict at the feel of teeth, long canines, biting into me. The boy's fear and shock were so intense, they robbed me of any kind of action. When I spoke, the words were harsh, whispered. "One, a female, took the boy. The other four, all males, moved into the house." The hunger grew, and with it the anger. And terror. Mind-numbing, thought-stealing terror. The boy's death struggles increased. The smell of blood and death and fear choked. "Both died within minutes."

I pointed again and Jane led me. The carpet squished under my feet. I knew it was blood, even with my eyes closed. I gagged and Jane stopped, letting me breathe, as well as I could in this death-house, letting me find my balance, my sense of place on the earth. When I nodded again, she led me forward. I could tell I was in a kitchen by the cooking smells that underlay the blood. I pointed into a shadowy place. "A woman was brought down there. Two of them . . . " I flinched at what I saw. Pulled my hand from Jane's and crossed my arms over me, hugging myself. Rocking back and forth.

"They took her together. One drank while the other . . . the other . . . And then they switched places. They laughed. I can hear her crying. It took . . . a long . . . long time." I blundered away, bumping into Jane. She led me out, helping me to get away. But it only got worse.

I pointed in the direction I needed to go. My footsteps echoed on a wood floor. Then carpets. "Two little girls. Little . . . Oh, God in heaven. They . . . " I took a breath that shuddered painfully in my throat. Tears leaked down my cheeks, burning. "They raped them, too. Two males. And they drank them dry." I opened my eyes, seeing twin beds, bare frames, the mattresses and sheets gone, surely taken by the crime scene crew. Blood had spattered up one wall in the shape of a small body. To the sides, the wall was smeared, like the figure of angel wings a child might make in the snow, but made of blood.

Gorge rose in my throat. "Get me out of here," I whispered. I turned away, my arms windmilling for the door. I tripped over something. Fell forward, into Brax. His face inches from mine. I was shaking, quivering like a seizure. Out of control. "Now! Get me out of here! Now!" I shouted. But it was only a whisper.

Jane picked me up and hoisted me over her shoulder. Outside. Into the sun.

■ ■ ■

I came to myself, came awake, lying in the yard, the warm smell of leather and Jane all around. I touched her jacket and opened my eyes. She was sitting on the ground beside me, one knee up, the other stretched out, one arm on bent knee, the other bracing her. She was wearing a short-sleeved tee in the cool air. She smiled her strange humorless smile, one side of her mouth curling.

"You feeling better?" She was a woman of few words.

"I think so. Thank you for carrying me out."

"You might want to wait on the thanks. I dropped you, putting you down. Not far, but you might have a bruise or two."

I chuckled, feeling stiffness in my ribs. "I forgive you. Where's Brax? I need to tell him what I found."

Jane slanted her eyes to the side, and I swiveled my head to see the cop walking from his car. He wasn't a big man, standing five feet nine inches, but he was solid, and fit. I liked Brax. He was a good cop, even if he did take me into some awful places to read the dead. To repay me, he did what he could to protect my family from the witch-haters in the area. There were always a few in any town, even in easygoing Spruce Pine. He dropped a knee on the ground beside me and grunted. It might have been the word "Well?"

"Seven of them," I said. "Four men, three women, all young rogues. One family, one bloodline. The sire is male. He's maybe a decade old. Maybe to the point where he would have been sane, had he been in the care of a mastervamp. The others are younger. All crazy."

For the first years of their lives, vampires are little more than beasts. According to the gossip mags, a good sire kept his newbie rogues chained in the basement during the first decade or so of undead-life, until they gained some sanity. Most experts thought that young rogues were likely the source of werewolf legends and the folklore of vampires as bloody killers. Rogues were mindless, carnal, blood-drinking machines, whether they were brand-new vampires or very old ones who had succumbed to the vampire version of dementia.

If a rogue had escaped his master and survived for a decade on his own, and had regained some of his mental functions, then he would be a very dangerous adversary. A vampire with the moral compass of a rogue, the cunning of a predator, and the reasoning abilities of a psychotic killer. I huddled under Jane's jacket at the thought.

"Are you up to walking around the house?" Brax asked. "I need an idea which way they went." He looked at his watch. I looked at the sun. We were about four hours from sundown. Four hours before the blood-family would rise again and go looking for food and fun.

I sat up and Jane stood, extended her hand. She pulled me up and I offered her jacket back. "Keep it," she said, so I snuggled it around my shoulders, the scent of Jane rising around me like a warm animal. She followed as I circled the house, keeping between Brax and me, and I wondered what had come between the two while I was unconscious. Whatever it was, it crackled in the air, hostile, antagonistic. Jane didn't like cops, and she tended to say whatever was on her mind, no matter how insulting, offensive, rude, or blunt it might be.

I stopped suddenly, feeling the chill of death under my feet. I was on the side of the house, and I had just crossed over the rogues' trail. They had come and gone this way. I looked at the front door. It was undamaged, so that meant they had been invited in or that the door had been unlocked. I didn't know if the old myth about vamps not being able to enter a house uninvited was true or not, but the door hadn't been knocked down.

I followed the path around the house and to the back of the grassy lot. There was a playset with a slide, swings, a teeter-totter and monkey bars. I walked to it and stood there, seeing what the dead had done. They had played here. After they killed the children and parents, they had come by here, in the gray predawn, and played on the swings. "Have your crime people dusted this?"

"The swing set?" Brax said, surprised.

I nodded and moved on, into the edge of the woods. There was no trail. Just woods, deep and thick with rhododendrons, green leaves and sinuous limbs and straighter tree trunks blocking the way, a canopy of oak and maple arching overhead. I looked up, into the trees, still green, untouched as yet by the fresh chill in the air. I bent down and spotted an animal trail, the ground faintly marked with a narrow, bare path about three inches wide. There was a mostly clear area about two feet high, branches to the side. Some were broken off. A bit of cloth hung on one broken branch. "They came through here," I said. Brax knelt beside me. I pointed. "See that? I think it's from the shirt the bloodmaster was wearing."

"I'll bring the dogs. Get them started on the trail," he said, standing. "Thank you, Molly. I know this was hard on you."

I looked at Jane. She inclined her head slightly, agreeing. The dogs might get through the brush and brambles, but no dog handler was going to be able to make it. Jane, however . . . Jane might be able to do something with this. But she would need a blood scent to follow. I thought about the house. No way could I go back in there, not even to hunt for a smear of vampire blood or other body fluid. But the bit of cloth stuck in the underbrush might have blood on it. If Jane could get to it before Brax did . . . I looked from Jane to the scrap of cloth and back again, a question in my eyes. She smiled that humorless half smile and inclined her head again. Message sent and received.

I stood and faced the house. "I want to walk around the house," I said to

Brax. "And you might want to call the crime scene back. When the vampires played on the swings, they had the family pets. The dog was still alive for part of it." I registered Brax's grimace as I walked away. He followed. Jane didn't. I began to describe the crime scene to him, little things he could use to track the vamps. Things he could use in court, not that the vamps would ever make it to a courtroom. They would have to be staked and beheaded where he found them. But it kept Brax occupied, entering notes into his wireless notebook, so Jane could retrieve the scrap of cloth and, hopefully, the vampires' scent.

Jane was waiting in the drive when I finished describing what I had sensed and "seen" in the house to Brax, her long legs straddling her small used Yamaha. I had never seen her drive a car. She was a motorbike girl, and lusted after a classic Harley, which she had promised to buy for herself when she got the money. She tilted her head to me, and I knew she had the cloth and the scent. Brax, who caught the exchange, looked quizzically between us, but when neither of us explained, he shrugged and opened the car door for me.

The vampire attack made the regional news, and I spent the rest of the day hiding from the TV. I played with the kids, fed them supper, made a few batches of dried herbal mixtures to sell in my sisters' herb shop in town, and counted my blessings, trying to get the images of the McCarleys' horror and pain out of my mind. I knew I'd not sleep well tonight. Sometimes not even an earth witch can defeat the power of evil over dreams.

Just after dusk, with a cold front moving through and the temperature dropping, Jane rode up on her bike and parked it. Carrying my digital video camera, I met her in the front garden, and without speaking, we walked together to the backyard and the boulder-piled herb garden beside my gardening house and the playhouse. Jane dropped ten pounds of raw steak on the ground while I set up my camera and tripod. She handed me the scrap of cloth retrieved from the woods. It was stiff with blood, and I was sure it wasn't all the vampires'.

Unashamedly, Jane stripped, while I looked away, giving her the privacy I would have wanted had it been me taking off my clothes. Anyone who happened to look this way with a telescope, as I had no neighbors close by, would surely think the witch and friend were going skyclad for a ceremony, but I wasn't a Wiccan or a goddess worshipper, and I didn't dance around naked. Especially in the unseasonable cold.

When she was ready, her travel pack strapped around her neck, along with the gold nugget necklace she never removed, Jane climbed to the top of the rock garden, avoiding my herbs with careful footsteps, and sat. She was holding a fetish necklace in her hands, made from teeth, claws, and bones.

She looked at me, standing shivering in the falling light. "Can your camera record when it's this dark?" When I nodded, my teeth chattering, she said, "Okay. I'll do my thing. You try to get it on film, and then you can drive me over. You got a blanket in the backseat in case we get stopped?" I nodded again and she grinned, not the half-smile I usually got from her, but a real grin, full of happiness. We had talked about me filming her, so she could see what happened from the outside, but this was the first time we had actually tried. I was intensely curious about the procedure.

"It'll take about ten minutes," she said, "for me to get mentally ready. When I finish, don't be standing between me and the steaks, okay?" When I nodded again, she laughed, a low, smooth sound that made me think of whiskey and woodsmoke. "What's the matter?" she said. "Cat got your tongue?"

I laughed with her then, for several reasons, only one of which was that Jane's rare laugh was contagious. I said, "Good luck."

She inclined her head, blew out a breath, and went silent. Nearly ten minutes later, even in the night that had fallen around us, I could tell that something odd was happening. I hit the record button on the camera and watched as gray light gathered around my friend.

If clouds were made of light instead of water vapor, they would look like this, all sparkly silver, thrust through with motes of blackness that danced and whorled. It coalesced, thickened, and eddied around her. Beautiful. And then Jane . . . shifted. Changed. Her body seemed to bend and flow like water, or like hot wax, a viscous, glutinous liquid, full of gray light. The bones beneath her flesh popped and cracked. She grunted, as if with pain. Her breathing changed. The light grew brighter, the dark motes darker.

Both began to dissipate.

On the top of the boulders where Jane had been, sat a mountain lion, its eyes golden, with human-shaped pupils. Puma concolor, the big-cat of the western hemisphere sat in my garden, looking me over, Jane's travel pack around her neck making a strange lump on her back. The cat was darker than I remembered, tawny on back, shoulders, and hips, pelt darkening down her legs, around her face and ears. The tail, long and stubby, was dark at the tip. She huffed a breath. I saw teeth.

My shivers worsened, even though I knew this was Jane. Or had been Jane. She had assured me, not long ago, that she still had vestiges of her own personality even in cat form and wouldn't eat me. Easy to say when the big cat isn't around. Then she yawned, snorted, and stood to her four feet. Incredibly graceful, long sinews and muscles pulling, she leaped to the ground and approached the raw steaks she had dumped earlier. She sniffed, and made a sound that was distinctly disgusted.

I tittered, and the cat looked at me. I mean, she *looked* at me. I froze. A moment later, she lay down on the ground and started to eat the cold, dead meat. Even in the dark, I could see her teeth biting, tearing.

I had missed some footage and rotated the camera to the eating cat. I also grabbed her fetish necklace and her clothes, stuffing them in a tote for later.

Thirty minutes later, after she had cleaned the blood off her paws and jaws with her tongue, I dismantled the tripod and drove to the McCarley home. Jane—or her cat—lay under a blanket on the backseat. Once there, I opened the doors and shut them behind us.

There was more crime scene tape up at the murder scene, but the place was once again deserted. Silent, my flashlight lighting the way for me, Jane in front, in the dark, we walked around the house to the woods' edge.

I cut off the flash to save her night vision, and held out the scrap of bloody cloth to the cat. She sniffed. Opened her mouth and sucked air in with a coughing, gagging, scree of sound. I jumped back, and I could have sworn Jane laughed, an amused hack. I broke out into a fear-sweat that instantly chilled in the cold breeze. "Not funny," I said. "What the heck was that?"

Jane padded over and sat in front of me, her front paws crossed like a Southern belle, ears pricked high, mouth closed, nostrils fluttering in the dark, waiting. Patient as ever. When I figured out that she wasn't going to eat me, and feeling distinctly dense, I held out the bit of cloth. Again, she opened her mouth and sucked air, and I realized she was scenting through her mouth. Learning it. When she was done, which felt like forever, she looked up at me and hacked again. Her laugh, for certain. She turned and padded into the woods. I switched on my flash and hurried back to my car. It was the kids' bedtime. I needed to be home.

It was 4:00 a.m. when the phone rang. Evan grunted, a bear-snort. I swear, the man could sleep through a train wreck or a tornado. I rolled and picked up the phone. Before I could say hello, Jane said, "I got it. Come get me. I'm freezing and starving. Don't forget the food."

"Where are you?" I asked. She told me, and I said, "Okay. Half an hour."

Jane swore and hung up. She had warned me about her mouth when she was hungry. I poked my hubby, and when he swore, too, I said, "I'm heading out to the old Partman Place to pick up Jane. I'll be back by dawn." He grunted again and I slid from the bed, dressed, and grabbed the huge bowl of oatmeal, sugar, and milk from the fridge. Jane had assured me she needed food after she shifted back, and didn't care what it was or what temp it was. I hoped she remembered that when I gave it to her. Cold oatmeal was nasty.

Half an hour later, I reached the old Partman Place, an early-nineteenth-century homestead and later a mine, the homestead sold and deserted when the gemstones were discovered and the mine closed down in the 1950s, when the gems ran out. It was grown over by fifty-year-old trees, and the drive was gravel, with Jane standing hunched in the middle. Human, wearing the lightweight clothes she carried in the travel pouch along with the cell phone and a few vamp-killing supplies.

I popped the doors and she climbed in, her long black hair like a veil around her, her thin clothes covering a shivering body, pimpled with cold. "Food," she said, her voice hoarse. I passed the bowl of oatmeal and a serving spoon to her. She tossed the top of the bowl into the floorboards and dug in. I watched her eat from the corner of my eye as I drove. She didn't bother to chew, just shoveled the cold oatmeal in like she was starving. She looked thinner than usual, though Jane was never much more than skin, bone, and muscle—like her big-cat form, I thought. Criminy. Witches I can handle. But what Jane was? Maybe not so much. I hadn't even known shape changers or skinwalkers even existed. No one did.

Bowl empty, she pulled her leather coat from the tote I had brought, snuggled under it, and lay back in her seat, cradling the empty bowl. She closed her eyes, looking exhausted. "That was not fun," she said, the words so soft, I had to strain to hear. "Those vamps are fast. Faster than Beast."

"Beast?"

"My cat," she said. She laughed, the sound forlorn, lost, almost sad. "My big hunting cat. Who had to chase the scent back to their lair. Up and down mountains and through creeks and across the river. I had to soak in the river to throw off the heat. Beast isn't built for long-distance running." She sighed and adjusted the heating vents to blow onto her. "The vamps covered five miles from the McCarleys' place in less than an hour yesterday morning. It took me more than four hours to follow them back through the underbrush and another two to isolate the opening. I should have shifted into a faster cat, though Beast would have been ticked off."

"You found their lair?" I couldn't keep the excitement out of my voice. "On the Partman Place?"

"Yeah. Sort of." She rolled her head to face me in the dark, her golden eyes glowing and forbidding. "They're living in the mine. They've been there for a long time. They were gone by the time I found it. They were famished when they left the lair. I could smell their hunger. I think they'll kill again tonight. Probably have killed again tonight."

I tightened my hands on the steering wheel and had to force myself to relax.

"Molly? The lair is only a mile from your house as the vamp runs. And witches smell different from humans."

A spike of fear raced through me. Followed by a mental image of a vampire leaning over Angelina's bed. I squeezed the wheel so tight, it made a soft sound of protest.

"You need to mount a defensive perimeter around your house," Jane said. "You and Evan. You hear? Something magical that'll scare off anything that moves, or freeze the blood of anything dead. Something like that. You make sure the kids are safe." She turned her head aside, to look out at the night. Jane loved my kids. She had never said so, but I could see it in her eyes when she watched them. I drove on, chilled to the bone by fear and the early winter.

Jane was too tired to make it back to her apartment, and so she spent the day sleeping on the cot in the back room of the shop. Seven Sassy Sisters' Herb Shop and Cafe, owned and run by my family, had a booming business, both locally and on the Internet, selling herbal mixtures and teas by bulk and by the ounce, the shop itself serving teas, specialty coffees, brunch and lunch daily, and dinner on weekends. It was mostly vegetarian fare, whipped up by my older sister, water witch, professor, and three-star chef, Evangelina Everhart. My sister Carmen Miranda Everhart Newton, an air witch, newly married and pregnant, ran the register and took care of ordering supplies. Two other witch sisters, twins Boadacia and Elizabeth, ran the herb store, while our wholly human sisters, Regan and Amelia, were waitstaff. I'm really Molly Meagan Everhart Trueblood. Names with moxie run in my family. Without a single question about why this seemingly human needed a place to crash, my sisters let Jane sleep off the night run.

While my sisters worked around the cot and ran the business without me, I went driving. To the Partman Place. With Brax.

"You found this how?" he asked, sitting in the passenger seat. I was driving so I could pretend that I was in control, not that Brax cared who was in charge so long as the rogue vampires were brought down. "The dogs got squirrelly twenty feet into the underbrush and refused to go on. It doesn't make any sense, Molly. I never saw dogs go so nuts. They freaked out. So I gotta ask how you know where they sleep." Detective Paul Braxton was antsy. Worried. Scared. There had been no new reported deaths in the area, yet I had just told him the vamps had gone hunting last night.

There were some benefits to being a witch-out-of-the-closet. I let my lips curl up knowingly. "I had a feeling at the McCarleys' yesterday, but I didn't think it would work. I devised a spell to track the rogue vampires. At dusk, I went to the McCarleys' and set it free. And it worked. I was able to pinpoint their lair."

"How? I never heard of such a thing. No one has. I asked on NCIC this morning after you called." At my raised brows he said, "NCIC is the National Crime Information Center, run by the FBI, a computerized index and database of criminal justice information."

"A database?" Crap. I hit the brakes, hard. Throwing us both against the seatbelts. The wheels squealed, popped, and groaned as the antilock braking system went into play. Brax cussed as we came to a rocking halt. I spun in the seat to face him. "If you made me part of that system, then you've used me for the last time, you no-good piece of—"

"Molly!" He held both hands palms out, still rocking in the seat. "No! I did not enter you into the system. We have an agreement. I wouldn't breach it."

"Then tell me what you did," I said, my voice low and threatening. "Because if you took away the privacy of my family and babies, I'll curse you to hell and back, and damn the consequences." I gathered my power to me, pulling from the earth and the forest and even the fish living in the nearby river, ecosystems be hanged. This man was endangering my babies.

Brax swallowed in the sudden silence of the old Volvo, as if he could feel the power I was drawing in. I could smell his fear, hear it in his fast breath, over the sounds of nearby traffic. "NCIC is just a database," he said. "I just input a series of questions. About witches. And how they work. And—"

"Witches are in the FBI's data bank?" I hit the steering wheel with both fists as the thought sank in. "Why?"

"Because there are witch criminals in the U.S. Sorcerers who do blood magic. Witches who do dark magic. Witches are part of the database, now and forever."

"Son of witch on a switch," I swore, cursing long and viciously, helpless anger in the tones, the syllables flowing and rich. Switching to the old language for impact, not that it had helped. Curses had a way of falling back on the curser rather than hurting the cursed.

I beat the steering wheel in impotent fury. I was a witch, for pity's sake. And I couldn't protect my own kind. Rage banging around me like a wrecking ball, I hit the steering wheel one last time and threw my old Volvo into drive. Fuming, silent, I drove to the Partman Place.

The entrance, once meant for mining machinery and trucks, was still drivable, though the asphalt was crazed and broken, grass growing in the cracks. The drive wound around a hillock and was lost from view. Beyond it, signs of mining that were hidden from the road became more obvious. Trees were young and scraggly, the ground was scraped to bedrock, and rusted iron junk littered the site. An old car sat on busted tires, windows, hood, and doors long gone. The office of the mining site was an old WWII Quonset hut, the door hanging free to reveal the dark interior.

Though strip mining had been the primary means of getting to the gems, tunnels had gone into the side of the mountain. The entry to the mine was boarded over with two-by-tens, but some were missing, and it was clear that the opening had been well used.

Brax rubbed his mouth, looking over the place, not meeting my eyes. Finally, he said, "I would never cause you or yours trouble, Molly Trueblood. I do my best to protect you from problems, harassment, or unwanted attention from law enforcement, federal NCIC or otherwise."

"Except you," I accused, annoyed that he had apologized before I blew off my mad.

He smiled behind his hand. "Except me. And maybe one day you'll trust me enough to tell me the truth about this so-called tracking spell you used to find this place. I'm going to check out the area. Stay here. If I don't come back, that disproves the myth that vamps sleep in the daylight. You get your pal, Jane, to stake my ass if I come back undead."

"Your heart," I said grumpily. "If you actually have one. Heart, not your ass."

He made a little chortling laugh and picked up the flashlight he had brought. "Ten minutes. Half an hour max. I'll be back."

"Better be fangless."

Forty-two minutes later, Brax reappeared, dust all over his hair and suit. He clicked the flash off and strode to the car, got in with a wave of death-tainted air, and said, "Drive." I drove.

His shoulders slumped and he seemed to relax as we turned off on the secondary road and headed back to town, rubbing his hand over his head in a habitual gesture. Dust filtered off him into the air of the car, making motes that caught the late afternoon sun. I rolled the windows down to let out the stink on him. We were nearly back to my house when he spoke again.

"I survived. They either didn't hear me or they were asleep. No myths busted today." When I didn't reply he went on. "They've been bringing people back to the mine for a while. Indigents, transients. Truant kids. There were remains scattered everywhere. Like the McCarleys, most were partially eaten." He stared out the windshield, seeing the scene he had left behind, not the bright, sunny day. "I'll have to get the city and county to compile a list of missing people."

A long moment later he said. "We have to go after them. Today. Before they need to feed again."

"Why not just seal them up in the mine till tomorrow after dawn," I said, turning into my driveway, steering carefully around the tricycle and set of child-sized bongos left there. "Go in fresh, with enough weaponry and men to overpower them. The vamps would be weak, hungry, and apt to make mistakes."

"Good Golly, Miss Molly," he said, his face transforming with a grin at the chance to use the old lyrics. I rolled my eyes. "We could, couldn't we? Where was my brain?"

"Thinking about dead kids," I said softly as I pulled to a stop. "I, on the other hand, had forty-two minutes to do nothing but think. All you need is a set of plans for the mine to make sure you seal over all the entrances. Set a guard with crosses and stakes at each one. That way you go in on your terms, not theirs."

"I think I love you."

"Stop with the lyrics. Go make police plans."

Unfortunately, the vamps got out that night, through an entrance not on the owner's maps. They killed four of the police guarding other entrances. And then they went hunting. This time, they struck close to home. Just after dawn, Brax woke me, standing at the front door, his face full of misery. Carmen Miranda Everhart Newton, air witch, newly married and pregnant, and her husband, had been attacked in their home. Tommy Newton was dead. My little sister was missing and presumed dead.

The attention of the national media had been snared, and more news vans rolled into town, one setting up in the parking lot of the shop. Paralyzed by fear, my sisters closed everything down and gathered at my house to discuss options, to grieve, and to make halfhearted funeral plans.

I spent the day and the early evening hugging my children, watching TV news about the "vampire crisis," and devising offensive and defensive charms, making paper airplanes out of spells that didn't work and flying them across the room, to the delight of my babies and my four human nieces and nephews. I had to come up with something. Something that would offer protection to the person who went underground to avenge my sister.

Jane sat to the side, her cowboy boots, jeans, and T-shirt contrasting with the peasant tops, patchwork skirts, and hemp sandals worn by my sisters and me. She didn't say much, just drank tea and ate whatever was offered. Near dusk, she came to me and said softly, "I need a ride. To the mine."

I looked at her, grief holding my mouth shut, making it hard to breathe.

"I need some steak, or a roast. You have one frozen in the freezer in the garage. I looked. You thaw it in the microwave, leave your car door open. I shift out back, get in, and hunker down. You make an excuse, drive me to the mine, and get back with a gallon of milk or something."

"Why?" I asked. "I don't understand."

Her eyes glowing a tawny yellow, Jane looked like a predator, ready to hunt. Excited by the thought. "I don't smell like a human. The older one won't be expecting me. I can go in, find where they're hiding, see if your sister is alive, and get back. Then we can make a plan."

Hope spiked in me like heated steel. "Why would the vampires keep her alive?" I asked. "And why would you go in there?"

"I told you. Witches smell different from humans. You smell, I don't know, powerful. If he's trying to build a blood-family, and if he has some ability to reason, the new bloodmaster might hold on to her. To try to turn her. It's worth a shot." Jane grinned, her beast rising in her. Bits of gray light hovered, dancing on her skin. "Besides. The governor and the vamp council of North Carolina just upped the bounty on the rogues to forty thou a head. I can use a quarter mil. And if you come up with a way to keep me safe down there, when I go in to hunt them down, I'll share. You said you need to replace that rattletrap you drive."

I put a hand to my mouth, holding in the sob that accompanied my sudden, hopeful tears. Unable to speak, I nodded. Jane went to get a roast.

I slept uneasily, waiting, hearing every creak, crack, and bump in the night. If we smelled differently from humans, would the vampires come after my family? My other sisters? Just after dawn, the phone rang. "Come and get me," Jane said, her voice both excited and exhausted. "Carmen's still alive."

I called my sisters on my cell as I drove and told them to get over to my house fast. We had work to do. When I got back with Jane, my kitchen had three witch sisters in it, each trying to brew coffee and tea, fry eggs, cook grits and oatmeal. Evan was glowering in the corner, his hair standing up in tousles, reading the newspaper on email and feeding Little Evan.

Jane pushed her way in, ignoring the babble of questions, and took the pot of oatmeal right off the stove, dumping in sugar and milk and digging in. She ate ten cups of hot oatmeal, two cups of sugar, and a quart of milk. It was the most oatmeal I had ever seen anyone eat in my life. Her belly bulged like a basketball. Then she took paper and pen and drew a map of the mine, talking. "No one'll be going into the mine today. Count on it. The vamps killed four of the men watching the entrances, and the governor won't justify sending anyone in until the National Guard gets here. Carmen is alive, here." She drew an X. "Along with two teenage girls. The rogue master's name is Adam and he has his faculties, enough to see to the feeding and care of his family, enough to make more scions. But if he dies, then the girls in his captivity are just another dinner to the rogues. So I have to take him down last. I need something like an immobility spell, or glue spell. But first, I need something to get me in close."

"Obfuscation spell," I said.

"No one's succeeded with that one in over five hundred years," Evangelina said, ever the skeptic.

"Maybe that's because *we* never tried," Boadacia said.

Elizabeth looked at her twin, challenge sparkling in her eyes. "Let's."

"But according to the histories, a witch has to be present to initialize it and to keep it running. No human can do it," Evangelina said.

"I'll go in with her," Evan said.

My sisters turned to him. The sudden silence was deafening. Little Evan took that moment to bang on his high chair and shout, "Milk, milk, milk, milk!"

"It would have to be an earth witch," Evangelina said slowly. "You're an air sorcerer. You can't make it work, either." As one, they all turned to look at me. I was the only earth witch in the group.

"No," Evan said. "No way."

"Yes," I said. "It's the only way."

At four in the afternoon, my sisters and Evan and I were standing in front of the mine. Jane was geared up in her vamp-hunting gear: a chain-mail collar, leather pants, metal-studded leather coat over a chain vest, a huge gun with an open stock, like a Star Wars shotgun. Silvered knives were strapped to her thighs, in her boots, along her forearms; studs in her gloves; two handguns were holstered at her waist, under her coat; her long hair was braided and tied down. A dozen crosses hung around her neck. Stakes were twisted in her hair like hairsticks.

I was wearing jeans, sweaters, and Evangelina's faux leather coat. As vegetarians, my sisters didn't own leather, and I couldn't afford it. I carried twelve stakes, extra flashlight, medical supplies, ammunition, and five charms: two healing charms, one walking-away charm, one empowerment, and one obfuscation.

Evan was similarly dressed, refusing to be left behind, loaded down with talismans, charms, battery-powered lights, a machete, and a twenty-pound mallet, suitable for bashing in heads. It wouldn't kill a vampire, but it would incapacitate one long enough to stake it and take its head. We were ready to go in when Brax drove up, got out, and sauntered over. He was dressed in SWAT team gear and guns. "What? You think I'd let civilians go after the rogues alone? Not gonna happen, people."

We hadn't told Brax. I glared at Evan, who shrugged, unapologetic.

"What are you carrying?" Jane asked. When he told her, she shook her head and handed him a box of ammunition. "Hand-packed, silver-flechette rounds, loaded for vamp. They can't heal from it. A direct heart shot will take them out."

"Sweet," Brax said, removing his ammunition from a shotgun and re-loading as he looked us over. "So we got an earth witch, her husband, a vamp hunter, and me. Lock and load, people." Satisfied, he pushed in front and led the way. Once inside, we walked four abreast as my sisters set up a command center at the entrance. Behind us I could hear the three witches chanting protective incantations while Regan and Amelia began to pray.

We passed parts of several bodies. My earth gift recoiled, closing up. There were too many dead. I had hoped to be able to sense the presence of the rogue vampires, but with my gift so overloaded, I doubted I'd be of much help at all. The smell of rancid meat and rotting blood was beyond horrible. Charnel house effluvia. I stopped looking after the first limb—part of a young woman's leg.

Except for the stench and the body parts, the first hundred yards was easy. After that, things went to hell in a handbasket.

We heard singing, a childhood melody. "Starlight, star fright, first star . . . No. Starlight blood fight . . . No. I don' 'member. I don' 'member—" The voice stopped, the cutoff sharp as a knife. "People," she whispered, the word echoing in the mine. "Blood . . . "

And she was on us. Face caught in the flashlight. A ravening animal. Flashing fangs. Blood-red eyes centered with blacker-than-night pupils. Nails like black claws. She took down Evan with one swipe. I screamed. Blood splattered. His flashlight fell. Its beam rocking in shadows. One glimpse of a body. Leaping. Flying. Landed on Jane. Inhumanly fast. Jane rolled into the dark.

I lost them in the swinging light. Found Evan by falling on him. Hot blood pulsed into my hand. I pressed on the wound, guided by earth magic. I called on Mother Earth for healing. Moments later, Jane knelt beside me, breathing hard, smelling foul. She steadied the light. Evan was still alive, fighting to breathe, my hands covered with his blood. His skin was pasty. The wound was across his right shoulder, had sliced his jugular, and he had lost a lot of blood, though my healing had clotted over the wound.

I pressed one of the healing amulets my sisters had made over the wound, chanting in the old tongue. "*Cneasaigh, cneasaigh a bháis báite in fhuil,*" over and over. Gaelic for, "Heal, heal, blood-soaked death."

Minutes later, I felt Evan take a full breath. Felt his heartbeat steady under my hands. In the uncertain light, my tears splashed on his face. He opened his eyes and looked up at me. His beard was brighter than usual, tangled with his blood. He held my gaze, telling me so much in that one look. He loved me. Trusted me. Knew I was going on without him. Promised to live. Promised to take care of our children if I didn't make it back. Demanded I live and come back to him. I sobbed with relief. Buried my face in his healing neck and cried.

We carried Evan back to the entrance, where my sisters called for an ambulance. As soon as he was stable, the three of us redistributed the supplies and headed back in to the mine. I saw the severed head of the rogue in the shadows. Jane's first forty-thousand-dollar trophy.

We had done one useful thing. We had rewritten the history books. We had proved that vampires could move around in the daylight so long as they were in complete absence of the sun. That meant we would have to fight rather than just stake and run. Lucky us.

There were six vampires left and three of us. By now, the remaining ones were surely alerted to our presence. Not good odds.

We were deeply underground when the next attack took place. Jane must have smelled them coming, because she shouted, "Ten o'clock! Two of them." Her gun boomed. Brax's spat flames as it fired. Two vampires fell. Jane dispatched them with a knife shaped like a small sword. While she sawed, and I looked away, she murmured, "Three down, four to go," over and over, like a rich miser counting his gold.

We moved on. Down a level, deeper into the mountain. Jane led the way now, ignoring some branching tunnels, taking others, assuring us she knew where we were and where Carmen was. Like me, she ignored Brax's questions about how.

Just after we passed a cross-tunnel, two vampires came at us from behind, a flanking maneuver. I never heard them. In front of me, Jane whirled. I dropped to the tunnel floor, cowering. She fired. The muzzle flash blinded me. More gunshots sounded, echoing. Brax yelled, the sound full of pain.

Jane stepped over me, straddling me in the dark, her boots lit by a wildly tottering light. I snatched it and turned it on Brax. He knelt nearby, blood at his throat. A vampire lay at his knees, a stake through her chest. My ears were ringing, blasted by the concussion of firepower. In the light, I saw Jane hand a bandage to Brax and pull one of her knives. Her shadow on the mine wall raised up the knife and brought it down, beheading the rogues; my hearing began to come back; the chopping sounded soggy.

She left the heads. "For pickup on the way out. The odds just turned in our favor."

I couldn't look at the heads. I had been no help at all. I was the weak link in the trio. I squared my shoulders and fingered the charms I carried. I was supposed to hold them until Jane said to activate them. It would be soon.

We moved on down the widening tunnel. Jane touched my arm in the dark. I jumped. She tapped my hand and mouthed, "Charm one. Now."

Clumsy, I pulled the charm, activated it, and tossed it to the left. The sound of footsteps echoed, as if we were still moving, but down a side tunnel. Then I activated the second charm, the one my sisters and I had worked on all day.

The obfuscation charm. It was the closest thing in all of our histories to an invisibility spell, and no witch had perfected it in hundreds of years.

Following the directions I had memorized, I drew in the image of the rock floor and walls, and cloaked it around us. I nodded to Jane. She cut off the light. Moments later, she moved forward slowly, Brax at her side. I followed, one hand on each shoulder. The one on Brax's shoulder was sticky with blood. He was still bleeding. Vampires can smell blood. The obfuscation spell wasn't intended to block scents.

A faint light appeared ahead, growing brighter as we moved and the tunnel opened out. We stopped. The space before us was a juncture from which five tunnels branched. Centered, was a table with a lantern, several chairs, and cots. Carmen was lying on one, cradling her belly, her eyes open and darting. Two teenaged girls were on another cot, huddling together, eyes wide and fearful. No vampires were in the room.

We moved quietly to Carmen and I bent over her. I slammed my hand over her mouth. She bucked, squealing. "Carmen. It's Molly," I whispered. She stopped fighting. Raised a hand and touched mine. She nodded. I removed my hand.

She whispered, "They went that way."

"Come on. Tell the others to come. But be quiet."

Moving awkwardly, Carmen rolled off the cot and stood. She motioned to the two girls. "Come on. Come with me." When both girls refused, my baby sister waddled over, slapped them both resoundingly, gripped each by an arm, and hauled them up. "I said, come with me. It wasn't a damn invitation."

The girls followed her, holding their jaws and watching Carmen fearfully. Pride blossomed in me. I adjusted the obfuscation spell, drawing in more of the cave walls and floor. Wrapped the spell around the three new bodies. The girls suddenly could see us. One screamed.

"So much for stealth," Jane said. "Move it!" She shoved the two girls and me toward the tunnel out. Stumbling, we raced to the dark. I switched on the flashlight, put it in Carmen's hands. Pulled the last two charms. The empowerment charm was meant to take strength from a winning opponent and give it to a losing, dying one. It could be used only in clear life-and-death situations. The other was my last healing charm.

We made the first turn, feet slapping the stone, gasping. Something crashed into us. A girl and Jane went down with the vampire. Tangled limbs. The vampire somersaulted. Taking Jane with him. Crouching. He held her in front of him. Jane's head in one hand. Twisting it up and back. His fangs extended fully. He sank fangs and claws into Jane's throat, above her mail collar. Ripping. The collar hit the ground.

Brax shouted. "Run!" He picked up the fallen girl and shoved her down the tunnel. The last vamp landed on his back. Brax went down. Rolling. Blood spurting. Shadows like monsters on the far wall.

In the wavering light, Jane's throat gushed blood. Pumping bright.

Carmen and I backed against the mine wall. I was frozen, indecisive. Whom to save? I didn't know for sure who was winning or losing. I didn't know what would happen if I activated the empowerment charm. I pulled the extra flashlight and switched it on.

Brax rolled. Into the light. Eyes wild. The vampire rolled with him. Eating his throat. Brax was dying. I activated the empowerment charm. Tossed it.

It landed. Brax's breath gargled. The vampire fell. Brax rose over him, stake in hand. Brought the stake down. Missed his heart.

I pointed. "Run. That way." Carmen ran, her flashlight bouncing. I set down the last light, pulled stakes from my pockets. Rushed the vampire. Stabbed down with all my might. One sharpened stake ripped through his clothes. Into his flesh. I stabbed again. Blood splashed up, crimson and slick. I fumbled two more stakes.

Brax, beside me, took them. Rolled the vampire into the light. Raised his arms high. Rammed them into the rogue's chest.

Blood gushed. Brax fell over it. Silent. So silent. Neither moved.

I activated the healing amulet. Looked over my shoulder. At Jane.

The vampire was behind her. Her throat was mostly gone. Blood was everywhere. Spine bones were visible in the raw meat of her throat.

Yet, even without a trachea, she was growling. Face shifting. Gray light danced. Her hands, clawed and tawny, reached back. Dug into the skull of the vampire. Whipped him forward. Over her. He slammed into the rock floor. Bounced limply.

Sobbing, I grabbed Brax's shoulder. Pulled him over. Dropped the charm on his chest.

Jane leaped onto the vampire. Ripped out his throat. Tore into his stomach. Slashed clothes and flesh. Blood spurted. She shifted. Gray light. Black motes. And her cat screamed.

I watched as her beast tore the vampire apart. Screaming with rage.

We made it to the mine entrance, Carmen and the girls running ahead, into the arms of my sisters. Evangelina raised a hand to me, framed by pale light, and pulled the girls outside, leaving the entrance empty, dawn pouring in. I didn't know how the night had passed, where the time had disappeared. But I stopped there, inside the mine with Jane, looking out, into the day. In the urgency of finding the girls and getting them all back to safety, we hadn't spoken about the fight.

Now, she touched her throat. Hitched Brax higher. He hadn't made it. Jane had carried him out, his blood seeping all over her, through the rents in her clothes made by fighting vampires and by Jane herself, as she shifted inside them. "Is he," she asked, her damaged voice raspy as stone, "dead because you used the last healing charm on me?" She swallowed, the movement of poorly healed muscles audible. "Is that why you're crying?"

Guilt lanced through me. Tears, falling for the last hour, burned my face. "No," I whispered. "I used it on Brax. But he was too far gone for a healing charm."

"And me?" The sound was pained, the words hurting her throat.

"I trusted in your beast to heal you."

She nodded, staring into the dawn. "You did the right thing." Again she hitched Brax higher. Whispery-voiced, she continued. "I got seven heads to pick up and turn in"—she slanted her eyes at me—"and we got a cool quarter mil waiting. Come on. Day's wasting." Jane Yellowrock walked into the sunlight, her tawny eyes still glowing.

And I walked beside her.

Faith Hunter was born in Louisiana and raised all over the South. "Signatures of the Dead" is a prequel to her Skinwalker series, featuring Jane Yellowrock. *Blood Trade*, the sixth Skinwalker novel, was recently released. Her Rogue Mage novels—*Bloodring*, *Seraphs*, and *Host*—feature a stone mage in a post-apocalyptic, alternate reality, urban fantasy world. The novels are the basis for the role playing game, *Rogue Mage*, that premiered in 2012. Under the pen name Gwen Hunter, she writes action-adventure, mysteries, and thrillers. As Faith and Gwen, she has more than twenty books in print in twenty-eight countries. She and her husband love to RV, traveling with their dogs to whitewater rivers all over the Southeast.

The Case: *A woman's ex-husband has physically assaulted her half a dozen times. Now he's threatening to kill her—tonight.*

The Investigator: *Sam Hunter—currently a Philadelphia PI, formerly a detective with the Minneapolis PD.*

LIKE PART OF THE FAMILY

Jonathan Maberry

"My ex-husband is trying to kill me," she said.

She was one of those cookie-cutter East Coast blondes. Pale skin, pale hair, pale eyes. Lots of New Age jewelry. Not a lot of curves, and too much perfume. Kind of pretty if you dig the modeling-scene heroin chic look. Or if you troll the anorexia twelve-steps or crack houses looking for easy ass that's so desperate for affection they'll boff you blind for a smile. Not my kind. I like a little more meat on the bone, and a bit more sanity in the eyes. This one came to me on a referral from another client.

"He actually try?"

"I can *tell,* Mr. Hunter."

Yeah, I thought and tried not to sigh. *What I figured.*

"You call the cops?"

She shrugged.

"What's that mean? You call them or not?"

"I called," she said. "They said that there wasn't anything they could do unless he did something first."

"Yeah," I said. "Can't arrest someone for thinking about something."

"He threatened me."

"Anyone hear him make the threat?"

"No."

"Then it's your word."

"That's what the police said." She crossed her legs. Her legs were on the thin side of being nice. Probably were nice before drugs or stress or a fractured self-image wasted her down to Sally Stick-figure.

Skirt was short, shoes looked expensive. I have three ex-wives and I pay alimony bigger than India's national debt. I know how expensive women's shoes are. I was wearing black sneakers from Payless. Glad I had a desk between me and her.

"Your husband ever hurt you?" I asked. "Or try to?"

"*Ex*," she corrected. "And . . . yes. That's why I left him. He hit me a few times. Mostly when he was drunk and out of control."

I held up a hand. "Don't make excuses for him. He hit you. Being drunk doesn't change the rules. Might even make it worse, especially if he did it once while drunk and then let himself come home drunk again."

She digested that. She'd probably heard that rap before but it might have come from a female caseworker or a shrink. From the way her eyes shifted to me and away and back again I guessed she'd never heard that from a man before. I guess for her, men were the Big Bad. Too many of them are.

It was ten to five, but it was already dark outside. December snow swirled past the window. It wasn't accumulating, so the snow still looked pretty. Once it started piling up I hated the shit. My secretary, Mrs. Gilligan, fled at the first flake. Typical Philadelphian—they think the world will come to a screeching halt if there's half an inch on the ground. She's probably at Wegmans stocking up on milk, bread, and toilet paper. The staples of the apocalypse. Me, I grew up in Minneapolis, and out in the Cities we think twenty inches is getting off light. Doesn't mean I don't hate the shit, though. A low annual snowfall is one of the reasons I moved to Philly after I got my PI license. Easier to hunt if you don't have to slog through snow.

"When he hit you," I said, "you report it?"

"No."

"Not to the cops?"

"No."

"Women's shelter?

"No."

"Anyone? A friend?"

She shook her head. "I was . . . embarrassed, Mr. Hunter. A black eye and all. Didn't want to be seen."

Which means there's no record. Nothing to support her case about ex-hubby wanting to kill her.

I drummed my fingers on the desk blotter. I get these kinds of cases every once in a while, though I stayed well clear of domestic disputes and spousal abuse cases when I was with Minneapolis PD. I have a temper, and by the time they asked for my shield back I had six reprimands in my jacket for excessive force. At one of my IA hearings the captain said he was disappointed that I showed no remorse for the last "incident." I busted a child molester and somehow while the guy was, um, resisting arrest he managed to get mauled and mangled a bit. The pedophile tried to spin some crazy shit that I sicced a dog on him, but I don't *have* a dog. I said that he got mauled by a stray during a foot pursuit. Even at my own hearing I couldn't keep a smile off my face to save my job. Squeaked by on that one, but next time something like it happened— this time with a guy who whipped his wife half to death with an extension cord because she wasn't "willing enough" in the bedroom—I was out on my ass. He ran into the same stray dog. Weird how that happens, huh? Long story short, I already didn't have the warm fuzzies for her husband. We all have our buttons, and when the strong prey on the weak, all of mine get pushed.

"Did you go to the E.R.?"

"No," she said. "It was never that bad. More humiliating than anything."

I nodded. "What about after the divorce? He lay a hand on you since?"

She hesitated.

"Mrs. Skye?" I prompted.

"He tried. He chased me. Twice."

"*Chased* you? Tell me about it."

She licked her lips. She wore a very nice rose-pink lipstick that was the only splash of color. Even her clothes and shoes were white. Pale horse, pale rider.

"Well," she said, "that's where the story gets really . . . strange."

"Strange how?"

"He—David, my ex-husband—*changed* after I filed for divorce. He's like a different person. Before, when I first met him, he was a very fastidious man. Always dressed nicely, always very clean and well-groomed."

"What's he do for a living?"

"He owns a nightclub. The Crypt, just off South Street."

"I know it, but that's a Goth club, right? Is he Goth?"

"No. Not at all. He bought the club from the former owner, but he remodeled it after The Batcave."

"As in Batman?"

"As in the London club that was kind of the prototype of pretty much the whole Goth club scene. David's a businessman. There's a strong Goth crowd downtown, and they hang together, but the clubs in Philly aren't big enough to turn a big profit, and not near big enough to attract the better bands. So, he bought the two adjoining buildings and expanded out. He made a small-time club into a very successful main stage club, and he keeps the music current. A lot of post-punk stuff, but also the newer styles. Dark cabaret, deathrock, Gothabilly. That sort of thing. Low lights, black-tile bathrooms, bartenders who look like ghouls."

"Okay," I said.

"But this was all business to David. He didn't dress Goth. I mean, he wore black suits or black silk shirts to work, but he didn't dye his hair, didn't wear eyeliner. Funny thing is, even though he was clearly not buying into the lifestyle, the patrons loved him. They called him the Prince. As in Prince of—?"

"Darkness, yeah, got it. Go on."

"David was more fussy getting ready to go out than I ever was. Spent forever in the bathroom shaving, fixing his hair. Always took him longer to pick out his clothes than me or any of my girlfriends."

"He gay?"

"No." And she shot me a "wow, what a stereotypically homophobic thing to say" sort of look.

I smiled. "I'm just trying to get a read on him. Fastidious guy having trouble with a relationship with his wife. Drinking problem, flashes of violence. Not a gay thing, but I've seen it before in guys who are sexually conflicted and at war with themselves and the world because of it."

She studied me for a moment. "You used to be a cop, Mr. Hunter?"

"Call me Sam," I said. "And, yeah, I was a cop. Minneapolis PD."

"A detective?"

"Yep."

"Okay." That seemed to mollify her. I gestured to her to continue. She took a breath. "Well . . . toward the end of our relationship, David stopped being so fastidious. He would go two or three days without shaving. I know that doesn't sound like the end of the world, but I never saw David without a fresh shave. Never. He carried an electric razor in his briefcase, had another at home and one in the office at the club. Clothes, too. Before, he'd sometimes change clothes twice or even three times a day if it was humid. He always wanted to look fresh. Showered at home morning and night, and had a shower installed in his office."

"I get the picture. Mr. Clean. But you say that changed while you were still together?"

"It started when he fell off the wagon."

"Ah."

"When I met him he said that he hadn't taken a drink for over two years. He was proud of it. He thought that his thirst—he always called it that—was evil, and being on the wagon made him feel like a real person. Then, after we started having problems, he started drinking again. Never in front of me, and he always washed his mouth out before he came home. I never smelled alcohol on him, but he was a different person from then on. And he started yelling at me all the time. He called me horrible names and made threats. He said that I didn't love him, that I was just trying to use him."

"I have to ask," I said, being as delicate as I could, "but was there someone else?"

"For me? God, no!"

"What set him off? From his perspective, I mean. Did he say that there was something that made him angry or paranoid?"

"Well . . . I think it was his health."

"Tell me."

"He started losing weight. He was never fat, not even stocky. David was very muscular. He lifted a lot of weights, drank that protein powder twice a day. He had big arms, a huge chest. I asked him if he was taking steroids. He denied it, but I think he was trying to turn into one of those muscle freaks. Then, about a year and a half ago, he started losing weight. When he taped his arms and found that his biceps were only twenty-two inches, he got really angry."

"David has twenty-two inch biceps?" Christ. Back in his Mr. Universe days, Arnold the Terminator had twenty-four inch arms, fully pumped. I think mine are somewhere shy of fifteen, and that's after three sets on the Bowflex.

"Not anymore," said Mrs. Skye. "He lost a lot of muscle mass. Really fast, too. I was scared; I told him to go to a doctor. I thought he might have cancer."

"Did he go to the doctor?"

"He said so . . . but I don't think he did. He kept losing weight. After six months, he didn't even have much definition. He was kind of ordinary sized."

"Was he drinking by this point?"

"I'm sure of it."

"That when he started putting his hands on you?"

"Yes. And he became paranoid. Kept trying to make it all my fault."

"How long did this go on?"

"Well . . . after the first time he, um, *hurt* me, I gave him a second chance. After all, he was my husband. I figured he was just scared because of his health. But then it happened again. The second time he knocked me around pretty good. I couldn't go out of the house for a few days."

"Was that when you left?"

It took her so long to answer that I knew what her answer would be. I've done too many interviews of this kind. If self-esteem is low enough then victimization can become an addiction.

"I stayed for two more months."

"How many times did he hurt you during that time?" I asked.

"A few."

"A few is how many?"

Another long pause. "Six."

"Six," I said, trying to put no judgment in my tone. "What was the last straw?"

She looked at her hands, at the clock, at the snow falling outside. If there'd been a magazine on my desk she would have picked it up and leafed through it. Anything to keep from meeting my eyes. "He choked me."

"I see."

"It was in the middle of the night. We were . . . we were . . . "

I almost sighed. "Let me guess. Make-up sex?"

She nodded, but she didn't blush. I'll give her that. "He'd been sweet to me for two weeks straight without getting mad or yelling, or anything. He acted like his old self. Charming." She finally met my eyes. "David has enormous charisma. He makes everyone like him, and he always seems so genuine."

"Uh huh," I said, wondering how that charm would work on a blackjack across his teeth.

"We sat up talking until late, then we went to bed. And in the middle of the night . . . things just started happening. You know how it is."

I didn't, but I said nothing.

"I was, um . . . on top. And we were pretty far into things, and then all of a sudden David reaches up and grabs me around the throat. I thought for one crazy moment that he was doing that auto-whatever it's called."

"Autoerotic asphyxiation," I supplied.

"Yeah, that. I thought he was doing that. He talked about it once before, but we'd never tried it. He's really strong and I'm pretty small. But . . . I guess I thought he was trying to change things, you know? Create a new pattern for us. A fresh start."

Naivety can be a terrible thing. Jesus wept.

"But it wasn't sex play," I prompted.

"No. He started squeezing his hands. Suddenly I couldn't breathe. It was weird because we were so close to . . . you know . . . and David kept staring at me, his eyes wide like he was in some kind of trance. I tried to pull his hands apart, but it just made him squeeze tighter. That's when he started calling me names again, making wild accusations, accusing me of destroying his life."

"How did you get away?"

Her eyes cut away again. This was obviously very hard for her.

"I threw myself sideways and when I landed I kicked him in the, um . . . you know."

I smiled.

"Good for you," I said, but she shook her head.

"I grabbed my clothes and ran out. Next day I drove past the house and saw that his car was gone. I had a locksmith come out and change the locks and change the security code on the alarm. I hired a messenger company to take a couple of suitcases of his clothes to the club. Next day I rented a storage unit and had a moving company take all of his stuff there. I used the same messenger service to send him the key."

"I'm impressed. That was quick thinking."

"I . . . I'd already looked into that stuff before. Until that last stretch where he was nice I was planning to leave him. I'd already talked to my lawyer, and I filed for divorce by the end of that week."

"What did David do?"

"At first? Nothing, except for some hysterical messages on my voicemail. He didn't try to break in, nothing like that. But after a while I started seeing his car behind mine when I was going to work."

"Where do you work?"

"I'm a nurse supervisor at Sunset Grove, the assisted living facility in Jenkintown. Right now I'm on the four to midnight shift. I've spotted David's car a lot, sometimes every night for weeks on end. I've seen him drive by when I'm going into the staff entrance, and his car is there sometimes when I get back home, cruising down the street or parked a block up."

"What makes you think he's planning to do more than just harass you?"

"He's said so."

"But—"

"He didn't say or do anything at first . . . but over the last couple of weeks it's gotten worse. About three weeks ago I came out of work and stopped at a 7-Eleven for some gum, and when I came out he was leaning against my car. I told him to get away, but he pushed himself off the car and came up to me, smiling his charming smile. He told me that he knew who I was and what I was and that he was going to end me. His words. *'I'm going to end you.'* Then he left, still smiling."

"Did anyone see this?"

"At one in the morning? No."

Convenience stores have security cameras, I thought. If this thing got messy I could have her lawyer subpoena those tapes. I had her write down the address of the 7-Eleven.

"That's how it went for a couple of weeks," she said. "But last night he really scared me."

"What happened?"

"He was in my bedroom."

"How?"

"That's it . . . I don't know. The alarms didn't go off and none of the windows were broken. I heard a sound and I woke up and there he was, standing by the side of my bed. He's really thin now and as pale as those Goth kids at his club. He stood there, smiling. I started to scream and he put a finger to his lips and made a weird shushing sound. It was so strange that I actually did shut up. Don't ask me why. The whole thing was like a nightmare."

"Are you sure it wasn't?"

She hesitated, but she said, "I'm positive. He pointed at me and said that he knew everything about me. Then he started praying."

"Praying?"

"At least I think that's what he was doing. It was Latin, I think. He was saying a long string of things in Latin and then he left."

"How'd he get out?"

"The same way he got in, I guess . . . but I don't know how. I was so scared that I almost peed myself and I just lay there in bed for a long time. I don't know how long. When I finally worked up the nerve, I ran downstairs and got a knife from the kitchen and went through the whole house."

"You didn't call the cops?"

"I was going to . . . but the alarm never went off. I checked the system . . . it was still set. I began wondering if I *was* dreaming."

"But you don't think so?"

"No."

"Why are you so sure?"

She fished in her purse and produced a pink cell phone. She flipped it open and pressed a few buttons to call up her text messages. She pointed to the number and then handed me the phone.

"That's David's cell number."

The text read: *Tonight.*

"Okay," I said. "Let me see what I can do."

"What *can* you do?" she asked.

"Well, the best first thing to do is go have a talk with him. See if I can convince him to back off."

"And if he won't?"

"I can be pretty convincing."

"But what if he won't? What if he's . . . I don't know . . . too crazy to listen to reason?"

I smiled. "Then we'll explore other options."

The Crypt is a big ugly building on the corner of South and Fourth in Philadelphia. Once upon a time it was a coffin factory—which I think would have been a cooler name. Less trendy and obvious. The light snow did nothing to make it look less ugly. When we pulled to the corner, Mrs. Skye pointed to a sleek, silver Lexus parked on the side street.

"That's his."

I jotted down the license plate and used my digital camera to take photos of it and the exterior of the building. You never know.

"Okay," I said, "I want you to wait here. I'll go have a talk with David and see if we can sort this out."

"What if something happens? What if you don't come out?"

"Just sit tight. You have a cell phone and I'll give you the keys. If I'm not out of there in fifteen minutes, drive somewhere safe and call the name on the back of my card." I gave her my business card. She turned it over and saw a name and number. Before she could ask, I said, "Ray's a friend. One of my pack."

"Another private investigator?"

"A bodyguard. I use him for certain jobs, but I don't think we'll need to bring him in on this. From what you've told me I have a pretty good sense of what to expect in there."

As I got out my jacket flap opened and she spotted the handle of my Glock.

"You're not . . . going to *hurt* him," she asked, wide eyed.

I shook my head. "I've been doing this for a lot of years, Mrs. Skye. I haven't had to pull my gun once. I don't expect I'll break that streak tonight."

The breeze was coming from the west and the snow was just about done. I squinted up past the streetlights. The cloud cover was thin and I could already see the white outline of the moon. Nope, no accumulation. Typical Philly winter.

I crossed the street and tried the front door. Place didn't do much business before late evening, but the doors were unlocked. The doors opened with an exhalation of cigarette smoke and alcohol fumes. There was probably an anti-smoking violation in that. Something else to use later if I needed to go the route of making life difficult for him.

It was too early for a doorman, and I walked a short hallway that was empty and painted black. Heavy black velvet curtains at the end. Cute. I pushed them aside and entered the club. Place was huge. David Skye must have taken out the second floor and knocked out everything but the retaining walls of the adjoining properties. The red and white maximum occupancy sign said that it shouldn't exceed four hundred, but the place looked capable of taking twice that number. Bandstand was empty, so someone had put quarters in to play the tuneless junk that was beating the shit out of the woofers and tweeters. Whoever the group was on the record they subscribed to the philosophy that if you can't play well, you should play real goddamn loud.

There were maybe twenty people in the place, scattered around at tables. A few at the bar. Everyone looked like extras from a direct-to-video vampire flick. The motif was black on black with occasional splashes of blood red. White skin that probably never saw the sun. Eyeliner and black lipstick, even on the guys. I was in jeans and a Vikings warm-up jacket. At least my sneakers and my leather porkpie hat were black. Handle of my gun was black, too, but they couldn't see that. Better for everyone if nobody did.

The bartender was giving me *the look*, so I strolled over to him. He knew I wasn't there for a beer and didn't waste either of our time by asking.

"David Skye," I said, having to bend forward and shout over the music.

"Badge me," he said.

I flipped open my PI license. "Private."

"Fuck off," he suggested.

"Not a chance."

"I can call the cops."

"Bet I can have L-and-I—Licenses and Inspections—here before they show. Smoking in a public restaurant?"

Another smartass remark was on his lips, but he didn't have the energy for it. He was paid by the hour and this had to be a slow shift for tips. I took a twenty from my wallet and put it on the bar.

"This isn't your shit, kid," I said. "Call your boss."

He didn't like it, but he took the twenty and made the call.

"He says come up." The bartender pointed to another curtained doorway beside the bar. I gave him a sunny day smile and went inside.

There was a long hallway with bathrooms on both sides and a set of stairs at the end. I took the stairs two at a time. The stairs went straight up to his office and the door was open. I knocked anyway.

"It's open," he yelled. I went inside; and as I looked around I hoped like hell that the office décor was not modeled after the interior landscape of David Skye's mind. The walls were painted a dark red, the trim was gloss black. Instead of the band posters and framed "look at who I'm shaking hands with" eight-by-tens, the walls were hung with torture devices and S-and-M clothes. Spiked harnesses, leather zippered masks, thumbscrews, photos from Abu Graib, diagrams of dissected bodies. A full-sized rack occupied one corner of the room and an iron maiden stood in the other, one door open to reveal rows of tarnished metal spikes. The only other furniture was a big desk made from some dark wood, a black file cabinet, and the leather swivel chair in which David Skye sat. He wore a black poet's shirt, leather wristbands, and a smile that was already belligerent.

"The fuck are you and the fuck you want?"

The man was a charmer. I could just taste the charisma his wife had mentioned flowing like sweetness from his pores.

I flipped my ID case open. "We need to have a chat. It can be friendly or not. Your call."

"Go fuck yourself."

So much for *friendly.*

"That whore send you?" he demanded.

I smiled but didn't answer.

He had a handsome face, but his wife was right when she said that he'd lost weight. His skin looked thin and loose, and he had the complexion of a mushroom. More gray than white.

"Did my wife send you?" he said, pronouncing the words slowly as if I'd come here on the short bus.

"Why would your ex-wife send me?"

His eyes flickered for a second at "*ex*-wife." I strolled across the room and stood in front of his desk. He didn't get up; neither of us offered a hand to the other.

"She makes up stories," he said.

"What kind of stories?"

"Bullshit. Lies. Says I slapped her around."

"Who'd she say that to?"

He didn't answer. He did, however, give me the ninja secret death stare, but I manned my way through it.

"What are you supposed to be?" he said.

"Just what the license says."

"Private investigator. Private *dick.*"

"Yes, and that was funny back in the 1950s. Why do *you* think I'm here?"

"She's probably trying some kind of squeeze play. The club's doing okay, so she wants a bigger slice."

"Try again," I said, though he might have been right about that.

"Oh, I get it . . . you're supposed to scare me into leaving her alone."

"Do I look scary?"

He smiled. He had very red lips and very white teeth. "No," he said, "you don't."

"Right . . . so let's pretend that I'm here to have a reasonable discussion. Man to man."

Skye leaned back in his chair and stared at me with his dark eyes. It was a calculating look, and I'm sure he took in everything from my slightly threadbare Vikings jacket to my cheap black sneakers. Put everything I was wearing together and it would equal the cost of his shirt. I was okay with that. I don't dress to impress. Skye, on the other hand, smiled as if our mutual understanding of my material net worth clearly made him the alpha.

I smiled back.

"What does she want?" he asked.

"For you to leave her alone."

"What is she afraid of?"

"She thinks you're trying to kill her."

"What do *you* think?"

"What I think doesn't matter. I'm not a psychic, so I don't know whether you're trying to kill her or if you're playing some kind of mindgame on her. Whatever it is, I'm here to ask you to lay off."

"Why should I?"

"Because I asked real nice."

He smiled at that.

"Because it's illegal and I could build a harassment case against you and you could lose your club and sink a quarter mil into legal fees. Because I know inspectors who can slap you with fifteen kinds of violations that will hurt your business. I can have your car booted by *accident* three or four times a week, every week."

"And I could have you killed," he said, the smile unwavering.

"Maybe," I said. "You could try, and I might fuck up anyone you send and then come back here and fuck you up."

"Think you could?"

"You really want to find out?" When he didn't answer, I took a glass paperweight off his desk and turned it over in my hands. A spider was trapped inside, frozen into a moment of time for the amusement of the trinket crowd. I knew he was watching me play with the paperweight, wondering what I was going to do with it.

I put it back down on the desk.

"Really, though," I said, "how long do we need to circle and sniff each other? We don't run in the same pack and I don't give a rat's ass what you do, who you are, or how tough you think you are. We both know that you're either going to stop bothering your ex-wife and go on with your life, or you're going to make a run at her—either because you have some loose wiring or because I'm pushing your buttons by being here. If you back off, we're all friends. I'll advise my client not to file a restraining order and you two can let the divorce lawyers earn their paychecks by kicking each other in the nuts."

"Or . . . ?" he asked. Still smiling.

"Or, you don't back off and then this is about you and me."

"Nonsense. You're no part of this. This is about me and—"

I cut him off. "I'm *making* this about you and me. Maybe I have a wire loose, too, but once I tell a client that I'm going to keep her safe, I take it amiss if anything happens to her."

"*Amiss*," he repeated, enjoying the word.

"But that's a minute from now. We're still on the other side of it until you give me an answer. What's it going to be? You leave her alone? Or this gets complicated."

"What were you before you started doing this PI bullshit?"

"A cop."

He grunted. "You sound like a thug. An asshole leg-breaker from South Philly."

"Thin line sometimes."

He steepled his fingers. It was one of those moves that looked good when Doctor Doom did it in a comic book. Maybe in a boardroom. Looked silly right now, but he had enough intensity in his eyes to almost pull it off. He gave me ten seconds of *the stare*.

I stood my ground.

His cell phone rang and he flipped it open, listened.

"I'm in a meeting," he said, and closed the phone.

His smile returned.

I heard the footsteps on the stairs even though they were quiet.

I sighed and turned. There were four of them. All as pale as Skye, but much bigger. "Really? You want to play that card?"

"It's one of the classics. Though, to be fair, it'll be more than a typical beating. I . . . hm, am I wrong in presuming you *have* had your ass kicked?"

"That cherry was popped a long time ago."

The four men entered the room and fanned out behind me.

"So, our challenge, then," Skye said, "is to put a new spin on this. Something surprising and fresh so that you'll be entertained."

"Mind if I take my jacket off first?"

"Go right ahead."

I heard a hammer-cock behind me.

Skye said, "You can put your jacket on my desk here, and take off your shoulder holster and put that—and your piece—on top of it."

"Sure, whatever," I said. I shrugged out of the jacket. I bought it the year the Vikings took their eighteenth division title. I'll buy a new one if they ever win the Super Bowl. Or when pigs sprout wings and learn to fly, whichever comes first. I folded it and set it down, unclipped my shoulder rig, set that down. If I was going to ruin my clothes, then at least nothing I was currently wearing had sentimental value.

I leaned on the desk. "Let's agree on a couple of things first, okay?"

"Sure," he said with a grin.

"When I'm done handing these clowns their asses, then you and I dance a round or two."

"That would be fun," he said, "but I doubt I'll have the pleasure."

"Second, if I walk out of here on my own steam, then it's with the understanding that you will leave the lady alone."

"If you walk out of here? Sure. But, tell me something," he said, and he looked genuinely interested, "Why do you care? What is she to you?"

"Maybe I'm the possessive type, too. Maybe now that she's asked for my help, it's like she's part of the family. So to speak."

"Part of the family? You fucking kidding me here?"

"Nope."

"You Italian? This some kind of dago thing?"

"I said it's *like* she's part of the family. My family," I said, "and I protect what's mine."

"That's it? It's just a macho thing with you?"

"No, it's more than that," I admitted. I gestured to the torture-and-pain motif in which his office was decorated. "But, seriously, I doubt you would understand."

"Mmm, probably not. I'm not into sentimentality and that bullshit. Not anymore."

"What happened? What changed you?"

His smiled faded to a remote coldness. "I learned that there was something better. Better than family, better than blood ties. Better than any of this ordinary shit."

"You found religion?" I said.

"It's a 'higher order' sort of thing that I really don't want to explain and I doubt *you'd* understand."

"I might surprise you."

"I don't think that's possible. But *we* might surprise you. In fact I can pretty fucking well guarantee it."

"Rock and roll," I said.

I straightened and turned toward the four goons. They took up positions like compass points. The office was big, but not big enough to give me room to maneuver. They were going to fall on me like a wall, and they knew it. The guy with the gun even snugged it back into his shoulder rig. They were *that* confident, and they were smiling like kids at a carnival.

"You shouldn't have bothered Mr. Skye," said the guy in front of me. He was the gun who'd holstered his gun. He stood on the East point of the compass. "You should have—"

I kicked him in the nuts. I really didn't need to hear the speech.

I'm not that big, but I can kick like a Rockette. I *felt* bones break and he screamed like a nine-year-old girl. Dumbass should have kept his gun out.

I stepped backward off of him and put an elbow into West's face. It had all of my mass in motion behind it. That time I heard bones break, and he went down so fast that I wondered if I'd snapped his neck.

That left South and North. South spent a half second too long looking shocked, so I jumped at him with a leaping knee—the only Muay Thai kick I know—and drove him all the way to the wall. By the time North closed in I'd grabbed South by the ears and slammed him skull-first into a replica of a torture rack. Blood splattered in a Jackson Pollack pattern.

I pivoted and rushed to intercept North, who was barreling at me with a lot of furious speed; so I veered left and clothes-lined him with my stiff right forearm. He did a pretty impressive back flip and landed face down on the black-painted hardwood floor.

If this was an action movie everything would switch to slow motion as the four thugs toppled to the ground and I turned slowly, looking badass, to face the now startled and unprotected villain.

The real world is a lot less accommodating.

I caught movement behind me, figuring it for Skye going after my gun, so I whirled and made ready to launch into a diving tackle.

Only it wasn't Skye.

It was East and West getting to their feet. West's face was smeared with blood from his broken nose, but he was smiling. As I watched he took his nose between thumb and forefinger and *snapped* it into place, then spit a hocker of blood and snot onto the floor.

North was chuckling as he rose; and behind me I could hear South shifting to stand behind me again. I turned in a slow circle. They were all smiling. They shouldn't have been *able* to. They should have been sprawled on the floor and I should have been giving some kind of smart-ass speech as I closed in to lay a beating on Skye. That was the script I'd written in my head.

What the hell was this shit?

"Surprise!" said Skye dryly.

"What the hell are these fuckers *taking*?"

"You wouldn't believe me if I told you?"

"Try me."

"Blood," he said.

"What the—"

And I looked more closely at the smiles. Lots of white teeth. Lots of long, pointy white teeth.

"Oh, balls," I said.

"Yeah, kind of cool, huh?"

"Vampires?" I said.

"Yeah."

"Actual vampires."

Skye laughed. The four—well, let's call a spade a spade—*vampires* laughed with him.

Even I laughed.

"Geez. When shit goes wrong it goes all the way wrong, doesn't it," I said.

"On the up side," said Skye, "you did win the first round. Nice moves."

"Thanks."

The four of them circled me. My pulse jumped from "uh-oh" to "oh shit." It was cold in his office, but I was starting to sweat pretty heavily.

"I guess I shouldn't be surprised," I said. "You're one, too? Am I right?"

"A recent convert," he admitted.

"So . . . that whole weight loss, going all weird on the missus, that was—?"

"A transition process. It's not like they show in the movies, you know. Takes weeks. The whole metabolism changes."

"No kidding."

One of the vampires faked a lunge to psyche me out and I jumped a foot in the air. I'm pretty sure I didn't yelp like a Chihuahua, but I wouldn't swear to that in court. They all laughed at that, too. I didn't.

"Which explains why you lost all that weight."

"Who needs steroids and free-weights," he agreed and spread his hands. "This package comes with honest-to-God super strength. I'm like Spider-Man and Wolverine rolled into one. Super strong and I heal from damn near anything."

"Could you be more specific on that last point?"

"Cute."

"Worth a try." I looked at them, at their grinning, evil faces. My nuts were trying to crawl up inside of my chest cavity. I mean . . . *fucking vampires?*

"Weird thing was," I said, "I was starting to build a case in my head about your wife. You losing weight and getting pale, blaming her for it all, and you saying you *know* what she is. Is she a vampire, too? Is she the one who bit you?"

Skye laughed. "Christ, no. And she's not a succubus, either. She's just a nagging, soul-draining, passive-aggressive, codependent bitch."

"Wow. You're really a chauvinistic prick, aren't you?"

"Better than being pussy whipped."

I dropped it. I had bigger fish to fry than trying to bring this macho jackass into the twenty-first century. Namely the fact that I was in a roomful of vampires.

I know I keep harping on that, but really . . . it's not the sort of shit that happens all the time to me. Or, like . . . *ever*.

"Say, man," I said to Skye, "any chance we can roll back this tape to the point where we were still friends? I just walk out of here and we all call it a day?"

Skye made a face as if pretending to consider it. "Mmm . . . no, I don't see that happening."

"You want to make a deal of some kind?"

"Nah," he said. "You got nothing I want. Except the O-positive."

"AB-neg," I corrected.

"Never tried that."

"You wouldn't like it. Goes right to your hips."

The wattage on his smile was dimmer. Jaunty banter can buy only so many seconds and then it's back to business.

I tried to keep my face neutral, but my pulse was like a jazz drum solo.

"I'm going to throw something out here," I said. I could hear a tremor in my voice. Fuck.

"Oh, please." He gestured to the four killers and they started forward.

"Wait! Just hear me out. What have you got to lose?"

The thugs looked at Skye. West gave a "why not?" kind of shrug.

Skye sighed. "Okay, what is it? Last words? A little begging?" he suggested.

"Mm, more like last threat."

"This I got to hear."

The five of them looked genuinely interested.

"Okay, so here you are, five vampires. That's some really scary shit, am I right? I mean creatures of the night and all that."

He nodded, nothing to disagree with.

"To most people that's enough to make them go apeshit crazy. I mean . . . vampires. Not your everyday thing. It opens up all kinds of metaphysical questions. If vampires exist, what *else* does? If there are supernatural monsters, does that mean God and the Devil are real? You follow me?"

"Sure. We get that a lot."

"And I'm outnumbered here. Five to one. Tough odds even without you fellows being the undead. So . . . why am I not scared?"

His eyes narrowed.

"I mean, yeah, my pulse is racing and I'm sweating. But do I look as scared as I should be? I don't, do I? Now . . . why is that?"

"So you put up a good front. It'll be a good anecdote later," he said. "For us."

"Maybe he's got a hammer and stake," suggested West.

That got a laugh.

"Nope."

My heart rate had to be close to two hundred. It was machine-gun fire in my chest.

"Coupla garlic bulbs in your pocket?" asked East.

"Nah. I don't even like it on my pizza."

"You don't have any backup," said North. "And you don't got your gun."

My blood pressure could have scalded paint off a battleship. I wiped sweat off my brow with my thumb.

"Okay, jokes over," snapped Skye. "What's the punch line here? Why aren't you as scared as you should be?"

I smiled.

"I'll show you."

The first time it happened, way back when I was thirteen, it took almost half an hour. I screamed and cried and rolled around on the floor. First time's always the hardest. Each time since, it was easier. My grandmother and her sister could do it in the time it took you to snap your fingers. My best time was during a foot chase back when I was with Minneapolis PD. I was running down the guy who'd beaten his wife with the extension cord. He saw me coming and ducked into his apartment. I kicked the door and he came out of the bedroom with a gun and opened up. I went through the change in the time it took me to leap through the doorway. Like the snap of my fingers. One minute me, next minute *different* me.

I tore the shit out of him. I lost my badge and pension and had to make up all sorts of excuses. On the plus side, I didn't die, which *would* have happened if I hadn't managed the change so fast. I'm only mortal when I look like one.

That night in Skye's office wasn't my best time. Maybe third or fourth best. Say, two, three seconds. It felt like an explosion. It hurts. Feels like my heart is bursting, like cherry bombs are detonating inside my muscles. It starts in the chest, then ripples out from there as muscle mass changes and is reassigned in new ways. Bones warp, crack and re-form. Nails tear through the flesh of my fingers and toes, my jaw shifts and the longer teeth spike through the gums. It's bloody and it's ugly and it hurts like a motherfucker.

But the end result is a stunner. A real kick-ass dramatic moment that wows the audience.

I think all four of the thugs screamed. They jerked back from me, looks of shock and horror on their faces. If I wasn't so deeply into the moment, I would have smiled at the irony. Monsters being scared by a monster.

I crouched in the center of the room, hands flexing, claws streaked with blood, hot saliva dripping from my mouth onto my chest.

It would have been cool and dramatic to have said "Surprise!" to them, the way Skye had said it to me, but my mouth was no longer constructed for human speech. All I could do was roar.

I did.

And then I launched at them.

Vampires are strong. Four or five times stronger than an ordinary human. Werewolves?

Hell, we're a whole different class.

I slammed into West with both sets of front claws. He flew apart like he was made of paper and watery red glue. North and East tried to take me high and low, but they'd have done better to try and run. I brought my knee up into East's jaw as he went for the low tackle and his head burst like a casaba melon. I caught North by the throat and squeezed. Red geysered up from the stump of his neck as his head fell away. South backed away, putting himself between me and Skye, arms spread, making a more heroic stand than I'd have thought. I tore the heart from his chest. Turns out, vampires *need* their hearts.

Skye had my gun in his hands. He racked the slide and buried the barrel against me as I leaped over the desk. He got off four shots. They hurt.

Like wasp stings.

Maybe a little less.

I don't load my piece with silver bullets. I'm not an idiot.

He looked into my eyes and I would like to think that he saw the error of his ways. Don't fuck with the innocent. Don't fuck with my clients. My clients are *mine*, like members of my pack. Mess with them and the pack leader has to put you down. Has to.

So I did.

She saw me coming from across the street, her face concerned and confused. I was wearing a different pair of pants and different shoes. My own had been torn to rags during the change. Stuff I was wearing used to belong to the bartender. He didn't need them anymore. He'd been on the same team as Skye and the four goons.

I opened the door and climbed in behind the wheel.

"Are you all right, Sam?" she asked, studying my face. "Are you hurt? Is that blood?"

I dabbed at a dot on my cheek. Missed a spot. I pulled a tissue out of my jacket pocket and wiped my cheek.

"Just ketchup," I said.

"You stopped for *food*?" she demanded, eyes wide.

"It was on the house. I was hungry. No biggie."

She stared at me and then looked at the club across the street. The snow was getting heavier, the ground was white and it was starting to coat the street.

"What happened in there?"

I put the key into the ignition.

"I had a long talk with your ex. I told him that you were feeling threatened and uncomfortable with his actions, and I asked him to back off."

"What did he say?"

"He won't be bothering you anymore."

"Just like that? He agreed to leave me alone just like that?" She snapped her fingers.

"More or less. I told him that I had some friends on the force and in L-and-I. Guess I made it clear that I could make his life *more* uncomfortable than he was making yours. He didn't like it, but . . . " I let the rest hang.

"And he *agreed*?"

"Take my word for it. He's out of your life."

She continued to study me for several long seconds. I waited her out and I saw the moment when she shifted from doubt and fear to belief and acceptance. She closed her eyes, sagged back against the seat, put her face in her hands, and began to cry.

I gripped the wheel and looked out at the falling snow, hiding the smile that kept trying to creep onto my mouth. I was digging the P.I. business. Fewer rules than when I was a cop. It allowed me to be closer to the street, to go hunting deeper into the forest.

Even so—and despite what I'd said to Skye—I *was* pretty rattled that he'd been a vampire. I mean, being who and what I am, I always suspected other things were out there in the dark, but until now I'd never met them. Now I knew. How many vampires were there? *Where* were they? Would they be coming for me?

I didn't have any of those answers. Not yet.

I also wondered what *else* was out there. I could feel the excitement racing through me. I wanted to find out. Good or bad.

I reached out a hand and patted Mrs. Skye's trembling shoulder. It felt good to know that one of the pack was safe now. It felt right. It made me feel powerful and satisfied on a lot of different levels. I knew that I was going to want to feel this way again. And again.

The snow swirled inside the thickening shadows.

Inside my head the wolf howled.

Jonathan Maberry is a Bram Stoker Award-winning author, writing teacher, and motivational speaker. Among his novels are *Ghost Road Blues*, *Dead Man's Song*, *Bad Moon Rising*, *Patient Zero*. His most recent novel for adults, *Extinction Machine*, fifth in the Joe Ledger series, was published earlier this year. Maberry's nonfiction works include *Vampire Universe*, *The Cryptopedia*, *Zombie CSU: The Forensics of the Living Dead*, and *They Bite!* His work for Marvel Comics includes *The Punisher*, *Wolverine*, *DoomWar*, *Marvel Zombie Return*, and *Black Panther*.

The Case: *Lord Abe no Yasuna's wife, Lady Kuzunoha, and their son, Doshi, are missing.*

The Investigator: *Yamada no Goji, an impoverished nobleman of Japan's Heian era, who—for a price—will do what needs to be done, especially if the solution to the problem isn't as simple as using a sword.*

FOX TAILS

Richard Parks

I was just outside of Kyoto, close on the trail of a fox spirit, when the ghost appeared. It manifested as a giant red lantern with a small mouth and one large eye, and blocked access to a bridge I needed to cross. While it was true that ghosts made the best informants, their sense of timing could be somewhat lacking.

"I have information, Yamada-san," it said.

"I'm not looking for information. I'm looking for a fox." I started to brush past it.

"A silver fox with two tails? Sometimes appears as a human female named Kuzunoha?"

The lantern suddenly had my full attention. "I'm listening."

"You're chasing a youkai pretending to be Lady Kuzunoha. You really do not want to catch it, if you get my meaning."

I did. As monsters went, youkai ran the gamut from "mildly annoying" to "slurp your intestines like hot noodles." By the time you knew which sort you were dealing with, it was usually too late.

"How do I know you're telling me the truth?"

The lantern looked disgusted. "The other rei said you were smart, Yamada-san. How? You can follow that illusion until it gets tired of the game and eats you. Or we can reach an agreement. That is up to you." The lantern pretended to look away, unconcerned, but having only the one eye made it very difficult to glance at someone sideways without him knowing it.

"You're saying you know where Lady Kuzunoha is? What do you want in exchange?"

"Two bowls, plus prayers for my soul at the temple of your choice."

"One bowl, and I haven't been inside a temple since I was seven. I'm not going to start on your account."

I knew it would all come down to just how hungry the ghost was, but I wasn't worried—I'd already spotted the drool. It was staining the lantern's paper. The thing grumbled something about miserly bastards, but gave in.

"Very well, but do it properly."

"Always," I said. "Now tell me where I can find Lady Kuzunoha."

The ghost knew I was good for it. Information was the lifeblood of any nobleman's proxy, and only a fool would cheat an informant once a deal was agreed. I wasn't a fool . . . most of the time.

"Lady Kuzunoha is in Shinoda Forest."

I sighed deeply. "I don't appreciate you wasting my time, rei. My patron already had the place searched! She's not there."

"If the idiot hadn't sent his army he might have found her. She had more of a romantic rendezvous in mind, yes? If you're really looking for her, that's where she is. Go there yourself if you don't believe me."

"All right, but remember—I may not be intimate with temples but I do have contacts. If you're lying to me, I'll come back with a tinderbox and a priest who specializes. Do you understand me?"

"She's there, I tell you. Now honor our bargain."

I reached inside my robe and pulled out a bag of uncooked rice already measured out. I took a pair of wooden chopsticks and shoved them point first through the opening of the bag and held the offering in the palms of my hands before the lantern.

"For the good of my friend . . . uh, what's your name?"

"Seita."

"—Seita-san."

The bag floated out of my hands and shriveled like a dead leaf in a winter's wind. In a moment the pitiful remnants of the offering drifted to the ground in front of the bridge and the lantern let out a deep sigh of contentment.

"Quality stuff," it said. "I hope we can do business again."

"Maybe, if your story proves true and Lady Kuzunoha doesn't send any more youkai after me."

"But Lady Kuzunoha didn't . . . ahh, please forget I said that."

For a moment I thought the lantern was just looking for another offering, but that wasn't it. The thing was actually scared, and there aren't many things short of an exorcist that will scare a ghost.

"If she didn't send it, who did?"

Just before it winked out like a snuffed candle, the lantern whispered, "Yamada-san, there isn't that much rice in Kyoto."

• • •

The servant who had come to my home the day before claimed to be from Lord Abe no Yasuna. At first I didn't believe him, but I wasn't so prosperous that I could chance turning down work. I also couldn't risk the potential insult to Lord Abe if the servant was telling the truth—even the Emperor would think twice before courting the Abe family's displeasure.

Like most members of the Court, the Abe family's ancestral lands were elsewhere, but they kept a palatial residence within the city to be close to the seat of power. Courtiers and supplicants waited two deep within the walled courtyard, but the servant ushered me right through. I didn't miss the raised eyebrows and muttering that followed in our wake. It didn't bother me; I was used to it.

Technically I was of noble birth since the minor lord who was my father lowered himself to acknowledge me. Yet he had met with misfortune and I had no inheritance, no regular patron, and no political connections, so the main difference between someone such as myself and your typical peasant farmer was that the farmer knew where his next meal was coming from. Yet, if it hadn't been for that accident of birth, people like Abe no Yasuna wouldn't deal with me in the first place, so I guess I should count my blessings. One of these days I'll get around to it.

I was ushered in to the Abe family reception hall. "Throne room" would have been a better description, and not too far from the truth. The Abe family counted more than a few actual royalty in their family tree, including the occasional emperor. The man himself was there, waiting for me. He was tall and imposing, probably no more than forty. Handsome, I would say. There was a peppering of gray in his black hair, but no more than that. He seemed distracted. Kneeling at a discreet distance was an older lady. At first glance I assumed she was a servant, but then I got a better look at her kimono, not to mention her face, and saw the family resemblance. It was unusual for a noblewoman to greet male guests save behind a screen, but perhaps the circumstances were unusual. I suspected they might be.

I bowed low. "You sent for me, lord?"

He studied me intently for several seconds before speaking. "Yamada no Goji. Your reputation for effectiveness . . . and discretion, precedes you. I trust it is deserved."

It was all I could do to keep from smiling. A delicate matter. Good—delicate matters paid the best. "I am at my lord's service."

Lord Abe turned to the kneeling woman. "Mother, I need to speak with Yamada-san alone. Boring business."

"Family business," said the old woman dryly as she rose, "but do as you will. It seems you must, these days."

Mother. Now I understood. I had heard of Abe no Akiko by reputation, as had nearly everyone in Kyoto. She had been a famous beauty in her day and, judging from what I could see of her now, that day was not long past. She also had a reputation for being a fierce advocate of her family's position at court and was rumored to have put more than one rival out of the game permanently. Still, that wasn't an unusual rumor for any courtier who'd lasted more than a few seasons. More to the point, she wasn't the one who had summoned me

Lord Abe was silent for a few moments, either collecting his thoughts or making sure his mother was out of earshot; I couldn't tell which.

"Have you ever been married, Yamada-san?" he said finally.

"I have not, lord."

"I was, for a while, to a lovely woman named Kuzunoha. I rather enjoyed it, but love and happiness are illusions, as the scriptures say."

I was beginning to get the drift. "Pardon my impertinence, but when did she leave?"

Lord Abe looked grim. "Two days ago."

"And you wish for me to find her?"

Lord Abe hesitated. "The matter is a bit more complicated than that, as I'm sure you've already guessed. Please follow me."

Despite Lord Abe's confidence I hadn't guessed much about the situation at all, beyond the obvious. Wives left husbands for numerous reasons, and vice versa, and this wouldn't be the first time I'd been sent after one or the other. Lord Abe's position was such that he had apparently been able to keep the matter quiet; I'd certainly heard nothing of it. Still, the situation was unfortunate but not a real scandal. I followed as Lord Abe led through a small partition leading to a tiny room behind the dais where Lord Abe had received me. We came to another screen that opened onto another courtyard, and beyond that was the roofed wall that surrounded the entire residence complex. There was another gate visible.

Lord Abe stopped at the screen. It took me a few seconds to realize that he wasn't looking beyond it but *at* it. Someone had written a message on the shoji screen in flowing script. It was a poem of farewell, but, despite its obvious beauty, that was not what got my attention. It was Lady Kuzunoha's confession, clearly stated, that she was not a woman at all but a fox spirit he had once rescued on the grounds of the Inari Shrine and that she could no longer remain with Lord Abe as his wife. The poem ended: "If you would love me again, find me in Shinoda Forest." The poem was signed "Reluctant Kuzunoha."

"My lord, are you certain this is your wife's script?"

"Without question. She always had the most beautiful calligraphy. She could copy any text of the sutras exactly, but when writing as herself her own style is distinctive."

That his wife had left him was one thing. That his wife was a fox was quite another. Pretending to be a human woman was a fox spirit's favorite trick, and Lord Abe wouldn't be the first man to be fooled by one. At the least, that could be somewhat embarrassing, and, in the rarified circles of court where favor and banishment were never separated by more than a sword's edge, "somewhat" could be enough to tip the scale.

"She knew I didn't allow servants in here, so none have seen this but my mother and myself. I will destroy the door," Lord Abe said, "for obvious reasons, but I did want you to see it first. I have already sealed the document granting you authority to act on my behalf in this matter." He pulled the scroll out of a fold of his robe and handed it to me.

I took the scroll but couldn't resist the question. "What matter, Lord Abe? Pardon my saying so, but if this confession is true, then you are well rid of her. Fox spirits are dangerous creatures."

That was an understatement if there ever was. One Chinese emperor had barely avoided being murdered by a fox masquerading as a concubine, and one poor farmer spent a hundred years watching a pair of fox-women playing Go for what he thought was an afternoon. They were tricksters at the best of times and often far worse.

"It wasn't like that," Lord Abe said quietly. "Kuzunoha loved me. I do not know what drove her to leave or to make this confession, but I was never in danger from her."

"You want me to find her, then?" I had to ask. There were at least as many fools among the nobility as elsewhere, and there was always someone who thought the rules didn't apply to him. I was more than a little relieved to discover that Lord Abe was not that stupid.

He shook his head. His expression had not changed, but his eyes were moist and glistening. "Lady Kuzunoha is correct that we cannot be together now, but she should not have asked me to give up Doshi as well."

"Doshi?"

"My son, Yamada-san. She took my . . . our son."

I was beginning to see what he meant by "complicated."

"I take it you've already searched Shinoda Forest?" That was an easy supposition to make. I already knew what he'd found, otherwise I wouldn't be there.

He sighed. "I should have gone personally, but I did not trust myself to let Kuzunoha go if I ever held her again. My mother suggested we send my personal retainers and in my weakness I agreed. They searched thoroughly, and I lost two good men to an ogre in the process. There was no sign of either Kuzunoha or Doshi." He looked at me. "That is your task, Yamada-san. I want you to find my son and return him to me."

"Again I must ask your pardon, Lord, but is this wise? The boy will be half-fox himself. Isn't there a danger?"

His smile was so faint one might have missed it, but I did not. "There's always a danger, Yamada-san. If we are fortunate we get to decide which ones we choose to face. I want my son back."

"By any means required?"

"Do not harm Lady Kuzunoha. With that one exception, do what you must."

At least my goal was clear enough. I didn't for one moment think it was going to be easy.

Another advantage of being of the noble class was that it entitled you to carry weapons openly, and Shinoda Forest was *not* a place you wanted to go empty-handed. The place had a deserved reputation for being the haunt of fox spirits and worse; most bandits even avoided the place, and any bandit who didn't was not the sort you wanted to meet. Yet here I was, for the princely sum of five imported Chinese bronze coins and one kin of uncooked rice a day, plus reasonable expenses. You can be sure I counted that payment to the red lantern ghost as "reasonable."

There was a path. Not much of one, but I stuck to it. There was a danger in keeping to the only known path in a wood full of monsters, not to mention it might make finding Lady Kuzunoha even more difficult, but I kept to the path anyway. Getting lost in Shinoda Forest would have done neither me nor my patron much good.

Even so, once you got past the fact that the woods were full of things that wanted to kill you, it was a very beautiful place. There was a hint of fall in the air; the maple leaves were beginning to shade into red, contrasting with the deep green of the rest of the wood. The scent was earthy but not unpleasant. It had been some time since I'd been out of the city and I was enjoying the scent and sounds of a true forest. Too much so, perhaps, otherwise I would never have been caught so easily.

I hadn't walked three paces past a large stone when the world went black. When I woke up, I almost wished I hadn't: my head felt like two shou of plum wine crammed into a one shou cask. For a moment I honestly thought it would explode. After a little while, the pain eased enough for me to open my eyes. It was early evening, though of which day I had no idea. I was lying on my side, trussed like a deer on a carrying pole, and about ten feet from a campfire.

Sitting beside that campfire were two of the biggest, most unpleasant-looking men it had ever been my misfortune to get ambushed by. They were both built like stone temple guardians, and their arms were as thick as my legs. Otherwise there wasn't much to separate them, save one was missing an ear and the other's nose had been split near the tip. One look at them and my aching brain only had room for one question:

Why am I still alive?

I must have moaned with the effort of keeping my eyes open, since one of the bandits glanced in my direction and grunted.

"He's awake. Good. I thought you'd killed him. You know an ogre likes 'em fresh."

There was my answer, though it went without saying that I didn't care for it. Maybe I could get a better one. "You two gentlemen work for an ogre?"

"Don't be stupid," said Missing Ear. "The ogre is just a bonus. Our employer wants you dead, and, since you're dead either way, we sell you to the ogre that lives in this forest. That's good business."

He clearly wasn't the brightest blade in the rack, but I couldn't fault his mercantile instincts. "So who are you working for?"

"You're dead. What do you care?"

"If I'm going to die, I'd like to know why. Besides, if I'm good as dead it's not like I'll be telling anyone."

"Well, if you must know—oww!" Missing Ear began, but then Split Nose leaned over and rapped him sharply on the back of his skull.

"You know what *she* said about talking too much," he said. "What if she found out? Do you want her angry at you? I'd sooner take my chances with the ogre."

Her. At this point there didn't seem to be much question as to whom they meant.

Missing Ear rubbed his head. He had a sour look on his face, but what his companion had said to him apparently sank in. "No. That would be . . . bad."

"So far we've done everything like she said. The ogre will see our fire soon and come for this fool, and that's that. We can get out of this demon-blighted place."

"You two are making a big mistake. I'm acting as proxy for Lord Abe. An insult to me is an insult to him." It wasn't much, but it was all I had. I was still surprised at the bandits' reaction. They glanced at each other and burst out laughing.

"We know why you're here, baka," said Split Nose when he regained his composure. "Now, be a well-behaved meal and wait for the ogre."

The bandits obviously knew more about this matter than I did. It was also obvious that they had searched me before they tied me up. I could see my pack near the campfire and my tachi leaning against a boulder only a few feet away. It was the only decent material object I owned, a gift from the grateful father of a particularly foolish young man whose good name I was able to salvage. It was a beautiful sword, with sharkskin-covered grip and scabbard both dyed black. The tsuba was of black iron and the blade, I had occasion to know, was sharp enough to shave with. If only I could reach it, I could demonstrate that virtue on my captors, but it was impossible. As close as the tachi was, it might as well have been in Mongolia for all the good of it. Try as I might, I could not get free of the ropes. I flashed back on something Lord Abe had said.

"Love and happiness are both illusions."

To which I could add that life was fleeing and illusory itself. I might not have been much for the temple, but the priests had that much right. The best I could hope for now was that the ogre was more hungry than cruel; then at least he would be quick.

There was a very faint rustling in the undergrowth. At first I thought it was the ogre coming for his supper, but then I couldn't quite imagine something that large moving so quietly. A light flared and I assumed someone had lit a torch, but the flame turned blue and then floated over the campsite and disappeared. Then, almost on cue, thirteen additional blue fires kindled in the darkness just beyond the campfire.

Yurrei . . . ? Oh, hell.

Ghosts were just like youkai in one important respect—there were ghosts, and then there were ghosts. Some, like the red lantern ghost Seita, were reasonable folk once you got to know them. Some, however, tended to be angry at everything living. Judging from the onibi and balefire I was seeing now, all three of us were pretty much stew for the same pot. Split Nose and Missing Ear knew it too. The pair of them had turned whiter than a funeral kimono, and for a moment they actually hugged each other, though Split Nose managed to compose himself enough to rap Missing Ear's skull again.

"You idiot! You made camp in a graveyard!"

"Wasn't no graveyard here!" Missing Ear protested, but Split Nose was already pointing back toward me.

"What's that, then?"

I was having some trouble moving my head, but I managed to see what they were seeing, not ten feet away on the far side of me. It was a stone grave marker, half-covered in weeds and vines, but still visible enough even in the firelight.

When I looked back at the bandits the ghost was already there, hovering about two feet off the ground. It might have been female; it was wearing a funeral white kimono but the way its kimono was tied was about as feminine as the specter got. Its mouth was three feet wide and full of sharp teeth, its eyes were as big as soup bowls and just as bulging. One of its hands was tucked within the kimono, but the other, pointing directly at the cowering bandits, bore talons as long as knives.

YOU HAVE DISTURBED ME. PREPARE TO DIE. The ghost's voice boomed like thunder, and the blue fires showed traces of red.

"Mercy!" cried Split Nose. "It was a mistake!"

YES. NOW PREPARE TO ATONE!

"Mercy!" they both cried again and bowed low.

The revenant seemed to consider. BOW LOWER, DOGS.

They did so. Then came two flashes of silver, and the bandits slumped over into a heap. In an instant the balefires went out, and the ghost floated down to earth, and then she wasn't a ghost at all but a woman carrying a sword.

My sword.

I glanced at the boulder and saw that the tachi was missing, though its scabbard still leaned against the stone. The grave stone was gone, but by this time I expected that. Fox spirits were masters of illusion. The woman turned to face me.

I had never seen a more beautiful woman in my life. A master painter could not have rendered a face more perfect, or hair so long and glossy black that it shone like dark fire. She seemed little more than a delicate young woman, but the ease with which she handled my sword and the twitching bodies of the two bandits said otherwise. She walked over to me without a second glance at the carnage behind her.

"Lady Kuzunoha?" I made it sound like a question, but really it wasn't.

"Who are you?" she demanded.

"My name is Yamada no Goji. Lord Abe sent me."

"I've heard of you, Yamada-san. Well, then. Let's get this over with."

She raised the sword again, and I closed my eyes. I would have said a prayer if I could have thought of one. All I could manage was the obvious.

This is my death . . .

I heard the angry whoosh of the blade as it cut through the air. It took me several long seconds to realize that it hadn't cut through me. Not only was I still alive, but my hands were free. Another whoosh and my legs were free as well, though both arms and legs were too numb from the ropes to be of much use to me at first. While I struggled to get to my feet, Lady Kuzunoha calmly walked back to the bandits and took a wrapping-cloth from one of their pouches which she used to methodically clean the blade. I had just managed to sit up when she returned the long sword to its scabbard and tossed it at my feet.

"I wouldn't advise staying here too long, Yamada-san," she said. "The ogre will be here soon."

"I'm afraid he's going to be disappointed," I said.

She shook her head, and she smiled. "Oh, no. Those two are still alive. We foxes know much of the nature of the spine and where to break it. They'll die soon enough, but probably not before they're eaten. The fools would have been eaten in either case, of course. Ogres don't make bargains with meat."

Her words were like cold water. If they couldn't totally negate the effect her beauty was having on me, at least they reminded me that I wasn't dealing with a human being. An important point that I had best remember. I got to my feet a little unsteadily.

"My thanks for saving me, Kuzunoha-sama," I said, "but I'm afraid that I have some business with you yet."

"So I assumed. The path is about fifteen paces ahead of you. Stay on it until you reach the river. You'll be able to hear a waterfall," she said. "I'll be waiting for you there."

Lady Kuzunoha moved quickly away from me. In a moment her image shimmered, and I saw her true form, a silver fox bearing the second tail that betrayed her spirit nature. She ran swiftly and was soon out of sight. I gathered my belongings and hobbled along the way she had gone as best I could.

I wasn't clear on a lot of things, not the least of which was why Lady Kuzunoha had bothered to save my life. After all, if she knew who sent me, then she knew why I had come and, if she'd been willing to surrender the boy in the first place, she could have arranged that easily enough while Lord Abe's men searched the wood. And if she *wasn't* willing to give up the child, why not just kill me? It's not as if I could have done anything to stop her, and if I had any doubts of either her ability or will in that regard, I had the wretched bandits' example to prove otherwise.

A lot of things didn't make sense, and if I wanted any answers I'd have to go much deeper into Shinoda Forest to get them. Part of me wondered if I might be better off taking my chances with the ogre. Then I heard a large crashing noise in the forest back the way I'd come and decided not. I picked up the pace as much as the headache and my tingling limbs allowed.

I'd been careless once and was lucky to be alive. This time as I moved down the path, I had my sword out and ready. I wasn't sure how much good it would do me against what I'd likely face, but the grip felt comforting in my hand.

I came to the place Lady Kuzunoha described and followed the sound of rushing water. A cold water stream rushing down the adjacent hill formed a twelve-foot waterfall into the river's rocky shallows. Lady Kuzunoha was in human form again. She stood directly underneath the rushing water, her slim fingers pressed together in an attitude of prayer, her long black hair flowing over her body like a cloak. Her hair was the only thing covering her. For a little while I forgot to breathe.

I knew Lady Kuzunoha's human form was an actual transformation and not simply illusion, else she would never have been able to bear a human child, but I also knew it was not her true form. Knowing this did not help me at all. The only thing that did was the sharp and clear memory of what she had done to those two hapless bandits; that was my cold waterfall. That left the question of why Lady Kuzunoha needed one.

When I finally managed to look away, I noticed Lady Kuzunoha's kimono neatly folded on top of a flat stone nearby. I'm still not sure why I turned away. Maybe it was my common sense, warning me of danger. Or maybe I had come to the reluctant—and relieved—conclusion that this little show was not being staged for my benefit. Lady Kuzunoha was preparing herself for something, but I didn't have any idea as to what that might be.

There was a small clearing nearby; I waited there. Lady Kuzunoha finally emerged, now fully dressed, her hair still wet but combed out and orderly. If anything she appeared more winsome than before. She looked sad but resolute as she approached the center of the clearing. In her sash she had tucked one of those slim daggers that high-born ladies tended to carry both as self-defense and a symbol of rank. She knelt beside me, looking away.

"I'm ready," she said. She drew the dagger and put the naked blade across her thighs.

I frowned. Maybe Seita the ghost was right about me, since what came out of my mouth then wasn't very intelligent. "I don't understand. Ready for what, Lady Kuzunoha?"

It was as if she hadn't even heard me. "I would send my love a poem but words are useless now. You may take back whatever proofs your master requires. Now stand ready to assist me."

The light dawned. The waterfall was a purification rite, which would explain the prayer but not much else. "You think I'm here to kill you!"

Lady Kuzunoha looked up at me. "Do not mock me, Yamada-san. I saved your life, and I think I'm due the courtesy of the truth. Did Lord Abe send you or not?"

"I have his writ and seal if you doubt me. But I am no assassin, whatever you may have heard of me."

Now Lady Kuzunoha looked confused. "But . . . what else? I cannot return. He knows that."

If Lady Kuzunoha was confused, I was doubly so, but at least I had the presence of mind to reach down and take the knife away from her. "First of all, assuming I *had* been sent to harm you, will you please explain why you're being so cooperative?"

She frowned. "Did my husband not explain the circumstances of our first meeting?"

"He didn't have to—I saw your message. You said that he rescued you from hunters . . . before he knew that you and the silver fox were one and the same, I mean."

"There was even more to it that he didn't know, Yamada-san. You see, I was already in love with Lord Abe, from the day his procession rode past Shinoda Forest three years ago. I came to the Inari Shrine in the first place because I knew he would be there. He already owned my heart, but from that day forward he owned my life as well. If now he requires that of me, who am I to deny my love what is his by right?"

Now it was starting to make some sense. No one had ever claimed that self-sacrifice was a fox trait, but I knew love made people do silly things, and it was clear even to a lout like me that Lady Kuzunoha, fox spirit or no, was still deeply in love with her husband. I had suspected that Lord Abe was deluding himself on that point, but now I knew better.

"If Lord Abe didn't know you were a fox, why did you leave him?"

"I didn't want to," Lady Kuzunoha said, sadly. "I tried so hard . . . You know what I am, Yamada-san. The body I wear now is real, but it is a sort of mask. Sometimes the mask slips; that's unavoidable. Yet it was happening to me more and more. In my foolishness I thought I would be spared this, but the burden of pretending to be something I am not became too much, even for his sake. It was only a matter of time before my true nature would be revealed and my husband and his family shamed. I could no longer take that risk. I am a fraud, but I was honest with my husband about why I had to leave. He did not come himself, so I assume he hates me now."

"He doesn't hate you, Lady Kuzunoha. He understands your reasons and accepts them, though he is very sad as you might imagine."

Lady Kuzunoha rose to her feet with one smooth motion. "Then why did my lord not come himself? Why did he send his warriors? Why did he send *you*?"

"My patron said he did not trust himself to let you go if he ever held you again. I can not fault him in this."

She actually blushed slightly at the compliment, but pressed on. "You didn't answer my other question."

"He sent his retainers and me for the same reason: we were looking for Doshi."

"My son? But why?"

"To bring him home, Lady. Lord Abe lost you. He didn't want to lose his son too. Maybe that's selfish of him, but I think you can understand how he feels."

"But I do *not* understand," Lady Kuzunoha said, and now the gentle, sad expression she had worn since leaving the waterfall was nowhere to be seen. She looked into my eyes and my knees shook. "Yamada-san, are you telling me that my son is missing?"

I fought the urge to back away. "But . . . you didn't take him?"

"I . . . ? Of course not! Doshi's blood may be mostly fox, but in Shinoda Forest that's not enough. He could never have made a home in my world! Doshi belongs with his father."

I took a deep breath. "If that's the case, then yes, Lady Kuzunoha—I'm telling you that your son is missing."

I'm not sure what I expected, but Lady Kuzunoha merely held out her hand. "Please return my dagger, Yamada-san. I promise not to use it on myself . . . or you."

I gave the knife back, carefully. "Do you have someone else in mind?"

Her smile was the stuff of nightmares. "That remains to be seen."

I had more questions, but Lady Kuzunoha was in no mood to answer them, and I knew better than to test my luck. She was kind enough to see me safely out of the forest before she disappeared, but it was clear she had other matters on her mind besides my well-being. I, on the other hand, could think of little else.

The bandit was right to call you a fool. You had no idea of how big a mess you were in.

The youkai that Seita had warned me about should have been my first clue. Still, if Lord Abe had sent me chasing wild foxfire, there still might be time to get on the right trail. I didn't like where I thought it was going to lead, but I had given my word, and that was the only thing worth more to me than my sword. I just hoped it didn't have to mean more than my life.

When I got back into Kyoto, the first thing I did was track down Kenji. It wasn't that hard. He was at one of his favorite drinking establishments near the Demon Gate. Technically it was the Northeast Gate, but since that was the direction from which demons and evil spirits were supposed to enter, the name stuck. Naturally someone like Kenji would keep close to such a place. He said it was good for business.

Business looked a little slow. For one thing, Kenji was drinking very cheap saké. For another, he was in great need of a barber; his head looked like three days' growth of beard. I found a cushion on the opposite side of his table and made myself comfortable. Kenji looked at me blearily. He had one of those in-between faces, neither old nor young, though I happened to know he was pushing fifty. He finally recognized me.

"Yamada-san! How is my least favorite person?"

"Terrible, you'll be pleased to know. I need a favor."

He smiled like a little drunken buddha. "Enlightenment is free but in this world all favors have a price. What do you want?"

"I need to seal the powers of a fox spirit, at least temporarily. Is this possible?"

He whistled low. "When all is illusion all things are possible. Still, you're wading in a dangerous current, Yamada-san."

"This I know. Can you help me or not?"

Kenji seemed to pause in thought and then rummaged around inside his robe, which, like him, was in need of a bath. He pulled out a slip of paper that was surprisingly clean considering from where it had come. He glanced at it, then nodded. "This will do what you want, but the effect is temporary. Just how temporary depends on the spiritual powers of the animal. Plus you'll have to place it on the fox directly."

"How many bowls?"

"Rice? For this? Yamada-san, I'll accept three good bronze, but only because it's you."

Reluctantly I counted out the coins. "Done, but this better not be one of your worthless fakes for travelers and the gullible."

He sat up a little straighter. "Direct copy from the Diamond Sutra, Yamada-san. I was even sober when I did it."

"I hope so, since if this doesn't work and somehow I survive, I'll be back to discuss it. If it does work, I owe you a drink."

He just smiled a ragged smile. "Either way, you know where to find me."

I did. Whatever Kenji's numerous faults as a priest and a man, at least he was consistent. I carefully stashed the paper seal and headed for Lord Abe's estate. I wasn't sure how much time I had left, but I didn't think there was a lot.

There was less than I knew.

Before I even reached the gate at the Abe estate, I saw a lady traveling alone. She was veiled, of course. Her wide-brimmed boshi was ringed with pale white mesh that hung down like a curtain, obscuring her features. I couldn't tell who it was but her bearing, her clothes, even the way she moved betrayed her as a noble. A woman of that class traveling unescorted was unusual in itself, but more unusual was the fact that no one seemed to notice. She passed a gang of rough-looking workmen who didn't even give her a second glance.

Once the density of the crowd forced her to brush against a serving girl who looked startled for a moment as she looked around, then continued her errand, frowning. The woman, for her part, kept up her pace.

They can't see her.

At that point I realized it was too late to keep watch at the Abe estate. I kept to the shadows and alleyways as best I could, and I followed. I could move quietly at need and I was as careful as I could be without losing sight of her; if she spotted me, she'd know that fact long before I did. I kept with her as the buildings thinned out and she moved up the road leading out of the city.

She's going to the Inari Shrine.

Mount Inari was clearly visible in the distance, and the woman kept up her pace without flagging until she had reached the grounds of the shrine. Its numerous red torii were like beacons, but she took little notice of the shrine buildings themselves and immediately passed on to the path leading up to the mountain.

Hundreds of bright red gates donated by the faithful over the years arched over the pathway, giving it a rather tunnel-like appearance. I didn't dare follow directly behind her now; one backward glance would have betrayed me. I moved off the path and kept to the edge of the wood that began immediately behind the shrine buildings. It was easy now to see why hunters might frequent the area; the woods went on for miles around the mountainside. There were fox statues as well, since foxes were the messengers of the God of Rice; they were depicted here in stone with message scrolls clamped in their powerful jaws. The wooden torii themselves resembled gates, and I knew that's what they were, symbolic gates marking the transition from the world of men to the world of the spirits, and this was the true destination of my veiled Lady. I didn't want to follow her further but I knew there was no real choice now; to turn back meant failure or worse. Going on might mean the same, if I was wrong about what was about to happen.

The woman left the path where the woods parted briefly to create a small meadow. I hid behind a tree, but it was a useless gesture.

"You've followed me for quite some time, Yamada-san. Please do me the courtesy of not skulking about any longer."

I recognized the voice. Not that there was any question in my mind by then, but there was no point in further concealment. I stepped into the clearing. "Greetings, Lady Akiko."

Lady Abe no Akiko untied her veil and removed her boshi. She was showing her age just a little more in the clear light of day, though she was still very handsome. "Following me was very rude, Yamada-san. My son will hear of it."

"Perhaps there is a way we can avoid that unpleasantness, Lady, if not all unpleasantness. You're here about your grandson, aren't you?"

She covered her mouth with her fan to indicate that she was smiling. "Of course. Family matters have always been my special concern."

Someone else entered the clearing. Another woman, dressed and veiled in a manner very similar to Akiko. "You said you'd come alone," the newcomer said. It sounded like an accusation.

"It was not my doing that he is here," Lady Akiko said. "And it will make no difference. Surely you can see that?"

"Perhaps." The newcomer removed her boshi, but her voice had already announced her. Lady Kuzunoha. She glared at me as she approached. Now she and Lady Akiko were barely a few paces apart.

"Yamada-san, this no longer concerns you," Lady Kuzunoha said.

"I respectfully disagree. My responsibility ends only when Lord Abe's son is found."

Lady Akiko glared at her former daughter-in-law. "And this . . . this vixen who betrayed my son knows where he is! Do you deny it?"

"Of course not," Lady Kuzunoha said haughtily. "I know exactly where my son is. As do you."

Lady Akiko practically spat out the words. "Yes! With the person who took him!"

"Yes," Lady Kuzunoha said grimly. She drew her dagger. "Let us settle this!"

"Pitiful fool!"

It turned out that Lady Akiko already had her dagger unsheathed, concealed in the sleeve of her kimono. She lashed out and Lady Kuzunoha gasped in pain. She clutched her hand as her dagger fell uselessly into the grass. In a moment Akiko had Kuzunoha's arms pinned at her sides and her dagger at the young woman's throat.

"One doesn't survive so long at court without learning a few tricks. Or, for that matter, giving your enemies a sporting chance. Now prove the truth of my words, worthless vixen! Tell me before this witness where Lord Abe's son is, and do not try any of your fox tricks else I'll kill you where you stand!"

"You will not taste my blood that easily, Old Woman."

The fight was far from over. Lady Kuzunoha's power was gathering around her like a storm; the air fairly crackled with it. Lady Akiko held her ground, but the hand holding the knife was shaking, and I knew it took her a great effort to keep the blade pointed at Lady Kuzunoha's throat.

"Tell Yamada-san where Doshi is if you want to live!" Lady Akiko said. "And no lies!"

"Why would he believe anything I say," Lady Kuzunoha said calmly, "if he does not believe what I have told him before now?"

I knew that, in a few seconds, anything I did would be too late. I stepped forward quickly, pulling out Kenji's seal as I did so. Both women watched me intently as I approached. "Lady Kuzunoha, do you know what this is?" She nodded, her face expressionless.

Lady Akiko wasn't expressionless at all. Her look was pure triumph. "Yamada-san, you are more resourceful than I thought. I will recommend to my son that he double your fee."

I gave her a slight bow. "I am in Lord Abe's service." I concentrated then on Lady Kuzunoha. "If you know what this is, then you know what it can do to you. Do you truly know where your son is?"

She looked resigned. "I do."

"That's all I need. Please prepare yourself."

Lady Kuzunoha went perfectly still in Lady Akiko's grip but before either of them could move again, I darted forward and slapped the seal on Lady Akiko's forehead.

"Yamada sarrrrrr—!"

My name ended in a snarl of rage, but Lady Akiko had time to do nothing else before the transformation was complete. In Lady Akiko's place was an old red fox vixen with three tails. Lady Kuzunoha stood frozen, blinking in surprise.

There was no more time to consider. My sword was in my hands just as the fox gathered itself to spring at Lady Kuzunoha's throat. My shout startled it, and it sprang at me instead. My first slash caught it across the chest, and it yipped in pain. My second stroke severed the fox's head from its body. The fox that had been Abe no Akiko fell in a bloody heap, twitching.

I had seen Lady Kuzunoha butcher two men with barely a thought, but she looked away from the remains of her former mother-in-law with a delicacy that surprised me. "I-I still had some hope that it would not come to this. That was foolish of me."

"She didn't leave me much choice."

Lady Kuzunoha shook her head. "No, your life was already worthless to her. Doubly so since you knew her secret. Speaking of that, how *did* you know?"

I started to clean my sword. "Lady Kuzunoha, I have just been forced to take a rather drastic step in the course of my duties. I'll answer your questions if you will answer mine. Agreed?"

She forced herself to look at Lady Akiko's body. "There is no reason to keep her secrets now."

"Very well. There were two things in particular. Someone put me on the trail of a youkai that was pretending to be you. Once I knew that you didn't send either it or those bandits, that left the question of who did. More to the point, you told me that Doshi was *mostly* fox, remember?"

She actually blushed. "Careless of me. I did not intend . . . "

I smiled grimly. "I know, and at first I thought you'd simply misspoken. But, assuming you had not, for Doshi to be more than merely half fox meant his father was at least part fox himself. How could this be? The simplest reasonable answer was Lady Akiko. Did Lord Abe know about his mother? Or himself?"

"No to both. Fortunately his fox blood was never dominant. Lady Akiko and I knew about each other all along, of course. She opposed the marriage but couldn't reveal me without revealing herself. We kept each other's secret out of necessity until . . . "

"Until Doshi was born?"

She nodded, looking unhappy. "I knew by then I couldn't stay, but I thought my son's position was secure. I was in error. There was too much fox in him, and Lady Akiko was afraid his fox nature would reveal itself, and disgrace the family. The position of the Abe family was always her chief concern."

"If the boy was such a danger, why didn't she just smother him in his sleep?"

Lady Kuzunoha looked genuinely shocked. "Murder her own grandson? Really, Yamada-san . . . Beside, it's easy enough to dedicate an unwanted child to some distant temple with no questions about his origin. In preparation, Lady Akiko had him hidden within the shrine complex; the Abe family is their foremost patron, so it was easy to arrange. Once I knew my son was missing it took me a while to follow his trail and to arrange a meeting."

"Duel, you mean."

She looked away. "Just so. While I may have hoped otherwise, it was destined that either I or Lady Akiko would not leave this clearing alive. Her solution to the problem of Doshi was quite elegant, but you were an obstacle to that solution and, once you found me, so was I."

"Which explains why she went to so much trouble trying to prevent me from finding you in the first place. Was she correct then? Won't Doshi be a danger to the family now?"

"Yes," said Lady Kuzunoha frankly. "Yet my husband already knows that. Perhaps not how great a risk, I concede, but I don't think that would deter him. Do you?"

I finished cleaning my sword and slid it back into its scabbard. "No, but as grateful as he's going to be at the return of his son, Lord Abe is going to be considerably less so when I explain what happened to his mother, proxy or no."

Lady Kuzunoha covered her mouth as she smiled. "Yamada-san, perhaps there is an 'elegant solution' to this as well. For now, kindly produce my lord's proxy seal and we'll go fetch my son."

That proved easily done. The presence of both the seal and Lady Kuzunoha herself was more than enough to send one of the shrine priests scurrying ahead of us to a small outbuilding near a koi pond. There we found Doshi in the care of a rather frightened wet nurse. Lady Kuzunoha paid off the poor woman generously, thanked her for her solicitude, and sent her on her way. The baby looked up, lifting its little arms and gurgling happily, as Lady Kuzunoha smiled down at him.

"Probably time you were weaned, my son." She turned to me. "Please take him, Yamada-san. You'll need to get him back to his father quickly; he'll have to make his own arrangements for Doshi's care. I will give you some writing to take to my husband before you leave."

I hesitated. "Don't . . . don't you wish to hold your son? This may well be your last chance."

She smiled a sad smile. "Thank you for that offer, but I can only echo the words of my lord in this, Yamada-san: if I held him again, what makes you think I could let him go?"

I had no answer to that, but I did have one last question. "One thing still bothers me: you were unable to maintain the deception of being human, but Lady Akiko had been in the family much longer than you. How did she manage?"

Lady Kuzunoha laughed softly. "Yamada-san, as I told you before: the mask will slip, and we cannot control when or how. For me, my right hand would turn into a paw without warning. For Lady Akiko, it was her scent."

I blinked. "Scent?"

She nodded. "Her true scent, as a fox. But the human nose is a poor tool at best. Those close to her would either miss the scent entirely or at worst mistake it for . . . something else," she finished, delicately. "Lady Akiko was simply luckier than I was."

That may have been so, but Lady Akiko's luck had finally run out. I was afraid that mine was about to do the same.

Lord Abe received me in his private chambers after I placed his infant son back in the care of his servants.

"Yamada-san, I am in your debt," he said. "I-I trust Lady Kuzunoha was not . . . difficult?"

From my kneeling position, I touched my forehead to the floor. "That relates to a matter I need to speak of. Lady Kuzunoha was quite reluctant, as you can imagine, but I was impertinent enough to acquire the assistance of Lady Akiko in this. They spoke, mother to mother, and Lady Akiko persuaded her."

"I see."

I could tell that he didn't see at all, but the die was already cast. I produced the scroll Lady Kuzunoha had supplied. "Lady Akiko told me of the . . . differences, between your wife and herself. That her intense desire to protect the family's name had perhaps blinded her to Lady Kuzunoha's virtues. To atone for this—and other burdens—she has decided to renounce the world and join a temple as a nun. She also sent a personal message to you."

Lord Abe was a Gentleman of the Court, whatever else he might be. He concealed his shock and surprise very well. He took the scroll I offered and unrolled it in silence. He remained intent on what was written there for several moments longer than would have been required to actually read the words. I tried not to hold my breath.

"My mother's script," he said, almost to himself. "Perfect." He looked down at me, his expression unreadable. "I don't suppose my mother revealed to you which temple she had chosen to join?"

I bowed again. "She did not so confide in me, my lord, though I had the impression it was quite far from here. She seemed to feel that was for the best. She hoped you would understand."

He grunted. "Perhaps she is right about both. Well, then, Yamada-san. I've lost both my wife and my mother, but I have not yet lost all. It seems I must be content with that."

I breathed a little easier once I'd been paid and was safely off the grounds. I wasn't sure how much of my story Lord Abe really believed, but if he didn't realize full well that Lady Kuzunoha had written that message, I'm no judge of men. Perhaps that was another choice he made. As for myself, I chose to be elsewhere for a good long time. Hokkaido sounded best; I'd heard that it's very sparsely populated and only a little frozen at this time of the year. But first I went to meet Kenji by the Demon Gate, since I'd given my word and now I owed him a drink.

I owed myself several more.

⟡

Richard Parks has been writing and publishing science fiction and fantasy longer than he cares to remember. His work has appeared in (among many others) *Asimov's*, *Realms of Fantasy*, *Lady Churchill's Rosebud Wristlet*, and several "year's best" anthologies. A Yamada novel, *To Break the Demon Gate*, is scheduled for release this year. A collection of Yamada stories, *Yamada Monogatari: Demon Hunter* was published earlier this year. He blogs at "Den of Ego and Iniquity Annex #3" (www.richard-parks.com).

⟡

The Case: *A voluntary human "blood donor" is found murdered in the kitchen of a vampire mansion during festivities celebrating the ascension of a new vampire leader.*

The Investigators: *Dahlia Lynley-Chivers—a savvy, sexy, centuries-old vampire—and Matsudo Katamori, vampire and former police officer.*

DEATH BY DAHLIA

Charlaine Harris

Dahlia Lynley-Chivers had been a woman of average height in her day. Her day had been over for centuries, and in modern America she was considered a very short woman indeed. Since Dahlia was a vampire, and was reputed to be a vicious fighter even among her own kind, she was usually treated with respect despite her lack of inches and her dainty build.

"You got a face like a rose," said her prospective blood donor, a handsome, husky, human in his twenties. "Here, little lady, let me squat down so you can reach me! You want me to get you a stool to stand on?" He laughed, definitely in the hardy-har-har mode.

If he hadn't preceded his "amusing" comment on Dahlia's height with a compliment, she would have broken his ribs and drained him dry; but Dahlia was fond of compliments. He did have to bear some consequence for the condescension, though.

Dahlia gave the young man a look of such ferocity that he blanched almost as white as Dahlia herself. Then she stepped pointedly to her left to approach the next unoccupied donor, a blond suburbanite not too much taller than Dahlia. The woman opened her arms to embrace the vampire, as if this were an assignation rather than a feeding. Dahlia would have sighed if she'd been a breather.

However, Dahlia was hungry, and she'd already been picky enough. This woman's neck was at the right height, and she was absolutely willing, since she'd registered with the donor agency. Dahlia bit. The woman jerked as Dahlia's fangs went in, so Dahlia considerately licked a little on the wound to anesthetize the area. She sucked hard, and the woman jerked in an entirely different way. Dahlia was a polite feeder, for the most part.

The blonde's arms squeezed Dahlia with surprising force, and she gripped a handful of Dahlia's thick, wavy, dark hair, which fell in a cascade reaching almost to Dahlia's waist. The blonde pulled Dahlia's hair a little, but she wasn't trying to pull Dahlia off . . . not at all.

At Dahlia's age, she didn't need to drink much at a sitting (or perhaps *at a biting* would be a more appropriate term). After a few pleasurable gulps, the vampire had had enough. Dahlia didn't want to be greedy, and she'd taken such a small amount that it would be safe for the woman to donate again on the spot.

Dahlia gave a final lick, and when the air hit the licked puncture marks, her natural coagulant set to work almost instantly. The blond woman seemed disappointed that the encounter was over and actually tried to hold on to Dahlia. With a stiff smile, Dahlia removed herself with a little more decision. The donor turned to the next vampire in line, who was Cedric. She would have to be stopped after that; most people who enjoyed being bitten enough to be listed with the donor agency simply weren't smart about when to stop.

"You could be a little nicer," Dahlia's best friend Taffy said reprovingly. "Would it have hurt to you tell the breather how good she was?" Dahlia would have ignored anyone else who ventured to give her advice on her manners, but Taffy was within two hundred years of being as old as Dahlia. They were the oldest vampires in the nest, and their friendship had survived many trials.

Taffy had been practically Amazonian during her lifetime, and she remained an impressive woman even now. Five foot seven and busty, Taffy's light hair exploded in a tangled halo around her head and fell past her shoulders. Taffy's husband Don was one of the trials they'd survived, and it was due to Don's preference that Taffy went heavy on the makeup and tight on the clothes. Don thought that was a mighty fine look on Taffy.

Of course, Don was a werewolf. His taste was dubious, at best.

Taffy waved at Don, who was over by the food table. Werewolves were always hungry, and they could drink alcohol until the cows came home—and then the Weres would eat them. A party with an open bar and a buffet was like heaven to Don and his new enforcer, Bernie. The two Weres were making the most of the opportunity, since politics demanded they be in the vampire nest for Joaquin's ascension celebration.

Dahlia noticed Don and Bernie casting contemptuous glances at the group of blood donors. Werewolves thought humans who were willing to give blood to vampires were from the bottom of the barrel. Any self-respecting Were would rather have his fur shaved off. Dahlia was sure Don didn't mind giving Taffy a sip in private . . . at least she hoped that was the case. During Dahlia's own brief marriage to the previous enforcer, her husband had not been averse to a little nip.

The demons and half-demons huddled together in a corner, and just after a very skinny female said something, they all burst into laughter. Dahlia looked for one half-demon computer geek she knew better than the others. With a frisson of pleasure, she spotted Melponeus's reddish skin and chestnut curls in the cluster. Their eyes met. The half-demon and Dahlia exchanged personal smiles. They had had some memorable evenings together in Dahlia's bedroom on the lower level of the mansion. The glitter in Melponeus's pale eyes told Dahlia that the demon wouldn't mind a replay.

She might retrieve some pleasure from this dismal evening, after all.

A few creatures Dahlia didn't recognize were scattered through the crowd. No fairies, of course; vampires loved fairies to death, literally. But there were other creatures of the fae present, and a witch. Joaquin had a reputation as a liberal, and he'd made up the party list and presented it to Lakeisha, who'd retained her post as the executive assistant to the sheriff despite the change in regimes. Lakeisha had sniffed at some of the inclusions, but she had obeyed without a verbal comment. All the vampires were walking softly and carefully until they learned their new leader's character. Since he'd lived on his own, not in the nest, until his appointment as sheriff, Joaquin was a largely unknown element.

As Taffy took Dahlia's arm to steer her over to the buffet to join Don, Dahlia said, "I'm not enjoying myself, though I ought to be."

"Why not?" Taffy asked. "The humans will be gone soon, and we can be ourselves. It's not like we haven't seen this coming. Cedric has been getting more and more set in his ways. He's lazy. He's sloppy. A waistcoat every day. So dated! He can't even pretend to belong to this century."

Like all successful vampires, Dahlia knew the key to surviving for centuries was adaptation. And the most conspicuous adaptation was following the trend in clothes and language. This had been essential when vampires existed in secret, so they could blend in with a crowd long enough to cut out their prey. Vampires were an increasingly familiar presence in business and politics, but they found society still accepted them more easily if they mimicked modern Americans. It was true, too, that old habits died hard. It had only been six years since the undead had "come out," and to vampires that was less than the blink of an eye.

"I did see that Cedric would have to be replaced," Dahlia said. "I don't know Joaquin well, and maybe I'm worried about how he will rule, and how living in the nest will be with him in residence. At least he had a very conventional ascension."

"It couldn't have been more standard," Taffy agreed. "And soon the guests will be gone and we can amuse ourselves. I'm pleased with Joaquin's first steps.

The mansion is looking beautiful, more beautiful than it did for my wedding." Taffy tapped the newly polished wooden floor with the toe of her boot. The reception room, which was large and full of dark leather furniture and scattered rugs, was at the back of the mansion and looked out onto the garden. Taffy had gotten married in that garden one memorable night. Though the night was chilly the fountain was splashing away in the dimly lit courtyard outside the French doors. The lights didn't need to be bright; vampires have excellent night vision.

Dahlia was proud that the mansion, which housed the vampire nest of Rhodes and was the area headquarters for all vampires, was polished and sparkling, clean and newly redecorated. However, Dahlia's pride had a certain nostalgic tinge. Though for decades they'd all tried to prod the old sheriff, Cedric, into installing new carpet and modernizing the bathrooms, she found that she missed the old fixtures. And she missed the former sheriff, too. Maybe he counted as an old fixture.

"I'm going to talk to Cedric," she said.

"Not the smartest move, homes," Taffy cautioned. Taffy always tried to use current slang, though sometimes she got it wrong or was off by five years . . . or ten.

"I know," Dahlia said. The new sheriff, Joaquin, was certainly keeping an eye open to see who approached Cedric; but Dahlia was not afraid of Joaquin, though she did regard him with a certain respect for his devious ways. The ousting of Cedric had been handled with a sort of ruthless finesse. Cedric, sunk into what he thought would always be his cushy job, had been foolishly complacent and unaware. "I'll join you later," she told Taffy. "Though I may stop to have a word with Melponeus, too."

"Playing with fire," Taffy said, grinning broadly.

"Yes, we did that last time." Even half-demons could produce fireballs. The memory caused Dahlia to have her own tight smile on her lips as she approached the former sheriff.

"Cedric," she said, inclining her head very slightly. Even Dahlia didn't care to provoke Joaquin by appearing to offer Cedric obeisance.

"Dahlia," he said, his voice laden with melancholy. "See how the peacock preens?"

Joaquin, in the center of a cluster of other vampires, was dressed to kill. Obviously Joaquin felt like the king of the world on his ascension night. In his thin, dark, hand he held a goblet of Royalty (a blend of the blood of various European royals, who could keep their crumbling castles open with the money they made by tapping into their own veins). His favorite artiste, Jennifer Lopez, was playing in the background. He was wearing a very sharp dark gray suit with a pale gray silk shirt, and in his crimson tie was an antique pearl stickpin. Fawning all over Joaquin was Glenda, a flapper-era vamp who had never been Dahlia's favorite nest sister.

"You could use a little preening, Cedric," she observed. Cedric was wearing fawn-colored pants and a white linen shirt with a flowered waistcoat, his favorite ensemble. He had many near-duplicates of all three pieces hanging in his closet.

Cedric ignored her comment. "Glenda looks good," he said. In the past Glenda had slipped into Cedric's bedroom from time to time, more to keep the sheriff sweet than from any great affection. Dahlia had often seen the two clipping roses in the mansion garden at night. They'd both been ardent rose growers in life— or at least, Glenda said she had been.

Glenda, who was no more than ninety, did actually look very tempting this evening in a thin blue silk slip dress with absolutely nothing underneath. She was smoothing Joaquin's shirt with the air of someone who knew what was underneath the silk. Dahlia harbored a certain appreciation for Glenda's cleverness.

"You know she's trash," Dahlia told Cedric.

"But such delicious trash." After tossing his head to get his long pale hair out of his way, Cedric took a pull on his bottle of Red Stuff, a cheap brand of the synthetic blood vampires drank so they could pretend they didn't crave or require the real thing. This was sheer affectation; Dahlia had watched Cedric approach a donor.

Red Stuff was a far cry from Royalty in a crystal goblet. Cedric's mustache drooped, and even the golden flowers and vines in the pattern on his waistcoat looked withered.

Having served their purpose, the human donors were being ushered out of the large reception room by a smiling young vampire. They'd be taken to the kitchen and fed a snack, allowed to recover from their "donation," and returned to their collection point. This had been found to be the most efficient method of dealing with the humans the agency sent. If they weren't shepherded every step of the way, these humans showed a distressing tendency to want to hide in the mansion so they could donate again and again. Some vampires weren't strong-willed enough to resist, and then . . . dead donors and unwelcome attention from the police followed.

The only donor left in the room was the young man who'd irritated Dahlia. He seemed to be in the process of irritating Don, Taffy's husband, packmaster of Rhodes. That proved his stupidity. Dahlia turned back to Cedric.

"Will you stay in the nest?" Dahlia asked. She was genuinely curious. If she'd found herself in Cedric's position, she would have packed her bags the second the king chose Joaquin.

"I'll find an apartment elsewhere, sooner or later," Cedric said indifferently, and Dahlia thought that this perfectly illustrated Cedric's drawbacks as a leader.

Though he'd been a dynamic sheriff in his heyday, Cedric had gradually become slow . . . and that was the nicest way to put it. This indolence and complacency, creeping into Cedric's rulings and decisions over the decades, had been his downfall. It was no surprise to anyone but Cedric that he'd been challenged and ousted. To the newer vamps, the only surprise was that Cedric had ever been named to the position in the first place.

"The situation won't change," Dahlia said. Cedric would make himself a figure of fun if he gloomed around the mansion during Joaquin's reign. "I'm sure you've saved money during your time in office," she added, by way of encouragement. After all, all the vampires who lived in the nest contributed to their sheriff's bank account, and so did the other vampires of Rhodes who chose to live on their own.

"Not as much as you would think," Cedric said, and Dahlia could not restrain a tiny gesture of irritation. Her sympathy with the ex-sheriff was exhausted. She excused herself. "Melponeus has asked to speak to me," she lied.

Cedric waved a dismissive hand with a ghost of his former graciousness.

While Dahlia strode across the carpet to the cluster of demons, not the least hampered by her very high heels, she glanced back to see Cedric open the door to the hall leading to the kitchen. He stepped through at the same time as Taffy and Don. Glenda called, "Taffy!" and passed through after them.

Then Dahlia stopped in front of Melponeus, his fellow demons clearing the way for her with alacrity. Though Dahlia was a straightforward woman by nature, she was also incredibly conscious of her own dignity, and she didn't care for the leering element in the smiles the demon's buddies were giving her. Melponeus himself surely knew that. After the barest moment of conversation, he swept Dahlia away to an empty area.

"I apologize for my friends," he said instantly. Dahlia forced her rigid little face to relax and look a bit more welcoming. "They see a woman as lovely as you, they can't regulate their reactions."

"You can, apparently?" Dahlia said, just to watch Melponeus flounder. He knew her better than she'd thought, because after a moment's confused explanation, he laughed. For a few minutes, they had a wonderful time with verbal foreplay, and then they danced. "Perhaps later . . . " Melponeus began, but he was interrupted by a scream.

Screams were not such an unusual thing at the vampire nest, but since this one came in the middle of an important social occasion, it attracted universal attention. Every head whipped around to look east, to the wing occupied on the ground floor by the kitchen.

"Don't move," called Joaquin to stem the surge of the crowd in the direction of the commotion. Somewhat to Dahlia's surprise, everyone obeyed him. She found that interesting.

Even more interesting was the fact that Joaquin searched the crowd until his eyes met hers. "Dahlia," he said, in lightly accented English, "take Katamori with you and find out what's happened." Katamori was something of a policeman a couple of centuries ago.

Dahlia had to work to keep her face expressionless. "Yes, Sheriff," she said, and jerked her head at Matsuda Katamori, a vampire who had an apartment near Little Japan. Katamori, who appeared just as surprised as Dahlia at being singled out, immediately glided to her side. They moved quickly to the door to the passage leading to the mansion's kitchen.

It wasn't a wide space, and the carpet had been installed to deaden sound, not to beautify. Both the vampires were alert as they moved silently down the passage to the kitchen. The swinging door had been propped open.

When the mansion had been built in the early 1900s, the builder could not have imagined that the kitchen would be used by non-eaters. The white tile floors and the huge fixtures had been maintained, even updated, once or twice during the century that had passed. When Cedric had bought the mansion at a bargain price (glamour had been involved), he'd left the kitchen as though it would still be needed to prepare a banquet. Normally, the stainless steel fixtures shone in the overhead lights suspended from the high ceiling.

Now the stainless steel was splashed with red. The smell of blood was overwhelming.

From where they stood just inside the doorway, Dahlia and Katamori couldn't see the body because of the long wooden table running down the middle of the room, but a body was undoubtedly there. The only thing living in the kitchen was one of the half-demons, a skinny girl Dahlia hadn't met before. The girl was standing absolutely still, very close to the corpse, if Dahlia's nose was accurate, and her hands were up in the air. Smart.

Dahlia enjoyed the smell of blood, but she preferred her blood to be fresh and its source living, as did every vampire but the rare pervert. Once the blood had been out of the living body for more than a couple of minutes, it lost much of its enticing smell, at least to Dahlia's nose. From the delicate twitch of Katamori's nostrils, he felt much the same.

The girl's feet were hidden from view by the old wooden table, originally intended for staff meals and food preparation. But the blood smell was emanating from the area around her, and red had splashed the gleaming range and refrigerator on the south wall. She was standing squarely in front of the refrigerator.

The half-demon girl opened her mouth to speak, but Dahlia held up her hand. The girl closed her mouth instantly.

"Is any of this blood yours?" Dahlia asked.

The girl shook her head.

Dahlia and Katamori looked at each other. Dahlia didn't have to look up far to meet his eyes. He waited for her instructions. She was the senior vampire. She liked this silent acknowledgement a lot. Dahlia said, "I'll go right, you take left." She didn't know much about Katamori, but she did know that his reputation as a fighter was almost as formidable as her own.

Without a word, the slightly built Japanese vampire began working his way around the north side of the table, his eyes and ears and nose working overtime. The north wall featured huge windows, now black. The effect was unpleasant, as if the night were watching the scene in the kitchen, but Dahlia was not about to be distressed by any nighttime creepiness. She herself was the thing that went bump in the night.

She began circling the table to the south side. The stovetops and ovens, a stainless steel prep table with pots and pans on a shelf underneath, and an industrial refrigerator and a freezer filled the wall. A few steps revealed the crime scene. The half-demon girl was standing stock-still on the edges of the pool of blood that had flowed from the victim. Dahlia took in the whole picture, then she began noting the details.

The corpse was that of the young man who had irritated her, the human donor she'd last observed having words with Don. The man's throat had been torn out. Dahlia had seen much worse in her long, long, existence, but she was irritated at the waste of the blood.

The half-demon girl had not a speck of blood on her, except for her shoes, which were red Converse high tops, now somewhat darker around the rubber sole. Dahlia raised her delicate black eyebrows, looked across the room.

"Katamori?" she said.

"Lots of people have been through," Katamori answered.

From this laconic response, Dahlia understood that he'd found nothing tangible on his side of the room, but that there were complex scent trails. That made sense. The north side of the kitchen was the natural route to take to get to the door on the far end of the long room. This door led into a mudroom with hooks for wet weather gear and gardening clothes. On the other side of the mudroom a heavier door opened out onto the broad apron marking the end of the service driveway. All the humans who'd come to the mansion to donate earlier in the evening had both entered and left the mansion through that door.

"Please stay where you are for the moment," Dahlia said to the half-demon, who bobbed her head in a series of sharp nods. Since the blood pool and the body took up the whole of the floor between the appliances and the table, Dahlia bent her knees and leaped over the table, landing lightly on her amazing heels on the other side.

She met Katamori at the end of the table, and together they looked back at the body. There was a series of bloody footprints leading away from the corpse, footprints too large to be that of the half-demon girl. These prints lead to the first exit door, the door to the mudroom. Together, they examined it. There were no bloody fingerprints on the knob or the glass panes. Dahlia bent over to sniff the knob, shrugged. "A bloody hand touched it, but that tells us nothing," she said, and pushed the door open. Katamori tensed, ready for anything.

The mudroom was empty.

The two vampires stepped into the small space. The floor was covered with a rubber mat, and there was a bench running along both sides. Underneath were stored a few pairs of boots, some of which had been there for forty years. A coat or two hung from the row of hooks mounted above the benches. At least one of the coats had been there for two decades, an elaborate black coat with a huge fur collar. "I don't think anyone will return to get this one," Katamori said, and pushed it with his finger. A cloud of dust rose up. Dahlia noticed that most of the hooks were similarly covered in dust. Only two of the hooks were shiny enough to indicate they'd been used recently.

The knob of the solid door that led to the outside was pristine to the eye, and when Dahlia bent to smell she got only a whiff of blood, a slightly weaker trace than that on the inner knob. "Left this way," she told Katamori. "Let's finish the kitchen, then we'll report."

They turned back into the kitchen.

Before they'd left, the humans had piled their plates and cups by the sink. Fainting humans were bad for business, so the agency had insisted the vampires take a tip from the blood bank in offering refreshments. Nothing to be found there; the victim hadn't approached that area.

"What do we have so far?" Katamori asked.

"There's a vampire smell in here, very recent," Dahlia said.

"Besides the half-demon, I'm getting humans, a werewolf, at least two vampires."

Werewolves. Dahlia's mouth twitched. But first of all, she had to interrogate the only living creature in the cavernous room. "Demon girl," she said, "explain yourself." Now that Dahlia spared a moment to take in the half-demon's ensemble, Dahlia's eyes widened. The skinny creature, whose short hair was dyed a brilliant lime green, was wearing black Under Armour from top to bottom. Her red sneakers were a fine clash with the lilac miniskirt and a buckskin vest lined with fleece.

"I'm Diantha," the girl said. And then she began a long sentence that was possibly in English.

"Stop," Katamori said. "Or I'll have to kill you."

Diantha stopped in mid-word, her mouth open. Dahlia could see how very sharp the half-demon's teeth were, and how many of them seemed to be crammed into her little mouth. Katamori would have quite a fight on his hands, and Dahlia found herself hoping it wouldn't come to that.

"Diantha, I'm Dahlia. Our names are similar, aren't they?" Dahlia said. She hadn't tried to sound soothing in a century or two, and it sat awkwardly on her. "You must speak so that we can understand you. Maybe it will help you to be calm if we tell you we know you didn't do this thing."

"We do?" Katamori knew the reason, but he wanted Dahlia to spell it out.

"No blood on her, except on her shoes." She didn't bother to lower her voice. Diantha's bright eyes were on her so intently that she knew the girl could read her lips.

"I'mtherunnerformyuncleinLouisiana," Diantha said. She didn't seem to need to breathe when she spoke, but at least this time she spoke slowly enough—at less than warp speed—that the vampires could understand her.

"And you are here at the ascension party because . . . ?"

"Rhodesdemonswereinvited, Iwasstayingthenightafterbringing—" And the rest of her sentence ran together in a hopeless tangle.

"Slower," Dahlia said, making sure she sounded like she meant it.

Diantha sighed noisily, looking as exasperated as the teenager she appeared to be. "Since I was here for the night, they invited me to come with them." She put an almost visible space between each word. "Nothing else to do, so I came with."

"You're visiting from Louisiana on a business errand, and you came to the mansion with the Rhodes demons because they were invited."

Diantha nodded, her green spikes bobbing almost comically. If Dahlia hadn't seen demons fight before, she might have laughed.

"How did you happen to enter the kitchen?" Katamori asked. During Dahlia and Diantha's conversation, he had circled the table to stand at Diantha's back. She had turned slightly so she could keep both vampires in view, since she was now bracketed between them. Despite Dahlia's assurances, the half-demon girl didn't like her situation at all. Her knees bent, and her hands fisted, ready for a challenge.

But when she spoke, her voice was steady enough. "I was going to the refrigerator," Diantha said, still making the effort to speak slowly. "You guys were out of Sprite, and I thought it would be all right if I checked to see if there were more in the refrigerator. Ismelledtheblood—"

Dahlia held up an admonishing hand, and Diantha slowed down. "I yelled because I smelled the blood as I stepped in it. "

"Not before?" Most supernaturals had a very sharp sense of smell.

"Smell of vampire had deadened my nose," Diantha said.

That made sense to Dahlia. Though the scent of vampire was naturally delightful to her, she had been told many times that it was overwhelming to other supernaturals.

"Was the blood still running when you came in?" The thicker trickles from spurting arteries were barely moving down the shiny surface of the appliances, and the cast-off drops that been slung away when the throat had come out had begun to dry at the edges.

"Little," Diantha said.

"Was anyone else here?" Katamori asked.

Diantha shook her head.

The two vampires glanced at other, eyebrows raised in query. Dahlia couldn't think of any more questions to ask. Evidently Katamori couldn't, either.

"Diantha, in a second you can move." Dahlia and Katamori closed in on each side of the body. "All right," Dahlia said. "Step out of the blood. Take off your shoes and leave them."

The half-goblin girl followed Dahlia's instructions to the letter. She perched up on the wooden table to remove her red high tops. She placed her stained shoes neatly side by side on the floor. "Stayorgo?" she asked, looking much more cheerful now that she wasn't so close to the corpse. Demons didn't often eat people, and proximity to the body hadn't been pleasant for her.

"I think you can go," Dahlia said, after a moment's thought. "Don't leave."

"Gobacktotheparty," the girl said, and did so.

By silent agreement, the two vampires bent to their task. With their excellent vision and sense of smell, they didn't need magnifying glasses or flashlights to help them analyze what they saw.

"The human donors came into the kitchen and ate and drank," Katamori began. "A vampire shepherded them."

"As always," Dahlia said absently. "And that's a vampire we need to talk to, because somehow this human got left behind, or he hid himself. Obviously, the shepherd should have noticed."

"A werewolf came through here, probably after the death. Perhaps more than one werewolf," Katamori continued. He was crouched near the floor, and he looked up at Dahlia, his dark eyes intent. His black braid fell forward as he bent back to examine the floor, and he tossed it back over his shoulder.

"I don't disagree," Dahlia said, making an effort to sound neutral. Any trouble which involved the werewolves would involve Taffy. "I think we should tell Joaquin that the shepherd needs to come here now, or as soon as he's returned."

Katamori said "Yes," but in an absent way. Dahlia went to the swinging door. As she'd expected, one of Joaquin's friends, a wispy brunette named Rachel, was waiting in the hall. Dahlia explained what she needed, and Rachel raced off. Cedric had forbade the use of cell phones in the mansion, and Joaquin had not rescinded that rule yet, though Dahlia had heard that he would.

In two minutes Gerhard, the shepherd of the evening, came striding down the hall to join Dahlia. She could tell by the way he walked that he was angry, though he was smiling. That perpetual smile shone as hard as Gerhard's short corn-blond hair, which gleamed under the lights like polished silk. He'd lived in Rhodes for fifty years, but he and Dahlia had never become friends.

Dahlia didn't have many friends. She was quite all right with that.

"What would you like to know?" Gerhard asked. His German accent was pronounced despite his long years in the United States.

"Tell me about taking the humans out of here," Dahlia said. "How did you come to leave this one behind?"

Gerhard stiffened. "Are you saying I was derelict in my duties?"

"I'm trying to find out what happened," Dahlia said, not too patiently. "Your execution of your duties is not my concern, but Joaquin's. The man is here. He isn't supposed to be. How did that come about?"

Gerhard was obliged to reply. "I gathered the humans together to leave. We came to the kitchen. I followed procedure by showing them the food and drink provided. After ten minutes, I told them it was time to go. I counted as we left, and the number was correct."

"But here he is," Katamori said, straightening from his crouched position by the body. "So either your count was incorrect, you are lying, or an extra human took his place. What is your explanation?"

"I have none," Gerhard said, in voice so stiff it might have been starched.

"Go to Joaquin and tell him that," Dahlia said, without an ounce of sympathy.

"Well, then." Gerhard became even more defensive. "This man and I had come to an arrangement. I left him here, because upon my return we were to spend time together."

"Though he had already donated this evening," Dahlia said.

"His name was Arthur Allthorp. I have been with him before," Gerhard said. "He could take a lot of . . . donation. He loved it."

"A fangbanger," Katamori said. Fangbangers, extreme vampire groupies, were notorious for ignoring limits.

Gerhard gave a jerk of a nod.

Neither Dahlia nor Katamori remarked on the fact that Gerhard had initially lied to them. They knew, as did Gerhard, that he would pay for that.

"He was my weakness," Gerhard said violently. "I am glad he is dead."

This sudden burst of passion startled Dahlia and disgusted Katamori, who let Gerhard read that in his face. Gerhard whirled around to leave the kitchen, but Dahlia said, "What time did you leave with the humans? Was anyone in here with the man Arthur when you took the others away?"

Gerhard thought for a second. "I bade them get into the vans at ten o'clock, since that was the time appointed by the agency that sent them. There was no one in here. But I could hear people coming down the hall as I waited for the other donors to exit. I'm sure one of them was Taffy."

Dahlia would have said something unpleasant if she'd been by herself. As it was, she was aware of Katamori's quick sideways glance. Everyone in the nest knew that Dahlia and Taffy were friends, despite Taffy's unfortunate marriage. Dahlia's own brief marriage to a werewolf had been forgiven, since it had lasted such a short time. But Taffy showed every sign of continuing her relationship with Don, and even of being happy in it, to the bafflement of the other vampires of Rhodes. "We'll have to find Taffy and Don and ask them some questions," she said. "Gerhard, would you request this of Joaquin?"

Gerhard gave a jerky nod and left, shoving the door with such force that it was swinging to and fro in an annoying way.

Dahlia turned her attention back to the spray of blood on the fixtures and the blood pooled on the floor, still wet. "In my experience," she said to Katamori, "It takes over an hour for blood to begin to dry. Given its tacky quality and the low temperature of this room, I believe the body has lain here for at least thirty minutes, give or take."

Katamori nodded. They were both experts on blood. They looked up at the clock on the kitchen wall. It read 10:45.

"If Gerhard did leave with the humans at ten o'clock . . . say it took him five minutes to encourage them to put their dishes by the sink, and to get them out the door . . . then this Arthur was left by himself at 10:05 or 10:10. I talked to Cedric, and then I danced with Melponeus." Dahlia was trying to figure out when the scream had brought the party to a halt.

"We heard Diantha at 10:30," Katamori said. With some surprise, Dahlia saw that he was wearing a watch, an unusual accessory for a vampire.

"And we were in here within a minute and a half of that. We've been investigating for perhaps twenty minutes. So someone entered the kitchen between ten minutes after ten and twenty-five minutes after ten, by the narrowest reckoning."

"And this Arthur died of his throat being ripped out," Katamori said.

"Yes. Though he may have been choked before that. Without the excised material it's hard to say."

"It's over here." Katamori pointed to a grisly little mound of skin and bone half-hidden under a chair.

Dahlia squatted to peer at the discarded handful. "This is so mangled, I still can't say whether or not he was choked. This tissue was tossed aside, not consumed."

Katamori made a moue of distaste.

Dahlia said, "I was thinking of the trace of werewolf, and all that that implies." Werewolves would eat human flesh, at least when they were in their wolf forms.

"Do you think we've seen everything there is to see, smelled everything there is to smell?" Katamori asked, tactfully bypassing the werewolf issue.

"Let's go through the human's pockets," Dahlia suggested, and Katamori squatted on the other side of the body. Dahlia had quick, light, fingers, and she was thorough. Folded and stuck in a pocket on her side of the corpse, she found a sheet from the donor bureau containing a rendezvous point and a scheduled donation time for tonight. Just as Gerhard had said, the donors were to picked up at eight, returned to the pickup point at ten.

Dahlia wondered if Gerhard had told Arthur to make sure he was included on the donor list. It couldn't have been a coincidence that Gerhard's favorite banger had been included in the donor party. In the last four years it had become a regular practice for the hosts of parties to which vampires had been invited to hire donors from a registered donor bureau, so they could be sure that all the human snacks on offer had been checked for blood-borne diseases and psychoses. There was a disease vampires could catch from humans (Sino-Aids), and donors been checked for hidden agendas ever since a donor in Memphis had brought a gun and opened fire on the assembled party-goers.

Dahlia opened Arthur Allthorp's wallet to check his donation card, which was perforated with seven holes. The card was punched every time the agency sent him out. After Dahlia had turned over the body to go through the other pants pocket, Katamori patted down Arthur's legs. To their surprise, he found a knife in an ankle sheath. *Very* careless. Gerhard's inefficiency was now a mountain rather than a molehill.

After a glance of silent agreement, the two stood, having gotten all the information from the body. They looked all around the vast kitchen for any clue they might have missed. The blackness continued to stare in through the big windows. The blood continued to cling wetly to the stainless steel surfaces. Arthur Allthorp, fangbanger, continued to be dead.

After Katamori deadbolted the outside door, he and Dahlia left the kitchen. Rachel had resumed her post in the hall, and Dahlia asked her to keep guard over the swinging door. "Let no one into the kitchen until we're sure we don't need it any more," she said. "No one will be able to enter from the outside."

Rachel nodded, her expression intense. She was still proving herself as a vampire, and Dahlia felt sure Rachel would stand her ground against anyone who wanted to see the body.

Back in the reception room, Joaquin had resumed his seat in the throne-like chair reserved for the sheriff. His ascension party had taken a definite downturn in tone. The festive atmosphere had degenerated to uneasy apprehension. The party-goers were milling around uneasily. The demons and part-demons had established a tight knot in one corner with Diantha in its center, and the fae (an oread, a rare nix, and an elf) clustered close to them.

Bernie Feldman, Don's enforcer, was watching the French doors with unmistakable worry. Bernie was standing oddly, as if nursing a hurt in his stomach. Dahlia followed his eyes. Approaching, obviously disheveled, were Taffy and Don. Taffy had her shoes in her free hand. The other hand was holding Don's, and the two were looking at each other with what Dahlia could only describe as "goo-goo eyes."

"Disgusting," she muttered, and Katamori glanced at the happy pair. "They went through the kitchen," he said. "We're going to have to question them."

"Better report to Joaquin first."

The two vampires went to stand in front of their new leader. Dahlia bowed her head a carefully calibrated angle. Katamori's head was perhaps a centimeter lower than hers. Joaquin accepted their gesture and waited for them to report. He looked better in the chair than Cedric had. Joaquin was slim and tall, with thin dark hair and large brown eyes. The new sheriff wasn't as old as Dahlia (only two of the Rhodes vampires were older than her), but jobs didn't always go to the oldest.

Glenda was draped over the back of the sheriff's seat as if being Joaquin's new fuck buddy gave her some special status. Dahlia eyed the vampire with no expression. Her dislike of Glenda went from vague to specific.

"What have you discovered?" Joaquin asked, giving the two investigators all his attention.

Dahlia was pleased with the mark of respect. "The human was named Arthur Allthorp. He was a pet of Gerhard's." Dahlia had already spotted the blond vampire, who was trying to look stoic, but only managing gloomy. "Gerhard allowed Arthur Allthorp to remain in the kitchen while Gerhard took the other donors back to their rendezvous point. I see that he has told you that." Gerhard was flanked by Troy and Hazel, the vamps Joaquin had named as his punishers.

"Furthermore," Katamori said, "I found a knife strapped to the human's ankle."

Another nail in Gerhard's coffin, perhaps literally.

"He died very quickly when his throat was torn out," Dahlia said. "We know he died in a ten-minute window, give or take a minute or two, between ten-ten and ten-twenty-five."

Katamori said, "Passing through the kitchen close to the time of death were the human donors, Gerhard, another vampire or two I can't identify, and at least one werewolf."

All eyes went to Don and Bernie, who had been whispering furiously into Don's ear. Don looked shocked and grim. Taffy was the only vampire standing anywhere close to them, and she took her husband's arm. He patted her hand to show her he appreciated the support. Bernie stood to Don's other side, and he had an expression Dahlia had seen before. It meant, "I'm ready to die, but I'd rather not."

"It won't make any difference to you, Joaquin, but I didn't do it," Don said in his deep voice. "I can't imagine why I'd have any reason to kill the poor bastard, though maybe motive doesn't interest you." If Dahlia had had a moment to do so, she might have advised Don that this was not the time for sarcasm.

"Don and I did go through the kitchen," Taffy said. "But we were on our way out into the garden to have a talk."

"What was that talk about?" Glenda asked.

"You were right on our ass, so you probably know already. But I don't answer to you," Taffy said, and the light of battle flashed into her eyes.

"Any vampire who spends time with a werewolf has degraded herself and has no status in the nest," Glenda said, straightening and taking a step away from the sheriff's chair.

Dahlia was instantly on the alert. If she let Taffy take on Glenda, Don would get involved, and the whole situation would get unnecessarily complicated. When Glenda took another step in Taffy's direction, Dahlia was ready. She leaped and kicked as hard as she could, and Glenda went flying through the air with her beautiful clinging dress whipping around her, as Dahlia landed gracefully and spun around to make sure Glenda was down. The crack of Glenda's ribs was audible as she met the wall. She slid down to collapse on the carpet, bleeding and whimpering.

Joaquin didn't move, but his eyes were blazing. From their positions flanking Gerhard, Troy and Hazel snarled. There was a long, tense, moment with all eyes on Dahlia.

"Excuse my preemptive punishment of Glenda, Joaquin," she said calmly.

"I acted without your permission, but I was incensed at her presumption. She has no right to make such a pronouncement with you sitting in front of us. You alone have the right to determine who belongs in our community and who doesn't. Glenda showed unforgivable disrespect."

Joaquin blinked. "Interesting interpretation of Glenda's words," he said.

No one went to help the fallen vampire. Possibly they were all afraid that Dahlia would consider them an enemy if they did so.

"She *was* presumptuous," Joaquin said after a moment's consideration, and the room relaxed. Dahlia could tell more than one vampire would have enjoyed seeing her deal out even more damage to Glenda, but she'd made her point and interrupted Glenda's accusation.

Joaquin continued, "Do you know who the other vampires were who passed through the kitchen at the vital time?

"One was Cedric," she said. "I know his scent too well to mistake it. And I witnessed Glenda following Taffy, Don, Bernie, and Cedric out of the room, but I'm not sure if she entered the kitchen or not."

Joaquin's heavy eyebrows flew up in surprise. He looked at his predecessor.

"I walked through the kitchen," Cedric said. He was leaning against the wall. "I was right on the heels of Taffy and her werewolf, but Glenda went out before me, not after. I wanted to talk to her."

"Why?" Joaquin said. He looked up at Cedric, whose blue-patterned waistcoat was rumpled up above his belly. Even Cedric's boots were scuffed, while Joaquin's loafers shone like mirrors. The contrast could not have been more unkind: Cedric the old catfish, Joaquin the sleek barracuda.

To the side of the room, Glenda moaned as she struggled to her knees to get to her feet. Very quietly, another vampire stepped over to let her drink from him. Dahlia noticed he was looking as neutral as possible, as if his arm just happened to be in the right place in front of Glenda's mouth for her to have a healing draft. He even kept his eyes on the floor so Dahlia couldn't meet them. Dahlia smiled inside. It was good to be feared.

"Why?" Cedric said. "Because I wanted to go outside, and I hoped she would walk with me, for old times' sake. Because, in case you hadn't thought of it, this is a very awkward evening for me, and I needed friendship."

The demons looked amused, the Weres embarrassed, and the vampires all looked elsewhere. An open admission of weakness was not the vampire way. Only Dahlia looked thoughtful.

Joaquin said, "Taffy, what happened out in the garden?"

Taffy bowed her head to her sheriff. "Of course I'll answer, if my sheriff asks it," she said graciously, reinforcing Dahlia's point. "We talked to Bernie, my husband's enforcer, about his lack of courtesy to one of the demons." She nodded her head toward Diantha. "Bernie was . . . uncouth enough . . . to make fun of her speech patterns. Don felt the need to teach Bernie a lesson about diplomacy. As you can see, Don made his point."

Now that danger had passed, Bernie had resumed his hunched-over position. He was clearly uncomfortable. He bobbed his head in acknowledgement, straightened, and winced. "My leader did correct me," he said.

"While we were in the garden," Taffy continued, "We remembered it was the site of our wedding, and we celebrated in an appropriate way." She smiled brilliantly at Joaquin, pleased that she'd phrased it so diplomatically. Taffy had never been subtle.

Don grinned at her and slung his arm around her shoulders. "We had a *great* celebration back in the bushes," he said. "Even if it was colder than a witch's tit."

The only witch present opened her mouth to protest, but Dahlia's head whipped around so Dahlia could look at the woman in a significant way. The witch's mouth snapped shut.

"But none of this offers any proof that the human didn't die at your hands," Joaquin said in the most reasonable of voices.

"We haven't got a speck of blood on us, Sheriff," Taffy said, holding out her arms to invite inspection. "When Don gave Bernie his etiquette lesson, he didn't break the skin. My husband knows the smell of blood is tough on vampire sensibilities."

"Would the killer be blood-spattered?" Joaquin asked Dahlia. "You saw the wound."

"I'll defer to Katamori," Dahlia said. "It's well known that Taffy and I are friends."

"A vampire moving at top speed, a vampire who had performed this kill many times, might be able to avoid the blood," Katamori said. "Anyone else would have had to change clothes." He walked over to the couple, examined them with minute care. "I see and scent no blood on Taffy and Don."

Dahlia's shoulders might have relaxed a fraction.

Gerhard said quickly, "I'll smell like blood because I took some from a donor this evening." It was Dahlia's turn to work, and she looked Gerhard over from stem to stern. She straightened to tell Joaquin, "He does have a trace of blood scent, and one pinpoint of blood on his collar, but nothing out of the ordinary."

Cedric said, "You may examine me, Katamori," though no one had suggested this. Katamori glanced at Joaquin, got no signal either way, and moved over to Cedric. He'd give Cedric a thorough examination, Dahlia knew. Katamori had never been fond of Cedric.

"I can't find any on Cedric's clothes," Katamori said. "Though he does smell slightly of blood."

Cedric shrugged. "I partook of the donors," he said.

There was a pounding on the mansion's front door.

Dahlia looked at the clock on the wall, just as a precaution. It was now eleven fifteen. Arthur Allthorp had been dead around an hour. The front doorkeeper for the evening, a young vampire named Melvin, came into the reception room so quickly that he skidded on the parquet floor. "The police are here, Sheriff," he said to Joaquin. "They say they've had a report of a body on the premises."

"How long can you delay them?" Joaquin snapped.

"Ten minutes," said Melvin.

"We'll need it," Joaquin said. "Go."

Melvin began walking slowly through the archway on his way back to the front door. He was looking at his watch.

"Katamori and I will dispose of the body," Dahlia said, and she and Katamori took off at top speed. As they passed Rachel, still on guard at the swinging door, Dahlia said, "Cleanup crew, right now!" Rachel moved so fast you could hardly see her go, and Dahlia could hear her call a few names in the reception room.

It wasn't the first time a body had had to be disposed of quickly in the mansion.

While Katamori unlocked the mudroom door, Dahlia pulled an ancient tablecloth from the linen closet. Together, the two vampires wrapped the body in the yellowing linen to prevent drippage. Dahlia took the feet and Katamori lifted the shoulders. They were carrying the body out while the cleaning crew swarmed through the swinging door. Conveniently, all the cleanup material was kept in the kitchen, and as Katamori and Dahlia took their burden through the mudroom and out the final door, she glimpsed the vampires on duty opening cabinets to pull out the bleach and turning the faucets in the sinks while others fetched the mops.

The dead man had been tall and heavy. Since Katamori and Dahlia were not too far apart in height they could bear the weight equally, and they were both immensely strong; so Arthur Allthorp's weight wasn't an issue. His bulk was. They carried the body through the large garden to the formal fountain with its deep raised surround, designed to form a pool. The statue in the middle of the fountain was a woman in flowing drapery. She was holding a tilted jug, out of which the running water splashed into the pool. At the side of the fountain farthest from the house, they laid the body down. Dahlia leaped up on the broad edge of the pool and craned over precariously to fish a key from the statue's drapery. It wasn't in the fold that usually held it, and she had a moment's severe jolt until she felt the metal edge in the next fold down. All the vamps in the house knew the key's location, and once or twice it had been misplaced. With a huge feeling of relief, Dahlia hopped down, a little wet from the experience.

She squatted to insert the key in the keyhole of a large panel in the base of the fountain. This panel looked as though it had been designed to give access to the plumbing and the fountain mechanism, but the vampires had designed it for another use. Though this body was somewhat bigger than most of the previous bodies that had been hidden there, and though the hole was partially obstructed, they had to make it work. Dahlia actually crawled in the space to pull on the body, while Katamori remained outside to stuff the legs in. Then Dahlia had to crawl out over the body, getting even more rumpled and a bit stained in the process.

By that time, she and Katamori could hear the police surging through the mansion.

"I can't be found like this," Dahlia said, disgusted, looking down at her dress.

"Then take it off," Katamori said, holding the "maintenance panel" open. "I have an idea."

When the police came out to search the garden, they found Katamori and Dahlia frolicking in the fountain stark naked. The sight froze them in their tracks. Not only was it fall and chilly, but in the moonlit garden Dahlia was white as marble.

"All over," said one of the cops, awestruck. "And he's just a shade darker."

"Did you need to talk to us?" Dahlia asked, as if she'd just noticed their presence.

Katamori, at her back, wrapped his arms around her. "I hope not," he said. "We have other things to do."

"Cold hasn't affected *him* much," muttered Cop Two. He was trying to keep his eyes off the vampires, but he kept darting glances in their direction. Dahlia could feel Katamori's body shake with amusement. Humans were so silly about nudity.

"No, no, you two are okay. No bodies in that pool?" asked Cop One, smiling broadly.

"Only ours," Dahlia said, trying to purr. She did a credible job.

"Probably a prank call," said Cop One. "Sorry we're interrupting your evening. We would have been here twenty minutes ago if there hadn't been a wreck on our exit ramp."

That was interesting, but they had to stay in character. "You're not disturbing us at all," Katamori said, bending his head to kiss Dahlia's neck.

"Let's look through the bushes," said Cop Two, scandalized, and the two policemen dutifully searched the paths and parted the bushes, trying not to watch the activity in the waters of the fountain while checking any place a body could be concealed.

Except for the one place it was.

But they made a slow job of it because they kept looking back to watch Dahlia and Katamori, whose cavorting progressed from warm to simmer to boil.

"Oh my God," said Cop One. "They're actually . . . "

"Did you know how *fast* they could move?" muttered Cop Two. "Her boobs are shaking like maracas!"

By the time the two marched back to the mansion's French doors, the two vampires were perched on the edge of the fountain, Katamori's legs hanging over the maintenance door while Dahlia sat in his lap. They both looked pleased, and were whispering to each other in a loverlike way.

Dahlia was saying, "I'm much refreshed. What a good idea, Katamori."

"I enjoyed that. I hope we can do it again. Even out here. Perhaps without an audience, next time. How many police were lined up inside, watching?"

"At least five, plus the two out here. Did you see what I found in the hiding place?"

"Yes, I saw. Joaquin will be so pleased with us. Surely the humans will leave soon. I think we did an excellent job of distracting them. Thank you."

"Oh, it was my pleasure," Dahlia said sincerely.

In half an hour, Joaquin himself came into the garden to tell them that the police had left. He was only slightly startled to find them still naked.

"I'm glad you've enjoyed each other's company," he said. "Did you have any problems concealing the body?"

"Let me show you what we found under the fountain when we opened it," Dahlia said, and reopened the panel to pull a bundle of clothing out. It was not her clothing, or Katamori's. She shook out the garments and held them up for Joaquin's viewing. He was silent for a long moment.

"Well," he said. "That's settled, then. Bring them in when you've readied yourself. Later tonight, I'll send Troy and Hazel out here to dispose of the body for good. I regret this whole incident." The new sheriff seemed sincere, to Dahlia. He turned and went into the mansion.

The two pulled on their own garments, though Dahlia hated resuming her stained dress. It had been a gamble leaving the clothes in a heap by the fountain, but it had been the right touch. Katamori and Dahlia checked each other to make sure they were in order. She tucked his shirt in a little more neatly, and he buckled her very high heels for her. They followed Joaquin back in through the brightly lit French doors.

The crowd had thinned.

"Where are the demons?" Dahlia asked Taffy, who was sitting beside Don on a loveseat.

"They left when the police did," Taffy said, running her fingers through her huge mane of hair. "They were smart to go while the getting was good."

"There's no harm in that," Dahlia told her friend. "Diantha was the only one involved, and we know she didn't do it."

"Melponeus looked sorry to be leaving without seeing you again," Taffy said slyly. "He did a little looking out the windows when the police seemed so interested in the garden. I think it sparked a few memories he enjoyed very much."

"You've had the demon?" Katamori was intrigued.

"Yes," Dahlia said. "The heat and texture of his skin made the experience very interesting. Nothing compared to you, of course." Dahlia could be polite when it mattered.

Joaquin and his bodyguards were waiting for Dahlia and Katamori to present their findings. All the Rhodes vampires gathered around when they entered. Joaquin, who had resumed his seat in his massive chair, waited impassively for their report. Cedric was still drinking Red Stuff and seemed even more unhappy, and Glenda, now completely healed, glowered at Dahlia. But they joined the throng with the rest. Even Don and his enforcer rose to join the crowd when Taffy did.

"That was an excellent strategy to distract the police," Joaquin said. "Now tell us what you've discovered."

"We found a bundle of bloody clothes hidden in the base of the fountain," Dahlia said, and a ripple ran through the crowd. "If we hadn't had to hide the body, if no one had called the police, we might never have found them. Since Arthur Allthorp's murderer was the one who called the police, hoping to get the nest in trouble, you might say he cut his own throat."

Joaquin held up the bloody bundle. The smell was really strong now, and the Weres' upper lips pulled up in a snarl of distaste. Even Weres liked their blood fresh. Joaquin, with a certain amount of drama, shook out the garments, one by one.

"Cedric, I believe these are yours," he said.

"That's not true," Cedric said calmly. He swept a hand down his chest. "Someone is trying to incriminate me. This is what I have been wearing all evening."

"Not so," retorted Dahlia. "The flowers on your vest were golden at the beginning of the evening. After the death of the human, the flowers were blue." She was almost sad to have to say the words, but out of spite Cedric had almost condemned the whole nest to hours in the police station, days of bad press, and the end of the regime of Joaquin before it had even really begun. "The clothes you have on now are your clothes you wear when you garden, the clothes you leave hanging on a peg outside. Including the boots."

Everyone looked down at Cedric's scruffy boots. They were certainly not footwear anyone would choose to wear to a reception, not even Cedric.

For a second, fear flashed in Cedric's blue eyes. Only for a second. Then he charged at Dahlia, a wild shriek coming from his lips.

She'd been expecting it for all of a couple of seconds. She stepped to the left quicker than the eye could track her, seized Cedric's right arm as he went past her, twisted it upward at a terrible angle, and when Cedric screamed she gripped his head and twisted.

Cedric's head came off.

There was silence for a moment.

"I'm so sorry," she said to Joaquin. "I didn't intend his decapitation. The mess . . . "

"He'll flake away and we'll get out the vacuum cleaner," Joaquin said, with a good approximation of calm. Before his elevation to the sheriff's position, Joaquin had been in body disposal, Dahlia recalled. "If the stain won't clean out of the rug, we'll buy another."

That was something Cedric would never have said, and Dahlia brightened. "Thank you, Sheriff. He almost surprised me," she said, and she could barely believe the words were coming from her lips. Perhaps she would miss Cedric more than she had realized.

"When the humans charge the police in order to be shot, they call it 'suicide by cop.'" Katamori bowed to his new friend. He said gallantly, "We will call it 'Death by Dahlia.'"

Charlaine Harris is a #1 *New York Times* bestselling author who has been writing for more than thirty years. After publishing two stand-alone mysteries, she published eight books featuring Aurora Teagarden, a mystery-solving Georgia librarian. In 1996, she released the first of the Shakespeare mysteries featuring amateur sleuth Lily Bard. The fifth (and last) of the series was published in 2001. Harris had, by then, created the Southern Vampire Mystery series about a telepathic waitress named Sookie Stackhouse who works in a bar in the fictional northern Louisiana town of Bon Temps. The first book, *Dead Until Dark*, won the Anthony Award for Best Paperback Mystery in 2001. The thirteenth and final novel in the series, *Dead Ever After*, will be published in May 2013. Alan Ball produced the HBO series based on the Sookie books, *True*

Blood, which premiered in September of 2008. Its sixth season aired earlier this year. Harris has also co-edited six anthologies with Toni L. P. Kelner. Personally, Harris is married and the mother of three. She lives in a small town in southern Arkansas in a house full of rescue dogs. "Death by Dahlia" features Dahlia Lynley-Chivers, who was introduced in the Sookieverse short story "Tacky," and has appeared in *All Together Dead* and several other short stories. Dahlia also "stars" in *Dying for Daylight*, an interactive PC game.

The Case: *Two men find death when they descend into the sea to recover the remains of a man who has lain dead ninety fathoms deep for five years. Meanwhile, terrifying sounds emerge from what was thought to be a watery tomb.*

The Investigators: *Sherlock Holmes, the world's greatest consulting detective, and John H. Watson, MD, Holmes's friend, assistant, and sometime flatmate.*

SHERLOCK HOLMES AND THE DIVING BELL

➤◆➤

Simon Clark

WATSON. COME AT ONCE. THAT WHICH CANNOT BE. IS.

That astonishing summons brought me to the Cornish harbor town of Fowey. There, as directed by further information within the telegram, I joined my friend, Mr. Sherlock Holmes, on a tugboat, which immediately steamed toward the open sea. The rapid pounding of the engine made for an urgent drumbeat. One that reinforced the notion that once more we'd embarked upon a headlong dash to adventure.

By the time I'd regained my breath, after a somewhat hurried embarkation, I saw that Holmes had taken up a position in the tugboat's bow. There he stood, straight-backed, thin as a pikestaff, hatless, and dressed severely in black. Every inch the eager seeker of truth. His deep-set eyes raked the turquoise ocean, hunting for what he knew must lie out here.

But what, exactly, was the nature of our case? He'd given no elaboration, other than that mystifying statement in the telegram. *That which cannot be. Is.*

I picked my way across the deck, over coils of rope, rusty chain, and assorted winding gear that adorned this grubby little workhorse of the sea. The vessel moved at the limits of its speed. Steam hissed from pipes, smoke tumbled out of the funnel to stain an otherwise perfectly blue June sky. Gulls wheeled about our craft, for the moment mistaking us for a fishing boat. Either they finally understood that we didn't carry so much as a mackerel or, perhaps, they sensed danger ahead, for the birds suddenly departed on powerful wings, uttering such piercing shrieks that they could be plainly heard above the *whoosh!* and *shorr!* of the engine.

Likewise, I made it my business to be overheard above the machine, too. "Holmes. What's happened?"

That distinctive profile remained. He didn't even glance in my direction.

"Holmes, good God, man! The telegram! What does it mean?"

Still he did not turn. Instead, he rested his fingertip against his lips.

Hush.

My friend is not given to personal melodrama, or prone to questioning my loyalties by virtue of frivolous tests. Clearly, this was a matter of great importance. Just what that matter was I'd have to wait and see. However, a certain rigidity of his posture and grimness of expression sent a chill foreboding through my blood. Terrible events loomed—or so I divined. Therefore, I stood beside that black clad figure, said nothing, and waited for the tugboat to bear us to our destination.

Presently, I saw where we were headed. Sitting there, as a blot of darkness on the glittering sea, was a large vessel of iron. What I'd first surmised to be a stunted mast between the aft deck and the funnel was, in fact, a crane. A cable ran from the pulley at the tip of that formidable lifting arm to a gray object on the aft deck.

In the next half hour Holmes would speak but tersely. "Steel yourself, Watson." That was his sole item of conversation on the tugboat.

The dourness of countenance revealed that some immense problem weighed heavy on the man. His long fingers curled around the rail at the prow. Muscle tension produced a distinct whitening of the knuckles. His piercing eyes regarded the iron ship, which grew ever nearer. And he looked at that ship as a man might who'd seen a gravestone on which his own name is etched with the days of his mortal arrival and, more disconcertingly, his departure.

The tugboat captain fired off two short blasts of the steam whistle. The leviathan at anchor gave an answering call on its horn. A mournful sound to be sure. Soon the tugboat drew alongside. A grim-faced Holmes took my elbow in order to help me safely pass from the heaving tugboat to the rope ladder that had been cast down for us.

My heart, and I readily confess the fact, pounded nearly as hard as the pistons of the tugboat. For, as I climbed up toward the guardrail fifteen feet above me, I saw an assembly of faces. They regarded me with such melancholy that I fully expected to be marched to a gallows where my noose awaited.

Panting, I clambered over the rail onto the aft deck. There, something resembling the boiler of a locomotive, lying horizontally, dominated the area. A pair of hawsers ran from this giant cylinder to a linking ring; from that stout ring a single hawser of great thickness rose to the crane's tip.

Holmes followed me on deck.

Immediately, a man of around sixty, or so, strode forward. His face had been reddened by ocean gales and the sun. A tracery of purple veins emerged from a pair of mutton-chop side-whiskers that were as large as they were perfectly white. Those dark veins appeared as distinct as contour lines on a map. Such a weather-beaten visage could have been on loan from the Ancient Mariner himself. His wide, gray eyes examined my face, as if attempting to discern whether I was a fellow who'd stand firm in the face of danger, or take flight. That assessment appeared to be of great importance to him.

Holmes introduced me to this venerable seaman. "Captain Smeaton. Dr. Watson." We shook hands. His grasp was steel. Holmes closed with the terse request: "Captain Smeaton, please explain."

The captain shared the same funereal expression as the rest of his crew. Not smiling once. Nevertheless, he did speak.

"Dr. Watson," he began in a voice long since made permanently hoarse from having to make himself heard above ocean storms, "I don't know what Mr. Holmes has revealed to you about our plight."

"Nothing." To avoid my friend's silence on this matter as being altogether too strange I added, "I arrived from London in something of a rush."

Captain Smeaton didn't appear concerned by my ignorance and continued swiftly. "You're on board the *Fitzwilliam*, a salvage vessel. Mr. Holmes spent the day with us yesterday, because . . . well . . . I'll come to that later, sir. I'll tell the story in plain-speak. There's no requirement for me to embellish with colorful or dramatic phrases, because what you'll witness is going to strike at the heart of you anyway."

Holmes stood beside me, listening carefully.

The Captain did as he promised, rendering his account in deep, whispery tones that were plain and very much to the point. "Five years ago, Dr. Watson, we were engaged by the admiralty to recover silver bullion from the *SS Runswick*, which lies ninety fathoms beneath our keel. The depth is too great for divers using Siebe Gorman suits. They can operate to depths nearing thirty fathoms or so—to go any deeper is certain death. So we use Submarine Chambers, such as this." He indicated the iron cylinder that occupied the deck. Moisture dripped from its massive flanks. Bulbous rivets held that hulking beast together in such a formidable way the thing appeared downright indestructible to my eyes.

"A diving bell?" I asked.

"As they are commonly known. Diving bells have been used since the time of the ancient Greeks, sir. Back then they'd simply invert a cauldron, trapping the air inside. This they'd submerge into the ocean. A diver would then visit the air pocket in order to breathe. That arrangement allowed sponge divers, and the like, much greater duration on the seabed."

"Remarkable," I commented, eying the huge vessel squatting there on the deck. "And this is the twentieth century descendent of the cauldron?"

"That it is, sir." Captain Smeaton's gaze strayed toward Holmes as if seeking permission to continue. Holmes gave a slight nod. "To get to the meat of the matter, sir, back in 1899 we used a diving bell to retrieve silver bullion from the sunken ship. One particular morning, I ordered that the *Pollux*, which is the name of the bell, be lowered to the ocean floor. On board was a man by the name of George Barstow. The diving bell was delivered to the wreck by crane, as you see here, sir. It is both lowered, and raised to the surface by means of a steel hawser. Fresh air is pumped down to the craft via a tube. Contact is maintained between the ship and the diving bell by telephone. I tell you, gentlemen, I curse the hour that I ordered Barstow to man the craft. Not a day goes by without me reliving those terrible events." He took a deep breath, his gray eyes glistened. "Initially, the dive went well. Barstow descended to the wreck without incident. His function was to act as observer and to send directions, via telephone apparatus, to my men on the ship to lower a grappling hook in order to retrieve the cargo. We successfully hooked five cases of silver and brought them to the surface. Then I noticed a swell had begun to run. This poses a risk to diving bells as it puts excessive strain on the hawser. I gave the order to winch the craft back to the surface." He paused for moment. "That's when Barstow spoke to me by telephone. He reported that the diving bell had become caught on the superstructure of the wreck. The thing had jammed fast. We tried every which way to free the bell. Meanwhile, waves had started to break against the sides of the ship. So I told the winch-man to use brute force and haul the diving bell free." He paused again. Trying to avoid melodrama, he said simply. "The hawser snapped. As did the telephone line and air pipe. That was five years ago. The *Pollux* became George Barstow's coffin. He's been down there ever since."

"And now you are trying to recover the *Pollux* and the man's body?"

"Indeed we are, Dr. Watson." He nodded to where a hawser ran along a steel channel to a fixing point on deck. Barnacles and brown kelp sheathed the hawser. "That's from the *Pollux*. We recovered it three days ago."

"It's still attached to the diving bell?"

The captain nodded his gray head. "The *Pollux* is held down there on the seabed. Probably the old wreck's doing. Even so, we made fast the cable on deck here. I'm going to do my damndest to haul that diving bell out of Davy Jones's locker and bring the blasted thing back to dry land, so help me." His hands shook as a powerful emotion took charge. "Or it'll be the death of me in trying."

I looked to Holmes for some explanation. After all, a salvage operation?

Surely that's a matter that doesn't require the intervention of the world's greatest consulting detective.

"Yesterday," Holmes said. "The diving bell's twin went in search of its sibling."

I turned to the vessel that so much resembled the boiler of a locomotive. On the side of that great iron cylinder was painted, in white, the name *Castor*. "And did it find its twin?"

"It did. The diving bell returned without apparent incident. However, the crew of two were, on the opening of the hatch, found to be quite dead."

"Quite dead!" thundered the Captain. "They died of fright. Just take one look at their faces!"

"What I require of my friend, Dr. Watson, is to examine the deceased. If you will kindly take us to the bodies."

"Holmes?" I regarded him with surprise. "A post mortem?"

"The simple cause of death will be sufficient, Watson."

"I can't, Holmes."

"You must, and quickly."

"Not unless I am authorized by the local constabulary, or the coroner."

"You must tell me how they died, Watson."

"Holmes, I protest. I shall be breaking the law."

"Oh, but you must, Watson. Because I am to be—" he struck the side of the diving bell, "—this vessel's next passenger!"

Before I could stutter a reply a sailor approached. "Captain! It's started again! The sounds are coming up the line!" His eyes were round with fear. "And it's trying to make words!"

That expression of dread on the man's face communicated a thrill of fear to my very veins. "What's happening, Holmes? What sounds?"

"We're in receipt of another telephone call." His deep-set eyes locked onto mine. "It hails from ninety fathoms down. And it's coming from the *Pollux*!"

Upon passing through a door marked *Control Room*, we were greeted by a remarkable sight.

Three men in officer's uniforms gathered before telephony apparatus on a table. Fixed to the wall, immediately in front of them, was a horn of the type that amplifies the music from a gramophone. Nearby, two young women stood with their arms round each other, like children frightened of a thunderstorm. Both were dressed in black muslin. Both had lustrous, dark eyes set into bone-white faces. And both faces were identical.

Twins. That much was evident.

The occupants of the room stared at the horn on the wall. Their eyes were open wide, their expressions radiated absolute horror. Faces quivered. They hardly dared breathe, lest a quick intake of breath would invite sudden, and brutal, destruction.

Holmes strode toward the gathering. "Are the sounds the same as before?"

An officer with a clipped red beard answered, but he couldn't take his bulging eyes from the speaker horn. "They began the same . . . in the last few minutes; however, they've begun to change."

A second officer added, "As if it's trying to form words."

The third cried, "Sir! What if it really is him? After all this time!"

"Keep your nerve, Jessup. Remember that ladies are present." Captain Smeaton tilted his head in the direction of the two women. Then he said, "Dr. Watson. Allow me to introduce you to Mrs. Katrina Barstow, widow of George Barstow, and her sister, Miss Claudine Millwood."

"Evidently," murmured Holmes, "this isn't the occasion for formal introductions."

For the women in black disregarded me; they hugged each other tight, desperate for some degree of comfort amid the horror.

"A series of clicks." Holmes tilted his head to one side as he listened. "Almost like the sound produced on a telephone speaker when a thunderstorm is approaching."

Jessup cried, "Or the sound of his bones. They've begun moving about the *Pollux*!"

Captain Smeaton spoke calmly. "Go below to your cabin, Jessup." Jessup fled from his post, and fled gratefully it seemed to me.

More clicks issued from the horn. The women moaned with dismay. Mrs. Barstow pressed a handkerchief against her mouth as if to stifle a scream.

Captain Smeaton explained, "After the hawser was recovered from the seabed, my crew secured it to a deck bollard. One of the ship's apprentices did what he was routinely supposed to do. He attached the *Pollux*'s telephone wire to this telephone apparatus."

Holmes turned to the Captain. "And that's when you began to hear unusual sounds?"

"Unusual?" exclaimed the red-bearded officer. "Terrible sounds, sir. They come back to you in your dreams."

I listened to the leaden clicking. Very much the sound of old bone striking against yet more bone. "Forgive me, if I ask the obvious. But do you maintain that the telephone line connects this apparatus with that in the diving bell, which has lain on the seabed for five years?"

"Yes, Dr. Watson. I fear I do." Captain Smeaton shuddered. "And I wish circumstances did not require me to make such a claim."

"And those clicks are transmitted up the wire from . . . " I refrained from adding *Barstow's tomb.*

Sherlock Holmes turned to me quickly. "Ha! There you have it, Watson. *That which cannot be. Is.*"

"Then it is a fault with the mechanism. Surely?"

"Would I have come aboard this ship, Watson, to attend to an electrical fault? They did not mistake me for a telephony engineer."

"But dash it all, Holmes—"

Then it issued from the horn. A deep voice. Wordless. Full of pain, regret, and an unquestionable longing. "Urrr . . . hmm . . . ahhh . . . "

Ice dashed through my veins. Freezing me into absolute stillness. "That sound . . . "

"Human?" asked Holmes.

"Decidedly. At least, it appears so."

"Fffmm . . . arrnurr . . . Mmm-ursss . . . "

The deep, shimmering voice from the horn trailed away into a sigh comprised of ghosting esses. *"Ssss . . . "*

The pent-up scream discharged at last. Mrs. Barstow cried, "That's my husband! He's alive. Please bring him back to me. Please!"

Her sister murmured to her, reassuring her, comforting her.

"No, Holmes," I whispered to my friend. "That's impossible. No mortal man could survive five years underwater without air."

"Survive? Or evolve? As environment demands? Remember Darwin."

"Holmes, surely you're not suggesting—"

"I'm suggesting we keep our minds open. As well as our eyes."

The voice came ghosting from the horn again. That longing—yet it appeared to come from the lips of a man who had witnessed the unimaginable. His widow wept.

Captain Smeaton said, "Perhaps the ladies should leave."

"No!" Holmes held up his hand. "Now is the time to unravel this particular mystery!"

The syllables rising from the *Pollux* became a long, wordless groan.

"Mrs. Barstow." Holmes spoke briskly. "Forgive what will be difficult questions at this vexing time. What did you call your husband?"

The widow's eyes, which were surely as dark as the coal that fired water into steam in this very ship, regarded Holmes with surprise.

"Madam, how did you address your husband?"

She responded with amazement. "His name? Are you quite mad?"

"Madam, indulge me. Please."

"My husband's name is Mr. George Barstow."

His manner became severe. "You were husband and wife. Surely, you gave him a familiar name? A private name?"

"Mr. Holmes, I protest—"

"A nickname."

Miss Millwood stood with her arm around Mrs. Barstow, glaring with the utmost ferocity at my friend.

"If I am to unravel this mystery, then you must answer my questions."

The groaning from the horn suddenly faded. An expectant silence followed. An impression of someone listening hard. A someone not in that room.

Still Mrs. Barstow prevaricated. "I don't understand what you would have me say, Mr. Holmes."

"Tell me the private name with which you addressed the man whom you loved so dearly. The name you spoke when you and he were alone."

A storm of rage erupted. Not from any living mouth there. It came from the speaker horn that was connected by some hundred fathoms of cable to the diving bell at the bottom of the ocean. The roar came back double, then again many-fold. It seemed as if demons by the legion bellowed their fury, their outrage and their jealous anger from the device. The pair of ship's officers at the desk covered their ears and fled through the doorway.

At last the awful expulsion of wrath faded. The speaker horn fell silent. Everyone in the room had been struck silent, too. All, that is, except for Sherlock Holmes.

"Mrs. Barstow. A moment ago you said these words to me: 'My husband's name is Mr. George Barstow.'"

"Indeed." Recovering her composure, she stood straighter.

"*Is*, Madam, not *was*?"

"*Is!*"

"Therefore in the present tense. As if he is still alive?"

"Of course." She pointed a trembling finger at the speaker horn. "Because he lives. That's his voice."

"Then perhaps you will tell me your private name for Mr. Barstow? The one you use when the servants are gone, and all the lamps are extinguished."

The blast of sound from the instrument almost swept us off our feet. A glass of water on the desk shattered. At that moment, the widow's sister stiffened, her eyes rolled back, and she fell into a dead faint. Holmes caught the woman to prevent her striking the floor.

Nevertheless, he fixed Mrs. Barstow with a penetrating gaze. "Madam. I am still waiting for you to reveal the name—that secret name only you and he knew."

"*Katrina. Stay silent. Do not say it!*"

All heads turned to the speaker. That voice! Waves of such uncanny power radiated from every syllable.

"George," she cried.

"Do not speak with Sherlock Holmes. He is evil. The man is our enemy!"

"You heard with your own ears!" she shouted, her fist pressed to her breast. "My husband is alive!" She turned to Captain Smeaton. "Send the machine down to save him."

Captain Smeaton's weather-beaten face assumed a deeper shade of purple. "I will not. Whatever's down there can no longer be George Barstow. Not after five years."

"He's immortal," she cried. "Just as my sister promised."

My friend's eyes narrowed as the widow voiced this statement. Quickly, he settled the unconscious form of Miss Claudine Millwood into a chair at the desk. I checked the pulse in her neck.

"Strong . . . very strong. She's fainted, that's all."

"Thank you, Watson," said Holmes. "And I rather think the pieces of our jigsaw are falling into place." He picked up the handset part of the phone and spoke into the mouthpiece. "Whom do I have the honor of addressing?"

"Barstow."

"For a man dead these last five years you sound remarkably vigorous."

"So shall I be when you are dust, sir."

Holmes turned to Captain Smeaton.

"You knew Barstow well. Is that his voice?"

"God help us. Indeed it is."

Mrs. Barstow clawed at Smeaton's arm. "Send the machine. Bring him to me!"

"No!" Captain Smeaton's voice rang out with fear, rather than anger.

"I agree with Mrs. Barstow." Holmes pulled on his black leather gloves. "Prepare the diving bell. I will visit the *Pollux* myself."

"Impossible."

"I insist. For I must see for myself who—or what—is the tenant of your lost machine."

Not many men thwart my friend, Sherlock Holmes. Ten minutes later, the crew had the *Castor* ready for descent. Holmes quickly returned to the control room. The twin sister still lay unconscious; the horror had overwhelmed her senses. The widow stood perfectly straight: her dark eyes regarded Holmes from a bone-white face.

"Mrs. Barstow," he intoned. "You do know that what you crave is an impossibility? Your husband cannot still be a living, breathing man after five years in that iron canister."

"I have faith."

"I see."

"Mr. Holmes, do you wish to hear that private name I gave my husband?"

Holmes spoke kindly, "That will no longer be necessary."

I couldn't remain silent. "Good God, man, surely you will not descend in that machine?"

"I have no choice, Watson."

"Please, Holmes, I beg—"

"Wait for me here, won't you, old friend?" He gave a wry smile. "Fates willing, this won't be a lengthy journey." He picked up the telephone's handset. "But first, one more question. Barstow?"

A sound of respiration gusted from the speaker.

"Barstow. Tell me what you see from your lair?"

"All is green. All is green. And yet . . . "

"And yet what?"

"The funnel of this wreck towers above the diving bell. Always I see the funnel standing there. A black monolith. A grave-marker. Do not come here . . . "

"It is my duty, sir. You are a mystery. I must investigate."

"No."

"My nature compels me."

"No! If you should dare to approach my vessel I will destroy you!"

"Sir, I shall be with you presently."

Holmes briskly left the room. The voice still screamed from the speaker: *"You will die! You will die!"*

We crossed the aft deck to the *Castor*. With utter conviction I announced, "Holmes. I'm coming with you."

He gave a grim smile. "Watson. I was rather hoping you would."

Moments later, we clambered through a hatch into the huge iron cylinder. In shape and in size, it resembled, as I've previously described, the boiler of a locomotive. Within: a bench in padded red plush ran along one wall. In the wall opposite the seat, a pair of portholes cast from enormously thick glass. They were set side by side, and prompted one to envisage the bulging eyes of some primordial creature. Above us, the blue sky remained in view through the open hatch. Captain Smeaton appeared.

"Gentlemen. You will receive fresh air through the tube. If you wish to speak to me, use the telephone mounted on the wall there beside you. God speed!"

"One moment, Captain," said Holmes. "When Watson and I are dispatched to the seabed, ensure that Mrs. Barstow and her sister remain in the control room with you. Is that understood?"

"Aye-aye, Mr. Holmes."

"Upon your word?"

"Absolutely."

"Good. Because their proximity to you might very well be a matter of life and death."

Then the hatch was sealed tight. A series of clanks, a jerking sensation, the crane lifted the *Castor* off the deck. A swaying movement, and I spied through the thick portholes that we were swung over the guardrail and dangled over the ocean; such a searing blue at that moment. "Castor and Pollux," I whispered, every fiber tensing. "The heavenly twins."

"Not only that. In most classical legends Pollux is immortal. Whereas—" he patted the curving iron wall in front of him. "—Castor is a mere mortal. And capable of death."

The shudders transmitted along the hawser to the diving bell were disconcertingly fierce. The sounds of the crane motors were very loud. In truth, louder than I deemed possible. Until, that is, the diving bell reached the sea. With a flurry of bubbles it sank beneath the surface. White froth gave way to clear turquoise.

Swiftly, the vessel descended. Silent now. An iron calf slipping free of its hulking mother on the surface.

"Don't neglect to breathe, Watson."

I realized I was holding my breath. "Thank you, Holmes."

"Fresh air is pumped through the inlet hose above our heads."

"Hardly fresh." I managed a grim smile. "It reeks of coal smoke and tickles the back of the throat so."

"At least it is wholesome . . . if decidedly pungent."

The light began to fade as we sank deeper. I took stock of my surroundings. The interior of the cylinder offered little more room than the interior of a hansom cab. Indeed, we sat side by side. Between us hung the cable of the telephone. The handset had been clipped to the wall within easy reach. And down we went.

Darker . . . darker . . . darker . . . The vessel swayed slightly. My stomach lightened a little, as when descending by elevator. I clenched my fists upon my lap until the knuckles turned white.

"Don't be alarmed," Holmes said. "The barometric pressure of the interior remains the same as that of sea-level."

"Then we will be spared the bends and nitrogen narcosis. The former is agonizing. The latter intoxicates and induces hallucination."

"Ah! You know about the medical perils of deep-sea diving."

"When a former army doctor sits beside a naval doctor at his club you can imagine the topics of conversation over the glasses of port." I clicked my tongue. "And now I tell you this so as to distract myself from the knowledge that we are descending over five hundred feet to the ocean floor. In a blessed tin can!"

Holmes leaned forward, eager to witness what lay beyond the glass. The water had dulled from bright turquoise to blue. To deep blue. A pink jellyfish floated by. A globular sac from which delicate filaments descended. Altogether a beautiful creature. Totally unlike the viscous remains of jellyfish one finds washed ashore.

Holmes read a dial set between the portholes. "Sixty fathoms. Two thirds of the way there, Watson."

"Dear Lord."

"Soon we should see the shipwreck. And shortly, thereafter, this vessel's twin."

"Twin?" I echoed. "Which reminds me. I thought the twin sisters we encountered today were decidedly odd."

"Ah-ha. So we are two minds with a single thought."

"And no doubt you deduced far more than I could from their dress, speech and retinue of subtle clues."

"Supposition at the moment, Watson, rather than deduction. Before I make any pronouncement on the sisters, or the singular voice emerging from the telephone, I need to see just who is in residence in the *Pollux*. Which, if I'm not mistaken, is coming into view below."

He'd no sooner uttered the words when a shadow raced from the darkness beyond the porthole glass. Silently, it rushed by.

"What the devil was that?" I asked in surprise.

"Possibly a dolphin or a shark . . . " He pressed his fingertips together as he considered. "Although I doubt it very much."

The mystifying remark didn't ease my trepidation. And that trepidation turned into one of overt alarm when a clang sounded against the side of the diving bell. The entire structure lurched, forcing us to hold tight to a brass rail in front of us.

"Some denizen of the deep doesn't want us here," observed Holmes. "Here it comes again."

The dark shape torpedoed from the gloom surrounding the diving bell. Once more it struck the iron cylinder.

"We should inform Captain Smeaton," I ventured.

"In which case he'll winch us back up forthwith. No, we must see the occupant of the *Pollux*. That is vital, if we are to explain what is happening here."

Darkly, I murmured, "Barstow didn't want us to call on him. He promised our destruction if we tried."

"Yes, he did, didn't he?" Holmes watched the cylinder resolve itself in the gloom beneath us. "So why does he—or what he has become—desire to remain hidden away on the seabed?"

"Hypothetically speaking, Holmes?"

"While we are in a speculative frame of mind: Barstow described his surroundings for us via the telephone. Be so good as to repeat his description."

"Let me see: Green. Yes, his words were 'all is green.'"

"Continue, pray."

"And he made much of the wreck's funnel. How it loomed over him. A grave-marker as he put it."

"What color is the seawater down here. Green?"

"No, it's black."

"Indeed, Watson. And as for the ship's funnel? A great monolith of a structure?"

"Where is the funnel? I don't see one."

"Because there is no funnel. At least there isn't one fixed to the wreck. It must have become detached as the ship foundered years ago."

"So, why did Barstow describe the wreck in such a way?"

"Evidently, Barstow cannot see the wreck as it really is, sans funnel. Nor can he see that the water at this depth is black—not green."

"So who did the voice belong to that we heard coming from the speaker?"

"It belongs to whoever is responsible for the deaths of those two men yesterday. And who will be responsible for our deaths today, if our wits aren't sharp enough." He clapped his hands together. "Pah! See the wreck. It's a jumble of scrap metal covered in weed. Barstow's description belonged to someone who has never seen a wreck on the ocean bed before. Instead, they based their description on pictures of ships that they see on sitting room walls."

"To repeat myself, Holmes, who did the voice actually belong to?"

"Ah, that can wait, Watson. Our descent is slowing. Soon we will look into Barstow's lair." He shot me a glance. "His tomb?"

The crane operator stopped paying out the hawser as we bumped against the bottom. Just a yard or so away lay the diving bell—the twin of the one we now sat in. Though confoundedly gloomy down here I could make out some detail. Kelp grew from the iron cylinder. The rounded shape was suggestive of some monstrous skull covered with flowing hair. Spars from the wreck had enclosed the diving bell like the bars of a cage, trapping it that fateful day five years ago. A grip so tight that the haulage gear had snapped the hawser as it strove to raise the doomed submersible to the surface.

Those black waters would reveal little. Not until Holmes closed a switch. The moment he did so, a light sprang from the lamp fixed to our craft. "Now we can see who resides inside the *Pollux*."

Holmes took a deep breath as his keen eyes made an assessment. "Are we of the same opinion of the occupant?"

Likewise, I took a steadying breath. I peered through our porthole and into the porthole of the craft trapped by the stricken bullion carrier, *Fitzwilliam*. "Now I see. But I don't understand how he speaks to us."

"Confirm what you observe, Watson."

"A cadaver. Partly mummified as a result of being confined in an airtight compartment. Inert. Lying on the bench at the rear of the vessel."

"The man would have been dead within a few hours of being marooned without an air supply. Is that not so?"

"Agreed."

"Notice that the hawser has been retrieved and snakes up to the surface. But notice, equally, that the telephone cable has been snapped at the point it should enter the *Pollux*. Barstow, alive or dead, never made so much as a single call once that cable had parted from the apparatus within his diving bell."

"So, who is responsible?"

"A creature of flesh and blood!" If it weren't for the confines of the diving bell an excited Sherlock Holmes would have sprung to his feet. "Miss Claudine Millwood! Twin sister of that man's widow." He inhaled deeply, his nostrils twitching in the manner of a predator catching scent of its prey. "You see, Watson, I shall one day write a monograph on an especially rarefied subject. Yet one which will be invaluable to police when interrogating suspects or, more importantly, discussing certain matters, within the hearing of a suspect. I have observed, during my career as a consulting detective, that the eyes of a human being move in such a prescribed way that they hint at what they are thinking. Strongly hint at that! With practice, one can become quite adept at reading the eye-line of a man or woman."

"Therefore, you studied Miss Claudine Millwood when you questioned Mrs. Barstow?"

"That I did, sir. In this case, as I spoke to the widow, I also took careful note of the direction of Miss Millwood's eye-line. When I mentioned Mr. Barstow by name the woman's gaze became unfocused, yet directed slightly downward and some degrees off center to her left. Trust me, Watson, how we arrange our limbs and direct our gaze reveals volumes to the competent observer."

"Therefore you could glean her unspoken thoughts?"

"To a degree. The direction of her gaze and the unfocused eyes told me that Miss Millwood was in the process of recalling a memory that is not only secret to her, but one she knew would shock or revolt right-minded individuals. That was enough to arouse my suspicions."

"And you divined this by reading the eye-line? Remarkable!"

"Just as you, a medical man, can diagnose an illness from subtle symptoms. Moreover! The woman couldn't bear to hear her own sister reveal that private, intimate name, which, once upon a time, she murmured into her husband's ear. A name that Claudine Millwood did not know."

"Millwood was in love with her sister's husband?"

"Without a shadow of doubt. Whether that love was reciprocated or not we don't know."

"And during the years Barstow lay in that iron tomb the love grew."

"Indeed! The love grew—and it grew malignantly. That obsessive love took on a life of its own. Millwood projected thoughts from her own mind into the telephone apparatus. She imitated the late Mr. Barstow."

"Why didn't she want us to venture down here?"

"That would have destroyed the fantasy. We would have returned to the surface, but not, however, with an account of finding a handsome young man full of miraculous life, still trapped within the diving bell. No! We would have returned with the grim fact that we gazed upon a shrivelled corpse." Holmes snapped his fingers. "We would have ruptured the fantasy. The woman has incredible mental powers, certainly—yet she is quite mad."

"So she killed the crew of the *Castor* yesterday?"

"In order to prevent them describing what we, ourselves, now see."

"Holmes, Captain Smeaton claimed they were frightened to death."

"Miss Millwood will have conjured some terrible chimera, no doubt."

"And the shadow that attacked us as we descended?"

"Millwood."

"Then she won't allow us to return to the surface?"

"No, Watson. She will not."

"Therefore, she won't stop at yet more slayings to keep her fantasy alive— that Barstow is immortal?"

"Indubitably. However, we do have recourse to the telephone." He picked up the handset.

"But the woman fell in a dead faint. I checked her myself; she's deeply unconscious."

"My good doctor, I don't doubt your assessment. However, recall the essays of Freud and Jung. Aren't the leviathans of deep waters nothing in comparison to those leviathans of our own subconscious?"

Holmes turned the handle of the telephone apparatus. At that precise instant, a dark shape sped through the field of electric light. This time the walls didn't impede its progress. A monstrous shadow flowed through the iron casing of the diving bell. Instantly it engulfed us. We could barely breathe as tendrils of darkness slipped into our bodies, seeking to occupy every nerve and sinew.

"Watson, I am mistaken! The woman's attacks are far more visceral than I anticipated."

"She's invading the heart. Those men died of heart failure. Ah . . . " A weight appeared to settle onto my ribs. Breathing became harder. My heart thudded, labouring under the influence of that malign spirit. "Holmes, you must tell the . . . the captain to distract her. Her flow of unconscious thought must be disrupted."

Holmes grimaced as he struggled to breathe. "A shock . . . how best to administer a shock?"

"Electricity."

With a huge effort Holmes spoke into the telephone. "Captain Smeaton. Ah . . . I . . . "

"Mr. Holmes?"

"Listen. We will soon be dead. Do as I say . . . uh . . . don't question . . . do you understand?"

"I understand." The man's voice was assured. He would obey.

"Is Millwood there?"

"Yes, she's still unconscious."

"Then rip the power cables from an electrical appliance. Apply the live wire to her temple."

"Mr. Holmes?"

"Do it, man . . . otherwise you haul up two more corpses!"

Then came a wait of many moments. Indeed, a long time seemed to pass. I could no longer move. The shadowy presence coiled about the interior of the diving bell as if it were black smoke. We sagged on the bench, our heartbeats slowing all the time. Another moment passed, another nudge toward death. That shadow was also inside of us, impressing itself on the nerves of the heart.

All of a sudden, a woman's piercing scream erupted from the earpiece of the telephone. Immediately, thereafter, Captain Smeaton thundered: *"Damn you, man, I've done as you asked. But you've made me into a torturer!"*

Instantly, the oppression of my cardiac system lifted. I breathed easily again.

Holmes was once more his vigorous self. "No, Captain. You are no torturer. You are our savior."

I leaned toward the telephone in order to ask, "Is she alive?"

"Yes, Dr. Watson. In fact, the electrical shock has roused her."

The black shadow in the cabin dissipated. I heaved a sigh of relief as I sensed that entity dispel its atoms into the surrounding waters. The diving bell gave a lurch. And it began to rise from the sea bed. The ocean turned lighter. Black gave way to purple, then to blue. Holmes, however, appeared to suddenly descend into an abyss of melancholy.

"We're safe, Holmes. And the mystery is solved."

He nodded.

"Then why, pray, are you so downcast?"

"Watson. I didn't reveal the purpose of my trip to Cornwall. I came here to visit an old friend. You see, his six-year-old daughter is grievously ill. No, I am disingenuous to even myself. The truth of the matter is this: she is dying."

"I am very sorry to hear that, Holmes. But how did that sad state of affairs bring you to investigate this case of the diving bell?"

"An act of desperation on my part." He rested his fingertips together; his eyes became distant. "When I heard the seemingly miraculous story that a man had been rendered somehow immortal I raced here. It occurred to me that Barstow in his diving bell had stumbled upon a remarkable place on the ocean bed that had the power to keep death at bay."

"And you came here for the sake of the little girl?"

"Yes, Watson, but what did I find? A woman who has the power to project a sick fantasy from her mind and cause murder. For a few short hours I had truly believed I might have a distinct chance of saving little Edith's life. However . . . " He gave a long, grave sigh. "Alas, Watson. Alas . . . "

Simon Clark has been a professional author for more than fifteen years. When his first novel, *Nailed by the Heart*, made it through the slush pile in 1994 he banked the advance and embarked upon his dream of becoming a full-time writer. Many dreams and nightmares later he wrote the cult horror-thriller *Blood Crazy*, and other novels including *Death's Dominion*, *Vengeance Child*, and *The Night of the Triffids*, which continues the story of John Wyndham's classic *The Day of the Triffids*. Simon's latest novel is a return to his much-loved Vampyrrhic mythology with *His Vampyrrhic Bride*. Simon lives with his family in the atmospheric, legend-haunted county of Yorkshire. His website is www. nailedbytheheart.com.

The Case: Two elderly men are found dead. Neither have identification. Otherwise, all they seem to have in common is a beautiful young hooker who was nearby when they died.

The Investigator: Tony Foster, one of three practicing wizards in the world and Second Assistant Director of Darkest Night, *the most popular vampire/detective show in syndication.*

SEE ME

Tanya Huff

"Mason, you want to move a bit to the right? We're picking up that very un-Victorian parking sign."

Huddling down inside Raymond Dark's turn-of-the-nineteenth-century greatcoat, Mason Reed shuffled sideways and paused to sniff mournfully before asking, "Here?"

Adam took another look into the monitor. "There's fine. Tony, where's Everett?"

Tony Foster took two wide shots with the digital camera for continuity and said, "He's in the trailer finishing Lee's bruise."

"Right. Okay . . . uh . . . " Adam was obviously looking for Pam, their PA, but Pam had already been sent to the twenty-four-hour drugstore over on Granville to pick up medicine for Mason's cold. He'd already sneezed his fangs out once, and no one wanted to go through that again. Tony grinned as Adam's gaze skirted determinedly past him.

Although he'd been the First Assistant Director since the pilot, this was Adam's first time directing an episode of *Darkest Night*—the most popular vampire/detective show in syndication—and he clearly intended to do everything by the book, including respecting Tony's 2AD status. Or possibly respecting the fact that Tony was one of the world's three practicing wizards. Even if he didn't get a lot of chance to practice given the insane hours his job required.

CB Productions had never had the kind of staffing that allowed for respect.

"I'm done here, Adam. I'll get him."

"If you don't mind . . . "

Chris on camera one made an obscene gesture. "Dude, he's with Lee."

Tony flipped him off as he turned and headed for the trailer that housed makeup, hair, wardrobe, and, once, when the writers were being particularly challenging, three incontinent fruit bats.

Halfway there, he met Everett and Lee heading back.

Everett rolled his eyes and cut Tony off before he got started. "Let me guess, Mason's nose needs powdering."

"It's a little ruddy for one of the bloodsucking undead."

"My sister's wedding is in *four* days," Everett growled, hurrying toward the lights. "I've already rented a tux. If he gives me his cold, I'm putting itching powder in his coffin. And you can quote me on that."

Tony fell into step beside Lee, who, unlike Mason, was dressed in contemporary clothing.

"I get that it's artistic, the real world overlapping Mason's angst-ridden flashback, but, after four seasons, I can safely say that our fans could care less about art and the only overlapping they want to see is James Taylor Grant," he tapped Lee's chest, "climbing into the coffin with Raymond Dark."

"Not going to happen."

"Jealous?"

Tony leaned close, bumping shoulders with the actor. "It's basic geometry. Mason's bigger than me and you and I barely fit." At the time, they'd been pretty sure they weren't coming back for another season and had wanted to go out with a bang. Tony still had trouble believing the show had hung on for four years. He had almost as much trouble believing he and Lee Nicholas had been together for over two years—not exactly out, although their relationship was an open secret in the Vancouver television community.

Their own crew had survived a dark wizard invading from another reality, a night trapped inside a haunted house trying to kill them, and the imminent end of the world by way of an immortal Demongate hired to do some stunt work. Relatively speaking, the 2AD sleeping with the show's second lead wasn't worth noting.

Tony handed Lee off to Adam and headed down the block to check out the alley they'd be using as a location later that night. Stepping off the sidewalk and turning into the space between an electronics store and a legal aid office, he switched over to the gaffers' frequency with one hand as he waved the other in front of his face. "I think we're going to need more lights than Sorge thought, Jason. There's bugger all spill from the . . . "

He paused. Frowned. The victim of the week was an impressive screamer. Pretty much simultaneously, he remembered she wouldn't be arriving for another two hours and realized that the scream had come from in front of him, not behind him.

Had come from deeper within the alley.

"*Tony?*" Adam, in his earbud.

"I'm on it." He was already running, muttering the night-sight spell under his breath. As it took effect, he saw someone standing, someone else lying down, and a broken light over a graffiti-covered door at the alley's dead-end. Still running, he threw a wizard lamp up into it. People would assume electricity.

The someone standing was a woman, mid-twenties maybe, pretty although overly made-up and under-dressed. The someone on the ground was an elderly man and, even at a distance, Tony doubted he'd be getting up again.

"Tony?" Lee, leading the pack running into the alley behind him.

"Call nine-one-one," Tony snapped without turning. He'd have done it himself, but these days it was best to first make sure the screaming was about something the police could handle. Like called to like, as he'd learned the hard way. Having Henry Fitzroy, bastard of Henry VIII, romance writer, *and* vampire based in Vancouver was enough to bring in the fine and freaky. Since Tony had started developing his powers, the freaky vastly outnumbered the fine.

Dropping to one knee beside the body, he checked for a pulse, found nothing, checked for visible wounds, found nothing. The victim wasn't breathing, didn't begin breathing when Tony blew in two lungfuls of air so Tony shifted position and started chest compressions.

One. Two. Three. Four. Five.

A smudge of scarlet lipstick bled into the creases around the old man's mouth.

Six. Seven. Eight. Nine. Ten.

A glance over his shoulder showed Lee comforting the woman, her face pressed into his chest, his arms around her visibly trembling body.

Eleven. Twelve. Thirteen. Fourteen. Fifteen.

The old man was very old, skin pleated into an infinite number of wrinkles, broken capillaries on both cheeks. He had all his hair but it was yellow/white and his teeth made Tony think of skulls.

Sixteen. Seventeen. Eighteen. Nineteen. Twenty.

His clothes belonged on a much younger man and, given what he'd been doing when he died—fly of his jeans gapping open, hooker young enough to be his granddaughter—he was clearly trying too hard.

Twenty-one. Twenty-two. Twenty-three. Twenty-four. Twenty-five.

Where the hell was the cavalry? There'd been a police cruiser at the location. How long did it take them to get out of the car and two blocks down the street?

A flash of navy in the corner of one eye and a competent voice said, "It's okay. I've got him."

Tony rolled up onto his feet as the constable took over, stepping back just in time to see Lee reluctantly allowing the other police officer to lead the woman away.

She was pretty, he could see that objectively, even if, unlike Lee, he'd never been interested in women on a visceral level. Long reddish brown hair around a heart-shaped face, big brown eyes heavily shadowed both by makeup and life, and a wide mouth made slightly lopsided by smudged scarlet gloss. Tears had trailed lines of mascara down both cheeks. Below the neck, the blue mini-dress barely covered enough to be legal and he wondered how she could even walk in the strappy black high heels. She wasn't trying as hard as the old man had been but Tony could see a sad similarity between them.

"She's terrified she's going to be charged with murder." Lee murmured as Tony joined him.

"Death by hand job?"

"Not funny. You don't know that she . . . " When Tony raised an eyebrow, Lee flushed. "Yeah, okay. But it's still not funny. She really is terrified."

"Sorry." Tony moved until they were touching, shoulder to wrist.

The police seemed a lot less sympathetic than Lee had been.

"I'm going to see if she needs help," he said suddenly, striding away before Tony could reply.

"This is not a reason to stop working," Adam called from the sidewalk at the end of the alley.

"Does anyone care that I'm fucking dying over here?" Mason moaned beside him.

Standing at the craft services table, drinking a green tea, and trying very hard to remember that the camera really did put on at least ten pounds, Lee attempted to ignore the jar of licorice rope. The memory of the woman in the blue dress had kept him on edge for two days and he kept reaching for comfort food.

Movement on the sidewalk out beyond the video village caught his eye and, desperate for distraction, Lee gave it his full attention. He'd have liked to have been able to tell Tony later that he was surprised to see the woman in the blue dress again, but he honestly wasn't. Grabbing a muffin and sliding a juice box into his jacket pocket, he picked his way through the cables toward her.

"These are for you." When she looked down at the muffin in her hand, a little confused, Lee added, "The other night, you felt . . . looked like you weren't getting enough to eat."

She had on the same blue dress with a tight black cardigan over it. The extra layer did nothing to mask her body but, he supposed, given her job, that made sense.

"So, the other night, did the police ever charge you?"

"No."

Something in her tone suggested he not ask for details. "Were they able to identify the old man?"

"No." Her hair swept across her shoulders as she shook her head. "I don't think so. They wouldn't tell me anyway, would they?"

"I guess not." He heard a hundred unpleasant encounters with the police in that sentence and he found himself hating the way she seemed to accept it. "I never got your name."

"Valerie."

"I'm Lee."

"I know." She smiled as she gestured behind him at the barely organized chaos of a night shoot.

The smile changed her appearance from attractive to beautiful. Desirable. Lee opened and closed his mouth a few times before managing a slightly choked, "Right. Of course." He glanced down, unable to meet her gaze any longer, noticed her legs were both bare and rising in goose bumps from the cold, looked up to find her watching him, and frowned. "Are you warm enough?"

Expectation changed to confusion and she was merely attractive again. "I'm fine."

"You sure? Because I could . . . "

"Lee!" Pam trotted up, breathing heavily, one hand clamped to her com-tech to keep it from bouncing free. "They're ready for you."

Tony watched Lee take his leave of a familiar hooker and follow Pam onto the section of street standing in for Victorian Vancouver. Tony met him just before he reached his mark and leaned in, one hand resting lightly against the other man's chest. "You okay?"

"I'm fine. I was just talking to . . . "

"I saw."

"Her name's Valerie."

"I know. Police let it drop when they questioned me about finding the body. They didn't charge her."

"Yeah, she said."

"Apparently you don't scream if you've just killed someone and there was still five hundred and twenty-seven dollars in the guy's wallet." Tony frowned "They said there was no ID, though."

Lee frowned as well, a slight dip of dark brows. Not quite enough to wrinkle his forehead. "They said a lot."

Tony shrugged. Past experience had taught him that a lot of cops weren't too concerned about maintaining a hooker's privacy, but he had no intention of getting into that with Lee. "She say why she came by? Are we on her stretch of turf?"

"No." Lee shook his head, careful not to knock James Taylor Grant's hair out of place. "Well, maybe. But I don't think that's why she came by."

"Get a room, you two!" Adam's shout moved them apart. "And Tony, unless you've been cast as Grant's new girlfriend . . . "

"And the Internet goes wild," someone muttered.

" . . . get your ass out of my shot."

Lee handed Tony his green tea, and visibly settled into his character as Tony moved back beside the camera. When he looked for Valerie, she was right where Lee'd left her, cradling the muffin in both hands. Suddenly becoming conscious of Tony's regard, she turned her head slightly and their eyes met.

Tony almost recognized her expression.

"Upon reflection," he said softly to himself, hands wrapped around the warmth of the paper cup, "I don't think that's why she came around either."

"You don't have to come in now, you know." Eyes half closed, Tony stared blearily across the elevator at Lee. Early mornings were not his best time. "Cast call isn't for another hour."

Lee waved it off. "Five thirty, six thirty—they both suck. But my car's back in the shop, it's too early to haul one of the drivers out when you're going in anyway, and once I'm there, I can always grab some shut-eye on the couch."

"I don't know." He sagged against the elevator wall, the stainless steel cold even through three layers of clothing. "We've been seen a lot together lately, and that roommates thing only goes so far."

"Tony, it's five o'clock in the morning, even the paparazzi are still asleep. What's up with you?"

"I've just been thinking about it, that's all. About the choice you're making for . . . " He waggled his coffee between them. " . . . us. And I want you to know that I appreciate it."

"What the fuck brought that on?"

Lee's eyes started to narrow, as if he could read the world *Valerie* in the space between them so Tony hurriedly muttered, "I don't know. Lack of sleep."

After a moment, Lee leaned in, gently bumped the sides of their heads together—a manly embrace for the security cameras—and stepped away as the elevator reached the parking garage. "You're an idiot."

Unlike Lee's expensive hybrid, Tony's elderly car seldom broke down, and Tony gave thanks that his ancient brakes worked as well as they did when he pulled out of the underground garage and nearly ran down a brown-haired woman in a short blue dress.

"Is that . . . ?"

"Yeah, I think it is." Lee twisted in his seat as she disappeared behind a panel van in the small parking lot. "Pull over."

"What?"

"I should talk to her."

"About what?"

"I don't . . . " Sighing, he faced front again. "Doesn't matter. She's gone. Maybe it's the way we met, maybe it's just that she's so vulnerable in spite of . . . everything. I think she needs a friend." When Tony glanced over, Lee was frowning slightly. "There's just something about her, you know?"

"Yeah." Tony could feel her watching from wherever she'd tucked herself and worked very hard at unclenching his jaw. "I know."

Finished at 4:30—almost like a person with a real job—and back home by six, thanks to traffic, Lee sagged against the minivan's seatbelt and muttered, "I should never have gotten rid of the bike."

Richard, CB Productions' senior driver, shrugged as he pulled into the condo's driveway. "Well, you got domestic."

"Jesus, Tony had nothing to do with it." Lee wondered which of them Richard thought had lost their balls. "CB *suggested* the insurance wouldn't cover me if I kept riding."

Richard shrugged again. "Yeah, that's a good reason too. You going to need a ride in tomorrow?"

"No, my car'll be ready in the morning; I'll drive. I've got a late call, it's all Mason and the . . . "

Girl. Woman. She was standing on the other side of the street. Watching him through the breaks in the rush hour traffic. Smiling. Looking good. Looking beautiful. Looking even better than he remembered, actually. The black sweater had fallen open and soft curves filled out the drape of the dress.

"Lee?"

Lee was already out of the car. "Thanks for the ride, Richard."

By the time the traffic cleared and he had a chance to get across the road, she'd disappeared. He crossed anyway, although he had no idea which way she'd gone or what he'd do if he caught up to her. He knew better. He was on a syndicated vampire show, for crying out loud, he'd had crazy stalking fans before. Not as many as Mason, but then, Lee wasn't the one actually wearing the fangs.

He wondered if she was homeless. The unchanging wardrobe suggested as much. There really wasn't much he could do, except give her money, but he found he wanted to do something. Be the hero.

He didn't get much chance to do that these days.

It had been another fifteen-hour day, and all Tony wanted was a chance to spend some time with Lee before falling into bed and starting the whole grind all over again in the morning. The flashing lights on the patrol cars and other emergency vehicles, not to mention the bored looking police officer approaching his car, suggested otherwise.

"Sorry, only residents are allowed into the building right now."

"I live here."

Her gaze flicked down to his car. When it flicked back up, she didn't even pretend to hide her disbelief. "Driver's license, please."

Tony handed it over and stared past her as she checked his name against a list. Two EMTs were rolling an elderly man wearing sweatpants and a UNBC T-shirt out of the building on a stretcher.

Tony knew dead.

He knew freshly dead.

He knew long dead and decaying.

He knew undead.

This guy, he was dead.

"Who is he?" he asked, as a man in a rumpled trench coat zipped up the body bag.

The officer glanced over her shoulder. "No idea, no identification. Custodian found him in the mechanical room." She handed Tony back his license. "ME says natural causes. You're good to go, Mr. Foster."

Lee was distracted that night but hey, dead guy in the mechanical room so Tony figured he had cause.

Hoped that was the cause.

Next morning, when Tony pulled into the studio parking lot, he found himself parking next to Constable Jack Elson's red pickup. Jack had started coming around when a bit player had died under suspicious circumstances, had hung in there when the circumstances had changed from suspicious to really fucking strange, and continued to come around because he was dating the production company's recently promoted office manager. Leaning on the tailgate, he was obviously waiting for Tony.

"Go easy in there," he said, as Tony joined him. "Amy's . . . "

"In a mood?"

"That'll do." Jack rubbed his hand over his head, ruffling his hair up into pale blond spikes. "I had to cancel on her again. I'm working a missing person case and unless he magically appears in the next twenty minutes there's no way I'll be free for lunch." Blue eyes narrowed. "He's not likely to magically appear in the next twenty minutes, is he?"

Tony rolled his eyes. The RCMP constable had been a part of what Amy liked to call "CB Productions and the Attack of the Big Red Demon Thing" where all cards had been laid on the table—and then incinerated—and was remarkably open-minded for a cop, while still managing to maintain his profession's suspicious nature. "Not as far as I know. Why?"

"He was seen four days ago in Gastown. You were in Gastown four days ago. Know a twenty-seven-year-old named Casey Yuen?"

"Name doesn't sound familiar." He rubbed the back of his neck. "You know they . . . well, we found a body in an alley down the street from our shoot?"

"The John Doe? I heard *you* found him. And I checked him out, but he's about seventy years too old."

"They found another elderly John Doe in the mechanical room at Lee's condo last night."

"I heard. You weren't there when it happened."

"You checked?"

Jack shrugged. "Things happen around you. But I also heard it was natural causes both times. And that the first guy's heart had a good reason to give out."

Valerie. Who he'd seen outside their building the morning of the day the old man had died. It hadn't even occurred to him to tie her to the second death until Jack's innuendo.

"The death occurred in the early evening," Jack pointed out after Tony filled him in, "and I think I'd have heard if it was a second death by hand job. That'd make it a pattern and we watch for those."

"Neither man had ID."

"That's not as uncommon as you might think." Jack studied him shrewdly. "I'll check to see if the second body gave any indication of recent sexual activity but I suspect there's another reason your working girl is hanging around. Lee was playing white knight at the scene and she showed up at the shoot later."

"How . . . " Tony cut himself off. "Amy."

Jack shrugged. "All I'm saying is that if the girl was outside your building, odds are good she was there for Lee not because she's been helping absent minded old men die happy."

"I'm not jealous."

"Did I say you were?" But he was thinking it. Tony didn't need to be a wizard to see that on his face. "Look, Tony, old men die. It happens. Sometimes they get confused and wander off without identification. Before he went into the nursing home, we got my granddad an ID bracelet, just in case. But, right now, I'm more concerned about that missing twenty-seven-year-old."

"I could . . . "

"No." Jack held up a hand. "I don't want you out there playing at Sam Spade with a wand. I just wanted to know if you knew him." *If you were involved* said the subtext. "If I run into any weird shit, trust me, I'll call you."

Tony didn't have an office. He had a corner of a table in one end of the soundstage near the carpentry shop where craft services occasionally set out the substantials rather than have cast and crew tromp through the truck. Barricaded in behind a thermos of coffee and a bagel, he alternated between working on a list of what he needed to do before they started the day's shooting and thinking about the woman in the blue dress.

Sure, Lee seemed taken by her, but Tony wasn't jealous.

He was suspicious. Not the same thing.

The old guy in the alley had five hundred and twenty-seven dollars in his wallet and was dressed to score. Tony remembered his initial impression of trying too hard and anyone trying *that* hard—not a lot of eighty-year-olds would shoehorn themselves into a pair of tight, low-slung jeans—hadn't been wandering around randomly.

When he called lunch, Tony reminded everyone to be back in an hour, then told Adam he might be late. That there was something he had to investigate downtown. If Adam believed the investigation was necessary to protect the world from a magical attack, well, Tony wasn't responsible for Adam's misconceptions.

Jack Elson could go fuck himself. Tony wasn't playing at anything. Two men were dead, Valerie had a connection to them both, and she was hanging around Lee.

And he didn't *have* a fucking wand.

The drive into Vancouver from Burnaby wasn't fun, traffic seemed to be insane at any time of the day lately, but Tony wanted the car with him, just in case. In case of what, he had no idea. Stuck behind an accident on McGill Street, he pulled out his phone and realized that of the three people he could call for advice, two of them would be dead to the world—literally—until sunset. His third option, Detective Sergeant Mike Celluci, would likely tell him the same thing Jack had. Stay out of it.

Lee was in it.

So was he.

As the car in front of him started to move, he pocketed his phone and hit the gas.

■ ■ ■

Gastown was a historic district as well as an area the city was fighting to reclaim and, in the middle of the day in late fall, the only people out and about were a few office workers hurrying back from lunch, a couple of bored working girls hoping to pick up some noon trade, and a man wearing a burgundy fake fur coat passed out in a doorway. The alley didn't look any better by daylight.

Tony walked slowly past the graffiti and the dumpster and the other debris he hadn't noticed that night. He walked until he stood on the spot where the old man's body had lain, checked to make sure no one was watching, and held out his left hand. The scar he'd picked up as a souvenir of the night in Caulfield House was red against the paler skin of his palm. The call wasn't specific; he had no idea of where the old man's identification was or even *what* it was exactly, he just knew it had to exist.

That would have to be enough.

Come to me.

It took Tony a few minutes to realize what he was seeing—that the fine, gray powder covering his palm was ash. He traced the silver line back to a crack where the lid of the dumpster didn't quite fit. Watched it sifting out and into his hand. There was quite a little stack of it by the time it finished. Mixed in with the ash were tiny flecks of crumbling plastic and what might have been flecks of rust.

The old man had ID with him. Someone had burned it then dusted it over the garbage in the dumpster. Even if they'd looked, the police would never have found it.

Tony flicked his hand and watched the ash scatter on the breeze.

Most modern identification was made of plastic.

It would take more than a cheap lighter to destroy it so thoroughly.

Lee wasn't exactly surprised to see Valerie standing at the end of the driveway when he headed out to work. He pulled over and unlocked the passenger side door. She stared at him for a long moment through the glass—although, given the tinting, he doubted she could see much—and then, finally, got into the car.

Enclosed, she smelled faintly cinnamon. He loved the smell of cinnamon. Her lips were full and moist, the lower one slightly dimpled in the middle. Her eyes made promises as she said, "I know places we can go where we won't be interrupted."

"That's not why I stopped."

"That's why everyone stops." A deep breath strained the fabric of the dress. "I can give you what you need."

"I have what I need." As a line, it verged on major cheese, but it was true. "What do *you* need?"

"What do I . . . ?" She blinked and the promises were unmade. "No one's ever asked me that before."

"I'm sorry."

She looked startled by the sympathy. He had a feeling no one had ever apologized to her before, either. Slender fingers tugged at the hem of her dress. "I . . . I could use a ride downtown."

"Okay." Lee pulled into traffic. "That's a start."

Amber snapped her gum and pushed stringy hair back off her face. "So you're not a cop?"

"No."

"Or some kind of private dick?"

Tony spread his hands. "I don't even play one on TV."

"Then why are you askin'?" She sagged back against the building and yawned. "You don't look like some kind of religious nutter. What'd this girl do for you that was so fucking great you need to find her?"

"It's not what she did for me . . . "

"Ah." Amber cut him off. "I get it. Jealous boyfriend." She laughed at Tony's expression. "Honey, you haven't looked at my tits once, and even the nutters check the merchandise. And—" her voice picked up a bitter edge "—you turn, just a little, when a car goes by. Enough that a driver could check us both. You've got a history. Afraid he's going to find out about it?"

"He knows."

"Uh huh."

Tony had no idea how this had suddenly become about him. "Look, I just need to find Valerie. Reddish brown hair, short blue dress."

"Black heels? Black sweater, kind of cropped? She just got out of one of them expensive penis-mobiles on the other side of the street," Amber added when he nodded. "At least someone's making the rent today."

Tony turned just in time to see Lee's car disappear around the corner and Valerie walk into a sandwich shop. He shoved the fifty he'd been holding into Amber's hand and ran across Cordova, flipping off the driver of a Mini Cooper who'd hit the horn.

The sandwich shop was empty except for the pock-marked, middle-aged man behind the counter.

"The woman who just came in here, where did she go?"

The man smiled, looking dazed. "I didn't see a woman."

"She just came in here."

His smile broadened. "I didn't see a woman."

The guy was so stoned he wouldn't have seen a parade go through. The only other door was behind the counter. When Tony moved toward it, he found himself blocked.

"Where the fuck do you think you're going?" Counter guy didn't look stoned now, he looked pissed.

"Look, I *need* to find that woman."

And the smile returned. "I didn't see a woman."

It wasn't magic, at least not magic Tony recognized, but it wasn't right.

"I gave her a ride, Tony, what's wrong with that?"

"Nothing's wrong with it." Tony paced the length of Lee's dressing room and back again, wishing he had another ten or twenty meters to cover. "It's just . . . she wants something from you."

Lee rolled his eyes. "No shit. But I'm not going to give it to her. I feel sorry for her. She's in a bad situation." He caught Tony's wrist as he passed and dragged him to a stop. "You should know about that."

Except this *still* wasn't about him. "I think she had something to do with those two deaths."

"Then why did she scream that night in the alley? Why did she scream and attract attention to herself if she had something to do with the guy's death?"

"She screamed because I was already on my way into the alley. She knew she was going to be discovered and screaming would shift suspicion away."

"You have any evidence to support this theory?"

"I found the old man's ID . . . "

"Tell Jack."

"It's been destroyed. I'm guessing that between the time he died and the time she screamed—and he was still warm so that wasn't long—something reduced his ID to a fine ash." Tony twisted out of Lee's grip. "Your average hooker couldn't do that."

"*You* could." From the look on his face, Lee knew exactly how that had sounded. "Look, you have no proof Valerie's involved in anything but bad timing. You're not a detective . . . "

"And you only play one on TV."

"Is this about me? Because I'm paying attention to her? For fuck's sake Tony."

"I saw how she looked at you."

"I'm an actor. Lots of people look at me."

Tony meant to say, *I think you're in danger,* but when he opened his mouth, what came out was, "I saw how you looked at her."

Before Lee could respond, Pam rapped on the dressing room door and called, "They're ready for you on set, Lee."

Lee took a deep breath and shrugged into the overlay of James Taylor Grant. "We're done talking about this," he growled, opened the door, pushed past Pam, and slammed the door so hard two framed photos fell off the wall.

"I think you're in danger," Tony said, staring at the broken glass. "Lee . . ."

"I've got that promo thing tonight." Lee shrugged out of Grant's leather jacket. "With the American affiliates. There's going to be a lot of liquor, so I'll probably get a room at the hotel."

Not the sort of hotel a basic streetwalker could score an entry to. "Okay." Tony held out the next day's sides. "You've got a ten a.m. call tomorrow."

Lee looked down at the paper, up at Tony, closed his eyes for a moment and sighed. "She's very beautiful and I'm not dead but I would never . . ."

"I know." And ninety percent of the time, he did.

If he wanted to talk to a hooker, Tony had to go back to where the hookers were. Back in Gastown, he wrapped himself in a notice-me-not and wandered along the sidewalks, searching for Valerie among the men and women who had nothing left to sell but themselves.

A little voice in the back of his head had started trying to tell him that she was with Lee when he spotted her outside the Gastown Hotel on Water Street. Same blue dress. She was standing by a car. A classic *Chevy Malibu*. Mid-sixties probably, jet black. Tony couldn't see much of the driver except for the full tribal sleeve tattoo on the arm half through the open window.

He was a block away on the wrong side of the street so he started to run. Stopped when she half-turned and looked right at him.

Her eyes widened and he had no doubt she could see him clearly.

As clearly as he could see her. Surrounded by traffic and people, she was entirely alone. Her need to be *seen* hit him so hard it nearly brought him to his knees.

Then she shook her head, got into the car, and by the time he reached the curb in front of the hotel, Tony couldn't tell which set of taillights he needed to follow.

Nine-thirty the next morning, Tony was out in the studio parking lot waiting for Lee, pretending he wasn't. He stepped back as Jack's truck pulled in and then stepped forward again when the constable stopped a mere meter away. "Listen, Tony, can you do me a favor. Tell Amy . . ."

"No."

"I'm just going to be late, that's all. I've got another missing person and my time is fucked."

Tony closed his hand over the edge of the open window. "This missing person, does he own a classic car?"

He got his answer from the look on Jack's face when he pushed up his sunglasses. "Tony?"

"Check around. See if an old John Doe with a tribal sleeve turned up. Left arm."

Jack glanced down at the paperwork on the seat beside him. "My missing person has a tribal sleeve. Left arm." When he looked up, his eyes had narrowed to the point where they were nearly cliché. "What do you know?"

"I spooked her and she got careless." He drew in a deep breath and let it out slowly. "And this isn't a police case."

Jack stared at him for a long moment and finally nodded. "You want me to call you when this old John Doe turns up?"

"You can."

"But I don't need to."

Tony shrugged.

"So while I'm dealing with this case that isn't a police case, what are you going to be doing."

"Research."

"Where do you research *this* kind of shit?"

"I work on a vampire/detective show, Jack." Backing away from the truck, Tony spread his hands. "I'm going to talk to the writers."

Lee half expected Tony to be waiting for him in the parking lot. They were used to spending nights apart—hell, they'd spent five weeks apart during hiatus while he was in South Africa shooting a movie—but this . . . He couldn't fucking believe they were fighting over a woman. Wasn't that what straight guys did?

When Tony finally appeared forty minutes later, Lee stepped toward him only to be yanked back into place by the stunt coordinator.

"Trying to keep you from breaking bones," Daniel growled. "Pay attention."

They moved directly from set-up to rehearsing the fight scene to shooting the fight scene.

By the time Lee was free and the crew had scattered for lunch, Tony was behind closed doors in CB's office.

"How long's he going to be?"

"Jesus, Lee, how should I know." Amy reached under a fall of matte-black hair to adjust her headset. "Stupid PA quit and it's not like I don't have the whole office to . . . " She rolled her eyes as the phone ran. "CB Productions, can I help you?"

His scene later in the day was all weird, esoteric dialogue, the vampire/ detective version of techno babble. He should go to his dressing room and run lines but all Lee could think of was brown eyes and chestnut hair and a blue dress. "I'm done until three. Tell Tony I've gone into downtown."

Amy nodded, rolled her eyes at whatever was being said on the other end of the phone, and waved him toward the door.

Valerie was waiting on the corner of West Cordova and Homer Streets. Well, not waiting for *him* but since he was the one who drove up beside her, Lee figured she might as well have been. "Hey!"

Her smile made him feel immortal.

"You hungry?"

"Hungry?"

Her confusion made him feel like pounding the men who'd all asked her a different question. "You *do* eat, don't you? Come eat with me," he continued, not waiting for an answer. "You and me. Just food. I promise."

"Just food?" She pushed her hair back off her face.

"Lunch." It felt like they were speaking two different languages. "I'll pay for your time, if that's what you're worried about."

"He went where?"

"Downtown."

"Son of a bitch!"

"Hey!" Amy lunged up from behind her desk, grabbed Tony's wrist and hung on. "You want to explain yourself!"

Faster to explain than fight. "Lee's hooker is something like a succubus."

"She's a demon? Tony, do not tell me we're starting that demon shit up again because we barely survived the last time they came visiting!"

"No, I'd know if she was a demon." After Leah and the Demongate, if there was one thing Tony could recognize, it was a demon. "I said she was something *like* a succubus. All her victims are men, probably men sexually attracted to her but . . . " He waved a hand. He didn't have a lot of actual fact although the show's writers had come up with a lot of theories. "Anyway, she's definitely sucking the life out of them and she wants Lee."

"Who doesn't," Amy muttered, using her grip to fling him toward the door. "Don't just stand here talking, move!"

■ ■ ■

The sandwich shop was not the place Lee would have chosen, but Valerie seemed comfortable there, so he tried not to think about health code violations.

"Why don't you want me?"

The upper curve of her breasts was creamy white.

"I do want you."

She gave him a twisted smile and stood. "Then why don't we . . . "

Lee reached out and pulled her back down into her chair, trying not to think about the feel of her skin. "Look, I want to *help* you. You can get out of this life. I know people . . . a person . . . who has."

It wasn't until she glanced down at the bracelet his fingers made around her wrist that he realized he was still holding on. When he let go, she frowned.

"Why are you doing this?"

He shrugged and went with the truth. "I can't stop thinking about you."

She licked her lips and he couldn't look away from the glistening moisture her tongue left on the pink flesh. "We should deal with that."

He gave her back a twisted smile. "I'm trying to."

Her laugh stroked him. "Not what I meant."

"I know. Why are *you* doing this?"

Suddenly, she was only Valerie again. "What?"

"You asked me, I'm asking you."

She stared at him for a long moment, and, just as suddenly, she wasn't Valerie, she wasn't anything he knew. To begin with, she was one hell of a lot older than mid-twenties and when she spoke, her voice sounded as though it came from very far away as well as from inside his head. "I take them into me but it never lasts and I'm alone again."

Over the last few years, Lee had seen a lot of things that terrified him. This wasn't one of them. "*. . . maybe it's just that she's so vulnerable, in spite of . . . everything.*" What he'd said to Tony still stood. A word like *everything* covered a lot of ground.

"You don't have to be alone." And he was back in the sandwich shop again, sitting across a grimy, laminate table from an attractive woman in a blue dress. "I think you could use a friend."

"A friend?" This expression, the staring like she couldn't believe what she was seeing, he recognized although he was usually the one wearing it. "You don't know . . . "

"I have a pretty good idea." He shrugged. "I'm the second lead in a vampire/ detective show. I read some weird shit. Not to mention, my life has gotten interesting lately."

"And you still think we could be friends?" She stared at him like she couldn't believe what she was seeing. All things considered, Lee found that kind of funny. "I'm a . . . "

"Hooker." He grinned when the corner of her mouth twitched. "Yeah. I know people who've got out of . . . *that*."

"That?"

"Something very like that. My partner's ex is kind of . . . " It was as if thinking of Tony magically made him appear. There he was, suddenly standing on the other side of West Cordova and even through the sandwich shop's filthy windows, he looked . . .

Terrified.

"There's something wrong." Lee shoved his chair back and tossed his card onto the table. "That's got my cell number on it. You can call any time. We'll work this out. But I've got to . . . "

"Go."

"Yeah." He gripped her shoulder as he passed, and ran out the door. "Tony!"

Tony'd found the car but he couldn't find Lee and his hand was shaking too much to use his phone and . . .

"Tony!"

He turned in time to see Lee start across the road toward him.

To see the SUV come out of nowhere.

To hear the impact.

To see Lee flung into the air. To see him land crumpled by the curb in a position the living could never hold.

Tony knew dead.

He froze. His heart shattered like Lee had been shattered. Then he took one step. And another.

She reached the body first. Stood there for a moment, searching Tony's face. Then she dropped her knees, gathered Lee up onto her lap and pressed her mouth to his.

"Oh my God! I didn't see him."

Panicked hands grabbed Tony's arms, fingers digging painfully deep in a grip he couldn't break.

"He was just *there*."

All Tony could see was a red face and wide eyes and a mouth that wouldn't stop moving.

"I swear I didn't see him. I wasn't going that fast. He didn't *look*. He was just *there*!"

Then other hands grabbed and other voices started to yell out words that stopped making sense and Tony finally managed to break free.

■ ■ ■

He found Lee sitting on the edge of road, his jeans were torn and there was blood on the denim, blood on his shirt, and a smear of scarlet lipstick on the corner of his mouth.

His heart starting to beat again, Tony bent and picked the blue dress up off the pavement.

Together, they watched a cloud of fine silver ash blow away on the breeze.

Tanya Huff lives in rural Ontario and loves country life. A prolific author, her work includes many short stories, five fantasy series, and a science fiction series. One of these, her Blood Books series, featuring detective Vicki Nelson, was adapted for television under the title *Blood Ties*. A follow-up to the Blood Books, the three Smoke Books, featured Tony Foster as the main character. Her degree in Radio and Television Arts proved handy since Tony works on a show about a vampire detective. Her most recent novel, *The Silvered*, was published in fall 2012. When not writing, she practices her guitar and spends too much time on line. Her blog is: andpuff.livejournal.com.

The Case: *A murdered Chinaman is just the beginning of intrigue involving a unicorn's questionable gift, a notorious madam, and a pushy little sorceress.*

The Investigator: *Natalie Beaumont, a hard-boiled used bookstore owner with a knack for finding things.*

THE MALTESE UNICORN

Caitlín R. Kiernan

New York City (May 1935)

It wasn't hard to find her. Sure, she had run. After Szabó let her walk like that, I knew Ellen would get wise that something was rotten, and she'd run like a scared rabbit with the dogs hot on its heels. She'd have it in her head to skip town, and she'd probably keep right on skipping until she was out of the country. Odds were pretty good she wouldn't stop until she was altogether free and clear of this particular plane of existence. There are plenty enough fetid little hidey holes in the universe, if you don't mind the heat and the smell and the company you keep. You only have to know how to find them, and the way I saw it, Ellen Andrews was good as Rand and McNally when it came to knowing her way around. But first, she'd go back to that apartment of hers, the whole eleventh floor of the Colosseum, with its bleak westward view of the Hudson River and the New Jersey Palisades. I figured there would be those two or three little things she couldn't leave the city without, even if it meant risking her skin to collect them. Only she hadn't expected me to get there before her. Word on the street was Harpootlian still had me locked up tight, so Ellen hadn't expected me to get there at all.

From the hall came the buzz of the elevator, then I heard her key in the lock, the front door, and her footsteps as she hurried through the foyer and the dining room. Then she came dashing into that French rococo nightmare of a library, and stopped cold in her tracks when she saw me sitting at the reading table with al-Jaldaki's grimoire open in front of me.

For a second, she didn't say anything. She just stood there, staring at me. Then she managed a forced sort of laugh and said, "I knew they'd send someone, Nat. I just didn't think it'd be you."

"After that gyp you pulled with the dingus, they didn't really leave me much choice," I told her, which was the truth, or all the truth I felt like sharing. "You shouldn't have come back here. It's the first place anyone would think to check."

Ellen sat down in the armchair by the door. She looked beat, like whatever comes after exhausted, and I could tell Szabó's gunsels had made sure all the fight was gone before they'd turned her loose. They weren't taking any chances, and we were just going through the motions now, me and her. All our lines had been written.

"You played me for a sucker," I said, and picked up the pistol that had been lying beside the grimoire. My hand was shaking, and I tried to steady it by bracing my elbow against the table. "You played me, then you tried to play Harpootlian and Szabó both. Then you got caught. It was a bonehead move all the way round, Ellen."

"So, how's it gonna be, Natalie? You gonna shoot me for being stupid?"

"No, I'm going to shoot you because it's the only way I can square things with Auntie H., and the only thing that's gonna keep Szabó from going on the warpath. And because you played me."

"In my shoes, you'd have done the same thing," she said. And the way she said it, I could tell she believed what she was saying. It's the sort of self-righteous bushwa so many grifters hide behind. They might stab their own mothers in the back if they see an angle in it, but that's jake, 'cause so would anyone else.

"Is that really all you have to say for yourself?" I asked, and pulled back the slide on the Colt, chambering the first round. She didn't even flinch . . . But, wait . . . I'm getting ahead of myself. Maybe I ought to begin nearer the beginning.

As it happens, I didn't go and name the place Yellow Dragon Books. It came with that moniker, and I just never saw any reason to change it. I'd only have had to pay for a new sign. Late in '28—right after Arnie "The Brain" Rothstein was shot to death during a poker game at the Park Central Hotel—I *accidentally* found myself on the sunny side of the proprietress of one of Manhattan's more infernal brothels. I say accidentally because I hadn't even heard of Madam Yeksabet Harpootlian when I began trying to dig up a buyer for an antique manuscript, a collection of necromantic erotica purportedly written by John Dee and Edward Kelley sometime in the sixteenth century. Turns out, Harpootlian had been looking to get her mitts on it for decades.

Now, just how I came into possession of said manuscript, that's another story entirely, one for some other time and place. One that, with luck, I'll never get around to putting down on paper. Let's just say a couple of years earlier, I'd been living in Paris. Truthfully, I'd been doing my best, in a sloppy, irresolute way, to *die* in Paris. I was holed up in a fleabag Montmartre boarding house, busy squandering the last of a dwindling inheritance. I had in mind how maybe I could drown myself in cheap wine, bad poetry, Pernod, and prostitutes before the money ran out. But somewhere along the way, I lost my nerve, failed at my slow suicide, and bought a ticket back to the States. And the manuscript in question was one of the many strange and unsavory things I brought back with me. I've always had a nose for the macabre, and had dabbled—on and off—in the black arts since college. At Radcliffe, I'd fallen in with a circle of lesbyterians who fancied themselves witches. Mostly, I was in it for the sex . . . But I'm digressing.

A friend of a friend heard I was busted, down and out and peddling a bunch of old books, schlepping them about Manhattan in search of a buyer. This same friend, he knew one of Harpootlian's clients. One of her *human* clients, which was a pretty exclusive set (not that I knew that at the time). This friend of mine, he was the client's lover, and said client brokered the sale for Harpootlian—for a fat ten percent finder's fee, of course. I promptly sold the Dee and Kelley manuscript to this supposedly notorious madam who, near as I could tell, no one much had ever heard of. She paid me what I asked, no questions, no haggling—never mind it was a fairly exorbitant sum. And on top of that, Harpootlian was so impressed I'd gotten ahold of the damned thing, she staked me to the bookshop on Bowery, there in the shadow of the Third Avenue El, just a little ways south of Delancey Street. Only one catch: she had first dibs on everything I ferreted out, and sometimes I'd be asked to make deliveries. I should like to note that way back then, during that long, lost November of 1928, I had no idea whatsoever that her sobriquet, "the Demon Madam of the Lower East Side," was anything more than colorful hyperbole.

Anyway, jump ahead to a rainy May afternoon, more than six years later, and that's when I first laid eyes on Ellen Andrews. Well, that's what she called herself, though later on I'd find out she'd borrowed the name from Claudette Colbert's character in *It Happened One Night*. I was just back from an estate sale in Connecticut, and was busy unpacking a large crate when I heard the bell mounted above the shop door jingle. I looked up, and there she was, carelessly shaking rainwater from her orange umbrella before folding it closed. Droplets sprayed across the welcome mat and the floor and onto the spines of several nearby books.

"Hey, be careful," I said, "unless you intend to pay for those." I jabbed a thumb at the books she'd spattered. She promptly stopped shaking the umbrella and dropped it into the stand beside the door. That umbrella stand has always been one of my favorite things about the Yellow Dragon. It's made from the taxidermied foot of a hippopotamus, and accommodates at least a dozen umbrellas, although I don't think I've ever seen even half that many people in the shop at one time.

"Are you Natalie Beaumont?" she asked, looking down at her wet shoes. Her overcoat was dripping, and a small puddle was forming about her feet.

"Usually."

"Usually," she repeated. "How about right now?"

"Depends whether or not I owe you money," I replied, and removed a battered copy of Blavatsky's *Isis Unveiled* from the crate. "Also, depends whether you happen to be *employed* by someone I owe money."

"I see," she said, as if that settled the matter, then proceeded to examine the complete twelve-volume set of *The Golden Bough* occupying a top shelf not far from the door. "Awful funny sort of neighborhood for a bookstore, if you ask me."

"You don't think bums and winos read?"

"You ask me, people down here," she said, "they panhandle a few cents, I don't imagine they spend it on books."

"I don't recall asking for your opinion," I told her.

"No," she said. "You didn't. Still, queer sort of a shop to come across in this part of town."

"If you must know," I said, "the rent's cheap," then reached for my spectacles, which were dangling from their silver chain about my neck. I set them on the bridge of my nose, and watched while she feigned interest in Frazerian anthropology. It would be an understatement to say Ellen Andrews was a pretty girl. She was, in fact, a certified knockout, and I didn't get too many beautiful women in the Yellow Dragon, even when the weather was good. She wouldn't have looked out of place in Flo Ziegfeld's follies; on the Bowery, she stuck out like a sore thumb.

"Looking for anything in particular?" I asked her, and she shrugged.

"Just you," she said.

"Then I suppose you're in luck."

"I suppose I am," she said, and turned toward me again. Her eyes glinted red, just for an instant, like the eyes of a Siamese cat. I figured it for a trick of the light. "I'm a friend of Auntie H. I run errands for her, now and then. She needs you to pick up a package and see it gets safely where it's going."

So, there it was. Madam Harpootlian, or Auntie H. to those few unfortunates she called her friends. And suddenly it made a lot more sense, this choice bit of calico walking into my place, strolling in off the street like maybe she did all her shopping down on Skid Row. I'd have to finish unpacking the crate later. I stood up and dusted my hands off on the seat of my slacks.

"Sorry about the confusion," I said, even if I wasn't actually sorry, even if I was actually kind of pissed the girl hadn't told me who she was right up front. "When Auntie H. wants something done, she doesn't usually bother sending her orders around in such an attractive envelope."

The girl laughed, then said, "Yeah, Auntie H. warned me about you, Miss Beaumont."

"Did she now. How so?"

"You know, your predilections. How you're not like other women."

"I'd say that depends on which other women we're discussing, don't you think?"

"*Most* other women," she said, glancing over her shoulder at the rain pelting the shop windows. It sounded like frying meat out there, the sizzle of the rain against asphalt, and concrete, and the roofs of passing automobiles.

"And what about you?" I asked her. "Are *you* like most other women?"

She looked away from the window, back at me, and she smiled what must have been the faintest smile possible.

"Are you always this charming?"

"Not that I'm aware of," I said. "Then again, I never took a poll."

"The job, it's nothing particularly complicated," she said, changing the subject. "There's a Chinese apothecary not too far from here."

"That doesn't exactly narrow it down," I said, and lit a cigarette.

"Sixty-five Mott Street. The joint's run by an elderly Cantonese fellow name of Fong."

"Yeah, I know Jimmy Fong."

"That's good. Then maybe you won't get lost. Mr. Fong will be expecting you, and he'll have the package ready at five thirty this evening. He's already been paid in full, so all you have to do is be there to receive it, right? And Miss Beaumont, please try to be on time. Auntie H. said you have a problem with punctuality."

"You believe everything you hear?"

"Only if I'm hearing it from Auntie H."

"Fair enough," I told her, then offered her a Pall Mall, but she declined.

"I need to be getting back," she said, reaching for the umbrella she'd only just deposited in the stuffed hippopotamus foot.

"What's the rush? What'd you come after, anyway, a ball of fire?"

She rolled her eyes. "I got places to be. You're not the only stop on my itinerary."

"Fine. Wouldn't want you getting in Dutch with Harpootlian on my account. Don't suppose you've got a name?"

"I might," she said.

"Don't suppose you'd share?" I asked her, and took a long drag on my cigarette, wondering why in blue blazes Harpootlian had sent this smart-mouthed skirt instead of one of her usual flunkies. Of course, Auntie H. always did have a sadistic streak to put de Sade to shame, and likely as not this was her idea of a joke.

"Ellen," the girl said. "Ellen Andrews."

"So, Ellen Andrews, how is it we've never met? I mean, I've been making deliveries for your boss lady now going on seven years, and if I'd seen you, I'd remember. You're not the sort I forget."

"You got the moxie, don't you?"

"I'm just good with faces is all."

She chewed at a thumbnail, as if considering carefully what she should or shouldn't divulge. Then she said, "I'm from out of town, mostly. Just passing through, and thought I'd lend a hand. That's why you've never seen me before, Miss Beaumont. Now, I'll let you get back to work. And remember, don't be late."

"I heard you the first time, sister."

And then she left, and the brass bell above the door jingled again. I finished my cigarette and went back to unpacking the big crate of books from Connecticut. If I hurried, I could finish the job before heading for Chinatown.

She was right, of course. I did have a well-deserved reputation for not being on time. But I knew that Auntie H. was of the opinion that my acumen in antiquarian and occult matters more than compensated for my not-infrequent tardiness. I've never much cared for personal mottos, but if I had one it might be, *You want it on time, or you want it done right?* Still, I honestly tried to be on time for the meeting with Fong. And still, through no fault of my own, I was more than twenty minutes late. I was lucky enough to find a cab, despite the rain, but then got stuck behind some sort of brouhaha after turning onto Canal, so there you go. It's not like old man Fong had any place more pressing to be, not like he was gonna get pissy and leave me high and dry.

When I got to 65 Mott, the Chinaman's apothecary was locked up tight, all the lights were off, and the "Sorry, We're Closed" sign was hung in the front window. No big surprise there. But then I went around back, to the alley, and found a door standing wide open and quite a lot of fresh blood on the cinderblock steps leading into the building. Now, maybe I was the only lady bookseller in Manhattan who carried a gun, and maybe I wasn't. But times like that, I was glad to have the Colt tucked snugly inside its shoulder holster, and happier still that I knew how to use it. I took a deep breath, drew the pistol, flipped off the safety catch, and stepped inside.

The door opened onto a stockroom, and the tiny nook Jimmy Fong used as his office was a little farther in, over on my left. There was some light from a banker's lamp, but not much of it. I lingered in the shadows a moment, waiting for my heart to stop pounding, for the adrenaline high to fade. The air was close, and stunk of angelica root and dust, ginger and frankincense and fuck only knows what else. Powdered rhino horn and the pickled gallbladders of panda bears. What the hell ever. I found the old man slumped over at his desk.

Whoever knifed him hadn't bothered to pull the shiv out of his spine, and I wondered if the poor SOB had even seen it coming. It didn't exactly add up, not after seeing all that blood drying on the steps, but I figured, hey, maybe the killer was the sort of klutz can't spread butter without cutting himself. I had a quick look-see around the cluttered office, hoping I might turn up the package Ellen Andrews had sent me there to retrieve. But no dice, and then it occurred to me: maybe whoever had murdered Fong had come looking for the same thing I was looking for. Maybe they'd found it, too, only Fong knew better than to just hand it over, and that had gotten him killed. Anyway, nobody was paying me to play junior shamus; hence the hows, whys, and wherefores of the Chinaman's death were not my problem. My problem would be showing up at Harpootlian's cathouse empty handed.

I returned the gun to its holster, then I started rifling through everything in sight—the great disarray of papers heaped upon the desk, Fong's accounting ledgers, sales invoices, catalogs, letters, and postcards written in English, Mandarin, Wu, Cantonese, French, Spanish, and Arabic. I still had my gloves on, so it's not like I had to worry over fingerprints. A few of the desk drawers were unlocked, and I'd just started in on those, when the phone perched atop the filing cabinet rang. I froze, whatever I was looking at clutched forgotten in my hands, and stared at the phone.

Sure, it wasn't every day I blundered into the immediate aftermath of this sort of foul play, but I was plenty savvy enough; I knew better than to answer that call. It didn't much matter who was on the other end of the line. If I answered, I could be placed at the scene of a murder only minutes after it had gone down. The phone rang a second time, and a third, and I glanced at the dead man in the chair. The crimson halo surrounding the switchblade's inlaid mother-of-pearl handle was still spreading, blossoming like some grim rose, and now there was blood dripping to the floor, as well. The phone rang a fourth time. A fifth. And then I was seized by an overwhelming compulsion to answer it, and answer it I did. I wasn't the least bit thrown that the voice coming through the receiver was Ellen Andrews's. All at once, the pieces were falling into place. You spend enough years doing the step-and-fetch-it routine for imps like Harpootlian, you find yourself ever more jaded at the inexplicable and the uncanny.

"Beaumont," she said, "I didn't think you were going to pick up."

"I wasn't. Funny thing how I did anyway."

"Funny thing," she said, and I heard her light a cigarette and realized my hands were shaking.

"See, I'm thinking maybe I had a little push," I said. "That about the size of it?"

"Wouldn't have been necessary if you'd have just answered the damn phone in the first place."

"You already know Fong's dead, don't you?" And, I swear to fuck, nothing makes me feel like more of a jackass than asking questions I know the answers to.

"Don't you worry about Fong. I'm sure he had all his ducks in a row and was right as rain with Buddha. I need you to pay attention—"

"Harpootlian had him killed, didn't she? And you knew he'd be dead when I showed up."

She didn't reply straight away, and I thought I could hear a radio playing in the background. "You knew," I said again, only this time it wasn't a query.

"Listen," she said. "You're a courier. I was told you're a courier we can trust, elsewise I never would have handed you this job."

"You didn't hand me the job. Your boss did."

"You're splitting hairs, Miss Beaumont."

"Yeah, well, there's a fucking dead celestial in the room with me. It's giving me the fidgets."

"So how about you shut up and listen, and I'll have you out of there in a jiffy." And that's what I did—I shut up, either because I knew it was the path of least resistance, or because whatever spell she'd used to persuade me to answer the phone was still working.

"On Fong's desk, there's a funny little porcelain statue of a cat."

"You mean the maneki neko?"

"If that's what it's called, that's what I mean. Now, break it open. There's a key inside."

I tried not to, just to see if I was being played as badly as I suspected I was being played. I gritted my teeth, dug in my heels, and tried hard not to break that damned cat.

"You're wasting time. Auntie H. didn't mention you were such a crybaby."

"Auntie H. and I have an agreement when it comes to free will. To *my* free will."

"*Break the goddamn cat*," Ellen Andrews growled, and that's exactly what I did. In fact, I slammed it down directly on top of Fong's head. Bits of brightly painted porcelain flew everywhere, and a rusty barrel key tumbled out and landed at my feet. "Now pick it up," she said. "The key fits the bottom left-hand drawer of Fong's desk. Open it."

This time, I didn't even try to resist her. I was getting a headache from the last futile attempt. I unlocked the drawer and pulled it open. Inside, there was nothing but the yellowed sheet of newspaper lining the drawer, three golf balls, a couple of old racing forms, and a finely carved wooden box lacquered almost the same shade of red as Jimmy Fong's blood. I didn't need to be told I'd been sent to retrieve the box—or, more specifically, whatever was inside the box.

"Yeah, I got it," I told Ellen Andrews.

"Good girl. Now, you have maybe twelve minutes before the cops show. Go out the same way you came in." Then she gave me a Riverside Drive address, and said there'd be a car waiting for me at the corner of Canal and Mulberry, a green Chevrolet coupe. "Just give the driver that address. He'll see you get where you're going."

"Yeah," I said, sliding the desk drawer shut again and locking it. I pocketed the key. "But, sister, you and me are gonna have a talk."

"Wouldn't miss it for the world, Nat," she said and hung up. I shut my eyes, wondering if I really had twelve minutes before the bulls arrived, and if they were even on their way, wondering what would happen if I endeavored not to make the rendezvous with the green coupe. I stood there, trying to decide whether Harpootlian would have gone back on her word and given this bitch permission to turn her hoodoo tricks on me, and if aspirin would do anything at all for the dull throb behind my eyes. Then I looked at Fong one last time, at the knife jutting out of his back, his thin gray hair powdered with porcelain dust from the shattered "lucky cat." And then I stopped asking questions and did as I'd been told.

The car was there, just like she'd told me it would be. There was a young colored man behind the wheel, and when I climbed in the back, he asked me where we were headed.

"I'm guessing Hell," I said, "sooner or later."

"Got that right," he laughed and winked at me from the rearview mirror. "But I was thinking more in terms of the immediate here and now."

So I recited the address I'd been given over the phone, 435 Riverside.

"That's the Colosseum," he said.

"It is if you say so," I replied. "Just get me there."

The driver nodded and pulled away from the curb. As he navigated the slick, wet streets, I sat listening to the rain against the Chevy's hardtop and the music coming from the Motorola. In particular, I can remember hearing the Dorsey Brothers, "Chasing Shadows." I suppose you'd call that a harbinger, if you go in for that sort of thing. Me, I do my best not to. In this business, you start jumping at everything that might be an omen or a portent, you end up doing nothing else. Ironically, rubbing shoulders with the supernatural has made me a great believer in coincidence.

Anyway, the driver drove, the radio played, and I sat staring at the red lacquered box I'd stolen from a dead man's locked desk drawer. I thought it might be mahogany, but it was impossible to be sure, what with all that cinnabar-tinted varnish. I know enough about Chinese mythology that I recognized the strange creature carved into the top—a *qilin*, a stout, antlered beast with cloven hooves, the scales of a dragon, and a long leonine tail. Much of its body was wreathed in flame, and its gaping jaws revealed teeth like daggers. For the Chinese, the *qilin* is a harbinger of good fortune, though it certainly hadn't worked out that way for Jimmy Fong. The box was heavier than it looked, most likely because of whatever was stashed inside. There was no latch, and as I examined it more closely, I realized there was no sign whatsoever of hinges or even a seam to indicate it actually had a lid.

"Unless I got it backwards," the driver said, "Miss Andrews didn't say nothing about trying to open that box, now did she?"

I looked up, startled, feeling like the proverbial kid caught with her hand in the cookie jar. He glanced at me in the mirror, then his eyes drifted back to the road.

"She didn't say one way or the other," I told him.

"Then how about we err on the side of caution?"

"So you didn't know where you're taking me, but you know I shouldn't open this box? How's that work?"

"Ain't the world just full of mysteries," he said.

For a minute or so, I silently watched the headlights of the oncoming traffic and the metronomic sweep of the windshield wipers. Then I asked the driver how long he'd worked for Ellen Andrews.

"Not very," he said. "Never laid eyes on the lady before this afternoon. Why you want to know?"

"No particular reason," I said, looking back down at the box and the *qilin* etched in the wood. I decided I was better off not asking any more questions, better off getting this over and done with, and never mind what did and didn't quite add up. "Just trying to make conversation; that's all."

Which got him to talking about the Chicago stockyards and Cleveland and how it was he'd eventually wound up in New York City. He never told me his name, and I didn't ask. The trip uptown seemed to take forever, and the longer

I sat with that box in my lap, the heavier it felt. I finally moved it, putting it down on the seat beside me. By the time we reached our destination, the rain had stopped and the setting sun was showing through the clouds, glittering off the dripping trees in Riverside Park and the waters of the wide gray Hudson. He pulled over, and I reached for my wallet.

"No, ma'am," he said, shaking his head. "Miss Andrews, she's already seen to your fare."

"Then I hope you won't mind if I see to your tip," I said, and I gave him five dollars. He thanked me, and I took the wooden box and stepped out onto the wet sidewalk.

"She's up on the eleventh," he told me, nodding toward the apartments. Then he drove off, and I turned to face the imposing brick-and-limestone façade of the building the driver had called the Colosseum. I rarely find myself any farther north than the Upper West Side, so this was pretty much terra incognita for me.

The doorman gave me directions, *after* giving me and Fong's box the hairy eyeball, and I quickly made my way to the elevators, hurrying through that ritzy marble sepulcher passing itself off as a lobby. When the operator asked which floor I needed, I told him the eleventh, and he shook his head and muttered something under his breath. I almost asked him to speak up, but thought better of it. Didn't I already have plenty enough on my mind without entertaining the opinions of elevator boys? Sure, I did. I had a murdered Chinaman, a mysterious box, and this pushy little sorceress calling herself Ellen Andrews. I also had an especially disagreeable feeling about this job, and the sooner it was settled, the better. I kept my eyes on the brass needle as it haltingly swung from left to right, counting off the floors, and when the doors parted, she was there waiting for me. She slipped the boy a sawbuck, and he stuffed it into his jacket pocket and left us alone.

"So nice to see you again, Nat," she said, but she was looking at the lacquered box, not me. "Would you like to come in and have a drink? Auntie H. says you have a weakness for rye whiskey."

"Well, she's right about that. But just now, I'd be more fond of an explanation."

"How odd," she said, glancing up at me, still smiling. "Auntie said one thing she liked about you was how you didn't ask a lot of questions. Said you were real good at minding your own business."

"Sometimes I make exceptions."

"Let me get you that drink," she said, and I followed her the short distance from the elevator to the door of her apartment. Turns out, she had the whole floor to herself, each level of the Colosseum being a single apartment. Pretty ritzy accommodations, I thought, for someone who was mostly from out of town. But then, I've spent the last few years living in that one-bedroom cracker box above the Yellow Dragon—hot and cold running cockroaches and so forth. She locked the door behind us, then led me through the foyer to a parlor. The whole place was done up gaudy period French, Louis Quinze and the like, all floral brocade and orientalia. The walls were decorated with damask hangings, mostly of ample-bosomed women reclining in pastoral scenes, dogs and sheep and what have you lying at their feet. Ellen told me to have a seat, so I parked myself on a récamier near a window.

"Harpootlian spring for this place?" I asked.

"No," she replied. "It belonged to my mother."

"So, you come from money."

"Did I mention how you ask an awful lot of questions?"

"You might have," I said, and she inquired as to whether I liked my whiskey neat or on the rocks. I told her neat, and set the red box down on the sofa next to me.

"If you're not *too* thirsty, would you mind if I take a peek at that first," she said, pointing at the box.

"Be my guest," I said, and Ellen smiled again. She picked up the red lacquered box, then sat next to me. She cradled it in her lap, and there was this goofy expression on her face, a mix of awe, dread, and eager expectation.

"Must be something extra damn special," I said, and she laughed. It was a nervous kind of a laugh.

I've already mentioned how I couldn't discern any evidence the box had a lid, and I supposed there was some secret to getting it open, a gentle squeeze or nudge in just the right spot. Turns out, all it needed was someone to say the magic words.

"*Pain had no sting, and pleasure's wreath no flower,*" she said, speaking slowly and all but whispering the words. There was a sharp click and the top of the box suddenly slid back with enough force that it tumbled over her knees and fell to the carpet.

"Keats," I said.

"Keats," she echoed, but added nothing more. She was too busy gazing at what lay inside the box, nestled in a bed of velvet the color of poppies. She started to touch it, then hesitated, her fingertips hovering an inch or so above the object.

"You're fucking kidding me," I said, once I saw what was inside.

"Don't go jumping to conclusions, Nat."

"It's a dildo," I said, probably sounding as incredulous as I felt. "Exactly which conclusions am I not supposed to jump to? Sure, I enjoy a good rub-off as much as the next girl, but . . . you're telling me Harpootlian killed Fong over a dildo?"

"I never said Auntie H. killed Fong."

"Then I suppose he stuck that knife there himself."

And that's when she told me to shut the hell up for five minutes, if I knew how. She reached into the box and lifted out the phallus, handling it as gingerly as somebody might handle a stick of dynamite. But whatever made the thing special, it wasn't anything I could see.

"*Le godemiché maudit,*" she murmured, her voice so filled with reverence you'd have thought she was holding the devil's own wang. Near as I could tell, it was cast from some sort of hard black ceramic. It glistened faintly in the light getting in through the drapes. "I'll tell you about it," she said, "if you really want to know. I don't see the harm."

"Just so long as you get to the part where it makes sense that Harpootlian bumped the Chinaman for this dingus of yours, then sure."

She took her eyes off the thing long enough to scowl at me. "Auntie H. didn't kill Fong. One of Szabó's goons did that, then panicked and ran before he figured out where the box was hidden."

(Now, as for Madam Magdalena Szabó, the biggest boil on Auntie H.'s fanny, we'll get back to her by and by.)

"Ellen, how can you *possibly* fucking know that? Better yet, how could you've known Szabó's man would have given up and cleared out by the time I arrived?"

"Why did you answer that phone, Nat?" she asked, and that shut me up, good and proper. "As for our prize here," she continued, "it's a long story, a long story with a lot of missing pieces. The dingus, as you put it, is usually called *le godemiché maudit*. Which doesn't necessarily mean it's actually cursed, mind you. Not literally. You do speak French, I assume?"

"Yeah," I told her. "I do speak French."

"That's ducky, Nat. Now, here's about as much as anyone could tell you. Though, frankly, I'd have thought a scholarly type like yourself would know all about it."

"Never said I was a scholar," I interrupted.

"But you went to college. Radcliffe, class of 1923, right? Graduated with honors."

"Lots of people go to college. Doesn't necessarily make them scholars. I just sell books."

"My mistake," she said, carefully returning the black dildo to its velvet case. "It won't happen again." Then she told me her tale, and I sat there on the récamier and listened to what she had to say. Yeah, it was long. There were certainly a whole lot of missing pieces. And as a wise man once said, this might not be schoolbook history, not Mr. Wells's history, but, near as I've been able to discover since that evening at her apartment, it's history, nevertheless. She asked me whether or not I'd ever heard of a fourteenth-century Persian alchemist named al-Jaldaki, Izz al-Din Aydamir al-Jaldaki, and I had, of course.

"He's sort of a hobby of mine," she said. "Came across his grimoire a few years back. Anyway, he's not where it begins, but that's where the written record starts. While studying in Anatolia, al-Jaldaki heard tales of a fabulous artifact that had been crafted from the horn of a unicorn at the behest of King Solomon."

"From a unicorn," I cut in. "So we believe in those now, do we?"

"Why not, Nat? I think it's safe to assume you've seen some peculiar shit in your time, that you've pierced the veil, so to speak. Surely a unicorn must be small potatoes for a worldly woman like yourself."

"So you'd think," I said.

"Anyhow," she went on, "the ivory horn was carved into the shape of a penis by the king's most skilled artisans. Supposedly, the result was so revered it was even placed in Solomon's temple, alongside the Ark of the Covenant and a slew of other sacred Hebrew relics. Records al-Jaldaki found in a mosque in the Taurus Mountains indicated that the horn had been removed from Solomon's temple when it was sacked in 587 BC by the Babylonians, and that eventually it had gone to Medina. But it was taken from Medina during or shortly after the siege of 627, when the Meccans invaded. And it's at this point that the horn is believed to have been given its ebony coating of porcelain enamel, possibly in an attempt to disguise it."

"Or," I said, "because someone in Medina preferred swarthy cock. You mind if I smoke?" I asked her, and she shook her head and pointed at an ashtray.

"A Medinan rabbi of the Banu Nadir tribe was entrusted with the horn's safety. He escaped, making his way west across the desert to Yanbu' al Bahr, then north along the al-Hejaz all the way to Jerusalem. But two years later, when the Sassanid army lost control of the city to the Byzantine emperor Heraclius, the horn was taken to a monastery in Malta, where it remained for centuries."

"That's quite a saga for a dildo. But you still haven't answered my question. What makes it so special? What the hell's it *do*?"

"Maybe you've heard enough," she said, and this whole time she hadn't taken her eyes off the thing in the box.

"Yeah, and maybe I haven't," I told her, tapping ash from my Pall Mall into the ashtray. "So, al-Jaldaki goes to Malta and finds the big black dingus."

She scowled again. No, it was more than a scowl; she *glowered*, and she looked away from the box just long enough to glower at me. "Yes," Ellen Andrews said. "At least, that's what he wrote. Al-Jaldaki found it buried in the ruins of a monastery in Malta, and then carried the horn with him to Cairo.

It seems to have been in his possession until his death in 1342. After that it disappeared, and there's no word of it again until 1891."

I did the math in my head. "Five hundred and forty-nine years," I said. "So it must have gone to a good home. Must have lucked out and found itself a long-lived and appreciative keeper."

"The Freemasons might have had it," she went on, ignoring or oblivious to my sarcasm. "Maybe the Vatican. Doesn't make much difference."

"Okay. So what happened in 1891?"

"A party in Paris, in an old house not far from the Cimetière du Montparnasse. Not so much a party, really, as an out-and-out orgy, the way the story goes. This was back before Montparnasse became so fashionable with painters and poets and expatriate Americans. Verlaine was there, though. At the orgy, I mean. It's not clear what happened precisely, but three women died, and afterward there were rumors of black magic and ritual sacrifice, and tales surfaced of a cult that worshiped some sort of demonic objet d'art that had made its way to France from Egypt. There was an official investigation, naturally, but someone saw to it that *la préfecture de police* came up with zilch."

"Naturally," I said. I glanced at the window. It was getting dark, and I wondered if my ride back to the Bowery had been arranged. "So, where's Black Beauty here been for the past forty-four years?"

Ellen leaned forward, reaching for the lid to the red lacquered box. When she set it back in place, covering that brazen scrap of antiquity, I heard the *click* again as the lid melded seamlessly with the rest of the box. Now there was only the etching of the *qilin*, and I remembered that the beast had sometimes been referred to as the "Chinese unicorn." It seemed odd I'd not thought of that before.

"I think we've probably had enough of a history lesson for now," she said, and I didn't disagree. Truth be told, the whole subject was beginning to bore me. It hardly mattered whether or not I believed in unicorns or enchanted dildos. I'd done my job, so there'd be no complaints from Harpootlian. I admit I felt kind of shitty about poor old Fong, who wasn't such a bad sort. But when you're an errand girl for the wicked folk, that shit comes with the territory. People get killed, and worse.

"It's getting late," I said, crushing out my cigarette in the ashtray. "I should dangle."

"Wait. Please. I promised you a drink, Nat. Don't want you telling Auntie H. I was a bad hostess, now do I?" And Ellen Andrews stood up, the red box tucked snugly beneath her left arm.

"No worries, kiddo," I assured her. "If she ever asks, which I doubt, I'll say you were a regular Emily Post."

"I insist," she replied. "I really, truly do," and before I could say another word, she turned and rushed out of the parlor, leaving me alone with all that furniture and the buxom giantesses watching me from the walls. I wondered if there were any servants, or a live-in beau, or if possibly she had the place all to herself, that huge apartment overlooking the river. I pushed the drapes aside and stared out at twilight gathering in the park across the street. Then she was back (minus the red box) with a silver serving tray, two glasses, and a virgin bottle of Sazerac rye.

"Maybe just one," I said, and she smiled. I went back to watching Riverside Park while she poured the whiskey. No harm in a shot or two. It's not like I had some place to be, and there were still a couple of unanswered questions bugging me. Such as why Harpootlian had broken her promise, the one that was supposed to prevent her underlings from practicing their hocus-pocus on me. That is, assuming Ellen Andrews had even bothered to ask permission. Regardless, she didn't need magic or a spell book for her next dirty trick. The Mickey Finn she slipped me did the job just fine.

So, I came to, four, perhaps five hours later—sometime before midnight. By then, as I'd soon learn, the shit had already hit the fan. I woke up sick as a dog and my head pounding like there was an ape with a kettledrum loose inside my skull. I opened my eyes, but it wasn't Ellen Andrews's Baroque clutter and chintz that greeted me, and I immediately shut them again. I smelled the hookahs and the smoldering *bukhoor*, the opium smoke and sandarac and, somewhere underneath it all, that pervasive brimstone stink that no amount of incense can mask. Besides, I'd seen the spiny ginger-skinned thing crouching not far from me, the eunuch, and I knew I was somewhere in the rat's-maze labyrinth of Harpootlian's bordello. I started to sit up, but then my stomach lurched and I thought better of it. At least there were soft cushions beneath me, and the silk was cool against my feverish skin.

"You know where you are?" the eunuch asked; it had a woman's voice and a hint of a Russian accent, but I was pretty sure both were only affectations. First rule of demon brothels: Check your preconceptions of male and female at the door. Second rule: Appearances are fucking meant to be deceiving.

"Sure," I moaned and tried not to think about vomiting. "I might have a notion or three."

"Good. Then you lie still and take it easy, Miss Beaumont. We've got a few questions need answering." Which made it mutual, but I kept my mouth shut on that account. The voice was beginning to sound not so much feminine as what you might hear if you scraped frozen pork back and forth across a cheese grater. "This afternoon, you were contacted by an associate of Madam Harpootlian's, yes? She told you her name was Ellen Andrews. That's not her true name, of course. Just something she heard in a motion picture—"

"Of course," I replied. "You sort never bother with your real names. Anyway, what of it?"

"She asked you to go see Jimmy Fong and bring her something, yes? Something very precious. Something powerful and rare."

"The dingus," I said, rubbing at my aching head. "Right, but . . . hey . . . Fong was already dead when I got there, scout's honor. Andrews told me one of Szabó's people did him."

"The Chinese gentleman's fate is no concern of ours," the eunuch said. "But we need to talk about Ellen Andrews. She has caused this house serious inconvenience. She's troubled us, and troubles us still."

"You and me both, bub," I said. It was just starting to dawn on me how there were some sizable holes in my memory. I clearly recalled the taste of rye, and gazing down at the park, but then nothing. Nothing at all. I asked the ginger demon, "Where is she? And how'd I get here, anyway?"

"We seem to have many of the same questions," it replied, dispassionate as a corpse. "You answer ours, maybe we shall find the answers to yours along the way."

I knew damn well I didn't have much say in the matter. After all, I'd been down this road before. When Auntie H. wants answers, she doesn't usually bother with asking. Why waste your time wondering if someone's feeding you a load of baloney when all you gotta do is reach inside his brain and help yourself to whatever you need?

"Fine," I said, trying not to tense up, because tensing up only ever makes it worse. "How about let's cut the chitchat and get this over with."

"Very well, but you should know," it said, "Madam regrets the necessity of this imposition." And then there were the usual wet, squelching noises as the relevant appendages unfurled and slithered across the floor toward me.

"Sure, no problem. Ain't no secret Madam's got a heart of gold," and maybe I shouldn't have smarted off like that, because when the stingers hit me, they hit hard. Harder than I knew was necessary to make the connection. I might have screamed. I know I pissed myself. And then it was inside me, prowling about, roughly picking its way through my conscious and unconscious mind—through my soul, if that word suits you better. All the heady sounds and smells of the brothel faded away, along with my physical discomfort. For a while I drifted nowhere and nowhen in particular, and then, then I stopped drifting . . .

. . . Ellen asked me, "You ever think you've had enough? Of the life, I mean. Don't you sometimes contemplate just up and blowing town, not even stopping long enough to look back? Doesn't that ever cross your mind, Nat?"

I sipped my whiskey and watched her, undressing her with my eyes and not especially ashamed of myself for doing so. "Not too often," I said. "I've had it worse. This gig's not perfect, but I usually get a fair shake."

"Yeah, usually," she said, her words hardly more than a sigh. "Just, now and then, I feel like I'm missing out."

I laughed, and she glared at me.

"You'd cut a swell figure in a breadline," I said, and took another swallow of the rye.

"I hate when people laugh at me."

"Then don't say funny things," I told her.

And that's when she turned and took my glass. I thought she was about to tell me to get lost, and don't let the door hit me in the ass on the way out. Instead, she set the drink down on the silver serving tray, and she kissed me. Her mouth tasted like peaches. Peaches and cinnamon. Then she pulled back, and her eyes flashed red, the way they had in the Yellow Dragon, only now I knew it wasn't an illusion.

"You're a demon," I said, not all that surprised.

"Only a quarter. My grandmother . . . Well, I'd rather not get into that, if it's all the same to you. Is it a problem?"

"No, it's not a problem," I replied, and she kissed me again. Right about here, I started to feel the first twinges of whatever she'd put into the Sazerac, but, frankly, I was too horny to heed the warning signs.

"I've got a plan," she said, whispering, as if she were afraid someone was listening in. "I have it all worked out, but I wouldn't mind some company on the road."

"I have no . . . no idea . . . what you're talking about," and there was something else I wanted to say, but I'd begun slurring my words and decided against it. I put a hand on her left breast, and she didn't stop me.

"We'll talk about it later," she said, kissing me again, and right about then, that's when the curtain came crashing down, and the ginger-colored demon in my brain turned a page . . .

. . . I opened my eyes, and I was lying in a black room. I mean, a *perfectly* black room. Every wall had been painted matte black, and the ceiling, and the floor. If there were any windows, they'd also been painted over, or boarded up. I was cold, and a moment later I realized that was because I was naked. I was naked and lying at the center of a wide white pentagram that had been chalked onto that black floor. A white pentagram held within a white circle. There was a single white candle burning at each of the five points. I looked up, and Ellen Andrews was standing above me. Like me, she was naked. Except she was wearing that dingus from the lacquered box, fitted into a leather harness strapped about her hips. The phallus drooped obscenely and glimmered in the candlelight. There were dozens of runic and Enochian symbols painted on her skin in blood and shit and charcoal. Most of them I recognized. At her feet, there was a small iron cauldron, and a black-handled dagger, and something dead. It might have been a rabbit, or a small dog. I couldn't be sure which, because she'd skinned it.

Ellen looked down, and saw me looking up at her. She frowned, and tilted her head to one side. For just a second, there was something undeniably predatory in that expression, something murderous. All spite and not a jot of mercy. For that second, I was face to face with the one quarter of her bloodline that changed all the rules, the ancestor she hadn't wanted to talk about. But then that second passed, and she softly whispered, "I have a plan, Natalie Beaumont."

"What are you doing?" I asked her. But my mouth was so dry and numb, my throat so parched, it felt like I took forever to cajole my tongue into shaping those four simple words.

"No one will know," she said. "I promise. Not Harpootlian, not Szabó, not anyone. I've been over this a thousand times, worked all the angles." And she went down on one knee then, leaning over me. "But you're supposed to be asleep, Nat."

"Ellen, you don't cross Harpootlian," I croaked.

"Trust me," she said.

In that place, the two of us adrift on an island of light in an endless sea of blackness, she was the most beautiful woman I'd ever seen. Her hair was down now, and I reached up, brushing it back from her face. When my fingers moved across her scalp, I found two stubby horns, but it wasn't anything a girl couldn't hide with the right hairdo and a hat.

"Ellen, what are you doing?"

"I'm about to give you a gift, Nat. The most exquisite gift in all creation. A gift that even the angels might covet. You wanted to know what the unicorn does. Well, I'm not going to tell you; I'm going to *show* you."

She put a hand between my legs and found I was already wet.

I licked at my chapped lips, fumbling for words that wouldn't come. Maybe I didn't know what she was getting at, this *gift*, but I had a feeling I didn't want any part of it, no matter how exquisite it might be. I knew these things, clear as day, but I was lost in the beauty of her, and whatever protests I might have uttered, they were about as sincere as ol' Brer Rabbit begging Brer Fox not to throw him into that briar patch. I could say I was bewitched, but it would be a lie.

She mounted me then, and I didn't argue.

"What happens now?" I asked.

"Now I fuck you," she replied. "Then I'm going to talk to my grandmother."
And, with that, the world fell out from beneath me again. And the ginger-
skinned eunuch moved along to the next tableau, that next set of memories I
couldn't recollect on my own . . .

. . . Stars were tumbling from the skies. Not a few stray shooting stars here and
there. No, *all* the stars were falling. One by one, at first, and then the sky was
raining pitchforks, only it *wasn't* rain, see. It was light. The whole sorry world
was being born or was dying, and I saw it didn't much matter which. Go back
far enough, or far enough forward, the past and future wind up holding hands,
cozy as a couple of lovebirds. Ellen had thrown open a doorway, and she'd
dragged me along for the ride. I was *so* cold. I couldn't understand how there
could be that much fire in the sky, and me still be freezing my tits off like that.
I lay there shivering as the brittle vault of heaven collapsed. I could feel her
inside me. I could feel *it* inside me, and same as I'd been lost in Ellen's beauty, I
was being smothered by that ecstasy. And then . . . then the eunuch showed me
the gift, which I'd forgotten . . . and which I would immediately forget again.

How do you write about something, when all that remains of it is the
faintest of impressions of glory? When all you can bring to mind is the empty
place where a memory ought to be and isn't, and only that conspicuous absence
is there to remind you of what cannot ever be recalled? Strain as you might, all
that effort hardly adds up to a trip for biscuits. So, *how do you write it down?*
You don't, *that's* how. You do your damnedest to think about what came next,
instead, knowing your sanity hangs in the balance.

So, here's what came *after* the gift, since *le godemiché maudit* is a goddamn
Indian giver if ever one was born. Here's the curse that rides shotgun on the
gift, as impossible to obliterate from reminiscence as the other is to awaken.

There were falling stars, and that unendurable cold . . . and then the empty,
aching socket to mark the countermanded gift . . . and *then* I saw the unicorn.
I don't mean the dingus. I mean the *living creature*, standing in a glade of
cedars, bathed in clean sunlight and radiating a light all its own. It didn't look
much like what you see in storybooks or those medieval tapestries they got
hanging in the Cloisters. It also didn't look much like the beast carved into the
lid of Fong's wooden box. But I knew what it was, all the same.

A naked girl stood before it, and the unicorn kneeled at her feet. She sat
down, and it rested its head on her lap. She whispered reassurances I couldn't
hear, because they were spoken as softly as falling snow. And then she offered
the unicorn one of her breasts, and I watched as it suckled. This scene of
chastity and absolute peace lasted maybe a minute, maybe two, before the trap

was sprung and the hunters stepped out from the shadows of the cedar boughs. They killed the unicorn, with cold iron lances and swords, but first the unicorn killed the virgin who'd betrayed it to its doom . . .

. . . And Harpootlian's ginger eunuch turned another page (a hamfisted analogy if ever there was one, but it works for me), and we were back in the black room. Ellen and me. Only two of the candles were still burning, two guttering, halfhearted counterpoints to all that darkness. The other three had been snuffed out by a sudden gust of wind that had smelled of rust, sulfur, and slaughterhouse floors. I could hear Ellen crying, weeping somewhere in the darkness beyond the candles and the periphery of her protective circle. I rolled over onto my right side, still shivering, still so cold I couldn't imagine being warm ever again. I stared into the black, blinking and dimly amazed that my eyelids hadn't frozen shut. Then something snapped into focus, and there she was, cowering on her hands and knees, a tattered rag of a woman lost in the gloom. I could see her stunted, twitching tail, hardly as long as my middle finger, and the thing from the box was still strapped to her crotch. Only now it had a twin, clutched tightly in her left hand.

I think I must have asked her what the hell she'd done, though I had a pretty good idea. She turned toward me, and her eyes . . . Well, you see that sort of pain, and you spend the rest of your life trying to forget you saw it.

"I didn't understand," she said, still sobbing. "I didn't understand she'd take so much of me away."

A bitter wave of conflicting, irreconcilable emotion surged and boiled about inside me. Yeah, I knew what she'd done to me, and I knew I'd been used for something unspeakable. I knew *violation* was too tame a word for it, and that I'd been marked forever by this gold-digging half-breed of a twist. And part of me was determined to drag her kicking and screaming to Harpootlian. Or fuck it, I could kill her myself, and take my own sweet time doing so. I could kill her the way the hunters had murdered the unicorn. But—on the other hand—the woman I saw lying there before me was shattered almost beyond recognition. There'd been a steep price for her trespass, and she'd paid it and then some. Besides, I was learning fast that when you've been to Hades's doorstep with someone, and the two of you make it back more or less alive, there's a bond, whether you want it or not. So, there we were, a cheap, latter-day parody of Orpheus and Eurydice, and all I could think about was holding her, tight as I could, until she stopped crying and I was warm again.

"She took so much," Ellen whispered. I didn't ask what her grandmother had taken. Maybe it was a slice of her soul, or maybe a scrap of her humanity. Maybe it was the memory of the happiest day of her life, or the ability to taste her favorite food. It didn't seem to matter. It was gone, and she'd never get it back. I reached for her, too cold and too sick to speak, but sharing her hurt and needing to offer my hollow consolation, stretching out to touch . . .

. . . And the eunuch said, "Madam wishes to speak with you now," and that's when I realized the parade down memory lane was over. I was back at Harpootlian's, and there was a clock somewhere chiming down to 3:00 a.m., the dead hour. I could feel the nasty welt the stingers had left at the base of my skull and underneath my jaw, and I still hadn't shaken off the hangover from that tainted shot of rye whiskey. But above and underneath and all about these mundane discomforts was a far more egregious pang, a portrait of that guileless white beast cut down and its blood spurting from gaping wounds. Still, I did manage to get myself upright without puking. Sure, I gagged once or twice, but I didn't puke. I pride myself on that. I sat with my head cradled in my hands, waiting for the room to stop tilting and sliding around like I'd gone for a spin on the Coney Island Wonder Wheel.

"Soon, you'll feel better, Miss Beaumont."

"Says you," I replied. "Anyway, give me a half a fucking minute, will you please? Surely your employer isn't gonna cast a kitten if you let me get my bearings first, not after the work over you just gave me. Not after—"

"I will remind you, her patience is not infinite," the ginger demon said firmly, and then it clicked its long claws together.

"Yeah?" I asked. "Well, who the hell's is?" But I'd gotten the message, plain and clear. The gloves were off, and whatever forbearance Auntie H. might have granted me in the past, it was spent, and now I was living on the installment plan. I took a deep breath and struggled to my feet. At least the eunuch didn't try to lend a hand.

I can't say for certain when Yeksabet Harpootlian set up shop in Manhattan, but I have it on good faith that Magdalena Szabó was here first. And anyone who knows her onions knows the two of them have been at each other's throats since the day Auntie H. decided to claim a slice of the action for herself. Now, you'd think there'd be plenty enough of the hellion cock-and-tail trade to go around, what with all the netherworlders who call the five boroughs their home away from home. And likely as not, you'd be right. Just don't try telling that to Szabó or Auntie H. Sure, they've each got their elite stable of "girls and boys," and they both have more customers than they know what to do with. Doesn't stop them from spending every waking hour looking for a way to banish the other once and for all—or at least find the unholy grail of competitive advantages.

Now, by the time the ginger-skinned eunuch led me through the chaos of Auntie H.'s stately pleasure dome, far below the subways and sewers and tenements of the Lower East Side, I already had a pretty good idea the dingus from Jimmy Fong's shiny box was meant to be Harpootlian's trump card. Only, here was Ellen Andrews, this mutt of a courier, gumming up the works, playing fast and loose with the loving cup. And here was me, stuck smack in the middle, the unwilling stooge in her double-cross.

As I followed the eunuch down the winding corridor that ended in Auntie H.'s grand salon, we passed doorway after doorway, all of them opening onto scenes of inhuman passion and madness, the most odious of perversions, and tortures that make short work of merely mortal flesh. It would be disingenuous to say I looked away. After all, this wasn't my first time. Here were the hinterlands of wanton physical delight and agony, where the two become indistinguishable in a rapturous *Totentanz*. Here were spectacles to remind me how Doré and Hieronymus Bosch never even came close, and all of it laid bare for the eyes of any passing voyeur. You see, there are no locked doors to be found at Madam Harpootlian's. There are no doors at all.

"It's a busy night," the eunuch said, though it looked like business as usual to me.

"Sure," I muttered. "You'd think the Shriners were in town. You'd think Mayor La Guardia himself had come down off his high horse to raise a little hell."

And then we reached the end of the hallway, and I was shown into the mirrored chamber where Auntie H. holds court. The eunuch told me to wait, then left me alone. I'd never seen the place so empty. There was no sign of the usual retinue of rogues, ghouls, and archfiends, only all those goddamn mirrors, because no one looks directly at Madam Harpootlian and lives to tell the tale. I chose a particularly fancy-looking glass, maybe ten feet high and held inside an elaborate gilded frame. When Harpootlian spoke up, the mirror rippled like it was only water, and my reflection rippled with it.

"Good evening, Natalie," she said. "I trust you've been treated well?"

"You won't hear any complaints outta me," I replied. "I always say, the Waldorf-Astoria's got nothing on you."

She laughed then, or something that we'll call laughter for the sake of convenience.

"A crying shame we're not meeting under more amicable circumstances. Were it not for this unpleasantness with Miss Andrews, I'd offer you something—on the house, of course."

"Maybe another time," I said.

"So, you *know* why you're here?"

"Sure," I said. "The dingus I took off the dead Chinaman. The salami with the fancy French name."

"It has many names, Natalie. Karkadann's Brow, *el consolador sangriento*, the Horn of Malta—"

"*Le godemiché maudit*," I said. "Ellen's cock."

Harpootlian grunted, and her reflection made an ugly, dismissive gesture. "It is nothing of Miss Andrews. It is mine, bought and paid for. With the sweat of my own brow did I track down the spoils of al-Jaldaki's long search. It's *my* investment, one purchased with so grievous a forfeiture this quadroon mongrel could not begin to appreciate the severity of her crime. But you, Natalie, you know, don't you? You've been privy to the wonders of Solomon's talisman, so I think, maybe, you are cognizant of my loss."

"I can't exactly say what I'm cognizant of," I told her, doing my best to stand up straight and not flinch or look away. "I saw the murder of a creature I didn't even believe in yesterday morning. That was sort of an eye opener, I'll grant you. And then there's the part I can't seem to conjure up, even after golden boy did that swell Roto-Rooter number on my head."

"Yes. Well, that's the catch," she said and smiled. There's no shame in saying I looked away then. Even in a mirror, the smile of Yeksabet Harpootlian isn't something you want to see straight on.

"Isn't there always a catch?" I asked, and she chuckled.

"True, it's a fleeting boon," she purred. "The gift comes, and then it goes, and no one may ever remember it. But always, *always* they will long for it again, even hobbled by that ignorance."

"You've lost me, Auntie," I said, and she grunted again. That's when I told her I wouldn't take it as an insult to my intelligence or expertise if she laid her cards on the table and spelled it out plain and simple, like she was talking to a woman who didn't regularly have tea and crumpets with the damned. She mumbled something to the effect that maybe she gave me too much credit, and I didn't disagree.

"Consider," she said, "what it *is*, a unicorn. It is the incarnation of purity, an avatar of innocence. And here is the *power* of the talisman, for that state of grace which soon passes from us, each and every one, is forever locked inside the horn—the horn become the phallus. And in the instant that it brought you, Natalie, to orgasm, you knew again that innocence, the bliss of a child before it suffers corruption."

I didn't interrupt her, but all at once I got the gist.

"Still, you are only a mortal woman, so what negligible, insignificant sins could you have possibly committed during your short life? Likewise, whatever calamities and wrongs have been visited upon your flesh or your soul, they are trifles. But if you survived the war in Paradise, if you refused the yoke and so are counted among the exiles, then you've persisted down all the long eons.

You were already broken and despoiled billions of years before the coming of man. And your transgressions outnumber the stars.

"Now," she asked, "what would *you* pay, were you so cursed, to know even one fleeting moment of that stainless former existence?"

Starting to feel sick to my stomach all over again, I said, "More to the point, if I *always* forgot it, immediately, but it left this emptiness I feel—"

"You would come back," Auntie H. smirked. "You would come back again and again and again, because there would be no satiating that void, and always would you hope that maybe *this* time it would take and you might *keep* the memories of that immaculate condition."

"Which makes it priceless, no matter what you paid."

"Precisely. And now Miss Andrews has forged a copy—an *identical* copy, actually—meaning to sell one to me, and one to Magdalena Szabó. That's where Miss Andrews is now."

"Did you tell her she could hex me?"

"I would never do such a thing, Natalie. You're much too valuable to me."

"*But* you think I had something to do with Ellen's mystical little counterfeit scheme."

"Technically, you did. The ritual of division required a supplicant, someone to receive the gift granted by the unicorn, before the summoning of a succubus mighty enough to effect such a difficult twinning."

"So maybe, instead of sitting here bumping gums with me, you should send one of your torpedoes after her. And, while we're on the subject of how you pick your little henchmen, maybe—"

"*Natalie*," snarled Auntie H. from someplace not far behind me. "Have I failed to make myself *understood*? Might it be I need to raise my voice?" The floor rumbled, and tiny hairline cracks began to crisscross the surface of the looking glass. I shut my eyes.

"No," I told her. "I get it. It's a grift, and you're out for blood. But you *know* she used me. Your lackey, it had a good, long look around my upper story, right, and there's no way you can think I was trying to con you."

For a dozen or so heartbeats, she didn't answer me, and the mirrored room was still and silent, save all the moans and screaming leaking in through the walls. I could smell my own sour sweat, and it was making me sick to my stomach.

"There are some gray areas," she said finally. "Matters of sentiment and lust, a certain reluctant infatuation, even."

I opened my eyes and forced myself to gaze directly into that mirror, at the abomination crouched on its writhing throne. And all at once, I'd had enough, enough of Ellen Andrews and her dingus, enough of the cloak-and-dagger bullshit, and definitely enough kowtowing to the monsters.

"For fuck's sake," I said, "I only just met the woman this afternoon. She drugs and rapes me, and you think that means she's my sheba?"

"Like I told you, I think there are gray areas," Auntie H. replied. She grinned, and I looked away again.

"Fine. You tell me what it's gonna take to make this right with you, and I'll do it."

"Always so eager to please," Auntie H. laughed, and the mirror in front of me rippled. "But, since you've asked, and as I do not doubt your *present* sincerity, I will tell you. I want her dead, Natalie. Kill her, and all will be . . . forgiven."

"Sure," I said, because what the hell else was I going to say. "But if she's with Szabó—"

"I have spoken already with Magdalena Szabó, and we have agreed to set aside our differences long enough to deal with Miss Andrews. After all, she has attempted to cheat us both, in equal measure."

"How do I find her?"

"You're a resourceful young lady, Natalie," she said. "I have faith in you. Now . . . if you will excuse me," and, before I could get in another word, the mirrored room dissolved around me. There was a flash, not of light, but of the deepest abyssal darkness, and I found myself back at the Yellow Dragon, watching through the bookshop's grimy windows as the sun rose over the Bowery.

There you go, the dope on just how it was I found myself holding a gun on Ellen Andrews, and just how it was she found herself wondering if I was angry enough or scared enough or desperate enough to pull the trigger. And like I said, I chambered a round, but she just stood there. She didn't even flinch.

"I wanted to give you a gift, Nat," she said.

"Even if I believed that—and I don't—all I got to show for this *gift* of yours is a nagging yen for something I'm never going to get back. We lose our innocence, it stays lost. That's the way it works. So, all I got from you, Ellen, is a thirst can't ever be slaked. That and Harpootlian figuring me for a clip artist."

She looked hard at the gun, then looked harder at me.

"So what? You thought I was gonna plead for my life? You thought maybe I was gonna get down on my knees for you and beg? Is that how you like it? Maybe you're just steamed cause I was on top—"

"Shut up, Ellen. You don't get to talk yourself out of this mess. It's a done deal. You tried to give Auntie H. the high hat."

"And you honestly think she's on the level? You think you pop me and she lets you off the hook, like nothing happened?"

"I do," I said. And maybe it wasn't as simple as that, but I wasn't exactly lying, either. I needed to believe Harpootlian, the same way old women need to believe in the infinite compassion of the little baby Jesus and Mother Mary. Same way poor kids need to believe in the inexplicable generosity of Popeye the Sailor and Santa Claus.

"It didn't have to be this way," she said.

"I didn't dig your grave, Ellen. I'm just the sap left holding the shovel."

And she smiled that smug smile of hers and said, "I get it now, what Auntie H. sees in you. And it's not your knack for finding shit that doesn't want to be found. It's not that at all."

"Is this a guessing game," I asked, "or do you have something to say?"

"No, I think I'm finished," she replied. "In fact, I think I'm done for. So let's get this over with. By the way, how many women have you killed?"

"You played me," I said again.

"Takes two to make a sucker, Nat." She smiled.

Me, I don't even remember pulling the trigger. Just the sound of the gunshot, louder than thunder.

Caitlín R. Kiernan is the author of several novels, including the award-winning *Threshold, Daughter of Hounds, The Red Tree, The Drowning Girl*, and, most recently (as Kathleen Tierney), *Blood Oranges*. Her short fiction has been collected in *Tales of Pain and Wonder*; *From Weird and Distant Shores*; *To Charles Fort, with Love*; *Alabaster*; *A Is for Alien*; and *The Ammonite Violin & Others*. Her erotica has been collected in two volumes, *Frog Toes and Tentacles* and *Tales from the Woeful Platypus*. Subterranean Press published a retrospective of her early writing, *Two Worlds and In Between: The Best of Caitlín R. Kiernan (Volume One)* last year. She lives in Providence, Rhode Island with her partner, Kathryn.

ACKNOWLEDGEMENTS

"Cryptic Coloration" by Elizabeth Bear © 2007 Elizabeth Bear. First publication: *Jim Baen's Universe*, June 2007.

"The Key" by Ilsa J. Bick © 2004 Ilsa J. Bick. First publication: *Sci Fiction*, August 11, 2004.

"Mortal Bait" by Richard Bowes © 2011 Richard Bowes. First publication: *Supernatural Noir*, ed. Ellen Datlow (Dark Horse Books).

"Star of David" by Patricia Briggs © 2008 Patricia Briggs. First publication: *Wolfsbane and Mistletoe*, eds. Charlaine Harris & Toni R. P. Kelner (Ace).

"Love Hurts" by Jim Butcher © 2010 Jim Butcher. First publication: *Songs of Love and Death: All-Original Tales of Star-Crossed Love*, eds. George R. R. Martin & Gardner Dozois (Gallery Books).

"Swing Shift" by Dana Cameron © 2010 Dana Cameron. First publication: *Crimes by Moonlight: Mysteries from the Dark Side*, ed. by Charlaine Harris (Berkley Prime Crime).

"The Necromancer's Apprentice" by Lillian Stewart Carl © 2004 Lillian Stewart Carl. First publication: *Murder by Magic: Twenty Tales of Crime and the Supernatural*, ed. Rosemary Edghill (Aspect/Warner Books).

"Sherlock Holmes and the Diving Bell" by Simon Clark © 2011 Simon Clark. First publication: *Gaslight Arcanum: Uncanny Tales of Sherlock Holmes*, eds. J. R. Campbell and Charles Prepole (Edge Science Fiction and Fantasy Publishing).

"The Adakian Eagle" by Bradley Denton © 2011 Bradley Denton. First publication: *Down These Strange Streets*, eds. George R. R. Martin & Gardner Dozois (Ace 2011).

"Hecate's Goden Eye" by P. N. Elrod © 2009 P. N. Elrod. First publication: *Strange Brew*, ed. P.N. Elrod (St. Martin's Griffin).

"The Case of Death and Honey" by Neil Gaiman © 2011 Neil Gaiman. First publication: *A Study in Sherlock*, eds. Les Klinger and Laurie King (Bantam).